0 028 462 38X

THE LAST DRAGON

By M. K. Hume and available from Headline Review

King Arthur Trilogy
King Arthur: Dragon's Child
King Arthur: Warrior of the West
King Arthur: The Bloody Cup

Merlin Trilogy
Prophecy: Clash of Kings
Prophecy: Death of an Empire
Prophecy: Web of Deceit

Twilight of the Celts Trilogy
The Last Dragon

M.K.
HUME

THE LAST DRAGON

SEFTON LIBRARY SERVICES	
002846238	
1341066/00	09/01/2014
AF	
SOUTH	£19.99

Copyright © 2014 M. K. Hume

The right of M. K. Hume to be identified as the Author of the Work has been asserted by her in accordance with the Copyright, Designs and Patents Act 1988.

First published in 2014 by HEADLINE REVIEW
An imprint of HEADLINE PUBLISHING GROUP

1

Apart from any use permitted under UK copyright law, this publication may only be reproduced, stored, or transmitted, in any form, or by any means, with prior permission in writing of the publishers or, in the case of reprographic production, in accordance with the terms of licences issued by the Copyright Licensing Agency.

All characters in this publication – apart from the obvious historical figures – are fictitious and any resemblance to real persons, living or dead, is purely coincidental.

Cataloguing in Publication Data is available from the British Library

Hardback ISBN 978 0 7553 7955 2
Trade paperback ISBN 978 0 7553 7956 9

Typeset in Golden Cockerel by Avon DataSet Ltd,
Bidford-on-Avon, Warwickshire

Printed and bound in Great Britain by
Clays Ltd, St Ives plc

Headline's policy is to use papers that are natural, renewable and recyclable products and made from wood grown in sustainable forests. The logging and manufacturing processes are expected to conform to the environmental regulations of the country of origin.

HEADLINE PUBLISHING GROUP
An Hachette UK Company
338 Euston Road
London NW1 3BH

www.headline.co.uk
www.hachette.co.uk

This book is written in memory of my dear friend, Robyn Jones, who passed away on 29 December 2010. She pulled me up when I was at my lowest, and simply would not tolerate cowardice or giving up when the going became tough.

She taught me that bullies only have power over us if we give it to them. At the table in her garden, she made me promise never to give up on myself, no matter what I was told – even when she was dying and my problems were as nothing to those she was carrying with quiet heroism. There are no words of sufficient eloquence that can repay such a gift.

People such as Robyn are true friends: those who speak the truth in hard times, but stay by your side to hold your hand in times of need.

My life is the poorer without you, my friend.

M. K. Hume

January 2014

ACKNOWLEDGEMENTS

When you write historical fiction, proof-reading is a long and tedious task that requires intense concentration. It's amazing how any number of people can read a manuscript and miss 'typos' hidden away in all sorts of strange places, but these 'bombs' will be found as soon as the novel has been printed, released and displayed on the shelves of a bookshop.

I try to get around this perennial problem by using (literally) a number of friends to do this difficult task for me, thus giving them an advance read of what takes place in the novels long before they are released for publication.

This process serves two purposes. In the first instance, we pick up most of the 'typos' at the right time in the production of the manuscript. But then, and probably more importantly, I get feed-back from superb readers on exactly how they feel about the content to which they have been exposed. Fortunately for my ego, their responses are usually favourable, but occasionally they come up with some major 'boo-boos' on my part, or sometimes on the part of Michael who handles all the editorial and production problems. I am always grateful for these discoveries, because repairs can be made *before* they become a source of acute embarrassment to me.

As an example of 'egg on your face', I utilised potatoes as one of the ingredients in a stew in one of the novels, set in sixth-century Britain. As potatoes did not find their way to the British Isles until about AD 1500, my recipe was about one thousand years out. I was totally humiliated by this error, because I knew in my own mind that Europe didn't have potatoes then. I just didn't pick up on it while in the frenzy of writing.

I thanked my correspondent, red faced, and have tried really hard to remove potatoes from my diet since then.

Similarly, I described the weaponry of Celtic warriors in another novel and mentioned that they were armed with the short Roman stabbing sword that had been used for many centuries by Roman legionaries. However, by the fifth century, the Roman legions were equipped with a longer form of the same weapon. Again, I was embarrassed by my own inadequacies. Fortunately, readers are nice people, so an apology was quickly provided to this knowledgeable critic.

And so my proof-reading friends are very important to me when we are in the final stages of producing each novel. I would particularly like to thank the following for their assistance with proof-reading and constructive criticism: Sue Carpenter, David Hall, David Stephenson, Peter Campbell, Suzanne Beecham, Pauline Reckentin.

To my publicist and source of corporate wisdom, Jolene Hill, my thanks.

I also thank my lovely agent and friend, Dorie Simmonds, who always gives me the confidence to go on, hopefully to bigger and better things.

And to the staff at Headline who always make me feel good about my work. Guys, the covers for the *Prophecy* trilogy were absolutely incredible. I thank you.

My best wishes and my thanks go to you, my friends.

M. K. Hume

DRAMATIS PERSONAE

Aelle	One of the Saxon thanes killed by King Artor. He was the father of Cymen (killed at Anderida), Wlencing (killed at Noviomagus) and Cissa who eventually became the leader of the Southern Saxons.
Ambrosius	High King of the Britons (Ambrosius Aurelianus or Ambrosius Imperator). He was the son of Constantine III and brother to Constans II and Uther Pendragon (all of whom were High Kings of the Britons). Constans II was succeeded in turn by Vortigern, Ambrosius, Uther and Artor.
Anna (Licia)	Queen of the Ordovice. She is the legitimate daughter of King Artor and Gallia, his first wife. Her identity was kept secret to protect her from those who would defile her and gain control over Artor. She was referred to as the king's sister to disguise her true relationship with the Dragon King.
Artair	The king of the Atrebates tribe.
Artor	High King of the Britons. The son of Uther Pendragon and Ygerne (the widow of King Gorlois of Cornwall). He fathered Anna (Licia) on his first wife, Gallia. He also illegitimately fathered Arthur on Elayne. The Saxons refer to Artor as the Dragon King.

Arthur	The illegitimate son of King Artor and Lady Elayne. She is the wife of Bedwyr, the Arden Knife, who fosters Arthur at King Artor's request. The boy becomes a warrior in his own right.
Bedwyr	Master of Arden Forest, and a member of the Cornovii tribe. Taken as a slave by the Saxons in his youth, he was instrumental in defeating the Saxon forces at the fortress of Moridunum. Later, in company with Galahad and Percivale, he became one of the three warriors who took part in the quest for the Bloody Cup. Married to Elayne, he has five children – Arthur (sired by King Artor), Lasair, Nuala, Barr and Maeve.
Blaise	Youngest daughter of King Bors Minor of the Dumnonii tribe and betrothed to Gilchrist (a grandson of King Gawayne), who will become a future king of the Otadini.
Bors Major	King of Cornwall. Nephew and successor to King Gorlois.
Bors Minor	King of Cornwall. The son of Bors Major and great-nephew of King Gorlois, he is a life-long ally of King Artor and, later, King Bran.
Bran	King of the Ordovice tribe. He is the son of Anna and the grandson of King Artor. He becomes Dux Bellorum of the West after the death of King Artor.
Cadwy Scarface	A notable Brigante warrior who was wounded at the battle of Moridunum. He served under Modred at the battle of Camlann and, later,

	fights in the battle of Calleva Atrebatum.
Caius	The foster-brother of King Artor, he is a famed warrior and also a psychotic who kills randomly. When found out, he is killed by Myrddion Merlinus with poison to avoid having to be tried by King Artor in open court.
Causus Gallio	A citizen of Deva when it was sacked by the Brigante tribe and the Pictish allies of Modred shortly before the battle of Camlann. He later becomes the Magistrate of Deva.
Cerdic	Thane and Bretwalda of the West Saxons.
Cernunes	The stag-horned god of Celtic polytheism. He is the leader of the Wild Hunt.
Cissa	Saxon king and Bretwalda of the Southern Saxons. His death was marked by a period of civil war in the south.
Crookback	Ednyfed and Cathella Crookback are peasant farmers on Bedwyr's lands inside Arden Forest. They and their family are killed by a band of pillaging Saxons.
Cymen	Son of Aelle, he is one of the influential Saxon thanes.
Cynric	Son of Cerdic, Thane of the West Saxons. Later to become a bretwalda in his own right. He captures Portus Adurni and Venta Belgarum in his father's name.
Deinol ap Delwyn	A Deceangli nobleman, kinsman of and successor to King Mark.
Don	The Celtic goddess representing the Mother. Out of superstition, her name was rarely

	spoken aloud. She develops some of the characteristics of the Roman goddess as well.
Eamonn pen Bors	Son of King Bors Minor and Queen Valda of Cornwall.
Ector	Son of King Bran, and great-grandson of King Artor.
Elayne	Wife of Bedwyr. Erstwhile confidante of King Artor. After a single liaison during a snowstorm, she becomes pregnant and bears Artor's child, Arthur. Bedwyr and Elayne raise the bastard child.
Enid (Queen)	Wife of King Gawayne. She is Gwyllan's mother.
Flavius Aetius	The last great general of the Roman Empire, he was murdered by the Western Emperor, Valentinian. With a coalition force of 200,000 Visigoth, Frank and Roman warriors, he fought an army of twice that size under the command of Attila the Hun at the battle of the Catalaunian Plains near Châlons. The battle took approximately one day, and he fought Attila's forces to a standstill in one of the great battles of all time.
Frith	The slave of Livinia at the Villa Poppinidii. She is the minder of King Artor's first wife, Gallia, and dies with her when the villa comes under attack.
Fortuna	The Roman goddess of chance or luck.
Gallia	King Artor's first wife, a woman of Roman lineage.
Gareth Major	The bodyguard of King Artor.

Gareth Minor	Son of Gareth Major. He becomes the confidant and bodyguard of Prince Arthur.
Gawayne	Son of King Lot and Queen Morgause, brother of Agravaine and Geraint. He is the king of the Otadini tribe.
Gerallt ap Cadwy	A Deceangli nobleman.
Germanus	A Frankish mercenary who is hired as arms master by Bedwyr to train young Arthur.
Gilchrist	The eldest grandson of King Gawayne, and heir to the Otadini throne.
Glynn ap Myrddion	Son of Myrddion and Nimue, and brother of Taliessin. His skills lie in medicine.
Gorlois	The Boar of Cornwall, king of the Dumnonii tribe. He is married to Ygerne, and is the father of Morgan and Morgause.
Gwyllan	King Gawayne's second daughter. Her name means 'Seagull', and she is the only one of her generation who suffers from the 'Sight'.
Havar	Commander of the Jute forces who fight alongside those of Thane Cerdic at the battle of Celleva Atrebatum.
Hengist	A Saxon aristocrat who serves under Vortigern as a mercenary for a number of years. He eventually rejoins the Saxons and becomes the Thane of the Kentish Saxons and, later, rules the lands to the north of the Wash.
Horsa	Brother of Hengist.
Idris ap Cadwy	Born Idris ap Gerallt, he has been fostered by Cadwy Scarface. He serves as his foster-father's equerry.

Ifor	Son of King Leodegran. He is the brother of Queen Wenhaver, the father of Tewdwr and the grandfather of Mereddyd.
Iseult	Wife of King Mark of the Deceangli tribe. The lover of Lord Trystan, she commits suicide after her capture while eloping with Trystan.
Lasair	Eldest son of Bedwyr and Elayne. Half-brother to Arthur, natural son of King Artor and Elayne.
Leodegran	Father of Queen Wenhaver and King Ifor.
Licia	Alternative name for Anna, daughter of Artor and mother of King Bran. She is Arthur's half-sister.
Lleywd	Master of the Villa Poppinidii.
Lorcan ap Lugald	Father Lorcan. A priest recruited to christen Bedwyr's newly born daughter. He becomes Arthur's tutor.
Lot	King of the Otadini tribe. He is killed by Modred with his wife Queen Morgause.
Luned	A descendant of Livinia. She becomes mistress of the Villa Poppinidii. She is the daughter of Livinia Minor and the wife of Llewyd.
Maeve	Youngest child of Bedwyr. She accompanies Blaise to Onnum when Blaise travels to become Gilchrist's bride.
Mareddyd	Great-nephew of Queen Wenhaver. Heir to the Dobunni throne, he is the sworn enemy of Prince Arthur.
Mark	King of the Deceangli tribe. He is a

	co-conspirator with Modred in the war against King Artor. He deserted his army after the battle where Modred lost his life.
Mark	Bishop of Glastonbury. He secretly buries King Artor at the church, and later allows Arthur to see the site of the grave.
Mary Martha	Abbess of her convent. She is Wenhaver, the widow of King Artor.
Modred	The Matricide. He is King Artor's nephew, the son of Queen Morgause, and is killed by Artor at the battle of Camlann.
Morgan le Fey	Elder daughter of Gorlois and Ygerne, sister to Morgause and half-sister to Artor, who becomes High King of the Britons.
Morgause	Daughter of Gorlois and Ygerne, sister to Morgan and half-sister to King Artor. Wife of King Lot and mother of Agravaine, Gawayne and Geraint.
Myrddion Merlinus	Merlin. He is named after the sun, and his name means Lord of Light. He is often referred to as the Demon Seed. He is a famed healer and is the confidant of King Artor and other influential rulers of his time.
Nimue	The Lady of the Lake. She is the widow of Myrddion Merlinus and the mother of Taliessin, Rhys and Glynn.
Nuala	Third child of Bedwyr and Elayne.
Pelles Minor	Son of Pelles Major. Commander of the archers in King Artor's army. He also serves King Bran.
Rab	Son of Crookback, a peasant farmer in Arden

	Forest, who is murdered by Saxons. He is Arthur's childhood friend.
Rhys ap Myrddion	Son of Myrddion and Nimue, and brother of Taliessin. He is a famed swordsmith and ironmonger.
Scoular ap Seosamh	King of the Brigante, who replaces Modred after the latter's death at Camlann.
Septimus	Cardinal. He took Lorcan to Rome and seduced him. The young Lorcan eventually killed him.
Stormbringer	A Danish captain who captures Arthur and his travelling party. His name is an alias.
Taliessin	Son of Myrddion and Nimue. He champions Prince Arthur.
Tewdwr	Son of Ifor and father of Mareddyd.
Trefor	A warrior from King Bors's cavalry who accompanies Arthur on the journey from Tintagel to Onnum.
Trystan (Lord)	Spymaster for King Artor. Lover of Queen Iseult. Killed and beheaded by King Mark for seducing his queen.
Uther Pendragon	The son of Constantine III and the brother of Constans II and Ambrosius Aurelianus, all of whom were to become High Kings of the Britons. Constans II was succeeded in turn by Vortigern, Ambrosius, Uther and Artor. Uther, in company with Ambrosius, returned to Britain after many years in exile.
Valda	Wife of King Bors Minor of Cornwall. She is of the hill people.
Wenhaver (Queen)	Second wife of King Artor, High King of the Britons.

Wlencing	Son of Aelle, one of the thanes of the Southern Saxons.
Ygerne	Ygerne is the wife of Gorlois, the Boar of Cornwall. After his death, she marries Uther Pendragon. She is the natural mother of King Artor.

MYRDDION'S CHART OF PRE-ARTHURIAN ROMAN BRITAIN

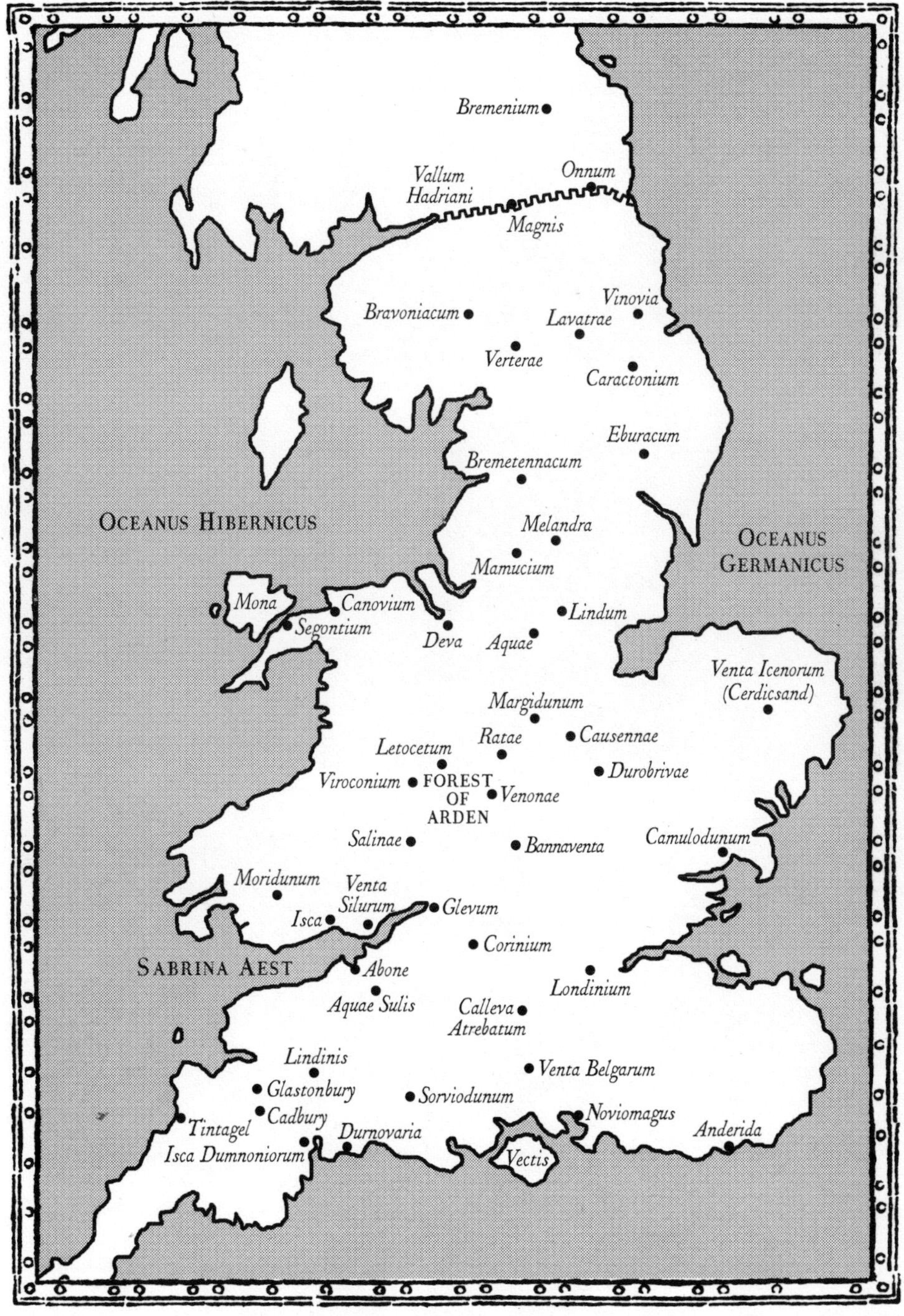

Myrddion's chart of the Celtic Tribal Areas

PROLOGUE

When passions come upon men in strength beyond measure, their gift is neither one of glory nor of greatness.

Euripides, *Medea*, c.431 BC

'Beware, children of Don, for the storm has come upon you and caught you unawares. Hide your faces in your cloaks and rend your tunics with your breast pins, for the Great Hunt is come and Cernunes with his stag's antlers harrows the skies and sets his hounds upon the children of Don. Blood and death ride on his storm, so your puny vaingloriousness will not save you.'

An old woman, a hermit by her long white hair and the skins that wrapped her thin, raddled body, stood upon the cracked pedestal in the marketplace of Mamucium, and her deep voice floated over the crowd of warriors, women and traders. Amid the hurly-burly of hawkers and touts, the cries of animals and the loud chatter of customers, the old woman should have been just one more oddity in the crowded marketplace, but her wild, exotic appearance struck men and women dumb with superstitious awe.

Her dirty, begrimed claws were raised upward so that her skeletal arms were exposed to the crowd before her. Her horny feet were also bared, but no man dared to laugh, for any fool could see that she belonged to the goddess in her crone form. With obvious authority she rounded on the warriors in their checked tunics and trews, and her flinty, pale eyes forced them to listen whether they chose to hear her or not.

'Woe unto you, children of the Brigante tribe, cowardly followers of a treacherous and cursed lord. You raised your swords against your lawful king, and stained Celtic earth with Celtic blood. The goddess has sent me to give you warning, for none of you will be spared in the years to come. You will know you are accursed, and yours will be the blood guilt that must be paid.'

One man, braver than most, climbed onto the shattered remnants of a marble king or god that had once stood on the pedestal in the days when the Roman legions had forced the Celts to obey their brutal, pragmatic rule. With one foot on the statue's breast and the other on its severed head, he stared the witch woman down and laughed derisively, making a rude, universal gesture of contempt with one hand. The sound of his voice was like the hoarse calling of crows fighting over corpses when a battle is done.

'Be silent, woman of the darkness! None may insult the warriors of this tribe. We owe allegiance to no one and nothing except our lawful king. So be gone with you and return to your hole in the earth lest we kill you like the toothless serpent you are.'

The younger men laughed nervously but several women pulled at their arms and tried to silence them, while the older, wiser warriors turned their faces away from the old seer's basilisk stare.

'Be gone, fool!' the old woman ordered. Then, by mischance or the goddess's will, the protesting warrior's boot slipped on the slick forehead of the sculpture and he almost fell. On one knee, he spat a curse at the old woman, but she was not yet done with him.

'Carrion will feed on you before three years have passed. Long will your wife search for your corpse, for the Saxons will feed you to their dogs when they finally hunt you down.'

Somewhere in the crowd, a woman wailed in a terrified voice that was high and shrill.

'Cry, widows. Beg the Mother to save you if you will, but you have slain her favourite, the Child of the Dragon, and she now turns her face away from you.'

The crone spun to face the cluster of warriors who surrounded their fallen brother and they could see that her eyes were filled with madness – or that she was possessed by the goddess. Superstition stilled the hands that had crept towards sword hilts and dried the saliva in their mouths. The eagerness for killing died in their eyes.

'When King Artor breathed his last, the Celtic kingdoms started to die. Nothing will save you now, not your wide lands, your fair Melandra, your warrior's swords or the strength of your arms. When you swore allegiance to the Matricide, you poisoned your own blood, and when you raised your swords against your brothers you damned your children to be slaves. The Saxons will devour you in the night, and no magical cup endures that can save you.'

More women began to weep and wail as they were caught up in the hysteria of the crowd. Warriors who had been at Deva, or had seen the Dragon King's insane charge across the ford, remembered how it felt to be a traitor, until their cheeks were stained with shame.

'No man is innocent.' The witch woman's voice was a whisper, but every person in the crowded, dirty marketplace heard all four words. The silence was absolute as the seer's message sank into their bones. No excuses would be accepted.

'Tell your children and your grandchildren, those of you who survive in the wild, high places in the bloody years to come. Do not forget the names of the heroes. Do not forget Modred, the Matricide, and what was done that bloody day when the Celts began their march towards death. You followed a man so crazed by vile ambition that he poisoned his own mother by stealth. And you knew it! You heard the rumours that damned the Matricide for ever – but he promised plunder, broad lands and power so you drowned your honour in the spoiled waters of greed. Warn your children that treachery breeds blood that must be paid before the darkness comes, and perhaps, if she believes you, the Mother will permit some children to survive for the Dragon's sake. But remember, when the Great Darkness comes and you forsake your heritage and your ancient lands, that the gods will not be mocked, or bargained with, or tempted. You must find some last rags of glory out of your betrayal if any of you are to survive the night that is coming.'

Then, as if the effort of speech had sucked the last blood from her veins, the old woman folded and fell, like a pile of old rags and threadbare furs. When one of the women dared to approach the prone figure, she discovered that the old hermit had breathed her last.

Her feet were scabbed and bloody from the long roads she had travelled, while her hollowed belly spoke of starvation and the travails she had undergone. Her flinty eyes had rolled up into her skull and only the whites could be seen between the swollen red eyelids. Her mouth was almost toothless and her flaccid breasts had surely never been young. Now that the Holy Spirit had deserted her, after having chosen her frail shell to bear the curse and the warning, she was a pathetic old woman once more.

Perhaps the Brigante might still be forgiven for raising their swords against the might of King Artor. Or perhaps they had not earned a moment's safety in the twilight world they had inherited.

The people of Mamucium remembered the witch woman's message, and passed it on to every person they met. They repeated the tales of shame to their children and grandchildren, and did not spare themselves in the telling. And, like all sensible men and women among their tribe, they turned their eyes to the east. And they waited.

CHAPTER I

RETRIBUTION

This ae nighte, this ae nighte,
– Every nighte and alle,
Fire and flet and candle-lighte,
And Christe receive thy saule.

From Brig o' Dread when thou may'st pass,
– Every nighte and alle,
To Purgatory fire thou com'st at last;
And Christe receive thy saule.

'The Lyke-Wake dirge'

When a great king dies, the earth shudders on its axis and even the sun and stars seem less bright and permanent. When King Artor died, no words were sufficient to describe the sudden stutter in the lifeblood of the Celtic nations. There was no time for mourning, only a terror of what would come, now that their protector had perished.

Ultimately, autumn followed a spring and summer of civil war between the Celtic tribes. The farmers obeyed the ancient laws of the earth and harvested their crops, storing grain in neat conical stone and mud granaries, while apples, fish, meat and vegetables were dried and pickled to see out the long winter. Furrows were dug in the bare earth, still crowned with the last dry stalks of an earlier crop, and birds came to feed on worms and beetles disturbed by the wooden ploughs. Careless of the fate of kings, the soil has rhythms that cannot be gainsaid by grief or hardship. Planting, weeding, harvesting and ploughing – the pattern will go on until the end of time.

In Deva, the violated streets and burned buildings still bore raw scars of the conflict that had ravaged a noble Roman city, one that had been an open metropolis for as long as men could remember. Those citizens who had escaped fire and sword crawled out of the rubble and began to set stone on stone and rebuild, for human beings are impelled to labour whenever everything they cherish has been desecrated. Build, destroy, rebuild . . . so the rhythm of cities mimics the patterns of the soil, for the trading ships would come again in the spring, bearing trade goods from the Middle Sea, and the lifeblood of Deva would begin to circle once more. But first, men must mourn their losses.

When the cold winds came, women wept for their empty beds and murdered children, while on Cadbury Tor an empty throne stood in the great hall of King Artor. No man, no matter how powerful or able, dared to rest upon the hard wooden seat. The Celtic warriors who patrolled the Roman roads harried the Picts back to their hollows beyond the Vallum Antonini, where they licked their wounds, smiled below their woad tattoos and waited, knowing that their old hatreds would finally bear fruit. The Warrior of the West had reigned for as long as most men had been alive, and few remembered the chaos of the Great Dragon's rule when the crazed Uther Pendragon had fought the invading Saxons until old age and madness left him brooding impotently in Venta

Belgarum. In those final years of inaction the Saxon barbarians had burned churches and torn down cities of stone before constructing their simple timber buildings and crude palisades in their place.

Later, under King Artor's long and peaceful rule, the Celtic peoples had prospered, but Artor had died by the hand of his nephew, Modred the Matricide, and no new king had yet been elevated to assume the throne of the Britons.

Pain and loss were followed by collective anger in the rhythm of men's hearts before hope could finally begin to grow. A rage for all things lost and broken, a fury for the uncertainty of the future and a realisation that the tribes had contributed to their own defeat scoured the spirits of the warriors, leaving a cleaner, brighter anger that demanded to be sated. Still disorganised, the Saxons had not dealt them their mortal blow. But Modred and his allies had killed their future and imperilled their homes, so the traitors must pay before the Celts could begin the healing process. Perhaps a new dragon would rise from dead, cold ashes.

The Matricide was dead. There was no body to display on the walls of Deva, for the High King's warriors had stabbed, torn, chopped and kicked at it on the battlefield after Artor had dealt the killing blow. Artor's own body had been spirited away by the three queens and taken down the long road leading to Glastonbury in the south, while his warriors took their bitter chagrin out on the Matricide's corpse. Modred was gone into the great darkness, and his remains were beyond the justice of his enemies.

But several of Modred's allies remained alive. They were free, breathing and cowering in hidden places, still hoping to escape the vengeance of the victors of the battle of Camlann. For those men whose anger burned the brightest, the greatest prize became King Mark of the Deceangli tribe, that ruler who had forsaken his oaths of fealty and been seduced by Modred's empty promises of land

and gold. This lordling was assailable, for his body had not been found when the battle was over.

Mark had fled the field when he became aware that Modred had been slain. Whether King Artor survived his wounds or not was of little importance to Mark, who ordered his surviving forces to retire behind their own borders in a hasty and craven retreat. No man, wounded or suffering, was spared during his mad dash to safety. The Deceangli had always prided themselves on the courage of their warriors, and on that numbing, bone-jarring ride the tribesmen cursed their failure on the battlefield and the cowardice of their king, who had determined that they must live for ever with the shame of their flight.

The Deceangli weren't alone in their shame and impotent anger. The tribes would remember Deva with the taste of wormwood on their tongues and they would dream of vengeance as they searched the north for pockets of Pictish resistance. In ruthless determination to salvage some shreds of honour from the civil war, the kings ground their teeth and vowed that someone would pay for the debacle. Mark knew he was living on borrowed time in his fortress beside the river at Canovium, and prayed that Artor's death would plunge the kingdoms into chaos. Which, of course, it did.

While Mark was a weak man with a coward's sense of self-preservation, he understood the frailties and self-delusions of other men. The power vacuum left by Artor's death weakened the alliance of kings, so each tribal group drew back to its own boundaries and watched its neighbours with untrusting, self-absorbed eyes. Mark wasn't forgotten, simply put aside until the wounds of his pursuers were cleansed and healing, and the old rhythms could reassert themselves.

For months, Mark hunkered down in the Canovium fortress, which possessed living rock from the heart of the mountains at its back, the river that rose near Dinas Emrys at its feet and huge ramparts of earth protecting his hall at its crown. Canovium had never suffered the ignominy of defeat, for it had been sited with self-defence as the prime consideration.

'Let them come,' Mark crowed at those times when he had drunk enough wine to numb his sharp, avian intelligence. 'They'll break their backs on my walls. That old bastard Artor is worm food now, so who is left to call me to account? Bedwyr? A Saxon slave in his youth, and now the master of nothing but trees! Gawayne? He's even older than his damned uncle, and his lands in Rheged are under constant attack from Saxon scum. He'll not leave his broad acres to settle old scores – not unless he's got a death wish. Who else is there to care who should live or who should die?'

But, drunk or sober, Mark did not forget the enigmatic king of the Ordovice, a tribe of great power in the west. Bran was said to be linked to the old king by blood, for ancient rumour had suggested that his mother, Anna, was King Artor's sister, but no man dared ask the question of King Bran outright. Reasoned, quiet and self-effacing on first acquaintance, Bran seemed too mild mannered to be a threat. Yet Mark worried about a steely glint that showed in the younger man's eyes when he was thwarted, and a natural talent for leadership which was surprising given that quiet demeanour. Mark was sharp and observant, or he would not have survived for so many years, and he recognised the adoration that the Ordovice warriors gave unstintingly to their king. Such worship couldn't be bought or borrowed: it had to be earned.

But word had come that Bran had been dangerously wounded in one of the early battles of Modred's campaign. Within his hall, Mark hugged himself in the cold and drew comfort from the younger man's illness. The wound would slow down any intemperate actions on Bran's part, even though his bitch of a mother had Uther Pendragon's long memory and was capable of leading a band of her warriors straight to the gates of Canovium. Fortunately, Anna was elderly and her brother was dead. She would be obliged to mourn Artor's loss.

Endlessly, Mark worried about his own safety as he watched the roads that led from the north and the south. Tortured and lacking the energy to rule, he waited as winter plunged the north into a prison of sleet, snow and black ice.

In those bitter days, the king often laughed or wept until his frightened servants were unable to discern the difference in the ugly sounds that came from his hall. At other times, he was heard talking to the empty chair where his wife had once sat in state, crooning endearments or cursing her vilely by turn. On these occasions, the servants and his personal guard shunned Mark lest he should see the contempt and pity in their eyes, for every soul in the fortress had heard how Queen Iseult, whose name meant *fair to look upon*, had broken her marriage vows to their king, judging him a lesser man than Lord Trystan, King Artor's spymaster and sworn servant, and had killed herself in front of her husband.

'Ah, Iseult, my sweet little bitch, you shouldn't have forsaken me. Don't you understand how you were the cause of everything's going wrong? I'd never have bothered with that madman Modred if it weren't for you. Why wasn't I good enough? What did Trystan have that I didn't? I had no choice but to punish you, and you knew it, woman. Else I'd have been a joke in my own hall. A man, especially a king, can't allow himself to be cuckolded in his own house.'

It was ten months since King Mark had returned to Canovium, and behind the wall hangings his servants crossed themselves or gripped their amulets with pious fingers as they listened to his crazy ramblings. 'I pray that our master dies and rots before the other kings turn their faces towards us,' his seneschal, Mellyr, whispered to the captain of the King's Guard. 'They'll kill us and burn Canovium to the ground if we continue to harbour him.'

The officer pretended not to hear the treasonous words of complaint, so the seneschal slipped away to dine with the house servants on mugs of ale and newly buttered flat bread in the kitchen of the fortress. The household regularly fed on gossip to quieten the steadily rising anxiety that came with each new day, for the roads remained empty of King Artor's troops or the warriors led by their neighbour, King Bran, who would soon be forced to call Mark to account for his treason. As Mellyr was fond of saying, every day the kings did not come was one day closer to the hour they would turn the road white with their dust.

Rather than grow complacent at the lack of immediate action, all sensible men in the fortress realised that the kings would never forget Mark's treachery. They would come. Their failure to arrive at once spoke only of their contempt for the Deceangli lord and his warriors, men who had cast aside their oaths of fealty and then deserted the field of battle.

'You were there when Lord Trystan and Queen Iseult died, Master Mellyr. Tell us about them,' one loose-lipped, heavy-bodied house servant asked, his eyes alive with excitement. The kitchens were warm and the ale was fresh and clean, so the servants found comfortable places to sit in anticipation of illicit entertainment, for they knew their king would punish any discussion of his queen and her infidelity. But talk of a local tragedy would divert their minds from what real disasters the morrow might bring. Outside, the winter winds battered at the fortress's upper walls and whistled through the bolted shutters as they sought to wind their cold tendrils into the empty rooms of Mark's palace.

'Who could not remember the tale of Queen Iseult and Lord

Trystan?' Mellyr's voice was warm with affection, for every red-blooded male in the fortress had fallen in love with Iseult's astonishing beauty, either as an ideal or as a fantasy. The other servants nodded, remembering coal-black hair with the midnight-blue gloss that was seen on the wings of ravens. Iseult's eyes had been an unusual colour, the irises so pale within their dark blue rims that they could have been grey or green, depending on the light. Her skin had possessed the perfect thick white texture of a statue rather than a living woman, so that she resembled someone carved out of ice or wax. She was so remote and so cold that she seemed almost inhuman in her unnatural calm and stillness, like a goddess out of old legends. Her servants agreed that such loveliness was both a blessing and a curse.

'And then Lord Trystan came to Canovium with his harp, his clever fingers, his glossy hair and his fine words,' Mellyr said softly. He remembered that first visit distinctly, recalling how Iseult had bloomed in response to Trystan's compliments. Under his bold, admiring stare, a delicate rose flush had stained the skin over her cheekbones and melted the ice in her blood. Her teeth, like small river pearls, had glowed within her parted red lips and she seemed to breathe faster as Trystan sang of perfect love. Iseult had been beautiful before Trystan's arrival, but on that night she had been incandescent. 'I never believed that love could strike so quickly, but I saw the queen open like a bud that has been frozen by a long, cold night and has been suddenly warmed by morning sunshine.'

'You're an old fool!' one of the household's oldest servants sneered. 'You sound like a bad poet or a fond father. You loved her too, so you should admit that you blame our king for her death, although any man would have been enraged if he had stood in King Mark's shoes.'

The sudden silence in the kitchen held the charged tension of an open conflict. The king's defender, Pedr, jutted out his chin aggressively while he bit into a torn slab of new bread with the intensity of a deeply affronted man. The servants weren't surprised, for if the king had an unswerving supporter in Canovium, that man was Pedr.

As the seneschal of Mark's household, a position of status earned over many years of service, Mellyr stiffened. 'Thank you, Pedr, but it is not your place to criticise where I place my affections. Aye, the queen did have a magical glamour that forced people to admire her, but she was a good wife to a husband who was thirty years her senior. She was obedient and respectful, like a loyal daughter or a granddaughter, but my position took me close to them and I saw that there was no love between King Mark and his wife. You should refrain from judgement, Pedr, because you insult your betters. Iseult didn't love her husband, but she served him as her position demanded. Any decent man would feel pity for her, for the poor girl suddenly felt the full force of physical love for a handsome young man when Lord Trystan visited the king's hall. I watched that storm of passion strike her when Trystan smiled at her and kissed her hand, and my attachment to her memory is born of an old man's longing to replace the ugly memories of her death with something fairer. Our mistress was doomed from the moment Lord Trystan cast his eyes upon her flower-fresh face.'

Pedr grunted over his cup of ale. 'I'm not saying you're right, Mellyr, and I'm not saying you're wrong. But a man must be able to believe that his wife will remain faithful.'

'Aye, Pedr. But our master bought her from her father, so there was a price on her body. Who can buy the heart, Pedr? Who can place a value on the soul?'

Disgruntled, Pedr nodded his head and the awkward moment

passed. The puzzled servants, who had watched the altercation with avid interest, settled back on their stools, ready for more entertainment.

'Whatever Queen Iseult's motives might have been, I watched her husband's face as I served him during the feast. You were the cup bearer that evening, Pedr, so you must have seen the way King Mark watched his wife whenever Trystan spoke to her. And you must have seen the way Artor's spymaster toyed with him! The young man flaunted his virility so bluntly that the king was forced to compare his old age with Trystan's youth. Trystan humiliated King Mark for his own amusement. He niggled at him, while joking openly that our king couldn't compete with him in physical contests. His whole attitude was fucking obvious . . . excuse me, ladies.' Mellor nodded in the direction of two kitchen maids who were pretending not to eavesdrop. 'In the foolishness of youth, Trystan flaunted his talents at every opportunity. I watched, and suspected from the start that the queen's new passion would eventually end in tears.

'Within a few weeks, I was forced to acknowledge that Trystan came to visit the queen in her apartments whenever Mark stirred out of his hall. And if the queen went riding, her retinue would gamble coin on whether Lord Trystan would appear, uninvited and charming, telling jokes that displayed a dangerous gaiety and effrontery. They were rarely disappointed. I also remember the times Lady Iseult stole away in the dead of night without even a maid to accompany her.'

Several kitchen hands made rude gestures with their hips, miming intercourse. They laughed crudely, but Mellyr silenced them with a single black glance.

'The poor girl was in love for the first time. Trystan was also smitten, although, if rumours are to be trusted, the young man had won more maidens than I've had hot dinners. The lovers weren't careful in their trysts, either. Inevitably, word reached King Mark, for the queen's beauty bred jealousy in the ladies of Canovium. I was with our king at Cadbury when he dared to order the High King to place a leash on his servant. I was certain that we would all be punished after such presumption, but the Dragon King made a wise response. He left our master in no doubt that it was *his* task to discipline *his* wife. He refused to intervene in what he felt was a family matter, but in doing so he forced Mark to face up to his own impotence so that, ultimately, he was easily tempted to join the cause of the Matricide, when Modred offered inducements of gold and power. I believe he felt there was a score to settle.'

An old man called Elystan, who had been dozing on the stool closest to the fire, raised his head like an ancient tortoise searching for the sun. Inside their web of sagging skin and wrinkles, the man's eyes were very sad.

'Weak men resent the voice that speaks their shame out loud. When the High King told King Mark to bring his wife to heel, our master knew he couldn't do it. And that made him feel even weaker. He needed strength, so he took steps to be strong in any way he could. Better to sit by a warm fire alone than suffer with a beautiful young wife who's been purchased with red gold. All men are fools in matters of love – even kings.'

'Aye. You have the right of it, Elystan, and we have to live with the consequences,' Mellyr agreed.

'And we're like to die of them as well,' Elystan answered, leaning towards the fire as if he felt a sudden cold. 'Don't be so foolish as to believe our master hadn't already met King Modred and become part of the conspiracy long before it became common knowledge. Mark travelled regularly into the south at that time, and only lacked an excuse to openly adopt Modred's cause. The High King gave him that excuse.'

The servants nodded their heads glumly and Pedr slammed his horn mug down on the table top so hard that the ale splashed on his neighbour. In retrospect, the romance between Queen Iseult and Lord Trystan was anything but a source of humour, for the lovers were damned as traitors when their liaison became common knowledge. Ostensibly, Mark made his decision to betray his oaths to the Celtic tribes because of the lovers' shameful behaviour and his own impotence, frustration and greed. But, inevitably, he would have betrayed the High King anyway, for he had been one of the first of the kings to voice his disapproval of Artor before the coronation at Venta Belgarum. Even Pedr, faithful as he was, could find no valid excuse for his master's actions.

'We can talk forever about why our master decided to act as he did on that fatal night, but all our wisdom can't change the past,' Mellyr continued. 'Such an adulterous passion couldn't be allowed to continue, and King Mark believed the queen had decided to cast away her status, her reputation and her crown to flee Canovium with her lover. Our King pretended to leave for the south. Queen Iseult . . .' The seneschal's voice faltered, and he crossed himself with Christian piety as he considered the events of that night.

'The queen arranged to meet Lord Trystan on the beach to make good their escape. I became aware that she intended to flee because she asked me to pack her saddle bags for a long journey. I swear that I said nothing to King Mark – nothing. I cannot tell how Mark became aware of her plans, but someone must have informed him of their intention to beg King Artor for sanctuary at Cadbury. Such public humiliation! They only reached the old ruined cottage at the headland to the north, where they planned to hide for the following day. On the night they eloped, a small troop of warriors was ordered to pursue them and surround their refuge, and our master and I went with them.'

Mellyr permitted the silence to stretch as his audience tried to imagine how the queen had felt. Excitement, a giddy sense of freedom and an overwhelming faith in the power of love must have made her feel invincible, even if only fleetingly. Every man and woman present could recall a time when their future seemed full of promise, only to have it dashed away as if by a pail of cold water thrown in the face.

'Mark managed to enter the hut on his own without alerting the lovers. It was late in the night, the witching hour before dawn when our blood moves slowly in our veins, and every man understands that evil things prowl at that time. Wickedness went into that hut with him, I swear, although Mark will tear out my tongue if he hears what I've said.'

'You'd do well to keep your mouth closed then, Mellyr,' Pedr threatened from alongside the guttering fire in the kitchens. 'No man should have to tolerate the betrayal of his wife with another man. By the goddess, I'd have killed them both if I'd been in our king's shoes.'

'Perhaps you have the right of it, Pedr.' Mellyr's mouth twisted as he spat into the red embers of the fire. 'But where's the honour in killing Lord Trystan from behind? You'd own that it's an unmanly thing to do. Although our master had the right to kill them both, I'd have preferred that he faced his betrayer man to man.'

'And how do you know he didn't face him, Mellyr? You're all hot air, for who can know the truth of what happened in that hut? I've heard more rumours about that night than I've had silver coins in my hands. You presume the master played false. Shame on you, Mellyr, for that man is our king!' Pedr's voice was harsh, and the seneschal remembered that the hulking tribesman had served the kings of the Deceangli tribe since boyhood, as had his father, grandfather and great-grandfather, back to the happy days when the Deceangli had been free of even King Vortigern's poisoned interference in their affairs. Pedr was a king's man to the horny soles of his feet, but Mellyr chose to reveal the truth as he knew it, and damn the consequences.

He raised his face to confront Pedr, his black eyes hard and unforgiving. 'I was the only man of the whole retinue who entered that hut – the only one who dared to see what really happened. Do you understand what I'm saying, Pedr? Were I not the Keeper of the King's Keys, and had the wars of Modred not intervened almost at once, Mark would have had me killed because of the things I witnessed. As it stands, I stay out of King Mark's way so he's not reminded of his deeds. I was there, and I know what I saw.'

Pedr was silenced. Mellyr had seen something that had destroyed his faith in his king so irrevocably that he was openly speaking treason. The tribesman's curiosity was sharpened.

'So? Out with it. What did you see?'

Like many poorly educated men who climb high in the world through their natural abilities, Mellyr had the natural gifts of a storyteller and the power to hold an audience by the seduction in his voice. Now that persuasive tone softened, and his fellow servants leaned forward to hear every word.

'I entered the hut because I heard the queen shrieking like a mad woman. King Mark was standing behind the corpse of Lord Trystan, who had fallen from his stool onto the floor. Clearly, Trystan had been sitting at a table with his back to the door, and his hands were empty of weapons. He had been killed from behind, unaware of Mark's presence. Iseult's warning came too late.'

'How did he die then?' one of the kitchen servants interrupted. His slack mouth was open and his eyes were gleaming as he enjoyed the vicarious violence. 'I heard he was beheaded!'

Mellyr felt a little disgusted. 'The king's blade had struck Lord Trystan at the base of the skull so that the point of the weapon was forced upwards under the bone. Trystan's bowels and bladder had voided but there was very little bleeding, yet our king had become spattered with blood. He must have twisted the knife with some force to be so soiled.'

The servants shivered deliciously as they imagined the gruesome tableau. Like all men who serve and have no power themselves, they were rapt, captured by the frailty and fallibility of their master.

'The queen knelt beside her lover and cradled his twitching body in her arms, careless of the blood and shit that soiled her skirts. No matter how I try, I can't forget her face. Her expression was so blank that she seemed unaware of what was happening. She had become a woman of ice again, so that her face registered nothing, not even grief. She knew what her fate must be, although I've often wondered whether Mark would not have killed her but instead brought her back to Canovium, bound and helpless, as proof that he was the better man. He is still besotted with her, even after her death, so who can tell? He might have spared her to slake his lusts and to answer any lingering doubts about his manhood. We'll never know, for Queen Iseult took her life into her own hands.'

His audience leaned towards him, even Pedr, who prided himself on not being easily convinced by honeyed words.

'She didn't speak; she didn't weep. When our master ordered her to leave the corpse, she obeyed, although she made a little cry of protest when King Mark sheathed his knife and drew his sword. I think I protested as well. It seemed an unworthy and unnecessary act to desecrate a corpse, but in the throes of his anger and spite our master felt no such qualms. He cut off Trystan's head, although he lacked the muscle to sever it with a single blow. He struck Trystan's throat twice with his blade before the head rolled free.'

Mellyr paused and someone pushed a horn cup of ale into his hands to oil his throat.

'"Where's your famed beauty now, Trystan, spymaster and whoremaster?" our master demanded. "Where's all your courage now?" But our queen said nothing. She flinched when Mark kicked the corpse, but her face seemed frozen, as if she were already dead.'

Mellyr could feel the eyes of the servants fixed on his face, so he gulped down half the ale in his cup. 'Then our queen drew a pretty little knife from under her travelling cloak. I can see it still in my mind's eye. It was heavily decorated with gold embossing and cabochon jewels, and didn't seem strong enough to do any damage. The blade was so very slender.

'"Would you kill me then, wife?" King Mark asked, and I confess I moved forward, ready to stand between them. But there was no need for me to intervene.' Mellyr paused for so long that his audience became restive.

'Well, finish your tale, man,' Pedr demanded, captured by the vividness of the story despite his determination to remain untouched by the queen's punishment.

Mellyr sighed deeply. 'Our queen was so beautiful that she could make even my old body stand to attention, and never more so than when she stared at her husband with her knife, a gift from her lover, held firmly in her hands. She was magnificent. "I'll not sully this blade with your accursed blood, Mark," she whispered. "I'm sorry that I'll not see you humbled, or live to watch your accursed, miserly soul dragged to judgement for your crimes – but death is far better than another moment of life as your possession." That's all she said, but the king's face became so pale that I believe he'd have killed her then for her insults, had he been given the chance. But Queen Iseult died the way she had wanted to live – on her own terms. She reversed the knife and used both hands to drive it into her breast, right here.'

Mellyr tapped his own chest to indicate where the queen had driven the blade between her ribs, and directly into her heart.

'She stood for a heartbeat, her eyes fixed on the king with an expression of such contempt that I'll never forget it. Then she pulled the knife out with the last of her strength, and folded as if her knees had collapsed under her weight. She died where she lay, and the expression of loathing in her eyes never changed.'

'What happened after that?' Pedr asked. The description had been so vivid that he was desperate to know the king's reaction. His long years of loyalty demanded some mitigating excuse in the tawdry tale of love, lust and revenge.

'I don't know. I fled like a coward, because I had seen what I should not have seen, and I feared the king's retribution. The rest you know. Trystan's body was set afire inside the hut and his remains were left for the scavengers, although Mark's warriors were disgusted by such undignified orders. Lord Trystan was a warrior of many gifts, one of King Artor's most trusted vassals, and to treat his corpse with such disrespect was a stain on their honour. We all knew that the Dragon would demand reparation for this murder – for murder it was, despite the provocation. But fortune favoured our king and Modred plunged us all into war before Artor could take action.'

'Yet he buried Queen Iseult with all the dignity of her status, despite the fact that she'd made him a cuckold. Surely that stands to his credit?' Pedr protested.

'Some women are so lovely and so compelling that they drive men mad, regardless of their characters or their intentions. Our queen was married to an old man when she was little more than a child, and before her adultery scarcely anyone in the Deceangli lands did not worship her for her piety, her goodness and her care for her people. I believe Mark dared not anger them by treating her corpse with disrespect.'

'That, at least, speaks well of him, although I'll admit that the murder of Trystan is a stain on his honour. Old men in love can be so very foolish,' Pedr said, and Elystan cackled his agreement from his stool by the fire.

In the dark corner near the hearth, a young boy pushed his cowl away from his sleepy head. Although he was exhausted from the labour of cutting wood and laying fires during the day, he had listened to the cruel story with interest. Hesitantly, he added his own mite to the story of the queen's death, making the blood of all the men present run cold with disgust.

'Why did our king keep her body for so long?' he asked naively. All eyes swivelled towards him. 'She was lying in the king's hall for over a week . . . until she started to smell too ripe to remain above ground. I set the fires for her every morning and evening and scraped out the ash. The king often visited her corpse while she was waiting for the burial rites.'

'What are you maundering on about, boy? It's normal to lay out an important personage so that her subjects can pay their respects.' Pedr added a cuff to the boy's ear to his scornful comments.

'Ow! What did you do that for, Master Pedr? I was only asking a question. You know that the king permitted nobody to come into the hall while the mistress was laid out there – just me. Everyone knows fires have to be lit and hearths cleaned, so no one notices me and my brushes. So why did the king . . . er . . . touch her?'

Pedr could think of nothing to say, and even Mellyr was momentarily lost for words at the awful implication of what the boy was innocently suggesting. Then, with a sudden indrawn breath, the seneschal found his voice. 'What do you mean, lump, when you say *touch*?'

The boy looked awkward. 'Our master stroked her body a lot when he forgot that I was there . . . and he talked to her as well. I saw him pulling down her skirts one day when I was going into the room. She was dead . . . so I couldn't understand what he was doing.'

Mellyr crossed himself and even Pedr swore a gross oath under his breath. In the hushed silence that followed, every man present wished he was somewhere else – anywhere but in this room.

Mellyr was the first to find his wits. 'You'll say nothing to anyone about this, boy, if you value your head on your shoulders. I don't care what you understand – or don't understand – just keep your mouth shut about what you saw, for all our sakes. Or we'll all swing for it.'

Shamefaced, the servants dispersed to their beds or their duties in haste, aware that their souls had been stained with something so unclean that no amount of water would wash away the unwanted knowledge. Even Pedr suddenly looked like the old man he was.

In the hall, Mark continued to berate the dead Iseult while tears of self-pity ran down his gaunt face. Outside, shivering with new-found knowledge, Mellyr checked that the guards were on duty, found a new flagon of wine in case his master should call for it, and then scuttled away to his cold, unhappy bed.

For the first time, the seneschal considered the possibility of flight. He was well over forty, his sons were grown and his wife had died of brain fever four years earlier. He knew he had reached the latter part of his life span and his tongue found a broken tooth in the back of his jaw that reminded him of his age. Soon he would be in his dotage. A daughter dwelled in far-away Pennal. Perhaps there, where the ocean winds scoured the black beaches clean, he could free himself from the filth he had seen and heard. Perhaps he could forget the scorn in Queen Iseult's dead eyes and this new horror could be cast out of his imagination and his memory.

'By Ban's head, I swear I can imagine what Mark was doing,' Mellyr whispered into the darkness of his narrow room, where his status allowed him to sleep alone. 'I can see his old man's hands stroking the queen's thighs, even though her flesh must have been cold and swelling. May God preserve us from such abomination!'

His mind flinched away from his new awareness. The darkness offered no possible justification for the king's actions, and the wind chilled the air in the narrow cell so that Mellyr shivered in his woollen robe.

'I think I'll steal away to my daughter's croft in the morning,' he said to himself. 'There's nothing to keep me in this place of pain and misery. At least, I'll not have to watch Canovium soiled by our king's downfall. Such a fate *will* come, because God doesn't permit such sins to go unpunished.'

Finally, when he had made his decision, the seneschal was able to sleep. No night terrors were visited upon him, and in the morning he awoke to a roll of thunder and the whispering wind of a growing storm.

Long after the seneschal had fled, and numbed by the boredom of endless servitude to a master who was too frightened to leave his citadel, the warriors of Canovium were caught unprepared when King Bran and his son Ector, nominated heir to Artor's throne, eventually arrived to smoke out King Mark. Nearly eighteen months had passed since the High King's death, but the council hadn't forgotten the treachery of the Brigante and Deceangli tribes. At a hastily convened meeting at Viroconium, the assembled kings had cast both tribes out of the confederation and then set a huge blood price of gold in punishment for Artor's death that must be paid promptly by the conspirators. Ultimately, the debt was paid by traders and landowners, even though they had taken no part in the decisions to break their oaths of fealty, because they feared another bloody conflict if they refused the kings' demands. The Deceangli debt was paid in full, but the southern kings still demanded the body of King Mark, preferably alive, so warriors were despatched under Bran and Ector to advance on the fortress of Canovium.

Mark raved and railed against the Ordovice king, swearing that he'd never open his gates and submit to Ordovice arrogance. Drunk and terrified, he swore he'd commit suicide in the forecourt of his fortress rather than submit to such oafs or permit them to drag him off in chains like a common felon. But the lords of his court and the merchants of Canovium knew that his end had come, so they sent a petition to King Bran in which they promised to deliver the person of King Mark – alive or dead – if the Ordovice warriors spared the town.

Politics always works to the same pragmatic pattern. When a ruler becomes a liability to trade and business, even the most faithful of his friends will look the other way as he is dragged down from his throne like a worthless slave. Mark was overcome by his own guard. His hands and feet were trussed together, despite his struggles, before he was delivered to King Bran on a spavined horse. Thus Canovium saw their loathed king no more, and the citizenry swore that the air became cleaner after his departure. The landowners of the tribe selected a distant kinsman with an honourable reputation to take Mark's place, and life went on for the Deceangli tribe as if he had never existed. Such is the realistic attitude adopted by men and women who must earn their bread through toil.

Ector was twelve and growing tall, although he had not yet won his place as a warrior. But he had watched King Artor die at Camlann with such gallantry that the boy's pride in his family name had increased tenfold. Too young to rule, regardless of King Artor's intentions, the lad nursed a fierce resentment towards the Brigante and Deceangli tribes, and the cowardice of King Mark had only served to heighten his loathing. Coldly, Ector suggested that the traitor should be imprisoned by the shattered citizens of Deva until the loyal kings could gather to decide his fate.

So Mark was locked in the darkest recesses of the old Roman prison of that city, where his jailers ensured that he should take no physical pleasure from continuing to live. The Romans had understood the indignity of pain, so Mark's cell was so small that he could scarcely move in the confined space. Rotten, vile-tasting food and stagnant, slimy water sustained his body, although the prisoner was forced to scavenge for vermin and insects in his cell to supplement his diet. He was aware that his jailers urinated and defecated in his water and thin gruel, but starvation robs even the most fastidious man of pride and he devoured what was given to him in an effort to stay alive.

Kept naked except for a filthy blanket, he was always cold. Lightless, his eyes forgot the warmth and vividness of the sun; verminous and filthy, he lost the power to smell his own stench. With pleasure, the people of Deva refused him any dignity or honour, and treated him worse than the Saxons treated their captives, for he was no longer granted the status of humanity.

So King Mark awaited his fate in torment, while around and above him Deva healed herself. Life went on.

CHAPTER II

JUDGEMENT

I am a brother to dragons, and a companion to owls.

Job 30:29

Life for life,
Eye for eye, tooth for tooth, hand for hand, foot for foot,
Burning for burning, wound for wound, stripe for stripe.

Exodus 21:23

Mark the traitor, erstwhile king of the Deceangli tribe and co-conspirator with Modred, the Matricide and Regicide, cowered under a filthy, flea-infested blanket in a deep cell in Deva. The golden city had suffered hideously in the War of the Matricide, when Modred had broken the laws of the High King and the tribes that had held sway since the legions had manned its venerable walls. For Modred had chosen to send a message to the kings that the ancient code of neutrality that had protected the port of Deva for so long no longer existed under his regime. No more moots would be held in Artor's circular hall, which had been built by that master of wild magic, Myrddion Merlinus, for the Picts had burned it to its foundations of stone, leaving the rafters gaping open towards the sky. The unarmed citizens had perished in its broad, straight streets where they were cut down like autumn grasses by the tyrant and his allies, the hated Picts, to the perpetual shame of his Brigante tribe.

The ruins of Artor's hall were sad reminders of the waste of human life. Close to the water, on land that overlooked the long neck of river which led to the open sea, the venerable Roman construction took advantage of a small area of flat land on a ridge that jutted over the wharves and the hustle and bustle of trade ships that had brought Deva her wealth and her protected status. Impious hands had never been raised against her stout walls and fine old buildings until Modred loosed the Pictish vermin upon their common enemies, the Latinised Celts, and raped the gracious, civilised town in a welter of fire and blood.

Standing beside his mother, Bran surveyed the ruins with a melancholy nostalgia for happier days. He had first seen his grandfather, Artor, High King of the Britons, on these cracked and broken stones, which had once served as the stage of a Roman amphitheatre. He had been a boy at the time, and had come with his father to a meeting of the kings, but no one had then informed him of his true relationship to the High King.

Through the eyes of a twelve-year-old boy, the other had seemed a living, breathing god. At the height of his powers, Artor had dominated the great men in the room by sheer force of intellect and personality, but Bran had been most impressed by his muscular grace and his clever manipulation of the squabbling kings who consistently opposed him. His armies had been fresh from their stunning victory over the Western Saxons in southern Cymru, but for all his military prowess Artor's proposal to restrict the Saxon advances along the mountain spine of Britain had been fought every step of the way by that fractious, ambitious group.

Bran sighed as he remembered the faces of men who had become legends through the telling and retelling of their exploits. His mother, herself enshrined in the songs of the poets, looked at her son's anguished face with concern. In this ruined place, she too was remembering, thinking of the tall, ascetic figure of Myrddion Merlinus whom the Saxons already called Merlin. The barbarians spoke of him with awe, for they believed him to be a magician and a wielder of wild magic. In their arrogance and simplicity, they could not imagine how Artor had defeated them, again and again, except through sorcery. With affection, mother and son remembered old Targo and stolid Odin who had stood at their master's back and protected the High King with their heart's blood. And there was Gruffydd, disreputable and irreverent as always, but holding Caliburn, the High King's sword. The younger Bedwyr, scarred by the Saxon slave collar but bearing deeper wounds that shadowed his eyes, stood in the background and expressed his disgust with the kings and their recalcitrance in every line of his whipcord body. Now all that strength and hope had gone into the shadows, or been defeated by time.

'This place is full of ghosts,' Anna sighed. 'If I close my eyes, I can still see them and hear them, but then the dreams are shattered when I gaze on these ruins. I am grown old, my son.'

'Aye, Mother. This hall was more than just a meeting place, at least to me. Three High Kings served the people here, in equality and duty, but all that was finest in their ideals was washed away by Modred's civil war. The amity has been broken for ever.'

Both looked up at the sky through the burned rafters that Myrddion had designed for King Ambrosius with such imagination and brilliance. Most of the circular wooden wall was irreparably damaged, as were the captured Saxon banners, looted and burned by the Picts and the Brigante. Charred timbers were evident in the tall ceiling, while cracked and fire-scarred stone was empty of the cushioned seats where the kings had lounged with their retinues. Bran stroked a broken stool that Artor himself had used, shunning panoply for efficiency, valuable now because it was all that was left of a grand idea.

'We shall judge Mark of the Deceangli here. Fitting, don't you think, Mother? It was Ector's idea, which surprised me. I never thought him to be a vengeful lad, but in the short time he knew King Artor he learned to worship him. And now he thirsts for Mark's blood.'

Anna sighed. As Artor's only legitimate child, she had the right to demand Mark's death as her own blood price, but many long years of secrecy had protected her real identity from the High King's enemies, and she had no desire to demand more bloodletting. She still feared for her grandson's future, for the boy had little of Artor in him, but much of his father. In her heart of hearts, Anna doubted that either boy or man had the necessary long view to defeat the Saxon advance, or the cold-blooded authority to save the Celtic people. They were, simply, too decent to do what needed to be done in the dark days that were upon them. She sighed. The times were bleak when goodness was a character flaw. She was loath to make this admission to herself, knowing that their futures lay in dutiful but ultimately futile hands. But none of her inner despair showed on her lined and tranquil face.

'Ector will soon learn that the actuality of judgement is very different from his desire for revenge. Any decisions made here will have repercussions which he must learn to endure. The boy is still very young to lose his childhood, but the Saxons won't wait until he becomes a man.'

'I have called the kings to Deva, Mother, and most will come of their own accord. The Brigante tribe has been ordered to attend with the gold they have gathered in reparation. Fortunately, their new king is little more than a boy and took no part in the civil war. In fact, Modred put a price on the boy's head, fearing that any living kinsman would threaten his grip on the kingdom. I've never met Scoular ap Seosamh but I hear the name is apt. He's overly educated, I'm told, and values old scrolls and knowledge from the past more than people. Obviously, he will lean on trustworthy Brigante lords, if there are any such persons, but he seems to mean well. Ironically, those butchers will now have a king who can write, which will be an interesting challenge for them.'

Anna laughed sardonically and her son was reminded that she was Artor's daughter, her thoughts very much like a man's, particularly in practical matters. 'But Luka was a Brigante. You never knew him, Bran, but he was full of laughter, fun and loyalty. Artor loved him very much and killed his murderers in a bloody display of personal grief. Don't allow yourself to damn the whole tribe because of Modred. He was his mother's son, only twisted, and Morgause herself was a creature of vanity, ruthlessness and cold ambition. Your kinfolk were terrible people.

'A little education won't hurt the Brigante sensibilities,' she continued reflectively. 'And it won't hurt them as much as being ruled by a madman like Modred. No, I wrong him. Modred was so full of his own importance that he willingly sacrificed the honour of his tribe for his own advantage. That's not madness: that's hubris in its worst form. Father always said to beware of hubris. Artor's own father was consumed by it, and many had good reason to know how brutal Uther Pendragon became. You should remember his legacy, my son, and stay free of the seductiveness of power.'

'Of course, Mother,' Bran answered, too easily for Anna's liking. Her son was quiet and self-contained, but he was proud too, and

Anna knew that this flaw was one of the deadly sins that could allow hubris to enter his heart, where it would flourish, grow and destroy his finer feelings. Regretfully, she set the topic aside. First things first, as Artor often said.

'When will the kings come? Deva can provide very little comfort or hospitality if we should receive too many visitors. The citizens will worry that they will fail as hosts, and I would like to allay their fears.'

Bran grinned appreciatively. 'You're always thinking about other people, Mother. You may tell the city fathers that the kings will provide their own victuals, wines and tents, for themselves and for their retinues. You can also assure the councillors that Deva will not be judged by its hospitality, given its suffering during the wars.'

Anna smiled in turn, and her son could see her agile mind prioritising a list of questions inside her head.

'The kings will begin to arrive within the week. For the sake of their continued safety, I hope the Brigante and the Deceangli kings come early, and that the last of the blood price arrives with them. There, Mother, is that what you needed to know?'

Anna nodded and her face cleared. 'I'll discuss your plans with the new magistrate when I speak to him later today. The previous incumbent was murdered at the city gates, so his replacement will be relieved to oversee the end of this matter. The sooner the Deceangli traitor is gone, the sooner we can all start to deal with the essentials of living. You'll have much to do before the start of the next Saxon summer. The barbarians will realise how weak the Celtic tribes have become by then, my son, so they'll attack in force this time.'

'I know. That is the next matter the kings must discuss after we have determined Mark's fate.'

So mother and son strolled in perfect amity between the ruined columns and the burned trees of Deva. The day was bright, with blue skies, scudding clouds like the tail of a white mare and a gentle warmth that coaxed flowers and nettles to bloom through the cracks in the marble paving. Both waited impatiently for the day when the full contingent of kings had gathered and the past could be laid aside – once and for all.

The kings came. Some tribal lords arrived with their wives and eligible daughters, hoping to arrange advantageous marriages if they could. Others, like Scoular ap Seosamh, were accompanied by a few old men who served as advisers. Surprisingly, the Brigante king's sole protection was two young warriors whose task was to guard a heavy wooden chest and a grizzled, scarred man who wore power like an invisible cloak. Bors Minor came from Cornwall, the land of the High King's mother, where the harpers still sang of the fair Ygerne and how her wild beauty drove Uther Pendragon to distraction. And the new Deceangli king came with a retinue of silent, solemn men who were unable to meet the eyes of their peers. After three days of arrivals, Bran called the assembled lords, their warriors and their wives to Artor's ruined hall so that justice could be dispensed at last.

Once the huge contingent was seated, wrapped in furs and wool to protect them from the draughts in the hall, Bran walked into the centre of the cleared space that had once been a Roman amphitheatre. Slowly, the massed crowd settled into silence. Some of the kings were eager for amusement, while others were anxious for revenge; some were simply irritated that they were still required to answer the ancient call of the High Kings, and they looked upon Bran as a usurper who wasn't worthy to stand where legends had once forced them into collective action. Bran felt their impatience.

Taking a deep breath to calm his nerves, he began the long and difficult task of bending these recalcitrant men to his will.

'The news from the east is worrying, and the union of kings hangs in the balance,' he began, pushing his long red-brown warrior plaits away from his careworn face. Although he had dressed with some thought, his appearance was sombre and funereal by comparison with his peers, who had chosen to display their status through finery and robes. 'We must arrive at a decision on how we are to meet the Saxon threat or there will be no land left for you to rule. The Saxon thanes multiply like ticks on a mattress and we lack the resources to stop them.'

'We know the situation with the Saxons as well as you do,' the hulking king of the Atrebates, Artair, muttered darkly while pulling his cloak tightly around himself. 'Why do we have to meet in these ruins? Venta Belgarum could have hosted this council, and the weather is far warmer in the south.'

Pelles Minor leapt to his feet, his short frame quivering with affront. 'Many years ago, Artor decided that Deva was to be our permanent meeting place. It was a good decision because it was central to all the tribes of the west and allowed these meetings to be held on neutral soil. The Celtic chiefs have met here and argued in this structure since long before I was born. These cracked stones remember *legends*, you oaf: history that came into being before the Atrebates were anything but Uther Pendragon's playthings.'

'With respect, sirs, this is no place or time for discord,' one old man grumbled from a prominent place in the forefront of the ruined hall. As Artair took exception to being described as an oaf, the interruption was timely.

The old man was surrounded by three strapping men, all seasoned warriors, and two women, who were quick to hand him a length of cloth when he began to cough. 'Excuse my infirmity, my friends, for I've caught a cold on the journey to meet you. My daughters, Gwenydd and Gwyllan, would prefer to have me cosseted in wool and seated at the fire like a grandsire, but I'd not miss a meeting such as this for the sake of my late uncle and my memories of old wrongs.'

'Thank you, King Gawayne.' Bran bowed towards the old man who had seen it all: the drawing of the sword from the stone at Glastonbury, the battles to free the west, and the whole tragedy and glory of King Artor's reign. 'We are honoured by your presence, my lord. You and your sons have travelled far to be with us, and we welcome you to this union.'

Polite grunts were aimed in Gawayne's general direction, which caused his sons to bridle a little at their lack of respect. But Gawayne grinned with the old insouciance that had won Queen Wenhaver's heart, and the intrinsic honesty that had made him so valuable to the success of his uncle's rule.

'Continue, Bran. We are listening to you.' Gawayne's blocked nose blurred his commanding voice, but the king of the Otadini tribe was incapable of speaking without the unmistakable confidence of power. As an aged aristocrat with a sense of humour and innate charm, Gawayne retained the gravitas that had made him a legend in his glorious youth.

The kings settled back into their seats, and in the back rows, where the women watched with quiet interest, Anna sighed gently. She knew that Bran would never have the force of personality that would silence strong and greedy men with a simple word or an irate glance. It was the truth; and it would always be Bran's weakness.

'Before we deal with the difficulties of our relationship with the Saxon invaders, we have some unfinished business to conclude.'

The crowd hushed. They understood exactly what Bran meant

by *unfinished business*, and each man present felt a twinge of relief that Bran's quiet, reasoned animosity wasn't turned in his direction. In his coldness, the king of the Ordovice was palpably Artor's descendant.

'Mark of the Deceangli tribe forgot his oath of loyalty to King Artor and the council of kings, and chose to follow his personal path of greed and resentment. In doing so, he allied himself with Modred the Matricide and our enemies, the Picts, in order to steal your lands, kill your men, lay waste your towns and burn your crops. He has been brought to Deva to be judged by you, the kings of those tribes who have suffered because of his treason.' Bran turned to the four warriors standing behind him. 'Guards! Bring out the traitor.'

Bran might not have possessed gravitas, but he had a spectacular sense of drama. The guards had been ordered to await his direct instructions before dragging Mark before the kings. When his dry, cold voice gave the cue, their footsteps were clearly audible to everyone in that tall, circular space. The dragging noises that accompanied their crisp march went some way towards preparing the audience for the filthy creature that was hauled into their presence.

Months below ground in the worst prison the Romans could devise had irreversibly changed the erstwhile king of the Deceangli tribe. His thin, narrow frame had always been elegant and self-contained, but now it was bent and skeletal. The black hair with the heavy swathes of white had always possessed an avian distinction, coupled with the long, prominent nose, jutting chin and ironic black brows, but the vile thing that entered the hall was no longer a hunting bird, or even a corvine scavenger. It was a travesty of a man, and each of the kings present was forced to turn away from what the jailers of Deva had created.

Mark's skin, his hair and the single ragged blanket that covered his genitals were the same uniform shade of grimy grey, as if even his colouring had deserted him. His emaciated body could barely stand, so that his guards were forced to half carry, half drag him to a stool where he could sit. The muscles in his legs and arms were wasted, so that his skin fell in loose folds over his bones. His belly was hollow, and every rib and vertebra was clearly visible. Partly healed cuts and scrapes covered his limbs and torso and his filthy grey beard had grown outwards before straggling down over his sunken chest. The uncombed hair on his head was rank, tangled and knotted into a bird's nest, while his sunken lips spoke of broken teeth that were rotting in his gums. Mark was pathetic; the traitor already smelled of death.

'This creature is the erstwhile King Mark, whom we accuse of treachery, albeit he is a distant kinsman to most of us. This man has conspired to revolt against the council of kings, and has now been brought before us for trial. Many among us have no doubt of his guilt, but to judge him and kill him out of hand would be an act comparable to those carried out by the Saxon barbarians who beset us. We are a civilised race, so we intend to try our brother in this place, where any man or woman may speak in defence or in accusation.'

Bran's words fell into the subdued silence like a stone flung into a very deep well. They had expected the Deceangli king to be dishevelled, dirty and cowed, but none of them had dreamed that Mark could be transformed into this subhuman bundle of stick-like bones.

A long sigh rippled through the crowd, half in sympathy, half in shock, as the former king stirred on his hard stool as if the pressure of sitting hurt his skin.

'Who will list the traitor's crimes?' Bran demanded. 'Who speaks against Mark?'

The room was silent, and Anna feared for a moment that the crowd's sympathies had been touched by Mark's physical decay. She looked across the room to the corner where the Deceangli contingent huddled behind their new king with their heads down in a wordless statement of collective guilt. Only one face was lifted and stared back at King Bran, with neither guilt nor anger imprinted on the bland young features.

'Who is that young man?' Anna asked her maid, the wife of one of Bran's advisers. 'The fair lad in the fourth row of the Deceangli attendants?'

'I don't know, madam, but I'll ask.' The woman rose and swept away in a swirl of heavy woollen skirts.

Bedwyr of the Cornovii had risen to his feet and joined Bran beside the sprawled figure on the stool. The atmosphere in the hall had a distinct taste and texture that was thick, expectant and almost sexually charged, as if bloodletting were a kind of orgasm. Bedwyr wore a heavy cloak of winter pelts taken from wolves he had killed with his own hands. A massy gold pin held the cloak together, and on the simple hand-span of gold a dragon reared its scaly head, reminding everyone within this ruined space that Bedwyr would be Artor's man until death, and beyond.

'I speak for Artor, who trusted Mark's word and handclasp when he said he would forgo the lure of gold and preferment in order to honour his oath of allegiance. Yet when Mark came to Cadbury, an attempt was made on Artor's life during a hunt held to entertain the visitors. Although the attack was unsuccessful, Artor was convinced that Mark had arranged for the bowshot to be taken. This treasonous attempt on the High King's life occurred before Mark had openly allied himself with Modred, demonstrating that perfidy and cowardice had been breeding in secret over a long period of time. Later, when Artor received his death blow during the Battle of the Ford, I saw Mark and his lords on Modred's side of the river in company with the Matricide. Mark's treason is beyond argument, so I demand his death.'

With a straight back and a rigid face, Bedwyr turned and resumed his seat. Once again, heavy silence descended over the assembly.

'Do the Deceangli lords deny the treason of their king and themselves? Do you have any justification for what you did?' Bran demanded, his thin lips curled in contempt.

The Deceangli king rose to his feet reluctantly. Of average height, weight and colouring, his gaze was direct and he stood with the confidence of a man who had no reason for fear or shame.

'My name is Deinol ap Delwyn. I am a distant kinsman of King Mark's father, but I have been living far from Canovium out of choice. I am not a warrior, and neither was my father, and we stayed in the mountains to preserve our lives from King Mark's depredations. Our ruler trusted no one, especially kinsmen. I cannot speak of the dreadful days that will live on in Deceangli memory for as long as we have hearts to feel shame, for I was not there. Therefore, I wish to call upon Gerallt ap Cadwy, a nobleman who was forced to comply with his king's demands. Let no sword be raised against Gerallt, for he has served his people well, regardless of the shame that racks him for the crimes carried out against the High King.'

'We will not harbour any animosity towards Gerallt ap Cadwy if he speaks out boldly and honestly,' Bran answered in his measured voice. Few men would readily walk into that small, circular space and be unaffected by the weight of all those judging eyes as they assessed him and determined his worth. Gerallt ap Cadwy stood slowly, bowed his shoulders a little under the scrutiny of so many accusing eyes, and then straightened his spine and strode forward to face his peers with a clear, untroubled face.

Gerallt was neither tall nor imposing in build, but his thick neck and heavily muscled torso spoke of years spent training with the sword or riding for many weary miles across dangerous terrain. He was forty if he was a day, but time had done little more than edge his black hair with a rime of white around the hairline and add a few more creases at the corners of his pale blue eyes. When he spoke, his voice had the smooth tones of a naturally charismatic man who was an inspired speaker.

'Gerallt ap Cadwy,' Bran repeated. 'Do not fear to speak, for it is the mark of a savage to harm the messenger who brings unwanted news.'

Gerallt bowed neatly, and then turned to the assembled kings and their retinues. Wisely, he ignored the resentment and red fury that lingered in the eyes of those warriors who still hated any man with Deceangli blood.

'I was born and bred in Deceangli lands, in Segontium that is now called Caer Narfon on the Menai Straits. The airs are strong there, and a man's word is weighed against the bite of the wind. We who were born a few miles from the beaches of Mona Island feel the weight of the gods pressing close to us, so we can distinguish right from wrong faster than those who live in softer climes.'

The crowd shifted restlessly and more than one king scowled with impatience.

'I tell you this detail so that you will know that I speak the truth, even though I besmirch my honour in the telling of it. No man willingly makes himself appear less than he is, unless the gods impel him to speak.'

'Get on with it then,' Gawayne ordered, then sneezed with a huge spray of expelled air. The kings around him cringed, but

Gawayne grinned wickedly. 'When you're as old as I am, there's nothing like a good sneeze. It's almost as good as sex,' he said to no one in particular. His daughters blushed.

'As you command, my lord, so I obey. I accompanied my king to Cadbury and we saw the great Artor in his hall. I heard my king attack his liege lord over the actions of the spymaster, Trystan, whom King Mark held accountable for the seduction of his wife, the Lady Iseult. King Mark became furious and threatened the High King when Artor refused to punish Trystan for what he deemed to be a family matter. I became concerned for my own safety and that of my companions, especially when an attempt was made on King Artor's life soon afterwards.'

'Do you know anything about that assassination attempt? Anything at all? Do not fear to speak, for I have already granted you immunity.'

Gerallt stared down at the filthy figure of his late master with a combination of pity and disgust clearly evident in his eyes. Mark felt the young man's gaze and stared up at his erstwhile vassal. The king's face was blank and uncomprehending, as if his senses had been driven out of his addled head, but Gerallt caught a flash of something crafty, as if a grey rat had scuttled across the bleak orbits of Mark's eyes, leaving only an impression of a long, scaly tail.

'I heard nothing of any such plot . . . not a whisper. But . . .'

The pause was evocative, as if Gerallt struggled with something internally.

'You must answer, regardless of how trivial the information seems with hindsight. No man here will blame you if you speak openly,' Bran repeated, as if he could read Gerallt's mind.

'The night before the assassination attempt, I undertook the task of evaluating the defensive ditches surrounding Cadbury . . .'

There was some muffled laughter as most of the listening men decided that the Deceangli warrior was either seeking out a willing woman or taking a piss, both good reasons to be abroad late at night. Gerallt pulled himself together and continued.

'I heard voices in a corner outside the king's hall, out of the wind. I could see Artor's guard posted on the entry gate to the forecourt, but I had thought I was the only other person outside on a cold night that was threatening snow. My curiosity was roused. Because of the hour, I used stealth to approach the place the voices were coming from, for a prudent man takes care when he is in a strange fortress.'

Bran nodded. Gawayne grinned knowingly and whispered something indelicate to his elder daughter, who blushed hotly. Meanwhile, Gerallt registered every flicker of emotion that crossed the faces of the assembled kings and drew strength from their obvious neutrality.

'As I neared the walls, I recognised Mark's voice. He was having a discussion with a man in a black cloak. There was no light so I couldn't see them clearly, but their shapes stood out against the brilliant white of a light snow cover. My king sounded very angry and was protesting intemperately. I heard him say that he'd have nothing to do with it, because he felt that it would fail. I confess I felt a twinge of suspicion, so I pressed myself back against the wall in case I was discovered. I couldn't hear what the other man said, but he laughed unpleasantly and my master sounded afraid. When they parted, I wished I could sink into the earth, because that cloaked figure radiated danger.'

'Did you recognise him?' Bran demanded hoarsely. Common sense told him that Gerallt must have been very close to the conspirators if he heard parts of the conversation. 'Can you prove what you say?'

'I saw Mark's face clearly and I know his voice, so I could not have made any mistake. Then, when the cowled man walked past the niche where I had concealed myself, a stray shaft of moonlight revealed the lower half of his face, which was clean-shaven. I would wager on the soul of my mother that he was Prince Modred, the bastard son of Queen Morgause of the Otadini tribe and the king of the Brigante.'

A storm of noise greeted this pronouncement and Scoular ap Seosamh cringed. The scar-faced warrior behind him cried out in disbelief, then Bran lifted one hand and the crowd gradually became silent. 'Are you absolutely certain, Gerallt ap Cadwy? There is no shame in doubting what you saw or heard on a dark and cold night near to three years ago, but if you have any reservations you must voice them now.'

'I'm certain, King Bran. I wished I weren't, for I had no desire to serve any man who would attempt to kill his sovereign lord by stealth. When word came to us that a bowman had tried to bring down the High King from a concealed position in a tree, I suspected that Mark and Modred had been plotting together, but I comforted myself with Mark's words of refusal when I overheard him arguing with Modred. I tried to tell myself that I had misunderstood the nature of the disagreement entirely but, try as I might, I could not rid myself of the suspicion that my master had been involved in treasonous discussions with Modred. When word came from Lady Morgan that King Lot and Queen Morgause had been assassinated, we had already left Cadbury and were safely back in Canovium. Like the other lords of the Deceangli tribe, I heard the rumours, but so much happened in such a short time that any further consideration of what I had seen and heard was driven out of my head. The king had just killed Trystan out of hand and Queen Iseult had committed suicide, so the palace was at sixes and sevens for some weeks.'

Bran brushed away domestic considerations with an impatient wave of his hand. 'When did you learn that you would be forced to fight with the Brigante and the Picts against your fellow Celts?'

For the first time, Gerallt hung his handsome head.

'The king called us to his hall. All the lords had been summoned, high and low, regardless of status. Any man with warriors at his command was ordered to attend the king in Canovium. Queen Iseult had only recently been laid into the ground, and Mark was ashen, angry and excited, all at the same time. We had no idea what would be demanded of us.'

'And what *was* demanded of you? Have no doubt, Gerallt alp Cadwy, the Deceangli people now stand low in the eyes of the people of the west. Some form of explanation would be prudent. Why should we try to understand your treason and your cowardice? Much hangs on the reason you are now called upon to give.' Bran spoke in his usual calm manner but Gerallt could see a softening in his eyes. Perhaps the rift between the Deceangli and Ordovice tribes could still be healed.

'Our king told us that Modred was the legitimate heir of Artor, who was old and like to die in the next few years. When we protested that King Gawayne stood higher in the chain of legitimacy, Mark brushed our words aside, saying that Gawayne was fully occupied in keeping the Saxons out of his lands beyond the wall. Modred was closer to our lands and had the backing of the powerful Brigante tribe. He told us that he had already made his mark on a treaty with the Brigante that would protect our borders, so we were already guilty of treason by virtue of that agreement. Whatever we did from that point onwards, the High King would try to destroy us, regardless of our feelings on the matter. We knew we were guilty by association, for Mark was our legitimate king. What were we to do? We argued among ourselves and wanted to defy him and to assassinate him if it was at all possible, but the guard was always present with their swords drawn and ready for use. Mark's unspoken message was very clear to all of us. We prayed for time to persuade our king to change his mind, but we were defeated by his show of force at every opportunity. We should have resisted him as a group, but we distrusted each other and he used our mutual suspicions against us. We swore to ourselves that we'd not raise our swords against our brothers, but we found ourselves far from home and in a Brigante camp before we fully realised what our king had done. By then, it was too late to mount a concerted protest.'

'Did you raise your sword against your kin, Gerallt?' Gawayne called from his seat.

'No, King Gawayne, I did not,' Gerallt answered firmly, his chin jutting aggressively as if he considered his word might be doubted. 'I was grateful when we fled from the battlefield behind our king, despite my shame. I had never believed I would ever run from combat, but better my hand should be cut off at the wrist than it should raise a weapon against a fellow tribesman. I led my warriors back to their homes in Caer Narfon and then waited on the judgement of the kings. I will willingly accept their punishment for my weakness and vacillation.'

Bran turned to face the shamefaced contingent from Canovium. 'And was this experience the same for all the tribal lords of the Deceangli?'

'I cannot swear for all my tribe, but it was true for most, if not every leader among our warriors.' Gerallt did not hesitate in his response, so his peers swallowed their fears and nodded in turn.

'We've received an object lesson that applies to every man in this council.' Bran addressed the assembled kings. 'This treason blossomed because good men became suspicious of each other and failed to stand forth to support the rightful High King because they feared reprisals against their families. If we are to have any hope of succeeding against the Saxons, we must present a united front and trust that our allies will come to our aid when we are imperilled. This man who stands before us has shown how easily he was cut away from like-minded peers until he ultimately found himself branded a traitor – without raising his sword in anger against those who oppressed him.'

The kings looked at each other with guarded eyes. Their understanding of Bran's message was clearly written on the faces of even the more conservative rulers.

'Do any of the Brigante lords have the courage to explain themselves?' Bran asked. 'I understand that their new king had a price placed on his head during Modred's rule, despite being far from the seat of power. I ask one of your leaders to stand forth and face your accusers. Some justification must be offered to explain your actions.'

As he spoke, the queen's lady slid back into her seat beside her mistress. 'I have been told that the young man who attracted your attention is called Idris ap Cadwy and he is the natural son of the Deceangli lord who was speaking just now. He was fostered some years ago to a Brigante kinsman called Cadwy Scarface, who is going to speak to this meeting.'

'He is a very interesting and attractive young man,' Anna whispered reflectively. 'He has the look of a fledgling eagle and the leashed energy of a good hound. He stands at the centre of two houses that are caught up in accusations of treason, yet his eyes are clear and his face is open to the scrutiny of anyone. He seems fearless.'

'His foster-father is about to speak.' The queen's servant pointed to a huge, greying warrior who had risen wearily to his feet and was lumbering towards the centre of the amphitheatre to face the tribal kings.

'The boy is watching him with his heart in his eyes,' Anna whispered, looking from Idris to the careworn, ugly face of the Brigante warrior. 'This Scarface cannot be a total monster if he has earned such adoration.'

The man raised his eyes to the assembled kings with an obvious effort, and Anna felt a frisson of admiration for the ageing warrior's courage. 'I am Cadwy Scarface. I'll not give my father's name, for I have brought shame on his memory. I stood with Bedwyr in the front line at Moridunum, where I got this love tap from a Saxon warrior. We brothers stood together in Artor's army, shoulder to shoulder and ankle-deep in blood behind the bodies of the Saxon dead. Those of us who were there on those three days when King Artor smashed the Cymru invaders for ever are linked by memories far more potent than tribal allegiance. Lord Bedwyr reminded me of this bond at the ford where Modred and Mark led us into perfidy.'

'Do you deny your part in the civil war that tore our realms apart?' Bran demanded.

Cadwy Scarface fell to his knees and raised his head to face the stares of his peers. 'I do not deny my part in the civil war. I was ordered by my king to make war on the High King and those who called him their master. I have served many kings with a good and trusting heart and I have grown old killing our Saxon enemies. My first loyalty is to my people, and I placed my love for the west second. Perhaps that preference is my greatest sin, for I do know that men must forgo their tribal concerns for the demands that will be placed on the heads of all Britons in the years that lie ahead. I can see the necessity, Lords of the West, but I cannot change my ways or influence the beliefs of other men. I sinned because I loved my tribe over all other considerations. For that patriotism, you may do with me what you will.'

'Don't kneel to us, Cadwy Scarface. My uncle, King Artor, would tell you not to be a fucking fool. He always understood the ways of the warrior, and defended men who served loyally regardless of the honour of their masters. He was fond of saying that if a good sword was wielded by a graceless fool, then the sword wasn't at fault. I, for one, have no argument with you, swordsman of the Brigante. We have fought together often enough.'

King Gawayne's speech was followed by a coughing fit that caused his younger daughter to produce honeyed wine and a goblet from her pack. Gawayne leaned back on his cushions. He was well pleased with his outburst, for several of his peers were looking guiltily down at their hands.

'Few men understand the ties of binding oaths and personal loyalties more keenly than Artor did.' Bedwyr added his voice to Gawayne's. 'For this reason alone, I acquit this warrior of treason and only hold him guilty of obeying his oaths of fealty when he knew they were wrong. I, too, have bled with Cadwy Scarface and have no desire to see him die because his master was a cur.'

'Nor I,' cried Pelles, quickly followed by Bors, two warriors who had served Artor long and well. 'We have all been guilty of deeds that caused us pain or shame for the sake of oaths given to our masters. Such is the cost of personal loyalty. Artor himself admitted that his actions at Melandra were prompted by his grief at the murder of his friend King Luka. Many of us were privy to his regrets. Yes, we who obeyed his orders sometimes believed that his actions were extreme, and were likely to cause resentment for decades to come. But we obeyed because Artor was our king and we were oath-bound to him. There is little difference between Cadwy Scarface and any one of us, except that his master was a murderous traitor while ours was a man of innate decency under his rage and loss.'

'We who remember the days of glory do not wish to sully Artor's memory with petty reprisals against worthy men,' Bors added, while around him other warriors remembered his long service to his kinsman over many years of warfare and tribulation. These men had earned the right to decide Cadwy Scarface's fate.

Bran bowed his head and assisted Scarface to rise to his feet. 'You are free, Cadwy, to add your sword to those of us who will mount the defence of the west. I hope we never reach this parlous state of affairs again.'

'I swear now that I will freely give my allegiance to all the kings of the Union of the West and hope for peace in the life that is to come,' Cadwy Scarface said in a voice so soft and emotional that few of those present heard all his words. 'May I die in the defence of all these lands, not just Brigante soil, for I and my fellow Brigante tribesmen already bear the curse of the Mother Goddess. Whatever comes to the Britons, whether it is shameful defeat, victory or a bloody death, I will always honour my oath.'

No man doubted him as he limped back to his seat in a hall that had settled into a thoughtful silence. Somehow the pleasure of laying all the blame for their losses at Mark's door seemed simplistic and mindlessly vengeful.

Then, from above, an owl screamed its hunting call of triumph and the air was filled with barred wings and sharp talons. The bird swooped over the assembled kings, its wicked claws spread to catch and kill, before it turned in mid-flight, as if the air had become solid. Then, with a few rapid beats of its wings, the great bird rose upward to the open roof in a long spiral before settling on a charred rafter. It gazed down at the humans below with unblinking yellow eyes.

'She is here,' Taliessin, the king's singer, said aloud in surprise. 'The goddess deigns to preside over this trial, and she is reminding us that our duties haven't been completed.'

Whether Christian or pagan, the kings touched their crosses or the runes at their throats in sudden dread. In broad daylight, at a time when such birds normally slept, the owl looked down at their upturned faces and swivelled its head to impale each one with its wide, yellow glare.

'We are reminded that she who must not be named has lost her favourite son, the Dragon's Child. Before us sits Mark, taking his ease while better men have admitted to their sins and errors.' Bran's voice was implacable and as cold as iron. 'What say you, Mark? Can you justify your treasons? Or will you go into the darkness, mute and cowardly?'

Shockingly, Mark began to giggle, the noise ugly in the context of the deadly punishment that lay over him. 'What does this nonsense matter? You'll do as you like anyway. I welcome death. Anything is better than having to spend another day in that pesthole in the ground.'

Then, sickeningly, he picked at his flesh with skeletal fingers tipped by talons that were every inch as long as those of the owl above him. Had the guard not cuffed him, he would have eaten the scabs from his own wounds.

'He's mad,' Gawayne muttered with a curse.

'He'd certainly like you to think so,' the Deceangli king muttered softly, but his voice was still loud enough for the kings near him to hear his warning. 'Mark is as he has always been, as cunning as a rat. He'll eat shit and drink piss if that keeps him alive. After all, he's survived when his master couldn't manage to keep his head.'

'I should have killed you when I had the chance,' Mark said conversationally to his kinsman. Then, with a speed that seemed impossible for someone so emaciated, he threw himself from his stool and lurched towards Deinol ap Delwyn with his skeletal hands outstretched to grip and tear.

But Mark had been weakened by the effects of starvation, and Deinol ap Delwyn's guard had no difficulty in intercepting him. A tall, red-haired warrior knocked Mark flat on his back while another warrior drew his sword and pressed it against the traitor's corded neck.

'Kill me then!' Mark crowed, with a voice as high as the cry of rooks in a distant wood. 'Prove how brave you are by killing an unarmed man,' and he pressed his throat against the sword point, forcing the warrior to lean away.

'No!' Deinol ap Delwyn ordered with unusual authority, for he was normally a passive and friendly young man. 'Too much Deceangli honour has been lost because of you, Mark. I'll not stain the consciences of good warriors with the guilt of your death, even if you sink those claws into my eyes. You disgust me.'

'Hold him down,' Bran ordered. 'He refuses to speak for himself in a rational manner, so I ask the kings to pass judgement upon him.'

'This is no court,' Mark snarled, rising shakily to his feet and dragging his blanket around his lean flanks. 'I've sat among you time after time and listened to you whisper treasons against Artor when you disagreed with his orders. You are hypocrites!'

Several kings looked away from his mad black eyes.

'None of you has the right to judge me. Given my choices, you'd have betrayed Artor for gold and land as readily as I did. You don't have the right.' The last words were howled almost maniacally, and spittle flew from his toothless, rotten gums.

'*We* have the right.'

A stern voice fell into the shocked stillness with the grating violence of a sword dragged along a metal breastplate. 'The citizens of Deva who were betrayed by you and your hell-spawn master have the right to call you to account and pass judgement on you.'

The man who spoke had stood at the back of the hall with a group of other men whose grave faces, half-healed wounds, amputations and plain clothing marked them as both ordinary citizens and victims.

'I am Causus Gallio, often referred to as the Gaul. My father was a member of the council of Deva, but in his youth he had served with the Romans in Gaul under Flavius Aetius. He retired to Deva as a trader in wool and lead, so I was born a Briton, and my children were also born on this hallowed soil. For generations, Deva has served as a sanctuary for all natives of these islands and as a conduit for the wealth that came from the new tribal traders of the Middle Sea. The Roman Empire may be dead, but Deva presented a sense of order and honour in an uncertain world. My wife is a Brigante woman, or she was until the Picts raped her to death in the fall of Deva. My father died at the city gates with the other members of Deva's council as they attempted to parlay with you and your evil master. They were unarmed. They were killed where they stood, like felons rather than true Britons. I claim the right to judge you and to be your executioner, as do my fellow citizens, those who have suffered and bled because of your greed.'

'I played no part in Deva's destruction,' Mark protested, as the men with Causus strode, limped and hobbled to the centre of the hall. But the words came out as a whine rather than an accusation. 'Modred chose to send a message to Artor which told the High King that the old ways were gone and finished. You were his victims, not mine.'

'But you said nothing to Modred that could have saved us,' roared an old-young man with wild eyes and a crazed expression.

His face had a red scar that ran from his right eyebrow across his nose to his jaw, while his arm had a wrapped stump where his forearm and hand had once been. 'I am Jacobus ap Lorweth, and my kin are both Roman and Deceangli. My mother was born within spitting distance of your accursed hall, Mark, and she was killed in her own house while surrounded by her grandchildren. Why did you permit the Picts to kill children, you traitorous bastard? Why did you turn your face away from your own people?'

'You have the right, citizens of Deva, to demand reparation from all of the Deceangli nobles assembled here.' Bran's voice was hard, for he had found it difficult to hear the stories of these two men and learn that they were true Britons who had been irreparably wronged by Modred and Mark.

'I have been appointed as the new magistrate of Deva since the old was executed by Modred,' Causus said slowly. He gathered his gravitas around his stocky form as if he were donning an invisible cloak. 'We have decided already that we will not call for judgement on anyone but Mark, a man who had the power to save our people, but chose to remain silent and comply with the orders issued by Modred. Perhaps the Matricide would have stayed his hand had Mark insisted. Perhaps it is Mark who should take the ultimate responsibility for the actions of the traitors.'

'Then you may announce your judgement,' Gawayne called from the Otadini camp. 'It is clear to me that you are owed a large portion of the blood price paid by Mark's and Modred's tribes, and that this traitor should be judged by the people of Deva.'

Voices rose in vociferous agreement. Inured to the predictable moral weakness of the kings, Bran smiled sardonically at their eagerness to pass on the unpleasant task of judgement to other shoulders. He was aware that many of them must be feeling a twinge of guilt at Deva's fate, for Artor was the only ruler who had made any attempt to save the city.

The men of Deva conferred briefly, and then Causus Gallio faced the assembly.

'Then we demand the body and soul of this creature. He would welcome death as a release, so we decree that he shall live. He dreads any return to the cells of Deva, so we decree that he shall rot there. I hope that he will remember the dead of our city until his last breath, and I pray that his victims visit him during the long nights and cluster around him until he howls to his gods for release. Even then, we will keep his husk alive to suffer as we have suffered. As my father often said: *So let it be written: so let it be done.*'

Mark began to shriek in a voice far more powerful than his ruined body should have permitted. As he was dragged away, he begged for a clean death, beating at the breastplates of his guards with ineffectual fists. When this tactic failed, he swore vile insults in a futile attempt to goad them into striking him down and killing him. The kings sat like stone, their faces turned away from Mark's shame, until the sounds of his despair faded and stillness returned to King Artor's hall.

Then, with a great beating of wings and a cry of exultation, the owl took to the air, swooped low over the heads of the assembled lords, and with unnatural speed swept upwards through the burned rafters until it disappeared into the sun-drenched daylight.

'The goddess has received her sacrifice and has departed,' Taliessin murmured, and ran his fingers over his harp strings with a sound identical to the beating of unseen wings.

The judgement of Mark, former king of the Deceangli tribe, had been completed. It was time now to begin the serious discussion of securing the future of tribal Britain.

MASTER BEDWYR'S FAMILY TREE

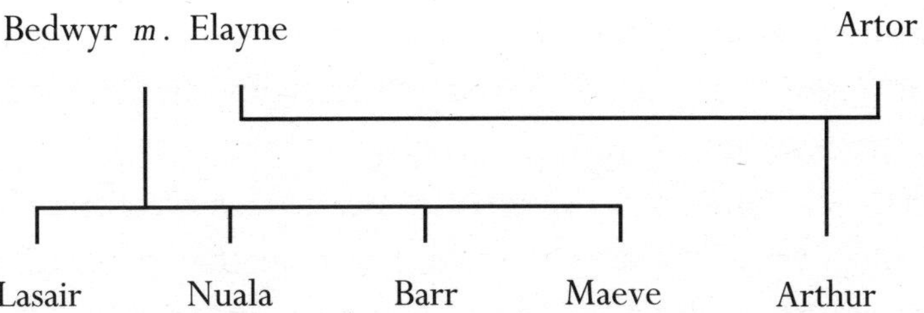

KING ARTOR'S FAMILY TREE

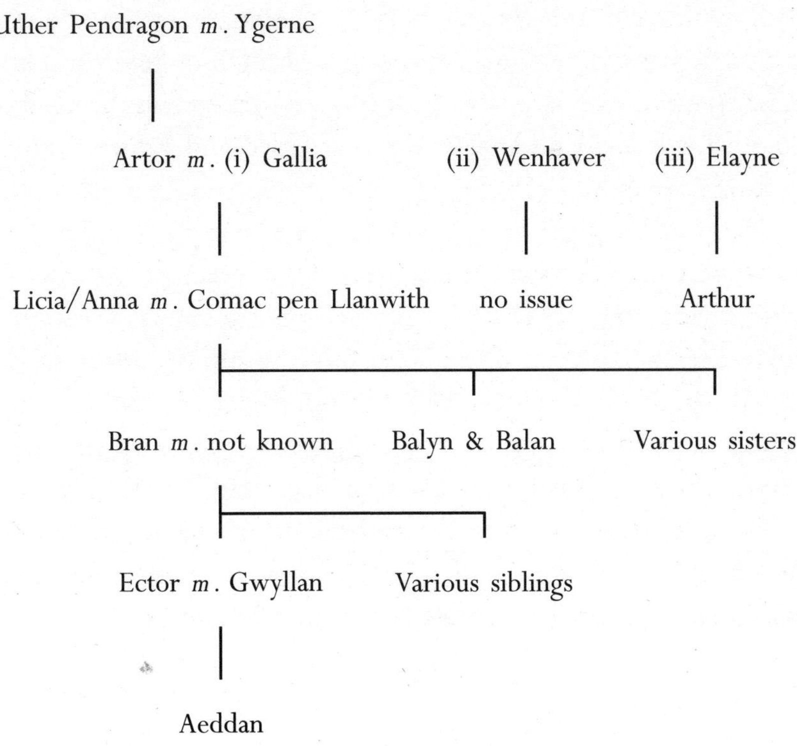

The Family Tree of King Bors Minor

N.B. Bors Major was the younger brother of Gorlois (married to Ygerne). She married Uther Pendragon after the death of Gorlois. Morgan and Morgause were sired on Ygerne by Gorlois, while Uther Pendragon was the sire of Artorex.

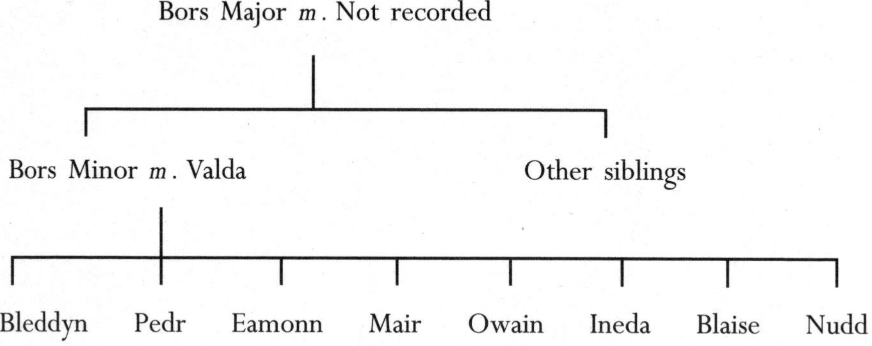

King Gawayne's Family Tree

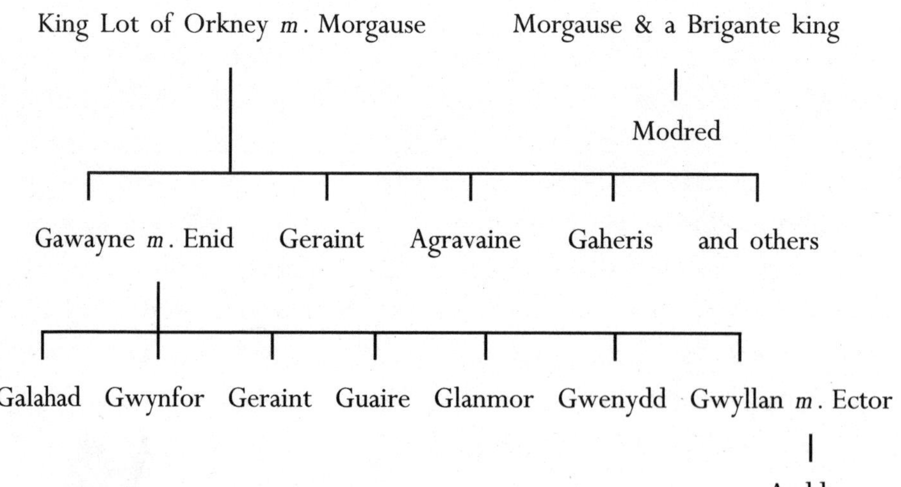

CHAPTER III

IDYLL

> A single sparrow should fly swiftly into the hall, and coming in at one door, instantly fly out through another. In that time in which it is indoors it is indeed not touched by the fury of the winter, but yet, this smallest space of calmness being passed almost in a flash, from Winter going into Winter again, it is lost to your eyes.
>
> The Venerable Bede, *Ecclesiastical History of the English People*

'Mother! Look!'

The shrill piping of pleasure came from high in an ancient oak, and for one short moment Elayne felt a thrill of fear for her wayward eldest son. He had climbed far too high for a boy of seven, and she could barely make out his wildly curling russet hair among the autumn leaves of the canopy.

Seven years! Such a long time, yet no day passed without a tangible memory of the man who had fathered her first child. As she stroked the weathered bark of the venerable oak, she was reminded of the mental strength of the last High King of the Britons. He had been strong, firm and age seared, like a tree that has seen every vicissitude of man: fire, the axe, and the destructive waste of the sword. But the heart of the man, like the tree, was still sound and growing. Time had taken away his keen eyesight and the strength of his arms, but nothing could dim the intelligence and the sympathy in his clear grey eyes.

How she missed their talks, those long afternoons when they had walked through the echoing halls of Cadbury. Artor had been the only man who had ever valued her talent for detecting guile and lies, who understood her as a person and not as a potential mother who could add to the glory of her tribe. Had he been younger, would they have cleaved to each other, thigh to thigh and breast to breast? But such thoughts were disloyal, unworthy and pointless, for Artor had gone into the great darkness while she was the wife of his most loyal vassal, Bedwyr of Arden. A single night, time out of time, when king and lady had been threatened by the coldness of death, had been all that fate had permitted. Yet Fortuna, or God, had ordained that one last gift should be proffered to a man who had given away everything of personal value. Before he died, he had known that he had fathered a son.

'Mother? You're not watching!' a petulant voice called out from the crown of the tree. 'Look up here, Mother! The world is quite different from upside down.'

Her wayward son was laughing as he swung on the wind, his knees hooked over a sturdy branch so that his long curling hair hung down below his merry, fearless face. With her heart in her mouth, Elayne tried not to reveal her panic. 'Come down, Arthur! At once! Your cousin Ector will soon be here with his betrothed. What will they think if they find you abed with broken limbs because you were showing off in a tree? You're not a little boy any longer.'

Arthur swung upward and gripped the branch with two dirty,

grass-stained hands that were large for a boy of his age. As agile as an eel, or the otters that frolicked in the rivers where the pools were deep and leaf dappled, the boy scrambled down the tree, his small face screwed up with uneasiness.

'You won't tell Ector, will you, Mother? He'd laugh at me for playing like a baby.' Arthur was so distressed that he slipped as he dropped from the lowest branch and a twiglet scored his forearm from elbow to wrist.

Although she was heavy with child, Elayne swung his strong, growing body into a warm embrace. He squirmed with embarrassment under her caresses, but nevertheless permitted his mother to wipe away the line of blood from his arm before kissing his cheek and releasing him.

'Your nurse is waiting, Arthur, and she will be cross if she lacks the time to bathe and dress you for Ector's visit. What will Ector's beloved think if you look like a beggar or an urchin, with leaves in your hair and your hands as dirty as the paws of a farmer's boy? Old Caitlin will be shamed before her king.' Although her tone of voice was mock-serious, the boy remained sunny tempered while Lady Elayne plucked a stray dried leaf from his curls and planted a kiss on his broad forehead.

'Besides,' she said with a secretive smile. 'We have a very special visitor coming with Ector on this occasion. Taliessin mentioned him when he visited us last winter, and you might have heard tales of his exploits. Then again, you may not know of him, because boys are notoriously bored by stories of old men.'

The lad looked closely at his mother with a narrow, measuring gaze that almost stopped her heart. Artor had examined faces just so, carefully and coldly, and she was swept back to another time and place, when she had been in great peril but had become gloriously and deliriously alive.

At such times, Elayne felt shame at the vividness of her memories. Here, in the Forest of Arden, they were untroubled by the world outside its borders. She was able to forget the first year of her marriage, the peril of Bedwyr's journey into the north with Percivale and Galahad, and the vicious hatred of Queen Wenhaver that had made her sojourn in Cadbury so dangerous. But the scent of the wind on icy mornings, the cry of a hunting hawk high above the trees, or even the smell of burning logs in the depths of winter, could speed her back to that other time, and that other Elayne, who had yet to learn the taste of womanly tears.

A tug on her sleeve pulled her back into the present. 'Are you playing with me, Mother? Who is our visitor? You haven't told me whom Ector plans to marry, so the stranger could be anyone. You just want me to be good and not complain about having to take a bath. But I'd have one anyway . . . because Ector is coming.'

'I always play fair with you, sweetling, but I *have* been teasing you. Ector is to marry Gwyllan, whose name means seagull. She is the daughter of . . .' Elayne allowed her voice to fade away, dragging out the pause until Arthur jumped up and down with impatience.

'Who, Mother? Who? You're teasing me again!'

His face screwed up and she saw a brief flash of anger pass redly through his grey-green eyes. But then it was gone as fast as it had appeared, to be replaced by a cheeky grin. 'Our visitor is no one important. You just want me to be good and remain quiet.'

'Ah, sweetling, the man of whom we speak is King Gawayne of the Otadini. He was the right hand of King Artor, and he was the west's greatest swordsman in his younger days.'

'Is he the father of Prince Galahad who sought and died for the Cup? The nephew of King Artor?' The boy's eyes were so wide that they were almost starting out of his head. 'Truly? King Gawayne is coming *here*?'

'Yes, Arthur, he is. King Gawayne is coming here, so be off with you to your bath, or he'll think you're a young Saxon rather than a true-born Celt.'

In fact, all the Cornovii lords, high and low, knew that Bedwyr had not sired the cuckoo in his nest, but none dared lay the name *cuckold* on such a noble warrior. Moreover, Lady Elayne was universally loved by all who lived in Arden Forest, so though the peasantry whispered around the winter fireplaces that young Arthur had been fathered by a great warrior, the most able in the land, no one was willing to name the dead high king. And so the boy grew without care for or knowledge of his birthright, exactly as his father had intended. The isolation of Arden Forest protected the lad from the scrutiny of those Celtic lords who would have guessed his parentage from a single glance at his wild hair. Bedwyr had even grown to like the boy, for in his grey-green eyes and calm face the Cornovii lord could see all that remained of his beloved master, now long buried in the wet earth of holy Glastonbury.

So matters stood in the year of our Lord 527, when Ector and his father led a loose confederation of western tribes that were seeking to keep the Saxon menace at bay. And now they had come to the Forest of Arden on a visit that would change the pleasant days of Arthur's childhood out of all recognition.

The retinue that rode up to the wooden hall and spreading house of Bedwyr Slave-scar was fine indeed. Ector of the Ordovice, the chosen heir of King Artor, was a young warrior of seventeen years whose dark hair and flashing eyes bore the stamp of otherness, that odd quality some men possess that sets them apart. He was a little above middle height, and had the unmistakable muscle of a skilled fighting man. He rode a large stallion of a rich dun colour that pawed the earth when he drew it to a halt, as if it were still eager to gallop wildly and only obeyed its master because it judged Ector's will to be stronger than its own.

Beside him, a woman sat astride a white hill pony. A long veil obscured her face and protected her complexion from the weak sun and the dust of the road. Fine kidskin gloves covered her hands, and the wool of her cloak was finely woven with a pattern of checks in dull green and dark blue. As Ector assisted her to dismount, she lifted her veil, and the crowd that had gathered in welcome saw the face of Gwyllan, the daughter of King Gawayne, for the first time. Their indrawn breath paid tribute to her beauty without the need for words.

Gawayne had always been a handsome, charismatic man, and elements of his blond beauty had been inherited by his daughter. Her skin was like his: fine and thin and very fair, with a light feathering of golden down that caught the light with a shimmer like gold dust. Her mother, Queen Enid, who had not made the long journey to the Forest of Arden, had been a dark, tiny beauty in her youth, and it was from her that Gwyllan had inherited the thick, dark brown hair that was as glossy as a horse's tail and braided in long plaits that fell almost to her knees. Her brows were also dark and fine over guileless blue eyes that, like Gawayne's, glowed with intelligence and sensitivity. Her fragile strength, her tiny voluptuousness and the delicacy of her bone structure brought out protectiveness in any man with red blood in his veins.

Gawayne must have been busy keeping the young bucks away from this one, Bedwyr thought with a wry smile. An appropriate punishment for a reformed womaniser! Bedwyr had first seen the girl at Deva when Mark had been brought to justice, but in the intervening years the daughter of Gawayne had grown into a beautiful woman, a female whose every movement spoke of sexual promise. Even Bedwyr felt the tug of that innocent invitation and his loins tightened against his will, so that the ageing warrior was reminded again that a man was forever prey to the devils of his sexual appetite.

Anna and Bran had accompanied the young lovers. Bran and Ector had visited Arden on many occasions, for Bedwyr was a trusted ally who guarded the approaches to the Ordovice lands. But, despite her liking for the forest master, Anna had never joined them before, for she had felt a certain apprehension at the likelihood of meeting Elayne and her son. However, the coming nuptials had forced the issue. Throwing caution to the winds, she decided to travel with the wedding party to visit their Cornovii allies. There, she could observe the boy and his mother, and perhaps satisfy her hopes that her father's old friend was happy at last.

'You have too many trees here, Bedwyr, not to mention rabbit holes that are determined to finish me off.' A booming voice drowned the jumble of courteous welcomes from Bedwyr and Elayne. 'Help me off this fucking horse. I'm an old man and long rides are becoming too difficult for me.'

The last great legend of the west, King Gawayne of the Otadini, dismounted with a boy's grace, putting the lie to his complaints of decrepit old age. Straightening his back slowly and surveying the stout defences set into a copse of mature oaks, Gawayne nodded and acknowledged the crisp, disciplined admiration of the warriors manning the palisades. In return, they honoured him with a wholly Roman salute, their fists thudding against the centre of their breasts.

Gawayne was as grey as an old lion, the creature he most resembled. His hair was a wild long bush around his head, resembling a mane, and his handsome features still retained the ghost of his old beauty, although his jowls sagged and deep pouches below his blue eyes revealed the many years he had lived. His gaze remained as open and as welcoming as ever, so women still blushed when he patted their cheeks, or other parts of their bodies. Even Elayne flushed as she acknowledged the flair of this man who had entranced three extraordinary women. Queen Enid of the north, Queen Wenhaver of the Britons and Mistress Miryll from Salinae were all great beauties, and while no one spoke openly of Miryll's pregnancy and death, many stories had been sung of Gawayne's legendary charm.

Introductions were made with due pomp and ceremony. With pride, Bedwyr introduced his eldest son, red-haired Lasair who was six years old and a fine, sturdy boy. The next child was a daughter, whom Elayne had called Nuala in honour of an aunt who lived beyond the Hibernian Sea. The small, red-haired girl was five and she giggled when Gawayne swept her up into his arms and tickled her chin. The youngest was another boy, Barr, who was little more than a toddler and darker in colouring than his siblings. He bowed low, and almost fell in his eagerness to demonstrate his new-found skill. Gwyllan was charmed and clapped her hands in congratulation, while little Barr blushed a bright, beetroot red.

'And this is Arthur,' Bedwyr said, without any further embellishment.

If Arthur was embarrassed at being ranked below his baby sister, it didn't show in his eager face. Like a miniature young man, he stepped forward and made his bow, producing a posy of wild flowers from behind his back and offering it to Gwyllan with a brilliant smile.

'These flowers are for my lady,' he murmured, 'but they are not as fair as you.'

Anna's heart stuttered with shock as she realised she had always suspected the truth. Indisputably, she recognised the wildly curling hair that had been forced into some kind of order, and the tall, loose-limbed grace that set him apart from his siblings. Anna paled a little and looked away.

'Goodness!' Gwyllan laughed gaily, unaware of a sudden undercurrent beneath the courtesies of the meeting. 'A little gentleman! Thank you, Arthur. How lovely your flowers are.'

Any awkwardness over Arthur's appearance was dissipated by the charm of his simple gift. Ector grinned proudly, and Bran nodded his approval. Only Anna and Gawayne were silent, and Elayne glanced at them nervously. She could tell by their expressions that they recognised the man in the face and form of the boy.

Gawayne had not been told that Artor had fathered one last child on Lady Elayne, so the presence of Arthur came as a shock. The boy he saw was tall for his age, wide shouldered and narrow of hip and with little of the baby fat that blurred the outlines of most children of seven. He had his father's red-gold hair, as wildly curly as Artor's had been, even into old age. Gawayne sensed his parentage at a glance, and felt a kick of love and presentiment under his breastbone. Then the boy turned to him with curious, measuring eyes and Gawayne felt like a young lad again under the fond regard of his own uncle. Although Arthur's eyes were different in colour, having a green rim around the irises, they examined the world with the same careful gaze. Gawayne returned the boy's bow, his face radiant.

Anna also felt her heart begin to ache. Her own hair had curled just so in childhood, and she recognised little mannerisms that had belonged to her father. The boy had cocked his head slightly to the right as he considered something, just as her father had done. She had feared this moment, this meeting with a child who could usurp the heritage of her beloved Bran and Ector, but she had not expected that the boy would be the image of her father.

'Hello, young Arthur,' she said softly, kneeling in the dust to look him in the eye. Fearlessly, he gazed back at her with a smile so wide it almost covered his face. 'Was it your idea to pick the flowers for Lady Gwyllan? If so, then you are a very courteous young man.'

'Mother says I'm an urchin, my lady. She says I will bring dishonour on the family if I don't mind my teachers. I can't see why anyone would care what I do, but Mother says everyone will be watching for me to make mistakes. Is that true, Lady Anna? Not that I think Mother would lie to me . . . but she might be exaggerating.'

'You're a little judge, I see!'

Listening, Gawayne smiled uncertainly, almost unwilling to believe that fate would leave this last cosmic joke to tease the Celts with what might have been. This exceptional boy was a bastard at best and not technically worthy to bear a sword.

'Your mother speaks the truth, Arthur,' he said carefully, for the child's eyes, compelling and clever, had turned to him. 'The world will watch you and look for any mistakes you might make. One day, your mother will tell you why you are a very important young man, and everything will then become clear to you. Meanwhile, your friends want you to grow to be a fine warrior who will bring great honour to your father's house.'

Gawayne had spoken quietly, but his voice carried to Bedwyr and Elayne who both flushed hotly, each reading correctly what Gawayne meant when he used the words 'your father's house'.

The moment was allowed to pass, and Bedwyr's home was soon boiling with servants preparing the obligatory feast. The master's hounds got under everybody's feet and the children were hustled away by their nurse. Like any good host, Bedwyr led the men to his personal room for a welcome cup of ale, while Elayne took Anna and Gwyllan to a small courtyard which she used for weaving and gossip with her women. Servants bustled to unpack the guests' saddle bags while ostlers saw to the horses and assisted the troop of cavalry who had escorted the guests. Meanwhile, the smell of roasting meat set mouths to salivating and nearly drove Bedwyr's hounds mad with anticipation. In a riot of colour, haste and energy, the day drew on.

Gawayne lifted his dirty boots onto a small table in Bedwyr's room and stretched his stiff muscles luxuriously. Although his body was at rest, his emotions were in turmoil at this new and unexpected development in the history of the west. Forever tactless, he was about to say the unthinkable and bring Bedwyr's secrets out into the light of day.

Smiling, he accepted a mug of ale. 'Bedwyr, my friend, you caught me by surprise when you presented your son to us, and I'm far too old to be given such a shock. It's none of my business, of course, but I thought I'd swallow the last of my few remaining teeth when I saw the boy.'

Appalled, Bedwyr stared back at his friend. So the secret was out. But then, perhaps it was best, after all, that Arthur's parentage should be considered by these three men, all kin to the boy, before he grew into manhood. He chose his words carefully.

'If you mean that Arthur is not my son, you are right, of course. I was angry at first . . . any man would be if he found himself in my shoes. But Artor and I had a long talk before the last battles, and he told me what had happened on the night of the snowstorm when Elayne was abandoned by Queen Wenhaver in that damned shelter and they were forced to lie together to conserve body heat. I was away with your son at the time, you remember. Of course, I knew that Elayne and Artor were fast friends and I was aware of the queen's jealousy, but I still believe that my wife didn't betray her vows willingly. Before you try to knock me flat on my backside, I'm not accusing the High King of rape, but when death seems very close few of us act normally. Elayne called that night "time out of time", and Artor was adamant that no blame should be cast on her. They had little protection from the storm during their hours of peril and both thought they would freeze to death before morning. I have come to believe that the pregnancy was the result of a single moment of weakness. Fate, if you like.'

Gawayne coughed apologetically and tried to hide a wry smile of self-knowledge. 'I never thought my uncle capable of that kind of weakness. He really must have thought that death was near. I never had any excuse when it came to the ladies, least of all imminent death.'

Bedwyr smiled briefly. 'I was angry for a long time, but Artor owned that the fault was his and pleaded for my forgiveness. You know what he was like. I couldn't stay angry with him when I considered the circumstances. He was only too aware of the implications of Arthur's birth, and, as usual, he tried to protect us all from any consequences of his folly. He wanted his son to grow to manhood without the burdens he had shouldered during his youth.'

'What a mess. No, really, Bedwyr, your boy is only seven years old and I could tell his lineage at a glance. Admittedly, there aren't too many men still living who can remember the young Artor, so time may be on your side, but what if the boy has ambitions? What if he seeks to raise himself above his station? He may be illegitimate, but he's the natural child of the last High King of the Britons.'

Bedwyr grimaced, but Ector came to his aid with the earnest sincerity of a fine young man. 'Arthur is a loyal little boy. He's been following me around like a puppy since he took his first steps. I don't believe for a moment that he'd try to steal my place or plot against my father. You only have to look into those changeable eyes of his to know that he's true and good, just like his father Bedwyr.'

'But Bedwyr isn't his father, is he? And the best youth can turn into a twisted man if he is robbed of hope,' Gawayne interrupted. 'Every boy hopes to exceed his sire in exploits and courage. How can he touch even a corner of Artor's greatness? Because he'll discover whose son he is, even if you manage to hide him until he's a grown man.'

He drained his horn mug in one gulp and then steepled his fingers in front of his face. 'I meant what I said to him, but really, of course, as a bastard he should be forbidden the study of weaponry and precluded from the role of a warrior. What would that mean to a young man like him? I remember when Myrddion Merlinus told me of the sense of loss *he* experienced as a boy when he learned that his birth barred him from full manhood. As a healer and a statesman, he became one of the most powerful men of our time, but that loss stayed with him into old age. You will have to be very careful in the way you raise the boy, Bedwyr.'

Bran had been silent throughout the conversation, but now he scratched his jaw and offered his opinion.

'Perhaps young Arthur should be told his whole history? And soon. If he is familiar with his birth and his background, it can't be used to poison his mind against us, or against others. Secrets can be fatal in the wrong hands. As for the status of warrior, why shouldn't he aspire to those heights? His birth has been shrouded in secrecy, so who will argue with Bedwyr if he decides his son should be trained to use sword, spear, shield and knife? And why not learn the use of the bow as well? Pelles would be happy to train the boy. I dare say he'd be overjoyed at the prospect, and he can be depended upon to keep his mouth shut.'

Gawayne frowned, and then grinned. 'Yes, Bran, you're right!

We will need every warrior we can find in the times that are upon us. Every Celt who dies in battle against the Saxons has taken twenty years to become fully grown, while ceols full of trained warriors keep arriving from Friesia and Saxony. If young Arthur has his father's skills, along with his looks, then he'll make a superb warrior for the west and help to lead us out of the wilderness. You're a cunning bugger, Bran. Just like your grandfather!'

Bran bridled a little at Gawayne's sardonic speech. He was genuinely fond of the boy, whom he knew to be forward and intelligent. He had been sure of his parentage from the first, not least because Artor's famed Dragon Knife had been taken by Bedwyr and passed to Elayne at Artor's express orders. Who but close kin would be chosen to receive such a gift? That knife had been owned by Artor since he was a very young man and was the only thing he had to give that was not entailed by the position of High King. If Gawayne's assessment was to be believed, the boy could be valuable to malcontents against the west, so it was far better that his skills should be used by kinsmen who cared for his best interests.

'Elayne loves the boy . . . all women worship their first-born child,' Bedwyr said. 'He reminds her of happier times. I'll not sacrifice Elayne's happiness, even for the sake of the west. Nor will I risk her peace of mind for you, Bran, or for you, Ector. She must decide if Arthur is to be told, because he is *her* son. You must agree that only Elayne has the right to make this choice for him.'

Anna wielded a long comb of fine carved bone and pulled the narrow tines through Gwyllan's long, lustrous hair. Her arm ached with the fierce insistence of approaching old age, deep in the shoulder joint, but she ignored the pain as Gwyllan purred under the rhythmic sweeps of the comb. This small duty was Anna's way of offering her own welcome to her new granddaughter by law, recognising that by this simple, pleasurable and domestic act she was building a bond between herself and the awed girl.

'My maidservant could have prepared my hair, Lady Anna. There is no need for you to trouble yourself,' Gwyllan protested, but Anna hushed her with a small sound.

'It is my pleasure to provide this small service to my grandson's beloved. We welcome you into our family in our various ways, my dear, and this small act is my gift. Your hair is lovely. It feels like fire-polished cloth, or the lovely fabric that Myrddion Merlinus gave me when I was a girl. He told me it came from far away in Constantinople, where the last of the Roman kings still reign in unbelievable luxury.'

'I have never heard of such a place,' Gwyllan whispered, and a world of longing lived in her voice.

'Do you so desire to fly, little seagull?' Anna asked, her voice sad and reflective, for women were unable to choose the directions of their lives. The higher her status, the less choice a girl had, so Gwyllan would never travel beyond the land of the Britons.

'Aye, Lady Anna, I do.' She smiled. 'I often dream of strange places in my sleep.' Then she covered her mouth with one hand as if she had spoken out of turn. 'Father will be cross if he learns what I have just said. Please, Lady Anna, don't tell him.'

Anna shook her head in confusion. The girl's large blue eyes were suddenly awash with unexpected tears, and Anna wondered what could trouble the girl so deeply.

'I don't understand, Gwyllan. Of course, I won't say anything to King Gawayne if you don't want me to, but why should your dreams distress him?'

'I have my great-aunt Morgan's gift of the Sight, and Father says I mustn't speak of it in case my husband learns of it. He is sure that Ector would cast me off if he knew about my affliction.'

Then the girl burst into a storm of weeping, just like a small child. Tears poured down her cheeks in salty runnels. Yet when other, less fortunate women would soon have red, puffy eyelids and blotchy cheeks, Gwyllan seemed even more attractive. Anna found the urge to protect the girl almost irresistible.

So this is glamour, she thought. The Lady of the Lake, the fair Nimue, had such a gift, but hers was the skill of persuasion. This child brings forth a protective instinct in both men and women. How very strange this gift is, and how foolish Morgan was to abuse it as she did.

'I cannot see how anyone could cast off a pretty little thing like you,' she murmured. 'Besides, such a gift can't be so very bad if it only comes in dreams.'

Gwyllan muttered something under her breath, but Anna could make no sense of the whispered words.

'Tell me, child. It's better you should tell me now than that I should hear about it later from someone else. Be brave, like the seagull, your namesake, and dare to speak aloud. Have you ever heard a quiet seagull? No one here will judge you.'

'I'm not always asleep when I have these dreams. Sometimes the feelings come when I least expect them and I'm wide awake. Oh, Lady Anna, you can't believe how frightening it is. No one else in the family seems to have inherited the curse. I've heard it said that Queen Ygerne had it too and passed it on to her daughter Morgan, but I never heard that King Artor knew what it felt like to see what is yet to be.'

Anna remembered her twin sons, Balyn and Balan, who had been cursed with a similar affliction so they had seemed to be one man divided in two. In the end, in a terrible misunderstanding, they had killed each other. Anna felt her throat thicken with an old sorrow.

'Truly, Gwyllan, we are kinfolk, distant but none the less real. My dead sons had an odd, extra sense that ultimately caused their deaths. Do you think I could hate and fear anyone who shared that wild gift? It would be like hating a part of my own self.'

Relieved, the girl threw herself into Anna's arms and hugged the older woman fiercely. 'I promise I will never harm Ector or any of your kin, Lady Anna. Ector is a lovely man, and a great warrior. I am sure that I will bear him sons, but sometimes I am fearful. I ask that you will forgive me if the curse comes on me.'

'You must tell me when the affliction is upon you, and I will protect you as best I can. If I should not be here to comfort you, then you must speak to the harpist Taliessin. He is the son of the Lady of the Lake and Myrddion Merlinus, so he understands what you feel. Nor should you consider your gift to be totally negative, for your family is very long lived. I have already outlived all of my childhood friends, while Morgan survived until her brain cracked. Your grandmother was poisoned, but she was preternaturally beautiful for a woman of her advanced age. Even King Artor was hale and vigorous at sixty when he died of wounds suffered in battle. God grants great strength to persons of your blood. Just look at Gawayne, who is near to seventy and still has all his wits. The Sight is merely a small part of this greater gift, but other men and women often feel terror when they hear of it, so you are wise to be silent. Nobody else must know of your affliction, even my grandson. Will you promise me, Gwyllan?'

The girl promised, just as Anna knew she would. Later, she couldn't understand what had impelled her to wring such an oath from Gwyllan, but somehow she knew it was important that the secret of the gift should be kept from all the other members of the family.

Then, as Anna heard the pipes and harps begin a shrill, wild melody that stirred her blood, she gave Gwyllan's hair one last pass of the comb so that the brown-black mane fell to the girl's knees in a sable wave. Finally, she used her thumbs to smooth away any trace of tears and ushered the maid towards the hall and the celebrations that had already begun.

That night and the following week passed with pleasure laid on pleasure. To supplement Bedwyr's winter stores, dwindling fast with so many extra mouths to feed, Gawayne suggested a hunt, which became a wild and wholly tribal celebration. Late into the night, the warriors ate, drank and danced wild ceremonies of the sword while the nobles looked on, their blood stirred by the wild gyrations. By day, the forest offered hunting and the pleasures of exploration, while the Cornovii king appeared with his retinue to bring further guests into Elayne's house. Heavily pregnant, yet like a general at war, she ran a team of servants who cooked, cleaned and foraged so that the forest's bounty of mushrooms, nuts, fruit and fish found its way onto her provident table.

The children ran like graceful hounds, hair flying and brown limbs flashing in the warm sunshine. Ahead of them all, fearless in his efforts to flush out game or birds for the noblemen's sport, Arthur proved his skill again and again, until Gawayne praised Bedwyr on the boy's woodcraft.

'Aye. He has a sense for the trees and an understanding of game. In the autumn, he keeps our pots full of rabbits and he has no fear of the task of killing his prey. Barr is more squeamish, but he's still a baby.' Bedwyr looked at the toddler with fondness as the child rolled and played among a pack of young puppies.

'You must teach the boy to ride soon. He'll keep your borders clean of Saxons if you give him the chance,' Bran suggested as he watched young Arthur lead Gawayne's huge horse by the reins, unafraid of the huge hooves and wild eyes of the battle-trained steed. 'He'll earn his keep if you make him a warrior. Just look at the size of his hands.'

Other people were also watching Arthur with careful eyes. Anna was searching for signs of the instability of temper that had blighted Balyn's life, but the boy remained sunny natured and excited by every aspect of the visit. Eventually, against all the unspoken rules of women of noble status, Anna decided to speak frankly to Lady Elayne.

She chose her time carefully. When the hunt was on, Elayne often snatched an hour or two with her feet up, for her pregnancy was tiring and her calves and ankles were swollen and painful. Elayne was always content to rest in her sheltered courtyard, surrounded by wooden walls that banished any stray winds. Here was children's clothing in need of mending and a distaff that sat in a rush basket with the washed lambswool that was waiting to be spun. Elayne would be relaxed and Anna might learn what she needed for her peace of mind.

After half an hour of hot, honeyed milk and desultory talk of weddings, babies and love, Anna asked her hostess if they could speak in private. Elayne eyed the older woman narrowly, for her quick intelligence guessed that her eldest son would be the topic of the proposed conversation. Reminding Anna of a mother wolf in her careful, guarded hostility, she dismissed her women and waited.

Anna looked at Elayne's stiff face and sighed. 'Before I say anything else, I must tell you that, contrary to established rumour, I'm Artor's daughter by a wife he took long before he married Wenhaver. I'm not a fool, Lady Elayne, and I remember my father in his youth. For that matter, I was young myself once, and my hair was much the same colour and texture as that mane of your son's.

I recognised Arthur's lineage the moment I saw him. How could I not know my own brother?'

'Bedwyr accepts that Arthur is our son,' Elayne said crisply. 'That is all you need to know, Lady Anna. I don't wish to be discourteous, but I don't owe you any explanations.'

Anna tried again. 'Please, Elayne? Your son and I share the same sire. Would you deny me?'

'I repeat, Lady Anna, that our household is happy and Arthur has a living father. He need never know otherwise.'

'Don't be naive, Elayne. I know you to be a woman of considerable common sense, because my father admired intelligence in his female confidantes and you would never have won his friendship without it. Your son is the heir of Artor, High King of the west. His very name could become a rallying cry, and unscrupulous men could capture him and claim the kingdom. You can't bury your head in the sand and hope that disaster won't come to your door.'

Elayne's face was perfectly blank, although when Anna looked into her host's green-gold eyes she saw no surprise in them. Elayne was obviously well aware of the dangers inherent in her eldest son's position.

'I have other concerns. King Bran and his son, Ector, are judged by the world to be all that is left of the glory of the west. Would you set your son up in opposition to them?'

'No. I'm not another Wenhaver who spends her days lusting after power, even from a cloistered nunnery. I merely demand the right to raise my eldest son in my own way. Surely Bedwyr and I have proved our loyalty to the west for time beyond reckoning.'

'I believe you, Elayne, so don't distress yourself unnecessarily. I did not imagine that you'd raise the boy to usurp the throne. But what of his future? Many men will see the boy and know his parentage at a glance. He will be branded as a bastard whatever you tell him. How will you protect him from the truth?'

Elayne's face was stricken with grief, and Anna felt a twinge of regret. Elayne had agonised over Arthur's fate since his birth, and all Anna had managed to achieve was to bring all her motherly terrors to the surface.

'May I advise you then, my dear? I have a solution, but you must believe that I'd never wish to harm my brother in any way. I like the boy and would be proud if he were mine.'

As Elayne muffled her sobs with her sleeve like a little girl, Anna hurried on. 'I think you must tell him everything. You must prepare him for the pitfalls and dangers that lie ahead of him. Don't coddle him, but raise him as a warrior so that he will be a credit to you, to his dead father, to his foster-father, and to those of us in the west who will need him in the future. Even now, you should keep his mind active, teach him to read, and watch always for the poison that lives in Artor's blood. My father battled all his life against the instability that came from both founts of his lineage. Queen Ygerne was lovely, but she suffered abominably from her demon Sight and the glamour that drew powerful men to her feet. Her daughter Morgan was a witch woman and her other daughter, Morgause, was the cruellest and most adamantine creature I ever met. As for Uther Pendragon, Myrddion Merlinus himself told me that Uther was a madman who was drunk on blood. He tried to kill his own son, both openly and in secret. Modred was a pederast, a sadistic monster and a traitor. Even Artor felt uncontrollable rage on several occasions, and was constantly forced to guard against the intemperate feelings that lay below his conscious emotions. Bedwyr knows. Ask him, because I don't believe he'd keep anything from you, including Artor's willingness to sacrifice anything and anyone for the cause of the west. Don't scowl at me, Elayne, for you know that he sacrificed himself too – and me, and he loved me as much as he loved anyone.'

'You've told me that Artor was your father, but you speak as if you hated him. Yet the world is still convinced that you are Uther Pendragon's bastard child and Artor's sister. Artor protected you – and your children – for as long as he lived. Your safety was more important to him than his need to see you, love you and honour you.'

Anne hugged herself and Elayne was shocked to see tears in the ageing woman's sunwebbed eyes. 'I know Artor loved me. He begged kisses of me when I was a tiny child, pretending to be my father's friend. He gave me my bride gifts, he cared for my twin sons and he mourned them with all his heart when they died. You were there, Elayne, and you washed their poor bodies and prepared them for the fire because I was too far away to do it myself. I have never had the opportunity to thank you for the honour you returned to them. I do so now.'

Elayne reached out one hand in heartfelt sympathy, but Anna had not finished. 'I was present when Artor died and I was able to tell him, at last, that I knew everything and forgave everything. Oh, Elayne, I would that I could spare you from the pain of silence – the long, empty years when you are without the person you love, and cannot admit to them that you love them. You must hold Arthur close and love him so much that the demons in his heritage are kept at bay. But, more importantly, you must raise him to be a man whom Artor would have admired. I have come to believe in the Christian God at last, and I am sure that Artor's spirit watches over everything you do. Give your son the chance to grow up clean and strong, because the world is wider than the Forest of Arden – and it will soon come knocking at your gates. Silence poisons. Silence kills, just as it slew my beautiful boys, Balyn and Balan.'

Then, because she remembered the twin grandsons of Artor in all their glorious youth, and because she had seen the High King almost destroyed by unspoken secrets that came to his gates and blew away all of his most cherished hopes, Elayne knelt at Anna's feet, gripped both of the older woman's hands and swore on the life of her unborn child that she would do as Anna asked.

'Even if he hates me for it, Arthur will learn the truth, I swear, and I won't spare myself in the telling.' Elayne pressed Anna's hand to the swell of her belly and, by chance, the child within her womb decided to kick vigorously, as if to acknowledge the oath.

Both women laughed rather tearfully and Anna helped Elayne to rise to her feet. 'I'm sorry to burden you so heavily, child, but persons who touch the edges of my family are often worn away by the skein of our blood. Fate weighs heavily on those unfortunates who love us, and I can't tell you why God or the Old Ones lay this burden on us – perhaps to shape some future for our land, or so I tell myself during those times when I see no purpose in so much suffering. I cannot say why we were chosen, but like it or not you are now caught up in a net that began to be woven generations ago. Even Morgan couldn't see the end of it, so may God protect you, my child. For my part, I will pray that Arthur grows straight and true as heaven has promised.'

Then Anna picked up Elayne's distaff and began to spin the undyed wool into thread, twisting the wheel deftly with her blunt-nailed hands. When Elayne's women crept back into the bower, the two noblewomen were sitting together amicably, mending and spinning, and the day had returned to its normal, predictable patterns. But Elayne had understood every word that Anna had spoken and pressed them close to her heart, even as she began to resent the web that held them all. Even with her oath fresh on her lips, she sought a way to save her child from the fate that the gods had laid upon him.

CHAPTER IV

THE BASTARD

> Be like a headland of rock on which the waves break incessantly: but it stands fast and around it the seething of the waters sinks to rest.
>
> Marcus Aurelius, *Meditations*, Book IV

With a calmness that she feared would shatter at a touch, Elayne tackled the problem of her son's birth head on, although she took the precaution of informing her husband of her decision later that night. Flank to flank, they lay in their shared bed, lulled by the rustle of the trees that whispered together with a sound like great, slow waves outside their house as the branches moved in tune with the night wind.

Bedwyr fumbled to find Elayne's hands under the blankets she had woven as part of her dowry. His sensitive finger pads found the calluses of years of spinning and weaving along her first two finger joints. He kissed the scars of her labours affectionately, and thanked his gods that he had been given such a clever and devoted wife. He knew the anxiety that she was facing; he understood her horror of risking her son's love with the truth; but he cherished her courage in facing a harsh necessity and doing what he would have feared to contemplate – dashing Arthur's image of himself.

'I love the boy, Elayne, even though he's not from my loins. This visit from the Ordovice and Otadini kings has given us some difficult decisions to make, so I've thought deeply in the past few days about things I can do to make your task easier.'

Elayne lifted her heavy body high on her pillows and opened her mouth to speak, but Bedwyr closed her lips with one sword-calloused finger. His eyes were dark, deep and affectionate. 'Be quiet, my sweetling, and think. Permit me to finish before you tell me that I'm without fault in this matter. When the kings arrived, I left Arthur to last in my introductions. I've done the same thing for most of his life, yet he's such a sweet, loving boy that he forgives me for overlooking him so casually. I was wrong to place such emphasis on his birth. The day I decided to raise my master's son, I forgave you *and* the boy for his existence, but still, in a corner of my heart, I have judged him for the sins of his father. I have been at fault, but . . . I swear, I will do it no longer. Bitterness could easily consume our eldest son, but it will not be because I place him below my natural sons in the pecking order of my affections. Never again, Elayne. I had planned to ride with Bran and Gawayne tomorrow towards our eastern boundaries, where they wish to acquaint themselves with the dangers we face from that direction. However, I will excuse myself from accompanying them, and hope they understand my reasoning.'

Elayne squeezed his hand and turned to examine his profile by a stray shaft of moonlight. Chronologically, Bedwyr was approaching old age, and his years showed in his grey-streaked plaits and the deep lines that scarred his face from nose to chin. His eyes were meshed in a fretwork of wrinkles that marked his tanned skin with fine, wire-like white lines. But his body was still hard and muscular, his eyesight and hearing were still acute, and while he might not be able to run for hours, as he had in his youth, few men could match his stamina on horseback or afoot. Elayne was very proud of her gallant old man, but she understood that his middle years were behind him and old age approached.

'I thank you, husband. I'm sometimes unwise and impetuous, which leads me into foolish errors. I spoke to Lady Anna today about our boy and she offered me advice on his future. She is wise in the ways of children, and as Arthur's sister she convinced me that I cannot ignore the truth by pretending that my poor son is just another boy. She pleaded with me to tell him the truth, because she learned from her own experience with Balyn and Balan that the ignorance that grows from well-meaning secrets can ultimately kill. Yes, I will find a way to be honest with him, although I fear the result. So rest now, my heart. Tomorrow will be difficult enough without a sleepless night.'

Bedwyr eased his wife carefully into his arms until her warm flanks and belly pressed against his side and he felt the unborn child kick against him. 'I love you, woman,' he whispered, and then kissed her with gentle passion. 'If I hadn't found you, I would have become Old Bedwyr, bitter and resentful of wrongs that had long passed. I owe you and Artor my thanks for everything that I cherish most. Sleep, dear heart, for I promise you that tomorrow will be the start of a new life for Arthur, and that all will be well for him.'

Elayne fell asleep with Bedwyr's promise nestling warmly in her heart. Although she had been certain that she would be unable to close her eyes all night, her grizzled old man had managed to ease her unquiet spirit.

Early the next morning, Elayne chose her moment to confront Arthur. After the kings had left on the long ride through the margins of Arden, Anna ushered Gwyllan into the bower. She had promised Elayne that she should have the privacy she needed to confide in Arthur for as long as she required.

Arthur was confused and a little surprised when his mother asked him to accompany her for a stroll. He would have preferred to set off with the riders, perched behind Ector on his huge horse, and his mother's request that he stay behind with the younger children had been a bitter disappointment. He had immediately wondered what he had done to cause offence, and now he expected that this talk with Elayne would be about some thoughtless action on his part. Unknown to both mother and son, Bedwyr was watching from the palisades as the couple walked in a fallow field thick with flowering weeds that stood almost as high as Arthur himself. Red head close to red-gold one, Elayne bent over her son with her arm protectively around his shoulders. Bedwyr could see the white smudge of Arthur's face above the green grass heads and the clumps of golden-brown flowers, and the Master of Arden wondered if it was his imagination that the boy's face seemed paler than usual, even at this distance.

Suddenly, the smaller figure shook off his mother's comforting arm and ran, quick as a hare, towards the forest. With a muttered oath, Bedwyr slid down the ladder to the ramparts and hurried through the gates, down the slight hill and into the field. Careless of his warriors who followed his hasty departure with alarm, and fleeter than most men of his age, Bedwyr reached his wife within moments. She was weeping soundlessly, the cowl of her cloak pulled over her face.

'He's upset that you aren't his father, my love. He didn't seem to care who his real father was, only that it wasn't you. Oh, what shall I do now? He believed me immediately, and his face, Bedwyr . . . his face!'

Elayne wrung her hands in a gesture of such distress that Bedwyr feared for her unborn child. For his part, Bedwyr acknowledged that he had been half expecting such a response, knowing Arthur's love of his brothers and sister, and his contentment with their stable family life. To lose that certainly of belonging would be like the amputation of a limb.

'I'll talk to the boy, Elayne. I promise that I'll bring him back, so go back to the hall and lie down for a while. My men will escort you, and this strong lad will carry you.' He indicated one of the warriors who had followed him. 'I don't want your pretty feet to touch the ground. The kitchens can manage without you, and Lady Anna will keep young Gwyllan amused. Please go, sweetheart, else I'll worry about you.'

She pressed his hand and watched wistfully as he strode away in the direction that Arthur had taken. The look in the boy's eyes when she had explained that he wasn't Bedwyr's son still haunted her, an expression of loss and betrayal that made her want to enfold him back into her body with her unborn child, so that nothing could harm him again . . . especially her own love, which had kept the secret of his birth for too long.

Bedwyr understood the minds of boys, so he knew just where Arthur would go. Boys always have secret places where they can dream large, ambitious dreams and take troubles too deep to be banished by a woman's cuddle. Bedwyr knew exactly where Arthur would hide in Arden Forest.

The trees were dense as Bedwyr forced his way between them. Had he still been standing on the palisades of his hall, he would have been able to see Arthur's destination, a forest giant that had sprouted from an acorn at least a thousand years earlier, and now raised its ancient branches above the canopy. Bedwyr was first and foremost custodian of the trees, so he was able to follow the faint trail left by Arthur's smaller body through the thick underbrush.

In his haste and distress, the boy had snapped the odd twig and his feet had carelessly scuffed the velvet moss on overturned logs. For those hunters who had eyes to understand the ways of the living forest, Arthur's state of mind was clearly written on broken ferns, crushed weeds and the small dark-loving things that he had disturbed during his wild, tear-blinded blunder through the woods.

From the forest floor, the oak seemed huge. A tangle of exposed roots spread around a base that was thick with a litter of rotting leaves, twigs and shredded bark. A boy could make a bed in such leaf mould and look up at the tree rising like a great wheel above him. Such a boy could send his mind far beyond the reach of his eyes and imagine the stars in even greater wheels, turning and turning, as ancient as time. Bedwyr shook his grizzled head to clear his mind of his own boyhood experiences, and his plaits flew like Medusa's locks around his ageing face. Oh, to be young and beginning all over again!

The giant oak tree bore small marks that were almost invisible to the naked eye where Arthur had set his feet in his climb up into the dizzyingly high branches. With an agility that belied his years, Bedwyr gripped a lower branch and swung himself upwards, finding almost imperceptible handholds as he went, until he reached the canopy and leaf-dappled sunshine.

'Arthur? Where are you, boy? One of these branches might break if I climb any higher. Your mother will need a new husband then, and you'll go begging for a father.' Bedwyr's voice was jocular and good natured, but he heard a small, strangled sob from above him.

'If you'll forgive my small show of cowardice, lad, I don't think I'll climb any higher. Take pity on your old father and come down a little so I can see you.'

'You're not my father.' Bedwyr could hear the misery in the boy's voice, which was quavering as Arthur resisted the urge to cry.

'Is that how it stands with you?' he asked calmly.

'No . . . no! I just don't want to be a bastard. I want you to be my father.' Arthur was sobbing now as the words came flooding out, until Bedwyr was afraid that he could lose his grip on the oak and tumble down from his perch to the unforgiving ground below them.

'Come down just a little so I can see you. I want you to look into my eyes and judge the truth of what I say for yourself. I won't lie to you, or try to soften what your mother has told you. I only want to explain things to you, and to tell you of some changes that will soon happen in your life.'

A rustle of leaves answered him and Bedwyr saw a pair of very dirty feet about ten feet above him. Arthur slithered down the trunk and settled into a fork with his back against the main trunk of the venerable oak, his feet stretched on each of the narrowing branches that formed his seat. Mournfully, Arthur looked down at his foster-father, who was almost close enough to touch the hardened soles of his feet had Bedwyr been so imprudent as to stretch one arm upward.

'Thank you, Arthur. I can talk to you properly now.'

Arthur's face was woebegone and the grime of his frenzied rush through the forest was streaked with runnels where tears had cut tracks through the dirt. Childishly, he brushed away the signs of his hurt with his forearm and looked down at Bedwyr with wounded, shadowy eyes.

'You can't say anything to change what is,' he whispered. Bedwyr had said much the same thing to his king on a bare hilltop in the teeth of a wind from the north. And now it was his turn to sigh for the past, as he leaned back against the sturdy trunk of Arthur's tree.

'I admit that I was angry when you were born. And I was hurt for a long time, because I had loved my king. In fact, I loved my king more than I loved your mother. Can you understand that type of love, Arthur?'

'No, I can't,' Arthur murmured, his eyes wide. This was man's talk, and the boy had no experience of the dark passions of adulthood.

'I loved your birth father because he was the finest and strongest man I ever knew – and the saddest. He had no heir to claim as his own – not even you, because to do so would be to shame your mother and place you in great danger. Do you understand that?'

'Sort of. But he was the king, after all. I thought kings were powerful men who could do as they willed.'

'They are . . . well, there are some things they can't do. Kings have to look after everyone, not just their own family. By the time you were born, King Artor was old and very tired. He can't have wanted to go to war, but he was forced to do it, wasn't he? He had to protect the ordinary people, like your nurse Caitlin, from a traitor who wanted to steal the land and make slaves of the peasants. He died for those people, although I know he'd far rather have been with you.'

'But he hurt you, and he hurt Mother – she said so.' Arthur's face was set in such a way that the planes of his adult features seemed superimposed over his boyish freckles and his tears. 'I hate him!'

'No, Arthur. If I don't hate Artor, and your mother doesn't hate Artor, then how do you have the right to hate someone you never knew? I can tell you, boy, that when I look at you I still see my dear master. I have to look away sometimes because I'm so frightened for you.'

'Then you do care about me a bit,' the boy exclaimed, leaping on the one part of Bedwyr's speech that he genuinely understood.

'Of course I do. I nursed you when you were a baby, so how could I not have loved you? King Artor might have quickened the seed that became you, but I'm still your father. Think of this tree, which was old when I was a boy. Now look just beyond its branches to that younger tree over there.' Bedwyr pointed to a small oak only twice the height of a man. 'Many years ago, I planted some of the acorns from this tree, and prayed that those seeds would shoot and grow. Can you understand that?'

'Yes, Father,' the boy answered cautiously, but his face was much happier than before.

'This large oak sired the smaller oak. A couple of years later, I came down here in the spring and found that a little sapling had broken through the earth and a baby tree had come to life. I cleared the weeds from around its roots and brushed them away from its trunk. Later, I brought water to it when the summers were very hot and its roots weren't deep enough to find underground moisture. I kept it alive. Who was the small tree's father? This old oak whose seed gave it life? Or I, who kept it alive?'

'You were, Father. I understand now.' Arthur's brows knitted together as his agile brain made the next move. 'You are raising me until I can stand alone, like the young oak over there.'

'Yes, Arthur, exactly so! Do you realise how many close kinfolk you have? King Gawayne, King Bran, Prince Ector – they are all tied to you by blood as well as by affection. Of course, we can never tell anyone outside our immediate family who your father was, but that doesn't mean that you can't talk to your new kinfolk about your sire, and discuss his true history with them. You should be aware that some wicked men will try to tell you falsehoods from time to time, but mostly you can rely on your kin to tell you the whole, blunt truth, warts and all.'

The boy slid down from his perch and balanced himself carefully next to Bedwyr, so the older man felt the touch of the boy's fingers, as light as a kiss, in his hair. The forest master closed his brown eyes with their flecks of gold and thought of the long journey through agony, enslavement, madness and suffering that had brought him to this safe, beloved harbour and the love of a child who wasn't his own. That love was the purest thing he had ever known.

'We must be careful, Arthur, or my old bones will slip and you'll have no father to help you learn your woodcraft. Let's go down to the ground so I can begin to tell you all the exciting new things you're going to learn about King Artor and your blood kin. I must admit I have waited for this day.'

So quickly and so lithely that he might have been the old god, Pan, the boy gave a whoop and began his descent at headlong speed. Bedwyr followed more slowly, his feet searching for the footholds that the boy had used, amazed that he had possessed the temerity to climb so high at his advanced age. 'A man must be mad!' he exclaimed to the oak trunk as he found the lower branches and finally saw the tangled roots with their shroud of deep leaf mould. Arthur was looking up at him and his small face was creased with concern, as if he feared that Bedwyr would fall.

Bravado made Bedwyr drop onto all fours from a branch nearly eight feet above the ground. Only chance prevented him from striking an uneven root and snapping his ankle like a twig.

'Are you hurt, Father?' Arthur asked, his eyes narrowed fearfully. 'That branch was too high.'

'Now you tell me, sprog. No, I'm unhurt!' Then Bedwyr surprised himself by throwing his arms about the boy, lifting him bodily off his feet and embracing him. Hesitantly at first, and then in a rush of strong emotion, Arthur clasped his own arms around Bedwyr's neck until the Arden Knife felt the boy's wet eyelashes on his cheek.

'Enough of weeping now,' Bedwyr mumbled, embarrassed by the flood of love and protectiveness that coursed through him. 'I've been far too reticent with you, lad, but that's going to change. From now on, I'd like you to bring any problems you have to me. So, you young scamp, sit yourself down so I can rest my bones, and I'll fill your head with snippets about some of your new family.'

'King Gawayne?' Arthur breathed, his eyes shining.

'Yes, Gawayne is your cousin, or I think he is. And Queen Anna is your sister. Gods, but your family's a fair tangle.'

Arthur's eyes almost started out of his head as he considered this astonishing relationship and he covered his mouth with both hands to stifle an oath that Bedwyr hadn't known he'd even heard. Then he remembered Gawayne's pungent language and realised that all his boys had probably learned some new forms of profanity since the old king's arrival.

I'll need to warn the little ones about Gawayne's more colourful turns of phrase . . . but later. First things first.

'But she's so old,' Arthur exclaimed, shocked despite his attempt at worldliness.

'I happen to know that Queen Anna has already agreed to tell you her story, including the tale of how King Artor married her mother when he was still a boy. At the time he was only a few years older than you are now.'

'So King Bran . . . and Ector . . . are . . .' Arthur's voice faded away and he used his fingers as he tried to work out the connection.

'Yes, young Arthur, despite being only seven years old, you are actually King Bran's uncle. And Prince Ector's great-uncle.'

Arthur started to laugh, and his glee was so infectious that Bedwyr also began to guffaw. Soon, man and boy were rolling in the leaf mould, paralysed by paroxysms of uncontrollable mirth, and Bedwyr realised that the crisis in his family was past. Each of them had stepped over a vast gulf, and potential disaster had been averted.

'Now, let me tell you what we've decided you have to learn. Let's see if you find that quite so humorous, young oak tree.' Bedwyr grinned and clapped the boy on the shoulder as father and son began to trudge back to the palisades where the people who loved them were waiting on tenterhooks. 'First, you must kiss your mother and remind her that you love her. She's been worried that you would be angry with her for betraying me with the king. When you're older and can understand a little better, she'll tell you how it all came about. But for the moment, she believes that you don't love her, and it's making her very unhappy.'

'But that's just silly,' Arthur protested, his eyes wide with surprise. 'How could I not love my mother?'

'So I told her, but that's how women think, my boy. Perhaps you'd best go to her quickly.'

'I will.' Arthur ran ahead, his eyes shining as if he had been given a gift beyond price.

'May the gods protect us all,' Bedwyr prayed ironically. Then he looked skyward. 'Where are you now, Artor, when I really need you? I've a feeling you'd be even more terrified than I am, if you had to deal with such a son.' Then Bedwyr paused, looked at his forest and smiled at his reservations.

'What a boy you've given me, Artor. What a boy you and Elayne have made between you! Well, I'll do my best, old man, because I've discovered I love him. He'd have spotted any lie in me, because he's so like you. Life will be interesting over the next few years – may the gods protect us all indeed!'

But his heart felt light and his spirits exhilarated as if he'd drunk too much fresh cider, and his steps were boyish and carefree as he hurried to his hall.

As he had promised, Arthur sought out his mother immediately. She was resting on the big, rough-hewn bed in Bedwyr's quarters and the boy could tell from her red eyes and her blotched complexion that she had been crying. Her eyes were closed and her hands were folded out of sight beneath the pillow that protected her aching neck and back. Lying down, she seemed small and delicate, perhaps because the swell of her belly made the rest of her frame seem too tiny to bear the weight of her unborn child.

Arthur tentatively reached out his right hand and wiped away the marks of tears on Elayne's pale face. Startled, she surged out of sleep with her hands raised to protect herself, and saw her son bending over her, his face glowing from within with the love that was clearly written in his pale eyes.

'I'm sorry to wake you, Mother, and I'm sorry for everything I said this morning. Father and I had a long talk and he explained everything to me. I love you, Mother, more than anything. More than Arden, or my brothers and sister, or anything! I'm really sorry, and I'm ashamed that I made you cry.'

Elayne tried to struggle into an upright position on the pillows, but needed Arthur's young strength to settle her weary, child-heavy body comfortably. She sighed with relief as her son tucked a blanket round her shoulders.

'Sit on the bed next to me, sweetling,' she murmured drowsily, still disoriented from a confusing, half-remembered dream of some appalling future.

'My hands and feet are filthy, Mother. I'll soil your bed,' Arthur protested, and she could see that he wasn't exaggerating.

'Never mind my bed, darling. I want my sweet boy to sit beside me.'

Without any further protest, Arthur sat on the edge of the bed with his feet dangling awkwardly over the edge. He's growing so big, Elayne thought with regret, and he'll soon be a man. She looked up at her son and sighed wistfully. 'I've been so worried, Arthur. I was afraid that you would think I was a whore for having carried Artor's child, and you would cease to love me.'

'I don't know what a whore is, but I'm sure I wouldn't think any such thing,' Arthur insisted, affronted. He raised his head so he could stare into her smiling face.

'Any woman who betrays herself and her kinfolk by lying with other men is called a whore,' Elayne explained carefully, determined that no secrets be permitted to fester between them, even such a simple matter as the meaning of an insulting word.

'Then you can't be a whore, Mother, because you didn't betray anybody. You told me you were half frozen, as was the High King, and you thought you were dying. I could never think of you as a whore, and I'll kill anyone who says such a terrible thing in my hearing.'

His face was so serious and so adult that she would have laughed had she not also detected the determination and potential violence of a man who possessed the capacity for unthinking rage. With Lady Anna's warning in mind, she was in no doubt that Arthur would indeed kill to protect the reputations of those he loved.

'I was so very angry when you told me that Bedwyr wasn't my sire that I wanted to kill something. There was a burning hot knot right here.' Arthur pointed to the centre of his chest. 'But now I feel very lucky. Now I have two fathers, don't I? One sired me and the other cares for my needs.'

Elayne smiled and hugged him, but then her face contorted in sudden agony. She tightened every muscle involuntarily and Arthur sat up, his face vulnerable with concern.

'What is it, Mother? What's wrong? Should I fetch Father?'

'Yes, sweetling,' she hissed through clenched teeth as a violent contraction rippled through her body like a sudden unexpected wave. Her forehead beaded with sweat from the shock of the pain, she set the plans for her labour into action. 'Fetch Bedwyr and Anna, my love. I think your brother comes early . . . and with considerable impatience.'

Frightened by the extreme pallor of her face, Arthur rose carefully from the bed so as not to disturb her further and then ran pell-mell through the wooden hall, bellowing for Bedwyr in a voice made higher than usual by his panic.

'What's amiss, lad?' By a lucky chance, Gawayne had returned early from the ride, and now stopped Arthur with one age-spotted hand on the boy's shoulder.

'Mother is in pain. She told me to find Lady Anna and my father. I must go, my lord.'

With a general's speedy assessment of an emergency, Gawayne swung into action. 'Lady Anna is in the bower, so go to her now and tell her that your mother is having labour pains. I'll find your father and fetch him to your mother's room. Don't fear, Arthur, for women are far braver than we men. If we had to bear the children, I fear that human beings would cease to inhabit the earth.'

Despite Gawayne's jocular attempt at comfort, fear loaned wings to young Arthur's heels, and his entry into the bower caused considerable concern because of his obvious urgency and his terrified eyes.

'Please come, Lady Anna,' he begged, gripping his sister's hand and tugging her towards the doorway. 'Mother says the baby is coming early, and she wants you there straight away. Lord Gawayne is searching for my father.' Then, because he was really only a little boy frightened for his mother's safety, Arthur's face contorted. 'It's my fault. I upset her,' he wailed.

Anna swung into action with the calm confidence of a woman who had brought many infants into the world. Leaving Arthur in Gwyllan's care, she bustled out of the bower with several of Elayne's women to collect bowls of hot water, swaddling cloth and all the other accoutrements of childbirth that Elayne had prepared in advance. Meanwhile, Gawayne had hunted out Bedwyr, who was scrubbing his dirty hands and face in a basin of cold water in the stables.

'You're about to become a father again, Bedwyr. My felicitations!'

'But the babe isn't due to be born for a month!' Then Bedwyr was gone, his long legs propelling him swiftly across the forecourt and into the house, concern written so strongly on his usually impassive face that the servants scattered out of his path as he ran.

Elayne sat in their huge bed with pillows piled high behind her back in an attempt to alleviate the force of the powerful contractions that had struck so suddenly. As Bedwyr surged into the already crowded room, she wiped her pale white face with a cloth while attempting to maintain a bright, confident smile for her husband's benefit.

'The pains came quickly, Bedwyr, much faster than with the other babes. I'm afraid that I might have affected the child by becoming upset, and he is retaliating by coming early into the world.'

Bedwyr's eyes flared with panic then, so she grinned to soften the alarming suddenness of her labour.

'Don't worry, husband. This is women's work, and with four living children I've proved I have a talent for it. The child will be born, and by the strength of his demands I'd swear he's a big strong boy.'

Then her grin changed into a grimace as another contraction gripped her. Anna and one of her ladies each held one of her hands and permitted Elayne to grip them so fiercely that her short nails left red crescents in their flesh.

'This . . . is no place . . . for you, my . . . love,' she panted, and Bedwyr felt as powerless as all men do in the wholly feminine world of pain, blood and childbearing.

'You've done nothing to harm the babe, and Lady Anna won't let anything happen to either of you,' Bedwyr whispered in a voice that wasn't quite steady.

'You must leave now,' Anna ordered crisply, releasing Elayne's hand as the contraction weakened. Firmly and kindly, she propelled the Master of Arden out of his own room with surprisingly strong hands. 'Young Arthur was already blaming himself for his mother's premature labour when I left him, so by now he'll be quite distraught! He's with Gwyllan in the bower.'

'Go to him then, beloved,' Elayne begged, before another contraction made her bite down on her hand until Bedwyr was sure she would draw blood. 'Make sure that the little ones are safe with their nurse. Kiss them for me.' She was panting heavily between the birth pangs, and Bedwyr fled.

Anna was accurate in her assessment of Arthur's feelings. The boy was pacing along the length of the bower and trying to hold back tears, while Gwyllan was attempting to calm him. Quelling his own doubts, Bedwyr grinned and briefly hugged his son.

'You're about to have a new brother or sister, so we must explain to the little ones that their mother will be too busy to put them to bed. Could you tell them stories, so that they aren't afraid before they nod off to sleep? Although your mother is as brave as a lion, women often cry out during childbirth, so you'll need to think of ways to explain any noises they hear that might frighten them. Can you do that? Good man! I knew I could depend on you.'

The tumultuous day came to an end, and just before the dawn Elayne was delivered of a sickly, mewling daughter who Anna feared was doomed to die.

'Not she,' Elayne whispered, for the birth had been accompanied by a great gush of blood that left her weak and deathly pale. 'She's strong and vigorous for all that the poor little thing was born so early.'

Anna's face said otherwise, so Bedwyr steeled himself to view his new daughter. The tiny babe had no protective layers of fat under her wrinkled skin, which fell in folds over the bone as if she were preternaturally old. Her features resembled those of a wizened old crone, and her skin seemed to be so thin that it was being worn away by the touch of her nurse's hands. A cap of thick dark hair was the only strong and vigorous part of the little creature's whole body.

'I'll find a priest,' Bedwyr said sadly. 'Elayne will take comfort if the child is christened.'

'The babe won't die,' Elayne insisted from her bed, while her women hastened to make her comfortable. She had heard his words with a mother's sharp ears. 'She survived the birth, so I swear she'll live, Bedwyr. This girl is special, and she deserves a name that will match her potential.'

Bedwyr kissed his wife and patted her hand to humour her, sure such a sickly child would be lucky to survive the day. 'I hope you're right, beloved, but I'll still send for a priest. Such a precaution can't hurt, can it?'

When Elayne nodded absently, Bedwyr kissed her again. He recognised the signs of complete exhaustion, and he pressed Anna to make sure that his wife could sleep without being disturbed before he left the room.

Anna used wide bands of heavy linen to strap Elayne's stomach, a remedy that Myrddion Merlinus had favoured to prevent dangerous haemorrhages. For a fleeting moment, she considered strapping Elayne's breasts as well to halt the flow of milk, but Elayne stopped her with a single burning glance.

'This child *will* live, Lady Anna, and Arthur *will* become a great asset to King Bran. When we are close to death, we sometimes see things more clearly than usual, and I have a powerful feeling concerning both my oldest and my youngest child. Unreasonable as it sounds, I know what I know – although you'll call it wishful thinking.'

'Not I,' Anna replied seriously. 'I'm old enough to have discovered that the more we learn and educate ourselves, the more we realise how little we really understand about the world. At any road, it's bad luck to presume that the child will die, so let's see if she'll take to the breast. If she can suckle, she will have a chance of survival.' She smiled down at Elayne before turning to the midwife. 'Woman, bring the child to Lady Elayne.'

The midwife obeyed, and despite her bone-deep weariness Elayne exposed her breast and pushed the little mouth towards her nipple. The child protested and turned her head fretfully away from the close, suffocating pressure of Elayne's flesh against hers.

'Persist, Elayne. She must suckle to gain strength. Perhaps she's too immature to be able to feed. Have you arranged a wet nurse?'

Elayne nodded tiredly. 'But she needs my milk at the moment, I know. Come, little one, don't resist your mother. I know what's best for you.'

The small battle of wills continued for some time, but at last the little girl parted her lips and Elayne popped her nipple into the toothless, old-woman's mouth. The child's unfocused eyes closed for a moment but Elayne stroked the tiny throat encouragingly until, snuffling like a little puppy, the babe discovered she could breathe through her nose. And then a miracle happened in the quiet room. She suckled.

'Ah, that's it! You're a good little girl,' Anna murmured in mingled surprise and satisfaction. 'She has a chance now,' she whispered, smiling down at Elayne.

The babe fed for only a few minutes before she fell asleep on the breast. Elayne had already drifted into slumber, so mother and daughter lay together, resting in the arms of the Mother in perfect trust.

'Stay with them,' Anna whispered to the midwife, 'and ensure that Elayne doesn't smother the infant by mischance. I'll send for the wet nurse.' Then she straightened her aching back and left the room, stretching her kinked muscles as she mentally prepared to take over the reins of the household until Elayne was well enough to resume her duties.

'What a night!' she muttered to the empty hallway. 'How strange fate is. In the space of a single day, my brother has discovered his true heritage and precipitated the birth of a new half-sister. I have seen many strange things in my life, but I've a feeling that this day past will be one to remember. I cannot tell whether good or ill is to be the outcome, but Taliessin would say that God moves all in inexplicable patterns.'

Anna found her way to Bedwyr's hall, where the men would soon be breaking their fast amid much jesting and tedious male chatter of coming hunts. As she raised her hand to push open the heavy door with its simple, woven leather latch, one last thought disturbed her so much that her fingers trembled on the carved knob over which the leather cord was secured.

If the gods are taking such an interest in Arthur and his newly born sister, then the children must be important in the games of power. But are they destined for good or for ill? And how are we poor mortals to discover the answers? Perhaps we will know if the fates allow the infant to live through the months to come.

Anna flushed with shame then, because these thoughts were unworthy of the daughter of Artor, the last High King. Taking her courage in both hands, she entered the hall to put in train her small part in the child's survival. A shaft of sunlight burst through the dull late-autumn dawning and lit the room through the opened entry at the far end, dancing down the flagstones to catch Arthur's hair in a net of gold.

He's wearing a crown, Anna thought, and shivered at the portent. Then Arthur grinned boyishly and the spell was broken.

A new day had begun.

CHAPTER V

A VERY STRANGE EDUCATION

> **teacher** 1. A person, either male or female, who instils into the head of another person either voluntarily or for pay, the sum and substance of his or her ignorance. 2. One who makes two ideas grow where only one grew before.
>
> The Roycroft Dictionary, MCMXIV

Miles from Arden's green heart, in a fold in the landscape between the fortresses of Ratae and Venonae, but out of sight of each, men were working to create a shelter that would not be obvious from the top of the hills that beetled over them. By their gait, their height and their weaponry, the interlopers were clearly Saxon or Angle.

Rather than the normal Saxon dwellings with their distinctive triangular appearance and steep roofs that almost reached the ground, the warriors were raising simple structures of soft wood made weather-tight by a simple rush covering laid over supporting branches. This rudimentary thatching, under the canopy of taller trees, made the impromptu village invisible from higher ground and minimised the chances of discovery by Celtic patrols.

Deep in the Celtic heartland, this tentative advance party would soon turn into a flood of infiltrators if their presence remained unnoticed. The Saxons had been ordered here by their thane, a wily old campaigner called Thorkeld Snakekiller, to prod at the Cornovii settlements in search of weaknesses. If they returned alive, then the way lay clear to the broad acres of the Cornovii and Ordovice tribes. If they were killed, then Thorkeld would be forced to search for another route. Grey of hair and eye, he was determined to find a way round the Celtic defences now that the fearsome Dragon King had finally made the journey into the shadows.

'This is our time. This land will be ours, sooner or later,' Thorkeld told the advance party. 'Know that our harpists will celebrate your courage when we build our hall where the fortress of Ratae now stands. Your route to the gods will be as straight as a true sword if they require you to sacrifice your lives, and you will banquet with the heroes for eternity. Go now, with Woden in your hearts.'

So the half-naked Saxon warriors worked in the autumnal sun and their pale skins reddened as the huts rose swiftly. Once their shelters had been built, they lit small cookfires within their closed and stuffy quarters, trusting that the encroaching darkness would cover the evidence that they waited within sight of the Celtic defences. In every warrior's heart, Thorkeld's message was repeated like the sonorous beat of a drum.

This is *our* time. This land will be *ours.*

When he had a clear understanding of what was needed in a crisis, few men in all the isles of Britain, whether Celt or Saxon, were as efficient or as single minded as Bedwyr, the Master of Arden. Caught up in the domestic drama, Gawayne gave permission for four of his best warriors to scour the cities and hamlets around Arden Forest in search of a priest who would consent to visit Arden, and Ector volunteered to ride to Glevum to recruit a suitable arms master for Arthur. The new birth had already determined that the visitors would be spending a few weeks longer in Arden than they had originally intended. Anna would not budge until the babe and her mother were out of danger.

'I don't begrudge the time,' Bran told her, and she could tell by his eyes that he was telling the truth. Amused, she understood his motives immediately.

'Of course not, my son. You will have the opportunity to assess Arthur's teachers and help to shape the direction of his education. What better way to ensure that he will remain loyal to your interests? Gawayne lingers here for similar reasons, although his lands are far away. Of us all, only Ector and Arthur are completely free of guile.'

Bran shook his head sardonically. 'Arthur is too young to be sly, but he's already asked me to tell him *all* my memories of King Artor, both the good *and* the bad. Such a balanced curiosity speaks well of the boy's promise, but it's also a warning that Arthur will be a very careful man. He will be difficult to fool as he ages.'

'He has made the same request of Gawayne and me. I know that Ector has already described the battle of Camlann as he remembers it. Bedwyr will need to think quickly when his son starts asking some of the more difficult questions.'

Bran grimaced. 'Do I reveal everything to him, Mother? Gallia, Livinia, and even Caius? Everything? He'll form a very odd opinion of his family if I do.'

'Honesty really is the best answer to questions from your uncle. And don't look so disapprovingly at me – he *is* your uncle,' she retorted crisply. 'You might be forty, but the relationship is real even if it's embarrassing to you. I'll handle the details of the Villa Poppinidii. If you can explain to Arthur what Balyn and Balan were like as young men and tell him what you remember of the High King's character, I think that would be all that's needed from you at this stage. We can flesh out the finer details later in his education.' She tapped her son on the nose with a confidence that Bran found intensely irritating. 'Don't allow your bad temper to show with the boy, Bran. It is one thing to be impatient with your mother, but Arthur is his father again, with something of Lady Elayne's balance to leaven the streak of instability that we knew so well. Whatever faults the boy is going to develop will be interesting to watch . . . but that's in the future, and I don't wish to stay here for months to evaluate them. You should be happy that the boy knows who he is, and we have already persuaded him to bond tightly with his larger family.'

Something feral appeared in Bran's face that was quite different from the calm, placid personality that was usually on show. 'All the same, I'd still sleep easier if he didn't exist.'

Anna was horrified. 'Shut away such thoughts, Bran. I'm not jesting. I'm sickened that you could even consider such a thing.'

Her hands had risen to the cowled neck of her simple homespun robe. Any stranger would believe her to be a house servant at first glance, but her face held authority and her eyes were like chips of hazel ice, glittering and stark. Bran stepped towards her hesitantly, regretting his ill-judged, improper comment.

'I didn't say I want him dead, I just wish he'd never been born. You know what I mean, Mother. I'm insulted that you'd even imagine I'd ever harm a kinsman.'

'I hope you're speaking honestly.' Anna's hard stare would curdle milk. 'Are you jealous of the boy, Bran? I could understand if you were. He's very like his father in many ways, but his life has been much happier than Artor's so far, and I have come to believe he will grow to be a productive, contented man.'

'Why should I be jealous of a bastard of seven? Now you're being ridiculous, Mother.'

'Maybe so.' She examined her son's face closely, until he was forced to turn away from her shrewd, troubled scrutiny. 'I love you, Bran, as the last of my strong sons, and as my king. I have always respected you as well, so I'd be devastated to discover that some of the taint of Uther Pendragon or Modred hid in your nature.'

Bran swore, but Anna cut him off by gripping his forearm tightly. 'They were your kin, as you well know. They are a part of your bloodline, so don't be so superior, boy, and don't even *think* about Arthur's death. The family would tear itself apart if anything were to happen to him. Ector would be heartbroken . . . and Bedwyr? Well, I'd rather not consider what the loss of Arden would mean to the remnants of the west. The Saxons would arrive on our doorstep in hordes without Arden protecting our flanks.'

'All this . . . this nagging because of a slip of the tongue, Mother. I'd never harm the boy, but life would be far more straightforward if he weren't here.'

'Yes, life can be very messy, Bran, especially family connections tied to power and inheritance.' Anna's voice was dry and suggested a hint of sardonic humour. 'We'll leave the conversation as it stands, my son. I've said what needs to be laid out for you, and the rest I'll leave to your own common sense. Ector is old enough to find a proficient arms master for Arthur's training, so trust his cool-headed intelligence and I will trust to yours.'

Her smile was conciliatory, but Anna was concerned at Bran's attitude to his newly found uncle. Unsettled by the conversation, she was unprepared for the sight of Gwyllan sitting disconsolately on a stool outside Bedwyr's apartments. When the girl saw Anna approaching, she leapt to her feet and waited for the older woman to reach her, while her hands twisted and tore at the overlong sleeves of her finely woven woad-blue robe.

Anna sighed inwardly. More problems. 'What can I do for you, Gwyllan? I can tell you're waiting for me, but come with me and we'll see Elayne and her new baby first. We'll find somewhere quiet where we can talk after I've made sure that mother and child are comfortable. Is that acceptable?'

Gwyllan ducked her head so that her long plaits fell forward to conceal her face, but she nodded and swallowed convulsively.

'This visit should be propitious, Gwyllan. As you're like to be a mother yourself in the next year or so, this experience will be instructive for you. Elayne has excellent mothering skills, which will assist her babe to survive. Watch and learn from her, for it will help you when your own time comes.' Anna smiled so sweetly and with such obvious pleasure at the thought of Gwyllan's future children that the girl dropped her eyes to the points of her embroidered slippers.

Gulping audibly, she followed the older woman into the room, which had been tidied and scented with fresh flowers that seemed to bloom on every flat surface. In clay pots, tin pans and even a goblet of rare Roman glass, late wild flowers of all types and sprays of greenery added splashes of vivid colour to the room. Daisies sprouted everywhere, raising their cheerful faces and yellow centres in posies of other blooms, even small, shy orchids collected from the deepest parts of the forest where they flowered secretly, high in the forks of tree branches.

Elayne was propped up on a mound of woollen pillows and appeared to be considerably better after a day of complete rest. She had been bathed, and her hair had been brushed and combed until the red-gold tresses glowed and then replaited into a thick coronet around her head. Only the deep purple shadows round her eyes spoke mutely of her recent ordeal.

'Arthur brought them. All of them! He is stripping every field and tree of flowers to brighten my day. I tell him there are only buckets left to put the flowers in, and the horses might object if they have no water, but . . . well, you can see what he does.'

'You're a lucky woman to be so well loved. Now, have you bled overmuch?'

Elayne and Gwyllan both blushed at the intimacy of the question, but Elayne shook her head. 'I have been strapped so tightly that my blood couldn't escape even if it needed to. I do thank you for assisting me during the birth, my lady, for only the good Lord will ever know if I'd have survived without your intervention. You have learned the skills of Myrddion Merlinus, and it is well known that he was the wisest healer in these isles. My little girl would have died without you. It was very good of you to help.'

'Nonsense, Elayne. What use would it have been to us if you had died? What good would Bedwyr have been to my son if he'd been left a widower with four small children? I often help at births when I'm at home, and such work gives me pleasure. We who bear the responsibilities of rule over others are obliged to serve our people when we have an opportunity to do so.'

Elayne blushed, but moved on to other matters. 'The little one fed three times during the morning. She can only suckle for five minutes or so, so I feed her often, especially since the wet nurse will arrive soon. She is still an ugly little thing, but her colour is much better already, don't you think?'

Anna moved across the room to a woven rush basket that sat in an improvised sling hanging from the ceiling. The air was warm, so the infant was lightly covered and her thin limbs and ancient, wizened features were exposed. Her eyes were the blue of many babies and Anna knew they were likely to change in colour. The babe's focus still wasn't sharp, but she stared intently at the giant face leaning over her. Unlike those infants who were so frail that the slightest ailment might carry them off, this one seemed untroubled. No fretful crying, no whistling breath and no clamminess in the hands and feet. Against all the odds, this child might yet live.

'See, Lady Anna? She's stronger than she appears, isn't she? I've chosen her baptismal name. Although it's not the custom, Bedwyr permits me to name my daughters.' Elayne's face glowed with affection and triumph.

Anna looked at the small, old-woman's face in the crib. 'She's certainly stronger, but a cold from a stray breeze could easily kill her. I'll pray to the Mother for her, if you'll not be offended. I'll not be happy until she's full sized and vigorous. What have you chosen as her birth name?'

'I've been presumptuous, but if fate permits her to live, then she's worthy of it. I've decided to call her Medb, which some men call Maeve. It's pretty, but I was told many years ago that it means intoxicating and bewitching, and my girl might need a powerful name at some time in the future. I've a feeling that she will become an important young woman as she grows to adulthood. Please don't laugh at my presumption, Lady Anna, but my aunt, who went to live with her husband across the Hibernian Sea, told me the tale of Medb, a great queen in Connaught. She was a war-like female and practised magic, but, most important, she wielded great power over men. We women need all the help that the Lord High God can give us, so although I'm now a Christian I've decided to name my new babe after a woman who ruled over her menfolk in a pagan world.' The triumph and challenge in Elayne's voice made Anna laugh and brought a frown of surprise to Gwyllan's face.

'The poor child will be saddled with the name of a notorious woman who broke the hearts, and other delicate parts, of any man who tried to press their claims on her,' Anna said. 'I hope little Maeve can live up to the expectations that such a name will place on her.'

'She will if I have any say in the matter,' Elayne replied. She was quietly determined under her giggles, and Anna reminded herself that this unassuming woman had been the confidante of the greatest of all the High Kings of Britain. There was far more to Elayne of Arden than mother and domestic chatelaine.

After some minutes of quiet conversation during which Anna satisfied herself that neither of her charges was suffering from a high temperature or other bodily ills, the two visitors excused themselves. One of Elayne's ladies showed them to the door with a low bow, and promised to inform Anna immediately if Elayne's condition changed.

Free now to discover what was bothering Gwyllan, Anna led the girl to a small orchard at the edge of the large clearing that was surrounded by Bedwyr's wooden palisade of sharpened tree logs. In the Roman fashion, Bedwyr liked to run a self-sufficient enclave that could survive for some time if the household should come under siege. Apple and pear trees clustered close to the wall, each carefully pruned and cleared of weeds that could trouble the harvesters. The apple picking was nearly over and only a few immature fruit remained, awaiting the last of the ripening. Here the air smelled clean and sweet, the grass was soft and mown short under the women's house slippers and no servants were nearby to hear their conversation.

'What troubles you, sweetness?' Anna began in a kind voice. Inwardly, she was impatient with Gwyllan's high-strung fancies, but she had instructed the child to come to her if she was troubled. She couldn't neglect her now simply because Bran had put her in a foul mood.

'I don't know where to start.'

'The beginning is as good a place as any,' Anna replied sharply, and immediately berated herself when Gwyllan coloured and was silenced. The girl bit her lip as she hunted for the right words to explain herself, her fingers playing with the nearest pear on the ancient tree above her. With one quiet hand, Anna stilled her unconscious movements. 'The fruit isn't ripe, child, so leave it be.'

'I'm sorry,' Gwyllan whispered, and gripped both hands together under her breasts. 'I know I'm being a bother when you're so busy with really important tasks. Don't worry about my silliness.' She gulped, and tried to wipe away tears that threatened to fall from her impossibly long lower lashes. 'My problems are too trivial to encroach on your time.'

'I'm sorry, child. I'm irritable and gruff today, but it's not your fault. Let's sit for a while. I confess I would enjoy some time to myself in peace and quiet. Men think that women's lives are easy, but we seem to spend hours of each day smoothing the ruffled feathers and bad tempers of our menfolk.'

Several mounds of hay had been brought to wrap around the tree trunks in preparation for the cold of winter. With her usual energy, Anna led the girl to the neat stacks of dried wheat stalks and threw her cloak over them. Gratefully, and with enviable flexibility, Gwyllan sat neatly on the impromptu seat. With a small pang of jealousy, Anna lowered her own bulk more carefully, frowning at the complaint from her older joints.

Ah, to be young again and able to use my body as I once did, she thought, suddenly envious of Gwyllan's easy strength and vigour.

I'm never going to be able to get up unless the child hauls me onto my feet.

'Now,' she began briskly. 'Did you have a dream, Gwyllan? Are night horrors bothering you?'

'No.' The whispered syllable offered no clue to the source of the child's discomfort.

'Did Elayne's childbirth upset you?' Anna guessed with a sudden flash of insight. 'Are you frightened of pregnancy?'

Gwyllan gave a strangled cry that lay somewhere between a sob and a laugh. 'I don't know how babies are made! I can't imagine how an infant ends up in here.' She patted her flat belly and then covered her face with her hands to hide a rich, ruby blush that spread upward from the neckline of her gown to stain her white throat and pale, porcelain cheeks.

'What? Are you jesting, Gwyllan? You come from a huge family, so you must have seen many infants born into this world. You've seen animals in rut, surely. Your mother must have explained the physical process of how babes are made?'

'No,' Gwyllan muttered, almost too embarrassed to speak. She was unable to meet the older woman's incredulous eyes. 'Father always says that when the time is right, he'll tell me all about it . . .' Her pause was very expressive. 'The time is surely right now, when I'm about to be wed, but I know less than Arthur, who seems to be aware of where babies come from. I'd ask him, but that would be too much shame and embarrassment for me to bear.'

Seeing the incredulous expression on Anna's face, the younger woman hurried to fill the shocked silence. 'I've seen babies being born, of course, and I was terrified. It's such a painful, messy business. I can't understand how a woman's body can stretch enough to expel . . . Oh, Lady Anna, I feel such a fool to be so ignorant and frightened!'

'Don't cry, Gwyllan. Everyone is afraid of what they don't understand – even your father. Of course you can't ask Arthur. I'm glad you've come to me, but I'm very surprised that your father has left you so unprepared. Really, Gawayne is like all men – ready enough to leap into any woman's bed, but woe betide the man who casts an eye on his daughters. I sometimes wonder whether they would prefer them to remain virgins for ever.'

Gwyllan's eyes were very wide as Anna began a detailed explanation of human sexuality. The girl looked quite revolted by some aspects of congress, and Anna wondered if Ector had the patience and sympathy to woo this ignorant girl with sensitivity. She made a mental note to talk to her grandson frankly, and soon.

Anna's description of conception rendered Gwyllan speechless. Sensibly, the older woman drew male genitalia in the rich brown dirt at their feet with a stick, and explained what Myrddion had told her of their function. 'Childbirth is not too bad, child. Elayne will tell you that once you hold your infant in your arms, you forget the pain you've experienced in birthing it. We're constructed for the role of mother – that's why we have such wide hips.' She smiled down at Gwyllan. 'You will find that the act of love which results in childbirth is just as pleasing to women as it is to men if their husbands understand what they're doing. Even if a man is inexperienced and clumsy, women find the act pleasant after the first occasion. Men may court sex more than women, but don't believe for one moment that we dislike it. Old wives' tales of pain and suffering are lies.'

Anna grinned conspiratorially and Gwyllan managed a rather damp smile in return, as if she were being told some exotic female secret.

'It sounds horrible, though,' she whispered. 'I've seen Elayne's baby, and even though she's tiny I can't imagine carrying something that big in my stomach . . . sorry, my womb . . . and least of all birthing it. It will kill me!'

'No, sweetheart, it won't. You're a delicate little thing, but so is your mother, and your hips, like hers, are womanly. How many children has your mother borne?'

'Ten,' Gwyllan murmured, her amazed eyes wide open. 'I never thought of that.'

'I often used to discuss childbirth with Myrddion Merlinus, and he always assured me that while it can be dangerous for the mother, the risks can be minimised if your midwife keeps you clean and regularly washes her hands with very hot water. He swore that hygiene was the key. I've no intention of passing into the shades for some time yet, so I promise I'll be with you when you have your first babe.'

'You promise?'

'Aye, child, I promise.' Anna crossed her heart in the homely children's gesture and Gwyllan managed the small smile of a conspirator. 'But if you find that the act of sex is difficult for you, or there's anything you don't understand, just ask me. You know I'll be honest with you.'

Back in the ladies' bower, where the younger woman continued her weaving of a fine shawl of rich red wool for her dowry, Anna amused herself by planning what she would say to thoroughly chastise Gawayne for his daughter's ignorance. The thought of embarrassing the great Gawayne maintained Anna's good mood for the rest of the afternoon.

One of Gawayne's warriors rode irritably up to the palisade, towing a donkey on which sat a tall, lanky priest, his cowl raised to obscure his face and his large, sandalled feet almost dragging on the ground. The warrior was in a thoroughly bad temper by the time the gate was eventually opened, and as the priest slid off his relieved mount he strode away to find King Gawayne and Lord Bedwyr. Over his shoulder, he shouted a brusque order for the priest to stay put until the masters arrived.

'Does anyone here have any wine? Ale? Even water would be better than nothing,' the priest bellowed at the guards. 'I've got a vile headache from dealing with yon laddie and his abysmal sense of humour.'

The guards looked at the priest incredulously. Once he threw back his cowl, he was certainly a surprising sight. He was an unlikely man of God in any circumstances, and if he was the best priest available, then Satan was winning the battle for human souls. One warrior said as much and the priest looked at him with eyes that were glacially green, reddened and unfriendly.

'Mind your tongue, idiot, or I'll tie a knot in it,' was his unpriestly reply.

'You're a drunken sot!' one of the guards called down superciliously. 'I can smell you from up here.'

'Can you then, lout? Come down and I'll show you what damage an unhappy, sober priest, smelly or not, can do to that huge wart on your face.'

'What wart?' the offended guard shouted back indignantly, as his friends laughed raucously.

'The feature that passes as a nose on most of us. If it's not a wart, then perhaps it's your dick, and the Lord God made an error in anatomy.' The man of the cloth then pumped his hips at the hapless guard with a suggestiveness that was as coarse as a slap in the face. 'Don't tell me you're frightened of a priest,' he sneered.

'You're not worth my time, arsehole,' the warrior shouted back, more mindful of Bedwyr's instructions to stay on watch than scared of the impudent priest below, who seemed devoid of any Christian decorum.

'So kiss mine, coward.' The priest turned round and bared his skinny backside to the warriors on the palisade, and then capped the insult with a wiggle of his buttocks.

The guard had to be restrained by several of his companions, and the hubbub of shouted oaths, barking dogs and even the distressed honking of the donkey greeted Gawayne, Bran and Bedwyr when they hurried up in company with the scowling Otadini warrior.

'Silence!' Gawayne roared in a voice that had the unmistakable tone of a master. 'You! Priest! If that's what you are! Cover your arse, for I don't find it remotely attractive. And you lot can get back to your watch immediately, or you'll feel the lash.' Belatedly, he realised he wasn't the master here, and apologised to Bedwyr for usurping his authority.

'No, my friend, please continue. My warriors are fully aware of the punishments that will be meted out if they don't obey any high-born lord.' Bedwyr looked up at his men on the palisades from under his greying brows and the guards suddenly became very interested in the landscape beyond the settlement, although the hostile glances darted down at the priest gave promise of future meetings when their lords wouldn't be present to ensure his safety. Unconcerned, the cleric examined his nails with studied insolence while one of Bedwyr's hounds spoiled the effect by sniffing at his stiff, filthy robe with friendly, inquisitive interest. The priest tried to shoo the huge dog away, but it was determined. Surprisingly, it licked the priest's grimy hand before leaning to one side to piddle against his leg.

'As for you, priest,' Gawayne snarled, spitting out the title in a hostile voice. 'What's your name?'

The priest turned his attention away from the dog to Gawayne's face, where he obviously recognised the arrogance of regal power. With his own form of impudence, he appeared to consider the question seriously before making a sketchy bow that encompassed all three nobles.

'I was born Lorcan, son of Lugald, but I've gone by several names since then. The Romans called me Lawrence when I was first made a priest. It's as good a name as any, I suppose. But I'll answer to *hey you* if I'm so inclined.'

Under the priest's insulting demeanour, Bedwyr detected a certain polish of accent and language that belied his crudity. Their visitor was a man who spoke fluently and displayed the confidence of a man who feared no one, regardless of whether they held a sword or simply possessed the power to push his face into the dirt. Around his tonsure his hair was coal black, and he obviously cared enough about his appearance to have shaved recently, for only blue-black stubble marred the clean lines of his grubby face.

'You're an insolent man, priest, whatever your name might be,' Gawayne retorted, and spat in the dust to register his disgust. He strode to within six feet of the priest and wrinkled his nose with contempt at the smell of an unwashed body, stale alcohol and donkey sweat. 'The guard's right: you do stink! Before we speak to you any further, and definitely before you enter the presence of the ladies, you will go with this warrior and scrub yourself, head to toe, and the servants will boil that thing that passes as a robe. My men will help you if you need any assistance or encouragement. Now, get out of my sight before I order you cleansed forcibly.'

'And who might you be, who orders me about as if I'm a slave and had me dragged out of a nice, warm tavern without a by-your-leave?'

The insolence of the question caused a collective gasp of shock from the onlookers. Gawayne might have been goaded into precipitate action had Bedwyr not stepped closer to the priest and made the necessary introductions, while keeping his own body between the volatile king and the difficult cleric.

'Shut your impertinent mouth and listen, you fool. This gentleman is King Gawayne of the Otadini tribe, nephew of the late High King. This other gentleman is King Bran, lord of the Ordovice tribe, and also a kinsman of the last King of the Britons. I am Bedwyr, also called the Arden Knife. I am Master of Arden Forest and all who dwell within it. You are here to christen my newly born daughter, who came before her time and could still perish. You are nothing more than the priest we need to welcome the child into your religious family, because my wife, the Lady Elayne, believes in the Jewish God. Do not tempt us to reject you and find another. I follow the old ways, so your faith means nothing to me and you might discover such a fate to be neither comfortable nor healthy.'

The priest said nothing. For once, his mobile features became blank and unreadable and he followed Gawayne's warrior, who expressed his disgust for his new orders by scowling blackly at his charge. The two men retreated from the small forecourt and Bedwyr heaved a sigh of relief. He realised he'd been holding his breath.

'Well,' he sighed. 'If that's a priest, he's a . . .'

'Horse's arse!' Bran added his curt opinion. 'What an argumentative son of a bitch!'

Gawayne agreed. All his instincts told him that this priest was unsuitable, impossible and lacking in any of the necessary qualities of compassion, tact and decency. But he possessed his uncle's capacity to read a man's nature through his outward appearance, and it warned him that Lorcan ap Lugald was not as he appeared at first sight. The cleric was a parody of a drunken, filthy failure, but something told the king that Lorcan was dissembling, or hiding his true self.

'What's worrying you, Gawayne? Something about that man has wormed its way under your skin.' With his usual perception, Bedwyr had placed his finger on Gawayne's reservations.

'His hands are scarred, callused and very large,' the king said reflectively. 'Did you notice how hard the muscle is on that skinny body? It's not a very priestly characteristic. I smell a warrior under that stink.'

'He suggested he'd been to Rome,' Bran added. 'He's a mystery, this priest, and he makes my palms itch.'

'He bears watching.' The Master of Arden spoke firmly, and Gawayne knew his friend's opinion was set in stone once his mind was made up. 'I don't trust him, but we only want him to christen the babe, so we don't have to spend much time with him.'

'Should we send him packing?' Gawayne asked. 'Why keep him around if we don't want him close to our women?'

'I've not decided . . . not quite,' Bedwyr said slowly. 'He's . . . a bit of a puzzle. He seems twisted by something or someone, hence his aggression and his sarcasm. He doesn't give a fuck what we think. He's not a *problem* for us, but I'm curious about him.'

'Then we'll wait until he scrubs up. At least he's broken the routine of the day,' Gawayne decided, his bad temper washed away by his inquisitiveness. He was ever a man who was amused by the extraordinary or the inexplicable, and this priest was an enigma that tweaked his desire for entertainment.

'He's provocative, deliberately so,' Bran muttered, as the three men strode away to compete against each other in a quickly arranged test of archery skills, a weapon with which all three men were relatively unpractised.

They had been enjoying an unequal contest, in which Bran's younger eyes gave him a decided advantage, when Arthur wandered into the courtyard where the servants had set up a target on a heavy bale of straw. As Gawayne had not learned archery among his wide-ranging warrior skills, precautions were always necessary, for the king's shots were invariably wild. With his deteriorating eyesight, he was likely to hit anything *but* the target.

'Forgive me for interrupting, Father, but there's an odd man wrapped in one of the servants' old robes shivering in the forecourt. He wants to know where you want him to go now that he is clean.'

'Hmn! Just when I was starting to understand how to aim the fucking thing.' Gawayne tossed his bow to a hovering servant with a grin. 'What did you think of him, Arthur?' Belatedly, he realised he had interrupted a conversation between father and son, so he apologised for his want of manners – again.

'No, Gawayne, there's no need to apologise,' Bedwyr said calmly. 'Your question was sensible.' He turned his attention to the boy. 'What *did* you think of the man, Arthur?'

'I like him,' Arthur answered readily. 'I don't know why, because he was rude to me and treated me like a little boy – which I'm not! But I *do* like him. He's a funny man, and much of his rudeness is his way of making a jest. I think he's very sad inside where no one can see it.'

'That's not the description that immediately leaps to my mind,' Bedwyr responded drily. 'But your opinion is interesting, lad, and I'll bear it in mind. Come, gentlemen, let's see if the priest's personality has improved now the dirt has been removed.' As he packed away the archery equipment, Bedwyr spared a thought for Arthur's perception. Long ago, at the battle of Moridunum, Arthur's father had seen through Bedwyr's rage and instability to the man who cowered within, after years of slavery under Saxon masters. Did Arthur have the same sensitivity as the High King? If so, the boy's opinion was very important.

The three men strolled back to the forecourt, their good humour much improved by their afternoon of pleasurable competition. The sight that greeted them was amusing.

A servant had found a large robe of homespun in an indeterminate shade of brown, and the priest had belted it with a length of rope and tied his rosary to the thick cord for safekeeping. Another pouch of leather was tied at the other side of his waist, and Bedwyr presumed that Lorcan kept his few personal possessions within it. Sandals protected his large feet, and without the disguising cowl his face was exposed to the view of anyone who cared to look.

Stripped of layers of accumulated grime, Lorcan was younger than the lords had expected. In fact, while he was a mature man, his face was almost unlined. It was neither handsome nor ugly, but it was full of character in the planes and bones of its strong features.

Black eyebrows arched over equally black eyes that snapped and crackled with intelligence. His nose was long, with flaring nostrils, and his mouth, which was wide with a thin upper lip, was saved from a pinched, miserly appearance by a fuller, almost voluptuous lower lip, at odds with the deep creases that scored the face from the sides of the broad nostrils to the corners of the mouth. As these wrinkles were the only marks on his face, their depth spoke of disappointment and prolonged sorrow rather than age. A firm jaw completed a face that scowled at the three nobles with a forthright and unfriendly expression.

The priest's body was less remarkable but equally puzzling. Bedwyr had met many servants of Jesus, including the current Bishop of Glastonbury, but none had possessed such overall control of their muscles as was evident in this man. Gawayne, on the other hand, immediately remembered the late lamented Lucius, former Bishop of Glastonbury, who had saved the life of the infant who would grow to become Artor, King of the Britons. Brave Lucius had concealed the sword and crown of Uther Pendragon for Artor to find and redeem at considerable personal risk. Lucius had also possessed the Bloody Cup, which had almost torn the tribes to pieces in civil war. Unlikely as it seemed, the bishop had been a Roman aristocrat during his youth and had become an officer and a skilled fighting man before he eventually gave his life to the Christ. Somehow, this unprepossessing man reminded Gawayne of Lucius.

'Have you ever been a warrior, Father . . . Lawrence?' Gawayne asked with greater courtesy than anyone present expected, including Lorcan, who eyed the king narrowly as if he expected some kind of trickery under the polite language.

'Call me Lorcan. I'm living in these isles now, so my Celtic name sounds better than other names I've used. Yes, I was a fighting man for a time. How did you know?'

'It takes one to know one,' Gawayne replied evenly, refusing to rise to Lorcan's bait.

'Tell us about your history, Lorcan,' Bedwyr asked, taking his lead from Gawayne and speaking more reasonably than he felt. 'I'm not being nosy out of vulgar curiosity. We all prize Lady Elayne and her daughter more highly than gold, and we would prefer to know the history of any man admitted into their presence.'

'I'm cold, my lord, and I'm hungry. I haven't eaten since your man took me into custody,' Lorcan retorted. He was obviously moderating his tone with some effort, causing Bedwyr to flush at his lack of consideration for one who would expect to be treated as a guest.

'Come into the hall then,' he said quickly. 'I'll arrange for one of the servants to find some bread and meat and a mug of ale for you. Our hospitality should also extend to some cheese and fruit that will put a smile on your face. We've forgotten the courtesy due to a priest, Lorcan, and for that I apologise.'

The three men ushered Lorcan into the hall, where a fire had been lit in the central fire-pit, and offered him a stool at one of the long trestle tables. A guard lounged unobtrusively against a wall within striking distance, alert to any signs of danger to his masters. Arthur found a stool at the end of the same table, and Lorcan winked at him conspiratorially while he waited for his food. Bedwyr's eyes narrowed in suspicion.

Two servants brought in a hastily prepared meal from the kitchens. A large bowl of porridge was placed in front of the priest, as well as a generous serving of honey, a real luxury in any household. A heel of fresh bread, newly baked that morning, a cut of venison, a small slice of hard cheese and a handful of nuts completed the meal. Then, joy of joys, a foaming mug of ale was placed in front of him. Without awaiting permission, Lorcan attacked the food and drink with the intense appetite of a half-starved man. When Arthur refilled his mug, he looked up from his meal and nodded his thanks before returning to his food with a hungry man's gusto.

Gawayne felt a twinge of guilt that no one, especially his warrior, had considered the priest's most basic of needs when he was first brought before the kings. 'When did you last eat?'

'I was about to start my first hot meal in three days when your man insisted that I leave with him. I'd even paid for it, but he was very impatient and persuasive. I could smell the food, and would have killed for it if he hadn't persuaded me that we were leaving immediately whether I liked it or not. You think me a drunkard because I arrived in a robe that had been soaked in ale. But what you don't know is that your warrior tipped a full jug of ale over my head. I seethed throughout the long ride here, and I was out for blood when we arrived. What can you do to me for speaking the truth? Kill me? Cut out my tongue? Go to it, then!'

'Let's presume we've just met,' Bedwyr intervened, for Lorcan's abrasive resentment was already causing Bran to raise his chin aggressively, while Gawayne, who was trying very hard to be understanding, was in danger of biting off his tongue in an effort to stay silent. 'We have been at fault, but some blame also lies with you for your lack of respect and your crudity. You desperately needed a bath, my friend.'

Bedwyr's change of tone caused the priest to grin. Good, Bedwyr thought. He has a sense of humour to go with his bad temper, so he's not entirely an oaf.

'We have need of your services, priest, so I'd like to encourage better communication between us,' Gawayne added evenly. 'Perhaps you could explain your history to us, Lorcan, son of Lugald. Meanwhile, we'll drink ale together and chat. Who knows, we may find gainful employment for you so that hunger is no longer an issue.'

Lorcan was puzzled. He understood that Bedwyr was desperate for a priest to christen his newly born babe, but he couldn't see a reason for the Master of Arden to need his services for any length of time. 'I've nothing to hide, so ask what you will.'

'Let's start with your birthplace,' Bedwyr suggested, careful to keep his face neutral.

'I was raised in a fishing village to the north of Dublin in the state of Midke near to thirty-four years ago, give or take a year or two. My father was a blacksmith, much sought after because his knives and ploughshares kept their edges and his fishing hooks were masterly. Simple folk have simple needs, you see. There was a monastery built on a small promontory at the far end of the village, a grey stone place, not very large, and ancient by the measure of memory in my old home. My father would care for the monks' animals and sharpen their tools during the winter. When I'm drunk and maudlin, I still remember the smell of peat fires and the heat of the forge, like a flame licking against one side of my body while the cold chilled the other.'

'You were fortunate. A simple life is no bad thing,' Bran said slowly, for Lorcan's story had touched him. Bran had never known a life without complications and his inner soul sometimes longed for the simple world which peasants inhabited so phlegmatically.

'We were luckier than most, for my father was never subject to the danger of drowning as were the fishermen who followed the shoals of herring in their flimsy coracles. Nor did we starve when unseasonal rains rotted the crops in the field. Aye, we were more fortunate than most. When times were hard, we never wanted for food, for men paid for my father's services with barter. I can still smell the fish in the curing house and taste the salt of the ocean in the air.'

He paused and Arthur ran for another jug of ale and refilled everybody's mug, even stealing a cup for himself, although all the children were familiar with Elayne's instructions on the use of homebrew, albeit her products were safer than water. Lorcan thanked him with a pat on the head, marvelling at the thick texture of the lad's spiralled curls.

'Fortune is an odd thing, masters, isn't it? We had enough to eat, but only just, for my poor mother was a good breeder and bore twelve living children. I think my father often prayed that some of us would die, but God was stubbornly good to us, although we were never quite satisfied after any meal. Mother wasted away when I was five, after bearing my youngest brother, who perished with her. Do you know, I can't remember her name? She died of weariness, I swear, being worn out and old by the age of thirty, with only a few teeth left in her head. I've already lived longer than she did. The babes had taken everything from her until she was scarcely a person any more – just a shapeless machine that created new life.

'Anyway, after she was put under the ground, we scarcely missed her except for the cooking and cleaning. I had no talent for either, nor could I fish or coax plants to grow. My father decided I should go to the monks, so one day he took me to the monastery and I didn't leave its walls for ten years, by which time I was nearly sixteen years old.'

'You've had a hard time of it, then,' Gawayne commented.

'Not really, masters. I was well fed, and the monks found that I had some intelligence, so they taught me to read and write. I laboured over my letters for the whole ten years, but I was rarely beaten and I found comfort in the crude stone and wooden sculptures of Jesus and the saints. I realise now that I was happy then.'

'Yet you left,' Arthur piped up, his childish voice causing Lorcan to raise his mobile eyebrows in surprise at the boy's impudence.

'Yes, lad, I did. I left with my master and a delegation that had been invited to travel to Tolosa, or Tolouse, where churchmen from many countries had gathered to shape the rules of the Holy Roman Church in the west. The Merovingian kings ruled their Frankish lands in splendour, but Tolosa belonged to the Visigoths. It was where I first saw the Pope, although as a minor cleric my sole task was to copy out my master's speeches and the long arguments over church doctrine.'

The three lords remained silent. In truth, they were stunned that their simple fishing expedition had caught such a prize as this man. And in the small town of Letocetum, of all places!

'Apparently my skills in copying Latin were superior to most of my peers', or so I was told when a church lord, a cardinal from Rome, demanded my services. The monks of my order were very flattered that a pupil of theirs was chosen for preferment, so I was handed over like a trifle or a gift that would win influence for my master with the church hierarchy. I was excited to see Rome, the place where Holy Peter died and the martyrs had perished for the glory of the faith. I was as a child among those wondrous souls.'

'You sound bitter, Lorcan, yet the places you have seen are remarkable, considering your age,' Gawayne said. 'Of all the men I have ever known, only Myrddion Merlinus travelled more widely than you, and he was a healer, so more doors opened to him than to other men.'

'Yes, I saw Rome in all her filthy decay. I met great men and evil men before I passed my seventeenth birthday, and I was too young to see that vice can flourish in the most holy of places. Ultimately, I ran away after two years and hid myself in Monza, north of Milan, where great mountains loom over the landscape and are perpetually shrouded in snow. I worked as a field servant while my hair grew out, and then I married a woman and bought fields of my own with coin I earned through hard labour. I was happy with my beautiful wife and my two babes for several years, but the wheel turned and war came to the north once again. Old Italia is racked with constant warfare. Petty kings and barons appropriate any land they can steal and, in turn, have it snatched away from them.'

'Did you lose your lands, Lorcan?' Arthur asked softly, his face shadowy with sympathy. Lorcan shrugged, but his shoulders hunched as if from a remembered wound.

'Aye, I lost everything in one bloody night. My wife, my little ones . . . all dead in the ashes of our house. The raiders thought I was dead too.' Lorcan grinned like a wolf and his canines seemed very white and sharp in his dark face.

'Over the next four years, I found every one of them. I killed them all – seventeen of the bastard sons of whores. I knew nothing of war and death when I started, but like my talent for languages, I found I had a gift for violence too. Later, I became a mercenary and took red gold to fight for any side that paid in coin. Sometimes I'd change sides, and later return to my original employers. And when my lust for revenge was finally satiated I realised I had become exactly what I hated most, and my conscience afflicted me with a wound that wouldn't heal.

'Once again, God showed me his mercy and I was taken in by a priest who was neither particularly good nor very kind. He had a wife and children, you see, a secret family contrary to all the rules of the church. He helped me to become sane enough to pass for a man rather than a monster. Although I had broken my vows, some ties cannot be forgotten and I donned my cassock again. He shaved my head into the tonsure and I was born again as Father Padraig, an Irish priest far from home on a pilgrimage to the holy places.'

'Why didn't you go back to your home?' Arthur asked. The older men shifted on their stools, bemused by Lorcan's abbreviated tale. He had seemed to speak honestly, but much of his story had been left unsaid. And perhaps it was better so.

'Why, young Arthur, I did go home. The monastery hadn't changed, but I didn't go inside. I couldn't bear to hear the name of Brother Lawrence, you see. The forge was still in the village, and one of my brothers had become the blacksmith when my father and four of my brothers died from the coughing disease two years earlier. My village was stranger to me than Tolouse, Rome or Monza had been. I learned the sad truth that we can never go back to the places of our childhood. We cannot start again.'

'So here you are, an unwilling man of the cloth in a land racked by fear of the barbarians,' Gawayne said reflectively, his chin resting on one hand and his eyes keenly assessing Lorcan for any sign of prevarication.

'Yes, here I am. Sometimes I drink too much when I remember my children, but I always try to recapture how I felt in the monastery when I thought I had a future and an ideal to follow. So far, I've only learned that I'm still a fool.'

So that's the reason for his aggression and his wildness, Bedwyr thought. He's a man who has lost everything and given himself over to hatred – just as I did. But there was no Artor to save Lorcan. I think I understand him now, he decided, and coughed to cover a lump that had suddenly appeared in his throat.

'If you are of a mind to agree,' he said, 'I am prepared to offer you employment, the chance to preach your religion and a comfortable refuge for as long as you choose to remain in Arden Forest. In return, I ask that you christen my daughter and care for the spiritual needs of my wife and any others who might convert to your way of life. Such an arrangement would be of great value to me at this time.'

Lorcan nodded. He could see the appeal of a respite from the tribulations of travel by accepting a winter in Arden Forest, so he readily agreed.

'But I want more of you. If I believed in providence, then I would say that Fortuna had spun her wheel in my favour when King Gawayne's warrior stole you out of Letocetum. My son, Arthur, needs a tutor. We have decided that he must learn to read and write Latin, and become proficient in geography and any of the other skills needed to make him an asset to my tribe. In return, I will pay gold for your services. By the time your task is finished, you will have sufficient funds to travel anywhere you choose without fear of having to beg for your supper.'

Lorcan began to refuse, but common sense withered the words in his mouth. Bedwyr could tell that he was seriously considering the offer.

'Please, Father Lorcan, I'm certain I would enjoy learning to read if you were to teach me.' Arthur added his persuasion to the discussion. 'It won't be very much fun if my teacher is dull and boring, but I think it might be very interesting if I were to learn my letters from you.'

'You think so, do you?' Lorcan retorted ironically. 'You'll soon learn that I'm a hard taskmaster, with *very* high standards. After all, I have been to Rome, and that means you have a distinguished tutor to ensure you mind your manners.'

'You're teasing me,' Arthur replied with a flash of temper. 'I'm not a little boy, you know.'

'I'll give you my apologies, young Arthur, when you prove that to me.' Lorcan turned to Bedwyr and bowed with a level of cynicism that caused the Master of Arden to cringe inwardly. 'You have purchased yourself a tutor, Master Bedwyr. If you come to regret your decision, it will be no fault of mine.'

With that parting shot, Lorcan crushed a nut in his hard, callused hand. Bedwyr sent a servant to find suitable accommodation for his children's new mentor, although he explained that Lorcan could build his own hut and church if he so wished. That night the first frost came, and Bedwyr wondered if Fortuna had sent him a gift that resembled a double-headed axe: the weapon was forged for both good and evil, depending on how you gripped the fish-skin haft.

The boy saw a fox treading carefully over the frozen ground of the forecourt, heading for the kitchens and the scraps that could be found in the rubbish pits beyond the orchard. Although Arthur's window was narrow and high, some instinct warned the animal that it was being observed. It looked upwards with glittering eyes and its nose tasted the night wind for potential threats. For a moment, boy and fox seemed linked together by a thread of kinship, as strong as iron wire, and then the momentary communication was broken as the fox disappeared into a black puddle of shadow.

CHAPTER VI

COLD COMFORT

'The angel of death has been abroad throughout the land; and you may almost hear the beating of his wings.'

John Bright, speech in House of Commons, 1855

Like all children, Arthur discovered that the concept of schooling was more pleasurable in contemplation than in actuality. Father Lorcan, as he insisted on being addressed, decided that classes should begin as soon as the family had broken their fast. Ector had not yet returned from his quest, but once an arms master was hired the afternoons would be taken up with learning to use a variety of weapons more complex than Arthur's sling and knife.

When Father Lorcan was introduced to Lady Elayne, those two very different persons found something of merit in each other, and Bedwyr was relieved that the priest was proving to be more affable than any earlier impressions could have predicted. Maeve was christened and the sterner name of Medb kept for occasions when she was naughty or fractious, and within a week Arthur felt as though he had been studying Latin forever.

'If you don't practise your letters, you'll never learn how to write,' Father Lorcan grunted crossly after Arthur admitted that he had failed to work with his chalk and slate as he had promised.

'But I was tired,' Arthur said, his face mulish and rebellious.

'Do you plan to be a man whose word is good, or a creature whose word means no more than a puff of wind?' Lorcan's face was set in uncompromising lines.

'But I . . .'

'The answer must be one or the other.' Lorcan's voice was very cold, and Arthur felt his stomach lurch in response. All his teacher's jesting manner had fled, leaving a chilly, disapproving sneer in its place.

'I want to be a man whose word is iron,' Arthur replied in a voice so small that Lorcan demanded he repeat his response.

'Yet you break your word to me the very first time I ask for it,' Lorcan retorted. Arthur scanned his face surreptitiously, but there was no softness there. 'What do you have to say for yourself, young Arthur?'

Lorcan waited while the silence between them dragged out ominously.

'I was wrong, so I'm sorry,' Arthur muttered reluctantly.

'Look at me when you admit fault, boy.'

Arthur's eyes were mutinous and glitteringly cold, but he apologised once again. Lorcan suddenly laughed, and Arthur's back stiffened in affront.

'You'd like to send me to the devil, wouldn't you? But this lesson will be important for the rest of your life, so I'm going to ensure you remember what I say. Your word is everything, Arthur, whether you give it in small things or in great matters of state. You must understand that there are no degrees of dishonour.'

'But, Father Lorcan, surely it's much worse to break your word to your king than to fail to practise your letters?' Arthur looked just a little smug, believing that he had discovered an answer to Lorcan's accusation that permitted him to retain some shreds of self-respect.

'Ahah! So now you're making judgements, are you? Any man who breaks his oath, no matter how trivial, is a man who is not to be trusted. Either your word is good, or it is not.'

'I don't understand, Father Lorcan. Truly, I don't.' Arthur was genuinely puzzled, and, knowing that even such a simple matter could be crucial to his development, Lorcan decided to take him to his father for arbitration.

Tutor and student approached Bedwyr as he discussed the last of the harvesting with his steward, a dour man whose rather shifty appearance was a trick of nature, for Budoc pen Gildas had a mind like an iron mantrap below his ferret-like features. As the noble visitors to Arden had cut deeply into Bedwyr's reserves of winter food, the master was irritated by the interruption, but he managed to hide the greater part of his impatience. Budoc looked skyward with a slight smile on his narrow features, a grin that simply added to Arthur's shame and his anger with his tutor.

Lorcan explained Arthur's reasoning. 'I have tried to explain that an oath given on a trivial matter is just as important as one that is offered in life-changing circumstances, but Arthur has not grasped the concept. Because I have been in the land of the Franks, I cannot think of a local example where trivial oath-breaking has led to greater sins, and I hope you can provide such an instance to aid his understanding.'

Bedwyr frowned in earnest now, and Budoc took a quick step backward to avoid overhearing the conversation. Arthur wished fervently that the earth would open up and swallow him, regretting that he had ever attempted to argue with his tutor. His eyes darted from Bedwyr's brown eyes to Lorcan's glittering black ones, but he found no comfort in either.

Bedwyr's greying brows knitted together and the look he shot at his son was both disappointed and angry. Suddenly, the finer details of the harvest no longer seemed important, so he dismissed Budoc swiftly and turned his full attention to his foster-son. Under his direct gaze, Arthur's eyes dropped and his sandals made little circles in the sod. The boy looked no older than his age, which Bedwyr found disconcerting and disappointing, because he had become accustomed to treating Arthur like a young man.

'You've heard of the Matricide, haven't you, Arthur?' he began, choosing his words carefully.

The boy nodded and raised his eyes to meet Bedwyr's direct stare. 'Modred broke his oath to the High King,' he answered. 'And his actions eventually started the civil war.'

The Master of Arden searched for the perfect words to drive Lorcan's message home. 'I remember when Modred first came to Cadbury,' he said at last. 'He lied constantly, even in small matters. Later, regarding larger issues, he avoided committing his warriors to King Artor's forces with one excuse after another, all of which were without any basis in truth. He was always eager to gossip and to twist circumstances to his advantage, but no one within the fortress believed a word he said and no one in Cadbury believed that he was a man of honour.'

'So he broke his word in small ways,' Arthur said slowly.

'Yes, boy, and he'd probably been telling falsehoods since he was very young. About your age, in fact. Let me give you a simple example. Everyone knew that his mother had refused to raise him, yet he suggested that he was raised as a Brigante out of some kind of personal choice. Now, Modred had some excuse for his lies because he had no living father or mother who was interested in teaching him how to behave honourably. You, on the other hand, have the advantages of loving parents and a tutor who will hold you to your word.'

'I think I understand,' Arthur said readily, but when Father Lorcan shot him a piercing glance his eyes dropped again and he said angrily, 'No, I don't, Father. I don't see how avoiding saying something or embroidering the truth as the Matricide did is anything like forgetting to practise my Latin when I promised I would.' His expression was mulish, and Bedwyr had to crush the urge to shake him.

'Well then, see if you can follow this example. You remember what your mother told you about the history of your birth?'

'Yes,' Arthur replied, confused by the sudden change of subject.

'What if you were told by a servant that everything your mother had said was a lie?'

'I'd not believe the servant because my mother speaks truthfully, even when it pains her.'

Bedwyr nodded. Both boy and man had forgotten the presence of the priest, who was very interested in the conversation. Lorcan had deduced some time earlier that his pupil was no ordinary lad, but he was now beginning to realise that Arthur might not be Bedwyr's natural son.

'What if your mother insisted that the servant had told a lie, and you then discovered for yourself, irrefutably, that the servant had told the truth? How would you then feel about your mother?'

Silence dragged out between Bedwyr and Arthur, while Lorcan held his breath, fascinated by this keyhole view into the family of his patron.

'I think I would forgive her . . . but I'd never believe anything she told me again. I'd always have to check what she said for myself.'

The words came out in a rush as Arthur dealt with an almost unimaginable betrayal.

'But would you believe her word in small things?' Bedwyr persisted.

Arthur thought hard. 'No, probably not. I'd worry that she was trying to spare my feelings.'

'What if she said you were the most handsome of all her sons?'

'I'd be happy,' Arthur answered, puzzled by yet another change of direction.

'But would you believe her?'

'I don't know. It would depend on whether I thought it was true or not,' Arthur admitted finally.

'In other words, you wouldn't believe your mother in any matter unless you already knew what she said to be true. Her word would be compromised because it had already been proved to be false.'

Lorcan saw comprehension begin to dawn on Arthur's face. As the boy had yet to learn how to hide his feelings, the workings of his clever brain were easy to follow and the priest knew that his student finally understood the meaning of personal honour.

'A lie is a lie, big or small, and we are judged by how truthful we are. If we give our word, we are obliged to keep it, even if it's hard.' Arthur's voice was firm at last and the wide, handsome brow cleared.

'Exactly so,' Father Lorcan said triumphantly.

Bedwyr hadn't relished the interview, but was pleased that Father Lorcan seemed to have the matter of Arthur's moral education in hand. He dismissed tutor and student and went away to find Budoc.

'You see now, don't you?' Lorcan said, trying hard not to betray his pleasure. Finally, Arthur had passed the test and come to a new understanding of oath-breaking, even if the priest wasn't quite sure what lay behind the conversation between Bedwyr and his son.

'Y-y-yes,' Arthur stuttered. 'I'm sorry I argued with you.' He was making a real effort not to cry. As he said, he was no longer a little boy, so he needed to act responsibly as a true son of his birth father. Father Lorcan's lesson had been very painful, but also very necessary.

'You were arrogant, Arthur,' Lorcan explained. 'Do you know what that is?'

When the boy shook his head, Lorcan explained that arrogance meant believing he knew better than anyone else, regardless of respective ages, experiences or birth. Arthur had the grace to look even more ashamed, if that was possible. For the next two hours, the priest had a very attentive and polite young student.

At the end of the lesson, Arthur lurched into heartfelt speech. 'Father Lorcan, I swear to study hard and practise my letters. I'll not make excuse or lie. If something stops me, then I'll tell you, honestly, and I'll take any punishment you give me without complaint.'

'Good,' Lorcan replied easily, giving most of his attention to putting a scroll into its casing. 'I would expect nothing less of a lad of your breeding. Now, go and enjoy the remainder of the day. You will begin your arms training soon, and you'll not have a spare moment.'

One day blended seamlessly into another and Arthur found that the learning went more easily. True to his promise, he practised his letters wherever he was, but Lorcan was too clever to show any overt approval of the boy's diligence. Praise, when it was offered, was for efforts beyond the ordinary, so Arthur strove even harder to please his tutor.

Maeve continued to thrive and Anna was sure that she could leave the babe in Elayne's capable, motherly hands, but Ector had yet to return.

'The boy is probably enjoying the fleshpots of Glevum or Abone,' Gawayne decided irritably, while Bran glowered at the old man for criticising his son.

'Ector takes his duties very seriously, Gawayne. I can guarantee that he will be sparing no pains to find a suitable arms master.'

'I hope he hurries then, for I can't remain in Arden for the winter. I'm needed at home before the first snowfall.'

'At least we should be safe from Saxon incursions in the months to come,' Bedwyr soothed. An all-out brawl between kings was unseemly and insulting to Bedwyr's status, so he reminded both parties that they were his guests and had no need for harsh words. 'I'm confident your journey north will be relatively uneventful, because those buggers usually stay put during the winter months. I think the danger time will be during spring and summer. They know Artor is dead so they'll attack in force then. The border lands have remained far too quiet, especially in the hives of old Corinium and the swamps of Durobrivae. I believe they'll make their move on Ratae and Venonae.'

'As long as you slow them down in the forest, I can smash them along the borders of Arden,' Bran replied confidently. And Bedwyr had no doubts that the Ordovice king would do exactly as he said. A great deal of political influence and many valuable acres depended on Arden's remaining an impediment to any Saxon advances from the east.

'At any rate, without insulting your hospitality, Bedwyr, which has been excellent, we must be gone in two days at the most. Despite Ector's continued absence, we still have to take the bride to Viroconium so that the nuptials can be completed.' Gawayne looked grumpy and dour, which was understandable in a man who had long outlived his time and whose every joint caused him pain. 'And then I can go home.'

'Of course, Gawayne.' Bedwyr understood immediately. After all, he too had passed his fiftieth year, and he felt all the aches and grumblings of a fighting man's body that had slowly grown old. 'We have been honoured to have your presence here for so long. As for the situation with Arthur . . . well, your help has been invaluable. You might be old, my friend, but you're not finished yet.'

Gawayne glared at his host from under his sandy-grey brows. 'I tell you, Bedwyr, Artor had the best of it. He died gloriously, having killed his enemy. Not for him the slow decay into blindness and senility. I envy him at those times when my bones ache so badly that my physician is forced to give me an infusion of poppy. But it's only a temporary cure. Would you believe that the great Gawayne would rather *talk* about seducing a pretty lass than bed her? Aye, it's true. And I'm ashamed that I've been reduced to this slow decline. Seeing young Arthur sometimes makes my heart hurt. Artor lives again, and who's to says he doesn't see us through the eyes of the boy? Fuck it, Bedwyr, getting old and into my dotage is almost more than I can bear.'

Bedwyr recognised that honesty rather than self-pity lay at the bottom of Gawayne's complaint, so he clapped his friend on the back. 'It comes to us all, Gawayne. I don't relish the prospect myself, but I scorn to wait passively to have my throat cut by the Saxons as I sit at my fireside. Let's pray that the gods will grant us a quick death with our swords in our hands.'

'Aye, friend. We can but pray that such will be our lot.'

So the Arden household and its guests heaved a sigh of relief when a small party on horseback, with Ector at its head, hove into view during the late afternoon. A very tall stranger in full battle garb stood out in the forefront of the troop, just behind Ector's sturdy figure.

'At last!' Gawayne muttered, *sotto voce*, as the gates opened to admit the troop. 'Ector has arrived at last, and with a barbarian arms master, if these old eyes don't betray me.'

Ector leapt off his horse with a young man's vigour and strode across the forecourt to greet Bedwyr and the two kings. Having observed their approach from the apple orchard, Arthur skidded to a halt before his kinsman.

'Ector, you've come,' he piped in his boyish voice. Ector ruffled the lad's wild hair absently and addressed Bedwyr with a broad smile.

'My apologies for my tardiness, but good arms masters are hard to find. However, I believe we've been lucky enough to secure a man well qualified to serve your purposes, Master Bedwyr, so allow me to introduce him.'

Ector motioned for the large barbarian to join them. The huge man had dismounted from his horse, and now strolled nonchalantly towards the kings. When he reached them, he bowed low and then stood at his ease, perfectly comfortable in his own skin.

'As I promised, this is Germanus. He insists on using this name and refuses to give his father's gens or nomen. He has sworn allegiance to the Merovingian king and also served the lords of the north. He was trained as an officer in the old Roman style of the Frankish kingdoms, which accounts for his moustache and his bare chin.'

'You are a mercenary then, Germanus?' Bedwyr asked bluntly, because a warrior for hire suggested a man who had no personal loyalty that led him to fight for a cause, payment in gold being his only motivation.

'No.' The flat syllable was unequivocal and Bedwyr raised his eyebrows in surprise.

'No?' The response from Gawayne was immediate, and Germanus swivelled his body to face this new questioner. He had already assessed the three men who stood before him with a warrior's practical eye for detail.

'I'm a professional, masters, and I go into battle to earn my coin. I sign on, or I did, to serve any master who pleases me. I do not sell my services to the highest bidder, and I resent any suggestion that I would.'

'No offence was intended,' Bran apologised. 'But we require an arms master for Bedwyr's son, young Arthur here, who may become an important man in the west in years to come. You must understand that few good things are spoken of mercenaries in this land, for most such men are famed for changing sides when it becomes expedient for them to do so.'

'Not me. I serve those masters who are worthy of my talents. I'm getting old now, so I came to Britain to settle down, marry and perhaps father a family. I've a tidy sum put by, so I don't need your coin. I am not yet convinced that I should waste my talents on a mere stripling.'

'Well, then, we must try to persuade you.' Bedwyr's voice was slow and reasonable. He had not taken to the barbarian, but the man was obviously powerful and the array of weaponry, both on his person and attached to his saddle, pointed at proficiency in a wide range of the instruments of death. He was tall, near to six feet three inches, and hugely wide across the shoulders. His legs were long, as were his arms, and his whole body was ridged with hard muscle.

'However, before I sing young Arthur's praises, I must ask whether you are Saxon, Angle or Jute in origin. As they are our sworn enemies, I'd be a fool to take one into my household.'

'Like Hengist and Horsa before me, I am Friesian on my mother's side, but I was trained in a Librone troop in the lands of the Salian Franks. I have no interest in local politics and wish to be left alone. The role of arms master would suit me well, for I've shed enough blood for one lifetime and wish to retire permanently. Does that answer satisfy you?'

'I suppose it must,' Bedwyr replied, and Germanus snapped his head back aggressively, a reaction which did the barbarian no harm in Bedwyr's eyes. Any man whose word was doubted would naturally be insulted.

Germanus's face was open, possibly because he was clean shaven except for a pair of bristling moustaches that were reddish-brown in colour. His hair was much lighter, tawny like a good ale, with highlights of blond like sun-kissed sand. His armour was workmanlike, very scarred on the leathers, while some of the iron plates were buckled. Gawayne noted that every item, from his sturdy gauntlets to his breastplate and groin guard, was polished and oiled. His boots were also clean, and very soft, to permit his feet to find purchase on any terrain, while the exposed hair on his bared head was neatly braided and ready for the unadorned helmet that rested in a pouch on his saddle. A spear, a long knife, a sword, a bow and a rectangular shield were also beautifully maintained and unembellished.

Arthur stared openly at the warrior who might teach him the martial arts. He was keenly interested, but disappointed that Germanus's accoutrements looked so plain, and surprised by Gawayne's obvious approval of these unadorned weapons. The old king had spotted the gladius that rested in a scabbard attached to Germanus's saddle, close to the Friesian's right hand.

'May I examine your gladius, Germanus? I sense that my request impels you to send me to the Christian devil, because you know it means I don't trust you yet. But only a foolish man would stand unprotected before a seasoned warrior until he knows the person he faces. Your blade will tell me much about you, if you are indeed a true master of weaponry.'

'My Minerva has only one master, but you may hold her as long as you do not harm her. As you may know, she is named for the goddess of the arts and wisdom, especially in weaving, and my beauty weaves death to those who presume to attack me or mine. She is wise enough to know a dishonourable hand and will turn on any man who tries to misuse her.'

Many men would have been amused, but Gawayne respected any man who worshipped his sword. A warrior's life depended on his weapons.

'I can promise you that your Minerva is as safe in my hands as she is in yours. Ah, but the scabbard is beautiful, my friend. The man who made this sheath knew his trade.'

From his position behind his father and the two kings, Arthur peered at the sword, still nestled in its scabbard, and tried to see what was so special about this very utilitarian object. As far as he could tell, the scabbard was made of metal, probably iron to judge by its colour, covered by some kind of roughly textured, dense hide which had been bound to the metallic surface with plain bands of brass polished to mirror brightness. The dark hide was almost black and mottled with brown, grey and amber. A neat, well-oiled clasp held the sword in place until it was released with a rapid flick of the thumb.

'This mechanism is lovely, and deceptively simple. I'd be willing to bet that the sword can't fall in the roughest gallop unless it's released, regardless of the most dangerous tumble.'

Germanus nodded economically, but Arthur would have sworn

that the large warrior was pleased, if the slight flush on his cheekbones was any indicator of pleasure. Gawayne reverently drew the gladius out of its scabbard. The metal blade hissed as it came free of its well-made sheath, revealing the sword in all its glory.

'See the clever mechanism?' Gawayne handed the scabbard to Bedwyr, who whistled softly in admiration of its weight and craftsmanship.

'Fish skin?' the forest master asked as his strong thumbs caressed the unfamiliar texture of the hide covering.

'Close – but not quite. This is the hide of a curious creature that lives in warmer waters and can hide itself in sand. It has two huge flaps of skin on each side that are shaped like triangles, and can grow to be six feet across. Its hide is very tough, and beautiful, as you can see, and the beast is armed with a vicious barbed spear attached to a long, narrow tail. It looks like no animal I have ever seen and it is called a manta, or devil fish. Its hide is perfect for a scabbard because it is so strong and long lasting.'

All the men showed their interest in Germanus's explanation, and Ector and Bran were impatient to feel the texture of the hide.

'It's not rough exactly, but it repels water,' Germanus added. 'It also prevents a hand from slipping in blood, and even the sharpest sword finds it difficult to cut.'

'You've used the manta skin on the hand grip of the gladius, too, over a wooden base, with the iron tang driven through to the pommel. It's a lovely design. May I examine the blade?'

Gawayne waited for Germanus's permission, and then the Otadini king swung the weapon in a circle, manipulating the blade into a deadly parabola of shining metal. Arthur was fascinated by the sound Minerva made as she cleaved the air. It was almost a hiss – but far more seductive.

'The balance is beautiful. Feel it, Bedwyr.' Carefully, Gawayne handed the gladius to the forest master, whose eyes showed a moment of pain.

'I've never seen or held the like – except for Caliburn, King Artor's sword. And that weapon will never again be seen by the eyes of men, for it lies deep in the icy waters of a tarn, guarded by Nimue, the Lady of the Lake.'

Germanus looked confused, so Bedwyr quickly explained and the barbarian's face cleared with understanding. 'Thank you for the compliment, my lord, but the man who wrought this blade deserves your praise rather than its owner. I simply saw the genius in an old swordmaker and I've had many reasons to thank the gods that he wrought Minerva for me.'

Bran ran his thumb along the double-edged blade and winced as its razor sharpness left a fine line of blood in its wake. 'Minerva is one sharp bitch,' he muttered. 'Like King Gawayne, I envy you such a lovely weapon.'

Germanus nodded his thanks with a strong man's phlegmatic economy.

'Have you ever changed sides in a conflict?' Bran asked softly. 'I suppose that's a disingenuous question, because you can lie and I would never know it. But I ask as one warrior to another. The boy, Arthur, is a kinsman and I would have him strong and well trained as my ally, once he is fully grown.' He pressed a scrap of cloth to his thumb to stem the bleeding from Minerva's kiss.

'Never, King Bran. Every man who earns his bread in battle must have his own personal code. I choose whom I fight for after I have ascertained the nature of the men who offer me coin, and I'll not risk my skin for a pretender, a traitor or a liar. My life is worth too much to me to be lost for an ignoble goal.'

'A good answer,' Bedwyr responded. 'How old are you?'

'I am near to thirty-five years, and I know my reflexes are slower than they were. I'm still a skilled warrior, especially in strategy and leadership, but from experience I am aware that my years will progressively slow me down until I am killed by a younger man. And in answer to your unspoken question, my trade has meant that a family of my own has been barred to me. A man pining for his wife is a liability on the battlefield. Part of the reason why I considered Prince Ector's proposition was that I could set down roots in this land, wed and eventually have sons of my own.'

Impressed, Bedwyr called Arthur to come and meet Germanus, who offered the boy his hand as if they were equals, thus winning the boy's immediate approval.

'I am pleased to meet you, young man. If your father and I come to terms, I believe we will rub together well, as long as you understand that I must be obeyed as your superior officer. Can you do that?'

'Aye, sir. My tutor has taught me not to be fractious . . . or hardly ever.' Then Arthur smiled and Germanus fell under the spell of the boy's charm. But like any other professional fighter's, his face said nothing.

'How old are you, boy, and what are your current skills?'

'I am seven now but I am soon to turn eight years of age. I am accurate with my sling and I can kill a hare without flinching, just as my father taught me. I can also use a small knife, although it's not good for much. I've sharpened it so I don't hurt the animals I kill.' Arthur handed over his old knife and Germanus tested the truth of the boy's assertion with the ball of his thumb. The blade was very sharp and worn, but Arthur kept it oiled ready for use. Not a speck of rust marred its surface.

'My son is modest. He is nearly as talented at tracking and woodcraft as I am,' Bedwyr said with pride.

Germanus examined father and son with a wise man's objectivity.

Bedwyr was obviously a skilled warrior, judging by the positioning of the buildings and defensive emplacements in his fortified home. As for the boy, there was something enigmatic about that open face, the grey eyes that were cold and warm by turn and the long-boned frame that was so full of promise. Never an overly imaginative man, Germanus suddenly visualised a double-bladed axe he had seen in Italia. To cover his confusion and puzzlement over Arthur's origins, he focused on the one fact that stood out above everything he had been told about his potential charge.

'You're very tall, young Arthur. If your hands and feet are any indication, you're likely to be as tall as I am – maybe taller.'

Arthur stared up at Germanus and grinned. 'Everyone calls me a beanpole, sir, so I'll have to take what the gods give me, I suppose. Mother says I grow out of sandals too quickly, but what can I do? I just grow and grow.'

Germanus felt as if the air shivered about the boy. Something impelled him to raise his hand to his chest in the shadow of a salute in the old Roman way. Then, embarrassed, he let his hand drop to his side. 'Fair enough, lad,' he said quickly to cover his unusual lapse of common sense, and then Arthur was dismissed so that the men could discuss terms and payment in private.

The royal visitors had been gone for a week when Arthur arrived at a run for his daily lesson in arms. To the boy's surprise, Germanus had concentrated on perfecting the skills he already possessed with the sling and the knife, and Arthur chafed at the slowness of his progress. On this particular day, he appeared carrying a very long bundle wrapped in a length of homespun that was unravelling a little at one end.

'What have you got there, lad? It's obviously a weapon of some kind. You've not been borrowing your father's knives, have you?'

Arthur was insulted at the thought. 'No, sir. I swear. My mother gave it to me recently and told me it is part of my inheritance and I should take great care of it. I wanted to show it to you, so you can tell me something about it.'

The boy's face was so open that his affront was clearly written for anyone who chose to see. Germanus nodded in understanding. 'I believe you, lad, so let's have it. Show me your treasure.'

'It's very long, sir.' As he spoke, Arthur unwrapped the bundle to reveal a knife that was almost the length of a short sword. It was distinguished by an unusual hilt, formed to represent a sinuous, malevolent dragon which protected the hand of the wielder with a mesh of outspread wings and serpentine coils. The decorative hilt was covered with a thin layer of pure Cymru gold.

'Gods!' Germanus breathed. 'What a superb weapon! May I feel its weight, Arthur? I've never seen the like of this before.'

Arthur handed the knife to Germanus, hilt first, and the arms master swore under his breath at the feel of the sharkskin grip and the beautiful balance of the weapon as it seemed to fit itself into his hand.

'The owner of this beautiful blade was a large man, I'm sure, and his hands were long and very fine. It was designed specifically for him, and the length tells me he was as large as I am, at least. And he would have held it just so.'

Germanus fell into a fighting crouch with his sword in his right hand and the Dragon Knife poised in his left, waiting for an opening so it could taste blood. The blade was beautiful, edged on both sides and curved just a trifle towards the point. Hours of care had been lavished on it, and the arms master could see that it had been honed and oiled over many years of hard usage. A tiny dent along one wing spoke of a hard sword slash averted by the web of iron that protected the owner's hand.

'This was Bedwyr's knife?' Germanus asked, a trace of incredulity in his voice, for this weapon was surely designed for a great king. Arthur was inclined to be insulted by the implied slight on his father, and he stiffened a little in anger. But then his innate honesty reasserted itself.

'No, master. This knife was an inheritance from my . . .' Arthur's voice trailed off in confusion. 'Oh, it's too complicated to explain. Bedwyr's hereditary weapon is the Arden Knife, which gives him his title, and you should ask to see it, but this weapon never belonged to him. Perhaps I shouldn't have shown it to you – I only did so because I wanted to boast that I owned such a beautiful object. My father might tell you its history if you ask him, but it's not my place to reveal secrets. I've been told that I must learn to use it as soon as I'm big enough to hold it properly. At present, I can barely lift it in my left hand.'

This whole situation is curious, Germanus thought as he tried to keep his face blank. This young boy possesses a truly great treasure, a completely original piece of art as well as a weapon that any warrior would kill to own.

None of his envy showed on his bland face, but he determined to bring up the subject of the Dragon Knife with Bedwyr as soon as possible, as training with this weapon would affect the schedule that Germanus was planning for his charge. The boy was already tall for his age, and he promised to be an extraordinary physical specimen when he put some years behind him. To wield such a knife, he would need to build up muscle in both arms. A good swordsman should always be able to use either hand with ease, but such ambidexterity was not possible for most men.

But, more important, the man who had used this knife did not use a shield. To hold off a skilled adversary with a sword and a knife alone left no room for error or carelessness. Arthur must be trained to become unusually fast to be worthy of this weapon, for only speed could counteract an unexpected blow if he had no shield to protect him.

And so, as he carefully planned Arthur's training strategy, Germanus decided to devote part of each day to exercises that would build up the boy's physical strength and speed. When asked, Bedwyr avoided explaining Arthur's relationship with the original owner of the Dragon Knife, so Lorcan and Germanus, the two outsiders in Arden, spent many fruitless hours speculating on the mystery surrounding their pupil. In the absence of any answers, except the fact that the boy must learn to use the knife, Germanus devised a regime specifically for that purpose. Weights would build muscle, so Arthur was given pieces of scrap iron that could be lifted and tossed from hand to hand whenever the boy was free of lessons. The size of the weights would be steadily increased as Arthur developed muscle tone.

But Germanus wanted more than simple muscle, for Arthur must become more than just a muscle-bound brute. The boy was also encouraged to climb and run, not that he needed very much urging to do what all lads love. In some ways, Arthur was disappointed that this regimen was considered work, but Germanus was clever enough to explain his strategy after observing his charge's daily activities. When Arthur understood the implications behind the differing modules used in his training, he soon became an eager and diligent student. The arms master began to appreciate Arthur's enquiring mind.

'So I need to build up my strength and speed,' Arthur repeated, his brows knitted with concentration.

'In a nutshell, lad, yes.'

'It seems wrong somehow to enjoy my training, don't you think, master? But I like my lessons in Latin, so I suppose it makes sense that climbing trees and running every day could be fun and still be useful. I *think* I understand what you want.'

This child is unnatural, Germanus thought. At his age, all I bothered about was mountains of food on my plate and endless play. What have the gods given me to work with? He sounds like an old man – but one who has charm, an even more dangerous gift than his physical strengths. He must be trained to understand the right paths that a man should follow to achieve his ends.

Germanus and Lorcan discussed their pupil on many occasions over jugs of ale, and both agreed that they were fortunate in being asked to mentor a pupil who was rarely argumentative or bad tempered. But Germanus remembered the mental image of a double-sided axe that had leapt into his mind when he met Arthur for the first time. Such a friendly, outgoing child seemed innocuous, but the arms master had seen both sides of his nature.

Animals loved Arthur. The huge, shaggy dogs that were so beloved by the Romans in times of war clustered around him, drawn by wordless communication with a boy who both ruled and loved them. His devotion extended to horses, donkeys, cats and even the small creatures of the forest that he killed as part of his hunting. But he never permitted any animal to suffer, even if it would ultimately flavour his stews. Animals killed for food died swiftly and relatively painlessly at his hands as he worked to keep their velvet eyes mesmerised by his own pale gaze. He believed that the guardians of Arden were duty bound to care for every creature, useful or otherwise, that dwelt within the boundaries of the forest.

Bedwyr had been concerned for some time that trap-lines were being set along the northern borders of Arden. While peasants needed to live, and the bounty of the forest was free to all men who needed to feed their families, he had come across a number of trapped beasts who had been left to die of thirst so that removal of their pelts was easy and trouble-free. Arthur had been with his father when they found the corpse of one obviously pregnant roe who had been caught by a leg-snare. The animal had broken her leg in her frantic struggles to free herself, and Bedwyr was forced to turn away from the terrified death-stare of the deer when he saw what had been done to the poor creature.

The hunter had left the simple twine trap that remained embedded in the flesh of her delicate foreleg, for its removal would take time and a replacement was easily made. Most of the carcass was untouched, although her hide with its faint, beautiful winter markings had been taken, and the hunter had carved away the choicest joints of venison.

Germanus, who was Arthur's shadow whenever they left the palisades of Arden, glanced down at the lad's pale face, and what he saw there concerned him far more than the barbarity of the roe's death. Under his sheet-white complexion, the boy's expression was set in uncompromising lines and his eyes were white with suppressed fury and horror. None of his mother's forest-green gentleness was visible in their unspoken desire to make the perpetrator of this crime pay for such cruelty. Germanus almost took an instinctive step backward at the repressed violence in the boy's fixed stare.

'I swear, Lorcan, if Bedwyr had caught the peasant who had killed that deer so casually, Arthur would have needed to be restrained. He'd have killed the hunter with that little knife he uses, regardless of how big his adversary was. I've occasionally seen that killing rage before, and I'm afraid for our pupil if he carries such a depth of aggression within him.'

'Our boy is as sunny tempered as a sweet spring evening,' Lorcan said, the poetry of his people in his blood overriding the responses of a practical, phlegmatic ex-mercenary. 'I've never seen what you describe, but I've heard rumours that he has a temper at times. We all do, so we shouldn't hold his occasional fits of anger against him. From what you describe, the peasant who butchered the deer deserves to be cuffed around a little.'

'You didn't see young Arthur's eyes, Lorcan, so you don't understand. They were like flat panes of glass, and I saw right through them to read the punishment he'd have meted out if he had the chance. What I saw in those eyes wasn't pretty – not remotely.'

'You're exaggerating, boyo,' Lorcan soothed. 'Any soft-hearted lad would feel the same as Arthur did.'

Germanus shook his head, rejecting the inadequacy of words to describe the subtle, murderous, violence that lived deep below the boy's charm. But he began to plan a series of exercises that would teach Arthur how to control his emotions, although even the boy's detractors would probably have denied that such precautions were needful to protect the world from a seven-year-old boy.

The weeks sped past and winter settled over Arden like a cloak of white. The snow came early and, with it, frozen mud and sleet. Suddenly, the daily runs ceased to be quite so pleasurable. With Germanus's blessing, Arthur began to range further and further from his home as he ambled towards the eastern margin of the trees in an effort to develop his growing stamina. Sundays, which should have been spent in practising his letters or in religious studies, saw him travelling deep into the forest clad in heavy furs and stout snow boots, a pouch of food slung over one shoulder. For protection, he was armed with the sharp knife on his belt, his sling round his neck, a collection of pebbles and a tinderbox in a leather bag, weaponry that should be suitable for any eventuality.

One particular Sunday, after a heavy overnight snowfall, Arthur broke his fast in the kitchen long before sunrise. The cold had forced him to break an icy plug that covered the surface of a barrel of water beside the kitchen doorway before he could fill a hide container to take with him during his ramble through the woods. Donning his trekking gear, he collected cold food for his pouch and set off with a cheerful wave to the disgruntled guards on the palisades.

'The young master's off again. Damn me, but he's growing like a weed, all legs and elbows and hair,' one of the guards grumbled to his companion to break the tedium of a freezing morning. Both men were looking forward to a bowl of porridge and hot, spiced wine to chase away the chill of the freezing winds. 'Why he'd want to go off gallivanting through the woods beats me. Fair enough in summer. Even autumn! But it's too fucking cold to be out in the wind at this time of day. Still, I suppose even a freezing wander through Arden Forest is better than lessons with that damn priest.'

His friend crossed himself at the blasphemy, for he was a Christian. Both men watched the lanky boy stride away between the trees and disappear into the morning darkness. They shrugged at the oddities of the great ones and soon forgot him.

Deep in the shadows of the trees, where the dawn's light couldn't reach, even when it stained the open sky, Arthur felt at one with his world. Within his cocoon of furs he was warm, and he liked the nip of cold air on his cheeks and nose, and the stirring of his blood when he breathed in the gelid air.

Around him, the silence was broken by cracks, growls, moans and thuds as tree limbs strained under the weight of snow like old men rising from their beds and shaking off their blankets. Large white lumps fell from high branches, causing thuds and clatters that continued down to the forest floor. In the distance, Arthur heard a smaller tree as it fell, ripped from the ground by the weight of accumulated snow that had fallen during the night. Every step the boy took broke the fresh white crust with a sharp little crunch as the animals of the forest began to stir in the early morning breeze that moaned through the sheltering trees.

Arthur looked up at the black sky through a net of bare branches and sighed with pleasure. Because he was loved and his time was fully occupied, he had no complaints about his life, but sometimes he longed to be completely alone. He had so much to try to absorb – so much to understand.

In a few short months, he had learned that his birth father was a greater man than he could have possibly imagined. He had met living legends like Gawayne and Lady Anna, and he had acquired two outstanding teachers. While the two men were very different, he liked them both, despite feeling that they chose to train him for the coin they earned for his tuition rather than affection for himself. In his cynicism, Arthur wasn't far off the mark, because Germanus was still cautious around him and Lorcan had ceased to care for anyone very deeply after the death of his family. None the less, Germanus admired something in Arthur's nature while remaining wary of his hidden depths, and Lorcan feared to become attached to him only because he knew he could never endure the loss of another person he loved.

The boy set forth towards the east, using the weak stain of the sun for navigation as he worked his way carefully through the woods, feeling the stretch and strain on his young thigh muscles as he avoided traps, hollows, fallen trees and hidden pits on the forest floor. His fertile imagination could conjure up the outcome of any fall: the snapping of a leg in a trap of hidden branches and the difficulties he would face in seeking assistance. Unlike most boys of his age, he took considerable care while he enjoyed his apparently aimless wanderings.

A tall oak tree claimed his attention, so he paused to climb its broad branches in order to fix his position. From the top, he had an unimpeded view of the forest and, beyond it, the rolling hill country that stretched out like a white blanket. Familiar as he was with the inhabitants of the area, he searched the landscape for the farm of Ednyfed Crookback, a peasant farmer who lived with his growing brood in a gentle fold in the hills. Crookback possessed a thriving little property where he grazed black-faced sheep and tended several acres of arable land.

Arthur observed a wisp of smoke above the tree line. Yes! He looked again. The smoke was in the general direction of the Crookback farm, but surely it was a little too dense and a little too black to be the normal result of a kitchen fire.

The boy felt a brief moment of concern. In winter, fire was the farmer's friend, for it warmed the circular fieldstone cottages and the barns and outbuildings. But thatched roofing could catch alight by accident, and wild sparks could transform warm comfort into deadly danger. Kitchens were usually partly covered lean-tos that were designed to prevent the spread of fire, but smaller fire-pits within the one-room cottages were used for warmth during the winter months. Astute farmers ensured that the pits were guarded from anything that could easily ignite, but accidents were part of daily living.

Arthur liked Ednyfed Crookback and Cathella, his fat, pretty wife. Their four healthy children were always excited when Arthur visited, especially their eldest son, Rab, who was of a similar age. Cathella always found a cup of milk for him and a slab of bread or an apple from their stores, and he would spend an hour or two with Rab and his brothers working at the homely tasks of a farmer before the long walk home to Arden. Each time he ventured so far, he would arrive back at the palisades after dark, to the annoyance of his father and concern of his mother, so these visits were sporadic and precious. Normally, he would never intrude on their hospitality in winter when food was scarce, but the blackness and density of that finger of smoke was beginning to worry him.

'I'll just make sure that all is well at the farm,' Arthur whispered to the tree trunk, before carefully making his way down to the ground again. Whistling under his breath, he set off in the direction of the finger of smoke.

Something itched in the back of his brain, a warning that told him he should exercise caution during this trek, and that dangers could lie in the forest around him. But like all healthy young animals, Arthur only believed the evidence of his five senses, so he had no hesitation in casting off the shivering alarms that lurked near the back of his skull.

Nevertheless, like a sharp fingernail drawn across the bones inside his head, the feeling of dread intensified as Arthur began to increase his pace. In the visceral part of his brain, he sensed that something was seriously wrong in the terrain that lay ahead of him. Keeping to the higher ground where the snow was thinnest, he trotted on with his mile-devouring young stride. The dark morning passed away and a pallid noon was close when the trees thinned and only the occasional copse remained to offer shelter.

The feeling of danger was strong at the back of his mind. The fingernail inside his head seemed to scratch his skull anew, and his hair stood on end at the base of his neck. With one hand shading his eyes from the glare of the snow, the boy scanned the hills below the finger of smoke that still rose, greyer and wispier now, before being dissipated by the light breeze.

There! Only young eyes could have seen it. And only someone who was already feeling a presentiment of wrongness would have bothered to look for it. Off to his left, along a ridgeline leading to a copse of trees at the crest of the small hill overlooking

Crookback's cottage, was a trail of footprints that were already blurring in the faint heat of the sun. He wasn't alone on this chill day. At least two other travellers were abroad, and their footprints remained as silent witnesses to their passage.

The smoke was nearly gone now, but it should still be rising if a farm fireplace was its source. Indecisive, Arthur stood on the edge of the forest. He knew that the wise course would be to go home and inform his father that something was amiss, but he was concerned for the safety of the Crookback family. He also feared to appear a fool if the family should be found, well and happy, the next morning. Finally, trying to convince himself he was imagining all sorts of disasters attached to the innocent footprints of passing strangers, Arthur set off to see what secrets lay beyond the hill.

The Landscape of Crookback Farm

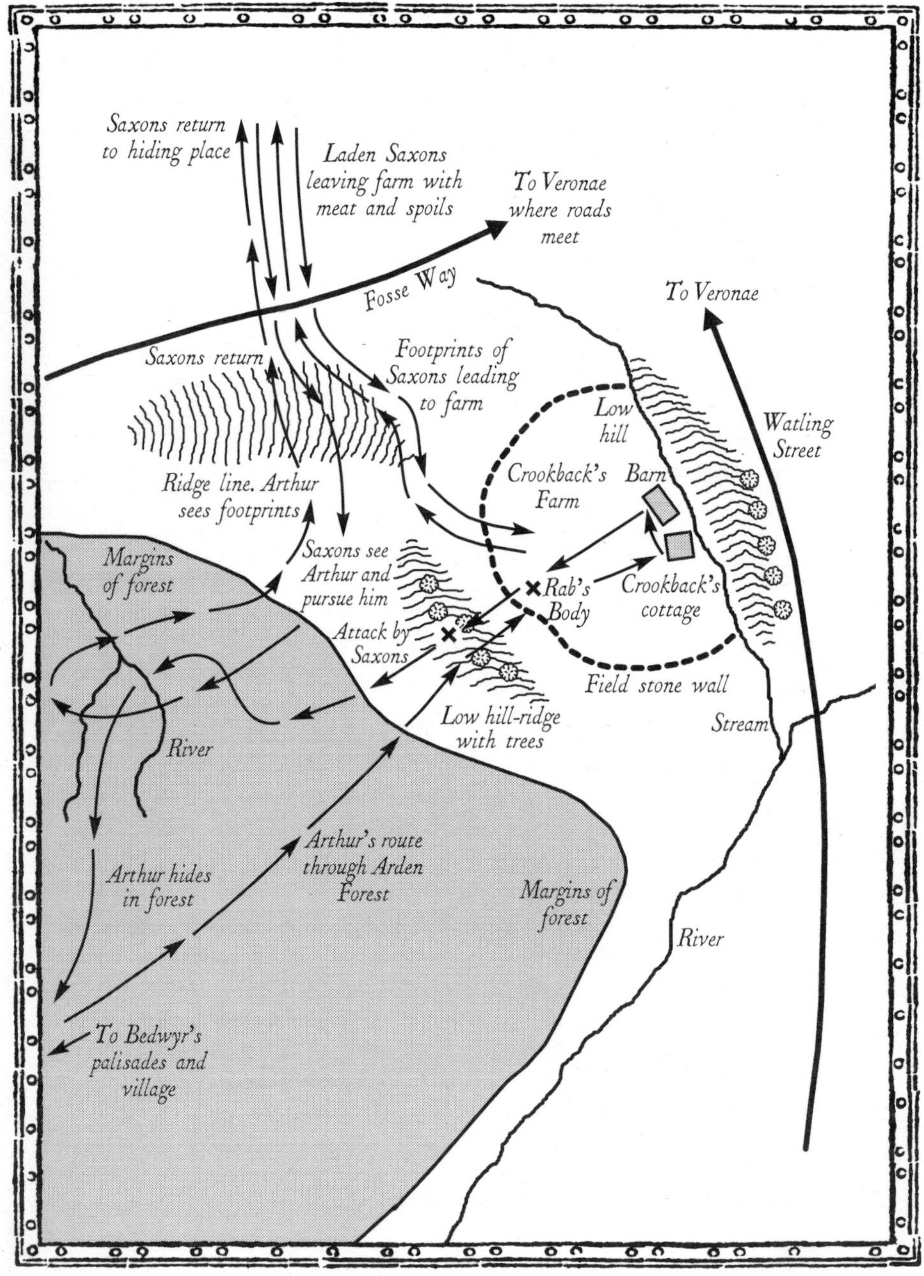

Saxons return to hiding place
Laden Saxons leaving farm with meat and spoils
To Veronae where roads meet
Fosse Way
To Veronae
Saxons return
Footprints of Saxons leading to farm
Low hill
Watling Street
Crookback's Farm
Barn
Ridge line. Arthur sees footprints
Saxons see Arthur and pursue him
Rab's Body
Crookback's cottage
Margins of forest
Attack by Saxons
Field stone wall
Low hill-ridge with trees
Stream
River
Arthur's route through Arden Forest
Arthur hides in forest
Margins of forest
River
To Bedwyr's palisades and village

CHAPTER VII

OUTLAWS

> Never break a covenant, whether you make it with a false man or a just man of good conscience. The covenant holds for both, the false and the just.
>
> Zoroastrian scripture, 'Avestan Hymn to Mithras', verse 2

Panting with exertion, thigh muscles screaming with strain as he ploughed into the cover of the small copse, Arthur launched himself onto flat ground and collapsed, prostrating himself behind a fallen tree trunk. With a quick glance back the way he had come, he saw the clear and unmistakable scars of his footsteps in the pristine snow. Swearing and sweating, he turned his attention to the farmland spread below him.

At first, the landscape appeared undisturbed. Low walls of fieldstone had been piled up to create rudimentary pens and to protect fields of grain that had long been harvested. A stream struggled through a long line of willows at the very base of the hill, its waters half frozen and silent. The croft rested near the stream on a small rise that would protect it from rising waters in the thaw. Off to one side was a barn where the croft's cows and single horse were stabled during the winter, along with Crookback's chickens and any sheep that were too young or too old to forage for themselves. Here the farmer kept his grain, which was milled downstream then stored in barrels for personal use or for trade and barter. Workmanlike, the farm had flourished for a century or more, safe in the knowledge that other fortresses kept outlaws, thieves and Saxons away from these hills and the quiet, bucolic existence of Britain's rural population.

At first glance, the farm seemed untouched, and Arthur sighed with relief. Then his eyes followed a last, dismal trail of smoke and saw that it was rising from the barn, not from the cottage.

Cupping his eyes with the heels of his hands, he struggled to shake off the snow-blindness that made details difficult to discern from a distance. There! The roof of the barn, which was made of crude wooden slabs instead of the usual thatch, was scarred along the highest point of the pitch.

'Everything is so still,' the boy whispered to himself to break the unnatural silence. 'It's all too quiet if the barn has caught fire. Surely there'd be signs that Ednyfed had fought the blaze.'

Even though an internal voice screamed at him to run for home, Arthur forced himself to scan the terrain below him. He could see several mounds at the front of the barn where the churned snow and what lay there had been covered with a thin dusting of pristine whiteness, but he refused to accept the evidence of his eyes and turned his attention back to the unnaturally silent cottage.

The door was firmly shut, but two ravens cawed raucously on the circular thatched roof as if warning the boy to come no closer. Superficially, the cottage seemed untouched, but many blurred footprints had poured in and out of the door, including one set that headed in his direction.

What to do? Reason told Arthur that he should run back the way he had come and raise the alarm, but the thought of Rab and his brothers steadied him. They could be hurt and bleeding, and his retreat might result in their deaths. Although his heart was beating painfully in his chest, he removed a store of pebbles from his pouch and loosened his knife in its scabbard. The weapon was little more than a toy and the blade was thin from honing, but Arthur knew it wouldn't fail him if it were needed.

If the farm had been attacked, why hadn't it been set alight and burned to the ground? Arthur's brain answered the silent question: the owners of those footprints don't want Ratae or Venonae to know that there are outlaws on the loose. If the heavy snowfalls continue all winter, the authorities might remain ignorant of what has happened here until the spring thaw.

But I don't know what *has* happened, Arthur's rational mind replied.

So you'll have to find out for yourself, won't you? And then you must let Father know as soon as possible.

Before he could change his mind, the boy thrust his knife between his teeth, touched the sling round his neck, clutched the pebbles in one hand and lunged down the hill on his belly, hoping that any watchers would thus miss his fast approach to the nearest wall of the farm. With his eyes darting from left to right, he leapt over the fieldstone and almost landed on Rab's corpse on the other side.

'Fuck!' Arthur swore when his foot skidded on the frozen head of his friend. Crouching, with bile in his throat and a silent apology to Rab on his lips, he turned the stiffened body onto its back.

Rab's eyes stared up at the grey sky with the distant glare of someone who has travelled far into the Otherworld. His skin was very white, and his eyes were set deeply back in his skull. Crystals of snow were trapped in his tousled hair, as well as in his dark eyelashes, while his mouth was still contorted in a scream of defiance or an agonised appeal. Rab had been caught at the wall where he had run with the desperation of a fleeing child. Arthur could see the spray of arterial blood across the black stones, telling him where Rab's exposed throat had been cut from behind with a casual slice of a knife or a sword. Rab's clothing was stained to the hems with his lifeblood, which had frozen stiff in the hours since his death.

'He was dead before I left the palisades,' Arthur murmured aloud for comfort. The body had been expertly searched, and even a bronze amulet that Rab had always worn round his throat as a talisman had been stolen. Under the frozen blood on his neck, Arthur could see a blue line in the white flesh where the leather cord had been snapped off by an impatient hand.

Arthur's every sense was on full alert as he made his way to the cottage, poised to turn and run at the first hint of threat. He kept low, bent almost double, and followed the half-filled trail of Rab's running feet until he reached the cottage door. He noticed the large, blurred shapes of the pursuer's footprints and guessed that the outlaws had worn the flat overshoes of wicker that made walking on snow so much easier. Back in his sleeping alcove in Arden, Arthur kept an old battered pair of these snowshoes, but such encumbrances were of little use in the forest so he had chosen to leave them behind. Now he wished he had brought them, for they would have been very useful on this flat, exposed stretch of ground.

With his mind cringing from images of his dead friend, he could guess at the scene that would greet him when he entered the cottage. But knowing and seeing were two very different things. If his information were to be of any serious use to Bedwyr, he must face whatever lay within, even if the child in him shuddered at the thought of what he might find.

Ednyfed Crookback had defended the small, one-room cottage with his hoe to the best of his ability. Inside the confined space, a spray of blood on the mud-daubed walls seemed to indicate that at least one of the attackers had suffered a wound. Ednyfed had done his best to bar the door, but his dishevelled nightwear spoke of a stealthy attack in the middle of the night. No warning had come from the farm dog, which was probably one of the snow-covered shapes at the front of the barn.

A hoe, no matter how sharp, could never be a match for swords, so except for the first lucky sweep Crookback had had little chance to protect his family. He had died from a long, looping sword cut under the arm that had wielded the hoe. The sword had cloven deeply into his chest, leaving a gross, gaping wound in its wake that gave the farmer no chance of survival. By the angle of the dead man's head and body, Arthur realised that Ednyfed had probably still been alive when his family had been slaughtered in front of him, and would have been in an agony of spirit far worse than any physical pain. The direction of his wide-eyed gaze led Arthur to the next victim. The boy had suffered a sword cut that almost separated his head from his body. Mercifully, the lad must have died instantly.

No quarter had been given to the other children, whose throats had been cut when they tried to hide behind their mother's skirts. For her part, Cathella had taken longer to die, although Arthur could barely understand the brutality of a rape that was followed by a casual knife thrust in the throat. The knife was old and rusty, and the warriors had left it in the fatal wound like an obscene brooch. Because of its aged, worn haft, Arthur thought the knife must have belonged to the cottage, and the outlaws hadn't even fouled their own weapons with Cathella's blood. She was less important than the farm dog in their eyes, a morsel to be tossed away when her purpose was done.

Arthur dragged his friend's shift down to cover her spread legs, even though it was stiff with her frozen blood. He had never considered the fate of women caught up in warfare before, but now he imagined his mother in such a position and a slow, red anger began to build in his chest, a visceral response to the arrogant, murderous force that had destroyed this place. In the silence of the bloodstained cottage, he realised that his breathing was ragged and tears were pouring down his cheeks. In a daze of pity, he tried to close the eyes of Cathella's staring corpse, but they were stiff and unresponsive. The hut stank of blood and urine, and he started to vomit weakly into the straw. Even as he retched, his brain began to sizzle with the growing tide of rage and he wished with all his heart that he was big enough to follow the outlaws and make them pay for the evil they had inflicted on these hard-working, gentle people.

Once he stumbled out of the cottage, Arthur took a grim pleasure in firmly closing the door to frustrate the still-cawing ravens. Reluctantly, he moved towards the barn. The snow-covered mounds proved to be the shaggy farm dog and several butchered sheep, while another half-dozen frightened beasts huddled in a corner of the simple wooden structure. The carcasses showed evidence that the outlaws had carved out the choicer cuts of meat to take with them when they departed. Conscious of the needs of the surviving animals, Arthur lugged a bale of hay out of a barred storage room inside the barn and spread it for them to eat until Bedwyr arrived. A few remaining chickens roosted on the highest rafters, but Arthur could imagine how easily most of the flock had been carried away after their necks were wrung. The birds flapped their wings in warning at the boy, but soon fluttered down from their safe perches when he scattered several handfuls of grain onto the hard sod floor.

Looking up, he saw the scars of burning in the sturdy oak beams of the barn where a stray spark from a torch had ignited the lighter roof staves. The ceiling had burned, but the tough oak rafters had resisted the flames, so only one corner at the back of the roof had collapsed. 'That's why the buildings seemed sound from the top of the hill,' he murmured to himself, taking comfort from the small sound of his own voice.

Then he heard a soft mewling from somewhere within the pile of fodder in the grain store. With apologies to the dead Crookback for further disturbing his handiwork, Arthur moved the barrels of grain to reveal what was left of a litter of kittens. New tears sprang to his eyes at this random act of cruelty. A snowshoe had crushed the babes while their broken mother lay in a tangle of smashed bones, defiant to the death as she had tried to protect her little ones. But there, in a far corner of the hay bales, a single kitten still lived. This was the strongest of the litter, one whose adventurous spirit had ensured it was out wandering in its restricted world when the marauders had come with death in their hands and feet.

In an unconscious need to ensure that something survived this charnel house, Arthur scooped up the small ball of fur. Despite an attempt to use its immature claws and teeth to puncture his hands when he thrust it deep inside his furs, the frightened kitten was quickly seduced by the warmth of its new nest. At first it nuzzled against his flesh in a fruitless search for milk, but then, unsatisfied, it curled into an indignant ball and promptly went to sleep.

'It's time to go, little one. Father must know what has happened so that Rab and his family can be given a decent burial, while the other farmers in the district must be warned that an enemy is on the move along the fringes of Arden Forest.'

Like his birth father before him, Arthur was quick to act once he had formulated a plan in his mind. Without a backward glance, he headed back to the farmhouse, hugging the ground as he used the footprints he had already created to retrace his steps. He hoped that if the outlaws returned they would be confused by this simple ploy, but he was clever enough to know they wouldn't be fooled for long. Once in open country, he would have to put his trust in the gods to hide his tracks during the dash to Arden, whither he must run as fast as the deep snow and his cumbersome furs permitted.

Still following his earlier trail, he reached the shelter of the wall and paused to close Rab's eyes, using two of his precious pebbles to hold the eyelids down. Several crows waited on the stones, examining him closely with their black beady eyes. They flapped their ragged wings just out of striking distance, but Arthur chased them off temporarily by using another pebble to kill one of them with his sling. However, he knew that the scavengers would be back as soon as he moved away, so he rolled Rab's shirt over as much of his friend's frozen face as he could before embarking on the muscle-straining climb to the top of the small hill, keeping his profile as low as possible. The warnings in his head still shrieked of danger. With a disconcerting feeling of being watched, he made his way doggedly up the slope, ignoring the strain that such strenuous exercise placed on his thighs.

He could see nothing amiss and his ears heard nothing that threatened danger, but still he took out his knife and clenched it in his mitten-clad palm, certain that peril was near at hand. His grip on the handle of the knife was impeded by the fingerless glove, so with mental apologies to his mother he stripped off the mitten and shoved it inside his shirt beside the sleeping kitten. Then, taking care where he placed his feet and keeping the noise of his passage to a minimum, he pushed his way up the last ten feet of the incline.

Within the protective shelter of the copse, Arthur took a deep, shuddering breath and dropped to one knee. The noise in his head suddenly became a solid wall of high-pitched keening, so he rolled backward instinctively. Whether he saw the sudden fall of blood drops from above or heard the scrape of boots on a tree branch, he had responded to the warning instantly, and his quick reflexes saved him. A fur-wrapped savage hit the ground awkwardly in the exact spot where he had been kneeling just a second before.

'You little bugger!' the outlaw swore in the common tongue as he grimaced with pain after his heavy fall. As if space had suddenly slowed to a crawl, Arthur had sufficient time to register that the man was bleeding sluggishly from somewhere in the fleshy muscles of his left thigh, which made him slow and awkward. The wound inflicted by Ednyfed Crookback on his killer was the only advantage Arthur held, for his adversary was over six feet tall, burly and thick bodied. Seeing the axe thrust securely into the man's sword belt, Arthur knew he was a Saxon.

Thanking the gods and the warning voice in his head, Arthur leapt to his feet with a boy's flexibility and tried to dodge around the bear-like figure blocking his path. He was too close to use his sling as a weapon, and if he came within reach of those huge, grasping arms he knew he would be finished. Like Rab, he would be left to lie in the snow, staring at the grey, darkening sky until the crows stole his eyeballs as a tasty morsel. Shuddering at the grotesque mental image, he crouched as close to the ground as he could and sought an opportunity to flee.

'My friends will be back for me shortly, you little Cornovii shit. Then you'll discover why this land will soon be ours, and how we'll drive you into the sea.'

The Saxon's eyes moved constantly in the manner of any seasoned warrior as he searched for external threats. He already knew this child was fast on his feet and surprisingly dexterous, for he had been concealed in the copse when Arthur had first approached, and had monitored his subsequent movements closely. Initially he had been deceived by the newcomer's height, for the lad already stood as tall as a short-statured man, and his furs gave the illusion that he was wider than he actually was. By the time he realised that his adversary was a stripling, the boy had slid down the hill and was out of reach. The Saxon had cursed Loki, the trickster god, for making a fool of him, and then decided to wait in a tree along the route he guessed the boy would follow on his return journey.

In face to face combat, Arthur knew his only advantage was his speed, but he also understood that the Saxon could easily bar his escape route. Effectively, the thick copse of trees that he had seen as an ally was now a barrier along the path to safety, one that provided no room for him to manoeuvre. The Saxon had time on his side, for the longer they tarried the closer they came to the moment his able-bodied friends would return for him.

Arthur decided to take a fearsome risk to break the impasse. He turned and ran back towards the farm, fumbling for his sling as he retreated. Once the weapon was in his hand and a stone was fixed in its pouch, a matter of seconds, Arthur whirled round and let the stone fly, despite being far too close to the target for the shot to be aimed effectively.

With a bellow of pain, the Saxon fell backward to the ground, clutching one wrist. He had raised his hand instinctively to protect his face when he saw the sling, so the stone had smashed his right wrist before being deflected into his left eye, momentarily impairing his sight. Cursing and raging, partially blinded and with his face streaked with a mixture of tears and blood, he struggled to get to his feet. Not giving himself a chance to lose his nerve, Arthur ran like a hare. He attempted to leap over the hunched figure, certain he could get a good start on the lumbering adult, but this was a trained warrior and not so easily defeated.

Confident that a mere child was no adversary, the Saxon hadn't bothered to draw his sword or his axe. Now his razor-sharp reflexes brought his uninjured hand up in an attempt to catch the leaping boy. He managed to snatch at Arthur's ankle and brought the lad tumbling to the ground, although he was unable to keep a solid grip on Arthur's flailing legs.

As Arthur struggled to his feet, shaking his head where he had struck a tree trunk during his tumble, the Saxon drew his knife and slashed viciously at his exposed belly, intent on gutting him like a fish. The blade caught Arthur as he leapt backward, slicing shallowly across his chest from one side to the other. The cut immediately released an oozing of blood that looked far worse than it was.

Fortunately for Arthur, his furs suffered the worst damage, but the terrified kitten, rudely awakened by the fall and the ensuing struggle, was digging its small claws into his flesh. Dimly, Arthur was aware of this, but he felt no pain. He had heard that warriors could suffer hideous injuries in the heat of battle yet fight on because they did not feel the agony associated with killing wounds. He hadn't believed such tales, but a part of his brain now registered that the stories he had heard might have been true.

Above the screaming in his head, the boy felt a red mist settle over him that was part anger and part fear. He threw himself bodily at the Saxon and clung to him like a limpet, his legs wrapped around the man's waist, seeing Rab's ice-sprinkled hair, Cathella's staring eyes and the agonised expression of Ednyfed Crookback superimposed over his enemy's snarling, bearded face. This animal was one of the men who had killed a harmless farmer attempting to protect his family as best he could. With a scream that matched the noises in his head, Arthur brought his own knife down again and again, striking blindly at any part of the furred hide in front of him he could reach until the writhing figure stopped pummelling his back with clenched fists.

When the man beneath him ceased to struggle, Arthur's brain slowly cleared and he realised that he was alive through sheer, blind luck. Fortuna had spun her wheel and made her decision against all reason. His suicidal charge had only been successful because the Saxon had dropped his knife in the abruptness of it, and then been slowed by his thigh wound until Arthur's blade, descending in yet another wild slash, had embedded itself in his eye.

Run, Arthur, run! They're coming for you!

As Arthur straddled the dead man, he heard the mental words of warning as if they had been spoken aloud. He struggled to his feet, his body one long ache of agony as pain finally cut through the heat of combat. Time was short, so he steeled himself to pull his knife from the Saxon's face. He knew he would always remember that sound, wet and sucking, as the weapon was withdrawn from the curdled eye and the brain behind it.

Bending to cut the snowshoes from the Saxon's belt, Arthur spent several minutes strapping the basketwork soles over his own boots: any time lost now would be regained once he started to run. Then, with every muscle protesting and his body demanding rest, he set off, skimming over the deep snow in a brisk, sliding gait that was faster than he could ever have managed without his purloined snowshoes.

Careless now of hidden traps in the snow under his feet, Arthur made good speed across the wide expanse leading towards Arden Forest and safety. Then, just when he thought he would reach the trees unobserved, he heard a muffled shout off to his right and a quick, snatched glance took in five warriors on the crest of the far ridge where he had seen those first footprints earlier in the day. One of the men stood and pointed in his direction. The group turned and began to plough through the snow with the obvious intention of cutting him off.

Although the band of warriors was still some distance behind Arthur, the men were moving fast, for they were as accomplished with snowshoes as he was. However, even as he mustered his failing strength to increase his speed, Arthur calculated that he would still reach the margins of the forest long before they did. But could he maintain the distance between them? The Saxons held a decided advantage, for Arthur's snowshoes betrayed his path at every step. They would be able to follow him with ease, even in the thickest parts of the forest.

'First things first!' Arthur murmured softly, remembering one of Bedwyr's favourite phrases. Reaching Arden Forest was the first goal, and he would worry about everything else once he was in the shelter of the trees.

'Help me, Artor! Help me, Mithras! Help me, Mother!'

Arthur called on every god and dead relative he could think of, but silently now, not daring to waste a single breath as he fled as fast as his immature legs would permit. He knew he was leaving a clear trail, but they could see him anyway and were moving swiftly in their effort to intercept him, so he concentrated all his energies on reaching the denser trees wherein lay his best chance of survival.

His light weight and his knowledge of the terrain worked in his favour, and he reached the sanctuary of Arden over a hundred spear lengths ahead of the Saxons. 'It's all downhill now,' his mind told him as if he were already free of his pursuers. Rather than waste time unfastening the straps, he sliced away the snowshoes from his boots. 'It's time to head for water.'

Arden was a lacework of streams and rivulets, wild, tangled and immeasurably old. One major river cut through the southern margins and led to Glevum, many leagues away. In addition, the forest was bound by two major Roman roads, Fosse Way to the south-east, running through Venonae and Ratae, and Watling Street to the north-east. The Crookback farm was situated before the intersection of these two roads at Venonae, and as Arthur moved over the forest floor he pictured the landscape in his head as if it were an unrolled scroll containing one of Myrddion Merlinus's charts. The outlaws had targeted this section of land, *this* farm, because it was close to the intersection of these two strategically important roads. Now, Arthur was even more certain that he had to reach Bedwyr alive, and as quickly as possible. Many lives would depend on this information reaching the kings of the west.

The forest held no terrors for Arthur, but the loss of blood from the long, shallow wound on his chest was steadily weakening him, for his rapidly beating heart was preventing any reduction of the blood flow. The urgency of his mission must take precedence over his own life, so if fate decreed that he should perish from his struggle to reach the palisades and Bedwyr, then so be it. As long as he arrived and passed on what he had seen before he died. The Saxons must not catch him, nor must he die of exhaustion, blood loss or exposure while on the run in Arden Forest.

'First things first,' he muttered again, and stopped to drink beside a streamlet so small that it was little more than a trickle down the side of a tree-choked incline. Then, moving the near frozen kitten to his outer fur, he dragged off his shirt, ripped off both sleeves and tied them together, before tearing the body of the shirt into two and making a large pad from one of the halves.

Conscious of the sounds of pursuit through the floor of the forest, Arthur hurried to bind the pad over the wound and across his chest with the knotted sleeves. Finally, he formed a sling out of the remainder of the material and tied it round his neck to carry the kitten. The knife could still be valuable, especially for climbing, so he thrust the weapon into his belt and set off again. Only cunning, understanding of the terrain and his ebbing strength could save him now.

Time passed slowly, but at length the short winter afternoon began to draw in and Arthur climbed painfully up the trunk of a large oak to obtain a final set of bearings in what was left of the fading light.

From his perch high in the tree, he caught an occasional glimpse of the outlaws following his trail and his heart sank at their nearness. Another tree was nearby and Arthur realised that he could reach one of its large, intertwining branches with relative ease. Wincing at the strain on the muscles crossing his chest, he forced himself to move from branch to branch, following a crazy route above the forest floor where, despite his wounds, he could move much faster.

Eventually, the encroaching darkness began to present new dangers for Arthur. He was marooned in the tree tops high above the forest floor, and he knew that any fall would be fatal. He had little room for error as he limped his way from tree to tree, and when he almost slipped after losing his footing in the deteriorating light he decided to huddle in one of the forked branches of a huge oak and rest during the hours of darkness. When he was sure he was secure, he made himself comfortable.

In his short, privileged life, Arthur had never known such a miserable night. Afraid to sleep in case he tumbled from his perch, he allowed the complaining kitten to suck snow from his hand for sustenance, and had reason to be grateful to the little creature whose constant demands kept him alert. During the madness of the day he had lacked any time to eat his casually packed lunch, even if his appetite could have survived finding Rab and his family, but now he chewed pieces of cold meat to soften them and fed the resultant mess to the irritable little cat. Fortunately, it had been started on solid food by its mother, although it wasn't quite weaned, and it attacked the chewed meat with inexpert enthusiasm.

Exhausted, in pain, and with eyes almost closing of their own accord, Arthur clung to his precarious perch for the long hours between dusk and dawn. In that dreadful time, he had the opportunity to think about his life. His mother would weep if he died, but she had other children to console her, no matter how much she cared for him. Bedwyr would also be very sad. Arthur knew his foster-father genuinely cared for him, but he also understood that Bedwyr saw the face of his dead friend in his son. Bedwyr had loved the High King more than any other person in his life, and Artor had represented those values that Bedwyr believed were worth dying for. No one else would really care, Arthur finally decided. And that was as it should be.

'We are all expendable,' he murmured with adult understanding, not realising how remarkable his thought processes were for such a young lad. What we are in childhood is potential. What we might have become is what should be mourned if we die young. What would Rab have become if he had been permitted to live? A master smith? He loved the idea of making objects with iron and fire. In killing the boy, the Saxons had killed the potential craftsman.

If I live, I will try to achieve my potential, Arthur vowed silently. The man who made the Dragon Knife fulfilled his, and created something that has lasted long beyond the fragile limits of a man's lifespan. During that long, dark night, Arthur became determined to make his life worthwhile, so he vowed to drain Lorcan and Germanus dry of every piece of knowledge they possessed. He owed that much to himself, and he owed it to Bedwyr and Elayne. He owed it to Artor, the man who had provided the seed that had given him life.

'I'll not die in this tree,' he swore. 'I'll reach the palisades and I'll see those Saxons dead for what they have done.'

When dawn came, he began the long journey to Bedwyr's hall once more, moving by instinct rather than conscious plan. He did not know it, but the Saxons had retreated during the night to pick the farm clean of food, grain and livestock for the winter months, hoping that the young interloper had died in the forest. In relative safety, therefore, but stumbling with exhaustion and loss of blood, Arthur returned to his home.

A number of Bedwyr's warriors had been organised into a search party that had begun combing the forest at first light. One small band of horsemen found the boy just an hour's walk from the palisades. They carefully lifted him onto a horse, where he leaned against the rider and allowed his exhausted muscles to relax. When the rescuers reached the hall, the boy was asleep in the saddle.

The next four hours passed in a dream – or a nightmare, depending on the point of view of the onlookers. Elayne supervised the warriors who carried her eldest son to his room, her face drawn and pale from worry, Father Lorcan close behind her. Arthur had scarcely been lowered onto the bed when Bedwyr arrived, dishevelled from searching along the forest trails during the night. He had heard the rumours that were circulating among his men as soon as he dismounted from his horse, and was eager to know how his son had been wounded.

'What's amiss with the boy? Where has he been?' he began. Lorcan had bared Arthur's chest to expose the rudimentary bandaging and had begun to soak the bloodstained pad from the flesh with warm water, while Elayne was nursing a very indignant kitten.

'Father,' Arthur croaked, trying hard not to cry from Lorcan's ministrations, even though the priest was attempting to be gentle. 'You must ride to the Crookback farm at once. It's really important.'

'Slow down, boy,' Bedwyr ordered, suppressing an urge to shake the lad for the worry he had caused his mother. 'Who gave you this wound?'

'A Saxon. Oh, Father . . .' Arthur was suddenly close to tears. 'I killed him with my old knife. He might have a wife and children at home, but I never thought of that. And it's too late now!'

Then, to his shame, Arthur began to weep as he suddenly realised the finality of death. All the horrors of the previous day swept over him in a wave.

Still burdened with the complaining kitten, Elayne bent over her son to comfort him, and Bedwyr noticed the little creature for the first time. 'Where did that come from? Get rid of it,' he ordered, and Arthur cried out in dismay.

'Please, Father, I've carried him all the way from the farm, and he's mine now. Please let me keep him. He's only making that noise because he needs to be fed.'

'Very well – someone take that damned cat and give it some milk,' Bedwyr decided quickly. 'Where did you go that put you in so much danger, lad? We've been worrying all night.'

'I went to the Crookback farm to see Rab. But he was dead . . . they're all dead . . . they were killed before I got there. I couldn't do anything to help them.'

'But Crookback's farm is only just beyond the margins of Arden, and it's within easy reach of Fosse Way. Who would dare to strike so close to our borders?'

'I think they were Saxons, Father – in fact I'm sure they were. The man I killed told me that I'd soon discover why they would eventually own these lands. I think there were six of them in the group that chased me, but there could have been more. They spent half the night searching for me in the forest, so they really wanted to stop me from spreading the news. If I hadn't decided to visit Rab, the murders might not have been discovered until the spring thaw. Oh, Father, it was terrible.'

'Oh, my love,' Elayne crooned, patting her son's shoulder. 'You must have been terrified.'

'I was so angry that I wanted to kill them all, Mother. I suppose the one I did kill is still there, unless his companions have taken his body away to prevent discovery. Do you think the spirits of the people we kill wait in the shadows to take their revenge on us? Old Berwyn says it's so, and he was a warrior for many years before he became too old to fight and became a gardener. He has told me tales of his life in the army of the High King. Will my Saxon haunt me?'

'Not if he tried to harm you first,' Father Lorcan whispered as he lifted the water-soaked pad from Arthur's chest to reveal the long slash, which was fast becoming inflamed. 'You're going to have an interesting scar to excite the ladies.' He whistled quietly in amazement at the length of the wound.

'I was lucky. He had already been wounded – it looked as though Crookback caught him on the thigh with his hoe – or he would have killed me. He was on the pathway, and I couldn't get past him.' Almost dry eyed now, Arthur described how the Saxon had died.

'It's more likely that his shade will be haunted by the spirits of Ednyfed Crookback and his family, so I doubt that he will be concerned over you,' Bedwyr said, for Lorcan was occupied with Arthur's wound. 'No, there is no need for you to fear the dead, Arthur.'

'Will you find them and kill them?' Arthur asked, his teeth clenched against the pain as Lorcan used hot water laced with stinging spirits to cleanse the cut. It was one of Myrddion Merlinus's techniques. Unfortunately for Arthur, the treatment was painful.

'I shall take great pleasure in destroying every one of them, Arthur. But for now you will remain in bed and rest. When Father Lorcan has completed his ministrations, I will get about the business of convincing the Saxons to stay well clear of my lands.'

In case his earlier words had been too gruff and unkind, Bedwyr gripped his son by the shoulder before ruffling his tangled, knotted hair. 'I'm very glad you survived this trial by combat, my boy, for your mother would never have forgiven me if anything had happened to you. You've been brave and true, so don't trouble yourself with guilt over the man you killed. He was a warrior and understood the risks of his trade.'

'Besides, he underestimated a weaker opponent,' Father Lorcan added. 'It is to be hoped that you will remember the lesson of this scar when you grow into manhood. A desperate creature will do almost anything to stay alive, regardless of how weak it might appear to be.' He smiled down at the boy. 'But for now, lad, I'm going to heat this small iron to cauterise the end of the wound under your arm. It's the deepest part of the cut and it is a little reddened, so it's better to be safe than sorry.' Father Lorcan grinned sardonically once more. 'This will definitely hurt you more than it hurts me.'

With a troop of twenty mounted warriors at his back, Bedwyr set out after the Saxons as soon as Arthur was asleep. Elayne kissed her husband before he mounted and made him promise to return safely, which he did while laughing down at her serious, worried face.

'I might promise to live, precious, but I can't actually guarantee it. As well you know! Take care of the boy.'

Then Bedwyr and his warriors trotted away from his hall in a flurry of snow. At the farm, the Cornovii warriors discovered that Arthur had been meticulous in his descriptions. Only a few dispirited chickens had survived the looting, for the Saxons had taken everything edible from the farm's stores, careless of the mess they made. Even though snow had fallen, their tracks were still visible, unusually deep because of the weight of meat and grain they carried.

'That greed will be the death of them,' Bedwyr told his captain drily as the troop set off in pursuit. Only when every Saxon was dead would Bedwyr take the time to bury Ednyfed Crookback and his family. The Master of Arden Forest was certain that Crookback would forgive him from the shadows where his shade was waiting for his murderers to join him.

Bedwyr's scouts found the Saxons' camouflaged campsite with relative ease and the Cornovii troop gathered above the fold in the hills. Bedwyr decided to attack during the hours of darkness, when his horses would have a devastating advantage. Any guards would be despatched by two warriors sent ahead on foot to clear the way.

Once the guards were eliminated the warriors would light a shielded torch, a signal that Bedwyr could begin the attack.

Although taken by surprise, the Saxons fought like berserkers, and several of Bedwyr's mounted warriors were killed as the troop cleared out the rats' nest that had infiltrated the hills between Venonae and Ratae. One wounded man was taken alive, but even the most creative measures used by the British warriors couldn't set the captive's tongue to wagging. He remained stubbornly mute to the messy end of his life.

Coel, Bedwyr's captain, was amazed at the fortitude of the hulking outlaw. 'These Saxons are brutes. They're too stupid to talk, even when they are faced with certain death,' he muttered as they cut the dead man free and flung his body onto the pile that had been prepared for burning.

'I wish they *were* brutes,' Bedwyr replied sadly. 'But they are still men. And they have a code of honour as strict as ours for all that they act like barbarians. They are what the Celts were before the time of the Romans, so who's to say that our culture is right and theirs is wrong? They are men who are seeking a homeland for their children.'

'They can have any homeland they want, as long as it isn't ours,' Coel countered, puzzled by his master's sad eyes when he should have been elated by the success of his plan.

'They grow confident, for they know that the Dragon King is dead. This is only the beginning, Coel. The darkness is gathering, and who knows whether there will be a dawn in our lifetime? Perhaps it is our tribes who will need to find another homeland before we go to the shades. Where will we go if our forests are barred to us?'

'But that won't happen,' Coel protested, and then his brows furrowed. 'It can't happen, can it, master?'

'How the fuck do I know? The gods will decide who deserves this land, rather than us mere mortals.' Then Bedwyr ordered the fire to be lit under the Saxon corpses and secured the Cornovii dead over their saddles before ordering the troop to return to Crookback's farm.

Coel watched his master carefully, and for the first time saw that Bedwyr had a new, and defeated, expression on his face.

The Saxon Attack on the Hospital at Caussenae

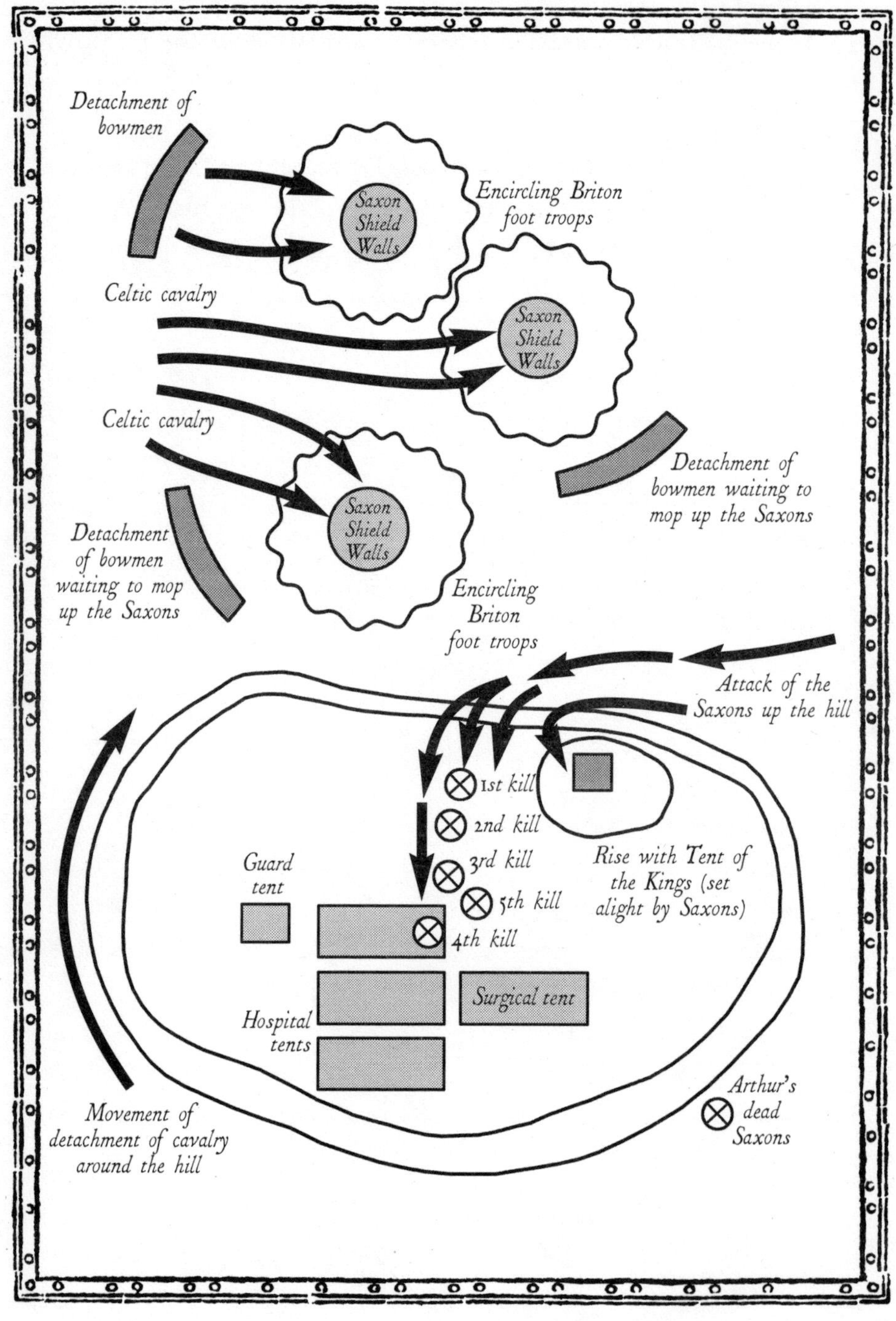

Detachment of bowmen
Saxon Shield Walls
Encircling Briton foot troops
Celtic cavalry
Saxon Shield Walls
Celtic cavalry
Detachment of bowmen waiting to mop up the Saxons
Saxon Shield Walls
Detachment of bowmen waiting to mop up the Saxons
Encircling Briton foot troops
Attack of the Saxons up the hill
1st kill
2nd kill
3rd kill
5th kill
4th kill
Rise with Tent of the Kings (set alight by Saxons)
Guard tent
Surgical tent
Hospital tents
Arthur's dead Saxons
Movement of detachment of cavalry around the hill

CHAPTER VIII

A TWILIGHT TESTING

He maketh wars to cease in all the
World: he breaketh the bow, and
knappeth the spear in sunder. And
burneth the chariots in the fire.
Be still then, and know that I am God:
I will be exalted among the heathen,
And I will be exalted in the earth.

Psalms 46:9

From his position on a hilltop to the north of Ratae, Arthur could see both the Fosse Way and the northern road that came from Londinium. On the fallow fields below, two small armies had met at noon and both sides were now exhausted and desperate as dusk began to settle over the hills to the west.

'I should be down there with Ector, Bran and Bedwyr,' Arthur growled at Germanus. 'I'm old enough and tall enough to fight those shaggy Jutes. How can I be blooded if I never take part in a battle?'

Arthur's face was set in lines of discontent as he stared down at the desperate conflict, so evenly matched that only the Christian God could distinguish friend from foe. At least the plain to the east of old Margidunum was free of the thick marshland and clinging, murderous mud that clogged the ground near old Caussenae, which had recently been put to the sword by the Jute invaders who had burrowed into the landscape like ticks, and would be as difficult to dislodge. The combined tribal invasion into enemy territory had been planned by Bran and Ector as a means of dissuading the Jute thanes from carrying out their regular forays towards Ratae. As Bran explained to Bedwyr, only a concerted show of force would pluck the tail feathers of the proud Jute roosters and convince them that the Britons still had teeth to bite.

'You're only thirteen, Arthur, even if you are almost as tall as me and have sprouted your first chest hair,' Germanus answered sharply. 'Impatient as you are to become a man, try thinking beyond your own desires. I'm as unhappy as you are to be stuck here in safety. But I've been barred from the battlefield in order to guard your back, so you should show a little gratitude to those noble kinsmen who love you. If Bran and Ector should perish on the field, you will be required to act as regent for Ector's son Aeddan. A significant weight of trust and responsibility has been placed on your shoulders, so stop whining.'

'I'm not whining,' the youth snapped back irritably, because Germanus was accurate in his criticisms. Arthur's voice sounded petulant, and he knew it held an unbecoming edge of childish complaint. 'I'm sorry you have to stay up here with me.'

'I know you are, because you hate it when I point out that you're in the wrong.'

Arthur swore creatively in Saxon and Jute, tongues he understood well courtesy of Bedwyr's insistence that he must be able to speak the languages of the enemy with some fluency. Unfortunately,

Germanus also had a passing knowledge of both languages and he cuffed his student lightly round the ear to remind him of their relative positions. So Arthur took refuge in the relative safety of silence and continued to survey the carnage below them, his large arms master standing phlegmatically at his shoulder.

The British forces had one major advantage over the Jutes and their Saxon allies: cavalry. On foot, the enemy's superior height, reach and longer arms could be decisive in close-quarters combat. Further, their lust for personal glory in battle often led them to carry out suicidal charges at their mounted foe, and they would then fight insanely until they were cut down.

The Jute berserker rage was terrifying, especially to young men such as Arthur who had never seen the crazed, mindless bravado of warriors consumed by blood lust. The sight of a half-naked lunatic charging at them, seemingly impervious to arrow wounds or the most hideous injuries, sometimes caused opposing warriors to retreat in superstitious terror. Arthur was able to understand a state of mind that overrode physical pain or human weakness, so he hoped he would not turn tail and run from the attack of a berserker, although he had a nasty feeling that the temptation might be almost irresistible.

He appreciated that cold reason won battles, and that courage was an important ingredient in the performance of a warrior, but he believed that the Roman legions had proved over the centuries that iron discipline could overcome the advantages of greater numbers and better weaponry in almost every battle. Their vassals, the Britons, had learned their lessons well, although many were contrary to the natural inclinations of the native-born tribal warriors. Ultimately, the British cavalry and foot soldiers adopted Roman techniques because their military tactics worked.

Inevitably, both Father Lorcan and Germanus had discovered

that their pupil was the natural son of King Artor, who had used native cavalry to smash the Saxons again and again. Neither man was particularly surprised. While Bedwyr was a man of many talents, the youthful Arthur was an exceptional student – too exceptional to be Bedwyr's son. At thirteen, he stood over six foot in height and possessed the muscular strength of a frame that had never been restricted by the awkwardness of most striplings. He read and spoke Latin like a native, was fluent in the northern languages, and devoured every scroll that came into his possession. His desire to understand the secrets of science, geography and history seemed insatiable. He was an exemplary student, usually calm, good natured and even tempered. Both Germanus and Lorcan agreed they would be hard put to it to find a better pupil.

But Arthur was far from perfect. During the last five years, his sense of dislocation had grown. He knew he could not claim any status through his sire, because any such assertion would bring shame to his mother. On the other hand, he needed to win acclaim in his own right if he was to fill the void that existed in his heart. His kinsmen were living legends, and he hungered to prove that he was a true scion of a great family. At the very least, he desperately wanted to win a name that would rival Bedwyr's, for all men knew that the Arden Knife was one of King Artor's bravest advisers.

And so his enforced inactivity on this bare hilltop above the battlefield almost drove him crazy with thwarted ambition. Germanus had explained the tactics employed by the Britons as the battle developed, and Arthur's quick brain had been fascinated by Bran and Ector's shared manipulation of the Jute warriors' weakness for personal display and heroism.

But the invaders were not wholly foolish, for cooler heads among them advocated the use of the shield wall, a defence that could only be smashed by concentrated cavalry charges or long and costly encirclements by troops deploying in a wedge formation to force open the protective rings. As Ambrosius, Vortigern, Uther Pendragon and Artor had learned to their chagrin, the shield wall was an effective tactic, especially as a last resort when the battle was at a desperate stage, as it was now. At worst, the wedge of warriors could be sucked into the enemy ranks and cut to pieces.

Arthur looked down at the pockets of vicious hand-to-hand fighting and cursed with impatience. He longed to experiment with some of the techniques explained so vividly by Germanus, tactics that had been inherited from the Romans, as well as those modified strategies that had served Artor, the Dragon King, so well for so long. But here he stood, his sword sheathed and the Dragon Knife unused, while other men fought desperately to ensure his safety. If it had not been childish to stamp his feet and grind his teeth, Arthur would have done both. Sometimes status can be very difficult to bear, he thought, and aimed a vicious underhand slash at a clump of flowering thistles with his knife, beheading them savagely and wishing they were Jutes.

But his studies during the last five years had made him acutely aware that he was still the veriest tyro, for all his young strength and height. Germanus had called him 'beanpole' for the past year or so, telling him that he still had inches to grow and muscle to build, and the boy knew that his prime task was to obey his tutors and learn from their expertise. Perhaps Arthur's best characteristic, from his masters' point of view, was his glum acceptance of his duty.

Secretly, Germanus worried how the lad would react when he was forced to kill an enemy in the heat of a pitched battle. He had been haunted by night terrors after the incident at Crookback Farm, but young warriors did not know their full capacity for violence until they were thrust into the chaos of battle and saw the blood of their victims on their weapons and their hands. Some men were racked by guilt, while others felt nothing at all – both undesirable traits for men who must serve on the Field of Mars. Germanus crossed himself surreptitiously, for he had become a Christian since arriving in Arden and the peaceful words of Jesus were at odds with the practical realities of a professional soldier's life.

'Who leads the Saxons on the field?' Arthur asked, intent on the carnage at the end of the shield wall closer to where they stood. The enemy force was obviously tiring and fewer than forty men were still standing behind the huge shields that offered their only protection against Ector's company of archers. Trained by Pelles Minor at Corinium, these bowmen peppered any careless or weary warrior who lowered his guard by even a fraction.

'Unfortunately, our spies have not been able to discover the names of their commanders and do not recognise their symbols, and we couldn't extract any response from the two prisoners we took earlier. As usual, they preferred to die rather than betray their oaths to their thanes.'

'I admire the fortitude of the northerners,' Arthur admitted. 'Their loyalty is absolute, and they'll not betray their masters regardless of the pain they must endure. They may be savages who destroy our holy places and kill our peasants, but they are also brave men.'

'Aye, boy. It's always a mistake to underestimate the enemy or to demonise him. The Saxons are men, like us, with families and children. He wants what I want: a cosy croft and a bit of land where he can keep his horses, sheep and cows – and some pigs. I like pigs.'

Arthur shot an incredulous glance at his tutor. 'You like pigs?'

'What's wrong with pigs? They're clean, and more intelligent than most men.' Germanus ignored Arthur's exaggerated shudder.

'The Jutes and the Saxons want security, land and somewhere to set down roots. They've been chased out of their homelands by other invaders and, by chance, they've found the isles of Britain. They won't retreat, Arthur. This will become their homeland, or they will die here.' He sighed. 'As a man who has no homeland, I can tell you that their honour demands they acquire this land. Although they might die in pursuit of their dream, they know that their sons, brothers and kinsmen will inherit what they've won.'

'I understand that too,' Arthur said. 'I almost wish I didn't, because I can see that it's difficult to kill a man you can sympathise with.'

'All too true, Arthur. As far as I can judge, the main differences between the Britons and the Saxons are your literacy and the way you use horses in combat. But to return to your question, we don't know who leads because we can't read the symbols on their banners. We send men into their settlements as spies, but the Jutes in particular are hard to fool because their colouring is so different from ours. Dark-haired men stand out. We hear a little of their plans, at the cost of many lives, but nowhere near enough for our needs. However, one name I know is that of Thorkeld Snakekiller. If he is in command, I'd expect to see a flag, a pennon or a shield with a dying serpent on it, but either my old eyes are failing or Thorkeld isn't involved in the current activity. Of course, he could be intelligent enough not to broadcast his position. Even King Artor used a plain shield in battle, because only a fool attracts danger.

'There is another name I've heard whispered in the halls of power, Arthur, and it's one that I think you'd best remember. Bran believes the Saxons are supporting the Jutes on the orders of Cissa, may his black heart rot and his conniving brain leak out of his ears. It was a sad day when Hengist and Horsa came to these shores, and after them that damned Aelle and his three sons. Aelle is dead, praise be to Jesus, for King Artor slew him when he secured his crown, but Cymen, Wlencing and Cissa have caused trouble for years. We know that Cymen died at Anderida when it was won back by the Saxons, and Wlencing perished at Noviomagus, but Cissa is still depressingly alive, although he's old now. Our best efforts have been unable to capture him and end his reign in the rich lands of the south.'

Arthur was fascinated by the history of the Saxon invasion of his homeland and picked up the threads of Germanus's tale as the arms master continued.

'Cissa was the youngest son, but he received a nasty sword cut during the battle that killed his father. Some men swear that Artor was responsible.' Germanus was pointing towards Arthur's genitals.

The younger man winced. 'And?'

'Rumour has it he still has his balls and enjoys women with an ardour akin to desperation since he gained his . . . interesting scar. But no child has been born from his unions, so the wound might have caused more damage than was originally thought, praise be to the Lord of Hosts. We have been told that his warriors don't dare to make jokes about Cissa's lack of children within the Saxon lands, but his death would be a huge relief to the Britons in the south who spend their lives under constant threat of attack by his minions. Cissa has a long reach and would be capable of uniting the thanes if he could create a lasting dynasty.' Germanus's dour face lightened for a moment in a sardonic grin. 'Let's hope that blessed sword cut something vital and his women stay barren. The Saxon lords won't tolerate a High King whose death could plunge their lands into the chaos we experienced when King Artor died.'

He realised what he had said as soon as the words were out of his mouth. He grimaced apologetically, but Arthur was still absorbed in the larger implications of Saxon politics and hadn't noticed Germanus's gaffe. The arms master hurried on.

'Cissa has had the audacity to rebuild Noviomagus using his own name, so the town is now called Cissa's Ceaster, would you believe. The man will always be a threat to our people, even if he is lacking half his teeth and a son.'

'Surely one man can't have so much influence here, so many leagues from Noviomagus?'

Germanus snorted drily. 'Aelle and his sons founded the Suth Seaxe, the southern Saxons, who rule from the east through to Noviomagus. Their reputations are unrivalled. Aelle was their first bretwalda, the supreme king of the Saxons, and his son, Cissa, has insisted that he is the second, even if he doesn't have the full backing of the northern Seaxe. I know bretwalda is a heathen word, but it's rather like our brit gweldig, so he had the gall to declare himself the king of Britain. You can think of him as the king of *Saxon* Britain, if such a thing exists, but your people still hold most of the western lands south of the Wall. The Saxons listen to Cissa in those lands that are under their control, and he is the brains behind the stealthy thrust towards our fortresses. We've underestimated the bastard since Artor killed his father, who had been the greater threat.'

'So you believe that we're caught in a stalemate and all King Artor's efforts came to nothing in the end?' Arthur growled in the back of his throat as he stared down at the fields below them.

'Fool of a boy!' Germanus cuffed his sullen charge across the back of the head. The Friesian knew that Arthur was angered by any implied criticism of his sire, but the arms master was voicing the talk among the common soldiers who saw the peaceful years of Artor's reign beginning to disintegrate. 'That remark demonstrates that you're not yet ready to understand strategy and political infighting. Cissa survives on the gloss of his father's superb good luck and his own grim determination to keep what his father won. If he should die without an heir, the Suth Seaxe will be swept from importance by civil war between the thanes as they struggle for the throne. Such a war could last for years unless a man of talent emerges.

'But King Artor didn't fight them in vain, for the Suth Seaxe will feel the loss of their best warriors during Artor's wars for many generations to come. Two of Aelle's sons died fighting Artor, as did their sire. In his wisdom, Artor fought for breathing space against the invaders, rather than make a futile attempt to win an impossible victory outright. Who can stop the wind? But a clever man can use that same wind, as Artor did. Because Cissa has learned from his experience of our way of life, the Britons of Noviomagus were not slaughtered en masse as the Celts of Anderida died in earlier battles. Cissa learned that even victorious Saxons need peasants to till the earth, for they'll not soil *their* hands with dirt and menial toil if they can avoid it. They learned because Artor won that precious commodity, time, which has been of some advantage to both sides in this conflict. Your reasoning is simplistic and you want to argue every order you are given, but at least you are beginning to listen to the voice of experience. Like the Saxons who were confronted by King Artor for thirty years, you have started to learn.'

Arthur grimaced. His arguments against blind obedience could be thrashed out with his tutors after the immediate threat to his kinsmen was eliminated by success on the battlefield.

In the conflict that was unfolding below him, the Britons had finally made inroads into the Saxon defences. By adopting the tactical wiles learned from his father and the strategies developed by King Artor, his great-grandfather, Ector had split the combined

Saxon and Jute forces into small, ineffective groups, and all that was now required was to mop up the last desperate resistance.

Saxon and Jute forces never surrendered, for retreat brought dishonour to each warrior forever, living or dead. Exhausted men perished when their shields were splintered and their swords were broken. Each man fought for his own survival and struggled with his foes like one possessed. Each life was relinquished with the maximum damage to their British enemies and Arthur felt a grudging admiration for these men of the sword who showed such courage in the face of certain defeat.

Deciding that further losses of his warriors would serve no purpose, Ector issued orders for an orderly retreat from the collapsed shield walls and their bloody survivors. Unwilling but obedient, the British warriors moved back, clearing the field so that the archers could fell the remaining Saxons without danger to their own men. Then the cavalry was released to finish off the killing. Ultimately, it was a hideous and rather inglorious slaughter, but the Britons finally won the field as twilight came in a rush of ruddy cloud.

'We've won, Germanus, we've really *won*.' Arthur leaped into the air like a boy cheering his friends after a game of physical skill.

'Aye, we've won, but the healers will fight for the rest of the night.'

Boy and man turned to look at the tents set up behind them on the brow of the hill. Since Myrddion Merlinus had first trained battle surgeons in the reign of Uther Pendragon, the role of healer had become a respected profession. Not far from the commanders' pavilion, a full tent hospital already housed wounded soldiers being treated by a highly trained corps of healers and herbmasters; another tent was used solely for field surgery.

'I'll say one thing for your tribesmen,' Germanus murmured

admiringly. 'Your field hospitals are as good as anything I ever saw in what was left of the Roman armies in the east. Your Merlinus must have been almost as good as your warriors swear he was.'

Arthur shrugged. 'I was much too young to have met him, but if Taliessin and his brothers are any indication of their sire, then the old man was a brilliant healer. Taliessin hasn't been in Arden for years, but he came every spring when I was a little boy. I wish he'd come again. He sings so beautifully, Germanus, and I would love you to hear his songs about the High King. He is said to look like his father, but all I remember is that he had long black hair with a white streak at the temples. King Artor is reputed to have loved Myrddion dearly and held him in high regard. Taliessin too, according to Mother.'

The pair stood quietly as a squad of six heavy-set peasants trotted past them, bearing lit torches and simple stretchers consisting of two poles with stout oiled cloth strung between them. As in the original system devised by Myrddion Merlinus, these bearers were the first of a band of strong young workers whose task was to bring the wounded back to the hospital and to do the heavy work required in nursing the sick. Only strong muscles could restrain a warrior requiring amputation of a leg or an arm, for no amount of poppy juice could deaden a man's nerves when the surgeon's knives began to saw through skin, muscle and bone to save the rest of the breached body.

Earlier that day, Arthur had heard the screams coming from the surgeons' tent and had paled when Germanus insisted that he should watch battlefield surgery at first hand. Viewing the effects of combat on healthy human flesh would stiffen the boy's sense of responsibility in conflicts that were yet to come, for most of the decisions he made as a commander would result in injury to those warriors who served under him. The whole experience had left

Arthur shaken, pale and awed by the skill of the men who sliced into human bodies to retrieve arrow heads or cut away compromised limbs. He had always imagined that healers were unsuited to serve as warriors, but he now saw that they must be as strong and authoritative as any military officer. A strong stomach and a vast store of knowledge were also essential.

The surgeons stood in pools of blood and other detritus from the human body that Arthur preferred not to recognise, while the women who assisted them toiled ceaselessly to clean the folding surgical tables and nurse the injured as best they could. Stripped almost naked, and streaked with blood that squelched in their sandals, the healers seemed to be dyed scarlet under the sanguine light of the torches that permitted them to continue their work long into the night. Some wore their unbraided hair long in imitation of Myrddion Merlinus, while others chose to shave their skulls for cleanliness. Regardless of their choice, they were eventually covered in blood from the top of the head to their toes.

Now, as he looked at the healers' tents in the twilight, Arthur had a nasty thought. 'If I were a Saxon thane, I think I'd have held men in reserve to attack the hospital now that the battle is finally lost,' he whispered, his eyes darting to the furthest reaches of the darkening hilltop. 'While the army is occupied down below with mopping up survivors, a small troop could badly hurt Bran and Ector's cause by killing the surgeons. How many warriors would perish if there were no healers available to treat their wounds in the next battles? Besides, such an attack would be a strategic victory, because it would strike at our hearts and mock our security.'

Against his will, Germanus's eyes began to search the undergrowth of the summit around them. 'You speak nonsense, lad. Saxons would consider war against unarmed men and women to be dishonourable. Besides, they never attack at night, and I can't imagine any of them having the discipline to hold back from the main engagement simply to strike a stealthy blow at us. They don't have the self-control.'

'Really?' Arthur replied doubtfully. 'But they kill priests and rape nuns willingly enough when they want to weaken our resistance, knowing that the murder of unarmed religious folk will always shake our confidence. So what's the difference? We change our strategies from time to time, so why shouldn't the Saxons change theirs if they think it would help them? Everyone used to say they never attacked in winter, but look at what happened at Crookback Farm.'

Germanus pretended to look scornful, but there was a nervous glint in his eye. Although he never spoke of it, he realised that his pupil had occasional flashes of brilliance when he grasped strategy in ways that were far beyond his years. Accordingly, the arms master stalked away from his charge and whistled piercingly into the darkness. A young warrior, barely sixteen years of age, came running with his sword clutched firmly to his side to prevent it from flapping against his knees. His young face was pale with excitement and the orange-brown freckles across his cheeks and his nose stood out in contrast.

Arthur couldn't hear the whispered conversation between the two warriors, but Germanus had obviously issued orders of some kind. As his fist thudded onto his new leather tunic in a hurried, self-important salute, the youngster began to run towards a picket line where several horses were tethered on a length of rope tied between two tree trunks.

'What was that all about, Germanus?'

'I've sent word to Bran to organise the deployment of half a dozen horsed warriors to patrol the margins of this hill – just in case you're right and the Saxons are brighter than I think they are. The hospital would be an easy target for an attack by stealth.'

Flattered, Arthur returned to his concentrated observation of the carnage below them. The bearers were working their way from the edge of the battlefield towards the central point where the resistance had been most intense, checking each body for signs of life. Bran had issued orders that wounded Saxon or Jute warriors were also to be taken to the surgeons' tent, although British warriors were to be given precedence over the enemy. He had learned at King Artor's knee that killing wounded enemies after a battle was a barbarian practice. 'We must portray ourselves as a civilised race,' Artor had told him. 'The only time when such barbarity should be permitted is when there are no other options, or we endanger our own warriors by saving the lives of our enemies. Only then is it expedient to kill wounded men.'

Bran had accepted his grandfather's words. The idealism that underpinned the pragmatic order affected him deeply, and ensured that many tribesmen survived after the last, ruinous battle against the Brigante who now fought against the Saxons at a time when they were truly needed.

The twilight was long and the healers laboured hard to save those men they could, until the night came quietly out of the east and the camp on the hill gradually became still and silent. Arthur could see the dim shapes of horsemen patrolling the perimeter of the field where the battle had taken place, for many dead lay where they had fallen and the next day would be occupied with burning and burying their remains. In the meantime, scavengers would be drawn to the reek of fresh blood and the dead were owed the dignity of protection from nature's cleaners. The soft jingle of harness gave Arthur comfort.

Germanus had instructed a small troop of warriors to wrap

themselves in their saddle blankets and sleep beside the field hospital, where they could defend the tents if they should be threatened during the night. Even without a planned attack on the hospital itself, the large, colourful pavilion pitched on the top of the mound would make a tempting target to the Saxons and Jutes. A small party of enemy warriors might wish to recapture some shreds of honour by killing a British king, even if they should die in the attempt. In fact, Bran, Ector and Bedwyr had chosen to stay with their men on the battlefield, devising the terms they would ask for the surrender of the enemy dead. The Jutes, superstitious as always, were prepared to pay for the return of the bodies of their warriors so that their souls could journey to Asgaard and the home of the gods, and gold would soon change hands.

Arthur had stripped off his armour and attempted to find a comfortable position on the stony earth, but sleep eluded him. He was overly excited, as any lad of thirteen would be after viewing his first battle, so his mind was churning and racing with what he had seen during that long and bloody afternoon. The sounds and smells of conflict had been a revelation, and now that he had time to reflect Arthur realised that he had nurtured a child's idealised vision of combat as something noble and heroic. The actuality of the stink of hot blood, voided bowels and vomit had shocked the boy when he smelled it for the first time in the tents of the healers. He was both horrified and fascinated by how much blood coursed through the human body. Death was a messy, undignified business which Arthur had never expected, for the singers glorified warfare and ignored the unpleasant physical side effects of violence. From what Arthur had seen, the warriors who received gross sword wounds emitted groans and pleas for release from their agony rather than grandiose speeches that tugged at the heartstrings. He would never again think of warfare in quite the same childish way.

'Do all men understand what can happen to them when death comes knocking?' he asked himself softly in the darkness. Something else to discuss with Germanus and Lorcan, he decided, and added it to a rapidly growing list in his head.

Then he heard a distinctive sound as a sandal slid across a patch of gravel and scree on the side of the hill below him. Arthur almost rose to his feet to greet one of the guards, but a sudden shriek in the back of his mind warned him that the noise was far too stealthy for a friendly warrior.

Sliding onto his belly and conscious of the traitorous light behind him from the tent hospital, Arthur peered carefully down the slope. At first, his eyes could see nothing but tussocks of coarse grass and silhouettes of saplings growing along the narrow gullies on the hillside. A troop of horsemen went by at the foot of the hill, visible only as vague forms that passed from pools of inky darkness into the feeble light of a nacreous moon. But as his eyes adjusted to the darkness and concentrated on the areas of deepest concealing shadow, he detected a betraying sign of movement.

There! A hump in the land that seemed more tussock than human shifted carefully for a few feet and then returned to stillness. One by one, twenty men betrayed themselves and Arthur felt a thrill of fear and excitement rush through his blood to his brain.

What should he do? Raise the alarm, you idiot, his mind shrieked.

Suddenly, under the pressure of reality, Arthur felt every inadequacy of his meagre thirteen years. By sheer chance, he had discovered the enemy as they made a careful, almost completely silent advance up the hill. From his limited observation of the Saxons in battle, he knew they would never surrender once he raised the alarm. They would fight until every one of them was dead, wreaking havoc on the hilltop before Bran and Bedwyr knew what was happening.

Don't think! Act! The order came from that instinctive part of his brain that had saved him in the past, and the young man obeyed its primal instructions immediately. Careless of discovery, he rose to his feet and rushed towards the commanders' pavilion to collect his weapons, shouting as he ran.

'Sound the alarm!' he yelled at the top of his voice. 'Awake! Saxons on the hillside! Alarm! Alarm!'

At the raised tent flap, he ran into a dishevelled Germanus, sleep clouded but gripping his sword and shield in his calloused hands. To save time, Arthur pointed back the way he had come.

'Twenty of them,' he spat out. 'Just below the brow of the hill.'

A lesser man would have wasted time in questioning him, but Germanus was an experienced veteran so he cast off sleep and loped away, yelling to alert the guard. Inside the tent, Arthur snatched up his knife and sword before struggling to buckle his iron-plated tunic into position. Leaving it half buckled and unable to find his helmet, he turned and ran back the way he had come in time to see Germanus already involved in a deadly struggle with a shaggy Saxon who had run up the last yards of the incline. More hulking shapes were beginning to materialise out of the darkness and Arthur realised that the hospital was under serious threat. Before he had time to think, he was confronted by a heavily armed Saxon warrior who grinned at him with a flash of white teeth in the dim light.

'Come to me, little boy,' the man sneered, beckoning with his left hand so that Arthur saw the axe dangling from a long thong looped around the wrist. 'Show me how much manhood you have.' The Saxon swung the axe into his hand. 'My sweetheart here will bring you dreams of peace and rest.'

'You talk too much,' Arthur replied, but his bravado was marred by the squeak in his breaking voice. His eyes darted over the huge man. The Saxon's face held no fear of the beardless youth before him.

The warrior laughed. Germanus had warned Arthur early in his training that most warriors used insults to unsettle their opponents and break their concentration, and that he would soon be among the walking dead if he responded by losing his temper. Ignoring the taunt, Arthur fell into the fighting crouch that the arms master had literally beaten into him with the flat of his blade.

The Saxon made a feint designed to force Arthur to overreach himself to counter it, the axe in his left hand cocked and ready to separate Arthur's head from his shoulders with minimal effort. But Germanus had made Arthur practise counter-moves so often that the response was second nature to him. With his feet planted firmly on the rough ground, he stepped backward to thwart the huge man's feint, leaving his adversary with two choices. The warrior could either advance towards Arthur or he too could step back, a move which would force the younger man to come towards him.

The Saxon's choice was never in doubt and the cold part of Arthur's brain anticipated it. Arthur was obviously an immature youth, so the warrior sensed fear in his backward step and advanced in a rush. One of Germanus's maxims flashed through Arthur's head. 'Make big men smaller,' the arms master had told him. 'Cut him off at the knees, and you'll bring him down to your level.' Arthur already stood over six feet in his bare feet, but his adversary was at least six inches taller and twice his weight.

Arthur stepped elegantly to one side and bent at the knee. The warrior's axe passed harmlessly over his head and the Dragon Knife found its mark, slicing through flesh and muscle and across the bone of the Saxon's leg.

With a howl of rage, the Saxon fell to his knees, blood spurting from what was essentially a trivial wound. With the speed of a striking snake, he lashed out instinctively with his sword, but Arthur was very fast. With a spin on his left foot that a dancer would have envied, he evaded the blow and positioned himself almost at the Saxon's back. The warrior had over-extended himself, and Arthur was able to avoid his enemy's boiled leather cuirass and stab with all his strength into his unarmoured side.

His sword slid under the Saxon's armpit and sweetly between the ribs, collapsing a lung in its passage and cutting the great vein leading to the heart. The years of practice on a straw-filled manikin finally bore fruit, and Arthur silently thanked Germanus for the hours of effort that made his actions second nature.

The Saxon collapsed like a felled tree, blood pouring from both his mouth and the wound. As Arthur stepped aside, sweeping his long curls away from his face, another Saxon appeared out of the darkness. Arthur reacted instinctively, raising his sword and taking the full force of an overhead axe blow on the blade. The weight of the attack drove the boy to his knees and he felt his weapon shiver in his hand before it snapped into two pieces.

He tossed the ruined sword hilt aside as the Saxon drew back for the killing blow. Faster than he would have thought possible, Arthur fell to the ground and rolled, careless of the blood from the first Saxon which was fouling the earth. Miraculously, the Dragon Knife found its way into his right hand and he drove upward with all his might, impaling the Saxon on the blade through the unprotected genitals, for few soldiers anticipate a blow from beneath.

The knife was almost wrenched from Arthur's hand by the

Saxon's paroxysms of pain, but he kept his grip on it and stabbed again from his back, using both hands as he aimed for the great artery in his adversary's thigh. Then, drenched in the dying man's blood, which spurted out like a fountain, Arthur clambered to his feet, appropriating the Saxon's sword as he rose.

Around him, the struggle was desperate. Armed only with staves and pikes, the stretcher bearers had joined the fray, led by the freckle-faced, youthful warrior and his four companions who were on guard duty. Although the stretcher bearers equalled the enemy numbers, the British men were untrained farm workers whose talents lay in their brawn rather than their fighting skills. The Saxon warriors carved through them as if they were made of straw and the night was soon alive with screams and prayers and the moans of the dying.

'Ring the alarm bell,' Arthur bellowed with a voice that broke in his mingled rage and fear. 'Ring the damned bell.' Someone in the hospital tent must have heard, because a bell began to toll with the desperate peal of muscles jerking frantically on the end of the rope. Suddenly, Arthur realised that Bran's tent had been set alight and the ruddy glow was illuminating the desperate conflict, giving him his first clear view of the entire scene. Good, he thought as he countered a vicious underhand sword cut aimed at his belly. Bedwyr will see and he'll come to our rescue.

Germanus was fighting a brace of Saxons with the concentration and strength of an automaton. His blade was sweeping in wide arcs that kept the enemy warriors at bay while his shield protected him from the wicked axe blows that had cut the stretcher bearers to pieces. Three of the guard had already fallen, including the freckled youth, but the remaining two protected Germanus's back, forming an effective triangle of iron that prevented most of the attacking force from reaching the hospital. The stretcher bearers had fallen, but they had slowed down and blunted the determined advance of the Saxons. Their deaths had not been an entire waste.

Nor were the healers totally helpless. Several of the enemy had bypassed the main struggle with Germanus and entered the nearest hospital tent with drawn swords. Now one of them suddenly reeled out of the tent into the night, his chest sliced open by a small knife. He was bleeding from a number of small wounds, and ineffectively trying to draw the weapon out of his breastbone with flailing hands. Arthur quickly finished him off with the Dragon Knife. A shaking, bandaged Briton followed him out of the tent, his body leaking blood from wounds that had reopened in the struggle. Armed with a surgeon's scalpel, the man wore the maniacal grin of a patriot still anxious to strike a blow at his enemy, even while in his extremity. Arthur helped him to lie down on the ground before he fell, and then turned to enter the hospital tent.

Pushing through the loose entry flap, Arthur came to an abrupt halt, for several women with sword cuts lay moaning on the blood-stained canvas floor. The warrior who had inflicted the damage was almost invisible under a heaving mass of nurses who had sworn to tend the sick and cause no harm. Arthur watched aghast as one woman screamed in triumph and held up a single blue eyeball in a blood-stained fist. Her long nails were thick with the man's blood from the cuts they had inflicted on him, and her face was vicious with the gleam of crazed revenge.

Then he felt a sting across the forearm, followed immediately by a crushing blow which felled him to one knee. As he rolled away from the Saxon who had attacked him from behind, he realised his right arm was broken. Thanking the gods that Germanus had taught him to use both hands in combat, he cast aside the stolen sword and sprang to his feet to meet the Saxon's second rush, the Dragon Knife in his left hand. Just as he reached him the Saxon stumbled, and in that moment's vulnerability Arthur slashed at his throat. The Saxon dropped like a stone, spurting arterial blood.

Arthur glanced down at the body, still twitching on the canvas floor, and saw a small dart-shaped object sticking out of the man's thigh. Either a healer or one of the women had thrown a surgical tool at him when they realised that Arthur was in imminent danger.

I'd be dead now if someone hadn't thrown that knife, Arthur thought, for the blow knocked the Saxon off balance. I never saw him coming, so I'll need to develop that fighter's extra sense that Germanus keeps talking about. I'll be fucking useless as a warrior without it.

Even though he didn't say it out loud, Arthur took heart and pleasure from the word, for it made him feel manly. But he knew his mother would have cuffed his ear for the curse, as would Father Lorcan, a man who swore like an ignorant savage at every available opportunity, his calling notwithstanding.

With a quick, muttered thanks to Fortuna and her caprices, Arthur left the tent and settled back into the fighting crouch which was now second nature. His right arm throbbed with a steady ache and screamed with outrage if he moved it, so he thrust his hand carefully into his iron-studded tunic to support it before parrying a savage thrust from a slightly smaller Saxon. Reckless with the thrill of battle, he grinned madly, although his knees were weak from loss of blood and he felt light headed. If he was destined to perish on this damned hill, he was grimly determined to take as many Saxons with him as possible.

Feigning an all-too-real weakness which caused the Saxon to rush at him and come within reach of the hungry Dragon Knife,

Arthur sliced at the warrior's face and saw it open and bloom like a strange, red flower. One hand holding his chin together and blood trickling down over his throat, the man charged again, maddened with pain and rage, so Arthur slashed again, opening the hapless warrior's face from the eyebrow to the throat, almost losing his grip on the Dragon Knife in the process. Then, as if by magic, the reeling Saxon disappeared under the hooves of a war horse and was swept out of Arthur's sight. And so, anti-climactically, the small battle at the top of the hill was over.

A troop of cavalry swept across the hilltop, their swords glimmering in the moonlight as they cut down the remaining Saxons. Bedwyr was in the van of the charge and could see his foster-son through the slits in his helmet as the boy swung the Dragon Knife around his head in a glittering circle. Arthur's face was as pale as newly bleached linen, and his hair was a wild nimbus around his head and shoulders.

The lad has turned into a man, Bedwyr thought. How will my Elayne feel now that her chick has grown into an eagle? But Bedwyr knew the answer already, for it is easier to stop the wind or the rain than it is to gainsay the nature of a young man. When Arthur's voice broke and his beard grew, Elayne's boy would be gone. And, if this momentary glimpse was any indication, he'd be off with the warriors.

In the aftermath of the attack on the British field hospital, Arthur was alternately lauded and castigated for his reckless bravery. White with reaction, Ector was far harsher in his treatment of Arthur than he had originally intended. 'You were foolish enough to face fully armed Saxons without a helmet, Arthur? Are your wits lacking? From what Germanus saw during the melee, your sword broke, you didn't consider using a shield and you didn't buckle your armour. Well? What excuses do you have for your execrable behaviour?'

'But there wasn't time. I had to . . .'

'Had to what? Didn't you consider for one moment that it would have saved many lives if you had alerted the guard? Instead, you took action without anticipating the results. Someone should have brought the warning to us at once, for we had a whole army at the foot of the hill. I've seen you run, Arthur, and for a great lump of a lad you're as fleet as the wind. You could have alerted the cavalry long before they heard the watch bell and saw my father's tent burning. How many stretcher bearers died because you wanted a piece of the glory?'

Even Bedwyr blanched a little at the harshness of the criticism, but the Arden Knife could see how much Ector had been rattled by Arthur's brush with death. He actually loves my boy, Bedwyr thought. He really does. It's not just a pose for political expediency.

'I didn't have time, Lord Ector. The Saxons were upon us before we knew they were there, and we only had a few armed men to protect the healers. I never thought . . .'

'You're right there, boy. You didn't think! Do you believe you can be replaced? Well, you can't! It takes generations to grow a man of your promise, and who knows what might happen in the future? If my father and I should die in battle, you're meant to become the fucking regent! My mother can't rule in Aeddan's place and my grandmother's too old. Who will protect my three-year-old son? Who will protect his sisters and his mother? So when will you face the fact that you are thirteen years of age – and your safety is of paramount importance to the future of the tribes?'

Against his will, Arthur felt tears begin to prickle at the corners of his eyes and he was terrified that he would cry. Such shame would be impossible to bear, so he steeled himself to listen to

Ector's insults, and told himself that he had earned every harsh word.

'I'm sorry, Lord Ector,' he replied steadily. 'But I was trying to do the right thing. How can anyone think of everything in the heat of a battle?'

'Welcome to the world of the leader and the warrior,' Ector snapped. 'That's what I must do, and that's what my father Bran does. It's what Bedwyr does. You *must,* as King Artor was known to say, get over the heavy ground as lightly as you can. You put yourself at risk, and your actions prolonged the battle.'

'I'm sorry.' Arthur brushed his eyes with his good hand. 'I'm sorry. I'll work harder and I'll try to learn everything I need to know. I'm sorry!'

'Enough, Ector,' Bran interrupted roughly. 'The boy has apologised.' Everyone present was surprised, because Bran rarely took Arthur's part, having a natural distrust of the youth because of his birth. 'The boy has admitted his fault like a man, as he should, but in his favour he alerted those warriors on the hilltop to the presence of danger, else the Saxons would have killed everyone up there before the watch realised the threat to the healers. He has never faced an attack in the darkness, and he had no idea how to respond. He might have put himself at risk, but you can't put old heads on young shoulders. The boy did his best.'

Ector ground his teeth, but then opened his clenched fists and visibly forced himself to relax. He even managed a slight grin. A little embarrassed by his emotional outburst, he reached towards the distressed boy, who was obviously on the point of weeping, and took him into his arms in a rough, comradely hug.

'I spoke harshly because we nearly lost you *and* the hospital. If truth be told, I'm also very angry with myself. I'd happily lose a thousand hospitals before I'd see you hurt, Arthur. It never occurred to me that anything like this would happen, because the Saxons usually avoid night attacks and I would have expected them to consider such a strategy to be a slur on their honour. But as commander I should have taken precautions, especially when Germanus asked for an armed troop to carry out patrols around the hill. Let's shake hands, Arthur, and we'll say no more about our lapses.'

Flushed and embarrassed, Arthur shook his kinsman's hand and swore allegiance with his whole heart, accepting the blame for what he had done at a time when most men would have been indignant or resentful at their treatment. Nor did he lose any honour by this free admission, for every man present knew that he would be a fine warrior and leader once he had learned to think before he acted. Secretly, Bedwyr's heart swelled with pride when he thought of the level-headed courage his son had displayed.

'Now get yourself off to the healers and have that arm seen to. I can tell from here that it's broken, and the love-tap on it will need to be sewn together.' Ector grinned like the boy he had been before care and responsibility started to create lines in his forehead at the grand old age of twenty-five.

'You've collected a respectable number of scars, Arthur, but I'd prefer you didn't try to collect any more,' Bran added with more kindness than usual. 'Tomorrow we bury our dead. If the Jutes wish to recover the bodies of their fallen comrades, as is their custom, they will pay for the privilege. As for the Saxons, their remains will be burned. I wouldn't leave them to scavengers, even though they fight like animals.'

'We ride the next day, son, so you must be ready to sit astride a horse,' Bedwyr said baldly. 'Can you do it? If need be, I can organise a place for you in a wagon.'

Arthur flinched at the idea and shook his head vehemently. 'No,

Father. I'll return to Arden like a man – even if I'm not one yet.' His final addition was accompanied by a rueful grin.

'Good lad.' As Arthur started to move towards the healers' tent, Bedwyr stopped him with a quick tap on the uninjured shoulder. 'Your birth father is swelling with pride in the lands beyond the shadows where the heroes dwell, for you are everything he would have wanted in a son. Although I'm not your sire, I'm unspeakably relieved that you're relatively unhurt, Arthur. I'm so proud of your courage that I could burst. Don't mind Ector's harsh words. He was horrified by the thought of how easily you could have been killed and he over-reacted. When you are a man and a leader, try to remember this day and how you felt when Ector berated you. Don't do it to anyone else.'

Then Bedwyr patted Arthur's cheek and cleared his throat in embarrassment before stalking off, leaving his son to wipe away a sudden gush of tears.

Few men in the British camp took Ector's jaundiced view of Arthur's part in the Saxon attack. Germanus was the centre of attention as he filled a bowl of half-heated stew, composed mostly of horsemeat, and regaled his eager audience with his recollections of the battle.

'I'd not say a word of praise to young Arthur's face, him being in training and only a student of the sword, you understand?' The listening warriors nodded their approval of such sensible treatment, for too much praise might go to the head of a stripling. 'I'd also prefer that he doesn't become too full of himself, if you know what I mean. I've seen many promising young warriors spoiled because they're told how good they are before they're ready to wear the mantle of hero. Damn me, but the boy was just so good.'

Once again, the audience of hard-bitten fighting men nodded in agreement, for soldiers understand the difficulties of training a lad with extraordinary talent, but they were curious to hear the whole tale of the battle on the hill.

'How good was he, Germanus?' a captain of cavalry, Selwyn of Glevum, asked eagerly. Normally, he gave Bedwyr's mercenary a wide berth, having little trust in barbarians, especially those who fought for coin. But his opinion had changed, for by all accounts Germanus had killed four men on the crown of the hill and proved himself to be a warrior of distinction.

'The boy predicted the Saxons would attack during the night some hours before it actually happened,' Germanus began, but when he saw several men cross themselves he hastily amended his statement. The boy needed no taint of superstition to damage his relationship with warriors who could, one day, come under his command in a future conflict.

'There was no magic – he saw a weakness in our defences and suggested to me that any Saxon who wanted to inflict major damage on us might attack the hospital. The boy is very sharp, so I had a word with the guard commander. He put five men on duty, purely to protect the healers. As it turned out, five men weren't enough, but without them I wouldn't be sitting here eating this slop.'

'Don't you be insulting my stew, Germanus. I guarantee you've eaten far worse in some of them heathen places you've been in. Iomhar ap Gwalchmal stands by his food, and I take exception to your rudeness. Now hand that plate back.'

'Don't be daft, Iomhar. I was only joking,' Germanus apologised quickly. 'The stew is fine and it'd be a pity to waste a dead horse. At any road, Arthur's still a boy, and like all lads he couldn't sleep after the excitement of the day. Old soldiers like us know better than to waste any time when we can be at rest, but this was his first battle.'

Germanus sighed, obviously reminiscing over the distant time when he too was a tyro in the arts of death. Respectfully, his audience permitted him his momentary return to his past, but cleared throats and impatient feet and hands soon indicated their eagerness to hear more. One enterprising young man filled Germanus's cup with ale, which he drained with obvious satisfaction.

'The first I knew of the attack was when I heard Arthur bellow the alarm. Damn me, but his voice is breaking young, and I remember thinking how odd the warning sounded. Then, when I was dressed and armed and came out of the tent, I was under attack immediately. The boy didn't even have a shield or a helmet when they came at him.'

'Heavens! He must have been crazy,' Selwyn murmured. 'I've got a lad of thirteen back in Glevum. He's training as a blacksmith because I don't want him dying young on the battlefield. He's got a good head on his shoulders, but he'd panic for sure in such a situation.'

'Young Arthur will be hearing from me about his failure to protect himself once his wounds are healed, because going into combat without a helmet is plain suicidal. Damn me, but he was daft. Still, he acquitted himself like a grown man.' Germanus smiled. 'I didn't have time to see anything much of Arthur as those buggers charged over the crest of the hill, but I watched him kill the first man who reached him. Very neat it was too. He took out the bastard's knee with that Dragon Knife of his before spitting him through the side with one stroke, just as I taught him to do. It was as good as you'd ever hope to see, and he didn't even pause to watch his man fall.'

'But he's just thirteen!' a voice exclaimed from the audience.

'Aye, but he's born for the warrior's trade or I'm a granddam in my dotage,' Germanus replied, ignoring several ribald comments as the listeners tried to imagine an old woman with bristling, greying moustaches.

'I saw him,' a bandaged warrior called from the edge of the audience. The man's face was grey and he had obviously received a nasty sword cut across his ribs, sufficient to break several and cause considerable loss of blood, but no lasting hurt. 'I was one of the guards . . . only two of us survived. I thank the gods that Arthur was alert, otherwise we'd all have been killed, including the thirty injured men in the hospital. Yes, I saw him with his amber hair spread out like a halo of blood in the light of the burning tent. I'll never forget it for as long as I live. For one moment there, it seemed as if the old Dragon King had come again to save us, just as he promised he would.'

Respectful room was made for the guardsman beside the fire and a comfortable stool was handed into the inner circle for him. The cook found another wooden bowl and filled it to the brim with more of his greasy horsemeat stew.

'Eat well, good sir. You need the warmth, and the meat will help to replace your lost blood. Ignore this Frankish oaf – it's very good.'

'Thank you, cookie. I'm famished and tired, both at once, but I don't believe I can sleep. Who would credit that the Saxons would attack at night?'

'Perhaps they're learning from us, or there's a thane with a little more sense than most of his kind,' Germanus muttered irritably. 'Tell us what you saw of my boy. I'll not comment on who his antecedents might have been, but he's a natural warrior when it comes to his use of weapons. And he doesn't show any strain when he's under pressure.'

'Not him! He took out his next man, a hulking brute who outmatched him in every way, breaking his sword in the encounter.

I was helping our commander, only a boy himself, but a kinsman of the Deceangli king. My lad had taken an axe blow that came near to taking his arm off at the shoulder. I knew he couldn't survive the wound so I dragged him out of the way in case I stepped on him. Your boy went down on his knees and attacked his opponent's balls from below, being outmatched in strength, reach and weaponry. Ah, but it was the sweetest thing I've ever seen.'

'He'll sing castrato from now on.' Selwyn offered his opinion with a black jest.

'Only if he does it in hell. When the brute clutched at his ruined manhood, young Arthur severed his artery with that knife of his. It could have been made for him, for all it's supposed to have belonged to the Dragon King.'

'So rumour has it. The boy killed five men – even more than you, Germanus. You'll need to keep your wits about you, old man, once the pupil starts to outstrip the master,' Selwyn said with a laugh. His companions followed suit, all of them awed by the actions of the thirteen-year-old boy.

'He'll be a master when he reaches his full height,' the wounded soldier decided, his voice firm with conviction. 'I'll happily serve under him if I should ever get the chance.'

'Best of all, Fortuna loves him,' Selwyn added. 'He has luck, and a man can go far when luck is on his side. I've been told he killed his first Saxon at seven years of age.'

When Germanus agreed that there was some truth to the rumour the soldiers were even more impressed, especially when the Friesian explained the whole story, and whispers spread that the Dragon King had come again. The tale was spread with superstitious fascination.

'Let's hope Arthur's luck continues.' Germanus had the final word, as befitted his position as a trusted servant. 'If the Saxons are learning new tricks, then we'll need all the help we can get, even from such a capricious goddess as the Roman bitch with her fucking wheel.'

His companions agreed, and as a bloody dawn began to light the battlefield and the grim mounds of the fallen the men drifted away to carry out their various tasks. Birds came and roosted on every available tree, trusting that these men who worked so hard to rob them of the spoils of battle would overlook the odd corpse. Scavengers dined well when men went to war.

Germanus finished his stew, his mind wholly occupied by what his charge still needed to learn. He knew that the years ahead would be difficult, but as one of his old commanders had been fond of saying, lives of peace and harmony were usually very dull.

'A little tedium might be a welcome change,' Germanus muttered to no one in particular before wandering off to find Arthur in the tents of the healers. Another red day had begun.

CHAPTER IX

THE ROAD TO MANHOOD

> Where there is much desire to learn, there of necessity will be much arguing, much writing, many opinions; for opinion in good men is but knowledge in the making.
>
> John Milton, *Areopagitica*, 31

Unaware of his burgeoning reputation, Arthur lived uneventfully in Arden, his mornings dominated by the prosaic patterns of reading and writing followed by earnest discussions of the scrolls that Father Lorcan seemed to conjure up out of nowhere. During the long afternoons, Arthur was equally occupied with a tiring regimen of exercise, weapons practice and weights that drove him to his bed in a haze of exhaustion.

Lorcan had stumbled upon a ready accomplice in the development of Arthur's mind, for the scrolls came from the library of Myrddion Merlinus in distant Caer Gai where they were personally selected by Nimue, the Lady of the Lake. Permitted to take notes from these rare and valuable histories, Arthur was gaining an unexpected knowledge of rudimentary Roman surgery, herb lore, mapping, siege machines and Myrddion's experiences as a physician in Rome, including symptoms and cures for the various plagues that spread throughout the known world from time to time. A normal lifespan was barely sufficient to learn a fraction of what Myrddion had accumulated during his seventy-odd years. Once studied, each scroll was swiftly returned to Caer Gai by one of Lorcan's messengers. Another was despatched immediately, for Nimue gave unstintingly from the vast storehouse of knowledge that had become the record of her husband's extraordinary life. With Nimue's assistance, another Artor would learn and flourish from the ashes of Myrddion's past.

'I don't understand all this talk of lead and defrutum,' Arthur muttered after a puzzling morning spent poring over the great healer's days in Rome. Arthur was already irritable, and the depth and breadth of Myrddion's mind always made him feel inadequate. 'Lead has been mined in the south of Britain for time beyond counting. How could such a useful metal be such a deadly poison when it's so essential to our lives? Myrddion Merlinus must have been wrong.'

Father Lorcan thought for a moment. 'Is lead truly essential? When do you use it? When does Bedwyr use it? I never heard of the Roman disease, as Merlinus names it. Other than iron and brass, lead is the most common metal used in the west because it's so soft and malleable. My only knowledge of lead comes from my years in the lands of the Middle Sea where it's used to make water pipes. Out of vanity, women in the Frankish lands use its powdered form to whiten their complexions. Didn't Lady Nimue describe how Queen Wenhaver used a powder of fine stone talc and lead to keep her skin fresh and pale? Perhaps that powder explains the queen's cruelties.' Lorcan scratched his unshaven chin reflectively, his horny nails catching on several days' growth of beard. 'I know that Elayne swears by her precious iron pots and the fired clay bowls that she uses for cooking in hot coals. I haven't seen any leaden materials used in Arden at all, not that I've really looked. However, I give some credit to the observations of Merlinus. Cases of his Roman disease still appear in places like Rome and Ravenna, although defrutum and sapa are rarely used any more. Perhaps that's the reason why this terrible disease has declined.'

'Or perhaps most of the users have died,' Arthur said sardonically.

Arthur loved his lessons with Lorcan because he discovered so much about the world beyond Arden. But, more important, they gave him an opportunity to learn more about his sire through the eyes of Myrddion Merlinus, who had loved the High King and only left him to be with Nimue. Arthur read the ancient history of his father's birth and discovered the story of another woman Merlinus had loved, Andrewina Ruadh, and how she had disappeared after delivering the infant Artor, son of Ygerne and Uther Pendragon, to the Roman villa of the Poppinidii family outside Aquae Sulis.

For some obscure, visceral reason that he didn't understand, this old story of devotion and duty touched Arthur more profoundly than larger tales of courage and battle. He thought of his mother's steadfast bravery when she revealed the details of his birth to him, and of the risk she had taken of losing her son's respect for ever. The courage of women was strange and incomprehensible to most men, so the long dead Andrewina Ruadh captured Arthur's imagination more powerfully than tales of Gawayne's heroism or Uther Pendragon's desperate battles. Andrewina Ruadh had travelled a lonely road with an infant not her own, pursued and in deadly peril. Where had she gone after completing her mission? Artor's foster-father had believed that Ruadh was close to death from a poisoned knife wound, but if she had perished her body had disappeared within the Forest Sauvage and never been discovered. Such a lonely end! Arthur tried to imagine being so far from her friends, the man she loved or the comforting touch of another human hand as she surrendered to death. Her need to protect the infant must have been greater than any thought for her own survival. Arthur began to appreciate the legends of Artor anew as he read the tales of a youth spent with his foster-brother Caius, a man of such inhuman instincts that he was eventually killed by Myrddion Merlinus, who abhorred murder.

'How confusing these people are,' he exclaimed. 'No one in these histories is completely good or completely bad. Even the best men say one thing with their mouths and, too often, suggest the opposite through their actions.'

'Yes, even the best men have weaknesses,' Lorcan agreed. 'A good and honest man learns what his flaws are so that his conscience can assist him to fight them for the duration of his life.'

Arthur grimaced. 'You make manhood sound very glum, Father Lorcan. It seems that when I'm not killing something, I'm supposed to ponder the sins that live in my secret heart. That's crazy, isn't it? I don't think I want to reach manhood in the near future.' He was only partly jesting. Since the Battle of the Hospital, he had searched for the reason for his many bad decisions and had finally come to the conclusion that his stupidity had stemmed from a hunger for fame. Above all else during that dark and terrifying night, he had wanted to prove that he was no longer a boy. The more he read about his renowned father, the more powerful grew his desire to follow in Artor's footsteps, to be the embodiment of his sire's civilisation. A large goal, made dangerous by pride. His ambition could easily become a dangerous weakness, Arthur thought regretfully. 'But I'll try not to forget Andrewina Ruadh, a courageous woman who won no fame from her sacrifice, and took her last breath alone and afraid, for a cause larger than herself. Perhaps if I tried to live like her I wouldn't succumb to hubris, a fault which Merlinus considered the greatest sin of all.'

'What are you muttering about, Arthur? Share your thoughts with me.'

'It's nothing, Father Lorcan. Just a private warning to myself to beware of pride.'

Lorcan scratched his jaw in the careless action that Arthur had learned was habitual when the priest was thinking. 'Hubris, you mean? It's been the death of many great rulers, so we'll read the Greeks tomorrow and see what the ancients have to say on the matter.'

Arthur almost groaned aloud, but he was learning to keep his thoughts private. More dusty scrolls, he thought drily. Still, I suppose I'll learn something.

He had already decided that Germanus was no Targo, whom he had read of in Merlinus's scrolls. For starters, Germanus had little or no sense of humour, while Targo had been a jester of a kind, teaching the young High King the ways of a warrior through a combination of humour and common sense. Merlinus had brought the Roman veteran to life in his writings, and Arthur could easily understand how Artor had learned to see the human condition through Targo's wise and sardonic eyes. He himself had no Targo to remind him of how less privileged people thought and acted. Perhaps, if Rab had lived, he would have provided that necessary viewpoint to keep him conscious of his wider duty. 'I'll worry about that later,' Arthur muttered to himself. 'I've got enough to be getting on with.'

That afternoon Arthur was required to lift a number of heavy weights designed to build slab-like muscles on his shoulders, upper chest and arms. Groaning, Arthur stripped to the waist to expose the still androgynous smoothness of a torso marred by only a few golden hairs, but saved from any appearance of softness by his scars, old and new. And thank the Christ for that, Germanus thought irritably, because he felt affection for the boy; he'll have troubles enough in life without being too pretty. That old slash Arthur had received across his chest as a boy had healed cleanly, and was now only a thin white line. High on his left shoulder, an angry red knot of scar tissue was a reminder of the battle that had taken place at the hospital. Elsewhere, his body was almost hairless apart from small swaths of golden down on his arms and legs and his pubic hair, which curled in spirals like the mane of hair on his head. Since the sneak attack by the Saxons, Bedwyr had shown Arthur how to plait his side curls, but his ministrations could barely tame a tenth of the young man's wild locks.

Germanus had filled a wooden trunk with old armour, river rocks and scrap iron. Handles at the sides of the trunk permitted it to be lifted to chest height, but only with considerable effort. Each time he tried, Arthur could feel his muscles tense to breaking point as they took up the unnatural strain on his growing frame.

'Today we try something new,' Germanus said blandly. 'You must lift the trunk above your head.' In response, Arthur began to estimate the moves needed to raise the weight above his shoulders. The real problem would be changing his grip halfway through the movement. He must release his hold on the handles to lift the trunk from underneath. Germanus watched with satisfaction as his pupil worried away at the problem.

'Have you worked it out yet, Arthur? If so – get on with it,' he said.

Arthur felt a worm of resentment grow in his skull. He gripped the trunk by the handles and snatched up the crushing weight until it was resting on his heavily muscled thighs. After several deep breaths to steady himself, he dragged the dead weight up to his chest, holding it there awkwardly by the handles while he tried to work out how to transfer his grip from the sides of the trunk to its base. His forehead beaded with sweat, and with his muscles shaking with strain, he forced his extended arms to lift the trunk higher with a jerky, swinging motion. His right hand released the handle and he tried to take the weight on his forearm as the trunk began to topple.

He failed dismally. Arthur dropped the whole weight to the ground with a dull, sullen thud that shuddered through the wooden staves that held the trunk together.

'Well, that didn't work very well, did it?' Germanus stated the obvious. 'Where do you go from here?'

'Back to the beginning!' Arthur hissed between his teeth as he tried to catch his breath. Lifting that deadweight so high had drained him so that his knees shook when he tried to lock them.

'Meaning?'

'I need to think.' The young man paced back and forth across the forecourt, while several warriors standing near the palisade called out helpful suggestions. Arthur would have wished them to the devil because they broke his concentration, but he knew that they meant well and were genuinely interested to see how he would approach such a seemingly senseless task.

Before he had fully thought out his next move, Arthur gripped the trunk at the base on each side. He had tried the handles, and knew he lacked the strength to transfer his grip from them to the bottom of the trunk. Now . . . did he have the strength to lift the trunk the hard way?

As he grappled with the awkward manoeuvre he was sure that he would never keep his grip on the smooth wooden planks, but he refused to surrender to a few pieces of scrap metal and wood.

Slowly, the trunk rose, and his back bent like a bow. Now his forearms felt like lead and his fingers clawed at the sides of the trunk. But the dead weight rose, although logic reasoned that he lacked the muscle to lift it. One foot. Two feet. Just a little more and he could rest with the weight of the trunk on his thighs and his slightly bent knees.

Panting and running with sweat, Arthur concentrated on the task before him. Inch by painful inch. Once the trunk was balanced on his thighs and the weight removed from his shoulders and lower vertebrae, he flexed his fingers and took a new grip with most of each hand safely below the trunk's base.

Now! Lift! he screamed at his traitorous brain. Lift the trunk up to your waist. You can rest it on your chest soon. Lift it, you son of a whore!

The trunk rose as Arthur took the full, crushing weight on his arms and shoulders. Fearing a cramp, he didn't dare to hurry, his eyes monitoring the slow rise of the trunk before him. I'll be damned, he thought irrelevantly, as his body and his will strove against the weight of scrap iron and stone.

Then the trunk was resting across his upper chest, although Arthur had to bend backward to accommodate the weight, setting his lower back to screaming at the sudden abuse. But now both hands were placed securely under the trunk.

Now! Before I lose my nerve!

The trunk rose above Arthur's head and he locked his elbows to hold it firmly in place. He had succeeded in the challenge. Bellowing in triumph, he stepped back and allowed the whole, meaningless collection of objects to fall to the ground where the wooden trunk shattered and spilled scrap iron and stone all over the courtyard.

'Good work, young Arthur. I didn't think you could do it. Now, go to the bathhouse and use hot cloths from the cauldron to wash your shoulders, hands and back. You're bleeding, boy.'

'Am I?' Arthur said blankly.

Then he realised that his nose had begun to gush, and Germanus felt a twinge of alarm. He had deliberately doubled the weight in the trunk to teach Arthur that some things couldn't be achieved. Unfortunately, the lad's fixity of purpose had lifted a weight that should have been impossible for a stripling of his age. Showing his student how to use his thumb and forefinger to pinch off the blood vessels in his nose, Germanus shepherded him off to the bathhouse.

The simple wooden hut was still thick with steam from an earlier group of bathers, but Germanus forced Arthur to sit on a wooden stool and douse himself with dippers of warm water while Germanus used hot cloths to release the strain in his pupil's back, shoulders and arms. Once the muscles began to relax, Germanus splashed oil onto his palms to massage the boy's shoulders and the two long ridges that ran parallel on either side of his spine. Arthur groaned under his master's ministrations, but Germanus was too nervous to check whether his pupil moaned in pain or pleasure. Once the muscles were at rest and he had satisfied himself that Arthur had taken no lasting hurt from his exertions, he slapped the young man on the back and ordered him to dress and then to rest for the remainder of the afternoon.

When Arthur was inclined to argue, Germanus explained. 'I made a serious error of judgement, Arthur, one that could have hurt you badly. You're as healthy as the best of your father's hounds – or his warhorse – so I should have explained that there was no shame in failing to lift that trunk, because I'd put more weight in it than usual. I intended you to discover that we all fail sometimes, in spite of our best efforts. But you succeeded, and in doing so you spoiled my lesson.' Germanus smiled. 'Damn me, boy, your stubbornness will be the death of you one day. You just hate to give in, don't you? Never mind – don't look so serious. It's a special talent you have, rather than a fault. I didn't recognise it in you, so the blame would have been mine if you had hurt yourself.'

For once, Arthur was too tired to argue. He staggered out of the bathhouse and made his way to his room, where he curled up under the coarse flax covers and fell asleep within moments.

As Germanus wiped his hand free of the clinging oil, a stranger slipped into the bathhouse and stared at him. Suddenly, the wooden slabs that walled the hut seemed closer and the whole structure seemed to shrink, such was the overpowering presence of the man who had entered so quietly. With an economical sweep of one arm, he bared his head of its disguising cowl.

Germanus had never met Taliessin pen Myrddion before, so he didn't recognise the long black hair with its single streak of white over the left temple. He saw a clean-shaven, ascetic face with beautiful, androgynous features and blue eyes that were shockingly pale against the stranger's black hair and eyebrows. Those narrowed eyes were contemptuous now, and Germanus felt his cheekbones flush at the stranger's lack of respect.

He studied the carefully closed face and body in front of him with a soldier's observant eye, and saw a stranger who was nearly as tall as he was, but physically more slender. The white streak in his raven hair made him look older than he really was, but Germanus decided that the interloper was probably in his mid-thirties. Those blue eyes were deceptive. They seemed crystalline and open, but nothing of the thoughts behind them was permitted to escape. The stranger stood as if he owned the timber bathhouse, and his opinion of Germanus was written all too clearly on his normally secretive features.

The arms master's eyes dropped to the stranger's hands. He was unarmed, but the fingers of both hands spoke of repetitive toil, with calluses built on the finger pads. No sword does that, Germanus thought, for the palms were comparatively unmarked. Then Germanus made the connection that explained the waxed hide bag slung over the stranger's shoulder.

'You must be Taliessin, the harpist. Who are you to show your contempt for me so openly, when you know nothing of me? Speak, man! If you have some argument with me, I'd prefer to hear it.'

'You have the advantage over me, soldier, for I don't know your name, and I don't know your place in the world of Arden. But I would be interested to know the name of the person who has mistreated this boy.'

Germanus laughed. 'You've been gone too long if you think of Arthur as a boy, Taliessin. Are you of a mind to play with Arthur as Myrddion Merlinus did with the lad's sire? Like father: like son? If that is your desire, then you're too fucking late. Arthur's grown now and he's no longer malleable, not by me, as today's exercise demonstrated, and certainly not by you. To answer your question, I am Germanus, arms master and tutor, and Arthur has been placed in my charge for seven years.'

'Then you shouldn't have taken such risks with him. His nose was bleeding by the time he released that trunk of scrap iron. He could have ruptured a major blood vessel in his head. He could have died – and something fated and wonderful could have been lost. I'm not my father and I don't claim to be half the man he was, but a blind man could see that those weights were far too heavy for any normal boy to lift.'

Taliessin's criticism was voiced in a lilting, attractive voice that was sharp at the edges, like shards of flint designed to cut and hurt. If such was the harpist's intent, then he failed. Germanus ignored him and picked up the used towels to wipe his arms and remove the last traces of oil from the raw wooden stool. His equally blue eyes closed down until they looked like milky marbles of glass within his heavy-boned skull.

'My reasoning was simple. Arthur had mentioned his fear of hubris to Lorcan, so I set a task for my charge that I thought couldn't be successfully completed. Where possible, Father Lorcan and I work together to devise problems that meet Arthur's intellectual development. He's not yet fourteen and he's already killed six men, which is a worrisome tally for a fully grown man, let alone a youth. The trunk was a mistake, because neither Lorcan nor I believed he would find a way to lift the bloody thing. He's suffered no lasting hurt, and by tomorrow he will have forgotten about it.'

Taliessin was slightly mollified, but his answer was so pedantic that Germanus wanted to shake him. 'You should have considered that possibility when you loaded the box.'

Germanus hawked and spat, showing his opinion without the need for words. 'He's not a dog who can be forced to do tricks for his master! He's the natural son of King Artor and he has the claws of the Red Dragon. He'll not submit to the will of others if he believes he has the strength and cunning to resist domination. Are you ready to discover your own weaknesses, harpist to a dead legend? He'll winkle them out, every one, and then you too will face the disapproval of other men.'

Taliessin had listened to every word, although his back was half turned to the arms master. He moved slowly to face Germanus. His eyes had changed and his body language was more conciliatory. 'Perhaps we should begin again, sir, for I have judged you unfairly. I am Taliessin, a poor harper who must sing for his supper at the courts of kings. You are Germanus, arms master to the young Arthur, and you come from . . . ?'

Curtly, Germanus described his history, including his recent marriage to the youngest daughter of an Ordovice landowner in Powys. Taliessin acknowledged the arms master's irrevocable ties to the cause of the Britons with a brief bow of his head.

'My felicitations, friend. May you have many sons.'

'Have you informed Master Bedwyr and Lady Elayne of your arrival, Lord Taliessin? Lady Elayne, in particular, will be overjoyed that you have come. She has often spoken of you during my time in Arden, but you have been busy elsewhere. Bedwyr, I'm sure, will also want to see you at once.'

Taliessin was aware that Germanus's eyes were still wary and flat, so he extended his considerable charm to win over this phlegmatic soldier, but his easy manner had little effect. Germanus was nothing like his mother's recollections of Targo, the High King's arms master and teacher, but perhaps that was no bad thing, depending on the nature of Artor's son.

With wholly feigned friendliness, the two men made their way to greet Bedwyr in Arden's hall, where the master awaited them. Taliessin was welcomed into the bosom of Arthur's family like a prodigal son. Wisely, Germanus decided to suspend all harsh thoughts concerning the harper until he knew Taliessin better. But he watched the tall, slender figure with eyes that never ceased to weigh the man's every action and word as he affectionately embraced his old friends Bedwyr and Elayne.

The arrival of Taliessin was the catalyst for unexpected changes in Arthur's life. Like all talented manipulators, the harpist took care not to be recognised as the source of the sudden upheavals taking place around him, but the hard-eyed master of arms understood Taliessin's ploys almost as well as he knew the palm of his own hand. A man with Taliessin's skills would never appear in a backwater like Arden without a purpose, especially after a six-year absence. All Germanus had to do was watch and wait for the harper's plans to be turned into action. Then he'd know. Germanus's curiosity would be slaked within two days.

At first, Taliessin was nonplussed by the changes in Arthur's life and education. He had been at odds with his own mother on the manner of Arthur's training, being in favour of permitting Arthur to grow to manhood in ignorance of his birth. Nimue had disagreed volubly, claiming that any half-clever boy would inevitably discover his family secret and resent the silence that had doomed him to ignorance. She reminded Taliessin that Myrddion regretted every day of the twelve years that Artor was untrained for the role that Fortuna had selected for him. Now, Taliessin was irritated that Anna, Elayne and Nimue had meddled in the perfectly acceptable plan he had put into action. The thirteen-year-old Arthur he had recently met had not turned out to be the lad he expected. This boy had killed trained warriors; this boy had been using his own father's histories to accumulate his knowledge; and this boy accepted that he might well have an important part to play in the future of the west.

Damn you, Mother, you didn't play fair with me, Taliessin thought. His mental criticisms were unjustified, however, because he too had not played the game according to the rules. In fact, both Myrddion and Nimue would have laughed if he had done so.

Taliessin had become a living legend. He was a genius and a thoroughly good man, but he wasn't free of vanity either. Under his calm, inscrutable face, his brain seethed. He hated being wrong footed by anyone, and he hated losing control of the game. Worse still, he was displeased to discover that two other men were shaping Arthur's thinking, particularly as the guidance came from

Germanus, a mercenary, and the upstart Lorcan from Hibernia. His dislike of Lorcan was immediate and reciprocated.

'After finally meeting you, I understand how your father must have appeared to the world,' Lorcan said with a guileless smile.

'Unfortunately, I don't have the same advantage,' Taliessin replied rather sharply, without considering the effect of his words. He sounded more irritable than he had intended and saw how Lorcan's mild dark eyes snapped at the oblique insult. Had the door to Lorcan's mind been visible, the harpist would have seen it slam shut.

Fuck! Taliessin thought in a most unpoetic fashion.

'I'm an open book, Master Taliessin, especially for a man of your advantages. I have been in correspondence with your mother for many years, and I have no objection if she decides to share my thoughts with you. We have similar aspirations for our boy.'

That's put me in my place, Taliessin thought. His eyes snapped as sharply as the Hibernian's had done, but he was unable to disguise the bubble of laughter that escaped his lips at the pissing contest he'd begun with both of Arthur's mentors.

The next evening, the men of the household sat at table for many more hours than usual, drinking clean ale and feasting on venison and hare caught during an afternoon of hunting. Without any apparent effort, Taliessin inserted the problems of the south into the conversation in such a fashion that only two of his audience recognised the ploy, and only two brains wondered at the intentions embedded in his words.

'The Saxon menace grows and grows on our northern borders. At first, only a few towns and villages fell to their roving bands, but Bremetennacum has now fallen and the Spine has finally been breached by the invaders.' Bedwyr spoke with a strong man's anger when faced with problems he cannot resolve. 'Unfortunately, there's little we can do about the growth of Mercia, as the Saxon scum call it, from here in Arden.'

'It's fitting that the Brigante lands should be the first to fall, just as the wild woman predicted,' Arthur murmured. 'I'm not superstitious, Father – or I don't think I am – but those traitors deserve to feel the lash of destruction and the loss of their homeland.'

'They fight desperately for every foot of land they hold, so you can be sure that they will not go quietly into the darkness. That's why we wanted to push the Jutes back during the spring,' Bedwyr replied. 'If the Jutes continue to gain concessions through treaties with Mercia . . . well, it doesn't bear thinking about, does it? The invaders hate us even more than we hate them, if such a degree of loathing is possible, but the tribes of Gwynedd, Powys, Dyfed and even southern Cymru send men to keep the borders clean of the rats, and Bran has sworn that Cymru will never fall into Saxon hands – never!'

Bedwyr's small speech was followed by a spontaneous burst of cheering from the warriors present, but Arthur's mind focused on the point of Bedwyr's impromptu zealotry and its real message.

'So Bran and Ector expect that all the Brigante lands will inevitably be lost. In fact, they are convinced that we will lose all our lands except for those areas north of the Wall, so they are preparing to protect Cymru at all cost. The Wall offers its own protection, and the kingdom ruled by King Bors is relatively easy to hold, but for the rest of us . . .'

'You're being unduly pessimistic, Arthur,' Bedwyr said.

'But realistic,' Taliessin added. 'The situation in the south is far more dangerous than it is here in Arden. The Atrebate tribe are feeling the pressure in Venta Belgarum. I wish that ancient scarecrow, Uther Pendragon, could see what his years of inactivity have cost us. The Suth Seaxe now own the roads leading to

Londinium, so Calleva Atrebatum shivers in the Saxon shadow, knowing that its survival depends on the goodwill of Bors, Pelles, Bran and Ector. Something must be done, not only to bind together what is left of the tribes, but also to tell the Saxons that they shall not move beyond a point that the Celts will determine.'

Bedwyr and the older warriors were cautious, but Arthur was set afire by Taliessin's words. Germanus was silently amused by the harpist's argument, for he was certain in his own mind that Taliessin was already planning for decisive action, although he obviously preferred that his part in the plot should remain secret. Arthur also saw Taliessin's motives clearly – and said so, setting the harper back on his heels.

Tough luck! Germanus thought, and grinned ironically in Taliessin's direction.

'In all seriousness, Father,' Arthur said eagerly, 'any policy which requires us to sit back and wait while the Saxons retain the initiative smacks of madness. We need to adopt an active strategy that will wrong foot the Saxons and keep *them* guessing and uneasy. Nervous enemies will make mistakes.'

'True, son, but we can't afford the smallest failure, because our losses will appear as weakness in their eyes. And we are weak, Arthur. That's the point. When we fight, our battles must achieve a measurable purpose.'

'So don't fight a battle,' Arthur suggested. 'If we were able to build a defensive ditch that would keep the Saxons out of British lands, it could become a major obstacle to Saxon advances while minimising casualties to British warriors.'

The men in the room paused in their eating and drinking to consider the plan that had been placed before them. Every man present knew Arthur's suggestion made sense, and his words won him another rung in his growing reputation. Outmanoeuvred by a thirteen year old who didn't realise the full strategic thrust of his proposal, Taliessin began to look for some way to take back the initiative, and immediately began to expand on Arthur's suggestion.

'You're saying that we should build a defensive ditch,' Bedwyr repeated slowly, after Taliessin had explained his thoughts. 'I don't understand the benefits of your plan, or how you intend to achieve it. Arthur seems to understand the points you're making, but I don't, although you've obviously been thinking about this for some time.'

'You'll acknowledge that we need to reunite the tribes and improve the morale of the British people,' Taliessin said, and Bedwyr nodded in agreement. 'I believe that a large project that is common to all the tribes would suit our purpose perfectly. And if that project should protect sections of Britain that are under threat, the more powerful our proposal would appear to both our friends and our enemies.'

Taliessin gazed across at his audience.

'I propose that we build a massive defensive ditch across a strip of land where the Dobunni, the Atrebates and the Catuvellauni tribes hold sway. Such a construction could prove to be an impassable barrier to our enemies while serving as a rallying point for the defence of our own people. We should dig the ditch deep into the earth and use the fill that is removed to form a huge dyke behind the ditch that would be too tall for a man to leap over. If we set sharpened stakes and mantraps into the front of it, we would have a construction that would confound our enemies.'

He paused to allow his words to bite. 'Built in a carefully selected defensive site, it could keep our enemies at bay for many years to come.'

'I understand what you're saying, Taliessin, and your plan makes good sense, but the Cornovii are only one tribe.' Bedwyr's face still wore an expression of polite amusement, a response which irked the harper far more than he was prepared to express. 'Why wouldn't the Saxons just walk round the undefended extremes of your ditch?'

'In my opinion, we should build the dyke from the hill fort at Maes Knoll to the Savernake Forest. The valley that lies between those two points is sealed off at both ends by large hills and forested areas that would be difficult for large parties of infiltrators to traverse, so the valley itself is the obvious route by which to penetrate the British defensive lines. The ditch would be built in two sections, one nine miles long and the other twelve miles, on either side of the River Avon. If we can seal off access to the stream we could slow down the Saxon advances for at least a generation – perhaps longer.'

'It's a wonderful idea, Master Taliessin,' Arthur breathed, his eyes glowing with excitement and commitment. 'I'd happily labour on such an undertaking, as would most of the young tribal warriors. We'd be building for our own future.'

Bedwyr considered the logistics of seconding young warriors to such a labour-intensive task under the supervision of older, more experienced leaders, and quickly decided that the concept was both workable and useful. Additional labour for the project could be recruited from the peasant classes, and the financial costs could be funded from the treasure chests of the British kings, including his own.

As he watched Arthur's brightly shining eyes, Bedwyr began to give serious consideration to the project. At least this plan would give the people some hope.

'Let those young men who are approaching manhood give a year or two of their lives towards building the Warriors' Ditch,' Arthur continued. 'No one would be lost from those troops who are currently defending the frontiers, and if the young men from all the British tribes came together they would soon have a good knowledge of each other's attributes and forge friendships that would last down the years. I remember Father Lorcan telling me of Myrddion's long view, and I'm certain that the great healer would have approved of Taliessin's plan.'

'Aye, boy, you have the right of it,' Lorcan agreed. 'Like father: like son.'

Bedwyr noticed how a red flush surrounded the harpist's neck at Lorcan's words. Taliessin needs to be reminded that there are other intelligent men in these lands, the Master of Arden thought with a sly grin of impish enjoyment. But, aloud, Bedwyr was determined to give credit to his son, although he knew Taliessin had fleshed out the concept for him. 'We'd have to convince Bran and Ector, who'll then have to convince the kings of the other tribes, but I think you've found a project that's worthy of you, Arthur. The Warriors' Dyke – yes, I like the idea.'

And so Taliessin saw his concept come into existence as an agreed plan, even though Arthur was given most of the credit. The harpist's one great regret was the status given to Germanus and Lorcan, who would have the task of protecting Arthur while he was labouring with the working party. Most of the kings agreed that their much-loved sons or grandsons should join the group, together with their own protectors, and so the plan for the Warriors' Dyke was set in motion. The project would bind together all the young aristocrats of their generation, with a supporting contingent of warriors, servants and peasants to care for them and assist with the manual labour involved in the actual construction of the defensive barrier.

Taliessin was amused. 'Well, Father,' he whispered softly to himself. 'I'm sure you'd be pleased at the outcome of my machinations to bring my little plot to fruition. I know you'd have told me in no uncertain terms that I've outsmarted myself. But Arthur will be forced to work with his peers, a role at which I am convinced he will excel. In years to come, Father, we may have many reasons to be thankful for the Warriors' Dyke.'

Spring had returned to the land once more when the young men of the tribes gathered, with much excitement and pleasurable anticipation, at a camp outside Abone where the hills met the skies in soft, downy pillows of white. Twelve months had passed, during which Taliessin had laboured to bring the tribes together in a common endeavour. He had copied his father's maps, especially those that related to the deep forests at the headwaters of Aquae Sulis's river and the line of low hills that marched across the entry to the softer, flatter lands of the west of Britain. The terrain was heavily wooded, much as the gods had made it, except for low hills that formed stepping stones for the deities who still traversed the river valleys. Here, where pilgrims had entered the golden land, Taliessin would build the Warriors' Dyke.

A holiday spirit prevailed as the young aristocrats settled into their bright tents, which had been painted and dyed in vivid colours. The fallow field chosen for the base camp looked as if a huge flock of butterflies had settled there.

By virtue of his long legs and extra height, Arthur stood out among the laughing, indolent throng. He had never had friends before, being the oldest boy in Bedwyr's forest nest, so the whole enterprise was hugely exciting for him. Now nearly fifteen and still growing, he towered over his peers, and several resentful young aristocrats took pleasure in grinding his nose into the ground over his inferior birth.

'What have I done to upset them? Mareddyd of the Dobunni

tribe doesn't know me at all, but he seems to think he is permitted to insult my father and myself with impunity.' Arthur sought the wise counsel of Lorcan and Germanus. 'I can hardly thump him, can I? He's two years older than me, but he's a foot shorter, so I'd be labelled a bully. What should I do?'

The two men conferred, and Germanus finally offered their joint advice. 'Accuse him of cowardice because you're not permitted to fight with him for the very reasons you've just described. You must never lie – especially if the truth works better. Mareddyd expected to lord it over everyone who answered Taliessin's call, which is a form of bullying in itself. He expected to be one of the oldest and best trained youths in the camp. He was wrong, so we think he's frustrated and angry. Speak the truth and watch him back down. If he does attempt to attack you, offer to meet him in combat using only one hand. Then use your height as an advantage, and beat the shit out of him.'

Lorcan added his own mite. Since the Dobunni prince was used to throwing his weight around and thrusting the younger aristocrats out of his way, he suggested that Arthur should make a habit of protecting the smaller boys.

'That won't be difficult,' Arthur said ruefully, pointing towards a group of three smaller lads sitting on their heels at the edge of the field. They were obviously waiting for their hero to finish speaking to the adults before clustering round him once again.

'You don't really mind them, do you, Arthur?' Lorcan asked, observing Arthur from under his shaggy brows.

'Apart from Rab, I never had a friend, Father Lorcan. I never had someone I could talk to, except for my younger brothers. Eamonn, Fiachra and Kieran are just like my siblings, so I don't mind having them underfoot at all. They're all thirteen and small for their age, so they aren't used to making decisions about anything.'

'Off you go then, and don't give this Mareddyd any opportunity to fight you unless you can turn the confrontation into a joke. Whose boy is he anyway? Is he the scion of someone important?'

'He says his great-aunt is the famed Wenhaver, the Queen of the Britons,' Arthur muttered. 'She could be, too. He's cruel enough. He likes to hurt the younger boys, but he's the only one of us who is likely to rule in his own right. All the rest of us are younger sons, or born on the wrong side of the blanket . . .' Suddenly Arthur grinned as the absurdity of the problem became obvious. 'He's like a half-grown rooster crowing over a motley collection of ducks, drakes, robins, chickens and turkeys.'

'And one peregrine,' Germanus added, his face set in serious lines.

'Don't be silly, Germanus. Peregrines are the birds of kings,' Arthur joked. 'There's no one here who fits that description. We're just a group of over-indulged young men.'

Lorcan and Germanus exchanged knowing glances with those guards from Arden who shared the knowledge of Arthur's heritage. 'It's so typical of the great folk,' one ageing warrior muttered to his mate. 'They think we have no eyes. I stood at the ford, shoulder to shoulder with the Cornovii troop, and watched the Dragon King as he rode across, flanked by his loyal warriors and those who loved him unto death. At the end, he'd lost all hope for the future and only his own bastard sons could be sufficiently trusted to guard him.'

'Aye,' the other guardsman, a younger man, agreed. 'I saw those fine boys and it's sad that so many of them are now dead. All of them, I suppose, for fate isn't kind to the bastards of kings. No one could mistake a son of Artor, not even Wenhaver if she stirred off her fat rump to see what had been going on over the years.'

'I heard she died,' Lorcan replied vaguely, and the guardsmen remembered their positions and prudently held their tongues.

Meanwhile, Taliessin was kept busy with the myriad administrative details of the fledgling project. With the help of his brother Rhys, he was kept fully occupied assembling materials and designing building plans. Discipline and the rules necessary for the efficient management of the encampment became an urgent prerequisite, for the task would absorb all the manpower from the nearby villages, as well as the warrior guards and any able-bodied volunteers who cared sufficiently for the west to offer their time and labour. A host of camp followers and prostitutes appeared out of nowhere, so the provident Taliessin put them to work on washing and hygiene duties, while the tinkers and hawkers of small trifles who came to fleece the princes were given a simple choice. They could work, or leave with a guardsman's boot to the backside. As these human leeches were planning to sell raw liquor to the young men or provide 'clean' girls for their enjoyment, Taliessin felt no qualms in confiscating their goods and sending them packing.

Feeding the workers and their guards, plus the peasants and tradesmen, was a major undertaking in itself, so the prostitutes were conscripted into performing many of the domestic duties within the encampment. Myrddion Merlinus had told his boys often enough that most girls in the trade were happy to leave it and work at almost any other occupation available to them, providing their pimps could be removed from their lives. These girls were very young, having been selected to cater for a youthful clientele, and most of them had been sold to their pimps by families who had fallen on hard times. Taliessin believed that the girls deserved a second chance and their pimps deserved none, for he considered the provision of children for sexual gratification to be an abhorrent crime. When asked, the girls agreed with alacrity to serve in the kitchens, and happily gave up the dirty, tawdry clothing of their trade without a second thought. At heart, these children of farmers were still babes.

The spring days were sun kissed in these pleasant regions of Britain, which rarely felt the full bite of winter. Arthur continued to study in the mornings, and arms practice with Germanus took place in the afternoon. Stripped to the waist, Arthur's body was beginning to show evidence of the long hours of exertion. Muscle ridged his abdomen and bulked out his shoulders so that his waist and hips seemed impossibly narrow. He stood head and shoulders above his peers at the encampment, and even Germanus felt short in his pupil's presence. The kitchen girls made every possible excuse to watch him as he practised the use of sword and knife in the complicated patterns that were more dance than violence, so that the afternoon light kissed his amber hair, covered his warm golden skin with a dusting of gilded freckles and danced along the honed edges of his weapons. The younger lads were mesmerised and took to copying Arthur's practice routines, so that Germanus soon found himself tutoring a good half-dozen striplings, all eager to win favour in the eyes of their hero.

Yet Arthur did not succumb to vanity, which would have been quite understandable, given the admiration that was lavished upon him. When one of the smaller lads, Eamonn of the Dumnonii tribe, was found weeping with frustration because he couldn't manipulate the short Roman sword that his father had given him, Arthur took the time to realise that the boy was naturally left-handed. Eamonn was distraught to discover that he favoured the sinister hand, for many men believed that such a trick of nature was the work of the devil, but Arthur explained that there was no shame in being left-handed, and the 'affliction' could actually be used to advantage.

'I'm speaking the truth, Eamonn. Most warriors train to fight right-handed opponents, so it's easy for a left-handed warrior to break through our guard if we lose concentration.'

Eamonn had brushed his forearm across his eyes to hide the tell-tale, shaming leak of tears. 'But I've seen you changing hands at will, Arthur. You can use right *and* left, but I don't have any choice in the matter.'

'Then it's better for you to stick to your left hand until such time as you become able to use your weapon with both. Your enemy will have to take greater care if he is to defeat you. I would feel much better going into battle with you at my back to protect my left side, Eamonn.'

'I'll always protect your back, Arthur. I swear to be your man until I die.'

Arthur didn't laugh, as many young men of his age might have done if confronted by a serious, tear-stained lad who promised lifelong fealty. With the generosity of a great man, he was able to accept the offer of everything that Eamonn had to give with the seriousness that such a holy gift entailed. He also possessed the imagination to see a future where such an oath could become a valuable asset. Coming from a younger son, the vow was worth little, but Arthur was so humbled by it that he agreed to remain friends with Eamonn forever. Within hearing distance, Taliessin managed to conceal a knowing smile.

Germanus missed nothing. 'This is what the harper intended all along,' he told Lorcan when they ate together that evening, free at last from the intrusive high spirits of the young men in the encampment. 'He wants Arthur to possess a corps of dedicated young peers from good tribes who have given him their personal loyalty. In many ways, Taliessin's planning smacks of treason: I know how Bran will react if he hears rumours of Eamonn's oath.'

'Taliessin will cause a world of trouble for Arthur and Bedwyr by playing these power games.' Lorcan scowled fiercely. 'He wants to replicate Myrddion's influence over the Dragon Throne by using our boy as his pawn in the game of kings. Arthur shouldn't be treated as an extension of his father. He's his own man and should be treated with the respect he deserves.'

'Not likely, given Taliessin's nature,' Germanus muttered. 'He's a poet rather than a warrior, so I doubt he recognises Arthur as a person, only as a character in a song he's writing. He loved Artor, but such devotion has left no room for anyone else. Making the son of the Dragon into another High King isn't treason in Taliessin's eyes. It's just a natural progression.' The arms master heaved a deep, regretful sigh. 'We must watch him all the time, Lorcan, or Arthur might be sacrificed because Taliessin has reached too high. But for the moment we'll say nothing, and allow the boy to enjoy building his dyke.'

A week later, construction began with much enthusiasm and the cheerful throwing of a great deal of mud. The ancient stone fortress sited on one of the hills became the starting point, and peasants, warriors and aristocrats were soon at work with shovels and primitive digging implements in a laughing, democratic bunch. In a relatively short period of time, a ditch eight feet deep and fifteen to twenty feet wide was excavated for a distance of some twenty feet. The soil was thrown onto the south-western side and formed into a mound rising some ten feet above ground level to ensure that the defenders would always look down on the attackers as they approached from the north and east. Mantraps would be installed at varying intervals to impede any attacking force. Below ground level, Taliessin's skilled workers shored up the earth with fieldstone collected from the site while sod was cut to cover the raw, muddy surface and consolidate the mound.

When Arthur stepped away from the ditch to evaluate Taliessin's initial planning, he could see the purpose of the earthworks immediately. From the bottom of the ditch, any attacker would be faced by a stone and sod mound rising nearly twenty feet above him. Once in the ditch, the enemy could be easily attacked from above, while the sloping banks provided protection for the defenders.

'See, Arthur?' Germanus explained, his dirt-stained hands indicating the deep ditch and the mound towering above it. 'If we set some dressed and spiked tree branches into the walls of the dyke, we could hold an army here and stop it getting through to the softer lands to the west. Look where the dyke will be built.'

Germanus pointed into the distance and Arthur saw what Taliessin had realised when he first came to the narrow valley that led into the west. Pilgrims had travelled along this route for hundreds of years, passing on to Glastonbury and Joseph of Arimathea's church via the easiest gaps in the mountain chain. 'See how small hills are aligned across the valley? We will build the dyke from hill to hill, across the river and the plain to the dense forest that protects the south. In such a way, we can control any enemy who tries to pass.'

'I understand. Taliessin is a clever man to pick this spot, for many great towns will be protected by this ditch. I see now that I referred to it as the Warriors' Dyke in a fit of stupidity. It should be named for its builders, rather than warriors, for only a small number of those will be needed in its defence once it is completed. The rest can be redeployed in other places.'

As the work advanced, Arthur became increasingly important. The labour was back-breaking, so the boys would have lost interest quickly if Arthur hadn't explained the dyke's strategic importance. 'We are working here to save our tribes from attack. Ask the

Atrebate warriors what it feels like to have Saxons living so close that you can almost spit on them. And they have no ditch to protect them.' He smiled at his awestruck audience. 'The work will become a little harder once we reach the flat lands, for the earth is soaked in water. According to the legends, Glastonbury was once an island in a great inland sea, and some farmers have found shells in the plains round here. If we are lucky, we might even find some ourselves.'

What lad could resist such a challenge? Try as they might, the young aristocrats found no shells, but in the vicinity of the fortress they discovered a number of bones, well gnawed by human teeth, and the remains of a number of broken, yellow-coloured clay pots. Arthur stared up at the ruins on the hill and imagined men throwing away the bones during the long watches of the night as they prayed to their gods to protect them from some long-feared enemies. Could those old defenders have been Picts, the blue-tattooed people who had been displaced so casually by the Celtic invasion? If so, the souls of those long-dead guards must have been rejoicing now in the shadows where they gathered to wait for their enemies.

The lads were fascinated by the tales that Arthur conjured out of the rubbish that was revealed by their toil. One week passed and twelve feet of wall and ditch was completed, leaving Taliessin to conclude that the dyke could take as long as five years to finish. If his figures were correct, it could be a wasteful and pointless exercise.

The next day dawned with grey skies and the threat of rain, but as Arthur told his young friends, the digging would always be hard work whether it was carried out in rain or sunshine. He examined a row of blisters on his palms and vowed that they could manage the next ten feet in no time at all. 'I have better things to do than work in the rain and the mud forever,' he explained.

Everyone but Mareddyd agreed with his assessment, but the bully had made himself so unpopular that nobody in the encampment cared what he said. He was totally ignored, and this was the worst punishment that could be laid on him. Isolated, the Dobunni heir smarted with indignation that a Cornovii nobody should be looked up to while he was not. For his part, Arthur took no part in the judgement of Mareddyd's peers, who roundly despised the prince for bullying the smaller boys and lording his superior birth and wealth over everyone around him.

The further the work progressed down the slope of the hill, the more the workers were hindered by mud. Arthur turned their hard labour into a game so that the young men struggled on, coated in heavy, clinging sludge which at least repelled the stinging insects that bred in these marshy lowlands. By comparing blisters around the campfire at nights and through Arthur's constant good humour, the aristocratic youngsters discovered they were enjoying themselves.

'Remember, friends,' Arthur explained one evening as he wrapped his abused palms with clean bandaging, 'the warriors and the peasants take their attitude to the dyke from us. If we are lazy, or if we complain about the difficulty of the work for no reason, they will follow our lead and also complain. This task is important, and we should be proud to play our part in it. I'm committed to what we're building, even if I know that peasants can do the digging faster and better than I do. When I'm an old man, I will look back at the Warriors' Dyke and say that I helped to build it and keep my people safe from harm. What are a few blisters compared with a goal like that?'

The nights passed in spirals of wheeling stars that seemed so close that Arthur could reach out his spread fingers and capture their chilly beauty in his hands. Although his muscles ached from the endless toil of digging, no mental screams of warning came to disturb his sleep and no threats of danger whispered from the back of his skull. Only the night breeze soughed through the fields of long grasses and sang melodies of ancient beauty in the leafy branches of young trees. Time stood still during those long, dreamy nights as the breezes brought the scents of spring and growing things to Arthur's senses, and he prayed that this stage of his life would never end. The peace of ordinary men and women came hand in hand with the cleansing honesty of toil that soothed the mind with a promise of long, warm days and sweet, refreshing nights.

So summer came to the flatlands leading to the heart of the west. The ditch was now almost three miles long and the peasants were filling its long, straight channel with sharpened stakes that pointed menacingly towards the east. Ahead lay the river, Taliessin's greatest challenge so far, although the waters were narrow here where the stream flowed down from high in the hills where it began its journey. Arthur waited for the day when Taliessin would explain how the ditch would intertwine with the singing, living water at the point where Taliessin had chosen to make his crossing.

Breathless, the world also waited in a hush of summer nights.

Plan of Warriors' Dyke

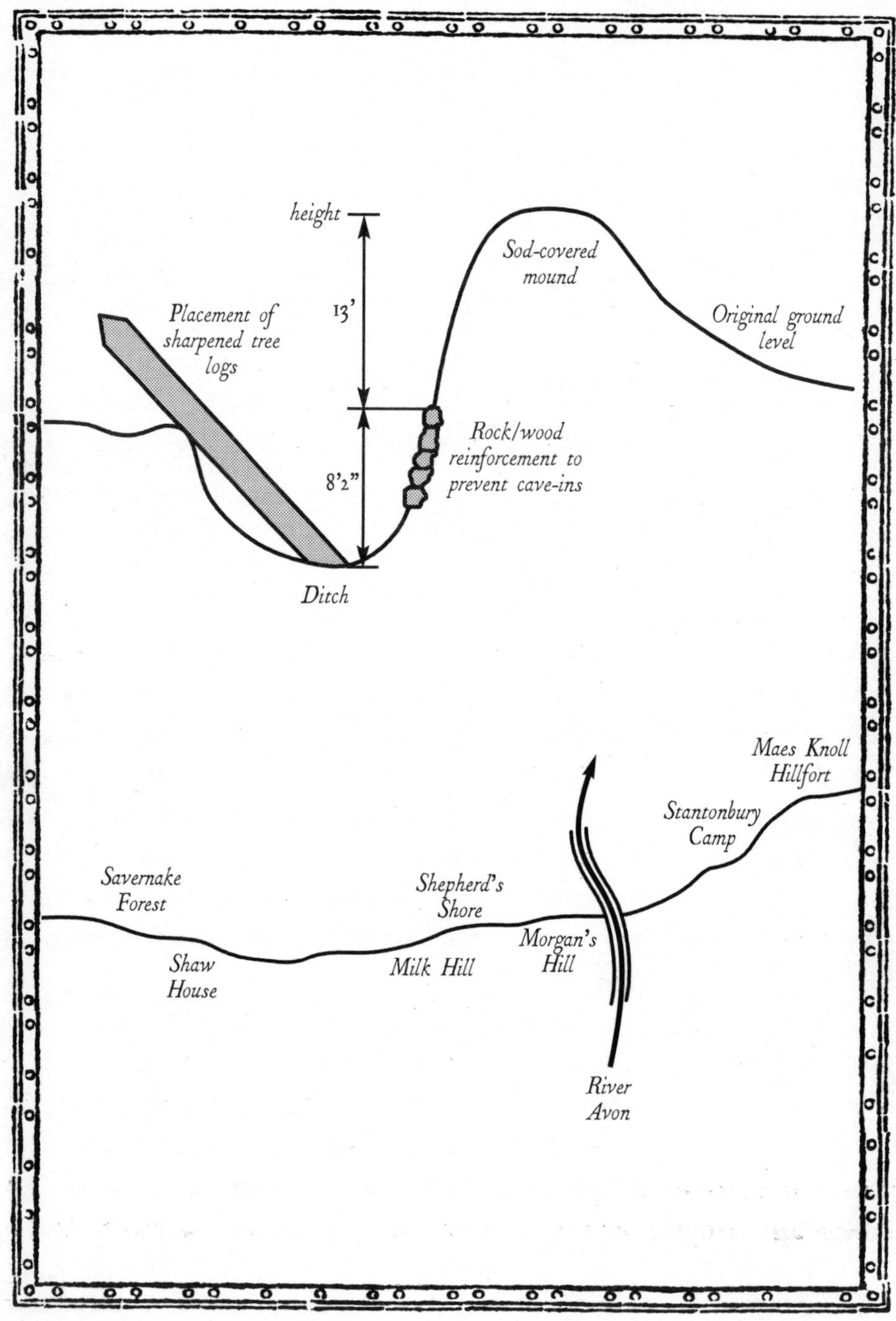

height
13'
8'2"
Sod-covered mound
Original ground level
Placement of sharpened tree logs
Rock/wood reinforcement to prevent cave-ins
Ditch
Maes Knoll Hillfort
Stantonbury Camp
Savernake Forest
Shepherd's Shore
Morgan's Hill
Shaw House
Milk Hill
River Avon

CHAPTER X

A DANGEROUS ENEMY

> The heart is deceitful above all things, and desperately wicked.
>
> Jeremiah 17:9

With a new stoicism, Arthur stared down at the dancing, gurgling waters of the river that could bring a year's labour to nothing. Not particularly wide nor overly deep, it still posed problems for the workers because marshland on both banks brought stinging insects and green clouds of gnats to feast on any exposed flesh.

'What's to stop the Saxons from loading rafts with their wagons and possessions and using the river to slip through into the west once we've gone? That's what I'd do if I were in their boots,' Arthur exclaimed to Taliessin when he saw the marshy banks.

Taliessin observed Arthur's serious expression with approval. He had been concerned by the younger man's enjoyment of company and his sense of humour, traits that Taliessin's earnest nature rejected as unnecessary. Arthur seemed to like everyone, and such fair, unprejudiced tolerance was not an ideal characteristic for a man who was born to rule.

'As always, Arthur, your questions are pertinent, but I would never waste months of my time building a dyke that could be easily bypassed. I have already solved the problem of how the ditch should cross the river.' Taliessin raised his hand and used his forefinger to emphasise the points he wanted to make by stabbing the empty air. 'First, we need to be aware of the Saxons' intentions in plenty of time to take action against them if they try to load their wagons onto rafts. A small troop of warriors will be based in this area and regular patrols will be carried out to monitor their movements. But in any case, the land is marshy upstream from the ditch and it would be almost impossible to load and launch any rafts from there.'

Arthur nodded. So far, Taliessin's reasoning seemed sound.

'Second, I plan to build a further obstacle to hold back the Saxons once our ditch has been completed. The small troop of Celts who will be left to guard this section of the wall will easily be able to handle the set of chains I intend to place across the river. The chains will be invisible under the water until such time as they are raised into position to block the channel.'

'Chains?'

'Yes, Arthur, chains. My father saw the great ropes of iron that seal off the harbour of the Golden Horn at Constantinople with his own eyes. As a boy, I tried to imagine the vast blue harbour shining in the sunlight and the network of chains that lay under the water. In times of danger, slaves would use huge pulleys to raise the chains up to bar the way of warships and prevent them from entering. Can you imagine the scale of it all? They used hundreds of yards of chain mesh, which is incredible when compared with our paltry thirty feet. Our small net is tiny by comparison, but it will be quite sufficient to achieve our purpose.'

Taliessin's eyes glowed with enthusiasm and his chill features were flushed with colour for the first time in Arthur's memory. Suddenly, Arthur wondered what he would have been like had he not been blighted by the last bitter days of Artor when he was little more than a boy. He was beginning to suspect that the harpist was determined to see the High King reborn and raised to his natural prominence in British life, whether the successor wanted such power or not. And he had a shrewd idea whom Taliessin wanted that successor to be.

Taliessin strode effortlessly along the marshy banks of the stream, his long black hair whipping in the strong breeze. 'Imagine, Arthur. The structure at Constantinople comprised a vast net of iron chains as thick as a man's upper arm that could block the harbour entrance. Father's account of it set me to thinking of what we could do here at our little river. A simple system of chains could immobilise any rafts or troops of horsemen that attempted to come downstream and block the easiest route into the west country. We would only need two men with a pulley system to raise and lower the chains. I've already drawn up the plans, and my brother Rhys has come to oversee the construction of the system.'

Arthur stared at the scrap of vellum on which the harper had sketched out the mechanical details of the chain gate. 'I'm awed by how easily you calculate the answers to difficult problems. By the grace of the gods, you have an enquiring mind that leaves other men stumbling through the darkness of ignorance.'

'The gods? Your mother is Christian, so I assumed that you shared her belief,' Taliessin said softly, with a blank expression that showed only polite interest. Under his bland demeanour, however, he was pleased that Arthur had no religious affiliations, for such neutrality reduced the chances of manipulative priests gaining ascendancy over his mind.

'I don't know what gods are out there.' Arthur gestured aimlessly with his hand at the sky and the distant hills. 'I don't know if the Christian God made everything, in which case he's to blame for much misery and ugliness as well as great joy and beauty. I can't guess which religion is correct, so I leave questions of faith to heads that are more clever and incisive than mine.' Taliessin shook his head and Arthur saw him wipe away the merest trace of a tear with trembling fingers. 'I'm sorry, Taliessin. I've upset you in some way that I don't understand. I'd take my words back if I knew what I'd said to hurt you.'

'You're very much like your sire, Arthur. At times like this it's easy to forget that Artor is long dead, because you look and think so much as he did. Many years ago, he once answered me exactly so to a similar theological question. He believed in purity of heart and goodness of action rather than the rhetoric and rituals of different faiths.'

'Then I'm glad that my lack of belief gives you pleasure as well as pain. It worries my mother sick, as if the afterlife would be barred to me if I were to die a heathen. I told her that any true god wouldn't care about the details if a man had lived a good life, but she's not convinced.'

'There's no need to fret about my feelings, Arthur. A man who feels no pain may as well be dead. As your father said, leave matters of religion to the priests. He lived his life by a very precise set of rules which he wouldn't break for any reason. Perhaps you'd not agree with all the commandments that he chose to keep over a long life, but they explain much about him and the ethics he admired. I believe our personal code of conduct explains us to any deity more truly than our choice of religion. I've never understood how a man can claim to be pure in the eyes of his god and yet kill the children of his enemies, as some priests suggest should be done. Children are not lice to be killed on sight. In fact, any religion that implies that some people have more right to live than others cannot be sanctioned by any god that I'd care to worship.'

Taliessin's voice was soft and almost seductive, and for the first time Arthur appreciated the potential for danger that lay beneath the harper's fair face. He was finally beginning to perceive the cause of the itch that Germanus felt whenever Taliessin was present. The Cymru poet did not possess the Sight, like his father before him, nor had he inherited Nimue's gift for reading others; but he sensed the skeins of power that ran intertwined through any group of persons, rich or poor, gifted or talentless, aristocrat or peasant. Taliessin saw potential in bands of colour, good and evil according to their relationship with others, and the ribbon of light coiling round Arthur was the red of hearts' blood, shading out to imperial purple.

Ignorant of what Taliessin saw so clearly when he looked at him, Arthur shook his head, showing his perplexity regarding the whole tangled question of the supernatural. Visibly confused, he put it aside to concentrate on more immediate matters.

'Who's coming this year, master? I'm looking forward to seeing Eamonn pen Bors again when he arrives. We had a wager when he left last autumn. He insisted that he wouldn't grow in the intervening months, so I laid my sling down in the hope that he'd be wrong. I think I have the better of the wager, for his big feet are one sign he's due for a growth spurt.'

'Yes, Eamonn is coming, and he's bringing his younger brother with him. Anyway, you young giant, who are you to speak about a growth spurt? How tall are you now?'

'By the Roman measurements, six feet and four inches,' Arthur replied with a grin. 'But I haven't grown for ages and my feet have stayed the same size for six months now. Mother is relieved, because my brothers already have a basket full of cast-off sandals that I've outgrown.' Arthur stared down at his long and slender feet. 'I'll be glad to stop growing. I'm sick of being treated like some kind of freak.'

'You're not a freak, Arthur, just a superb specimen of manhood. Don't be melodramatic! Your friends will be here soon and the skies are clear of rain clouds, which is surprising for the start of spring. Everything in our world is lovely, so you must learn to search for beauty. I remember well how your sire would pause on his horse to watch a dragonfly skip across a few inches of filthy water. He told me that the glories of the world almost stopped his heart sometimes, but it was the little things in nature that he loved most passionately.' Taliessin shook his head to dispel a cherished memory. 'You'd best set up your tent before the other lads arrive.'

As Taliessin turned brusquely away, Arthur felt as if he had been dismissed. The few minutes of shared intimacy seemed to have embarrassed the older man, and now he followed his show of affection by donning a cold, curt mask. What could Arthur do but obey this strange, other-worldly man who seemed to desire something of him, but steadfastly refused to tell him what it was.

As usual when he was puzzled or upset, Arthur went to his tutors for advice. Germanus and Lorcan were setting up their plain but comfortable tent on the margins of the meadow in company with the other mentors and servants of the princes who were already appearing at the encampment, wide with smiles and laughing over-loudly with the enthusiasm of young children on holiday.

Arthur thrust his head and shoulders into the opening of the tent and apologised for interrupting their work. Both men turned away from their unpacking, each with the same look of patient affection.

'What's worrying you, young Arthur? You've been looking forward to spring for months, and you've near to driven Arden crazy with your longing to be gone.' Germanus carefully stored his armour in its fleece bag on a peg attached to the main tent pole, although Arthur couldn't imagine any situation where the warrior would need full battle gear in this place. 'I like to be prepared,' Germanus answered his unspoken question. 'Now, what's stung you on the arse, boy? Out with it!'

'Else we'll never be unpacked,' Lorcan added. Germanus scowled at the interruption, for Lorcan always liked to have the last word, and the two teachers had argued over this on many occasions, rather like a pair of old lovers. However, both men would have been mortally insulted if they were made aware of the appearance of their affectionate squabbling.

'I've been speaking to Taliessin, and there are times when I don't understand him at all. On occasion I seem to make him . . . well, angry . . . that's the only description that feels right. He becomes so impatient with me that I can tell he wants to shake me. I'm almost certain that he has some sort of purpose planned for me, but when I indicate that I don't know what it is he becomes even angrier. I *think* he intends me to follow in the steps of my father, although I'm younger and stronger than Artor was when Taliessin knew him. Am I right?'

'Yes, but don't be misled by his motives, for there's nothing sexual in it,' Lorcan replied casually, and bit into a huge apple with obvious pleasure. Germanus glared at his friend, and Lorcan turned on him. 'What are you looking at, Germanus? You've gone all Saxon and stiff necked on me!'

'You need to mind your tongue, Lorcan, especially when you're talking about the actions of your betters. The High King never dishonoured Taliessin or vice versa, from what I've ever heard. And we would have heard it, because soldiers have bugger all to do but talk about their masters. Not that the High King found anything distasteful in the love that some men feel for others of their own sex. Master Bedwyr told me that King Artor regretted how little love existed in the world and how important it was to cherish true devotion wherever it was found. You're confusing Arthur, you clod.'

'I'm confusing him? You're turning a simple sentence into a dissertation on human sexuality.' Lorcan tossed the apple core at Germanus, who caught it easily because the Hibernian used little force and no anger in the throwing of it.

'Father Lorcan, Germanus . . . I'm confused and you're not helping. Are you saying that Taliessin was physically in love with King Artor? He's certainly never made any advances of that nature to me. I'm not such a baby that I'd misunderstand him. It's as if he becomes angry when I speak or act in ways that don't conform to his idealisation of the High King.'

'He loves the romance of what you are, Arthur,' Lorcan answered carefully. 'He was very young when he met his father's friend, and the High King was already a living legend. He was entranced by the tragedy of Artor's life and was full of hope for the future when he discovered that you'd been born. Even so, in the aftermath of the Battle of the Ford, he thought everything was lost. He was heartbroken when Artor died, for he loved him for his sense of duty and his courage. If you want to understand Taliessin's soul, all you have to do is listen to him when he sings of the death of the king. Taliessin worships no god, for Artor represented everything that Taliessin judges to be fine in the human spirit. When you deviate from Taliessin's view of his hero, he sees you as a traitor to the memory of Artor, so he's angry. He can't help it, so don't be irritated with him. He's a man who has lived with legends and has become one himself. His life has no meaning unless he can contribute to the formation of further legends, and he intends you to become the ultimate saviour of the west.'

'He doesn't want much, does he? Besides, I don't think the west can be saved,' Germanus added drily.

'Are you suggesting the harper is a little mad?' Arthur asked, his grey eyes wide. Taliessin was one of the great heroes of the age, a man who crossed borders at will and perpetuated the legends that had grown around the name of his famous master, Artor.

'Most great men are a touch crazy, because they have wide-ranging dreams and see the future far more clearly than do ordinary men.' Lorcan began to munch reflectively on another apple. 'You shouldn't blame Taliessin for his dreams concerning you. He cares about you deeply, and he knows you might be the key to the future of your people. He'd like you to live his way to achieve his aims, rather than your own. It's wrong-headed thinking, I know . . . but you must try to understand his motivation.'

'I get sick of being the one who has to understand,' Arthur snapped sulkily. Germanus could tell from his tone of voice that Arthur really was tired of being used by powerful men, and the arms master's sympathies went out to a boy who was yet to become a man, one whom everyone expected to act with calm reasoning and sensitivity to the needs of others when he was still only a stripling. There are special burdens placed on the tall and the strong, Germanus thought with a pang of memory for his own childhood experiences. He has needs too, and he only has fifteen years behind him. To break the mood, Germanus tossed an apple in Arthur's direction, and then peered through the tent flap.

'Eamonn has just arrived with a large retinue.' Germanus's eyes gleamed with impish humour. 'And I do believe that the young man has gained a little height. Oh, and before I forget it, the Dobunni heir is here as well, although without his followers: apparently his train was so large it fell behind and won't be here for a day or two yet.' The arms master tossed another apple in Arthur's direction. 'That's a prize for winning your wager. Now, get you gone, Arthur, and leave us old men to set our tent in order.'

Within days, the friendships and pleasures of life under canvas had re-established themselves as the young aristocrats of the southern tribes recommenced their backbreaking work on the Warriors' Dyke. The toil was rendered more interesting by the building of two small circular stone huts to conceal the pulley system that would raise and lower the network that would block off the channel. Taliessin's brother Rhys, a gifted blacksmith, was spending every daylight hour creating a series of graduated, interlocking chains that would complete the complicated structure. Arthur found a passion for the forge growing in him, and he took any opportunity to spend his free time running errands for Rhys and learning the rudiments of the blacksmith's trade from the hands of a master.

Everything in Arthur's life would have been exciting and fulfilling but for the presence of Mareddyd, heir of the wealthy Dobunni tribe and a natural stumbling block to any pleasant and friendly occasion. Mareddyd was now a warrior, and his blond hair was pulled back into plaits held together with ostentatious clips of gold. Although he had nominally come to the ditch to work, according to the scroll sent to Taliessin by his father Tewdwr, any bystander would have assumed he was there in a supervisory role.

Tewdwr had few illusions about the son who would one day be the ruler of the tribe that would benefit most from the construction of the Warriors' Dyke. The kings of the Dobunni had always been odd, having succumbed to Roman ways very quickly after Caesar's invasion. Leodegran, Wenhaver's father, had been a notable epicure and was even rumoured to have been one of Morgan le Fey's many amours. In contrast, his son Ifor, father of Tewdwr and grandfather of Mareddyd, was a man of iconoclastic leanings and simple tastes.

Ifor had originally been given the name of Fidius, Leodegran substituting the name of a Roman god for a Celtic title in order to glorify his son and heir. But Ifor refused to countenance such pretension and chose a good Celtic name to be his nomen. Ifor's dislike for all things Roman and epicurean had not declined during a long and stern life. Now in decline, Ifor saw in his grandson the same flamboyance, greed and amorality that had infected Leodegran and Wenhaver. Tewdwr feared that unless Mareddyd was given a lesson in manners, the Dobunni king might cut them both, father and son, out of the succession before he died. Thus Tewdwr's scroll to Taliessin begged that his son be forced to perform his share of the dirty work, and punished if he became a disciplinary problem.

From the first night at the encampment, the Dobunni heir flaunted his status as a fully fledged man. He was seventeen and of a good height, standing over five feet ten inches. His hair grew straight upward from the scalp so that his plaits refused to fall neatly from the crown of his head, and he made up for this small deficiency by binding the end of each braid with a small golden clip set with a river pearl. To risk such pretty baubles in the mud of the Warriors' Dyke seemed foolish to everyone but himself.

The members of Mareddyd's entourage were as objectionable as he was, and Arthur had wanted to box their ears last season when he heard them make fun of the smaller lads or torment poor

Declan, a younger son of the Atrebates king who was yet to lose his puppy fat. Roly-poly Declan was an easy target for unkind comments. The fact that his blushes were an unattractive plum colour didn't help, and when he was nervous he developed an unsightly rash.

But Arthur had taken the time to get to know him and had soon realised that the boy was clever and quick witted under the plumpness. Left to his own devices and free from teasing, there were few problems that Declan couldn't solve. Even his father knew that he would never be a successful warrior, but he had the clear, logical reasoning that made an excellent strategist and a careful king. Arthur had said as much to him and had been surprised by the gratitude and devotion in the young lad's eyes.

'Sooner or later, Mareddyd and I will probably come to blows,' Arthur muttered to Eamonn on the afternoon of the third day in camp. They were telling exaggerated versions of the truth about their winter exploits, as young men will. Arthur had hunted and killed the largest deer in Arden's history, while Eamonn had discovered a secret way into an underground cavern below Tintagel. After much boasting and hyperbole, their conversation gradually settled into more prosaic exchanges.

'I take it the Dobunni bastard hasn't improved over the winter?'

'Nah. He's more obnoxious than ever now he's a warrior,' Arthur murmured. 'He's still picking on poor Declan of Calleva Atrebatum. The boy's as plump as a stuffed goose, bless him. He hardly eats a bite, but his waist seems to get wider every time I look at it. Still, maybe Mareddyd's bad temper is caused by lack of sleep. He's been bunking down with whoever would have him, but his retinue is due to arrive tonight.'

'Couldn't Mareddyd's tent get lost en route? I was in Declan's shoes last year until you had words with the Dobunni thug. What did you say to him?'

Arthur examined Eamonn with his head cocked to one side. The year before, Eamonn had been a thin little squib who looked as if he'd blow away in the first strong wind. Now, he'd filled out so that his chest and torso were square and powerful. His legs weren't much longer, but slab-like muscle had built on the heavy bones of his thighs so that Arthur could see in Eamonn traces of the Boar of Cornwall, that powerful and honourable man who had refused to surrender his wife, Ygerne, to Uther Pendragon in the distant past. The scrolls of Myrddion Merlinus had included detailed descriptions of Gorlois, a man he obviously admired, so Arthur had little difficulty in recognising the ancestor in this young scion of a noble family. Even Eamonn's left-handedness had become a mental advantage, and he was finding weapons practice much easier when compared with the disasters in the past. He now possessed confidence, personality and physical dexterity, and Mareddyd would never consider bullying someone of such growing and formidable strength.

'You don't need to know. Anyway, he won't try anything this season. Look at the size of you!'

'I was an idiot, Arthur, and I thank Jesus you made me see the error of my ways. I began to enjoy weapons practice once I realised that I had it arse about. So then I was constantly hungry, and with all the food I ate I started to gain weight and . . . well . . . look at me now.'

'I am. Do I detect a certain preening under the masculine scruffiness? I know what's happened.' Arthur laughed, a little enviously. 'You've had a woman.'

Eamonn's toes made little circles in the dirt as he looked, shame faced yet proud, at anything but Arthur's keen-eyed face. 'Aye. But then, so have you, haven't you?' He was shocked when Arthur didn't answer. 'You're so tall, and all the girls follow you with their eyes. Shite, man, I've seen how the servants queue to watch you sluice off after a day's work is done. And you haven't had a woman? You're not . . . ?'

'No, Eamonn, I'm not.' Arthur's response was fast and clipped. 'Arden has fewer women than you might think and they all know me – too well, in fact. I've as much chance of bedding a woman in Arden as I have of growing wings and flying to the moon.'

Eamonn apologised sincerely to his friend for any embarrassment he might have caused, but Arthur waved away his sympathy. 'Never mind. I intend to set my tutors to work to ensure that I learn everything I need to know about the arts of love. Working on the dyke is probably the only chance I'll get, while I'm far away from home. It's one subject that I can't discuss with my mother and father.'

The two young men nodded glumly and swung their legs like children as they sat on a felled tree trunk. Arthur demanded a full account of Eamonn's experiences, and the conversation became ribald, centred as it was on the sketchy information that Eamonn had learned from a young street whore who had been hired by his older brother to educate him. Eamonn admitted that he found the whole experience rather humiliating, and couldn't understand why men turned to whores unless they had no choice.

'There's something embarrassing about paying for such a natural function. And the girl was paid to pretend. Can you imagine having to do that just to earn sufficient coin to survive? Afterwards, I felt ashamed, as if I'd done something morally wrong.'

Arthur had no idea how to respond to Eamonn's confidences. He'd never thought of the implications of purchasing a girl's services, nor could he imagine his body being invaded by another person, so he kept his mouth shut lest he expose his ignorance.

'Shite, Arthur, if I'm honest, I still don't know what to do. Prostitutes are such good actresses that I could have been useless. I probably was, since I had no idea what I was doing. The poor girl tried not to look bored, but I suppose she was just being kind.'

'Could a man die for love? Is sex worth all the songs that the harpers sing?' Arthur's idealistic view of the holy wonders of intercourse was crumbling away with every confidence that Eamonn shared.

'I'm sorry, Arthur, but I don't think so. From my limited experience, sex is all very well as far as pleasure goes, but I'd not choose to perish for a moment's physical satisfaction.' Eamonn grinned deprecatingly and Arthur found himself admiring the Dumnonii prince for his innate honesty. Few men can laugh at their lack of physical prowess, but Eamonn, at fourteen, was already showing more maturity than most fully grown men. 'No, I can't think of anything I'd die for, and certainly not a few moments of release. Sex is like a good sneeze, or scratching an itch.'

Eamonn giggled like a young boy, but his eyes were wise and thoughtful. 'That's all it is, for all we blow it up into some irresistible force that we can't live without. Aphrodite, Venus, the Mother, Mary Magdalene – I think we men are just scared and resentful of women. We want what they've got, but we hate the idea of admitting how dependent we are on them so we rape and trivialise them. It's sad, really, because love is the best part of us. I imagine that I seemed like a fumbling, pathetic boy who was tiresome and awkward, but the girl never made me feel bad or inadequate. She was generous, and when I hear the other lads making silly jokes about women I will feel a bit ashamed from now on.'

Bemused beneath the bravado, the young men whiled away a few free hours exchanging winter stories and the usual thoughtless pleasantries of young men. They watched as the field gradually filled with newcomers, raising their fists in greeting and calling out affectionate insults to fellow workers from the previous season, and each felt the bond of a common experience and a shared companionship with their peers. As they slouched on their log, they saw Mareddyd hurrying to meet his entourage, who had just arrived with a showy tent packed onto a heavy cart that was soon bogged down in the sticky mud of the field.

When the use of the lash and the screams of frustrated fury directed at the team only served to dig the wheels of the heavy cart deeper into the sod, Mareddyd took over a huge area around the terrified carthorses and ordered his servants to set up camp there, in a high-handed, arrogant manner that brooked no argument. Arthur and Eamonn noted that he was clad in the colours reputed to be favoured by his great-aunt, Wenhaver, whether out of preference or as a reminder of his regal connections. He was resplendent in sky-blue, a very expensive shade which was much embellished with gold thread and luxuriant fur of sumptuous thickness and gloss. Like Wenhaver, he was handsome except for a bullish flush of colour whenever his temper was roused, which was often.

His weapons, which he thrust into the hands of a young body-servant for cleaning, were very ornate. Arthur pursed his lips at the liberal use of gilt on the sword, with its complex hilt and large crosspiece in the Frankish style, and cabochon gems set into the engraved haft.

'It's very pretty,' he murmured softly, turning away. Eamonn raised one eyebrow in surprise. 'Far too pretty to be particularly useful. That blade is likely to break with one kiss from my Dragon Knife. My father Bedwyr swears that the greater the display, the poorer the workmanship.' Eamonn kicked him hard on the ankle. 'What's the matter? It's true.'

'And of course, you're an expert, *boy*,' Mareddyd snapped from behind them, his voice hoarse with offence. It was obvious from the bright spots of colour high on each cheekbone that he'd heard every word of Arthur's criticism, and Arthur realised how childish and ill natured his comments had been. He hadn't seen the blade in question, but had made his assessment only on the hilt, so his insults were both foolish and tasteless.

'Please accept my apologies, Lord Mareddyd,' he said sincerely, for he recognised that he had been at fault. 'I was ill mannered, loutish and jealous of your position. You have every right to demand recompense from me, for I have shamed my father's name.'

Arthur thrust out his hand as a sign of contrition, but Mareddyd roughly thrust it away. 'Keep your apologies for one who wants them, tree dweller. I'll see you this evening, directly after the evening meal. Perhaps you should bring your Dragon Knife with you and we'll see how its *kiss* compares with a blow from my sword.' Mareddyd's voice dripped with scorn, and Arthur was left in no doubt that the Dobunni prince would make him pay for his error of judgement. When Mareddyd spoke again, his voice was oddly elated, as if he had already achieved what he desired. 'My weapon is Frankish, and it was forged by a Merovingian swordsmith who served King Clodio long and well. The Salian Franks survive in old Roman Gaul because they are tough and battle hardened. Their weapons are beautifully crafted. Ostentation doesn't mean weakness to the Franks, whatever your father says, so you will need a new knife after tonight.'

And with his mouth pursed into a line of fury and triumph, the Dobunni heir stalked off to his slowly rising tent. His temper was already scarified by the shaming letter that his father had sent to Taliessin. The harper had punctiliously read the missive to

Mareddyd, and the young man was eager to vent his outraged feelings on his most hated enemy, Arthur of Arden. Mareddyd's dislike was personal: the prince was enraged by Arthur's size and strength and the natural charm that drew the other boys to him without any effort on his part. Mareddyd passionately wanted to be accepted as the natural leader of the young aristocrats, but Arthur was a tall barrier to his aspirations. Just thinking about the upstart caused Mareddyd to grind his teeth in fury, knowing he couldn't take any physical action against the younger boy without being branded either a coward or a bully.

'Now you've done it,' Eamonn said cheerfully as Arthur kicked at an immature clump of brambles with a vicious sideways swipe of his sandalled foot.

'It's my own fault, Eamonn. If the Dragon Knife is broken I will be to blame, because I have been vain and arrogant. I have allowed my prejudices to overcome my good manners. Hubris and vanity really are great sins.'

'It's only a knife, Arthur,' Eamonn said, trying to calm his friend's tense mood. 'Knives can be easily replaced.'

'Not this one. My mother will be very angry with me if anything should happen to the Dragon Knife, and Bedwyr would quite justly hold me up to ridicule in Arden. The knife is a holy and princely gift that I'm supposed to preserve from all harm. Instead, my boasting has brought about the biggest threat that the knife has ever faced. Perhaps Mareddyd will release me from my debt of honour if I abase myself in front of the whole group at the evening meal.'

Doubtfully, Eamonn looked across to Mareddyd's ostentatious tent and tore at the back of the trunk they were sitting on, stripping off the last of the bark with nervous fingers. 'I think you've got as much chance as a snowball in a fire-pit if you expect reasonable behaviour from Mareddyd. It's not his way.'

'And why should he be generous? I was the one who insulted Mareddyd's new status – I knew the sword was a gift from his father for attaining his manhood, and I belittled it. He may have been a horse's arse last season, but I was the rude one today.'

When the long twilight began and the kitchen women had ladled steaming servings of stew, flat bread and slabs of beef onto coarse wooden platters, Arthur kept his word. He knew he would be the butt of many coarse jokes, regardless of the outcome of his public apology to Mareddyd, but an honourable man had no choice other than to follow his conscience. Nervously, Arthur waited until the meal had begun before approaching the Dobunni prince in as humble a manner as he could muster. In case his plea for forgiveness failed, he had brought the Dragon Knife to the communal eating tent. Swathed in soft cloth to protect it from prying eyes, the heirloom would be displayed if necessary to show Mareddyd and the other aristocrats just how precious it was to the Britons.

When Arthur pleaded for a less confrontational settlement of his debt of honour, Mareddyd laughed. Suddenly aware that the knife concealed in the bag in Arthur's hands was probably far more important than he had originally imagined, he realised that there was a way he could have his revenge while minimising any accusations of dishonourable conduct that might be levelled against him.

'I'm not unreasonable, Arthur, and some of our disagreements in the past have been my fault. There, I admit it! We're like two bantam cocks in the same hen house. But I can afford to be magnanimous, now that I'm a man and a warrior. Since it's the reason for our disagreement, I have decided that you should hand your trifling knife over to me. I will then consider all matters of honour between us to have been settled. You say that the weapon is an heirloom, so I will ensure that it is kept safe in my house. In point of fact, it will be safer there than in yours, for you have put it at risk through a silly bout of boasting. But I require your acknowledgement of my magnanimity, given the insults that were directed at me. I suggest you consider your options, and advise me of your decision after everyone has finished their meal.'

Arthur flushed red along both cheekbones, until his pale eyes seemed to stare out at the world from a narrow mask of white skin. Rage flooded his body so potently that he could barely speak, aware that he had no room to manoeuvre in this nasty exchange. To the listening warriors and young aristocrats Mareddyd's terms seemed reasonable and Arthur knew it. But the audience wasn't aware of the significance of Artor's Dragon Knife, which had disappeared at his death and was now largely forgotten. If Arthur bared the knife now, he risked shaming his mother and drawing attention to her relationship with the late High King. But if he didn't show the knife to the audience, he risked losing his family's most precious heirloom as well as the goodwill of his peers.

Ignorant of his enemy's dilemma but confident that he would capitulate, Mareddyd had turned away to show his contempt. Only the unmoving shadow of Arthur's tall form warned the Dobunni warrior that Arthur had stayed rooted to the spot. He turned back to face the younger man.

'No,' Arthur stated flatly. His voice offered no hope of eventual capitulation.

Somehow, Mareddyd had managed to impress some of the watching warriors. His calm, reasonable tone of voice, even the length of time he allowed Arthur to think about his demands, sounded generous. Even Germanus was impressed with the young warrior's words, although he knew that the Dragon Knife could never be handed over to a mere prince of the realm. Arthur's single word of refusal was curt, abrupt and threatening.

'I will not relinquish the Dragon Knife to anyone. This weapon was passed to Bedwyr by King Artor, High King of the Britons, at his death. The Dragon Knife was his to give and Bedwyr has been magnanimous in allowing me to train with it. I proved my childishness through boasting, for which I apologise again to everyone involved, but I cannot give up a weapon that does not belong to me. As I have shamed my family's greatest link with the late High King, I believe I must demonstrate that Mareddyd's demand to own this knife is deliberately designed to humiliate and enrage me at a time when he knows that I cannot comply with his wishes, even in defence of my honour. Therefore, behold the Dragon Knife of King Artor, High King of the Britons.'

With an innate sense of drama, Arthur rolled back the dark fabric to reveal the golden hilt and long blade. He rested the blade on his palms and held it at shoulder height, while turning so that every person in the open tent could see the glorious weapon in the fading sunlight.

A collective exhalation of breath told Mareddyd that Arthur had eluded him once again – by his simple use of the truth. No single man could ever again own the Dragon Knife, so it couldn't be given away, lost or allowed to be stolen.

Arthur turned to face Mareddyd again. 'You have been very generous towards me, lord, and you have the right to heap any form of indignity upon me.' Arthur bowed his head, accepting that Mareddyd could demand anything else of him that he chose. But Arthur had won the approval of a large slice of the crowd through his honesty, and Mareddyd knew it. The Dobunni heir's stomach roiled sourly with his undigested meal and he longed to beat the submissive face of his enemy into a bloody paste.

'Then I demand satisfaction, man to man and face to face,' he shouted to the assembled audience. 'This Cornovii is unnaturally tall for his years so there is no advantage on my side, although I am the older. In fact, he has the longer reach and the stronger thighs. I will trust to Mithras to determine the outcome of this combat. The warriors' god will see through this boy's pretensions of nobility and expose him for the charlatan he is.'

'I will accept any terms determined by Lord Mareddyd, but I ask to fight without weapons. As I have said, I own that the fault for this breach of good fellowship is mine because of the jealousy generated by his fine sword.'

Young men love a fist fight and this audience was no different in the pleasure it derived from the prospect of a test of physical strength without any fear of serious injury to either combatant. Within a moment, the tent floor was cleared of trestle tables and long plank seating. The central area of green sward, not yet churned to mud by the movement of many feet, was swept clean, and all dropped pottery, wooden platters and any other detritus that could cause harm was picked up and removed. Germanus took the Dragon Knife and rewrapped it out of sight of avaricious eyes, while Lorcan helped Arthur out of his leather jerkin and stout work sandals, for Germanus had already decided that having a good footing on the slippery grass would be more important than the odd broken toe caused by Mareddyd's heavy boots.

Several enterprising warriors were taking wagers on the outcome of the bout and when Taliessin arrived, intent on stopping the fisticuffs, he realised that he would find it easier to clean their makeshift stables with his mother's eating spoon than to stop what had now turned into unexpected entertainment. Trusting that Arthur wouldn't be hurt too badly, Taliessin laid down some rudimentary rules and instructed the captain of the dyke's guard to maintain order within the makeshift fighting circle.

And so the two combatants prepared for battle after the

Cornish captain insisted that each youth bare his sleeves to ensure there were no hidden weapons. 'For you are supposed to be gentlemen, sirs,' he warned with a wide grin. 'Remember, no honourable man bites another man's balls, or tries to gouge out his eyes, but there be no further rules to worry you. Fight fair, and we'll let the gods decide.' Then the elderly warrior winked and rubbed his thumb and forefinger together. 'I'd be obliged if my choice would win, as well. I've a tidy sum riding on one of you, though it wouldn't be fair to say which one. So be at it, young men, until I call for a break.'

Niceties were in short supply in tribal fisticuffs, although their Roman masters had raised the brutal sport to the level of sanctioned, skilful murder. Neither Mareddyd nor Arthur had received any formal training in the sport, as it was not deemed suitable for aristocrats. Mareddyd had watched a number of contests, bloody, drawn-out affairs that had been conducted between professionals for coin, but Arthur had never seen a fistfight in his life, other than the odd scuffle between warriors during drunken sprees. However, Lorcan had received some unusual training in the monasteries of Rome where the use of personal defensive measures was condoned, and Germanus had also given his young charge some preliminary instruction in how to fight an opponent after being disarmed.

Lorcan's simple moves required practice and involved the knowledge of pressure points on blood vessels that could be used to incapacitate an enemy. He had shown Arthur how the ball of his palm, or the calloused outer edge of the hand, could be used to render someone unconscious with relatively little effort. There was no doubt that Arthur, with his superior height and excellent tutors, should have enjoyed an edge over his opponent, but Mareddyd outdid him in one thing.

He hated – and he hated hard!

From the moment the Cornish captain stepped aside, the Dobunni prince went for Arthur with the express intention of causing him permanent bodily harm.

He struck his opponent as soon as Arthur's hand began to drop from the customary handshake at the start of the bout. The swift blow to the face blinded Arthur for a moment, and the prince wound his fist in his enemy's curly hair and proceeded to pound the side of his head with his fist. Arthur would have lost at this point but for his experience of dealing with drunken warriors. Trusting that his skull was thicker than Mareddyd's, he head-butted the other boy, using the heavy bone of his forehead as a ram. The skin across Mareddyd's eyebrows split open like an over-ripe melon, exposing the red pulpy flesh inside.

Both boys fell onto the grass while their supporters screamed for them to regain their feet. With little skill but much enthusiasm, the pair rolled, kicked, bit and thumped each other whenever any uncovered flesh appeared. When Arthur managed to drag himself to his feet, Mareddyd rose with him because the Dobunni heir had wound his legs round Arthur's hips and was pummelling him crazily on the back. When Arthur shook him off with the strength of a bear, Mareddyd was sent careering across the floor before he stopped his wild tumble by winding an arm round a tent pole.

And so the conflict would have continued, half ferocity and half farce, had the Dobunni prince not lost his temper. Arthur's reasonableness had always eroded Mareddyd's nerves like pieces of glass grinding together, and now its effect on the young warrior was volcanic.

'This is stupid, Mareddyd,' Arthur panted as they circled each other. He was bleeding from a swollen lip and a split along his hair line but, so far, his golden looks were still undamaged. Likewise, except for the cut on his brow, a thick ear and a bent nose, Mareddyd's only serious injury was a mortal wound to his pride. 'I'll apologise to you again if that will stop this nonsense. Think, Mareddyd. We're only going to hurt each other for no purpose if we continue. We should be killing Saxons.'

'I won't be surrendering to you – ever,' Mareddyd screamed, and Arthur understood that he must finish this fight quickly before something tragic happened.

He feinted with each hand and then moved forward to pin and lift Mareddyd like the shaggy golden bear he resembled. Consolidating his grip, he began to squeeze. The Dobunni prince realised he had to break free of those iron-hard arms or he would be forced to surrender. But Arthur had spent years pitting his strength against the hard muscle of Germanus, a full-grown man. Nothing short of death would break his hold on Mareddyd.

Mareddyd slid his right hand downwards towards his foot, even as his other hand clawed at Arthur's eyes. Arthur automatically responded to the tearing fingernails by closing the lids to protect his eyeballs, and Mareddyd managed to reach back and down and pull out a curved, narrow knife that had been secreted in his boot.

'Knife!' Germanus's roar rose above the cheers and jeers of the crowd, most of whom had not yet seen the narrow, glittering weapon.

Germanus had survived the worst of encounters in the lands of the Franks and the Goths. While he could never hope to teach Arthur how to counter even half the dirty tricks he had seen during his wanderings, certain rules could be learned that would help a warrior in many desperate situations. He had taught Arthur that the moment he heard the word *knife* he must remove himself from proximity to his attacker and keep him at greater than arm's length.

Both eyes leaking tears and blood, half-blinded by Mareddyd's raking nails, Arthur reacted immediately. With reflexes honed by years of practice, he tossed the Dobunni prince like a piece of kindling clear across the tent the moment he heard his sword-master's warning.

But he was already too late. Warriors such as Mareddyd trained as assiduously as Arthur to react instinctively when under threat, and he contrived to slash across Arthur's abdomen even as he began his involuntary flight across the tent. The captain of the guard stamped hard on the weapon before it could be used again.

Arthur felt the sting across his belly: not particularly painful, but sharp. Through streaming eyes, he looked down and saw a long slash through the leather trews that were laced into place on the outside of each leg. The brown leather had been neatly split from his hipbone across the full width of the body, although only a sluggish trickle of blood was staining the scuffed, worn edges. His heart in his mouth, Arthur used both hands to explore the wound while Germanus and Lorcan exploded out of the crowd to reach their charge. No, he hadn't been disembowelled – and yes, his manhood was still in place.

'What the hell have you done to yourself this time, boyo? Are you determined that your father should behead both of us because you've gotten yourself killed?' Lorcan's voice was harsh, but his hands were gentle as he forced Arthur to sit on the churned grass. 'Do you have a competent healer in this place, Taliessin?' Only the stridency that lay under Lorcan's even voice warned those who knew him that the Hibernian was beginning to panic. Serious abdominal wounds were invariably fatal.

'He's already coming,' Taliessin answered in a tense voice. Around him, the audience quietened as they recognised his obvious concern. 'My brother is the only healer here, but he was trained by my father. Arthur could not ask for a better.'

Germanus grumbled something inaudible within his large moustache as he used his knife to cut the side lacings of Arthur's trews. The leather fell apart and revealed a wound that was obviously meant to kill. The point of Mareddyd's blade had entered Arthur's body on the edge of the hipbone in a long sweeping motion designed to gut him like a staked deer. Fortunately, the blade had barely penetrated the skin as Arthur tossed Mareddyd away from him, but although the wound was superficial it presented considerable danger because of the threat of infection. Even the untried boys present understood the peril that Arthur faced, and realised that something shocking and dishonourable had taken place.

'Let's have a look at this wound of yours, young Arthur,' a rich, seductive voice demanded. Despite his reluctance, Arthur bared the sluggishly bleeding wound for the second time. 'Well, well, young man, you've clearly gained the sympathy of the goddess. In this part of the body the major organs are close to the skin, but you're scarcely bleeding, which tells me that nothing vital has been breached. Fortuna obviously has a purpose for you.'

Arthur opened his eyes and saw Glynn ap Myrddion, brother of Taliessin, for the first time. The healer's hair was blond and he wore it in a long flaxen braid that fell almost to his waist. In colouring, Glynn was his brother's opposite, for his eyes were as black as jet. Glossy, impenetrable and intelligent, they were as shocking under his sandy brows as Taliessin's blue ones were in his pale face.

'Thank you, Master Glynn,' Arthur muttered, completely overawed by proximity to the scions of one of Britain's greatest men. When he was alone, it was easy to forget the prestige of Taliessin's father when the extraordinary skills of the harper in the fields of music, poetry and science were considered. When Taliessin was joined by Glynn, the healer, and Rhys ap Myrddion, whose skills encompassed ironwork, agriculture, science and mathematics, every man present knew he was in the company of greatness.

Without touching it with his naked fingers, Glynn checked the depth of the wound and placed a heavy pad of gauze over the torn flesh. 'Take him to my tent and I'll treat him there,' he muttered to Lorcan. 'While this blow was meant to kill, I doubt it will cause any lasting problems, except to leave yet another large scar. How old are you, Arthur?'

'Almost sixteen, my lord,' Arthur mumbled, his eyes wide with awe. Most of the boys at the Warriors' Dyke felt the same awe for Taliessin, but Arthur had known the harper since birth and he was no longer struck dumb in the presence of King Artor's poet.

'Well, you're as scarred as any warrior twice your age. That's an unenviable boast. As far as I can tell from such a brief examination, at least three people have tried to kill you before you've reached manhood. So it's off to my tent with you! It'll do you good to walk, but you should keep the wound covered. Evil humours entering the body through such an injury can often cause death. No one, not even my father, could save you if your blood became poisoned.'

In company with the healer and his two tutors, Arthur limped out of the tent to be treated. He shuffled away on his own two feet, a clear indication that the healer expected his patient to live. As they left the tent, Taliessin went to stand before Mareddyd and allowed the room to quieten. Behind his back, the aristocratic youths and their entourages were left gape mouthed and confused at the way their entertainment had terminated in the attempted murder of one of their own without the saving grace of a believable excuse. Fifty men had watched the prince attack his younger opponent with a weapon when Arthur was clearly unarmed, and fifty pairs of eyes were now avoiding his hot gaze as he dragged himself to his feet. And fifty mouths would later speak freely of Mareddyd's behaviour during the contest, a lapse of honour that would stay with him for the remainder of his life. All honourable men detest cheating in combat, but to draw a weapon on an unarmed opponent was despicable cowardice.

'What are we to do with you, Mareddyd pen Tewdwr, proud heir of a great family and descendant of kings? You have broken the rules of combat. The cause of this unseemly brawl was trivial even for a fist fight, young man. You chose to roll on the sod like a peasant because a silly youth criticised your sword. From all reports, only one other person even heard this minor insult, so you were not held up to public ridicule. Arthur apologised immediately, and you heard him repeat that admission of fault this evening before everyone present. Most of these young men had no idea what your argument was about, but Arthur knew he had spoken with a boy's rancour and jealousy when he uttered the insult. Would you have given up your sword in the same situation, Mareddyd? Of course not! Then, as clearly as if you had shouted your intention aloud, you tried to steal his knife for yourself because it was of value to him and his family. Finally, during a battle of honour, you drew a hidden knife to avoid being defeated in equal and fair combat. The whole camp saw what you did. Unfortunately, I am a mere harper and not one of your peers, so I am not permitted to punish you. Nor would I suggest that you be judged for your actions by your fellow warriors. This whole distasteful incident is best ended here. But it won't be swept aside, because every person present will remember today's treachery.'

Taliessin rounded on the audience, his ascetic, cold-blue eyes riveted upon both aristocrats and seasoned warriors. 'I know that you'll talk like gossiping old granddams behind your hands, and enjoy the telling of this evening of shame. But if you speak out of turn, and I discover you have lied or invented anything, then Taliessin will become an enemy of your house. Do you understand me?'

Shamefaced, the men present nodded or looked down in agreement. No one spoke to defend Mareddyd, and the young man felt the revulsion of the warriors enclose him like chains of iron as they stepped away from him, leaving him in a cone of silence. Furious, humiliated and afraid, he burst into intemperate speech.

'The Cornovii pig has always sought to wound or insult me. From our first meeting last season, I knew he would harm me if he could. I armed myself because I expected him to try to kill me with his bare hands. I thought he intended to break my back. I had no intention of harming him in return. I just wanted to stop him from killing me.'

No one stepped forward immediately to defend Arthur's good name. Although every boy who had been present the previous season knew that Arthur had never used insults against anyone, least of all Mareddyd, and many knew too that Arthur had ignored Mareddyd's own frequent insults to avoid the charge of bullying someone who was smaller than himself, they remained silent for fear of reprisals. Every man and youth there waited for one of their companions to do the noble thing.

Finally, Eamonn mustered the courage to answer Mareddyd's slurs against Arthur's character. 'The whole argument was a trivial matter, as Master Taliessin explained, and I think we were all actually enjoying the prospect of a fair fight,' he began. 'I, for one, longed to see Mareddyd thrown down on his skinny arse, because he spent most of last season making my life miserable. Didn't many of you feel the same way?'

A murmur of agreement soughed through the tent – softly at first, but growing louder as the audience grew bolder.

'But we allowed Arthur to fight our battles for us because he was bigger than we were. Our cowardice seemed harmless, for we thought that Arthur was strong enough to bear the brunt of Mareddyd's resentment. We should have fought our own battles. By the gods, I've said a thousand more insulting things about Mareddyd and his lack of character than Arthur's single fall from grace. So why did I let him face an older man who was a warrior in his own right? Why did I even permit the contest to take place? Yes, between us all we could have stopped the fight if we had made our feelings known. But we were afraid, and would not accept that united we are strong. Worse still, we were excited by the prospect of seeing Arthur grind Mareddyd's face in the dirt. If we accept Mareddyd's feeble excuses for his treachery, then we are just as guilty as he is because we know his words to be lies.'

Even Taliessin was surprised by the edge of command in Eamonn's voice. He might have been only fourteen years old and still far from his full growth, but his words were so compelling that every man present responded, even Mareddyd, although the warrior flinched at the contempt in Eamonn's tone.

'You called me every foul name imaginable last season, and I never demanded recompense. By your rules, Mareddyd, I should have called you to account a hundred times for your slurs about me. But, out of cowardice, I didn't utter a word of complaint against you. Once only, out of all the times you deserved censure, did Arthur say anything that could have insulted you – only once – and that was today when he scoffed at your sword. For someone who claims he was frightened of the situation he found himself in, you had several opportunities to ensure your personal safety. Arthur apologised often enough and you could have retreated with your honour intact on several occasions. A frightened man wouldn't have faced Arthur in physical combat. But then, in the way of the coward, you decided to be certain of winning by secreting a blade in your boot.'

'You Cornish squib! You can't match me in birth or in learning, so you seek to blacken my name by accusing me of cowardice. If I attack you now, or call you out, you'll charge me with being a bully. You're using your lack of height to demean me.'

'Yet you've used your lack of height to demean yourself. You felt you could use a knife on Arthur because he was bigger than you.'

Mareddyd's face was flushed with fury and guilt. But years of swaggering braggadocio was a habit that was impossible to break, now that he was a man. 'You have no right to criticise me, you bag of hot air. You're nothing, Eamonn! Even the women in my family stand tall. My great-aunt was a queen!'

'My father's great-uncle was married to the legendary Ygerne, and the High King himself was my cousin, so you should beware how you toss family connections around,' Eamonn snarled back at him. 'There are many lads here whom you have scorned who can claim a finer bloodline than you. Assumptions of grandeur matter little here, Mareddyd, for the history of our people has no bearing on the character we display to those who know us. I'll speak to you no more, whether you choose to stay at the Warriors' Dyke or not. Belatedly, I stand for Arthur.'

Then Eamonn turned his back on Mareddyd and waited beside the tent flap, leaving the accused to continue the diatribe of justification that had served him so successfully in the past. One by one, the young tribal aristocrats rose and turned their backs on him, before leaving the tent to join their entourages. Eventually, Mareddyd fell silent in a room where only three men still faced him – the captain of the guard, the enigmatic, judgemental Taliessin and the youthful Eamonn beside the tent flap.

'Since this is the way you allow these curs to taunt me, I will have none of any of you, Taliessin. Everyone present tonight should dread the time when I become the ruler of the Dobunni tribe, especially if their people should have any need for strong allies. I'll see all the tribes of the Britons turned to ashes for the insults that have been aimed at me this night. I'd prefer that the Saxons ruled our holy places than to offer aid to any of you. And you can tell that piece of shite, Arthur, that he'd best watch his back from now on. He's my sworn enemy until death takes one of us.' Then Mareddyd laughed, and the sound was an ugly, grating expression of contempt. 'You too, Eamonn! You too! Your head will decorate my hall before my life is done. You shamed me and I will not forget you.'

'You can only be shamed by what other men believe if guilt already lives in your heart,' Taliessin whispered, knowing that he was wasting his time. 'Go now, and make any excuses you choose to explain your return to your father. No one here will argue with any version of events that is not a direct lie. But you should be gone quickly, before the guards of some of these young men decide that you're a danger to their masters. They may decide to protect their charges from your threats in a more permanent fashion. Arthur is well liked, and you are not.'

Mareddyd spat on the sod, leaving the vile globule of phlegm lying at Taliessin's feet. Then the young man turned on his heel and approached the captain of the guard, his hand outstretched to receive his confiscated blade. The captain placed the knife in his hand. Then he stepped away from Mareddyd, turning his back on the heir to the Dobunni throne with the studied insolence of a trained warrior, and left the tent.

'You'll regret this day,' Mareddyd promised in a soft voice, his face bone-white and his clenched fists trembling with an anger that was barely contained. The childish threat was frightening because the Dobunni's voice was utterly flat, belying the physical signs of powerful emotion revealed by his body. The air seemed cleaner once he had left the tent.

Ostentatiously, Taliessin placed his boot on the globule of phlegm lying on the grass and ground it into the sod. 'This wasn't a good day's work, Eamonn. With luck, Mareddyd will forget this silly incident when he grows to adulthood, but perhaps he won't. However, the dyke still needs to be built and Arthur will be upset if his injury slows down its construction. We return to work tomorrow, and we will still boast with pride that we worked together on the Warriors' Dyke.'

Slowly, man and boy left the tent, leaving behind broken trestle tables and overturned stools, and the servants hurried in to clean the eating area before the light failed and night settled around them. Outside, a wind began to rise and set the forest to moaning as the breeze grew to a small gale, bending the smaller trees and forcing the predators of the night to scurry to safe cover as heavy rain began to fall.

'May the heavens protect us,' one of the older servants, a peasant farmer hired by Taliessin for the season, crossed himself in the Christian fashion, and stroked a runic amulet round his neck for added luck.

'What's your problem, Cobb? It's just an early storm, not a reason for worry,' a fellow villager answered as he staggered under a pile of used wooden platters, notable for the scraps of food left upon them by the aristocracy. The dogs would dine well this night.

'Can't you smell it?' Cobb asked bluntly. 'The storm reek, but worse, that only comes when the Wild Hunt is abroad and

Cernunnos goes hunting for human souls.' Everyone experienced a fleeting mental picture of the stag-horned god, huge and menacing, as he led the harrowers from hell. Even the Christians felt a frisson of horror at the thought.

'You're supposed to be a Christian, Cobb. The baby Jesus has driven the Old Ones out of this land, so how can the Hunt even exist?'

'You'll see, Brud,' Cobb snapped, and his fingers strayed to the protective amulet again. 'Men carry the Wild Hunt in them, so Cernunnos has been called up by men. I'll take my chances with baby Jesus and my runes. Perhaps both will protect me.'

'You're right about one thing: there's a storm coming,' Brud answered drily. 'So move your arses, mates, or we'll still be cleaning in the dark while the nobs are sound asleep under their warm dry furs.'

Aye, but we'll not all sleep this night, Cobb thought bleakly. Something frightening is coming. The dark years are beginning now, just as the Witch Woman warned the Brigante people. The Dragon King has been dead too long and the peaceful days are over. I had hoped to be safely in my grave before the bad times came again, but such is not to be my lot. Ah, Cobb, it's the very devil to live in the shadows of great men, and the poor peasant always suffers, pays and dies. Hours later, the farmer's thoughts were still bleak and dark as he made his way to his damp bed in the crowded servants' tent.

Outside, the black sky was riven with forks of white and yellow fire while the earth rumbled and shook with thunder. The trees cried as they were ripped from the ground by unusually strong winds, and even the nocturnal owls were forced to seek safe places where they could survive the terror that came from the heavens.

Had anyone cared to look, the stars were blotted out, one by one, as the storm marched across the sky, so that heaven itself became invisible. Under his warm furs, with his wound stitched, treated and covered, Arthur slept with the innocence of a healthy animal, unaware that the margins of his world were shrinking as time turned Britannia into a cauldron of trouble.

CHAPTER XI

OF LOVE AND WAR

The soul is placed in the body like a rough diamond and must be polished, or the lustre of it will never appear.

Daniel Defoe, *Of Academies: an Academy for Women*

That season was to live in Arthur's memory as the last months of his boyhood, the period before time, war and violence swept away everything he valued. His wound healed swiftly, leaving a spectacular new scar so that he now had two white lines running parallel across his body, occasioning much curiosity when they were compared with his healed shoulder wound.

Arthur hated being confined to his bed, so while he recovered he was permitted to carry out light duties working at the forge with Rhys ap Myrddion. A horrified Glynn was quite colourful in his description of Arthur's fate if the wound tore open and permitted the invisible evils of infection to creep beneath the skin. So graphic and ghastly were Glynn's word pictures that Arthur actually spent most of his time in his quarters until the wound was nothing but a pink-red scar stretching from one side of his abdomen to the other.

After that, he enjoyed his daily sessions at the forge where the iron was melted for the construction of Taliessin's chains. Once he could move freely, Rhys permitted him to ply the huge leather bellows that kept the fires white hot. Where Taliessin had found the large store of iron scrap needed to complete their task was beyond Arthur's imaginings.

'Your brother must have prised every nail and scrap of iron out of the tribes, not to mention pillaging Roman sites, to find such a store of metal. Is our little dyke worth all this effort?'

Rhys grinned with a white and charcoal smile that was much brighter for the glare of flame that surrounded them. 'My brother is . . . strange, as you are no doubt aware, but he's rarely wrong when he obeys his instincts. And those instincts led him to you, Arthur, just as our father was led to King Artor a generation or two ago.' He withdrew a long ribbon of iron from the forge as he spoke, and Arthur thought it resembled a coil of white rope that gradually flushed to cherry red as it cooled. With a sharp iron chisel in one hand and a wooden-handled hammer in the other, Rhys cut the pliant cord of iron into three . . . four . . . five regular strips a little longer than a man's hand. From his position at the bellows, Arthur found it impossible to raise his eyes from Rhys's deft gloved fingers. He watched as Rhys put down the chisel to pick up a set of long tongs and replace one of the short pieces of iron in the forge before nodding to his assistant. Using the muscles in his back and upper arms, Arthur brought the red-hot coals to shimmering life until the short thread of iron glowed white again. 'I, on the other hand, have no gifts beyond those things that are perceived by my brain, my hands and my curiosity.'

Rhys fed the glowing thread of iron through the last completed link in the chain, then twisted the white-hot metal into a perfect oval around the horn of the anvil. Using another set of tongs and his heavy hammer, he pounded the ring with perfectly judged force until small chips of red metal sparked in the hot, dry air and the two raw edges of cooling iron joined perfectly.

'I consider myself to be a free man,' Rhys added, and twisted the iron ring off the anvil and placed it in a wooden barrel of cold water, where it sizzled momentarily before changing to the grey of dead men's lips.

'You're a natural man,' Arthur said slowly as Rhys placed the next thread of iron on top of the hot coals.

'So are you, boy. I see no sign of a white streak in that curly mop of yours, and you do not appear to be haunted by dreams or strange images in your head. We're the lucky ones.' Rhys lifted the end of the growing chain from the barrel and laid it on the anvil while the new thread became white with heat. Then he took the newly cooled ring at the end of the chain in his gloved left hand, bent the hot iron thread through the oval loop with his long-nosed pliers and wound it round the horn of the anvil. A few quick strikes of the hammer sealed the half-formed circlet, and the chain continued to grow.

At last Rhys pulled off his gloves and used a tin dipper to douse his head with water from the barrel. Sighing with pleasure, he turned back to Arthur, taking in the broad shoulders, the keen eyes and the thick bones of wrist and ankle and lamenting the loss of the master smith who lived within this lad, who was still as malleable as the iron he was forcing to bend to his will.

'I hear a screaming at the back of my skull, just there, when I'm in danger.' Arthur tapped the back of his head with his knuckles. 'Sometimes it starts with an itch, or a word or two, but whenever I'm in danger it just seems to come from nowhere.'

Rhys leaned back against his anvil and crossed his arms across his belly, not in dread or out of a need for protection, but with the ease of a man who has always lived with wonders.

'Your gift seems useful to me, even if it's only in your imagination. Given your kin, I wouldn't be surprised by anything you came up with in the way of talents we cannot see. Father was fascinated by those strange gifts, although he hated his own talent for prophecy. He lost it in middle age in some type of unholy bargain and it didn't return until his last years, but growing up it seemed perfectly normal to me to have a father who spoke of flying ships of iron and journeys to distant stars. I've thought hard about some of Father's more improbable weapons of war and I'm convinced they could be made to work by great and inventive minds.'

'Your father was a living legend. Neither my mother nor my father has any such talent, but I understand exactly what you are saying.'

'To Father's best knowledge, Pridenow was the earliest of your family to bear this unseen affliction, although he managed to hide his fits from others.' Rhys eyed Arthur carefully as he spoke, hoping the young man was mature enough to understand his colourful background. 'Father's stories say that Pridenow had cruel headaches which were passed on to his daughter, Ygerne, a woman who possessed true glamour and the power to draw men to her. No one ever thought of harming Ygerne, not even Uther Pendragon, who seemed to have been prepared to kill almost everyone else, regardless of their station. Morgan was obviously tainted, and gloried in it, while Morgause had a talent for long life, childbirth and power. I know that sometimes these gifts don't seem to be anything more than odd coincidences, but you and I both know that they are real. Don't you feel the oddness in your sister Anna? Doesn't Ector's wife sometimes make you wonder? Is it so odd then that you imagine warnings when you're in danger? Be grateful for it, but tell no one about this particular skill, for they might make connections which could do you harm. Do you understand me, Arthur?'

'I understand, Master Rhys. I must admit that I wish I was free to choose a craft. How fine it would be to become a smith, or to learn the rudiments of healing. I try to imagine the freedom of choice, but I don't believe that the sons of masters can ever have free will, for we are all born to serve our tribes. Such is the privilege and the punishment of leadership. We have a soft bed, food for our bellies and servants to smooth our lives, but in return we must serve our people, giving our whole selves to the welfare of the weakest, the least able and the most elderly as a sacred duty. Bedwyr believes this service to be an absolute obligation and so does my mother. I have thought about it a lot, and I have come to believe that they are correct. Power and wealth are only transitory, and their pleasures must be paid for. The voice in my head might be a part of that payment.'

Rhys wiped his dripping face with a twist of old cloth. 'You could be right, lad, but my brother expects his chain to be finished by the time the season is done, so it can be set in place before winter comes. Back to the bellows with you, young Arthur, and exercise your muscles in the service of the west. This chain must hold back the Saxon boats.'

The approach of winter was scarcely noticeable in the fair but slightly tawdry city of Aquae Sulis. The wind was cold and the trees were relinquishing their leaves in sodden piles of brown sludge, but the walled gardens encircling every public building were still quite green, while the Roman predilection for fountains found full expression at every crossroad and in every courtyard.

At first, Arthur was embarrassed by the baths for which the city was famed, for both sexes bathed there on a regular basis, separately and together. He had nothing against swimming – but in public? And naked? He felt sick at the very thought of baring his whole body for the amusement of a crowd of men, servant girls and food vendors. Huddled in his towel, he watched incredulously as Germanus and Lorcan oiled their bodies and used their strigils to clear the accumulated grime out of their pores before plunging into the hot pool, where they stood and jeered at their student. Sheer embarrassment drove him to oil his skin in imitation, but the strigil seemed shaped to cut and nick his underarms and upper thighs. He obviously lacked the necessary familiarity and dexterity with the implement.

'Hadn't you better get in the water before you bleed to death?' Lorcan demanded, his dark eyes dancing with humour.

'Is he yours?' a portly citizen asked as Arthur waded awkwardly out towards them, his face contorted as the hot water rose up his thighs.

'He's ours, in so far as we're his teachers,' Germanus replied cautiously, his eyes lazily scanning the affluent-looking, well-fed gentleman who watched Arthur so intently. 'Why do you ask?'

'I organise gentlemen's amusements. Wrestling, boxing – you know the type of thing. I don't suppose . . . ?'

'No!' Lorcan and Germanus said as one, grimacing, as Arthur slid under the water, emerged again and moved into the tepidarium with visible relief.

'Such a pity,' the citizen murmured as he took in Arthur's sculpted shoulders, mane of dripping hair and beautifully etched, muscular abdomen. 'The scars, I mean,' he added hurriedly. Lorcan grinned wickedly.

'You may be of some use to us, sir, if you're of a mind to assist strangers in your city,' he said. The two tutors looked at each other with unholy glee. 'We have a duty as the boy's mentors . . .'

'But in an unfamiliar city . . .' Germanus's voice faded away.

'And as a priest, my experience in these matters has been quite limited . . .'

'Oh, you're looking for a good brothel?' the portly gentleman said, the confusion clearing from his plump features. 'Of course, your lad will need the very best.'

'Of course,' Lorcan and Germaus chorused in unison.

'The house you need is Aphrodite's Altar. There's no better brothel in all of Aquae Sulis, for it's Roman in style,' the citizen murmured appreciatively, and licked his pink lips.

'Shaved?' Germanus asked.

'Waxed!' the citizen answered, and shuddered deliciously.

He told them where the brothel could be found, and the tutors clapped him on the back in thanks before sliding into the tepidarium like large pale seals.

'Come. It's time you learned what it is to be a man, young Arthur,' Germanus said in a jovial voice that held more than a trace of mockery.

'But first we must bathe in cold water,' Lorcan added, 'and put a comb through that mop you call hair.'

Bemused, Arthur tried to make sense of his tutors' teasing. Then, with another hot flush, he began to understand. 'But I don't know what to do, and I haven't any money. You can't just dump me in some brothel and hope I figure out what I'm doing. Can you?'

'It's time you learned, laddie. You're a great lump of a boy, all hair and teeth, so let's see if the ladies can soften you a little.' Lorcan patted him affectionately on the head. 'You need to become a man, so we've organised an excursion for you.'

Arthur blushed and looked terrified. He had not forgotten the tales of his friend, Eamonn pen Bors, who had been taken to a street prostitute by his cheerful older brother. He felt his stomach settle somewhere around his bare, bony toes.

'Never mind. All you need do to impress the ladies is speak the truth, compliment them often and be very, very grateful,' Germanus told him. 'Women are different from men and they don't think the way we do. You'll learn that their minds can dance around a half-dozen different subjects without wasting time on logic. Bless them, we men can rarely understand them.'

'So maybe we should put off this meeting to a later date,' Arthur suggested desperately. 'I'll forgo the experience. After all, I won't miss something I've never had.'

'And spoil our amusement? No, it's time you met your fate, young Arthur. The servant girls come close to raping you every time you take off your tunic to wash that torso of yours. If I were a few years younger, I'd be jealous.' Lorcan's face became serious as he beckoned over a merchant who traded in ales, ciders and wines. Economically, he raised three fingers to indicate the number of drinks he wanted to purchase. Arthur watched in amazement as he fished a copper coin out of his mouth and washed it casually in the frigidarium before handing it over to the vendor.

Small tin mugs of some pungent brown liquor were thrust into the hands of Lorcan and Germanus, who handed the third to Arthur. The lad sniffed the liquor doubtfully, but Lorcan swallowed his draught in one gulp. The priest shuddered convulsively and his eyes immediately began to water. 'Damn me, Germanus, but that's excellent liquor. It's some kind of country brandy, but I'd rather not ask too many questions about how it's made. Drink up, Arthur, because it will turn your adventure into great fun.'

Arthur sipped at the liquid and almost choked as its power took his breath away. Fearing he'd disgraced himself entirely with the small group of naked men who were already smiling knowingly at him, he tossed the rest down in one determined gulp. When he stopped coughing and spluttering and managed to catch his breath, he could feel the liquor spreading hotly through his veins, warming his stomach and making his fingertips tingle.

Lorcan winked. 'Oh, and try not to upset any of the girls if you can avoid it. Women have much nastier dispositions than men and take offence at any little thing. All whores carry knives and they're likely to gut you if you say the wrong thing.' He paused, then added seriously, 'Don't insult them, and don't laugh at them, for their lives aren't easy.' It was a flash of sensitivity that Arthur would never forget.

Then, dawdling through nervousness, Arthur and his companions dressed and left the baths, following the portly gentleman's directions until they came to a villa where two tall body-servants carrying cudgels and staves guarded the entrance. Judging by the bulging biceps and oiled upper torsos of the guards, the house was both secure and discreet. No signs, loud music or drunken customers lowered the tone of the quiet lane. A large sculpture of Priapus erect was the only indication of the purpose of the establishment, and Arthur blushed once again.

Lorcan and Germanus swaggered into the open atrium of Aphrodite's Altar. A group of girls sat around in various stages of undress, several of them playing desultorily on flutes, citharas and small brass finger cymbals. The resultant sound was not harmonious, because the girls were amusing themselves rather than playing in unison, but it invested the scene with gaiety. The girls' flimsy draperies and wide smiles added to the festive air of the evening, a mood that Arthur found easy to absorb and enjoy. He felt his face fill with heat at a glimpse of a rosy, painted nipple, or a hennaed palm lingering on a delicate, plump thigh.

With easy charm, the lady of the house greeted them. She was a jolly woman whose plump frame and double chins suggested motherliness and good humour rather than overt sexuality, although Lorcan detected a sharp edge of calculation in her limpid brown eyes. She was a businesswoman and she did not choose to hide it.

'Greetings, gentlemen. Welcome to Aphrodite's Altar. I am Crislant, the proprietor of this establishment, and I personally guarantee the cleanliness, charm and graciousness of all my girls. You'll not be robbed or cheated in this establishment and the young ladies are accomplished, for I insist that they should be educated. After all, a girl can't remain young for ever.'

There was no appropriate response to this obvious truism, so Lorcan explained their visit with a few well-chosen words.

'A virgin!' Crislant squealed excitedly, and the girls suddenly became more animated, especially when Arthur moved into the lamplight. Nine pairs of eyes ringed with long blackened lashes took in every inch of his tall frame, lingering on the breadth of his shoulders and the flatness of his abdomen.

'My, but you're an excessively handsome young man,' Crislant whispered throatily as she looked up at his hair and features. 'What should we call you?'

Arthur blushed in earnest now, for Crislant's hands wandered embarrassingly across his back and down to the tautness of his buttocks. Short of slapping her hands away, he couldn't think of a single means of extricating himself.

'I am Arthur,' he whispered after a valiant effort to clear his throat. 'Your young ladies are very attractive, Mistress Crislant – as are you,' he added, remembering Lorcan's hint that women love praise. As he spoke, he raised the brothel owner's plump, painted paw to his lips and kissed her knuckles with nervous charm.

The woman patted his cheek with her hand. 'I'd love to be young again, and I'd surely give these lasses some competition. Now, Arthur, is your preference for fair hair or red? Blue eyes or brown? You only have to ask, and Crislant will find someone to meet your needs.'

'I don't really know how to answer you, mistress. I already feel a little bit foolish, so I'll place myself in your capable hands.'

'You're a clever boy, young Arthur. Did anyone ever tell you that you have a look of the last High King? I met him many, many years ago, and it's said he grew to manhood just a few miles from here. But don't blush at me, boy. If you share in the bloodline of King Artor you have no need to feel shame, whatever side of the blanket you were born on.' She smiled at him. 'Arduinna?'

Crislant's voice had suddenly become crisp and businesslike. A tall girl, probably a few years past her twentieth birthday, uncoiled her long legs and rose sensuously to her feet. Her hair was the colour of aged oak and it fell straight from her hairline to her waist without a trace of curl or kink, even at the ends. Something golden seemed to shimmer just below her pale skin. That same gold found its way into her hazel eyes, so that the irises seemed to be made of amber and yellow topaz and the black pupils appeared unnaturally large and jetty. Her eyes guarded her thoughts well and Arthur, who had been taught to read the expressions of opponents, had no idea what she was thinking behind her smooth, unlined face.

Arduinna took Arthur's hand and led him along a tiled passageway leading to a small, spartan room whose only concession to luxury was a high, narrow window that let in the sounds of the night. Arthur felt as if every nerve ending in his body was exposed and sensitive, and he was suddenly less frightened of the coming experience than excited by the prospect of it.

Trying to take the initiative and not sure how to do it, he attempted to put his arms about Arduinna, but she slithered out of his embrace, giggling. The sound was mellow and warm like thick golden honey and Arthur luxuriated in that intoxicating laughter, although he had no idea what to do now that Arduinna had refused his embrace.

'Allow me, master,' she murmured throatily and began to strip off his cloak and tunic, carefully releasing the catches, the cloak pin with its bronze spike decorated with Bedwyr's tree symbol and his heavy leather belt, whose green and white buckle bore a similar locking device.

'You wear the trees of Arden, master?'

'Aye. And what of you, Arduinna? What is that necklace?'

She lifted a small golden figure that hung from a length of red-dyed cord. It lay between her breasts like a golden eye.

'This is the goddess of the forests of my home across the water. We share the same name and she is a huntress. The Romans called her Diana, but we know who she really is, don't we?' She crooned to the tiny figure of a boar, vicious and charging. Somehow the idea of this lovely, golden woman and a hunting beast didn't seem incongruous in the soft warm night, sweetened with the last fruits of autumn.

'You're still a virgin, my lord. All whores dream of teaching the art of love to a man like you, for no man will ever forget his first woman. He will love many women in his lifetime, but the first is special. So, my lord, you only need to obey Arduinna and I will make you into a man. You should have no fear that I will think you foolish or ignorant, and I shall not mock you. On this night I am blessed, and I thank you for the gift I am about to receive.'

Then Arduinna proceeded to teach Arthur the delights of manhood. Amazed and surprised by his lesson, Arthur learned quickly that women are creatures of subtlety, so neither force nor aggression gives them pleasure. She showed him that time spent wooing a woman was worthwhile, for at first women are less ready for lovemaking than men. She explained every small action and every trivial caress so that Arthur understood the effect of what men do so casually for their own enjoyment, thoughtless of the woman between whose legs they lie. She taught him in those long hours that sexuality is a gift, a tool and a weapon, depending on who wields it, and why.

'But we are the lucky ones, aye? You and me: Arthur and Arduinna. We do not love each other, so we can give to each other without shame or pain. I will give you knowledge and you will give me pleasure. Do you see what I mean? Some gods demand the sex act as part of worship, and I can understand why the ancients thought in that fashion, because we can be ennobled by such worship. But where the heart is cold and power is all that is desired, we women are despoiled and become creatures of the darkness. You must remember that women are what you make of them. If you treat them with less respect than your horse or your dog, they will turn on you as all abused beasts do. And, sweet Arthur, you must remember that women are your lovers, your wives and your mothers. If a whore can be all those things to a man, surely she is worthy of some respect.'

She smiled down at him, and a stray shaft of moonlight played halo-like with her glowing hair. 'You're a sweet boy, Arthur, but the time has come when you must leave me. I hope I never see you again, so I remain young and beautiful in your mind for ever.'

'You will always be beautiful, Arduinna, both in my memory and in fact. Everything about you is golden and lovely, and I would take you away from here if I could. My heart hurts in my breast to think of you as the prey of the men who frequent this place.'

She laughed gently, but sadly too, and when Arthur raised his fingers to her face he could feel a narrow track of tears snaking from her eyelids to her jawline.

'I will grow old quickly. Women do in my trade. If I am fortunate, I will save enough money to move to a village far from here with sufficient coin to lead a respectable life. If I am not, I will lose my teeth and my looks, and survive as best I can. Whores don't live long, sweet Arthur.'

'But you are Diana, the Huntress, and she survives without men, Arduinna. I have no doubt that you are clever enough to do so too. After all, Crislant chose you to educate me in your arts. I don't think she'd have picked a foolish young girl. I'm not being vain, but my father was a close servant of the High King.'

'All men have heard of Bedwyr of Arden.' She laughed, and the sound had humour and hope in it. 'Perhaps you're right, Arthur. I will think on it, but now you must go back to your life.'

Only one thing still teased at Arthur's mind as he dressed, even while he joked with Arduinna as they walked hand in hand back towards the atrium where desultory music was still playing.

'What is it, Arthur? Is something still bothering you?' Then she gasped and began to giggle in earnest, masking the sound by covering her rich, full-lipped mouth with her fingers.

'Don't laugh at me, Arduinna. Please. You're making fun of me . . . and I can't help making a fool of myself.'

'You were as all boys are when they learn the ways of love for the first time, my dear. I'll not lie to you. But you were very sweet and you were eager to learn. If you practise hard, I know you will become a wonderful lover.' Then she punched him on the shoulder, as if she were an older sister, before kissing him on the lips.

In the atrium, Germanus and Lorcan were sleepily waiting to go to their beds, although neither man was prepared to admit that he had grown so old that a good night's slumber was preferable to the fleshpots. When Arthur sheepishly entered the room with Arduinna on his arm they rose creakily to their feet, winked at the mistress of the brothel and began to make their farewells. Arduinna kissed Arthur quickly on the cheek and ordered him not to look back when he departed. He obeyed her. Had he chosen to turn his head at the door, he would have seen that the girl with amber eyes had begun to weep quietly against the wall.

Morning came as the three men recovered from their entertainment in a pleasant inn on the outskirts of Aquae Sulis. There was a promise of rain in the air, and grey clouds scudded across the sky from the direction of the sea. Even in these temperate climes, the light breeze held a hint of cold to show it had teeth ready to bite the unwary. Arthur looked through the drawn shutters of their shared room and remembered Crislant's casual comment that the High King's youth had been spent near this town.

'Germanus? Master?'

Germanus was still asleep. Spring and summer had been hard work at the Warriors' Dyke, as the young aristocrats and their entourages had made one last push to complete the major section of the ditch before the onset of winter, when the frozen earth would be impossible to penetrate with their crude implements. Other groups would build off the main construction in the coming years, but, as Taliessin explained, those secondary walls and ditches could be constructed at any time. Meanwhile, the five major tribes of this area had agreed to provide a rotating guard of twenty warriors who would live and work at the Warriors' Dyke itself.

Germanus was really too old to be digging vast expanses of ditch, especially in deep and clinging black mud, but he was the only person to find one of the truly ancient sea shells. While digging, he had felt his hoe strike a hunk of indigenous rock.

Carelessly, he had thrown it onto the bank behind him and the clay had fallen away to reveal an odd circular shape.

'What's this, Germanus?' Arthur had asked as he lugged a length of chain to a half-built hut which, when completed, would house the equipment used to raise and lower the defensive barrier.

'It's just a bit of rock that was buried in the clay,' Germanus had answered casually, but Arthur, ever-curious, had soaked it until the last of the soil had washed away, revealing its true nature.

When Arthur hailed him, Germanus raised his hand instinctively to the petrified shell hanging round his neck on a chain of fine brass. Back in the far reaches of time, someone had drilled a small hole through the spiral shell, presumably in order to string it on a piece of hide. Now it rested on the greying chest hairs of Germanus, a mercenary born far from this ancient land.

'Do we have to begin our journey back to Arden today, master?'

Bleary eyed, Germanus eyed his student warily. He had drunk too much wine the night before and felt both guilty and hung over, while Lorcan had conveniently disappeared. 'Why?' the mercenary demanded irritably, being fairly certain that Arthur wanted something of him that would be either time-consuming or physically taxing.

'I'd like to see where King Artor grew to manhood,' Arthur replied candidly. There was no point in lying to Germanus, who was far too astute to be fooled. The tutors had known Arthur since he was a boy, so they could usually guess at his questions before he asked them.

'Seems fair. I've heard he grew up at a Roman farm called the Villa Poppinidii, only an hour or two from here by horse. I believe it still exists, although it's run down. Where's Lorcan?'

Arthur shrugged, saddened that such an important place had

been neglected over time. As he grew older, all the places that had seemed so real and inviolate during his youth were disappearing. Since that day on the snowy hill overlooking Rab's farm, Arthur had lost any faith in the firmness of the earth under his feet. The loss of his childhood meant he could never be quite certain that any day was perfectly safe. But the legends had seemed real. Now, the decline of the Villa Poppinidii would underline the decline of the tribal world, legends included.

Just then Lorcan entered, whistling tunelessly through his teeth. He looked as disreputable as ever, with mud caught between his dirty toes within his scuffed leather sandals. Arthur found it almost impossible to believe that not much more than twelve hours earlier Lorcan had been clean, sweet smelling and newly released from Aquae Sulis's most luxurious bathhouse. It was hard to imagine what he had done in the intervening hours to become as untidy as an unmade bed, but Lorcan never stayed neat and well dressed for long. Oddly, no one ever held his appearance against him, as if slovenliness were an easily discarded coat, non-essential to the man who lay beneath the surface untidiness.

'You're both awake,' Lorcan said unnecessarily, oblivious of the mud he had tracked into the room. 'Aquae Sulis is only so interesting, Germanus. There's a limit to what I can find to amuse me in a post-Roman city that doesn't really care what visitors think of it. Have you eaten?'

Germanus groaned and carefully shook his head. On the other hand, Arthur felt his stomach rumble at the mention of food. 'I would happily eat a horse,' he answered hopefully. 'You'll need sustenance, because you're about to embark on a journey with me to the Villa Poppinidii where King Artor spent his childhood. I have a yen to see the shadows of the past.'

'Let's not go,' Germanus mumbled. Putting a cushion over his head, he tried to pretend his companions had vanished into some silent, empty void.

Lorcan looked interested. 'I've heard talk about a very special garden that grows near the villa, and I'd be interested in seeing it. Up, Germanus! Arthur has given us something profitable to do with our day, rather than ride back to Arden or watch you spend your free time sleeping.'

With a quick burst of energy, he tore the woollen blanket off his fellow tutor, baring Germanus's hairy legs and a rucked-up tunic which he had slept in after tumbling, half drunk, onto his pallet. 'For the sake of the Christus, Germanus, spare the blushes of a priest by covering your hairy arse.'

'You weren't acting like a man of the cloth last night,' Germanus grumbled, but he yawned hugely and clambered to his feet, stretching his long, northern arms to show an alarming expanse of narrow flank. 'I know you're going to make my life miserable until I give in, so I'd best get dressed and join you.'

Then, with an old soldiers' efficiency, Germanus dressed, packed his saddle bags and was ready to leave before either of his companions. He was chewing charcoal to clean his teeth when the others joined him.

'Take it from me, boy,' he mumbled through the charcoal, 'look after your teeth, especially if you're going to be a fighting man. The inability to chew makes us old and weak faster than anything else I can think of. Rotten teeth can kill, not to mention giving you breath that stinks worse than a week of sweating. Bathing is all very well, and quite pleasurable, but good teeth beat cleanliness hands down.'

Arthur nodded, his face showing attention, while his mind travelled ahead to the villa and what he might see there. He had heard Germanus's opinion on oral hygiene many times and always cleaned his own teeth with a small twig after every meal, although the habit had earned him some good-natured ridicule at the Warriors' Dyke.

'Come on, old man. I'm eager to see the place that nurtured Artor. Perhaps I'll understand him better after I've seen the villa,' he urged, dancing in excitement like an overgrown boy. Under the tidal wave of his enthusiasm, the two older men were herded to the innkeeper to settle their account. It included the cost of stabling their horses, a sum which proved to be greater than the charge for their own quarters. As Germanus drew on his coarse sheepskin gloves, from which the fingers had been cut off at the first joint for dexterity, he carefully checked the three mounts and the packhorse and pronounced himself satisfied with the care they had been given.

Then, in a flurry of fallen leaves, the trio spurred their horses into a brisk trot through the crowded streets. Arthur felt elated at the thought of becoming his own man again after three seasons digging in the mud and slush of the Warriors' Dyke. Now all he needed was to prove his worth in battle. To outstrip the deeds of his father was an impossible ambition, but a part of Arthur that he kept well buried yearned to become a person of note in his own right. At the moment, he was a pale copy of a great man. He was happy, but he hungered to be a warrior renowned for his own deeds rather than those of the formidable Bedwyr, his ostensible father, and his sire whose name could never be spoken aloud. As he set off on the journey to the Villa Poppinidii, he was hopeful that this historic place might begin to fill the hole in his heart.

After two hours on the road, the three men were less cheerful than at the outset of their adventure. The terrain was rendered interesting by rolling hills, all of which were suitable for agriculture, as the farmer in Lorcan recognised immediately. A huge, menacing forest lay to their right, and Arthur told Germanus the tales of this sullen and forbidding place that the great Myrddion had included in his scrolls.

'Apparently, there's a garden around a ruin near that part of the farm where the villa's land abuts onto the forest. Myrddion speaks of Artor's first wife living and dying there when the High King was still a young man, but he is very hesitant to reveal much of what happened in those far-off days. I don't really understand why this Gallia was deemed to be unsuitable as a wife for the heir of Uther Pendragon.'

Lorcan snorted as his eyes searched the rolling land in front of them for signs of the villa. 'I asked about the history of the family when I was wandering through Aquae Sulis. One of the old women in the market was quite forthcoming, and she told me that Artor's first wife was the daughter of a Roman fish trader. It seems the family was very rich, but any merchant's daughter would have been considered unsuitable as a queen in those days. As she would today.'

Arthur's spine stiffened. 'Do you think that Artor would have cast her off to become High King?'

Lorcan recognised the autocratic note and moderated his tone immediately. 'No. The scrolls of Myrddion Merlinus tell us that he'd have refused the throne if he'd been forced to make a choice. I think Master Myrddion was very glad that he didn't have to face the issue and that mad old Uther killed his daughter-in-law before one of Artor's friends – himself, for instance – was forced into the same position.'

As Arthur gaped, shocked by the ruthless demands of power, Lorcan continued with his impromptu lesson. 'Quite apart from her father's trade, the tribal kings would never have accepted her Roman lineage. The queen had to be a tribal woman, one like Wenhaver.'

'Can we leave ancient history in the past?' Germanus asked plaintively, for he cared not a jot for the history of the tribes, except as it affected his lad. 'I believe the villa is in sight on the top of that hill. We should be watching for a path that leads off the road.'

The way to the villa was soon found. The gates were hospitably open, and the three horsemen began to ride in a long slow arc up the gravelled track to the house on the hillside. No one still lived who would remember the other three visitors who had come to the Villa Poppinidii when Artor was twelve years old, in search of a wild-haired boy called Artorex. Dozens of men and women had died in that quest by the time the lost child had eventually been found in this bucolic place. Now another Artorex was riding up to its doors.

The companions could tell that the walls of the villa had once been whitewashed until they shone in the sunshine, but neglect had allowed them to become so earth coloured that the lines of the building disappeared into the hill. As they neared the house, they saw chickens, ducks, several dogs and two young children playing in the courtyard, but almost immediately a servant hurried through the scarred wooden doors, ordered the children inside and straightened upright to demand the identities of the uninvited visitors.

Arthur announced his name and the names and callings of his companions. Mention of Bedwyr raised the man's eyebrows, and he begged the visitors to dismount and wait for just a moment. 'There's water in the pail and a dipper hanging beside the well. Help yourselves, gentlemen, while I fetch the mistress.'

'Our thanks, good sir,' Arthur replied courteously, and swung off his horse with an easy grace. A tow-haired boy appeared out of nowhere to take the reins. Arthur noted that the boy's eyes were pale blue, and he wondered how such northern eyes had a place in a Roman villa.

A woman came to the forecourt with the soft murmur of house slippers on stone as Germanus and Lorcan joined their master afoot. Her warm brown hair was neatly bound into matron's plaits at the base of her neck, although several curling tendrils had escaped and were moving softly in the light breeze. With pale hazel eyes, she scanned her visitors and lowered her head in the briefest of acknowledgements.

'I am Luned, daughter of Livinia Minor and wife of Llewyd, master of this villa. What is your business here?'

'I apologise for any concern that our sudden appearance has caused, Mistress Luned. I am kin to Artorex, who was the foster-son of the master of this house many years ago. I'm also kin to Queen Anna who was called Licia at her birth, and to her son, Bran, and her grandson, Ector. I have long wished to visit the home of my forebears and to see the garden of Gallia with my own eyes. We will take our leave if we are intruding, for I have no desire to make you uneasy or uncomfortable.'

With the same formality, Lady Luned dropped into a low curtsey. 'Lord Arthur, you couldn't intrude on us by visiting the Villa Poppinidii, where even the stones themselves remember the footsteps of the Great Ones. So enter and rest yourselves. My husband is absent with the grain harvest, but after you have taken refreshment I will escort you to the garden. You and I are also kin, remember?'

Arthur thought of the female line that ran back through the family to Lady Livinia Major, who had served as Artor's foster-mother when he was known as Artorex. As he struggled to remember the details, Mistress Luned seemed to read his mind.

'Yes, Lord Arthur, it's a tangled history, isn't it? And it's had more than its fair share of family tragedies. But let's not dwell on what we can't change. Join me in a jug of the sweet cider we brew with our own presses. My cook will find some of the tiny cakes that the slave woman, Frith, made to tempt the appetite of Artorex when he was a boy. Aye, it's odd to live with legends, isn't it? And stranger yet to treat them with easy familiarity while the rest of the world marvels . . . at least, those who can still remember.'

Mistress Luned's word was good and sweet cider appeared in cups of coloured Roman glass, ancient and infinitely precious. 'We have no Falernian wine nowadays, nor even the Spanish wines that my mother favoured. Our water source is clean and pure so, like any provident countrywoman, I make my own cider and ale. Please, drink . . . eat.'

As they enjoyed her hospitality in the ancient triclinium, Arthur's mind was buzzing with half-remembered details from Merlinus's scrolls, and a familiar feeling of *déjà vu* came over him when he saw the verdigris-covered bronze fish that had been so carefully described by both Artor and Merlinus. The atrium had changed very little in the intervening decades, for nature wears well with the passage of years, although the single tree was taller now and the vegetables that grew like exotic flowers around the pool and fountain were sparser than those described by Myrddion. Time plays tricks with even the greatest minds, Arthur thought, and applied himself to amusing Luned with tales from the building of the Warriors' Dyke.

Afterwards, the mistress of the house led the three companions across freshly ploughed fields that had been prepared for the spring crop. Around them, the farm was a hive of ordered activity: the fruit trees and nut shrubbery near the main house, the vegetable gardens beside the old slave quarters, and a small flock of sheep in a fallow paddock not far from the stables which housed the farm livestock. Even the number of beehives indicated careful husbandry on the part of the master.

'The villa may have seen better days, but this is a still a snug, well-managed farm. I've rarely seen better. And Arthur's doing well. He's a natural courtier for a boy who's never been anywhere much,' Germanus whispered to Lorcan, who nodded thoughtfully. Both men had remained silent throughout the refreshment at the villa, watching Arthur carefully as he carried the weight of the conversation. None of the social niceties had been neglected: another test had been passed.

Gallia's garden was set around the ruins of a small villa. The fire-cracked stones of the courtyard were decorated with dried flower heads, mosses and artfully ordered natural plants surrounding a small pool with a huge monolith at its centre. Rudimentary designs had been chiselled out of the weathered, lichen-slick surface of the ancient stone, including a complex pattern of channels and an odd off-centre cup. Despite the warmth generated by their vigorous walk across the fields, Arthur felt the hair rise on the back of his neck.

'May I touch the stone, Mistress Luned?' he asked, for an itching had begun at the back of his skull.

'Of course, Lord Arthur. This monument is called the Mother Stone and the older servants swear that Artor ordered it to be brought from the Old Forest to decorate his forecourt. I can't vouch for the truth of it, but it is certainly far older than anything else at this villa.'

Careful not to disturb the large fish that lurked under the water weed in the pond as it waited for an unwary dragonfly to skim too close to its watery home, Arthur leaned out to touch the surface of the rough-cut stone.

The itch became more pronounced, but he felt no threat, only a cold, heavy watchfulness, as if the monolith had seen rites so old and arcane that human memory had blotted out any memory of them. It seemed to recognise him – or someone like him – and the sensation was strange but not unpleasant. Like his father before him, he wondered what that tilted cup had been designed to hold, and instinct told him that the stone held a significance far beyond his understanding. Regretfully, he drew his hand away and moved through the forecourt to examine the remnants of walls that were thick with climbing roses and clematis, the crumbling stones bound together by great drifts of ivy and briar.

'See? That urn is rumoured to hold the earthly remains of Targo, while the ashes of Gallia and her woman Frith lie under the wild red rose over there. Across the forecourt, you can see a seat of old limestone which is perfectly placed for contemplation. Ector Major is inhumed beneath its plinth. As Artor's beloved foster-father, he earned his place among the noble dead who originally inhabited the villa. Men who are far more knowledgeable than I have said that the High King wished to lie here as well. Only Caius, the last of the Poppinidii gens, lies elsewhere, for Artor refused to permit his murderous foster-brother to befoul his loved ones. I speak frankly because I assume that you are all privy to the High King's secrets, judging by your speech. If I do wrong, then the good God will punish me, but I feel no censure in any of you.'

While Arthur wandered through Gallia's garden, Germanus and Lorcan sat with Mistress Luned, and were told much of the history of the Villa Poppinidii. She had met Artor on several occasions during her youth, for the High King could never completely forget the place where he had spent so many happy years. Whenever he was forced to travel to the north, he always contrived to deviate to the villa on the hill and the gardens that lay beyond.

As the sun lowered in the sky, heralding the approach of twilight, a man came running towards them from the villa. Luned rose from Ector's seat, straightened her skirts and waited for him to reach the small group.

'Ah, Gareth, I should have called you myself. Arthur has come to visit the family. You may have heard of him? He is the son of Lady Elayne and Lord Bedwyr of Arden Forest.'

Lorcan and Germanus exchanged glances. Clearly this Gareth was not privy to the secret of Arthur's birth.

Gareth was younger than Arthur and not as tall, standing at six feet and one inch. His wide shoulders and narrow hips indicated a superb physical specimen, but his blond hair, blunt-cut at the shoulders, was unplaited, so he had yet to attain the status of a warrior.

'Gareth?' Lorcan queried. 'One of King Artor's famed bodyguards was called by that name.'

'Aye, he was my father. I was born in his old age, after the death of his master. It was a time when he felt that his life belonged to him again. I am a direct descendant of Artor's nurse, old Frith, and my father's ashes lie beneath the daisy bank where they placed Targo's urn. They were friends for most of their adult lives.'

'It is a pleasure to meet you, Gareth,' Lorcan said smoothly, grateful for Myrddion's scrolls which had helped him to sort out the tangled skeins of familial relationships that the High King of the Britons had left in his wake.

Gareth's tanned, boyish face lit up as Arthur joined them, his blue eyes so wide with surprise and pleasure that Arthur was amazed that they didn't pop out of the boy's skull. 'My father was right, Mistress Luned,' he said. 'My day has come, just as Father said it would.'

'We can discuss your father's predictions later.' Luned sounded a little irritated by the interruption. 'What has brought you to us in such haste?'

'A courier from Aquae Sulis has just arrived, my lady. He is rousing the countryside and calling on the levees to assemble.'

'The levees?' Luned's face suddenly became ashen with concern.

'Lord Ector and King Bran have called all good Britons to assemble at Cunetio in the hills. The Saxons have invaded Calleva Atrebatum and the city is besieged. Our ancient enemy has attacked in force, and in winter, which is against all their usual practices. Massed warriors from Mercia have also been intercepted heading into the south. Our intelligence tells us that the true prize is Venta Belgarum, which they intend to take after Calleva Atrebatum falls. The Saxon kings have decided to strike deep into the heart of Britannia in an attempt to drive us into the sea.'

He panted out the last words. 'All men are urged to come to Cunetio. The Britons go to war.'

SAXON ADVANCES INTO SOUTH-WEST BRITANNIA

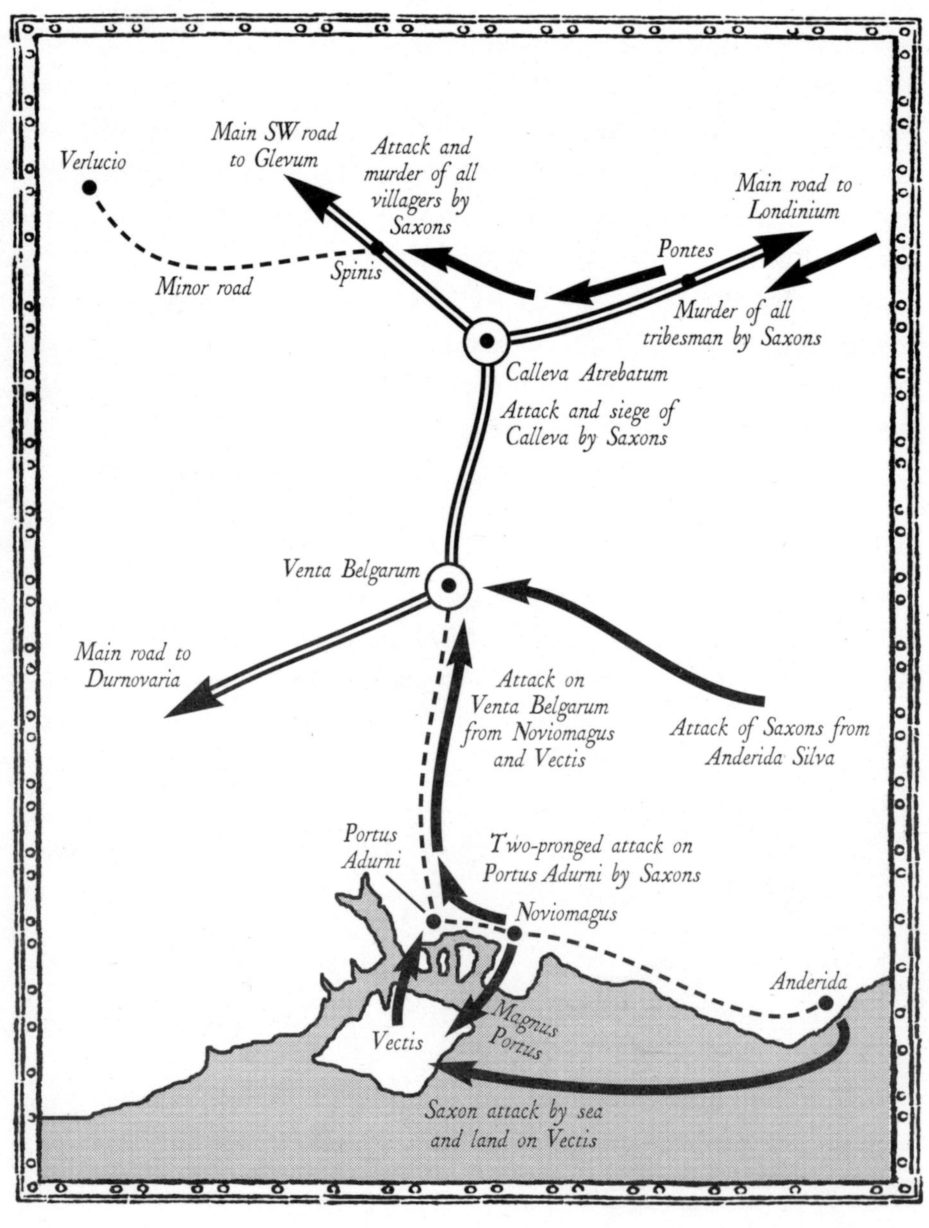

CHAPTER XII

THE CHURCH AT SPINIS

What I say is that "just" or "right" means nothing but what is in the interest of the stronger party.

Plato, *The Republic,* Book 1

In Roman times Cunetio had been a small, fortified town in the hills not far from the headwaters of the Tamesis river, but the long skeins of civilisation had worn very thin in the century since the legions had left Britain's shores, and now the ramshackle township had reverted to the tribal village it had once been. The meadows outside its low walls had been appropriated by foot soldiers and cavalry from as far away as the lands of the Selgovae, north of the Vallum Hadriani. Gawayne had finally succumbed to old age and death, and the new king of the Otadini was still feeling his way in his role, but he too had sent a small cohort of warriors as a reminder that all Britons should stand together against the Saxon interlopers.

Their banners flew in the winter wind, a little bedraggled by sleet and frost. On their stiff, frozen surfaces, representations of lions, leopards, griffins, serpents, sea-monsters and mailed fists rioted with other images and threatened the dark air. The largely illiterate foot soldiers and archers found their allocated areas by dint of these pictorial devices, while many other leveed troops wore their tribal devices on their ox-hide breastplates to identify them without the need for words. Although the encampment lacked the ordered efficiency of a Roman camp in that empire's heyday, the Britons indicated their unity of purpose and the serious nature of the coming battle by the absence of tribal arguments over old, unforgiven resentments.

At first, the Brigante and the Deceangli had expected to be ostracised for their part in the rebellion against King Artor in the civil war, although they were among the first to answer Bran's call to arms. However, the ever-diplomatic Ector gave express orders that the two tribes were to be treated as if no enmity had ever existed, and for the most part he was obeyed.

'We're done with petty squabbles over right or wrong. Ancient Calleva is like to be destroyed by the Saxon invaders, so the past is the past, and any man who raises his hand against any member of these tribes will answer to me.'

Excited, but rather frightened, Arthur and his tutors had left the Villa Poppinidii to travel directly to Cunetio, judging the call to arms too urgent to detour via Arden. They would have ridden that evening, but Mistress Luned had insisted that they rest so their mounts would be fresh for the journey. When she produced a rough map that showed the Roman roads leading directly to their destination via the village of Verlucio, Lorcan was amazed.

'Ector Major, who was the patriarch of the family and King Artor's foster-father, developed a passion for maps when he studied with Myrddion Merlinus. When Artor fought his twelve great wars, Ector recorded the details for posterity. Mother said that Ector used to show her and Licia the places where the king had fought. We all gained an understanding of the world and how we fitted into its wonders through Ector's maps and charts. As you can see, Father Lorcan, the track from Aquae Sulis runs directly to Cunetio. You couldn't be better placed to arrive swiftly at your destination.'

Later, she led Arthur to a small, sparsely furnished room not far from the scriptorium and explained that this monastic cell had been King Artor's room when he was a boy.

'Such a wonder. The room seems unchanged,' Arthur murmured, amazed that a man of such greatness had spent his boyhood days in such basic surroundings.

'We have other accommodation for guests, but I thought you might like to sleep where Artorex spent his nights,' Luned said. Arthur was touched.

'That would be wonderful, mistress. Thank you for your kindness.'

'Our hypocaust is still in use, so you may bathe if you wish. We have a ready supply of fresh water so you needn't fear to leave us wanting,' Luned added. 'Perhaps I can find a wide-toothed comb to handle your mop of hair. I think there's one in Lady Livinia's box that belonged to Artor when he was just a nameless boy with untamed hair. I'll see if I can find it.'

As Arthur tied to express his gratitude for so much unexpected hospitality, Luned brushed aside his words and glided away down the colonnade on silent feet.

Arthur availed himself of the baths, taking time for a thorough soak and to wash his wild hair until it was squeaky clean. He enjoyed the entire solitary process, and jumped when the lad called Gareth entered the dressing room carrying a coarsely carved wooden comb and began to untangle the mat of his amber curls.

'I'm old enough and ugly enough to service my own needs, Gareth, but I appreciate your efforts on my behalf,' he said, punctuating his words with a smile for the benefit of the young lad.

'My great-grandmother Frith used to untangle Artorex's hair just so, my lord. She bound our whole family to Artorex long before anyone now living in this villa was even born, but the oath still stands to this day.'

Being a sensible young man, Arthur admitted to himself that Gareth's deft ministrations were far more effective than his own usual efforts. The wide tines of the comb seemed to be made for his hair, so easily did it glide through the tousled mane.

'Yes, lord, Frith carved this comb with her own hands when Artorex was barely six years old. I would have known you anywhere, master, for your hair and your height are legends within my family. We are hand-fasted to you and yours for as long as the sun shines and the rain falls.'

'But that's hardly fair. No one has the right to own another person, least of all children who are yet unborn,' Arthur replied. He was genuinely surprised by Gareth's air of pride and purpose at the closeness of their respective kin.

'I belong to *you*, master. My father prophesied that you would come to the villa one day and that I would have a great man to serve, as he had, until death came to take me. I admit that there have been times when I doubted that such a person even existed. Even if you were alive and well, I could not see how you would ever find me in the backwaters of Aquae Sulis. But you are here now, and my father's promise was true.'

The boy was so proud and so clean in face and body that Arthur was ashamed. How could such a strong and intelligent youth desire, above all else, to serve him and his heirs for a lifetime? Arthur was no fool, for all that he was only sixteen years old. He was aware that the duties of high birth could be onerous for a young man, but never more so than when other people were happy to enslave themselves because of an accident of birth or the nature of his dead sire.

'When do we leave, master? Gareth asked.

'Do you plan to leave here with me?' Arthur yelped, aghast. He had only recently come to the full realisation that he already had two men in his service, Germanus and Father Lorcan, two men who were tied to him by bonds of respect and friendship. To have another servant was a terrifying prospect. 'I can't ask you to do that. We are off to war, and we could be travelling to our deaths.'

'I have been raised to serve and guard you, master. What else am I to do with my life? My father saw that I was trained with all weapons so that I could stand at your back. He sold his jewels to purchase the best armour available for me, and he ensured that I could read and speak sufficient Latin to be a credit to you. I have no other purpose than to serve you, and if you reject me I will have failed the ancient vows of my blood.'

Something obsessive in Gareth's eyes suggested to Arthur that the boy might do something desperate if he was refused. He considered his options. 'But you can't just leave Mistress Luned. You're her servant first, rather than mine. Besides, I don't have servants. I don't even believe in owning other people's labour.'

'I'm paid for any work that I do in the villa. My father amassed great wealth in gold and gems during a lifetime as King Artor's bodyguard, he spent little during a long lifetime of service. I am my own man and can go or stay where I choose. I must follow after you regardless of your wishes, so you might as well surrender.'

Such arrogance would normally have infuriated Arthur, for he hated being manoeuvred into decisions he disliked. But Gareth smiled so widely and with such evanescent joy as he offered his ultimatum that Arthur was helpless. From Gareth's point of view, he had found his purpose in life, one promised to him by his father from his earliest days. Arthur found that he envied the boy who was so close to him in age, yet so much more certain of his place in the world.

'You'll follow me, even if I refuse to allow it?'

'Yes, Arthur. My task is to protect you from harm and to serve you for the rest of my life, whether you like it or not.'

Arthur snorted with disgust. 'Why did your great-grandmother saddle you with such a curse?'

Quickly, Gareth outlined the family history. Frith had been Livinia Major's nurse, and when the infant Artorex had come to the villa she had looked after him, although she was already an elderly woman. She had loved Artorex with her whole being and had cared for his wife Gallia and their daughter, Licia, with great pride. She had given her own grandson, Gareth, to young King Artor as his protector, swearing that her house would serve King Artor and his heirs for ever. With a sinking heart, Arthur realised that his real opponent was a wizened, white-haired old woman who had been dead for nearly sixty years.

'If you wish to come, then I suppose I can't stop you,' he responded at the end of the tale. 'But you're not permitted to call me master, or lord, or any other servile form of address. I won't tolerate it. Hear me, Gareth? You will call me Arthur. And you will respect Father Lorcan and Germanus, for they are my friends as well as my tutors. I have known them for half my life and I love them like kin. Do you understand my terms?'

'Yes, master . . . Arthur.' Gareth smiled. 'I'll keep Frith's comb, although I suppose you'll object if I attempt to tidy your hair.'

'Exactly so!' Arthur said with a grin of his own. 'However, you can help me to plait this mess as I'm going to have to purchase armour that fits – and a discreet helmet.'

'Wait one moment, lord . . . Arthur. I think I can solve some of your problems.'

Gareth strode away on long legs that obviously wanted to run, but were held in check by the lad's natural dignity, and returned within five minutes, lugging a heavy wicker chest over one shoulder. With a flourish, he swept open the lid and drew out a helmet. 'This was my father's armour. He was wearing it on the day the great king died.'

The plain helmet was shaped like a centurion's helm with a corresponding crest of stiff, red-dyed horsehair. The nose plate and cheek guards were smooth and undecorated to give no purchase to any attacker's descending blade. The neck protection flanged outward to deflect blades in the same way, but on the back of the head an artisan had enamelled a huge red dragon to spread its wings protectively across the back of the neck.

'This helm is beautiful, Gareth, and you've kept it in excellent condition. But I can't accept this armour. Your father intended it to be used by you.'

'I have my own armour, Arthur, designed specifically for me by a master metalsmith. This chest contains the armour that was presented to my father by the High King. As far as I can see, it originated with your father and is rightfully being returned to his son.'

'A master smith made these too,' Arthur murmured as he examined the mail gloves, as flexible as superfine hide and lined with fine lambskin. The helmet was cushioned with the same fine leather. A breast and back plate, buckled at the shoulders and the sides, was made of smooth, beautifully crafted metal, undecorated except for the red dragon rampant across the chest, and the shirt of mail worn under it was so light, flexible and strong that Arthur was sure that, in all the land of the Britons, only Rhys ap Myrddion had the skill to produce armour of a like calibre.

A short knife, a shield, dragon cloak pins, greaves, a codpiece and an odd short spear that was used for stabbing rather than throwing completed the items in the wicker chest. 'They're all yours, Arthur, by my father's express bequest. He always knew you'd come, and that my life would have purpose. He left me his sword, for he knew you would wish to find your own. I also have a series of gifts that the High King showered on him over nearly forty years of service. They are mine to give, so if you should want any or all of them, you only have to ask.'

'Don't be foolish, Gareth. I'll become cross if you so much as hint that you should give me your birthright. I'll accept the armour with thanks, because I'm sure you'll be difficult if I don't – and I'll need it in the battles ahead. But I won't touch what your father gave to you under any circumstances.'

Gareth bowed his head. 'Yes, Arthur.'

'Well then, we shall be leaving shortly after dawn in the morning, so you'd best make all your goodbyes before you go to bed. It would be impolite to wake the house early on our behalf.'

'We keep farm hours here, Arthur, so I don't believe there'll be any problem with leaving at any time suitable to you.'

When Gareth had gone, Arthur lay staring at the same whitewashed ceiling that Artorex had gazed at sixty years earlier. He smelled the same scents of wood smoke and stew on the ovens as Artorex had. The rough wood slats, the leather straps on the bed that creaked whenever he moved, the sliver of light that shone through the primitive latch from the colonnade were all the same, as if the room had waited for its master to return and was now happy that it once again had a purpose.

Lulled by the past and the strength of his fertile imagination, Arthur fell asleep.

* * *

At Cunetio, Arthur quickly settled into the old pattern of life that had shaped him in Arden and honed his skills at the Warriors' Dyke. Tired and stooped with arthritis, Bedwyr was a grey-muzzled old wolf, but only a fool would look into his hooded eyes and assume that great age had finished him. The Arden contingent was large, but Bedwyr had left his borders adequately guarded during his absence. He was fully aware that any competent strategist would attack at just this time and cleave their way into the centre of Britannia like a hot, sharp knife through new cheese.

Not since the last call by King Artor to crush Modred and his conspirators in the civil war had so many tribesmen gathered in one place. And only a matter of the greatest urgency could have prompted the tribes who lived far away in relative safety behind the Walls to risk their best warriors in a major battle.

Calleva had been an important city for many generations before Caesar had brought the Romans to Britannia. The Atrebates had ruled all of southern Britain from it because of its plentiful water, the excellent defences of the hill on which it was situated, the forests that surrounded it and the mild and healthy climate.

The Romans came and judged that the Atrebate kings had been clever in their choice of capital. Plentiful firewood fired industry, the city had a formidable wall which the Romans built even higher with an accompanying ditch and, when they built their road network, the site was perfect as a natural crossroads that was easily defended. One road headed north-west to Corinium, another south-west to Durnovaria near the coast; another road headed east to Londinium while, to the south, a fourth road headed straight and true to Venta Belgarum and, from there, to the port of Magnus Portus.

But Calleva Atrebatum, as it had been called during Roman times, was in a gradual decline, slow but inexorable. Venta Belgarum had eclipsed it as a British centre during the reigns of Ambrosius and Uther Pendragon, perhaps because the brothers had a nervous need to have an escape route at their backs following their terrifying childhood experiences. However, the political situation had changed in recent times, and with it Calleva Atrebatum had regained much of its lost prestige: so much so that it was now under siege, in winter, by a determined Saxon force.

Cissa, the king of the Suth Seaxe, had finally died, leaving no offspring to take his place. In the power struggle that ensued, the more ambitious thanes began to consolidate their hold on the broad, rich lands of the south between Londinium and Noviomagus that had been in Saxon hands since King Artor had been a boy. The power vacuum which should have been a blessing to the British actually marked the beginning of a slow and terrible slide into irrelevancy for the old tribes of what was increasingly being called *Angleland*. The thanes of old Verulamium and Camulodunum, on the other hand, the Western Saxons, backed by the lords of Mercia, welcomed it. The invaders knew that many rich acres of land covered with black-faced sheep were there for the taking. The wealth of the old Roman cities lay open for strong arms to take, and so, lest the tribes organise in the wake of Cissa's death and use a civil war within the Suth Seaxe to strengthen their hold on the south and the west, the thanes struck boldly. Had the climate not been so mild, the advent of winter would have crushed their plans, but that year had brought no snow before the solstice, and the Saxons' gods promised them a great victory over their enemies. Pontes, west of Londinium, had long been a town where Britons and Saxons had co-existed amicably for the sake of trade, but now the thanes ordered the tribal citizens of Pontes to be put to the sword, the churches burned and the town placed under the banner of the White Dragon of the East.

Havar Havarsen, the White Dragon of Jutland, had come to Camulodunum in search of land for his people who were streaming in from the north of Europe. The huge, savage Dene had invaded Jutland and soon carved out a kingdom for themselves that left the Jutes homeless and lost. Bereft of pride, Havar and the thanes who had settled to the north of Londinium were quick to recognise the strategic advantage of taking and holding Calleva Atrebatum. They were unconcerned about the lateness of the season, for in Jutland the land was always covered with deep snow, and famines were common. For the Jutes, Britannia was a warm, ripe apple that dangled tantalisingly within their reach, so Havar and his Saxon allies encircled Calleva Atrebatum and settled down to wait.

Arthur was under no illusions. The Saxon force expected them. They were dug in and waiting for them in great numbers and he knew that the Britons had no choice but to do battle. But even success at Calleva would only ensure a little more breathing space, a little extra time before the inevitable destruction of the tribes as they were inexorably driven towards the sea. Arthur shuddered within his crude sheepskin coat, thrust roughly over his armour, as he watched the encampment prepare for the long task of moving to do battle at Calleva.

Bedwyr came up behind his stepson on deceptively silent feet and thrust a tin mug of hot water, herbs and honey into the lad's hands. 'Warm your fingers, boy. You'll need every one of them where we're going. We've too little cavalry and too few archers. Pelles has done his best, but you can't pluck men out of thin air. Still, according to the intelligence that's come from Calleva, the

Saxons continue to see no need for cavalry and archers, so it's an edge. It's small, but real.'

'I'm confused, Father. I'm excited because I know what a battle is like, and I know I'll kill many men. But I don't know how I should feel about it. Our enemies have wives and children, mothers and siblings – people who will grieve for them when they die. To be a successful warrior is to kill, but I know I will regret the deaths of strangers at my hands.'

Bedwyr's face suffused with colour and he slapped Arthur hard across the cheek with an open palm.

'Did that blow hurt? Good! You're talking weak-bellied shite, Arthur. We'll be at the gates of Calleva Atrebatum tomorrow, and we'll kill every Saxon warrior who faces us – or we will die ourselves. It's as simple as that, you fool. Who's been putting these nonsensical ideas into your thick skull? If it's Gareth, I'll shake his head clean off his shoulders.'

'No, Father!' Arthur's voice was strident with alarm. 'No one's been talking to me, least of all Gareth, who's just as anxious to kill Saxons as you are. I've just been considering what a waste of time it all is.'

Bedwyr looked at his wife's son with blank incredulity.

'Don't you remember what happened to Rab and the Crookback family? Answer me, you young fool! Don't you remember them?'

'Yes, of course I do. But our peoples are caught up in a killing spiral that is impossible to break. Sooner or later, we'll be forced to sue for peace.'

Bedwyr snorted in disgust. 'I want you to come with me, you fool, for there is something you must see if you are beginning to think such nonsense as this. Lorcan!' he roared, and nearby foot soldiers and archers flinched at the tone of his voice. 'Where the fuck are you, Lorcan?'

Seemingly out of nowhere, the tutor appeared in his homespun robe, his fine onyx and pearl rosary attached to the raw flax of his belt.

'Inform Lords Ector and Bran that I will be absent until nightfall. This prize idiot of a son of mine needs an object lesson in the form of what the Saxons left for us at Spinis.'

'Aye, lord. But . . .'

'Don't interrupt me, Lorcan, and don't ask questions. If your pupil is to have any chance of survival when we meet the Saxons, whether it's tomorrow or next week, then he has to have an incentive to fight. He must learn what the enemy is capable of, peace or not. Tell them we are going to Spinis. With luck we'll be back in about seven hours. Arthur, you'll need a decent horse. Now hurry, because you've made me seriously angry.'

Confused by his foster-father's attitude and running to find his sword and a horse, Arthur refused Gareth permission to accompany him. He knew his servant's presence exacerbated Bedwyr's temper, although he had no idea why.

'No, Gareth. You don't know Bedwyr the way I do. For some reason, he's as angry with me as I've ever seen him. If I allowed you to accompany me, he'd be even more furious than he is now. I'll have to face the demons in Spinis by myself.'

'You need me with you, Arthur. Heaven only knows what your father wants of you.'

Gareth's mouth was set in an uncompromising line, so Arthur knew that he ran the risk of angering his new servant as well as his stepfather. 'Sorry, Gareth, but if you ask Germanus and Father Lorcan, they'll tell you that Bedwyr is formidable when he's in a good mood and an unstoppable force when his temper is strained. I've done or said something to upset him, so I must hurry. Being late would be the final insult.'

Choosing the horse with the best staying power, Arthur joined Bedwyr beyond the picket line.

'When we ride, Arthur, oblige me by being silent. I spent too many years as a Saxon slave to be able to listen to your generous view of these animals. I watched them kill my friends in an unspeakable way and then they raped me. Once I was grown, I was forced to become their dog and ill treatment drove me to madness. I swear that only the faith of King Artor and the unqualified love of your mother gave me the strength to face my demons, else I couldn't have borne to hear you say what you did. You will now remain silent until I permit you to speak.'

Still confused, but aware that he had deeply hurt Bedwyr, Arthur nodded his head and they began to ride. Fortunately for their continued safety, heavy forest flanked both sides of the narrow road, so they could almost have been in Arden under the thick canopy of oak, elm, yew and hazel. Bedwyr knew the Saxon mentality as few men could, so he insisted that they ride through the thicker parts of the forest, rejecting the road as a death trap. Even so, Arthur felt eyes boring into the back of his neck throughout the whole journey, although his nerves were quietened a little by the absence of the early warning screams inside his head.

Spinis was a timber-cutting centre, where sawn logs were lashed together and sent down the river to nearby towns to be used in construction. It had always been a small settlement, although its isolated population boasted a small monastery and nunnery, and thus far the need for lumber had also blessed it with a certain degree of neutrality, although in time its sawmills would undoubtedly have fallen into Saxon hands as the invaders extended their trade in the district. Nevertheless, Cerdic, the king of the West Saxons, had recently decided to hasten the invasion process and send a clear, unequivocal message to all Britons that their days in the south were numbered.

Bedwyr and Arthur smelled Spinis well before they arrived. Any soldier recognises the stink of old death, which is green, sweet and sour by turn. The vile waves of sickly rot caused their horses to bridle long before Spinis came into view.

'Behold,' Bedwyr hissed as he dismounted and lashed his reins to a stout sapling. 'The Saxon response to a peaceful surrender.'

The trees suddenly gave way to a small clearing within which was a low-walled compound. An open gate hung on rickety hinges, but Arthur could see no evidence that it had been broken open by force. The smell was worse now, thick and cloying. Bedwyr wound a length of cloth around his mouth and nose. 'Look around, Arthur! See the answer that Cerdic gave to the abbot when that worthy, peace-loving churchman surrendered the monastery to him.'

Within the compound, a small wooden church took pride of place, attached to a small building housing the common eating area by a small cloister. The distinctive nave and apse made the church's Roman antecedents very clear.

The rest of the compound consisted of small circular structures made of unmortared stone roofed with thatch. These building were no wider than a man's outspread arms and were barely tall enough for a small occupant to stand upright. Arthur glanced inside one, half expecting to find a swollen body within the cramped quarters, but the tiny cell was empty except for a pallet stuffed with grass. This was a place where a monk prayed and slept in those times when he wasn't working at his labours from dawn to dusk. These men lived a spartan existence, one that gave them time for reflection and perfect silence.

'The monks were in the church praying for their abbot, who had left his altar to confront Cerdic's men.' Bedwyr's voice was sad and gentle. 'When we became aware of this atrocity, we found a lay brother who had managed to escape, although he was badly wounded. He told us what had happened in the church. Personally, I believe the Saxons permitted him to escape so that the story would circulate among our foot soldiers and peasants. The message was very clear: *Our gods are stronger than your gods, and we will prevail!* I'm not a Christian any more. My faith was burned away many years ago, but I admire bravery, and the abbot showed his balls when he faced an armed troop of Saxons and Jutes with only his crucifix to defend him.' Bedwyr frowned. 'He held some hope that these men had come in peace, I imagine, for the monastery possessed nothing of value except the food they had stored for the winter. And they would have given it all away without a second thought, so their deaths were pointless. Go, my son, and see what the abbot's prayers have earned him.'

Arthur suddenly noticed the silence of the monastic compound. No birds stirred in the meagre vegetable patch or sang in the pruned fruit trees beyond the church. When he looked skyward, none were flying in the air over the compound. The stillness was eerie.

The young man moved forward carefully and gazed at the body where it had been left by the Saxon warriors. The church was constructed out of split wood on a plinth of roughly laid stones, and the abbot's headless corpse lay across the steps leading up to the plinth. His head, with its contorted face under a roughly cut tonsure, was lying four feet away where it had rolled, trailing a slime of gore. Around the body, blood had jetted from the severed arteries so that the steps and plinth had been sprayed with an arc of sanguine red. The abbot's hands were empty. He was unarmed.

Within the miniature basilica, the monks had prayed as they

waited to die. Even those capable of resistance had obeyed their abbot's exhortation and gone to their deaths on bended knees, their hands folded before them in prayer. Before the altar, they had been cut down like kindling in a callous disregard for human life that was staggering in its coldness. Rumours of Saxon murder and looting of churches had been rife for decades, for the Saxons had no respect for any religion other than their own, but this slaughter was a special atrocity, because these monks offered no threat whatsoever to the attackers.

Sickened to his soul, Arthur couldn't leave this scene of horror, although every instinct told him to run to Bedwyr and admit that his foster-father's judgement was correct. He was unable to tell whether curiosity or sick revulsion kept his eyes riveted on the still forms, which were bloated with corruption and covered with clouds of iridescent flies. Yet within his brain something cold and calculating could discern exactly what had been done to the victims.

The closest corpses belonged to a huge, hulking man who stood over six feet tall and a smaller, elderly monk of very small stature. The older man was obviously a victim of some kind of bone deformity, for his spine was twisted so that his head poked upward from between his hunched shoulders like a curious tortoise.

The larger man had attempted to protect the elderly monk using his own body as a shield, an action that should have won admiration from his attackers, but such had not been the case. Men with huge swords and sharp, double-headed axes can finish a conflict against unarmed men in seconds, but Cerdic's warriors had chosen to extend the murder for their own entertainment. The large man had died slowly, probably from loss of blood, and every breath must have been agonising. An arm that had been almost severed at the wrist was raised in a futile attempt at protection, and Arthur could see how the blood had pumped out across the kneeling forms of both victims. A sword wound had pierced the larger man's gut, but the blow was clearly designed to inflict pain rather than to kill. Arthur could imagine the big man attempting to hold his ruined hand in place over his friend while hunching his body to protect his wounded belly.

The Saxons had tried to break the bond of peace and love that had obviously existed between the two victims. In the eyes of their killers, death was not sufficient. Christians claimed that love was the greatest rule of their order, while the second commandment was the promotion of peace among all people, regardless of race. Bedwyn was right: Cerdic had set about using the monks' instincts of self-preservation and their sheer terror to prove that their religion was a fraud. There was a reek of cruelty in the tiny church that was even more powerful than the smell of corruption.

Arthur could read Cerdic's thinking in the bodies that lay, swollen and inhuman, under their coverlet of parasitic insects. He could see the daggers proffered by the warriors to each of the monks and could hear the whispered temptations. *Kill him, and I might let you live.* Most men would leap at the chance to breathe a little longer, but the large monk took his vows seriously. And every time he refused to harm his companion, he was wounded again by his tormentors. How easy it was to see this pattern repeated again and again by the Saxon warriors as they approached pairs of monks before the altar. Had the single survivor, the lay brother, submitted to the primal instinct to save his own life? One thing was certain: that brother would never whisper his sins to his fellow tribesmen, even in his sleep.

The large monk hadn't surrendered his loyalty to his friend. Pierced by half a dozen wounds and bleeding freely from each breach of his hard, muscular flesh, he had continued to position himself between the Saxons and the elderly brother. Finally, he had been pushed impatiently to one side. Then, although the old man's hands were still outspread with the palms upward in supplication, his throat had been cut when the murderers had tired of their cruel game. With the last of his strength, the larger man had crawled to his friend and fallen down beside him as he died. The tragic story of courage and love was clearly visible for any intelligent man to read.

'Do you understand now, Arthur? Do you *see?*'

'Yes. How could I not?'

The game had continued as the attackers turned the small basilica into a charnel house. Eviscerated and half strangled, one man had been crucified on the altar in a nasty parody of the Christian ritual. The Holy Book had been torn to pieces, the pages defecated and urinated upon before being jammed down the throat of one of the victims, choking him. One by one, the monks had died in increasingly painful ways as Cerdic's men tried to force the servants of the Christian God to betray their faith. Ironically, they had saved their most creative and frustrated punishments for the few Saxon-born converts present, the perception of racial betrayal no doubt adding to their frenzy. As a final insult, some wit had drawn an upside down cross on the whitewashed walls, yet in the end, as their cracked and broken voice boxes mumbled prayers as they died, the monks effectively defeated their murderers by not surrendering to terror.

How Cerdic must have raged, for Arthur could see the mark of a heavy boot on the side of one dead monk's face – a pathetic voicing of the Saxons' impotent fury. Then the Saxons had left the monastery. But they were far from finished with Spinis.

Later, when Arthur and Bedwyr arrived at the small nunnery on the other side of the village, the young man was greeted with a scene that would remain burned into his brain for the rest of his life. Cerdic had not bothered with tests of loyalty from the nuns, for they were women and unworthy of any dignity. After viewing their corpses, Arthur came to the realisation that everything about Christianity must be anathema to Saxons and Jutes. He began to understand also that a refusal by the able-bodied to defend themselves was deemed to be cowardice by Cerdic's warriors. But the violent rape and evisceration of helpless women, old and young, was beyond Arthur's comprehension. A potent and ugly illustration of human evil was openly displayed in the small cells where elderly women had perished, raped by any implement to hand, including birch brooms, swords and even the large crucifix that had stood in the basilica. The younger nuns had been dragged away for the pleasure of the Saxon foot soldiers. None survived.

Finally, Arthur couldn't bear the litany of violence any longer. He was only sixteen, and he could find no excuse for what he saw, even cultural differences, hatred and ignorance. He began to vomit uncontrollably until his belly was empty and he could no longer stand without assistance. Such had been Cerdic's contempt for the citizens of Spinis that nothing had been permitted to live, not even livestock or domestic dogs. Nor had the bodies been buried or burned. They had been left in their filth and blood to teach the Britons what their fate would be in the conflicts to come.

'You should be able to see now that no honourable peace can ever be brokered with such men,' Bedwyr murmured as Arthur leaned on the side of his terrified horse.

'I do, Father. The animals who did this can't be true warriors by any definition, and they would regard any offer of peace as weakness on our part.' But although he did not say so, Arthur was sure that not all Saxons could be the same, and they should not be treated as if they were.

Fortunately, Bedwyr was ignorant of his son's private thoughts. 'Can you see now why I was so angry with you? Sooner or later, Arden will fall to these savages, or else we may find ourselves starving to death within its boundaries. Can you imagine your mother in the hands of men such as these? Your sisters?'

'No, Father, I can't,' Arthur murmured. He hid his eyes in distress. 'Surely we should bury these poor people. I will dream of their corpses for the rest of my life. Can we dig a grave for them?'

Bedwyr shook his head and spurred his horse back into the forest until Spinis was a place of darkening shadows behind them, and the scavengers slunk out of the shadows to continue their feeding. Arthur was forced to follow.

'We will come back and bury what is left with honour and respect when spring comes and the Saxons we now face are dead. They don't respect us, you see. They deem civilised behaviour to be weakness, and their gods are devoted to courage, duty, war and strength. These attributes are not bad things, but taken in conjunction with their loathing for change and any culture other than their own they become very dangerous.'

'They must have some weak points,' Arthur reasoned. 'Otherwise there's no point in our struggle. Better we should leave for the wild places as the Picts did before our ancestors drove them out of Britannia. I don't believe we should allow our entire culture to be destroyed in a pointless struggle to survive.'

Bedwyr pulled his horse to a halt under a huge oak tree that must have first broken the soil nearly a thousand years earlier. Mistletoe and other symbiotic plants clung to its ancient branches and scarred trunk, but although it had been rent by storms and lightning over the centuries and was now withered by age, it was still strong, healthy and growing at its heart.

'Look at this tree, Arthur,' the old man said, his white brows furrowing as he spoke. 'That's us! I finally understand what Artor meant when he explained that all his struggles and all his battles were not in any expectation of winning ultimate victory, but because he wanted breathing space for the Saxons to grow and change.'

'I can understand what he meant, but the warriors who attacked Spinis were just savages. Perhaps they've learned nothing in the last hundred years.'

'I'd wager that many of the men involved in the attack on Spinis were recent arrivals to these shores. Did you see the corpses of the Saxon monks who were slaughtered with their brethren in the basilica? Those Saxons had changed their ways, as have many others. In this case, time is both our friend and our enemy.'

'Then the battle for Calleva Atrebatum must be won,' Arthur muttered. He put heels to his horse, his thoughts fixed on the army of Britons who would move towards the battlefield on the morrow.

'Yes. The battle for Calleva Atrebatum must be won, or else the Britons are finished,' Bedwyr muttered. His words were soured by anxiety but his heart was beating quickly with new hope, for Arthur's eyes were no longer more green than grey. They were wintry now, alert and aware at last, and as pitiless as a shark caught in a net that still snaps and tears at the hands that are trying to kill it. And, in Arthur's face, Bedwyr could see his reward for nourishing and loving the fruit of his wife's shame and his own weakness.

'Perhaps there is still some reason to hope,' he murmured, and spurred his horse to follow Arthur into the darkening forest.

Taliessin's Plan of Calleva Atrebatum

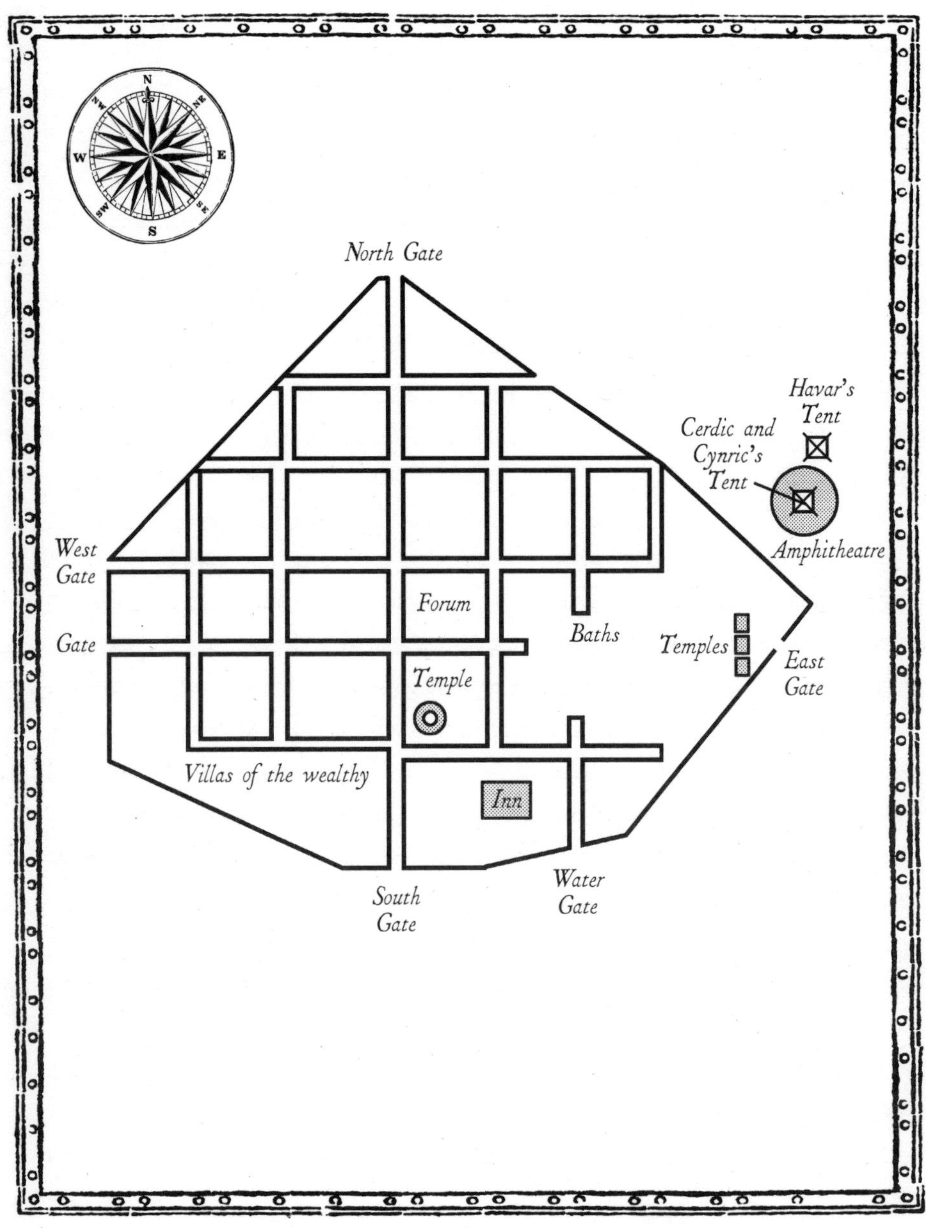

CHAPTER XIII

A TEST OF STRENGTH

Militarism . . . is fetish worship. It is the prostration of men's souls and the laceration of their bodies to appease an idol.

R. H. Tawney, *The Acquisitive Society*

The army moved ponderously through the low mountain range that separated Cunetio from Calleva. Deep forest encroached on their path along the river, masking the movement of the cavalry from Saxon scouting parties, but causing problems for the foot soldiers, the healers and the huge carts of provisions. Bedwyr, Ector and Cadwy Scarface led the cavalry contingent, chosen because all three were experienced in battle and understood the movement of men and horses through unforgiving terrain. Bors, Pelles, Tewdwr and the king of the Atrebates, Artair, led the bulk of the army. Bran was the overall commander, a role won by his blood link with the Dragon King and his years of battle against the Saxons from one end of Britannia to the other.

Old Calleva had been built on a long hill that commanded the surrounding countryside, the city walls enclosing the entire crown of the hill. This part of the countryside was blessed with plentiful supplies of underground water which flowed through beds of gravel. Perfectly filtered and unsullied by pollution, the precious liquid was sweet and clean in a world where water couldn't be universally trusted. The necessary elements of security were here in abundance: clean water and all-round views that stretched far into the distance.

The forest lay within a mile of Calleva's northern wall and supplied charcoal and fuel for ovens, forges and kilns. The Romans had turned Calleva Atrebatum into an industrial and administrative centre boasting a large forum, public baths, and *insulae* built for the town's workers, temples and basilicas.

Unusually for a security-minded town, Calleva possessed seven gates. The northern gate gave on to the wide road that swept east to Londinium. The main western gate opened to a road leading to Corinium in the north-west and another road leading to Durnovaria in the south-west. A smaller gate, suitable only for foot traffic and positioned very low in the surrounding terrain, serviced the outer town that existed around Calleva's flanks. Another small gate led to the east and the lower town, while an even smaller gate, the Water Gate, was positioned nearby.

Outside the east gate, and to its left, was the amphitheatre, which was now being used as the headquarters for the combined force of Saxon and Jute warriors besieging the British defenders. A large tent housed Cerdic and Cynric at the very centre of the amphitheatre in an attempt to gain a bloodless victory over their cocksure ally, the huge Jute, Havar, who was new to this land yet conducted himself like the heir apparent to Cerdic's throne. Havar had gone so far as to place his own campaign tent at the highest point of the amphitheatre, so that it overlooked Cerdic's tent.

'Havar has begun to style himself as the White Dragon, Father,' Cynric snarled. 'Who in the name of Odin does he think he is?

You're the bretwalda, not him. He's a Jute oaf who's been chased out of his homeland by the Dene and has now come to these lands with a cap in his hand to beg for a share of our victory.'

Cerdic was old in Saxon terms, for these warriors longed for a short and glorious life. Well over fifty, he had lost half his teeth and suffered some nasty burns around his feet, calves and thighs that forced him to walk with a stiff gait, although he was still formidable in battle. Rumour suggested that he had tribal blood in his veins, but no one dared to speak such heresy aloud. Cerdic's temper was quick and vicious.

His son, Cynric, was a handsome, tall man with sweeping red-gold moustaches and eyes that were a particularly guileless shade of blue. Ultimately, his pleasing demeanour was a honey trap, for Cynric was cold, calculating and ruthless to a fault.

When Havar had landed with his thanes and followers at old Venta Icenorum, Cerdic had seen the potential in having such a brutal, battle-hardened man to supplement his forces. Havar had survived a dozen dangerous raids and was accustomed to using his muscle rather than his brain to overcome any opposition. Cerdic and his son had decided, even before Havar had joined them, that he would be a perfect tool to break the hearts of the Britons and leave the Saxons to mop up the survivors. If Havar should die in the conflicts to come, Cerdic would be rid of a dangerous and ambitious interloper.

'Havar obeyed my orders to the letter at Spinis,' Cerdic pointed out. 'He works well on a loose rein but, frankly, I'd rather not play such brutal games, even though I know the effect they have on our common enemy. Better he should learn to understand that the British tribesmen will not easily surrender. We'd not even be having this conversation if the Dragon King was still alive.'

He began to cough uncontrollably, a hacking, painful cough

that came from deep in the lungs. Cynric fetched ale for him, concern softening his face, for he knew his father would soon be departing this earth.

'Havar was unmoved by the passive resistance displayed by the monks,' Cerdic murmured, when he could speak. 'He didn't understand their courage at all. Since he feels such scorn for tribal values, we'll let him bear the brunt of the British cavalry. He might live long enough to learn that if old men die slowly and hideously without surrendering, then armed warriors will take their revenge.'

Cerdic permitted himself a short laugh and began to cough again, and Cynric saw that the cloth he used to wipe his lips came away with traces of blood on it.

'Let's pray that Havar has a fatal introduction to British horsemen when they arrive here, Father,' Cynric agreed. 'He has much to discover about our enemy, and this lesson might be the death of him.'

'I've told him already that the tribesmen make useless slaves. The most bitter of them will wait years to cut your throat when you begin to forget they're there, and the women may beguile our men but can never be owned. Better to rape the bitches, and then kill them.' Cerdic laughed again. Both men knew that the Britons would ultimately lose these pleasant lands, but they would never become a captive race. Some might live beside the Saxons for generations, as had been the case at Pontes, but they never relinquished their culture – never.

As a talented commander, Havar had taken the precaution of inserting sentries into the forest along the approaches to Spinis and Calleva, but Bedwyr had no difficulty in finding them and diverting his horsemen along other routes. Ector would have preferred to kill the sentries outright and be done with them, but Cadwy Scarface watched Bedwyr's upright back as his horse picked its way through the thickets towards a wooded hill that overlooked the Saxon army and put his finger to his mouth to warn his master to be silent.

'I remember how Bedwyr set about hunting sentries many years ago in the forests of Moridunum,' he told Ector later. 'A special skill is needed if a scout is to kill men who expect to be approached by friends rather than enemies. Bedwyr lulled them into a sense of false security because he spoke their language like a native-born Saxon. Anyway, he believes that the time to kill them is when we decide to move. Meanwhile, the enemy won't get close enough to attack us without warning, if I know old Bedwyr.'

Cavalry and foot soldiers positioned themselves on the plain on the western side of the Saxon encampment. Like a well-oiled machine, they worked as one to raise their tents while the healers set themselves up on the highest point of the landscape. No sooner had the tents been erected than Bran and Ector ordered every man, regardless of station, to begin digging.

'We're back at that fucking ditch again,' Arthur muttered under his breath to Germanus as he added huge piles of soil to the growing wall that faced the main camp of the Saxons. Canny as always, Bran had used Artair's superior knowledge of the area to find two disused wells, which were quickly recommissioned. As in the old days of the Dragon King, pits were dug and disguised on the field and a supply of fish oil was collected to create nasty fire-traps that could crisp the unwary, while the cavalry occupied themselves with cutting down stakes from the forest to insert in the wall. Several of the kings grumbled as they took their undignified turns on the shovel-line, but no able-bodied man was exempt except for the archers and the healers, whose hands would prove vital in the coming campaign.

'I don't really mind digging,' Scoular ap Seosamh of the Brigante said to Artair as they struggled with their shovels beside Causus of Deva and Deinol ap Delwyn of the Deceangli, for Bran had decreed that erstwhile enemies should work together to restore the bonds of yesteryear. 'I'm just not very good at it.' He rubbed his blistering hands together in his sheepskin gloves. 'Then again, I'm also useless with a sword. But I'm quite effective, apparently, at organising supplies, so Bran gave me a list some time ago of the equipment we might need if Cissa and the Suth Seaxe decided to go to war with us. I don't think he expected Cerdic of the West Seaxe to grasp the advantage when Cissa died. Fortunately, I managed to obtain most of the items that Bran asked for well in advance of his projected need for them.'

'Cerdic of the West Seaxe has always had a brain in his head. He's not an impulsive leader,' Cadwy Scarface grunted as his ageing muscles hefted another shovel-load of the gravel onto the mound on the bivouac side of the ditch. 'Unless something unpleasant gets under his skin like a burr beneath a horse blanket.'

'Havar, the White Dragon, has managed to stir up the West Seaxe since he arrived. Our intelligence tells us he was responsible for Spinis, while Cynric was only an observer.'

'That accounts for the barbaric nature of that raid,' Arthur interrupted. 'But the brains behind the torture were Cerdic's. I wouldn't absolve Havar, but he must be having his own problems with Cerdic if he is being used to deliver the message.'

The young man quickly realised he was speaking out of turn, and should have remained silent in such exalted company, but he made such sense that the kings nodded in agreement and wondered silently what type of man was Bedwyr's eldest son, this cuckoo who had been sired in a forest nest.

'I don't care what Havar is, because I've got a few surprises for him when he joins battle with our main force,' Scoular said, looking very pleased with his prospects. 'Taliessin's brother has constructed a few little somethings that will spoil the plans of both Cerdic and Havar. The harper says they're Roman in design but all Briton in practical use.' All his life, the awkward, unattractive Scoular had been lacking in self-esteem, and half of his kingdom had now been stolen away by the Saxons of Mercia through infiltration. Yet Bran had looked beneath the outward appearance of the scholar to find an organised mind beneath the uncoordinated body. Anna, though now ailing and frail, had given good advice to her son over many years, and insisted that he should make good use of Scoular's talent for organisation in the Saxon push which was certain to come.

Actually, Scoular had enjoyed finding the peculiar items that Bran had requested, especially the salt, bitumen, pitch and saltpetre required for Rhys ap Myrddion's special programme. Nasty little shards of metal and even broken pieces of precious glass had been obtained as ammunition for the strange iron contraptions that Rhys had constructed. Other terracotta containers that seemed to have no purpose had also been found, a purchase that left Scoular intrigued. But Bran's list was mundane as well, for he instructed Scoular to collect a secret store of weapons and food, sufficient to supply an army of five thousand men for at least six months. Scoular had complied with his instructions and the supplies were currently sitting in secure storehouses. He could now sit back with wagons at the ready to answer a call that might never come.

Perhaps, if Scoular could contribute to the destruction of the West Seaxe, he could forget the loss of fair Melandra, the jewel of the Brigante lands, which had been razed to the ground by the new breed of Mercian kings. The fortress would endure only as a song and a memory of great beauty.

But I saw Melandra before it was destroyed, even though it was already in decline, Scoular thought as he hefted the shovel to move a large load of wet gravel. He grunted with the effort. Melandra was a fair dream, which has now gone. But it will survive in my mind for as long as I live. Why must the Saxons destroy everything that is beautiful?

Scoular's mobile, rather ugly face settled into lugubrious lines and the men around him fell silent. As a hopeless warrior with no strategic skills, and as the legitimate heir of Modred the Matricide, he should have been disliked by his peers, but few men could resist Scoular's shaggy brows or the brown eyes that danced with fascination at the world and its wonders. He could have been a joke, for his coordination was abysmal and he constantly fell over his own feet, but his natural charm, generosity and kindness more than made up for his awkwardness.

Arthur patted Scoular's back, although to do so was a social solecism. The Brigante king outranked him and was older in years, knowledge and experience. Fortunately, Scoular took no offence and smiled gratefully up into Arthur's golden face.

'Cheer up, my lord. I promise to make the Saxons pay for your distress. What I saw at Spinis precludes any leniency on my part.'

Germanus kicked Arthur's shin hard to shut him up and then, begging the pardon of the group, asked when battle was likely to be joined.

Causus of Deva, a Gaul, smelled the wind and leaned on his wooden shovel, grateful for a brief respite from the back-breaking task of digging. 'They could attack in the next five minutes, and if I were in their place I would. It depends on how confident they are, for they outnumber us. They have a hundred-odd of the largest Jutes I've ever seen, and most of the Saxons outweigh and outreach us. Except for this huge lump, of course,' Causus added for Arthur's benefit, although the white smile on his dirty face robbed the insult of any personal bite. He remembered the old Dragon King and his personal bodyguard of bastard sons, and was beginning to wonder who Arthur really was.

'Aye. If the Saxons weren't so sure of themselves, they'd attack earlier rather than later,' Cadwy agreed. 'They can see what we're doing, but they have no idea what use we'll make of it. Hades, I don't know myself, so how can they?' Cadwy was being uncharacteristically optimistic, judging that if his time had come to die, then this battle would be a memorable opportunity for a warrior to win renown. He genuinely wished to atone for his treason in the civil war, and his heart was light with the promise that the slate would soon be wiped clean.

A shadow intruded between Cadwy and the setting sun. Idris ap Cadwy, his foster-son, was standing on the mound in front of a new crew of diggers which included Bors of Cornwall. 'Shift change, Father . . . my lords. Bran has decided that we will work through the night so Scoular's boxes of tricks can be prepared under the cover of darkness.'

With relief, the workers downed tools and climbed wearily out of the growing trench. Fresh diggers were taking their places right along the line, and Bran's work continued apace.

As Arthur and Germanus walked away, Cadwy gripped his foster-son's arm. 'Ask him now, boy, for I have to know,' he hissed. 'By the gods, if Artor came again in the body of a true son, we could drive these Saxon lice back to whatever shithole they come from.'

'I think you're wrong to make this offer, Father. Your intentions could be misunderstood and you could be dead wrong . . . so many things could come back to bite you. Please . . .'

'Idris, I love you as a son, which is why I trust you to grant me this favour. I'd go myself, but too many people know me and would wonder why I sought out Bedwyr's lad. I need this task done properly, Idris, and you are the only man who can do it.'

Unhappy, Idris trudged away after the rest of the diggers, the line of his shoulders indicating his discontent.

'I need to clean myself of this muck, Germanus,' Arthur muttered. 'Isn't it odd that ditches seem to have dominated our lives for the past few years? Judging from our experiences at the Warriors' Dyke, this ditch is likely to fill with water in a day or two, so we need to get the stakes in quickly while we can still see the bottom of the trench.'

Hesitantly, Idris ap Cadwy joined them. His dark good looks and whipcord-thin physique were the perfect foil for Arthur's golden height and strength. 'May I join you, gentlemen, while you wash? I would like to speak to you on a matter of some importance.'

Arthur brushed his spiralled curls, rendered even wilder by mud and dirt, out of his eyes and examined Idris carefully. No warning itch or noise disturbed his mind. 'Of course, Master Idris. I would be honoured.'

By this time they had reached one of the wells situated deep within the British camp. Germanus and Arthur stripped to their loincloths and used buckets to sluice themselves from head to toe, the water running down their bodies in rust-coloured runnels. Germanus finished before Arthur, for his long, thinning hair was quickly cleaned, whereas Arthur's mane alone required half a dozen dowsings to remove the accumulated grime and muck that seemed to have been ground into his scalp.

'Damn this digging. I don't think I'll ever be clean again,' Arthur said to no one in particular, enjoying the feeling of his freshly washed toes on the rough stone edging to the old farm well. He bent to pick up his filthy clothes and scrubbed them in a bucket of water as well. Once he was satisfied that his tunic and trews were as clean as possible, he returned the bucket to its place, picked up his sodden clothing and began to walk towards the tent he shared with his three companions.

'You're welcome to break bread with us, Idris. Lorcan, my tutor, is our nominal cook, but I must say his ability is limited at best. The last time I saw him, my companion Gareth was guarding the picket lines, but he'll appear, ghost-like, just when we least expect him. And this large gentleman here is my arms master, Germanus. He's my teacher – and my friend.'

Idris was impressed by Arthur's easy introductions. The young man was indicating clearly that these men, whom other aristocrats would dismiss as servants, had roles far more important than mere service, and he'd not permit them to be insulted or embarrassed. He offered his hand to Germanus, who took it easily. The three men wandered through the tent town to a small hide structure just large enough for four pallets stuffed with fresh grass. Outside, over a rudimentary fire-pit made of river stones, several bars of old metal had been purloined by Father Lorcan to serve as a fireplace. A large iron pot held a stew of rabbit, turnips, parsnips, carrots and, miracle of miracles, strips of fresh cabbage.

Idris was struck dumb with amazement. Around him, groups of warriors were trying to turn dried meat into something remotely edible, using any greens they had foraged on the journey to Calleva. The bounty available to Arthur and his friends was a very pleasant surprise. He felt his mouth begin to water.

Arthur grinned at the expression on his face. 'We received news of the war while on a visit to the Villa Poppinidii, outside Aquae Sulis. Gareth has lived there all his life, so our hostess loaded us down with as much fresh food as we could carry, including a haunch of venison. We devoured that at Cunetio.'

'Arthur learned to kill rabbits with a slingshot almost as soon as he could walk. Living off the land is routine in the Forest of Arden,'

Germanus added laconically as Lorcan entered the tent. 'Hey, Lorcan, I need a favour. My hair is thinning and I'm beginning to look like an old man. When hair isn't useful, it becomes dangerous. It's too easy to obtain a handhold, and I've a mind to look young and beautiful for the Saxons.'

'If I have the time! Where's young Gareth got to? If we give him a foot, he'll take your whole leg. Where are the bowls? The wooden ones, Arthur. I'm taking the stew off the fire now, so we can heat it again in the morning.'

Then, using the point of his knife, he scraped away the coals to reveal a blackened tin. Lorcan prised off the lid with his blade and exposed a browned *something* that he tipped onto a wooden platter, where it steamed enthusiastically.

'What's that?' Arthur asked.

'It's a form of bread made from flour, water and salt. It hasn't much taste, but it will sop up the stew and put some meat on your bones. Now let's get inside and we'll eat like kings.'

'I have quite enough meat on my bones, thank you,' Arthur replied tartly, until Lorcan broke the rough circlet of dough into five equal portions that smelled warm, homely and delicious. 'Of course, I can change my mind, being the master around here.'

The four men each took a hunk of bread and a bowl of stew and went into the tent to hunker down on the pallets. Lorcan brought the remaining stew into the tent and lidded the pot. 'I draw the line at feeding the camp dogs and any other scavengers,' he explained. 'Fortunately, it's winter so nothing goes bad.'

Arthur snorted. 'Excuses! It's a poor cook who blames the weather for the quality of his meals.'

Lorcan clipped Arthur's ear and Idris was touched by the family atmosphere that underscored the relationship between the three men. But he barely had time to register their affection before a handsome youth in partial armour entered the tent and picked up the bowl of stew and the slab of camp bread that Lorcan had put out for him. He raised one eyebrow in Idris's direction, and the look of distrust in his arctic blue eyes was startling for a lad who could only be fourteen at most. Idris hastily looked away, addressing Father Lorcan.

'Ignore this cub, Father Lorcan. I'll wager your stew is the finest to be had this afternoon in either the British or the Saxon camp, and it's a privilege to be here. I'd venture to say no cook in Calleva could rival it either, given the primitive conditions in which you're forced to work your magic. You've missed your calling.'

Lorcan laughed and ruffled Idris's hair, an action that should have been a mortal insult, but somehow seemed sincere and affectionate rather than patronising. 'You're a liar, Master Idris, but I'll accept the compliment with pleasure.'

When the meal was finished, Gareth carried off the empty platters to the well to scour them clean with a handful of the sand that Lorcan kept in a hide container. Lorcan would have preferred to boil them, but time was never flexible enough for the chores that needed to be completed in any day's chaos. If they stayed in bivouac for any length of time, he would make other arrangements for hygiene.

With only a few regrets, Germanus was preparing to have all his remaining hair cut away to protect himself during the coming battle, despite the natural reluctance of a warrior to be parted from his plaits. As the tent quietened, Idris asked if he could speak to Arthur in private.

The two men moved out of the tent and strolled through the camp. Winter reduced the hours of daylight so the nights were long and bitterly cold, although no snow threatened.

'Thank you for the hospitality, Arthur. In fact, I have rarely eaten a meal that I enjoyed more. Your generosity is far greater than this stranger deserves.' By the light of a nearby fire, Arthur could see a fine network of lines around Idris's eyes. The foster-son of Cadwy Scarface was far older than his slender physique and well-shaped features suggested. 'I should explain that when I was about your age I was present at the judgement of King Mark of the Deceangli tribe. That memorable meeting took place at King Artor's hall at Deva, although it was a burned-out shell after Modred was through with it. It must be fourteen years ago now.'

So Idris ap Cadwy was about twenty-nine years old, Arthur thought; a man sliding towards middle age, although he seemed little older than Arthur.

'I was less than a year old at that time and Gareth was yet to be born.'

'Time passes quickly,' Idris said softly.

'Gareth will join us soon, I'm afraid. He's bound by some kind of archaic oath to guard me and he takes his self-appointed task very seriously.'

'Hmn,' Idris replied. 'I'd prefer we were alone.'

'I assure you that Gareth would die before betraying me. You can speak freely. Of course, if you say anything that Gareth considers to be a threat towards me, he might try to cut your throat.' Arthur smiled as he noted the expression on the face of his guest. 'No, I'm only jesting – don't look so alarmed.'

With a long, indrawn breath, Idris began his prepared speech in a rush, before he could lose his courage. 'My foster-father, Cadwy called Scarface, fought under the Dragon King when he was a young man. He has a very long memory and now he is greatly troubled.'

Oh, dear, Arthur thought. This is exactly what Anna feared most all those years ago. My sister may believe she has nothing of the family gift of sight, but she's altogether too clever. There are still some people alive who knew Artor when he was a young man, so it seems I may have to create a plausible story.

'Father swears to me that you must be the son of the last High King. He knew King Artor when he still wore his hair in warrior's plaits and he described your curls very accurately, Master Arthur. He also believes your size and bearing are unmistakable, although he thinks the High King was perhaps an inch taller. But, as he says, you are far larger than most Roman or tribal warriors. He assures me that your face is the image of the young King Artor, although your eyes have more green in them.'

Arthur cleared his throat. 'Why didn't Cadwy come to me with these crazy suspicions? Does he think to hide behind his foster-son?'

'He has been shamed, my lord, for he truly believes he betrayed your kinsman at the ford. He cannot meet your eyes.'

Arthur was impatient and a little frightened by the obsessive expression in Idris's eyes. 'I'm sorry, but you're speaking nonsense, Idris. King Bran has issued an order that the civil war is to be forgotten, and I obey my king. Please don't call me master or lord, for I'm half your age and have had none of your experience. I'm not even a warrior yet.'

'Cadwy asked me to press you to make your claim to the title of High King of the Britons. The tribes need you. We need a figurehead who will give heart to the ordinary warriors who can be expected to die on this plain. We all need you!'

Arthur's skin was paper-white, his eyes flat and deadly like pale holes burned into his skull. Behind him, Gareth readied himself for trouble and Idris heard the boy slide his sword up and down in its scabbard to check that it wouldn't jam. Only the greatest exercise of will prevented him from drawing his own weapon in response, an action which would have precipitated disaster for them all.

'I'll not raise my hand against King Bran and Lord Ector, who have given their youth and their lives to protect the tribes. Nor would I usurp the position of the rightful rulers of this land even if your deductions were true. I'll not be King Bran's Modred! Do you hear me, Idris? I should separate your head from your torso for even suggesting that I could be a traitor.'

Idris examined Arthur's face and decided that the young man spoke in deadly earnest. He knew he must repair the damage Cadwy had wrought out of love for the British people, but how could he convince this fierce young man that his foster-father harboured no traitorous intent? He fell to his knees and bared his neck in supplication.

'You may kill me if you believe I suggested treason, master. Cadwy wished with his whole heart to find a tool that would assist King Bran to defeat the Saxons. He is no traitor, although I can understand how it must have sounded to a stranger. You don't know Cadwy, but he worshipped your father, and would die happy if he could see you lead the Britons. Please try to imagine how he feels. He stood with Modred and so was partially responsible for the death of the High King and a thousand tribal warriors who cannot be replaced in this time of need. He looks at the ever-expanding gains made by the Saxons and his guilt is more than he can bear.'

Arthur paced, his muscles tensed and pumped for action in this trial by fire. More easily than he had expected, he resisted the temptation to strike and waited for Idris to go on.

'My foster-father is not a wise man, but he is good,' Idris continued. 'I tried to explain to him how his petition would sound, but he couldn't understand what I meant. He has no treason in his heart, only a longing for a chance to redeem the errors committed in his past.'

Gradually, Arthur's breathing and his frenetic pacing began to slow. Germanus came to the tent flap to check on the commotion, but Arthur waved him away. The fewer men who knew about Cadwy's foolish offer the better, even men he trusted as implicitly as his tutors.

'We'll speak no more of this matter, Idris. Get on your feet, man, for I'm unlikely to behead you after you've eaten at my table. You can tell your foster-father that I bear him no ill-will for his lack of understanding of my character. I am Bran's man and Ector's man until my death. Even if I were Artor's natural son, he could not have wished me to be High King. You must understand, Idris ap Cadwy, that I'll not be used by anyone, even men who have given their lives to the cause of the Britons. Finally, I beg that you never discuss this matter with anyone, else great harm might come to innocent men and women.'

'Thank you for your understanding, Lord Arthur. I'll persuade my foster-father to be prudent, but don't be surprised if he wishes to offer his fealty and his apologies in person.'

'If Cadwy Scarface approaches me, I'll not spurn him or make him feel any guilt. But leave him in no doubt where my loyalty lies.'

So Arthur passed an unexpected and disconcerting test of honour. Cadwy Scarface sought Arthur out on the morrow and embarrassed the young man by lying before him face down and full length in the mud with his arms outstretched in a cruciform position. Passing warriors stared at the odd tableau and the tall young Cornovii gained an extra gloss of reputation because of it.

'I'll remain your man until my death, Arthur,' the old man murmured. 'If the gods take pity on me, I will win the opportunity to die well in this campaign. Forgive me, Arthur, for I should have guessed that you would be a man of unimpeachable honour, one fit to be the son of the greatest man I have ever known.'

The old man was broken, and tears streamed down his scarred face in such profusion that Arthur took pity on him. 'All is forgiven, Cadwy, and I will pray that you join your master soon. Now stand on your feet like the true man you are, knowing that all is forgiven.'

But Arthur could not forget his test of integrity as he drifted off to sleep for the second night in the bivouac.

And, although the Britons were not hiding, the Saxons still did not come.

The Battle of Calleva Atrebatum – the Cavalry Charge

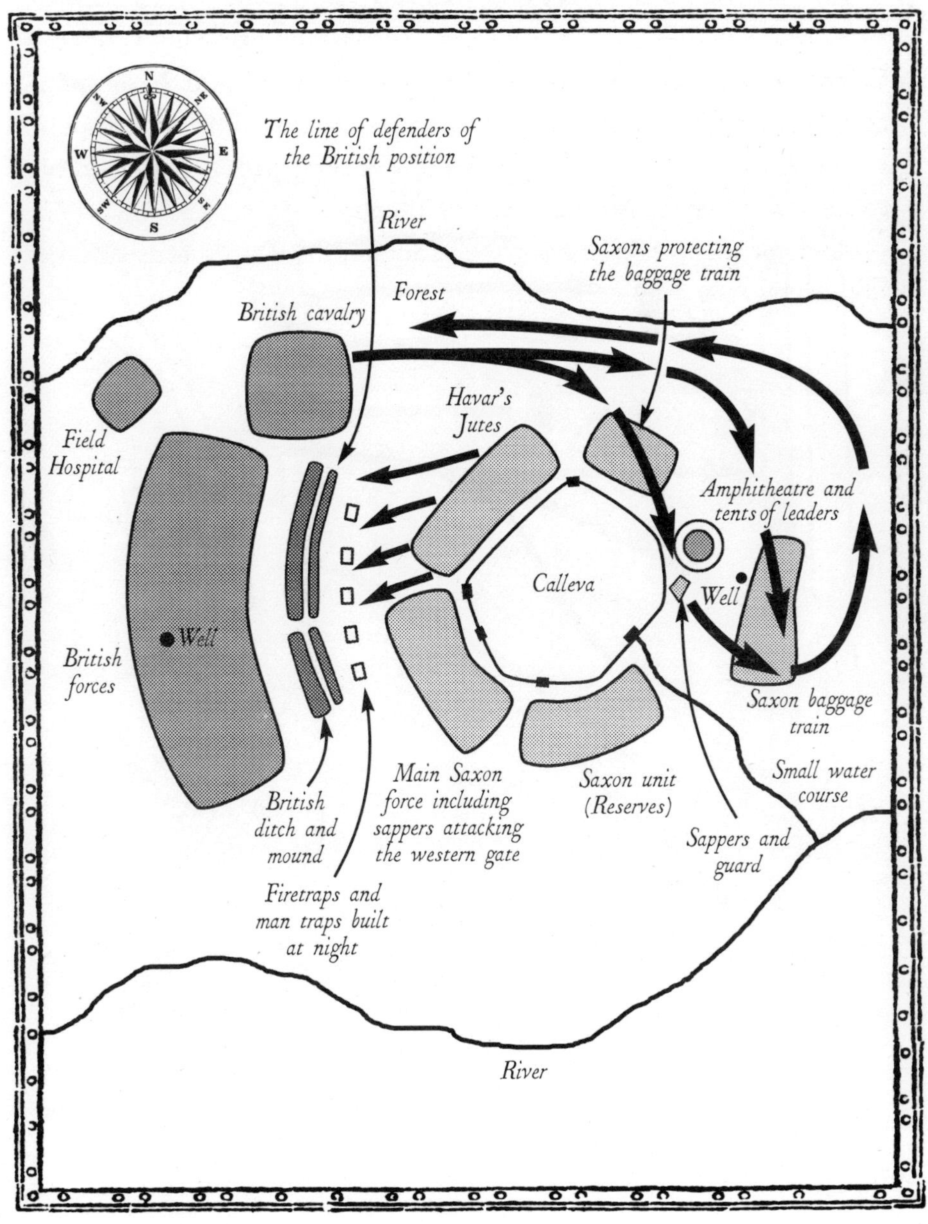

The Battle of Calleva Atrebatum – Stage One

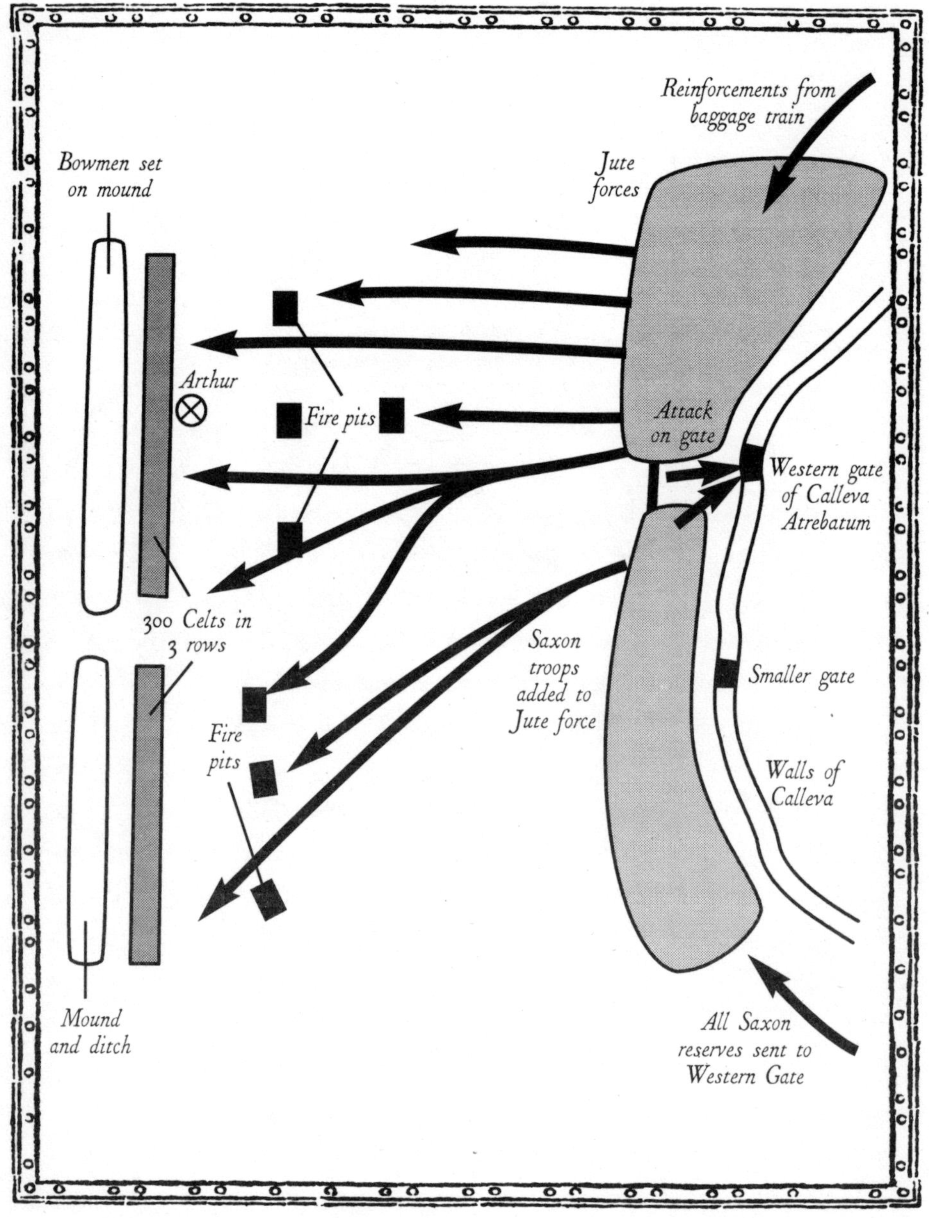

CHAPTER XIV

THE LAST MAN STANDING

Man, false man, smiling, destructive man.

Nathaniel Lee, *Theodosius*, Act 3, Scene 2

Three days passed while nothing in particular actually happened. Inside Calleva Atrebatum, the citizens looked down at the Saxon hordes, busily digging at the base of the eastern gate, and dropped hot pitch and boiling water on them. The activity was much the same on the main western wall, but there the besieged townsfolk could see the Britons in the relieving force as they worked like ants along their own trench, now clearly in two sections divided by a narrow causeway leading to a gap in the wall behind it. The spirits of the townsfolk were cheered by the energy of their allies. A few embittered persons complained that both Saxon and British forces seemed to be settling in for the winter but, largely, a celebratory mood fuelled optimism in the population of old Calleva.

For those with eyes to see, the Saxons showed less efficiency than the Britons in the complicated logistics of a protracted siege. Latrines were rudimentary, and should the months stretch out for too long, then disease would kill more Saxons than Bran's warriors. Saxons disliked sieges because they demanded patience rather than the glorious red work of hand to hand combat. There was little glory in starving an enemy to death.

In the abandoned amphitheatre outside the city walls, Havar was in the midst of a Jute tantrum, an awesome sight when the warrior in question was immensely tall, broad and prone to shouting to win any conversational disagreement.

'We should have scoured out those little black rats two days ago,' he roared, one arm pointing at Calleva and the British camp beyond it. 'Fighting men do not sit on their thumbs waiting for the gods to give them the victory.'

'What would you have me do, Havar?' Cerdic responded in a dangerously quiet voice, while his personal guard stood straighter with malignant red glints in their eyes.

'We outnumber the bastards and they know it. Attack them and they'll run like rats. Calleva will then be forced to surrender.'

Cynric smiled from behind one hand while his father stared blandly into Havar's congested face. 'And what strategy would you pursue, Havar? You should remember that this Bran, the king of the Ordovice tribe, is a kinsman of the Red Dragon who used Roman tactics against us for thirty-odd years. We never defeated him in all that time, regardless of how much we outnumbered his forces.'

'So that's why we're cowering here? You're afraid we'll lose the coming battle because Bran's a kinsman of the Dragon King? Artor's dead and rotting. You don't need to be frightened of a ghost.' Havar's tone was insulting, and Cynric's face was stripped of its condescending smile. 'No matter how many times the Dragon King beat you in the past, he's just a collection of old bones. If we attack in force, the Britons will break.'

'I considered attacking them as soon as their relief column started digging their ditch, but we didn't have the time to marshal all our troops before they were securely behind their wall. I'm left wondering now what they have in store for us. Everything I've heard of this Bran suggests that he's a cautious planner but an audacious fighter, which is a dangerous combination. I have survived as your bretwalda in this land because I also remain cautious, and I use the enemy's skills against him. Calleva is just one miserable city. We fight for larger stakes: for Venta Belgarum, and the mortal blow to the Britons when the city falls.'

Cerdic coughed. It was a hacking and painful sound, but the Saxon king hadn't finished.

'Calleva Atrebatum is as nothing in the scheme of things. I'd wait for a year outside this fleapit if it gave us the time for our troops from Noviomagus and Vectis to take Portus Adurni. The Britons believe that Venta Belgarum is special because those Roman fucks, Ambrosius and Uther Pendragon, used it as their capital and the Dragon King came to power within its walls. Think, Havar, for once in your life. Calleva is just a ruse, a feint, but it's one that seems more important than it really is because of the roads that it commands. In fact we can do without the roads, and when Portus Adurni, Magnus Portus and Venta Belgarum fall, it won't matter a shit what happens to Calleva Atrebatum.'

'But the Britons grow stronger with every day we wait. They were joined by a contingent from Venta Belgarum today. The gods know those cringing cowards have been hiding behind their walls for months since you claimed Vectis, but now they grow over-bold, and are crowing that their Red Dragon king has come again to save them.'

'You're still not listening, Havar,' Cerdic answered with a sigh. 'You're thinking with your balls rather than your brain. Let the

British make a stand here and there'll be fewer warriors for us to fight at Venta Belgarum. I don't care if they dig in here for months, although I'd not be overly happy about it. I'm prepared to lose half my forces at Calleva if it keeps the British tribes focused on this minor town rather than Venta Belgarum, where the real battle will take place. The Britons move like the wind. They're not rats, Havar. They're not cowards and they're definitely not stupid, although you seem to think that their brains are measured by body size. They'll be the death of you if you continue to underestimate them.

'And what of this Red Dragon we keep hearing about? Bran's spies are using our own fears and superstitions against us. They know the effect of the Dragon King on our thinking. By Baldur's balls, the man was unstoppable, and I thank the gods he's dead. But a number of his advisers are still alive, and Bran is a kinsman so something of the dragon lives on in him. If they've found yet another bastard they can use I'll be worried, mainly because it's difficult to defeat an idea. The ghost of King Artor of the Britons could become both an idealisation and a rallying call. If this Red Dragon truly exists, Havar, you have my permission to kill him by any means at your disposal. I don't want a new hero appearing out of the ruins of Calleva Atrebatum or Venta Belgarum to give the tribal kings someone new to rally around. They still won't win, because we possess too many of Britain's broad acres now, but it would slow us down, and we'd only inherit smoking ruins. So tell me: what have you heard about this Red Dragon?'

'According to one of their scouts who was caught behind our picket lines, a fresh young King Artor has come to Calleva to set the city free. You know better than I do how true these rumours can sound, but there's no doubt that a very tall warrior has been seen working on the ditch they've been digging. Apparently he's about my height, which makes him extremely tall for one of the

Britons.' Havar paused. 'Their scout died, but he was defiant to the end. I agree with you – I don't think we can afford to allow any rumours about a new Red Dragon to grow. I will kill this man personally, if necessary.'

Cerdic gazed into Havar's eyes to judge the Jute's worth. 'I will give you one thousand warriors to support the two hundred warriors who make up your personal guard. You can attack in the darkness just before dawn. As the Britons have chosen to mass their troops only on the western side of the city, I will move the bulk of my men there to intimidate the Celts as they attempt to repel your attack. The reserves can remain beside the west gate and watch your victory. They need only be pressed into service when you have breached the ditch. Does my strategy please you, Havar?'

That evening, the itch was screaming a warning at the back of Arthur's brain. Fortunately, he was saved from the embarrassment of having to explain his fears to King Bran when an indiscreet Saxon scout strayed too close to the picket lines. Bedwyr brought the hobbled, spitting captive to Bran's tent, with the added intelligence that the Saxon scouts watching the cavalry were all moving closer, probably to make accurate assessments of the strength of the British forces.

Bran was already pondering a message sent by mirrors from the southern gate of Calleva. Bedwyr had given Arthur permission to attend the strategy sessions of the kings on the proviso that he kept his mouth shut and his mind open. As Gareth was his ever-present shadow, the lad seated himself near the tent flap and tried to look as inconspicuous as anyone who stood a head taller than most warriors could manage.

'Lord Myrddion set up a spy network decades ago,' Gareth

hissed at Arthur. 'Part of the training for members of the group was the use of mirrors to transmit messages. Someone in Calleva Atrebatum has been feeding information back to Bran using some form of code.'

'Ah,' Arthur whispered softly. 'So he's been aware of the Saxon troop movements from the very beginning. Clever Bran.'

'Clever Myrddion! Taliessin has been reading the messages as fast as they transmit them.'

Gareth probably knew more about British battles of the past than anyone alive, Arthur decided as he rested on his heels and listened with excited, boyish attention to the plans discussed by the inner circle of commanders.

'The Jute and Angle troops under the command of Havar began to move as soon as darkness fell. Their bivouac was close to the amphitheatre, but they have reinforced one-third of the whole Saxon line between the north gate and the west gate. I'm certain that an attack will come from that direction, but our scouts tell me that the troops defending the amphitheatre are also on the move. I don't understand these tactics, not with several thousand men already in bivouac south of the west gate. I know that Cerdic must have some strategy, but I'm damned if I can fathom what it is. Some details of the Saxon battle plans don't make any sense, and any detail I can't understand makes me nervous,' Taliessin told them. His voice was dry and dusty, as if words of warfare had no place in the vocal chords that produced his beautiful songs and poetry.

He gazed around the expectant faces of the commanders in the tent and his eyes were lambent with regret. 'The Saxons expect to be attacked in strength by your cavalry. The men in this combined force are the tallest and the most ignorant of our enemies. I'm certain they've never faced a cavalry charge before and know little about what will happen, apart from word-of-mouth advice from knowledgeable friends. I suspect that Cerdic has arranged this move for some purpose of his own. He will let the Jutes fight under the banner of this Havar, and he'll try to pin us down here.' Taliessin stabbed at a piece of hide laid out on Bran's camp table. Arthur couldn't see that Taliessin's elegant finger had pinpointed the northern perimeter of the British force, but he could picture what Cerdic planned. 'As long as they can't read the mirrors, Cerdic won't know that we will be expecting them. No doubt they'll attack at dawn.'

'Before dawn,' Ector interrupted briskly, for he was quite certain of his facts. 'Saxons prefer daylight for their battles, but Jutes live in a world where daylight only comes for six hours a day in winter. They don't fear the dark quite as much as the Saxons do. I believe they'll attack when they think we least expect them in an attempt to catch us off guard.'

'Granted,' Bran concurred, and the other kings nodded their agreement. Bran's forehead was puckered, for above all things he hated being unprepared for any element of a coming battle. His cautious nature screamed at him that there was too much about the Saxon plans he didn't know.

'Cerdic must expect the cavalry to crush Havar as soon as it's light enough for them to ride,' Taliessin murmured.

'What is the distribution of Cerdic's troops on the eastern side of Calleva?' Bran asked the room in general.

'There's a thousand men camped to the south of the amphitheatre near where Cerdic has sited his command centre,' Bedwyr answered. 'I've seen the area with my own eyes. There are another five hundred men guarding the baggage train to the east, not counting the troops on the move as we speak that are joining up with Havar's force of Jutes. Fifty sappers are digging under the walls of Calleva north of the eastern gate, and Cerdic's personal guard are positioned to move as soon as the wall is breached. A similar troop of engineers is undermining the walls near the western gate, and a further thousand men are stretched from the west gate to the south gate, so that Calleva is effectively surrounded.'

'Can you be certain of this information, Bedwyr?' Bran asked carefully, for much depended on the accuracy of the figures he was given, even if he insulted Bedwyr by demanding reassurance.

'My Saxon is rusty, but it's good enough for normal conversation, and I can still do a good impression of a disreputable Saxon servant,' Bedwyr replied a little stiffly. 'I spent a few hours behind the Saxon lines, and learned everything I needed to know. The Saxons don't believe that our spies can infiltrate their ranks. We have three other men in place even as I speak, all inserted among their troops along the south-western perimeter.'

'I've asked you on many occasions not to risk yourself so casually, Bedwyr. We need you alive and difficult, not spitted to roast on a Saxon fire,' Bran snapped, his brows furrowed in exasperation. 'However, I trust your assessments. So you would agree that Cerdic expects the cavalry to attack the Jute and Saxon forces when the sun comes up?'

'What are your wishes, Father?' Ector asked. He would lead the cavalry charges in company with Bedwyr and Scarface, and hungered to know what glory would be offered during the coming morning.

'You will not attack the Jute forces. I expect Artair, backed by the Ordovice reserves, to hold the northern sector of the ditch at all costs. A small force of our troops will form up before it and lead the Jutes into disaster. When they attack, our warriors will retreat through the gap in the wall.' Bran smiled, and turned towards the back of the tent. 'Arthur? I know you're there in the back near the tent flap. Stand up, boy.'

Embarrassed, Arthur clambered to his feet.

'I've heard rumours within the camp that you're believed to be the ghost of King Artor, come back from the shades to lead us to victory. Everyone has heard the prophecy that the Dragon King will come again when his people need him, so let's use a little superstition to stiffen the spines of our own foot soldiers and frighten the shite out of the Saxons. I want you to stand, tall and prominent, in the middle of the front line where you can be easily seen. We will arrange for someone to find a red cloak for you to add to the dramatic effect. And you must plait that mane of yours, for you're a warrior now.'

'Yes, my lord, of course,' Arthur stuttered, and sat down abruptly before his legs collapsed and he fell down. Taliessin turned his back on the gathering. Only Deinol of the Deceangli saw the anger and chagrin on the harper's face, and he wondered what under-currents were at play in what sounded like a simple plan. Bedwyr's expression, too, was mutinous. Bran was using Arthur for his own advantage, and Bedwyr knew it. But before he could voice his objections, Bran issued his orders.

'The cavalry will carry out a lightning attack on the amphitheatre, the engineers working on the eastern wall of Calleva and the troops guarding the Saxon baggage train. You will inflict maximum damage on the sappers and the baggage train by using some of Rhys and Taliessin's boxes of tricks. Thanks to Scoular, who collected the materials to create it, Myrddion Merlinus has sent us a little gift from the Shadows. Let's see what the Saxons make of Marine Fire.'

The room was perfectly still. Legends of the liquid that burst into flame and killed indiscriminately abounded in many lands, although most scholars considered that the ancient recipe had been lost for many centuries. It was appropriate that Myrddion Merlinus had discovered it during his sojourn in Constantinople. He had added it to his scrolls in a private code known only to himself and Nimue, for after discussing the ethics of such a fearsome weapon with his beautiful wife he had determined to keep the recipe secret for fear that this scourge would destroy the world as he knew it. The situation must be truly grave if Nimue now permitted such a terror to be unleashed on an unsuspecting world.

'Meanwhile, our warriors will hold the northern ditch at all costs. Do you hear me? We must hold the ditch; a major breach of the line would be a disaster. The Saxons must fight us on our ground, on our terms, so they must not be allowed to form a shield wall. From the mound above the battlefield, our archers should be able to keep them from breaking through our lines. We have a considerable supply of arrows at our disposal and some of our peasants will make regular collections of used missiles during lulls in the battle. The archers' targets will be the largest concentrations of Jute and Saxon warriors. The bulk of our army will wait behind the mound until Cerdic himself comes against us – and then hell itself will be summoned forth.'

Bran gazed around at his silent audience. 'May all the gods be with us in the coming conflict, for it will mark the end of the west if we do not prevail.'

'What in the name of all that's holy is Marine Fire?' Arthur asked Germanus as soon as he reached their tent, Gareth hot on his heels. He had hurried through the camp as if the Ferryman was after him, ready to drag him off to the River Styx. Excitement, nervousness at the role allotted to him, and the feeling that he had been manoeuvred into a situation not of his choosing made his strides so long and swift that even Gareth's lanky legs could barely keep pace with him.

'Marine Fire? I've heard of it. It was the ultimate sea weapon used by the Greeks in centuries past,' Germanus answered, and Lorcan swore colourfully. 'It was described to me as the work of the Devil.'

'The battle is expected to start before dawn tomorrow so you must have our weapons prepared for what is to come. But Bran told us that our commanders have access to a supply of Marine Fire that will be used on the enemy. I'd like to know what the fuck it is, but no one seems to know very much about it.'

Germanus raised his head, now polished and bare under the light of a fish-oil lamp hanging on a chain from the tent pole. Although he still had his huge blond moustaches, the absence of his thinning braids made the arms master look years younger. However, his expression registered his disgust at the mention of the fearsome weapon, while his unease was palpable.

'Marine Fire was invented by the Greeks for use in sea battles against the Persians and the Phoenicians. It cannot be quenched by water, which seems to make it spread, and it sticks to any surface it finds with murderous, unquenchable heat. Only earth or dry sand can extinguish it. As you can imagine, any warrior dowsed with the flaming liquid would suffer a hideous death.'

'The weapon would be a hell's brew,' Arthur muttered. 'Do you know how it's made?'

'No, Arthur, I don't. And as far as I know, nor does anyone else, although I heard that it was used on a number of occasions by Emperor Anastasius of Constantinople to put down revolts. He used it as a weapon of last resort some twenty years ago, but after that his commanders refused to damn their souls again. As far as the scholars know, the secret had been lost for a hundred years until the emperor rediscovered the recipe. Fortunately, it was never made known to the Romans, for they'd have left little of the world unburned. I spoke to an old apothecary once who told me what he believed to be the ingredients, but he didn't know the proportions or how it was mixed. Marine Fire is made from quicklime, saltpetre, bitumen, sulphur, resin and pitch. My source thought there might be other ingredients that he didn't know, but I never heard what they could be.'

'A Greek historian, Thucydides, described such a substance near to a thousand years ago,' Lorcan added. 'Praise be to God, the secret of the weapon he described has been lost.'

'But obviously not permanently. Bran has managed to get his hands on *something*!' Arthur said quietly. He left the tent, determined to find Taliessin and discover how a poet could countenance the use of this liquid fire, a weapon that would appear to contradict any warrior's idea of honourable combat.

He was in luck. He found Taliessin in Bedwyr's tent beside the picket line, involved in what had obviously been a prolonged and passionate argument. A folded red cloak lay at Bedwyr's feet, and as Arthur edged into the tent both men turned their hot eyes to take in his bent form, while he apologised for the unexpected interruption.

'Don't ask, Arthur, for I can guess what you want to know. Like Bedwyr, you're confused by Bran's need to use Marine Fire. Correct?' Taliessin's voice was cold, but under it Arthur could detect a plea for understanding. 'Only the direst situation would force me to approve the use of this weapon, and nothing will persuade Rhys to part with the knowledge of how to make it. He would die first.'

Bedwyr began to protest, but Taliessin silenced him with his raised hand. 'Arthur deserves to know, as he will be in the forefront of our army, only yards from the ditch where, we hope, Cerdic will be forced to make a final massed attack on our defensive position. When the Saxon has no other choice, Arthur's presence will be used to lure these poor souls to a hellish death. He deserves to know, Bedwyr.'

'Very well, but keep it short.' Bedwyr answered, every line of his body voicing his disgust. 'I need some time with my son.'

'My father owned a collection of Greek scrolls that he used to study the healing methods used by the ancients. In the process, and quite by accident, he stumbled upon references to Marine Fire and how to treat injuries caused by its use. You are probably ignorant of my father's skills, but he had a masterful knowledge of languages and he collected scrolls wherever he went. In his youth, he visited Constantinople where he heard tales of the emperor's use of this dreadful invention during a rebellion that threatened the safety of the eastern Roman Empire. You knew Myrddion well, Bedwyr, and you are aware that while he was devoted to saving life, he also possessed a savage curiosity that could never be quenched. In his final years, before his sight failed, he studied his scrolls in detail, including the documents collected in Constantinople, and discovered how to make this hellish brew. I remember hearing a conversation between Myrddion and my mother where he said that some things should never be known. He believed that once a secret is learned, it cannot be unlearned. Myrddion asked Mother to promise that only in the face of the likely destruction of our people should the weapon ever be used. It was Bran who convinced her that such a day was coming. Mother trusts no one fully, especially ambitious rulers, so she has ensured that the secret of its recipe has not left the family. King Bran believes that the supply she gave him was prepared by her loyal family retainers, but that's not true. Only Rhys and I know how the ingredients were mixed. When Mother and I spoke of her decision to aid King Bran, I swore to her that it would be used once, and once only, because I knew that the deaths of those who perished would be on my conscience for the remainder of my life. We have since burned all my father's scrolls on dangerous weaponry. What lies in the containers of clay that hold the Marine Fire is all that will ever be provided from our sources – at least in these isles.'

Taliessin paused momentarily. 'Even now, I wish I could undo what my brother and I have done. Better we should fight and die with clean, honourable hands than live with the certain knowledge that the weapon we provided came from the realms of darkness.'

The tent was silent except for the noise of a freshening breeze as it shrieked through the trees around the picket lines. It sounded as if the Mother was keening already for her dead sons.

'I wish with all my heart that Bran did not know that Marine Fire exists, for I don't fully trust him,' Taliessin added. 'But he might easily be the last ruler of our tribe, and this night could be our last time together, so we must be honest with each other. At least Arthur's enemy, Mareddyd, will not be defending the ditch, so we don't have to fear treachery from that direction.'

'Mareddyd? The Dobunni brat? That upstart is one of the cavalrymen in my troop. What's his argument with my boy?'

Arthur realised that the call to war had come before he returned to Arden from the Warriors' Dyke, so Bedwyr was still ignorant of his disagreement with Mareddyd. While Taliessin described Arthur's close call at Mareddyd's hands Bedwyr insisted on viewing the scar, and both Taliessin and Arthur could tell that the mood of the Cornovii had not improved.

'If Bran knew that the Dobunni heir was Arthur's sworn enemy, then my son would probably find that young man standing beside him in battle,' Bedwyr growled. 'Or, worse yet, defending the lines behind him. Bran may be considered by some of our tribe to be a fine man, but Artor had excellent reasons for keeping his son's birth a secret from his own kinfolk. Few men are free of the sin of envy and Bran feels its sting no matter how he tries to like my boy. When Arthur was barely seven years old, Bran perceived him as a threat to the realm. Since then, Arthur has grown into the image of my dead master. At times, in tricks of the light, I almost fall to my knees before you, boy, so greatly do you resemble your birth father. But if Bran knew you as I do, he would have no fear of you. The violence of Uther Pendragon that overshadowed Artor's whole life is well buried inside you, for your mother's love has driven any taints in your heritage far away. My Elayne could make nothing that was wicked or false, so Bran should hold you close as one of the few men who will support him through thick and thin.'

Bedwyr gnawed at one fingernail and his hooded eyes gleamed with a slow red anger. 'But men always judge others by what they see in themselves. Bran is a good ruler and a cautious man, but like his grandfather and his great-grandfather before him he has a ruthless streak that will always sweep obstacles out of his path. Artor wasn't always fair or good. Those men at fair Melandra who saw Artor's punishment meted out on the men who murdered his friend and mentor King Luka observed the worst excesses of the Dragon King. That monstrous rage lives within Bran as well – but in our king it's cold, icy and considered. Bran will not weep if Arthur should perish tomorrow. In fact, he is making my boy a target by insisting that he should wear that bright red cloak you brought, Taliessin. A clever ruse! Praise God that Cerdic has very few bowmen with him, else Arthur would be turned into a pincushion as soon as the battle begins.'

Taliessin was aghast at the message inherent in this statement. 'Are you suggesting that our king would deliberately kill his kinsman out of jealousy?'

'Yes,' Bedwyr replied harshly. 'He has no love for my boy, for he fears that Arthur is too much like his birth father. Envy devours him.'

'But . . . but why?' Arthur asked, and Bedwyr's heart ached for Arthur's sudden education in weakness. The understanding of family inheritance was a hard lesson to learn, even for grown men with few illusions. Arthur loved his kinfolk without reservation and it had never occurred to him that they might not feel the same affection for him.

'He fears you might want his crown or, worse still, declare your intention to be crowned High King of the Britons. Other men would follow you, simply because of your appearance.' Bedwyr was brutally frank, but he knew that Arthur must be warned of the danger in which he had been placed.

'It's a good thing I have Gareth, Germanus and Lorcan to guard my back.' Arthur smiled, although he'd really have preferred to cover his face with the cowl of the fine red cloak and weep.

Taliessin embraced Arthur and whispered words of affection and hope into his ear, then left father and son to their private conversation.

'Does Bran really hate me, Father? I couldn't raise my hand against him, even now when you say he'd prefer it if I was dead. Have I done anything to antagonise him? Lorcan says I rattle out the first thing that pops into my head without thinking – is that it? Surely Bran knows I'd never want to steal his throne.'

'You're so like your mother, Arthur.' Bedwyr cupped Arthur's face with his right hand and felt the firm, smooth flesh and warm curls of the handsome, vigorous young man who still scarcely needed to shave. 'Like my Elayne, you see the good in others first. It's to be hoped that you won't become bitter, because you will meet many people who are false. I can assure you that most souls are good at heart most of the time, or at least they try to be. We are betrayed again and again in this life, but when we look for kindness it's there as well. Think of the people you've met in the past year. This Mareddyd appears to be a vicious bully, but how many other boys did you encounter who were like him?'

'Aye. I understand what you're saying, Father. Bran is just one member of the family, and I shouldn't judge the whole by one of the parts.' Arthur laughed. 'In fact, I could have been guilty of all the treasons he suspects without raising a hand in rebellion.' He told his father about Cadwy Scarface's misguided offer, careful to word his description of Scarface's pleas so that Bedwyr would not be left with the impression that Cadwy could still be a traitor, and after a glass of wine, coupled with several pieces of hard cheese from Elayne's cows and a fresh apple from the Villa Poppinidii, Bedwyr's temper finally settled. But the old man still had other matters to share with his son, and Arthur was touched when he brought forward a sword-shaped package wrapped in coarse cloth.

'You'll not have the opportunity to enjoy the feast I would have liked to give when you became a man, nor will your mother have the pleasure of plaiting your warrior's locks for the first time, but you must at least have your own sword in this coming battle, one that celebrates your reaching the responsibility and honour of manhood, and winning the warrior's mantle. This blade was prepared for the day when you would eventually reach manhood, and your mother and I are proud to present you with the best weapon that your family can provide.'

Bedwyr unwrapped the package while Arthur's eyes grew wider and wider – and began to moisten with tears. The young man's emotions were stretched this way and that, so that he hardly knew what to think any more. But he was certain of one thing: his parents loved him. Bedwyr's gnarled hands were trembling as they unwrapped the sword and then, surreptitiously, the old man wiped his eyes with his forearm when he thought Arthur wasn't looking.

'Elayne insisted that I find the best swordsmith in the west to create a weapon that was fitting for our eldest son. I found the best: Rhys ap Myrddion, who made this blade especially for you. We named it Oakheart, a plain name perhaps, but wherever you travel with it you will remember Arden, and us, with love.'

Then Bedwyr handed the sword to his son.

Oakheart was plain, to match its name. The blade was very long, as befitted a weapon made for a tall man. Only its name, inscribed in Latin on the base of the blade, provided any decoration, but the metal glowed almost blue in the strange, rippling light.

'Rhys said this iron came from the stars and is stronger than any other blade he has made. He kept the ore for a long time, until he had a project worthy of a gift from the gods. Furthermore, he used all his skills to fashion it and would accept no payment for its making, saying that you had been useful on the bellows – whatever that means,' Bedwyr told his son.

The tang slid sweetly and without seam into a short, blunt iron hand guard that possessed no cross-piece or decoration. The hilt itself was bound with layer on layer of fish skin, sealed with glue made from deer hide and bone, a process that was repeated again and again to form a surface that was hard wearing and beautiful as well as easy to hold, whether wet or dry. A single cabochon pearl was set into the end of the hilt, a strange, misshapen thing like a blinded or diseased eye. It should have been malevolent, but Bedwyr explained that the pearl was from Arthur's mother and asserted that Lady Elayne would give nothing that was soiled or evil.

'King Artor once wore this pearl on his thumb. He told me it had an ugly history and I believed him, for it had been soaked in blood on several occasions during the many years of his reign. When his grandsons Balyn and Balan died so horribly, your mother washed their bodies and gave them an honourable and dignified cleansing. King Artor was moved to give her this ring, not out of love, but out of gratitude for her service to his family. Although I was very angry with Artor when I discovered that Elayne was bearing his child, and would have thrown the ring back in his face, he told me that Elayne's purity of spirit and greatness of heart would cleanse the demons in his family's blood. I think he meant that you, too, would be born clean of the darkness that he had always recognised in himself.'

'What can I say, Father? The sword is beautiful, simple and pure. I can't find the words to express my love and respect for both of you. If I'm fated to die tomorrow, I could not have wished for a better father. I promise you that your name will not be sullied by any action of mine in tomorrow's combat. I am Arthur ap Bedwyr until I die, and proudly so. Let Bran and his ambitions go to Hades. Living in Arden is more than enough for me and I swear that I will fight tooth and nail to ensure that it remains Cornovii so that your birth son Lasair can hold it in your stead when you eventually go to the fires.'

'I will hold you to that, boy. Damn you, son, but you've made this soft-headed old man weep. Oh, well, tomorrow will be a trial for all of us, but tonight I am as happy as any man could be. Bran is a fool, and Artor may have sensed it, although I saw no sign of it. Poor exercise of power is a failing that the best rulers can succumb to, but I have no fears for you. You are what your birth father should have been had he been raised with love. Go with God, and let this old man try to pray – if I can remember any of the words.'

When Arthur chuckled to hear his father admit that he might have recourse to the Christian God at such a great age, Bedwyr chortled as well. Both men were soon laughing like loons, until the cavalrymen in the nearest tents shouted for quiet and some of the horses began to whicker nervously along the picket lines.

'Waiting is the worst part of any battle,' Germanus whispered quietly through the darkness. Three hundred men were crouching in three rows with one hundred men in each, with their tall, rectangular shields lying beside them as they huddled in position in the darkness. On the mound behind them, every archer in Bran's army was waiting expectantly under the command of Pelles and his two sons, Pincus and Peredor, the elder of whom was named for the legendary family patriarch, now long dead, a one-eyed scoundrel who had fought in a group of mercenaries led by King Artor. The High King had always referred to them as the Scum. Now that Pelles had nothing to prove, he had called his son by the common Roman name used by those long-dead warriors.

Dawn was still far away. To the untrained eye the Britons were simply tussocks of grass covered with a rime of heavy frost, and a casual observer from the direction of Calleva or the Saxon lines would never spot the band of men who waited before the ditch, their faces muffled to prevent even their warm breath from betraying their presence in the freezing morning air.

'We're going to look fucking stupid if the Saxons don't attack,' Germanus whispered from Arthur's right side.

'They'll come. See, Arthur? There's a light coming from Calleva, near the gate,' Gareth hissed from his master's left. 'Someone inside the walls has mounted the palisades and is holding a lantern to warn us. It probably means the Jutes are moving.'

Word came down the line barely ten minutes later to that effect. Absent from the fray, the king of the Atrebates sent an inspiring message by courier that all true Britons should fight to the death for the honour of their tribe on this auspicious day.

Germanus grunted his disgust. 'Since when did good British kings leave their men to fight and die without their leader at their head? Bedwyr plans to ride with his cavalry, as do Scarface and Ector. At least they have sufficient honour to risk their lives with their warriors. Where are the tribal kings who should be here? I've no doubt they'll be safely at Bran's command post.'

'King Artor would writhe with shame if he were to see what has become of his kings and their honour,' Gareth agreed scornfully. 'He always led the Britons into battle from the front where he could be seen. Always! And my father was always there, right behind him.'

'We are living in brutal times when honour is becoming nothing more than a dusty memory blowing away in the winds of time,' Arthur said, rather embarrassed by his own poetic metaphor. 'The Jutes and the Saxons are our immediate problem. I am happy to trust my life to the men who'll stand with me against the enemy. In fact, I'm proud to stand with them.'

Around him, other warriors had heard the conversation. And those who survived the coming battle would repeat it many times in the months ahead, for a glimmer of glory would shimmer over references to the battle of Calleva even considering the horrors of Marine Fire. Men would be proud to boast that they had stood with Bedwyr's son before the mound and the ditch – and that they had bravely held the line, one of only three hundred, against a thousand enemy warriors.

'So the Jutes really are going to attack in the darkness,' Arthur murmured. 'Their tactics are different from those of the Saxons, and I don't believe those differences will work in our favour.'

Then word came down the line to maintain silence, so the tribal warriors rose on one knee and prepared to leap to their feet, lock their shields into position and repel their giant adversaries.

Earlier that night, after four brief hours of sleep, Lorcan had embraced each of his three friends in turn and had left for the healers' compound, where it was his intention to offer hope to the living and comfort to the dying, regardless of what gods they worshipped. Then the three warriors had begun their final checks on their arms and equipment. Using Artor's comb, Gareth had taken particular care with Arthur's hair, plaiting the whole head and using the braids to protect the skull under the helmet with its rampant dragon and horsehair plume. He had polished the breastplate until it shone, while Arthur donned a soft woollen vest, the mail shirt and simple arm guards. When breast and back plates were buckled into place, Arthur marvelled at how light the armour actually was. He felt a little silly wearing the iron codpiece under his trews, but Germanus had set him straight with a pithy comment.

'Do you wish to spend the battle fearing you'll sing falsetto for life? Or do you bury your scruples and protect your cock in a case made of good iron? Many good men have been brought down while trying to protect their balls.'

For the sake of speed, Arthur rejected the stiff greaves over the shins that would slow him down considerably. However, he accepted the oddly shaped plates that covered his soft leather boots because Germanus pointed out, once again, that a foot wound exposed a man to real problems in a shield wall. 'Because that's what we'll be doing. Effectively, we'll be initiating our own shield wall. And the Saxons know everything there is to know about that strategy, because they invented it.'

'But the Dragon King held the shield wall at Moridunum and broke the back of the Cymru Saxons,' Gareth said in his soft, musical voice. 'My father told me about it, and he described it as one of the finest battles the Britons ever fought. They were called the Army of the Dead afterwards.'

'Aye. My father Bedwyr stood on that line beside Cadwy Scarface when they were young men,' Arthur chipped in. 'I've heard the tale a thousand times, and now I'll know what it feels like.'

Then, as they waited for the call to arms, Arthur had shown his companions the sharpened upper rim of his shield. He explained how Bedwyr had used that deadly edge to slice open unwary throats from below. Silently, Germanus and Gareth decided to sharpen their shields as soon as they were free to do so.

Now, tense and sick of waiting, the line crouched at the ready. Almost every man jumped when an owl called from the coppices where the cavalry waited in the darkness, its scream unnaturally loud in the silence of the night. Meanwhile, a heavy blanket of fog began to roll across the frozen ground so that the waiting warriors could barely recognise the faces of the men beside them. Silence hung heavily around them, as dense as the fog itself, while the earth seemed to hold its breath.

Then an arrow sang over their heads, followed by another. The arrow heads were wrapped in oily rags that were burning fiercely, aimed to land about a hundred yards ahead of the waiting line of Celtic warriors, and dimly lighting an area of about six feet around them. Shadows appeared in the area where the arrows were landing, large shadows that moved quickly until the flames were extinguished.

'Here they come,' Germanus said in his normal voice as the front defensive line rose swiftly, locked shields and braced for the coming impact. More flaming arrows hissed overhead with a sound like the whirr of giant gnats and lit the flat ground between the Britons and the north-western wall of Calleva, which had suddenly become alive with running figures that loped through the fog like golems or spirits of the dead as they hunted down anything with red blood pumping through its veins. For a moment, Arthur's heart almost stopped with sudden, superstitious panic.

'Breathe through your nose as deeply as you can, Arthur.' Germanus's voice was steady and calm as he sensed his student's sudden panic. 'Now! Brace your legs, because a running man the size of these devils can knock you off your feet if you're not ready for him.'

A scream, primal and shrill, cut through the unnatural silence. 'One of the Jutes has found a fire-pit. May he enjoy the warmth,' Gareth hissed callously. On cue, another brace of arrows streaked through the fog. One of them struck the pit and a vicious fire fuelled by pitch and oil leaped up to turn one scrambling figure into a pillar of flame, hair streaming like a red comet and highlighting the mass of men who were pouring past him, oblivious of his agony. Another man fell as the ground opened up under his feet and another who had been running at his heels tripped over him. Soon the falling arrows were lighting human torches who capered and danced in a blur of moving, blazing flesh until a casual knife thrust or axe blow from their peers put them out of their misery.

And then the Jutes were upon them, coming out of the fog like wraiths that seemed twice the size of mortal men. The shock of their meeting, round Saxon shield against rectangular Roman one, shook the line until it seemed the defence would crumble.

Arthur had been well taught. Ignore everything but the man who came for you. Stab, slash and push with every ounce of muscle until the enemy slipped on the icy grass and fell. Without pausing to think, Arthur stabbed down with his new sword and felt it cleave through mail, ox hide and flesh before he wrenched it free, and a great spurt of blood sprayed up from slashed arteries. Then, concentrating on the next comer, Arthur kept his shield high to protect Gareth on his left while Germanus on his right protected him. Safe in this cocoon of repetitive movement, Arthur faced the next warrior, and the next, until the earth was slick with blood. Maintaining his footing became the difference between life and death.

Behind him, arrows continued to sing from bowstrings, filling the lightening sky with sheets of iron-tipped wood which sent many men to their knees before they reached the waiting line of Britons, who managed, somehow, to remain on their feet under the massive weight of the huge Jutes. If one defender fell, another seamlessly took his place, for even the passage of fifteen years hadn't changed the iron discipline and strategies developed by the Dragon King. And all the while, a weak sun struggled to rise through the fog that swirled around the dead and the dying like a river of blue-grey ice.

In such a desperate struggle, Arthur decided it was probably best that he could see very little. The faces of his adversaries were always the same; lips drawn back over teeth in a howl of bloodlust; eyes wide and staring with that special madness of men so fired by adrenalin that they scarcely felt their own fatal wounds as they threw themselves upon the sword blades of their enemies. The screaming in his brain had resolved itself into a single voice that cried out, 'Sword up. Shield up. Slice through to the chin. Make him bleed.' And Arthur obeyed rhythmically, as a bloody sun rose slowly and the fog began to lift. Around him, the line of tribal warriors was becoming painfully thin, while the Jute corpses formed a wall of dead. Still, the Jutes continued to attack.

The man directly in front of Arthur was as tall as he was, but older and battle hardened, with a face blistered raw by the flames through which he had passed. He must have strayed too close to the fire-pits, Arthur's brain told him as Oakheart slid cleanly upward between the plates of iron on the Jute's chest and penetrated his mail shirt as if it was made of wool rather than tiny rings of iron. Then his mind suddenly shrieked at him, and his shield was twisted out of his grasp by a wicked blow from one side.

Immediately, Gareth used his own shield to cover Arthur, baring his body to attack, but Oakheart chose to sweep in a wider arc, seemingly of its own accord, as if it enjoyed having room to manoeuvre. The Dragon Knife found its way into Arthur's left hand of its own volition, and the long-practised patterns of the dance of death began automatically. As the sun broke through the mist it caught Arthur in its feeble, ruddy light. Saxon and Celt paused momentarily and stared at the figure that emerged from the line of defenders to fight such a vicious individual battle. Then the warriors returned to their own deadly rituals of combat.

But, far away on a hilltop, Cerdic saw Arthur clearly, as if his old eyes had suddenly been cleared of the rheum of old age. The citizens of Calleva Atrebatum also saw the figure in the red cloak and a wave of excitement swept through the besieged town.

'The Dragon King has come again,' the whispers began, and the word was passed from man to man, growing louder and louder with each repetition. 'You can see him from the ramparts whenever the mists clear. He bears a knife and sword as always, and has no recourse to a shield. Our enemies are dying all around him. See! The Dragon King has come again, just as he promised!'

On his hilltop, Cerdic cursed, coughed and spat blood on the earth as he watched the tall, cloaked figure whose weapons wove such complex patterns of death that they were almost too fast for the Saxon's eyes to follow. 'I know he's dead,' he murmured, so quietly that only his son could hear him. 'I could dig the bastard up if I went to Glastonbury. No one, not even the Red Dragon, can defeat death.'

But fear clutched at the heart of the Saxon bretwalda as blood and sputum caused him to spit once again so he could breathe more easily.

Then, in a mad thunder, he heard the British cavalry come at a gallop, not to attack Havar and his sacrificial Jutes from the rear, but towards the amphitheatre, the engineers and the troops guarding the baggage train.

'Let him be dead, Loki,' Cerdic swore as the Celtic cavalry cut the sappers to ribbons and swept on. 'Stop playing tricks with me.'

Then the morning light dazzled his eyes and Cerdic was forced to lean against his son's strong body for support.

Below him, the murder began.

THE BATTLE OF CALLEVA ATREBATUM – STAGE TWO

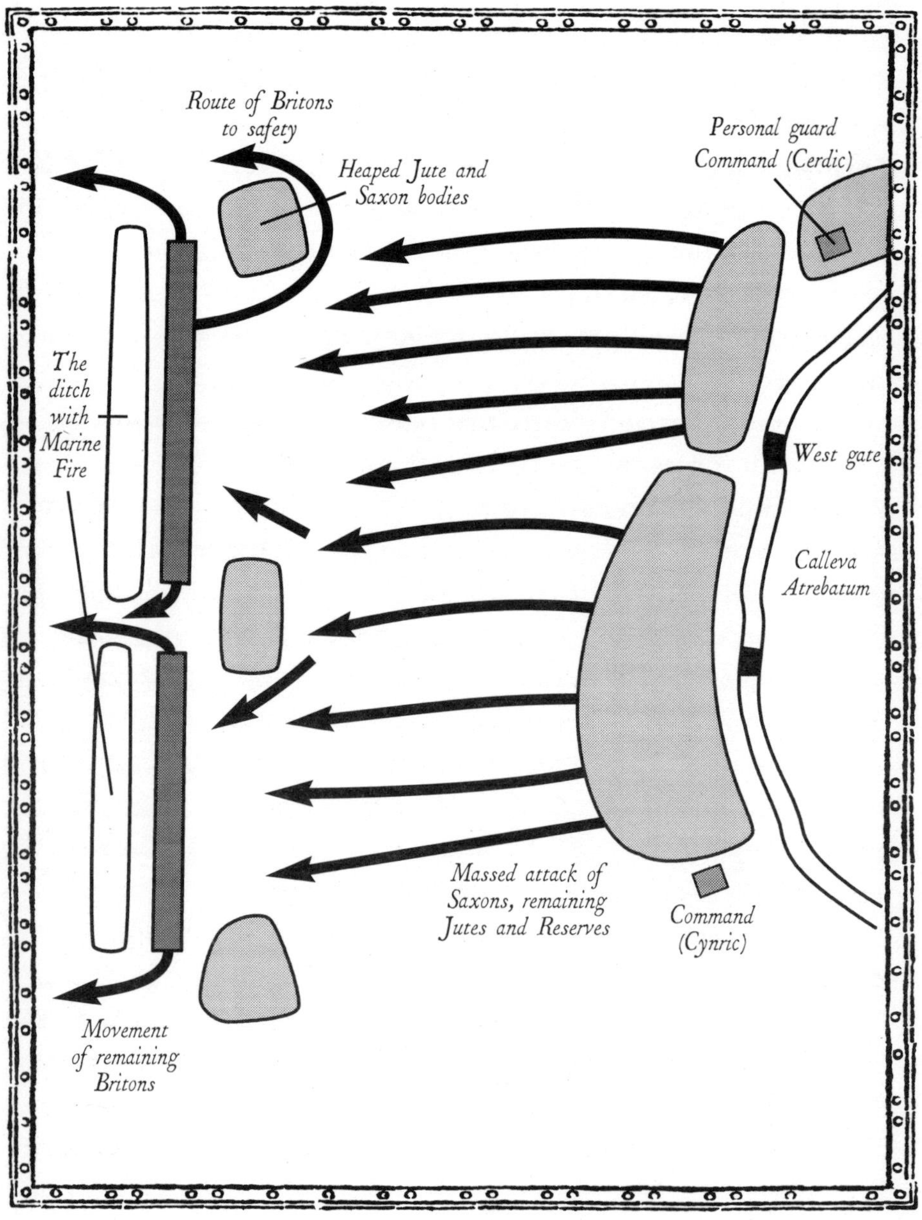

CHAPTER XV

THE FIRE THAT WILL NOT DIE

Truth sits upon the lips of dying men.

Matthew Arnold, 'Sohrab and Rustum'

As the sun began to rise over the killing fields to the west of Calleva Atrebatum, Bedwyr's cavalry struck beyond the eastern gate. The first dozen horsemen rode to the gate and killed the sappers there while the remaining cavalry headed for the warriors guarding the baggage train. Before them lay the well that supplied water to the Saxon forces. Caught off guard, the foot soldiers looked up at the horses, terrified by the sudden appearance of the cavalry out of the last shreds of the dissipating fog. One rider in particular was riding very carefully in the saddle as he clutched a container of raw, unglazed terracotta to his breast, his face as white as any of the enemy. His terror was written clearly in his colour, his expression and his wide, gasping mouth. Then, at the last instant before the horsemen would strike the enemy, the solitary rider veered away and hurled the cylinder towards a cluster of men who had been drawing water from the well. It smashed open on the hard ground and a spray of liquid fire engulfed the Saxon warriors.

As he watched from his vantage point high above the walls of Calleva Atrebatum, Cerdic could scarcely believe the explosion caused by that single container of *something*. Clearly the fruit of the chaos demons, whatever it was seemed to set the air itself on fire and over twenty men were suddenly transformed into columns of flame in front of him.

Then another white-faced rider appeared out of the mist with his accompanying guards. This time, in the chaos and with his companions clearing the way, the cavalryman rode towards the heart of the milling group of warriors by the baggage train and set his container soaring over their heads. As he spurred away, the lid of the terracotta urn became dislodged and the liquid hit the cold air, igniting in an arc of flame. Horses ran madly, oxen trampled men underfoot as they struggled to escape, and the earth itself began to blaze, regardless of the cold fog that should have hampered its spread – but had no effect on the raging fire from hell.

Attempts were made to use buckets of water to extinguish the flames, but the hellfire grew, feeding on the water and claiming new victims as it spread. Meanwhile, Bedwyr's cavalry rode back through those Saxons who had avoided the flames and were trying to flee from the vicinity of the well, their weapons forgotten in the primal instinct to be as far as possible from these unnatural flames that refused to be extinguished. Resisting the instinct to cut them down where they milled, Bedwyr ordered his troops to ride away from the eastern gateway as the fire finally started to die down, some of the more intelligent foot soldiers using handfuls of earth to smother the flames enveloping the twitching mounds of melting flesh and bone.

From his position on the hilltop, Cerdic watched the destruction of over two hundred of his men and writhed with rage as if he too was burning. 'Halt the attack!' he yelled to one of his runners. 'I must think! They have some kind of weapon the like of which I've never seen.'

The Jute force pulled back to a position just out of bow-shot, and Havar sent another runner back to Cerdic, begging for some of the reserves who were waiting by the western gate. He had lost over four hundred men in his frontal attacks, and had yet to understand how this catastrophe could have occurred. He stared impotently at the British lines and his eyes burned red with the berserker rage. With difficulty, he kept some control of his reason, recognising that now was the time for cool tactical decisions. He looked towards Calleva and the oily black smoke that rose ominously behind the town. The stench, even from this distance, had carried on the freshening cold winds, and Havar's stomach roiled with his recognition of cooked human flesh.

Standing in a small semicircle of dead and dying Jutes, Arthur came out of an odd kind of trance. He had been conscious of everything that had gone on around him with a jewel-bright precision, but a clear glass barrier had stood between him and his emotions so that many of the horrors he had witnessed had seemed to be happening to someone else.

The day hovered on the verge of misty rain, but so far the weather had not had any particular effect on the pattern of the battle. The fog had been clammy and every surface seemed to be damp, but the defenders of the ditch and mound had been spared the discomfort of fighting in the sleety rain that early winter often brought. Arthur stared up at some overflying geese as they moved in a wedge formation, far above the low, scudding clouds so that they were only intermittently visible. He could imagine the proud, barred wings that reminded him of old Pictish men covered with dark tattoos commemorating battles beyond counting, and he wished he could be flying with them, away from this place and the death that surrounded him.

When Havar retreated, teams of men from the Celtic reserves poured across the causeway between the ditches and began to move the bodies of the dead Saxons into large piles. Arthur was appalled when he saw an Ordovice tribesman casually cut the throat of one Jute warrior who was still twitching, deftly avoiding the jet of blood that arced from the carotid artery.

'Are we animals then, that we act like the Saxons whom we so revile?' Arthur muttered as he watched another warrior, an Atrebate, strip massy golden arm-rings from a dead thane, and he turned his head away when the same man lifted a flaccid hand with golden rings on the thumb and index finger. Without being told, Arthur knew immediately that this corpse robber would cut the digits from the hand to collect his trophies.

Arthur looked across at Germanus. He was still only half aware of the world around him, but sickened to the core by what he had seen. Germanus showed more sangfroid, having watched men act like brutes on the Continent for twenty years, but he understood the shock experienced by Arthur and Gareth, both of whom were profoundly ashamed of their own people and their avaricious behaviour.

'Your shield, Arthur. I'd rather you didn't go without it again. You could have been killed – or one of us could as we attempted to cover you,' he said mildly, to draw Arthur's attention away from the growing piles of corpses. Arthur's fey mood made the arms master nervous, worried about this peculiar blankness that had come over his charge in the middle of a major battle. He ordered Arthur to sit and the young man did so, settling himself on a patch of soil so bloodstained it looked as if the earth itself was wounded.

'What's that?' he asked vaguely, pointing at a coarse cloth bag on which Gareth was sitting. Germanus decided that the boy was in a kind of odd survival shock as the automatic responses to danger that had saved him during the battle slowly began to dissipate.

'It's a gift from Father Lorcan. A sand bag. We may need to use it if an accident occurs with the Marine Fire,' he replied quietly, as if to a child. Arthur had fought like a demon in the battle, inhuman in his speed and deadliness, and the arms master was now convinced that this boy-man had been born specifically to salvage what was possible from the destruction of the west. Like a demon-spawn, he had ignored minor slashes and injuries while attacking the most crazed and vicious fighters and killing with machine-like precision. Perhaps God was allowing him this short period of confusion during the lull in the battle so he could begin to accept the blood he had shed in the early hours of the dawn. Arthur's fellow warriors on the British line were already treating him cautiously, as if he was mad or had been blessed with the frenzy of the gods. Germanus watched Gareth cleaning the sticky, clinging mud from his pupil's sword and the Dragon Knife until they seemed untouched and unsullied, and wished he could do the same for their master.

At the very limit of the bowmen's reach, Havar paced and raged as he waited for Cerdic's orders. Havar had never felt the true sting of failure in his life, and now that he knew its taste he found the flavour to be as bitter as gall or wormwood. Worse yet, he felt as though he was a smaller man in the eyes of his thanes because of his failures. Cerdic had called them back from the enemy. Havar had been instructed to retreat. Unthinkable! 'By the jokester god's balls, they're only Celts!' he roared at a hapless warrior who was trying to replait his locks during the hiatus. 'Where did they get the strength to do this to me? And who the fuck is the warrior in the red cloak?'

No one answered, because no one knew. Besides, sensible men made themselves scarce when Havar lost his temper.

From his vantage point, Havar scanned the front line of the British defenders. Finally, he found three oversized men together, two of them caring for the largest of the three. In size they could have been Jute or Saxon, or even Dene, who were taller yet, but their armour showed their allegiance very clearly, now that Havar had the luxury of examining them at his leisure.

'Can you see the device on that clod's chest, Erikk? It's something in red,' Havar said, irritable because thirty-five years had robbed his eyes of their clarity.

'It's some form of winged creature,' the boy answered. Erikk was Havar's eldest son and this battle was his first taste of blood. 'I've got it! It's a red dragon with its wings outspread.'

'So the White Dragon battles the Red, Erikk. It seems that legends still walk the earth.'

Perversely, the symbol of the Red Dragon emblazoned across his enemy's chest comforted Havar. All men knew that the dragon was the favoured beast of the gods: no ordinary adversary had defeated the Jutes.

While Havar waited, Cerdic examined the results of the British cavalry attack in person. Men had literally cooked within their armour, and survivors were anxious to tell him that water did not quench the strange fire but seemed to feed it, sending out blazing particles that set fire to other men nearby. The fire stuck to a man's skin, like sap or gum, and ate through skin, flesh, muscle and bones. Sickened, Cerdic knew that he was looking at the work of a demon, a force that no man or king had the right to wield.

'Cynric!' he called. More and more, he could feel fluid building in his lungs, and he knew that his life span would soon be cut short. But his brain still worked with efficient clarity, like the wooden cogs of a Roman war machine he had once seen, the wheels and great, notched gears working seamlessly together to kill and maim. Cerdic knew his mind was like that machine, only faster and sharper, and he determined to set it to work against this great evil. In a wholly northern way, he cursed those who wielded this fury – the madmen who had stolen the fires of Udgaard.

'The Britons cannot be allowed to control this devil's brew. Up till now, we've made it easy for them to use it against us, because we have kept our troops away from theirs. The fire itself makes no distinction between Saxon or Briton. Look, Cynric – just two containers of devil's fire did this.'

Cerdic's arm swept across the scorched ground around the well, and the blackened lumps that lay beneath the scattered piles of soil used to drown the fire, fists raised and skulls opened like strange flowers of bone as the brains boiled within them. Anything human in those lumps of carbon had vanished in a slice of the Christian hell transported to earth.

Besides the destruction of most of their supplies, too many men had perished for Cerdic to forgive his enemy. The devastation was far beyond the normal losses inflicted during warfare. Bran had turned this war into a personal conflict, and Cerdic and his son would not rest until the Britons paid the full blood price for their hideous murders. Over two hundred men had died – a fraction of his force, but a terrible blow to the morale of the rest.

'They will not be able to use this weapon on our warriors if we can gain entry to Calleva, or if we can force them to fight us at close quarters in the ditch and on the mound. I doubt they are prepared to kill their own men.'

Cynric waited patiently. He understood the sharpness of his father's wits, and appreciated that Cerdic's decisions would almost certainly determine the fate of his army in the next phase of the battle.

'The reserves to the south of the eastern gate are to be placed under Havar's command and he must be ordered to take the northern sector of the ditch and mound at all costs. Do you understand, Cynric? Havar must win.'

'Yes, Father. I will ensure that Havar is told of your orders. But what shall we do with the reserves to the south-west?'

'They must be ready to move as soon as they are ordered into the attack. I want them to maintain pressure on the ditch where it is thinly protected along the southern section, at the points where Havar has yet to mount a sustained offensive. You, son, are in charge of penetrating the ditch and the mound. Once through the defensive line, you will destroy the command tents and crush the British reserves that remain behind the mound. Let Havar absorb the main thrust of the British defences while you set your men into a wedge and break through. Is that understood? Everything will depend on it. You must break through their lines. I am putting almost every man into the fray, so don't fail me.'

Cynric looked dazed. 'But we'll be risking everything, including our lives and our freedom, on these worthless fields, Father. There'll be no reserves, and no support. What if Havar fails? What if I fail?'

'You must not fail, Cynric! The devil's fire must not be used upon us again. You must be so close to the Britons that they won't be able to use that . . . that monstrous potion without killing their own warriors. We've stood toe to toe against Bran of the Ordovice on many occasions. He's not the Dragon King – and we outnumber the Britons by about two to one. What more do you want? They might have the advantage through the firestorm at this moment, but nothing is certain in a battle.'

Cynric agreed, but every instinct told him that his father was wrong. Cerdic had panicked because of the nature of the weapon used against them and the hellish deaths it had caused. But Cerdic was the bretwalda. Who was Cynric to question his father's decisions? Cerdic had earned the right to call himself king of the Saxons through skirmish and battle, although Cissa had vied with him for the title. But Cissa was dead, and Cerdic now ruled the lands that stretched from the Wash to the Litus Saxonicum. He would be obeyed without question, even if he led his warriors to destruction in this new and grotesque hell. But nothing in Cynric's orders demanded that all of his force should attack at once. Cynric determined to divide his troops into two groups and keep half of his men beyond the range of the Celtic bowmen until he was sure that Cerdic's strategy would work.

Yes, he would wait. After all, how could that hurt?

Two hours is an eternity on the battlefield, especially if you are waiting for your enemy to make up his mind. The Jutes beat their sword hilts against their shields and screamed insults at the Britons, inviting them to leave the safety of their little ditch and fight them man to man, instead of hiding behind their shields and their bowmen. Meanwhile, the Britons stood or sat in their rows, bolstered by the unseen men from their reserves who were waiting behind the mound. The veterans drank copiously from their ale or water bottles, and took what pleasure could be got from gossip, singing or telling ribald stories about their officers or the tribal kings.

Arthur had gradually come out of his odd period of weakness and had shaken his head when he saw the bloody piles of dead stacked at the northern end of the ditch. Much evidence of the conflict had soaked into the ground, or had been scattered on the churned earth. An earring torn out of the lobe that had held it was trodden into the mud. Across a puddle of half-congealed blood, a broken sword waited for the familiar hand of its owner to lift it once again. Arthur stared at the relics of violent death and began to vomit.

After Arthur's stomach had emptied, Gareth used a clean corner of the ruined red cloak to cleanse his mouth.

'I'm sorry,' Arthur said, and realigned his blood-spattered chest plate. 'I must have killed many men to find myself in this state, but it's only now that I realise how much butchery we've carried out this day. I'm not making much sense, am I? This was your first battle too, Gareth, but you're not acting like a silly child. So what's wrong with me? I vaguely remember losing my shield and using the Dragon Knife instead. Someone else seemed to be fighting inside my body. I don't understand.'

Germanus heard the ragged edges in Arthur's voice. The enemy was still very close, far too close for his charge to have self-doubts at the start of another sortie. He knew they would come again – there was no doubt of that – so Arthur must be patched together or he'd perish while worrying whether he was, in fact, a madman.

'Every warrior is different when he first stands shoulder to shoulder with his friends and tries to kill his enemies. Some, like Gareth, see it as a task that must be completed. For him this battle is the culmination of years of training with his father. His mind is razor sharp because he has been prepared to expect every detail.'

'I was also trained, as well you know,' Arthur interrupted. 'I was prepared just as carefully as he was. You were my master.'

'And I passed on to you everything I learned over twenty years of killing and surviving. But other factors came to light on the battlefield today, factors that do not concern Gareth. You are the son of a warrior, the grandson of a warrior, the descendant of warriors back as far as you care to look along your bloodline – and all those warriors were kings. You are measured by a higher standard than Gareth. Those members of your family who were too generous, too caring or too sensitive died before they could father children. Even the women of your blood are warriors. But you, Arthur, are a good, kind and happy man at heart. You don't love the killing fields, and you draw people to you because you have no real desire to inflict harm on anyone.'

Arthur looked to one side. Germanus had been making sense until the last part of his explanation. A flake of dried blood marred Arthur's thumbnail and he flicked it away in disgust. Good? Kind?

'Some part of you is determined to survive and to do what must be done to ensure it. It is your heritage and it is an inescapable part of you. If the conscious part of you shudders from killing, the deeper, atavistic part of you will do it willingly. What do you think the berserkers are? They are men who deliberately call on that hidden, deeper part of their souls so that they feel no wounds and can draw effortlessly on their training. You were a kind of berserker when you fought earlier. You acted consciously at first, but then you fell back on your instinct for survival when you lost your shield. You may find what I say hard to face, but almost every part of you, from the wild hair that protects your skull to your long, flexible feet which keep your body balanced, is bred for warfare.'

'Yes, I understand what you're saying,' Arthur murmured slowly. 'I remember the killing as if someone else was doing the fighting.'

'When the enemy comes against us again, you'll know what to expect and you'll fight with the full knowledge of what you do. Don't worry, Arthur. I've never lied to you, and I won't start now.'

Arthur looked a little happier. He had remembered his *voice*, that itch at the back of his head, the screaming that warned of danger, and he wondered if it was his training taking over when he was in a kind of shock composed of fear and dread. Had that inner instinct come out to save the body that nourished it? He shuddered at the thought, but he could understand such intervention.

Like his birth father before him, Arthur was fearful of madness, for his kinfolk were fully aware of the manifold weaknesses that had been apparent in the bloodlines that produced Uther, Morgan and Balyn. He had often been reminded that he should never forget the violence inherent in his family. Nor should he forget the blessings he had received from them, such as his great height. Inwardly, Father Lorcan and Germanus had disapproved of the constant emphasis placed by Anna and Bran on his mental state, for it had made the boy determined to be generous, reasonable and kind; to prove to himself that he hadn't been cursed by the family flaws.

In the light of his new-found knowledge of King Bran's feelings towards him, Arthur began to wonder whether the king had meant to cause him harm from the time when he first became aware of Arthur's birthright. Neither Bedwyr nor Elayne had spoken of this seam of cruelty within Arthur's bloodline, and both swore that Artor had been the fairest ruler of his age. But any man can be killed without a blow being struck if he is convinced that he suffers from a debilitating flaw or weakness. Survival in battle depended on one's ability to handle violence: perhaps Arthur had been taught to distrust his own capacity in that regard so that he might be slaughtered when he faced an enemy for the first time, and thus pose no threat to his kin? Would Anna do such a thing to her brother?

Regretfully, Arthur put the thought of family betrayal aside. He had no choice if he wanted to survive. More was at stake than the life of a landless warrior whose only distinction was that he looked like the Dragon King.

Done with talking, Germanus, Arthur and Gareth unslung the leather pocket of food each carried on the back of his belt, where it would be out of the way during combat. Wise soldiers refreshed themselves in any pause during a battle, for who could say when another opportunity might come to fill their bellies, and Lorcan had insisted that they take bread, the last of the cheese, an apple and a handful of nuts from their store. Around them, other Britons ate and drank in a mood reminiscent of a grim picnic, a strange comparison given that they were in sight of a huge pile of Jute bodies. Their own dead and wounded had been taken through the narrow gap in the mound and were now in the care of the healers and the priests. Arthur wondered briefly how Lorcan was faring.

Two men in helmets came from the causeway dividing the ditch and walked the length of the line, passing on various pieces of information to the British warriors. They eventually reached Arthur, Germanus and Gareth, who recognised the messengers as Ector and Idris ap Cadwy. Ector's face had aged in the course of the day, and Arthur was just thinking how glad he was not to be in a position where he was forced to make decisions which cost so many lives when he was called out of the line and Ector draped one arm affectionately around his shoulder. As his kinsman spoke, Arthur watched a small force, not much more than two hundred men, positioning themselves in front of the southern sector of the ditch.

'The mirrors tell us that the Saxons are moving. One contingent is being sent towards Havar, so Father presumes that his enlarged force will attack here, where your force will be standing at the front of the ditch. It is the point where the majority of our losses have been suffered so far. Incidentally, Arthur, please accept our congratulations. Father is very pleased. You and your men inflicted massive casualties on Havar – enough to keep him smarting for some time, but we're sure he'll be back to get his revenge as soon as Cerdic gives the order to attack again. That Saxon bastard keeps all his thanes and allies on short leashes. Cerdic's other reserves, the group you see stretching from the western gate down to the southern gate, are also preparing to move forward. We presume they will attack the southern end of the ditch, where we have placed another three hundred men.'

Arthur smiled wryly. Ector's estimates seemed optimistic, because he was sure there weren't three hundred poor sods positioning themselves along the southern part of the ditch. Even if there were, they would already be outnumbered, judging by the size of the Saxon bivouac south of Calleva's western gate, but Arthur would eat his left boot if there were two hundred Britons on the line, all green young men like himself, expected to hold back a thousand or more fully trained warriors.

The itch began in the back of Arthur's skull.

'We're keeping the bulk of our reserves to link with your force so that your wounded can be replaced,' Ector said, as if he could read Arthur's mind. 'They must be used to prevent the Saxons from breaking through. The plan is to engage all of Cerdic's forces on the field, so we'll be hideously outnumbered in every defensive position.'

'So? We will just fight until they run, or we die,' Arthur said softly. The situation was dire, and it was no time for self-delusion. For some reason, Bran was keeping most of his experienced warriors in reserve while those that filled the front lines were mainly of tender years. Why?

'No. Once Cerdic's troops are committed to an attack, our warriors must start to leave through the gap in the mound, not quickly at first or else the Saxons will smell a rat; they should give the impression they are deserting their posts from fear of their attackers. The southern troops will go round the end of the ditch and take up a defensive position to stop the Saxons from outflanking our line and surrounding us. But your troops here must run through the gap and take up positions behind the mound. You'll hear our trumpets sound and that's your cue to retreat, and may

God help you if you can't get through, for we'll be throwing the containers of Marine Fire into the ditch, where the water will help to spread the liquid. That's all the detail you need to know, but you must appreciate the urgency of that trumpet call. Make sure you move, kinsman, for that liquid fire is a hellish way to die. I saw it during the cavalry charge and it's something I'd like to forget. And promise me you'll be careful, for I'd miss you if anything were to happen to you.'

Arthur stared into Ector's eyes and acquitted him of any desire to harm him. Germanus, Gareth and Arthur had already discussed their positioning in one of the most dangerous positions on the whole battlefield and decided that Bran's actions were odd at best, but Arthur was determined that he would bring no shame to his father's name by disobeying an order or complaining of the dangers involved. Good men stood around him who could not demand a safer role. However, Ector's eyes were free of any guilt and they met Arthur's even gaze without shame. If Bran wished harm to Arthur, then he'd not shared his decision with his son.

Nodding, Arthur swore to stand until the trumpet call, when he would personally ensure that those Britons who had not already escaped ran for their lives. He was smiling, but only Germanus realised how shallow that smile was and that his eyes, more grey now than green, showed no hint of amusement or affection. Arthur was going through the motions while his mind burrowed away at the problem of avoiding the barrage of Marine Fire that would soon be unleashed. As soon as Ector and Idris had departed to speak to the southern contingent, he crouched close to the ground and drew a plan of the battleground on the cold, wet earth. Germanus immediately placed his finger on the discrepancies in Bran's arrangements.

'He expects six hundred men to run through one gap? King

Bran is mad. It'll take half an hour to get the troops through the mound to safety. What's more, the way round our end of the ditch is partially blocked by the Saxon and Jute dead stacked there.'

Arthur called the section commanders to an impromptu meeting, where he explained the problem with the use of his drawing on the cold earth. 'There'll be fuck-all time to get away once those trumpets sound, so we have to retreat in good order if we want everyone to reach safety.'

'Agreed,' a grizzled veteran replied. 'But you just can't fit that number of men through that space in that short a time. Can't be done!'

'Then the men at the end must go round the piles of Saxon corpses. If needs be, our stragglers may have to hide themselves among the Saxon dead. But no one will get out of this trap if we are all trying to pour through one narrow entrance.'

Germanus added his bit. 'Have you noticed the odds we're up against? Something doesn't make sense and this old soldier's nose smells something rotten under Bran's planning. It makes me wonder what the hell is happening here.'

'You too?' the veteran, whose name was Eanraig Four-Fingers, replied with a sour expression around his drawn-down mouth. 'Count the number of men sent to guard the southern part of the ditch.'

'There's not many of them,' Arthur answered, scanning the thin ranks from his greater height.

'Fewer than two hundred and fifty! And there are fewer than four hundred of us here to defend our bit. That tells me we're expendable, and part of the story is being left out. By my guess, Bran is determined to keep us in the dark.'

'I'll find out,' Arthur snapped, his slow temper igniting at last.

'You shouldn't go,' Gareth protested. 'Bran could say you're deserting your post.'

'No, he won't! Don't worry about it! I'll find out what's going on.'

Arthur strode through the narrow gap between the northern and southern sections of the ditch. He had barely covered twenty feet before Taliessin appeared out of nowhere and gripped his arm so hard that Arthur was certain the skin would be bruised.

'What are you doing here, Arthur? You're supposed to be on the front line.'

Organised chaos reigned behind the mound as five small wooden machines were pushed into place halfway up the incline and wooden chocks placed against the wheels to ensure they remained stable.

'What are they?' Arthur asked, his face darkening.

'Catapults – ballistas. They'll throw the Marine Fire out at the enemy when they're about halfway between here and the walls of Calleva.' Arthur blinked. He'd been told that the liquid fire would be used in the ditch.

'When will the trumpets sound to indicate that it's time to begin our withdrawal from the line? I don't much care for the idea of being burned alive.'

'I've not heard about any trumpets. The front lines are expected to run when the catapults fire the first of the containers. They'll allow for a count of fifty to give you time to escape before volunteers on the mound start to throw containers of Marine Fire into the ditch. The enemy will be caught between two fires. Don't you know this? You're volunteers, after all, and Bran says you are the pride of the army because you've chosen to risk yourselves for your homeland. You will be luring the Saxons into making a full frontal attack into the throat of our newly acquired weapons, and Bran will achieve a great victory at little cost. After your escape, all that will be needed is for the cavalry to mop up the survivors.'

'It's a pity, then, that no one told us. It seems odd that we weren't actually given the opportunity to volunteer!' Arthur's voice rasped as if it belonged to a man twice his age.

'What do you mean? Bran said that . . .'

'I don't care what Bran says. He lies! We were told to wait until the trumpets sound before we retreat, and now you tell me there are no trumpets. Six hundred good men are expected to get through one narrow escape route because the space at the northern end of the ditch is effectively blocked by Saxon corpses – put there on Bran's instructions! We make very effective bait, and we're expected to die for the sake of realism. Thank you for your honesty, Taliessin. I'll go now and warn my troops that we've been deemed expendable.'

Taliessin now looked thoroughly alarmed. 'You'll need to smear earth all over your bodies. It might stop some of the fire sticking to you. I swear I had no knowledge of any of the bad aspects of this plan. Take care, Arthur, because our men need you.'

'I don't think our leaders feel quite the same way,' Arthur replied sardonically as he started to make his way back to the ditch and the forward line. To make matters worse, the Saxon and Jute troops were beginning to stir like a vast ant nest tormented by a giant child with a large stick. There was too little time left to avoid the annihilation of the entire front line.

Arthur quickly outlined the real battle plan to Eanraig and his small corps of veterans. 'Our departure from the field must look like a poorly disorganised retreat rather than a planned strategy, so don't hold your breath waiting for that trumpet call. It won't come. As soon as the catapults throw the containers into the air, move the back two rows of the northern defenders through the gap in the mound at a run. The southern contingent must run towards the far end of the ditch as if the Christian Satan was pursuing them, and the front rank of the defenders on the north side should make a rush round the pile of Jute corpses. They'll probably have to fight their way out of the trap. But I have just been informed by Taliessin that Bran's warriors on the mound intend to hurl the next containers directly into the ditch behind us – at a count of fifty after the catapults fire the first salvo! We will be caught between two lines of fire. You must be ready to run as soon as I give the order, for this treachery has already been arranged by our glorious masters. Taliessin believed that we knew of Bran's intentions, and that we had volunteered to risk our lives for the greater good.'

One sour-faced veteran, the senior officer of the southern contingent, raised a hand. 'I've got nothing but green boys in my troop, including some who've been used for baggage train duties. The Jute charge will be pure bloody murder. They'll do their best, because they're good lads, but they'll never keep their heads. One escape route isn't enough.'

Arthur thought hard. 'Very well, count off the first fifteen men in each line out of those closest to the centre of the mound. That's about ninety men, yes? They must be sent through the centre gap. The rest of your boys, inexperienced or not, will then have plenty of space to manoeuvre round the south end of the ditch, although I suspect that the men on the north side will be trapped between ditch, corpses and trees. We have to move the largest number of men through these three gaps as quickly as possible, so be prepared to begin the evacuation the moment the opportunity arises.'

Arthur's voice dropped and his eyes turned opaque, almost white. 'This will be cold-blooded murder, my friends. Shite, I'd have volunteered if I had been asked. But to be tricked into being used as the bait in a nasty and dishonourable trap . . . I feel sick to be a British warrior on this wicked day.'

'I'd never have believed that Lord Ector could be false,' Eanraig said dourly. Arthur's information had come as a shock to the veteran, who was used to cleaner tactics in the time of the Dragon King.

'I'll swear that Ector didn't know. He is my kinsman, and I saw no lies on his face. It showed no deception at all. He believes what he told us.' Arthur's face showed new lines between the eyes, and Germanus swore inwardly to see his charge's loss of faith in the men who should have earned his trust. 'In the meantime, cover yourself with raw earth. Taliessin swears it will help to control the burning. We have a bag of sand here and I'd recommend that every man tries to find something similar to protect them against the flames.' He looked toward the Saxon lines. 'If the enemy gives us the luxury of time.'

Havar had been given his extra men and was chafing at the bit to begin his attack, confident that this new force would drive the pitiful defenders back into their own camp. All he needed now was the order from Cerdic. He watched closely as Cynric rode like the wind to reach the southern reserves before dismounting and calling the captains together. With his thousand men and the thousand reserves near the south gate, he knew that Bran's pitiful defence would be turned into bloody shreds of meat within the hour.

Pacing and swearing, while praying to Odin for the strength and resilience of the god's hammer, Havar waited with his whole mind set on exacting his revenge. He had heard the unspeakable details of the carnage that had routed the baggage train from his reserves, but his mind rejected the concept of such a weapon. He refused to believe that his warriors could be terrified into hiding behind their defences.

The battle call came with a scream from an ancient ram's horn used to rally the Saxon troops from time immemorial. Cerdic wore the instrument on his belt, even though he no longer had the lung power to blow it, for the horn was plated with precious beaten gold. A grandson, come to his first battle, blew on it lustily and the sound echoed along the walls, even carrying as far as the waiting Britons.

'They're coming,' Arthur yelled. 'Pass the word along to your brothers. You must fight as single warriors . . . hear me? No lines, because it will be too hard to disengage when the time comes to run. Be ready to move on my order, or when the first catapults fly. Give the bastards hell, so they'll think twice before they try to steal our lands again.'

Dirty, muddy and reminiscent of earth golems, the Britons waited in front of their ditch. For ease of retreat, the front row had moved forward and given themselves room to manoeuvre. Even with their hurried preparations, Arthur knew that many British warriors would die as collateral damage in the butchery that Bran intended to inflict on the Saxons. In the depths of his mind, he was aware that this carnage was designed to ensure a period of peace for the towns of the south-west, to give them time to consolidate their fortifications, but the betrayal hurt him nevertheless.

'Good Britons should be prepared to die for the greater good,' Gareth murmured at his side. 'Like you, I would have volunteered willingly if I had known what was to happen, but Bran would have been wise to be frank with his warriors and then ask for volunteers. He'll have difficulty regaining our trust after this treachery.' The young warrior's voice was calm and emotionless, although he must have felt some anger at being used so ruthlessly. 'War's a dirty game, but it should still be played as honestly as possible. I've never had any real illusions, because my father told me that Artor was as noble as was possible during his reign, but still accepted that men must sometimes be sacrificed for the sake of the rest.'

'Steady!' Arthur howled, interrupting him. 'Now! On your guard! They're on the move!'

Sword and knife raised, Artor's son stepped forward to meet the approaching Jutes who were loping towards the British line, their faces crudely painted to represent devils and beasts out of legend. He barely had time to glance towards the southern defenders, who were so thoroughly outnumbered and demoralised, when the first of the Jutes reached him and tried to decapitate him with a looping swing of his single-bladed axe, exposing his own torso in the process. Arthur evaded the overhand blow with ease and the Jute was caught off balance. A quick manoeuvre with the Dragon Knife and the warrior fell, neatly disembowelled. Battle had been joined.

As he engaged the enemy, Arthur felt no vagueness or lack of concentration. His mind was crystal clear, probably because he was so blazingly angry at Bran's treachery. Once again, Germanus's painstaking lessons with sword and knife bore fruit, and he found himself able to watch other aspects of the battle while he fought. As he downed another Jute warrior, whose impetuous forward rush came to an abrupt halt when Oakheart spitted him, Arthur saw the line of Britons holding the southern ditch begin to waver and break apart. They were so cruelly outnumbered and outreached that Arthur's anger grew even hotter as he watched the thin line of troops chopped to ribbons. He also registered that half of the southern Saxons had stopped short of the fire-pits and seemed to be awaiting instructions. Then he saw the vicious load from the first catapult hurtle over the defender's heads and land within the mass of charging Saxons.

'Retreat!' Arthur roared as loudly as he could, even as he despatched a Jute warrior who was attempting to pin Germanus down. 'Retreat! Pass the order! Retreat!' Then, with pumping legs, the two men ran towards the end of the ditch.

The ground shook as a second container of Marine Fire

exploded as it struck the ground. Some enterprising engineer, with a mind honed to gruesome efficiency by his long-distance view of war, had added small shards of iron, lead and glass . . . anything that would melt in the extreme heat. What was already a devastating weapon was rendered hideous by molten glass and metal that stuck to unprotected skin. Arthur could barely imagine the agony of it. He ran, making sure that Germanus and Gareth were with him, cutting down any Saxon or Jute who tried to engage them with a ruthless efficiency that he had never known he possessed. Other Britons ran with them, trusting to the young lord's luck to save them, while confusion reigned in the Jute ranks from one end of the ditch to the other. Where could they run? Back into the hell fire? Or should they follow the Britons who were fleeing before them into the heart of the enemy camp? Milling and thoroughly confused, they had no chance of escape. In the chaos of fire that rained down from above, the Saxon and Jute commanders lost all control of their warriors.

Eanraig was directing his troops through their single gap with admirable speed. He raised one hand in salute and disappeared as Arthur reached the pile of dead bodies at the northern end of the ditch, a gruesome memorial to all lost causes. Men were fleeing in single file between the bodies and the ditch, their eyes wide and horrified at how close they were to the innocuous, gravel-bottomed ditch with its harmless pools of water that would become deadly the moment the Marine Fire began to rain down on them.

'Go round the corpses. It'll take longer, but it's better than being too close when the fire starts.' Arthur's voice was clearly audible as the sudden whizzing sound of a catapulted container passed directly over his head. He ducked instinctively.

One after another the catapults fired a second volley, a little closer to the ditch, and were immediately reloaded. As the spreading fire cut through the rearguard of the Saxon attack, panicking warriors ran forward, away from the ugly, writhing death that burned men into shapeless lumps of charcoal and carbon.

Bran is a cold and clever bastard, Arthur thought, as he turned to block a wicked sword thrust that would have parted his spine if it had landed. The Saxons and Jutes were following Arthur's line of retreat out of an instinctive belief that the Britons knew a way to survive the hell that had set the air on fire. Even Havar had belatedly accepted that these Britons would not run, and knew the retreat was not cowardice.

Breathlessly, and with his heart pounding in his chest, Arthur reached the end of the mound. Disregarding his heavy armour, he gave one last burst of speed and plunged forward just as a wall of fire, taller than the tallest Jute, raced down the dyke like a wall of flood water. Arthur would have continued to run had Germanus not tackled him round the knees and brought him crashing to the ground.

Spluttering and protesting, Arthur found himself suddenly dowsed in sand and mud as he belatedly discovered that he was on fire. The Saxon at his heels was also on the ground and Gareth was dousing him in sand and dirt as well, patting down smouldering cloth and pulling off the man's armour as the buckles sizzled and parted company. Germanus checked Arthur for burns and discovered that only a small section of his leather trews had caught fire, leaving only minor lesions that would soon heal.

'Did all our men escape?' Arthur asked later. His own burns dressed, he was watching the Saxon warrior being led away. 'I think I was one of the last through the gap.'

'Our Saxon friend was the last one through and he's being taken to the healers on the orders of Taliessin himself. He's swearing and cursing us in his heathen tongue, and he describes us as monsters from hell and devoid of all honour. Us, would you believe! After Spinis?' Gareth sounded mortally insulted, but Arthur's sympathies were with the Saxon, especially when, having climbed to the top of the mound, he surveyed the chaos that remained on the battlefield.

The southern contingent of Celts had been forced to leave their wounded behind, and those who had tried to carry their friends to safety had been caught by the wall of flame. Already outnumbered and hacked to ribbons by Cynric's Saxons, they died horribly as they tried to reach their own lines.

The range of the catapults had been readjusted so that the last of the enemy fleeing back to the relative safety of Calleva still remained under fire. With unimaginable and hideous death both before and behind them, Saxons and Jutes ran in all directions, desperate to do anything to escape the missiles that rained down on them. Bran had ordered the reserves into the field in the south to block any escape from the leaping flames, and burning men were running crazily among their fellows, spreading the fire until they fell to the ground. Only Cynric's men, the ones he had ordered to halt before they reached the fire-pits, remained a viable force, and Arthur watched as a single mounted man, probably Cynric, called all the survivors to form around him. Grouped into compact squares, they began to lope away in the distinctive Saxon run that could cover miles with ease.

Arthur turned to Germanus and Gareth, who had joined him on top of the mound. 'May their gods be with them. Mithras will take his revenge on us for what we have done today. I'm ashamed to have been a part of it.'

At the northern end of the battlefield, the British cavalry waited. Once Bedwyr would have been desperate to pursue the invaders, for he held an unquenchable desire to blot out the memory of his early dealings with the monsters of Caer Fyrddin, but even

Bedwyr's long enmity towards the Saxons had weakened and now, in the wake of such hideous suffering, he found that he had no stomach for the murder of frantic men, reduced to flight by mindless, unimaginable panic.

Amazed, Arthur watched as the scene unfolded before him. He saw Havar die in a suicidal charge, but the White Dragon perished for nothing. Of Cerdic and Cynric there was no obvious sign as the Saxon warriors retreated into the distance, but after an hour of watching the slaughter Arthur's keen young eyes made out a second contingent of Saxons riding hard and fast towards the south.

'There goes Cerdic and his son,' Arthur hissed with disgust. 'At least Cynric raised his sword against the enemy. But Bran and Cerdic contrived to stay safely behind the action while watching worthier men die.' Arthur was so bitter that Germanus felt a worm of concern twist in his mind. 'When I heard that Havar was responsible for what I saw at Spinis I thought he was the cruellest, most barbaric creature alive, but at least he was prepared to get his own hands dirty. This . . . this abomination is an affront against our noble forebears and against the gods themselves . . . and we will pay dearly for it.'

Germanus laid his large, calloused hands on Arthur's shoulder and pressed gently. The warmth of the older warrior's body was a comfort, but Arthur was weary of pretences. He was certain now that his existence was an embarrassment to many of the people who had professed love for him. He acquitted Bedwyr of any sin, for not by word or deed had his foster-father ever shown himself to be false. But Bran? Even Taliessin, who wanted the best for him, saw Arthur as a pawn in a greater game.

'The Dragon King would cower in shame at what we have done today. Any justification we invent for our actions will consist of convenient lies. It's like Lorcan's story of the two mothers claiming one baby, so the child was ordered to be cut in half: we don't deserve to possess this land if we're prepared to turn it into ashes rather than relinquish it.'

'You are speaking treason, Arthur,' Gareth interrupted, his eyes jerking towards the temporary platform where Bran was surrounded by his captains. 'So be silent.'

'Treason?' Arthur shouted, and every man on the dais turned his head in their direction. 'Treason is standing here shamelessly and watching while murder is done.'

Then he turned on his heel and trotted down the mound to reach his quarters in the midst of the sea of tents. When Germanus and Gareth arrived later, they found him asleep on his pallet, still in his armour and entangled in the wool coverlet. He thrashed in his sleep, cursing invisible enemies and thrusting at them with nerveless, fumbling hands.

Germanus pointed at Arthur's shield, sword and knife where they lay on the camp table in the afternoon light.

'He has cleaned his weapons. Although he was heartsick with shame, he still cleaned his weapons. Whether Bran wanted to kill him or not, he has created a *weapon* that he can never control again. He has been a prize fool.'

'Then Arthur will have an even greater need to keep us by his side,' Gareth responded drily. 'Crucibles don't only melt metals so that we can skim off the dross. Today, Arthur was tested in a crucible of fire. I cannot guess what is to become of him, but I will follow him anyway.'

'And I,' Germanus sighed. 'To death, if need be. The good God has a purpose for Arthur, so we must ensure that his promise is fulfilled.'

'Aye,' whispered Gareth, and his young eyes were very old.

CHAPTER XVI

THE WHEEL TURNS

Hic iacet Arthurus, rex quondam rexque futurus.
(Here lies Arthur, the once and future king.)

Thomas Malory, *Le Morte d'Arthur*

Bells rang loudly and raggedly with the arrival of morning. The basilica in Calleva Atrebatum celebrated the town's deliverance in joyous song as a light snow began to fall. Out on the battlefield, where workers from the British baggage train attempted to determine which charred corpses were Saxon or Jute and which were Briton, the sounds were oddly comforting and the snow was a godsend. It hid what must be concealed.

After the battle, Rhys ap Myrddion had vomited until his stomach and throat were raw. He swore by everything he believed was true and pure that he would serve Bran no more, and the secret of Marine Fire would be lost for ever in these isles, even if he should be tortured for the recipe. He and Taliessin had wept together, for like most intelligent and gifted men they had never expected Bran to actually use their father's weapon of last resort so ruthlessly. Together, they decided that their mother must not be told what she had been made a party to, for Taliessin appreciated that the ageing Nimue would demand recompense from King Bran for the men he had murdered so casually. By demanding reparation, the Lady of the Lake would place herself in peril in these days when honour was superficial. Taliessin had passed on to Rhys the substance of Arthur's accusations against Bran, and the smith would have been sick all over again if his stomach had still held anything.

'We betrayed those fine young men. Not deliberately, but just as certainly as Bran betrayed them when we gave the Marine Fire to him. We didn't want to know. Father would say we were too pleased with ourselves for having solved the puzzle of Marine Fire to consider for a moment the outcome of our gift. We were arrogant.' Rhys began to weep silently, and Taliessin had no words of consolation in him.

'Aye, Rhys, we were, but mine is the greater guilt. I knew these powerful men, while you did not. We have become that thing we have fought so hard against – all to maintain a little power for ourselves. I am more ashamed than I can bear.'

Arthur stood on the mound as the snow began to fall. He was clean and scrubbed now, although he had had to break the skin of ice that lay over the water bucket before he could wash away the dirt. When he had finished, the water had the dirty, red-brown colouring of old blood. Dressed in full armour and clean clothes, he had rinsed his soiled possessions like a common soldier, desperate to remove every trace of his clash with the Saxons and Jutes.

Sleepily, Germanus had tried to convince him that he had fought cleanly and fairly. He assured him that he would never be called to account for anything he had said the previous day, adding that whispers were already passing through the camp of his courage and the cruel ruse that had been played on the defenders at the ditch by Bran and the other rulers.

So Arthur had gone out into the grey morning feeling almost at peace, if not happy. Once outside, he avoided the churned mud that threatened to mar his clean boots until he reached the mound. There, he was content just to watch the hard labour of the muffled peasants as they dealt with the detritus that had once been two thousand fighting warriors. It felt right to be here as the field was cleansed, almost as if he could put the betrayal and dishonour behind him if he saw the battle through to the very end.

A sweet cacophony of sound rose behind him, reedy and eerie, as a Hibernian warrior played an odd musical instrument consisting of a bellows and pipes. Its sound was a tuneful wail, the perfect accompaniment to a simple reed flute played by another gnarled warrior of uncertain antecedents. The third man in the cloaked group was Taliessin, and Arthur spied his brother Rhys standing behind him as he marked out the dolorous beat on a small drum.

When the four men reached the top of the mound, Taliessin began to sing of loss, guilt and betrayal. His song had no name and referred to no particular place or time, but in it a warrior lamented his betrayal of his honour by cheating to win his heart's desire from another suitor. The words were ambiguous, but Arthur spotted the relevance of the dirge immediately, and hoped that Bran was not abroad to hear it. The sweet, light notes of the harper, who had chosen to leave his instrument in his tent, rose over the killing field as his voice changed to that of a woman swearing to desert the man she loved because his honour had been besmirched by his love for her.

Arthur shuddered as the pipes wailed and Taliessin's voice wept for happier times. Then the woman, the cause of the dishonour in his song, chose to die because two fine men had been destroyed because of her. Although innocent, she blamed herself for a tragedy brought about by her deceptive, unwanted beauty. She tore at her thick white skin and cut her long, raven hair. Then she pressed a knife against her snowy breast as she sang. Arthur could see it all.

Snow, fall upon my gravestone and erase it.
Cover every mention of my name,
Or else some other foolish girl will read it
And envy my dishonour and my shame.

Beauty is the curse of foolish creatures,
Empty, useless and beyond our feeble will.
Let me lie, and lay no flowers upon me
For beauty such as mine will surely kill.

Winter winds, come freeze the earth around me,
And drive away all memory of my fame.
Forgive those souls who sinned because they loved me
And let me be forgotten with my blame.

Then Rhys, in a voice rusty with disuse, sang a simple country song about a man who loved his cat and mourned it with a terrible weeping when it finally died. Only at the end of the song did the listener realise that the owner of the cat had accidently killed his pet while seeking to poison his wife.

Arthur didn't know whether to laugh or to weep, but the song seemed appropriate as he watched the stoic peasants divide the grotesque bodies of the two armies into two unequal mounds. In this damp weather cremation would prove difficult, and one wit below the dyke joked crudely that it was a pity that all the Marine

Fire had been used, as a little fire-starting fuel would be a useful tool for their labours. To their credit, his friends turned their backs on him.

Both Saxons and Jutes had fought with courage against a weapon that could not be countered with muscle or skill. Arthur had seen many heroic acts performed by the enemy from his position before the mound as the attacking warriors sacrificed themselves for friends or kinfolk, daring to rip blazing armour off a suffering warrior and burning their own bodies in the process. Still more hardy souls had bravely faced superior numbers of cavalry with fire behind them, so that there was nowhere for them to run. These courageous men included Havar, a man whom Arthur had previously loathed.

'If the gods were to ask where the greater honour lies, I'd rather stand with the dead than live in the fading, degraded shadows of what we once were,' he said to the falling snow.

'So that's how you feel, Arthur?' a voice murmured silkily at his back. 'I thought so.' Bran had come up behind him, free of his usual guards for once. He had clearly heard Arthur's words.

A few inches shorter than Arthur, the king was irritated because he was forced to look up to see directly into his uncle's eyes. He was conscious that a few strands of grey hair streaked his plaits and suggested infirmity. Suddenly Bran felt old as he stood beside this boy, so tall and strong, with the certainty of youth shining in his eyes.

Arthur swivelled so that he half faced his kinsman and swallowed hard. Bran saw the Adam's apple jerk convulsively and made the crucial error of assuming that Arthur was afraid of him. In truth, Arthur was having considerable difficulty in coping with the screaming noise in his head and in resisting an almost primal urge to strike the king's smug, handsome face.

'Many less generous men would read treachery into that comment,' Bran added. His smile was open, frank and friendly, but Arthur knew his family very well, their superior intelligence, their talent for subterfuge and a shared charismatic charm. Bran was the least adept at wielding the family social skills, having been shy and retiring in his youth, but once he stepped out of the Dragon King's shadow and became the last hope of the tribes in the struggle to preserve their way of life he had gradually gained in confidence and ambition. Even Ector, Artor's chosen successor, had initially been considered a threat by his father, but Ector had failed to live up to Artor's expectations, not because he lacked ability, but because the time of High Kings of Britannia was over. Artor had made these isles shake and brought all men to their knees, but now Ector, his heir, was only another tribal claimant. Bran was now the supreme commander, the Dux Bellorum of the army of Britain, so he could gaze on Arthur with equanimity.

'You may read what you want into my words, Bran. You showed by your use of me yesterday that you have little liking for me. If we weren't worth the truth when we were in the line facing the enemy, why do you care what I think now?'

Two spots of colour appeared on Bran's cheekbones. 'Are you accusing me of trying to arrange your death on the battlefield?'

In his inexperience, Arthur found he was actually enjoying this bitter exchange. He was learning that having the opportunity to speak his mind released the anger that burned within him. 'I don't need to accuse you of anything, Bran. Every onlooker, every fellow warrior on the line and every cavalryman on the battlefield had their opportunity to observe and judge your behaviour. So were the other kings judged, and found wanting for their avoidance of danger. Don't frown, Bran! As the overall commander, your personal courage is not in doubt – but men such as Artair clearly avoided their duty. I don't need to say a thing. The king of the Atrebates was too cunning to command his troops from the front and chose to remain behind the lines in relative safety. Essentially, he left a boy of sixteen in charge of three hundred warriors and, by default, so did you, although you ordered Artair to the line. Furthermore, you ordered me to make myself a target by wearing that red cloak at the front of my warriors. Why?'

'You are similar in appearance to my grandfather,' Bran replied candidly. 'The very name of the Dragon King inspires fear and awe in the Saxons, for they deem him to be magical because they couldn't defeat him. As I told the council, I decided to use you to remind them of his promise that he would return one day when the Britons were in need of him. I decided to let the Saxons sweat a little by suggesting that the great man lives again. Was I wrong to use their superstitions against them?' Bran's light eyes were direct and demanded an answer.

Arthur considered the question for a moment. 'No. I would do the same in similar circumstances, but I should have been told what your plans for me entailed. I'd have volunteered anyway – most of the men would – but you didn't give anyone that chance.' Suddenly, the whole conversation began to sicken him. He felt physically ill, and this verbal exchange was no longer fun. 'Anyway, all I really want of you is an explanation. You pretended to value me as a kinsman and you acted as if you loved me, when it is clear you consider me to be some kind of threat. I loved and trusted you, Bran. I respected you as the head of the family and I would have done anything within my power to further your cause. I feel like a fucking idiot now, because I fought for someone who could release those horrible weapons on an unprepared enemy – and me!'

Bran sighed. 'We won, Arthur – we did what we had to do. We

don't have sufficient men to lose a single battle from now on, but more Saxons are crossing the Litus Saxonicum every year. Yesterday I was forced to kill as many as possible for the smallest losses on our part. If you don't like the methods I use, that's too bad. In my place, you would have done the same thing. The difference is that I shoulder my duty and try not to whine about it.'

Would I have done the same, Arthur wondered? Perhaps I would if my back was to the wall, but I'd have called for volunteers rather than sacrifice novices just because they'd be the least missed. And so, out of innate honesty, Arthur chose not to answer his kinsman, who shook his head with irritation.

'Think what you like, then, but don't try to take anything that belongs to me,' Bran responded coldly. 'We will remain civil at all times, for family ties mean something to me, regardless of what you believe. Remember what you are. You are a landless bastard and you'll only hurt your family in Arden if you cause me trouble.'

'You warned me often enough about the poison in our blood – I was almost paralysed on the battlefield with the terror of it. I never expected to see that madness in you, Bran, for you always seemed the most reasonable of men.'

Arthur had finally hit a nerve, and Bran paled. His canines were exposed by his sneering lips as his handsome features were twisted into ugliness by active dislike, leaving just an angry, ageing and embittered man.

'I don't want anything of yours, my lord. I never did. When I swore allegiance to you, I did so for life. And that oath remains strong, despite what I know of you now. Leave me be in Arden, Bran, where I will happily support my brother when he becomes the king of the forest. Please understand that I have no ambitions – none. I have seen the responsibility for our people twist you out of shape and I want nothing of it. You can assure my sister that she should never doubt my loyalty, but from this point onwards I'll not dance to anyone's tune unless I know the steps.'

Bran laughed. 'You're so melodramatic, Arthur, like a bad harpist's song. I won't pursue you, because too many people would notice. Believe it or not, I care for you. I've watched you grow to manhood. I'd prefer that you were short and fat, with two left thumbs and bad coordination, but in these days when all glory and beauty is going you're a reminder of what the Britons were in days gone by.' The truth shone out of him. Arthur remembered Bran's history and wondered if he could have borne Bran's burdens. 'I'll be forgotten in the destruction that is to come. I'll be just another Dux Bellorum trying to maintain the status quo in a time of rapid change. I wish I could stop the wind, or halt Fortuna's wheel, or whatever fancy metaphor Taliessin would use to describe these times. But I'm just a man who has had the great misfortune to be the last heir of a legend. Even Artor failed, and soon all this beautiful land will be in the hands of Cerdic and his ilk. Yet you look at me with scorn because I have used dishonourable means to even the odds. Don't be a baby, Arthur, for the Dragon King would have understood. I swear to you that if it was in my power I would use Marine Fire in every Saxon town until I had burned them all – alive or dead! I'd not lose a single night's sleep over it. You may call me mad if it makes you feel better, but I know exactly what I'm doing. I don't have the luxury of honourable scruples, because too many people depend on me. When you've walked in my shoes for a while, come back and tell me again that I'm a dishonourable monster.'

Bran was breathless with unleashed passion when he finished his speech, and Arthur gaped at him. He had never considered the demands of kingship, having a boy's glamorous and sanitised vision of total rule. He had comforted himself with the idea that Bran was crazed with hubris: he had never considered that Bran understood what he had done and had chosen this way because he believed it to be the least damaging answer to a hopeless dilemma. For the first time, Arthur saw traces of nobility and real courage in his kinsman. His face must have shown his sudden understanding because Bran turned away.

Bran had seen something in Arthur as well, something Arthur had no idea of. His eyes had caught the flat grey panes of Arthur's stare and he realised that he'd seen a similar expression many years earlier. Artor had worn that same look, and the High King had never lied. He had never wished to be High King. Cautiously, for Bran was a wise man despite his acquired bitterness, the king of the Ordovice tribe drew back from intemperate action, his face smoothing almost magically with his decision to let Arthur live.

'Very well, Arthur. Enough has been said between us – probably too much. I will hold you to your word, so just keep out of my sight.'

As Bran strode away through the thickening snow flurries, Arthur wondered what had brought the king out in such inclement weather to see the results of his decisions. Perhaps decency was not quite dead in Bran. Perhaps he had spoken the truth, in which case he was to be pitied, and Arthur had simply lacked the sensitivity or the years to understand.

'But I don't care either way,' Arthur whispered to himself. 'This dishonour will be punished. Neither the Saxons nor the gods will be mocked. Such weapons cannot be stolen and used with impunity.'

The population of Calleva Atrebatum ventured out from their houses and viewed the cost of their deliverance. Some of the citizens had watched the carnage from the walls of the town and felt odd about the means used to save them, but most of the townspeople were happy just to be alive. When the Saxons had arrived on their doorstep, Calleva had known what would happen to it if the walls and gates should be penetrated. So, out of gratitude for the raising of the siege, the inhabitants stripped the surrounding woods of dry firewood to finish what the Marine Fire had started, the cremation of the dead.

Given the steadily falling snow, Calleva put on her shiniest face to welcome her benefactors. Citizens huddled in bright woollen blankets and knitted gloves pressed fresh bread, dried fruit, sticky honey sweetmeats and garlands of ivy, green foliage and holly on the relieving warriors. One woman passed a silver ring into Arthur's hand. The large fish adorning it had a single eye, a freshwater pearl. He tried to return this bounty but the woman was swept away by the crowd.

Many of the celebrating citizens recognised Arthur as the tall lad in the red cloak in the centre of the line at the front of the ditch. Somehow, they had discovered his name and he heard it shouted adoringly by a hundred voices. The experience was very odd, but pleasant. The young man basked for a few minutes in the praise of the common folk as he rode with his friends among the foot soldiers who had held the line at the mound, until he realised how few they were. Eanraig looked up with a cheerful, twisted grin for Arthur, which the young warrior returned with a gaiety he didn't feel.

'Old men and boys – that's what we were. A ragtag of an army!'

'But the ragtag showed Bran how men can fight and die when they are committed to an ideal,' Germanus whispered to his pupil. Only then did Arthur realise that he had spoken aloud.

'Wave to them, Arthur,' Gareth suggested from his right side. 'The girls love it – and they love you as well.'

So Arthur waved and the girls did indeed love him, if only for that cold, pure afternoon. Their eyes shone and their rosy cheeks were glossy with youth and pride. They ran, skirts swirling to reveal knitted stockings and sensible boots, as they followed the young warriors to the forum. Arthur was ecstatic to discover that the heroes of the hour had been billeted in the public baths, which courtesy of the hypocaust were warm even in the midst of winter. With a crow of pure enjoyment, Lorcan claimed a space for their possessions in one of the dressing rooms, while Germanus took their horses to an area close to the inn at the southern gate where picket lines had been set up. There was insufficient stable room to house the cavalry mounts, but the hardy beasts would survive happily within the city walls, as long as blankets covered their withers and a plentiful supply of hay and water was available.

Arthur and his fellow warriors enjoyed the pleasures of the baths and of the glossy red-cheeked girls in the quiet of the more private places within the confines of that public building. But they were also forced to endure the questions of the townsfolk, who suddenly found that the need for cleanliness overrode their dislike of bathing in public. They had seen the explosions of Marine Fire and the after-effects, and they were eager to know what it was, where it had come from and the likelihood of its being used again in future battles. Arthur tried to be frank, but he judged any detailed description to be unnecessary. After all, why should he do Bran's work for him?

So the days turned into several weeks, until the citizens of Calleva Atrebatum began to wish the hungry army would take itself elsewhere. Winter was never a good time for an army to be eating its way through a town's supplies, even a wealthy place like Calleva. Long ago, the Romans had set up potteries, iron workshops and sawmills here, and a large sector of the current population still worked at these skilled employments. Four- and five-storey *insulae* had been built close to the business centre, and now the lives of the inhabitants were affected by the squads of swaggering and drunken warriors who clogged the heart of the town.

Meanwhile, on the outskirts, where the villas of the richer citizens were surrounded by fruit trees, the populace also felt the onerous effects of supporting an army, for these richer citizens had the excess food and space to quarter the kings and their retinues, all at no cost to their guests. Hospitality becomes grudging when an occupying army makes no move to leave its comfortable billet and return to its home. Gratitude wears thin. In a spirit that was far less charitable than Bran expected, the citizens began to duck their heads so the warriors couldn't see the active dislike that darkened their expressions.

Arthur would have left in the first week, but Bedwyr asked him to stay with the remnants of the army. 'I'm not sure why Bran chooses to remain here in Calleva. To all intents and purposes, we're waiting for Cerdic and his son to reappear, probably somewhere near Noviomagus.' Bedwyr grimaced in disgust. 'I refuse to call it by that Cissa name, even if it's only old men like me who still call it by its Roman title. Anyway, Bran expects reprisals from Cerdic and Cynric once they have made good their escape. When Cerdic departed he took only six hundred warriors with him, but that is still the basis of an army, especially if he can find reinforcements in the south and the east, so Bran is becoming increasingly nervous. And we won't have Marine Fire to back us up in any future battles.'

Arthur grinned and Bedwyr wondered when his son's smile had become so cynical and world-weary. 'It serves Bran right to be worried. Cerdic's single most important aim will be to destroy the army of the Britons, and Bran in particular. I'd still prefer to leave this gilded cesspit and go back to Arden, because I can only enjoy so many Roman bathhouses. Besides, the riff-raff is fouling the pools.' Bedwyr laughed, exactly as his stepson intended. 'The people of Calleva want us gone even more than I want to leave, Father. And I can't really blame them.'

'I agree. They're being eaten out of house and home and none of their women are safe. I'd like to think you haven't contributed to the disgrace of some of Calleva's daughters. I've seen the way they look at you, my boy.'

'Father, one advantage of reaching manhood is that I've discovered how to take advantage of willing and generous ladies. Don't worry – I have no intention of seducing any innocent young girls. I have too much to learn, and there are lovely matrons and widows enough to keep me more than happy.'

Bedwyr covered his ears, but Arthur saw his lips twitching. Then the Arden Knife began to laugh, the first honest mirth the old man had shown since before the battle. The two men ended up rolling on the tessellated floor of the baths, where Lorcan was guarding their possessions while Germanus and Gareth were off on some nameless business. The priest watched with avuncular amusement while father and son wrestled like overgrown children.

Given Bedwyr's reservations, Arthur wasn't surprised when a courier rode up to the south gate of Calleva Atrebatum shortly after the town gates had been closed for the night. The evening was perfect, clear and bright, with deep snow and no breeze to burn the eyes, although the heavy cloud cover had been blown away by gale force winds in the upper air. Stars shone whitely on a velvety black background, while from the top of the wall the scars of Marine Fire were covered by deep blankets of soft, unblemished snow. Into this peaceful scene the courier's frantic knocking with the hilt of his knife was an intrusion, and its sound was only drowned out by his bellowing demand to be allowed to enter the compound.

Eventually, the gatekeeper emerged from his small lodge and opened a door set into the large, latched gate. Swearing vilely, the courier was forced to dismount, lead his horse through the entry, and then remount before insisting on being taken directly to King Bran.

Arthur observed the courier's arrival from the walls. He had taken to going to the south gate for a few hours every night to relax and watch the tracks that met at this ancient crossroads. He had a feeling that circumstances were rushing together, as if their actions at Calleva had finally been judged in some higher court and punishment was about to be meted out by the gods. He chose the south gate because that direction seemed the most likely to deliver news of the Saxons. When he saw the courier approaching, he immediately tasted something metallic in his mouth, as if he had bitten his tongue. He sensed the promise of difficult times ahead.

In the grand villa that had been taken over by Bran and Ector, lamps were soon lit and warriors were despatched to the adjoining villas where the other kings were billeted. Arthur saw Bedwyr coming at a shambling run, and decided to join him. He might not trust Bran, but he might as well find out what was going on.

'Where did the courier come from, Father? I saw him approaching from the south.'

Bedwyr put his forefinger over Arthur's mouth to silence him. 'Keep your tongue between your teeth, boy. Listen if you must, but this courier comes from Venta Belgarum and there's no likelihood of good news from that quarter.'

The villa's atrium had been selected for the meeting, for the open space was large and possessed a number of stone bench seats and an area of dry, brittle grass where other men could sit on cushions. Bran had already ensconced himself on a marble seat beside the pool, over which a melancholy, immature willow tree was drooping as if in mourning for the loss of the old ways. When the leaders of the tribes had been seated, including the younger generation such as Mareddyd and Eamonn, Bran rose to his feet.

'I have just received distressing news from Venta Belgarum.'

The room buzzed with sudden consternation, as if a hive of bees had been disturbed.

'Cerdic reached Vectis over a week ago, and although he was sick with a lung infection he ordered his sons to crush all opposition at Magnus Portus, Portus Adurni and Venta Belgarum itself. Reinforcements from Noviomagus and Anderida had been summoned in readiness even before he besieged Calleva Atrebatum. We fell into a well-conceived trap when we threw our weight against the forces surrounding this town, because the whole Saxon plan was a feint to bring us into the field here. Venta Belgarum had been the real goal all along.'

A bubble of unholy laughter began to form at the base of Arthur's throat as he sensed Bran's embarrassment. Knowing his boy, Bedwyr elbowed him hard in the ribs.

'So, do we attack the Saxons who have besieged Venta Belgarum? If we imagine a large city surrounded by even more enemy warriors than there were here, the situation will immediately become clear.' Bran's voice was sardonic, as if the honest part of his nature was belatedly admitting the potential problems that the Britons faced. 'We shall hold a council of war tomorrow morning, after we have slept on this new information. We will consider our options before I issue my orders. Taliessin! Rhys! You will remain here, for I need to speak to you in private.'

Arthur and Bedwyr waited outside in the shadows of the trees surrounding the villa to discover how the sons of Myrddion would fare with Bran. They had to wait for some time.

The night was freezing, as if the absence of cloud cover permitted the god of winter to place his long, blue fingers on the earth to chill it. Every surface was burning to the touch and the snow was a crisp, stark blanket over all. The stillness seemed to enclose all of Calleva in a glass globe, invisible but ultimately fatal as the soft air was sucked out of the wintry town. Arthur felt the familiar itch settle into his head.

Eventually, just when Bedwyr was becoming seriously concerned about Taliessin and Rhys, the brothers stormed out of the mansion with their cloaks swirling around their shoulders in their haste and rage. Arthur and Bedwyr fell into step beside them and all four men returned to Taliessin's spartan billet in the forum.

'What did Bran want?' Bedwyr demanded without preamble. 'He's obviously made you very angry. So tell us, master harper, in case Bran tries to enforce his decrees on you.'

Taliessin lowered himself onto a stone bench. Although he was still only thirty-six and at the peak of his powers, he moved like a much older man. This weariness was echoed in his powerfully built brother, who was near to three years younger than his sibling. Both men had obviously been dealt a vicious blow, and were now mentally licking their wounds until they could bring themselves to consider Bran's ultimatum.

'I look at Bran and I see traces of Artor in him – and my heart is sickened by the likeness,' Taliessin began hesitantly.

'Oh, spit it out, brother! Neither of us ever expected Bran to treat us like traitors. Nor did we believe he would threaten us – and *Mother* – if he doesn't get his hands on more Marine Fire,' Rhys snapped, his rage burning white-hot behind his dark eyes.

'Are you going to obey him?' Arthur asked carefully. He was

appalled at the thought of such a monstrous weapon in Bran's hands once again, not because Arthur believed the king was evil, but because Bran imagined that its use would save the Celtic people. Bran would do as he threatened, and burn every Saxon settlement to the ground.

'No, we will not comply with his wishes,' Taliessin replied for both men. 'We will need to flee to Caer Gai, fast and hard, so that Mother can be warned and the hill people mustered to protect her. We don't wish to go to war with Bran, but we will if he threatens Nimue again.'

Bedwyr nodded. 'Without the use of Marine Fire, the south will fall and our people will be forced to abandon their lands, so I'm glad I don't have to make your choices. As for now, do you need assistance to escape from Calleva? If you do, we can help. In fact, I've already had an excellent idea about how to mask your departure, but you'll have to begin your preparations now.'

Wisely, Bedwyr was ignoring the underlying problem. As the possessors of the secret of Marine Fire, the sons of Myrddion were the only ones who could determine the fate of the Britons in the south-west. On them lay the harsh weight of thousands of lives, which must be weighed against the moral and ethical cost of utilising such a fearsome weapon.

And they decided to ensure that the key to the liquid was lost for ever.

The brothers packed speedily and moved down into one of the cellar rooms in the foundations below the baths. Tonight, Bedwyr reasoned, Bran would leave the brothers to stew over his demands. Tomorrow would see them quietly arrested, and the terrified kings would raise no objections. It was vital that Taliessin and Rhys should have made their escape before Bran came searching for them.

'Stay here, regardless of the dangers, and ignore everything you hear unless it comes from us,' Bedwyr warned them.

Above ground, the master of Arden began to make his preparations. 'Arthur, Lorcan . . . all of you, let the populace know what lies in wait for them in the immediate future. Bran plans to leave Calleva to its fate, now that the south has fallen to the Saxons. Make sure they understand that Cerdic is angry beyond reason with Calleva because of his burned warriors, and he intends that the entire population will feel the lash of his rage. Believe me, within hours the citizens of Calleva will have made a decision to abandon their town and run. It will start as soon as the gates open, and quickly become a flood as people try to escape to the west with all the possessions they can carry.'

'How does that help Taliessin and Rhys?' Arthur asked, and then his intelligence showed him the answer. 'Ah, the roads will become clogged as the wealthier citizens try to take as much with them as they can, and they'll be able to escape in the resulting chaos at the gates.'

Bedwyr nodded. 'It's time to spread some rumours. Are you up for it? Can I depend on your garrulousness?'

'Give me a couple of mugs of ale and I'll be as indiscreet as you want,' Father Lorcan answered with a wicked laugh.

'And I,' Germanus replied more seriously. 'I've become heartily sick of King Bran over the last ten years. I never liked his attitude towards our boy and now he's proved what kind of man he really is.'

'I will enjoy elaborating on the Saxons' probable thirst for blood,' Gareth said with a twist to his thin upper lip. 'I detest the destruction of British decency that we have experienced here. After the battle was over, I watched one of our peasants cut the fingers from a dead Saxon's hand to steal his rings. Not one of our warriors tried to stop him, and I began to wonder where their pride had gone. Peasants will be good or bad, as will all men, but we warriors have a code. The Dragon King once decimated a cavalry troop to find the murderer of Nimue's mother, because the slaughter of a pregnant woman was against all the rules of humanity. What of the destruction of the Severini gens in Aquae Sulis for the murder of children? Artor wouldn't close his eyes to the affair because the Severini were of noble blood, as others had. When did we Celts begin to shirk the rules of honour that all warriors are instructed to follow? King Bran has presided over the collapse of the entire warrior code.'

Arthur felt they were being harsh in their assessment of Bran. Through their dislike for the king, they were damning the citizens of Calleva to either homelessness or death, but Arthur could see that the choices available to his kinsman were so hard that the tribulations of his fellow Britons were no longer of prime importance.

'Good!' Bedwyr purred. 'Then we must get to work. After the arrival of the courier a number of rumours will already be spreading through the town. If your stories are added to the mish-mash, the population will soon be making their decisions to leave. I'd like to smuggle Taliessin and Rhys out among the evacuees as early as possible, for I smell trouble on the winds!'

As the five men rose to their feet, Arthur called his stepfather to one side. As soon as his companions were out of earshot, he whispered, 'Where will you go if Arden should fall to the Saxons, as it eventually must? I shall worry if you have no plans, for we need a place the children can run to when the Saxons come for them.'

'There's a forest to the south of Deva. Caer Gai lies high above it in the mountains, and tributaries of the river that nourishes Deva flow through it. The forest has sufficient river-bottom land in the flatter areas for sheep and light agriculture. I have already taken the precaution of speaking to Deinol ap Delwyn and Causus Gallio. Neither the Deceangli tribe nor the people of Deva will object to our presence on that land. When I return to Arden, I will send a troop of warriors there under the command of Lasair, who will be fully grown by then. He will establish our settlement and begin the process of building a fortress within the new Arden. Don't worry, Arthur. I won't permit any of our honourable traditions to die. Gareth was right when he spoke of a moral decline in our people. We're not what we were even ten years ago. I can only hope that God will help us in the trials that lie before us.'

'I can't fight for Bran, Father. I just won't do it! I intend to ride to Tintagel to see my kinfolk there, although Eamonn and Bors are still a part of the alliance. I also have a desire to see Glastonbury, and perhaps the priests will show me the grave of the Dragon King. But I have no wish to see Cadbury, which Mother has described so vividly, for I know I would be disappointed with its present state after years of decline. Have no fears for me, Father, for I'll be home within a year. But I must wash the taste of Calleva out of my mouth and strip the stench of it from my skin. Tell Mother that I love her.'

'Just don't be too long, my son. I'm an old man now, and I can't last for ever.'

Arthur laughed. 'You are immortal, Father. You and Nimue are the last living legends who possess memories of the Dragon King during the prime of his life. Taliessin only knew the older Artor, as did King Bran. You're the last of the true believers.'

Whispers had already circulated through the army long before dawn came with swirls of sleet. Nothing is secret when couriers can be tempted by spiced wine and a warm woman, so the courier's female companion soon became aware of the contents of the message delivered to Bran and she had no hesitation in fanning the rumours leaked to the eager ears of prostitutes and denizens of alehouses. When a further rumour described the desperate packing engaged in by the owner of the town sawmills, the very man who had provided accommodation to King Bran, panic began to grip both rich and poor. The man was determined to take everything but bricks and mortar with him, so all his servants and slaves were pressed into service to assist with the preparations for a frantic departure. The great wagons used for logging were brought in from the countryside as the timber merchant stripped his villa bare, literally under Bran's nose. Even the sculpture in the atrium, the marble benches and the prized glassware were strapped down or crated on the ox-drawn carts. Beefy guards loaded a succession of strongboxes while his wife and daughters fluttered their hands, but still managed to carry away everything but the tesserae on the floors. By mid-morning, without a word of apology to his noble guest, the timber merchant had departed for Abone. From there his party would travel to a smaller holding he had selected in the Forest of Dean.

Happy were those servants who were deemed necessary to protect the timber merchant's person, his family and his possessions, for they would accompany their master during the trek, and were even permitted to take a reasonable amount of their own personal property with them. Almost as fortunate were the workers from his mills who were indispensable to the running of the business enterprises in which the timber merchant had invested his money. While there were still a number of vehicles capable of transporting the tools and machinery that would prove useful once the new businesses began to operate, there was also a great deal of surplus equipment that must be disposed of prior to departure. With one eye over their shoulders and in a panic to begin their journey, the workers ensured it was sold off or abandoned in the shortest possible time.

The ordinary citizens of the town woke to see the wealthy deserters passing through the gates. The rich understood the practical results of warfare, and were fully aware of the punishments that the Saxons meted out to the populations of those towns where they experienced opposition. And while winter is never a good time to flee a town for the bleak countryside, those with money always have somewhere to go. Sorviodunum was the chosen destination for most of the businessmen who had trading ties with the centres of Aquae Sulis, Lindinis and Glevum, so the western gates were the first to be thrust open when the carts began to roll. Even Bran was unable to demand that Calleva stood firm, for since short memories are another trait of wealthy citizens in times of war the town fathers didn't hesitate to tell him that their predicament was his fault. The same men who had praised Bran for the salvation of their town now damned him, conveniently forgetting that they would already be dead were it not for his intervention.

Meanwhile, the poor too began to desert their homes, with handcarts for their possessions if they were fortunate or taking only what they could carry if they were not. The trickle became a flood by noon, and Bran became seriously concerned by the development. Short of using his army to stop the evacuation through bloodshed, he had no alternative but to watch as the town quickly emptied.

The disappearance of Taliessin and Rhys ap Myrddion was a further blow to the king's prestige. Like his grandfather before him, he felt their desertion keenly, for his warriors were unable to find the brothers, or so they reported when they explained their failure to hunt them down. Bran had no clear idea whether he would have carried out the threats he had uttered, but they had infuriated him to the point where he could barely speak for rage. Even Ector's calm reassurance gave him no comfort, for Bran was a realist and there was a pressing need in this time of political disintegration for a calculating mind and an accurate assessment of the diminishing British power base.

Meanwhile, wrapped in old cloaks to disguise their distinctive faces, and with mufflers around their mouths to protect their mouths and chins from the driving sleet, Taliessin and Rhys joined the slowly moving crowd as it passed through the north gate. Their hearts were in their mouths at the proximity of Bran's guards, who were stalking about the town in a growing fury of impotence. Standing on the wall some distance from the gate, muffled in a dark cloak to hide his own identity, Arthur watched the two brothers break free of the crowd at the gates and trot off on anonymous horses along the crowded road, heading north. Once out of sight of the town, they would leave the road and follow a cross-country route via Cunetio to the Fosse Way and the roads that led to the north-west. With a crow of satisfaction, Arthur watched them go.

Disaster, when it comes, is not necessarily loud, noisy or bloody. The worst defeats are often anti-climactic and bloodless, at times when both warriors and officers can lose hope in the future. Bran ruled the largest and strongest of the remaining tribes except for those held under the iron hand of King Bors of Cornwall. Mountains protected the Ordovice, but should this natural barrier be penetrated the Britons would be slaves of the Saxons for ever. Bran had publicly vowed that he would die before he permitted Saxons to stand on his soil. Privately, he knew that such a fate was inevitable.

Calleva emptied while Bran raged at all that was happening

around him. Then the ruler of the northern tribes approached him, begged his pardon and informed him that they would be returning to places of safety. They had considered the options available to them and had deemed the entire south now lost to the Britons. With every man who left them, the army was weakened and less viable as a fighting force. Bran understood the northern tribes' decision, but his outward demeanour remained angry and betrayed.

Ironically, Bran was being defeated through collective fear without Cynric's having to strike a blow, and he knew it. Now Bran's caution was to become his greatest enemy, for he was paralysed by indecision. Should he disperse the troops and return to Viroconium without attempting to slow the Saxon advance? He would be forced to watch his borders gradually whittled away by an encroaching Mercia. Or should he go to Venta Belgarum and risk the last army of the west?

He called Bedwyr and his son to a private meeting as Calleva turned into an echoing ghost town where looters removed anything of value before they themselves deserted the city. Bran permitted their worst excesses, for he believed the richer citizens of Calleva deserved nothing if they had the good fortune to be able to return to the town at some future time. Bedwyr and Arthur watched the blatant theft as they approached the inn where Bran was now staying. The innkeeper didn't quite have the arrogance to depart while King Bran was in residence, and cursed the timber merchant who had foisted the king onto him when that wily trader had made his flight from the city with all his possessions intact.

'The town is full of thieves, my lord, and there'll be nothing left at this rate,' Bedwyr began. 'What do you intend to do now?' The master of Arden had expected to feel some triumph, but he was overwhelmed by sadness as the town continued to empty.

'I'll release the troops soon and allow them to return to their tribes. There'll never be another army of the Britons. I don't regret my use of Marine Fire, because it saved many tribal lives. I've called you here to tell you my plans, which will allow you to make your own arrangements. Arden is more important than ever, but I wish to caution you of probable future events, Bedwyr, in gratitude for your long service to my family. Arden cannot stand alone for ever, so don't permit the Saxons to outflank you or you'll be trapped and I'll not be able to save you. I have drawn a line in the sand stretching from Deva to Viroconium and onward to Glevum. I will defend everything west of this line. The Britons are finished now and our defeat will come quickly.'

Then Bran looked directly at Arthur, whose eyes were discreetly turned downward. 'Most of what you accused me of was correct, Arthur, but I stand by what I chose to do. My plan was always risky, but I realised a long time ago that I had to save as many of my warriors as I could. You may be right in thinking that I resented you for your resemblance to Artor, but I believe that I would make the same decisions again if I were given the same choices. Perhaps I should have let Calleva burn while I waited to discover Cerdic's intentions, but I hate waste. At least give me the credit for the escape of the townspeople. They have a chance of survival now, which they didn't have before I used Marine Fire. We'd never have beaten the Saxons here without it.'

Arthur considered Bran's confidences seriously and nodded his head. 'I understand, kinsman, but I can't forgive you entirely. You should have trusted me, and you should have called for volunteers to serve on the line.'

'Should I? But the best and the bravest would have fought to participate in the action. How would that help the cause of the Britons? Losing my best troops was never a part of my battle plan. I suggest that you think about this conundrum in the years ahead. Perhaps you'll change your mind with the benefit of experience. In any event, King Artor once told me that a king must be prepared to sacrifice his own moral code if such action would serve to save his people. I believe he was correct. Think about that when we are strangers in our own lands.'

He smiled a conciliatory and bitter smile at the young man standing before him. 'Now, kinsman, you are free to leave. I'll not expect you to watch the disintegration of King Artor's army. It will be hard enough for me to bear; there is no need for you to share the pain.'

Bowing silently, father and son left Bran to his demons. Bedwyr was in tears as they crossed the threshold of the inn, and Arthur asked him why he wept for one such as Bran.

'He has proved to be a noble man. If there is a world beyond the shadows, and if our spirits endure beyond death, then Artor will be proud of Bran. His road has been hard, and the worst is yet to come for him.'

Arthur shook his head in genuine perplexity. 'I don't understand politics . . . I really don't. You were angry with Bran and resented his lack of honour in using Marine Fire – yet now you are weeping for him.'

'I thought the Britons had a future then. I was a fool.'

And no matter how Arthur coaxed him, Bedwyr refused to elaborate on his words.

For two days, Bran did nothing, while Calleva emptied around him like smoke in a strong wind. Then he called together the remaining kings and captains, and ordered that the army should disperse.

But one last task remained before Calleva was left to wither and die. To punish the population if ever they should decide to return at some future time, Bran ordered that all the wells should be poisoned, their walls collapsed and the holes filled in. Long-lasting contaminants were used to ensure that the water supply could never be used again, either by the Celts or by the encroaching Saxon hordes. Thus, Bran decreed, Calleva Atrebatum would remain deserted until the end of time, and neither Saxon nor Briton would ever again live in the ghostly mansions or walk the silent streets that had once been alive with industry and vigour.

Then Bran rode away, his head held high. He did not look back.

CHAPTER XVII

THE WAY TO THE NORTH

No state can exist without the confidence of the people.

Confucius, *Analects*, 12:7

'Look, Arthur. There it is, Tintagel the fair,' Eamonn cried, one arm pointing over the green, rolling land towards a grey headland thrusting out into an equally grey ocean. The companions were still too far away to mark any details of the fabled fortress, but the word *fair* had not immediately leapt into Arthur's mind.

'I'm at your disposal, Eamonn. Lead the way.'

Three horses and a hardy pack beast were spurred into a steady trot as Eamonn, Arthur and Gareth moved steadily through the long, brittle grasses of winter. From where they rode, the grim cliffs appeared to plunge straight down into the sea.

'Father will return before too long, Arthur, but before he does I'll have a chance to show you this wondrous place. It has never fallen to its enemies, even to Uther Pendragon, who was forced to use a ruse to enter the citadel. My home is as timeless and as defendable as any place on this earth, as you'll soon see. We don't have to tease ourselves with fear of the destruction of all we love.

Nothing is gained by it, and what Bran chooses to do can't be changed by any of us.'

Behind Eamonn's back, Gareth grimaced. His experiences of Cornwall thus far had convinced him that this country was perfectly safe from any Saxon ambitions. 'It's the far end of nowhere,' he had told Arthur privately in camp the previous night. Arthur had defended the magic of Cornwall, for many great men and women had emerged from its rolling countryside, deep-set wells, vestigial forests and foam-edged cliffs beetling over stony and precarious beaches. This timeless earth had nurtured Gorlois, a warrior of unimpeachable virtue; Ygerne had lived in Tintagel for much of her life and died in a nunnery not far from where they were now, and her beauty still echoed down the passage of decades; King Artor had been sired here, and what man had not heard the heroic tales of the Dragon King? And who could forget Morgan and Morgause, those two women who were superficially very different and yet were the most influential and feared women of their age other than Wenhaver and Nimue. This strange, glamour-drenched country had spawned legends and Arthur was certain that more would be born from its green and grey magic.

Besides, in the quiet reaches of the night when his companions were asleep around the campfire and the stars were so brilliant that Arthur felt he could reach out his hand and grasp them, he knew that in Cornwall he needed no one to guard his back. Here, friends were true and strangers didn't automatically earn his suspicion. Bran's arm was long, but Arthur was safe with Eamonn in this powerful tribal state.

Calleva Atrebatum was a memory now, one that lay six months behind Eamonn and Arthur. The erstwhile friends had met again as the last of the army disbanded and began to head north and west into an uncertain future. Eamonn's father had promoted him into manhood early and the lad had ridden in the second cavalry charge, but he seemed untouched by the horrors of that gruesome, unequal fight and Arthur envied his air of nonchalance and enthusiasm. When they bumped into each other at the west gate, Arthur had been struck immediately by Eamonn's impressions of the battle, Bran's behaviour and the use of Marine Fire. Eamonn had obviously seen totally different aspects of the conflict from those Arthur had observed, and Arthur had found his view very interesting.

'How lucky you were to stand in the line,' Eamonn had said with genuine envy. 'Not only did you have the opportunity to see the Jutes up close, but you also had the chance to be heroic. I only saw horses' arses from where I was positioned in the rear rank of the charge. I struck out at a few Saxons, but Jesus alone knows if any of my blows landed.'

'You were lucky then, my friend,' Arthur replied with a bitter, sardonic edge to his normally pleasant voice. 'That day spent facing totally unprepared Jutes who were surrounded by Marine Fire is graven into my memory. Bran was very foolish to have used such a weapon.'

'But consider the number of casualties we would have suffered if our forces hadn't had access to it. We were outnumbered by at least two to one, and even though Cynric has moved into the south he will spend years replacing the warriors he lost at Calleva. He'll curse Bran's name for decades.'

Marvelling at how men's perceptions varied when their experiences in the battle were considered, Arthur let the topic drop. He'd not really considered the lives that had been saved by the use of the terror weapon, and he was struck by Eamonn's compelling argument. Lives *had* been saved, probably thousands of them, and saved manpower mattered in the larger context of a deadly war of attrition. However, Arthur couldn't separate the practicalities of the battle of Calleva from the honour of those whose ethical considerations had been compromised. Eamonn would have explained, in his usual cheerful fashion, that they were fortunate not to have to make such difficult decisions. A king could not afford to be a man: a man could not understand the duties that lay on the shoulders of a king.

Besides, in a convoluted, wholly British fashion, Eamonn and Bran were related through the bloodlines of Queen Ygerne, the Flower of Tintagel. Best, Arthur decided, if Eamonn kept his illusions for as long as possible.

Calleva had provided one more piece of news before the friends had left its silent streets, where leaves and detritus were already piling in dark corners after being chased there by the winter winds. Ghosts already seemed to inhabit its deserted houses, which held the expectant air of rooms awaiting a mistress who has merely stepped outside for a moment, and will soon return to her duties.

Then, surprisingly, a rider came to the city gates with bittersweet news.

Cerdic had died on Vectis. The old monster had finally drowned in blood from burst blood vessels in his lungs. He had perished before Cynric had brought him the news that Venta Belgarum had fallen to the Saxons without a blow's being struck, so he didn't live to see the sacking of the town's ancient church, or the refugees who clogged the roads leading to the west. So many of the poor perished in that brutal winter that the rout of Venta Belgarum was remembered as the Flight of the Innocents, a fanciful title, for most of the souls who perished hardly fitted that description. For months before the siege, the more respectable citizens, accepting the inevitability of invasion, had fled with their strongboxes and their prized possessions. The whores, innkeepers, day labourers, thieves and frightened poor chose not to run, or had been unable to leave what little they had, so the toll upon them had been very high when Cynric had stripped them of everything of value and cast them out. Their frozen bodies were buried along the roadways, to be exposed in pitiful rows when spring finally returned to the land.

There were no harpers to sing of the loss of Venta Belgarum, Portus Adurni and Magnus Portus. There were no songs of courage, no fierce battles and no great outpourings of grief at these disasters. What had begun with the death of the Dragon King was now advancing inch by inch, and the land and its masters were changing. 'Britannia' was dead. When Arthur heard the name Angleland being used to describe his homeland for the first time, something seemed to burst in his chest and he began to understand Bran's frustration.

To preside over the land and to be both king and Dux Bellorum at a time when the tribes were being chopped up piecemeal and driven into the sea was worse than torture. Bran suffered the ignominy of following generations of heroes whose spirits were pressing him to save their people – and he did not have the resources to do so. Whatever he did, the erosion of his power filled his nostrils with the stench of decay. If he was considered at all, he would be remembered as the king who lost the kingdom of Britain.

Unseen by any Britons except those unfortunates on Vectis kept as slaves by the Saxons, Cynric sent his father to the gods with all the mourning and grandeur a bretwalda deserved. On a ceol piled high with treasure and a pyre built from aromatic woods, Cerdic's desiccated corpse was laid out in his most beautiful armour, his sword under his hands and the corpse of his favourite hound at his feet. Then, as the sun flamed just above the Litus Saxonicum, Cerdic's soul was set free as the lovely, narrow ship slipped out with the receding tide. The wood of the ship had been soaked in oil before the pyre had been set alight, and the ceol burned fiercely until only the hull remained, to disappear with the last of the sun's rays into deep water where no man could disturb Cerdic's perfect peace.

Father Lorcan and Germanus had retired from their long service to Arthur when he set off on the journey to Cornwall. Germanus had a wife at home in Arden whom he had barely seen since the first season of work on the Warriors' Dyke; to all intents and purposes she was a widow whose husband still lived. But to send Germanus back to his home alone would insult and hurt the old warrior, so Arthur decided that he would release Father Lorcan from his duties as well. He explained his reasoning to Lorcan in the privacy of his tent outside Calleva after drinking potent tipples of cider, and the priest reluctantly agreed. Wisely, he understood that Arthur was determined to have his way, regardless of arguments.

But Gareth was another matter altogether. Nothing would induce the young warrior to accompany the tutors to Arden Forest, and Arthur reluctantly accepted that he would not be swayed. When an avid young man such as Gareth had been raised to believe that he had a special destiny, Arthur learned, feeble excuses would not deter him. Gareth intended to travel to Cornwall, with or without Arthur's approval. If he must, he would follow the friends at a discreet distance, a plan that would leave them all looking foolish.

And so the small party set off for Durnovaria and Isca Dumnoniorum, exploring the gentler coasts to the south of Britain and enjoying the soft landscapes that Ygerne had so loved. After viewing the beaches of yellow sands, which were broken by tussocks of hardy grasses and yellow-flowering shrubbery, and the white cliffs that rose out of the green landscapes, the companions turned once again towards the west. The landscape was a strange and changeable living entity, where Arthur saw small stone circles and rows of monoliths that appeared out of fields like crooked fingers.

As a young man attuned to the land and its patterns, Arthur could easily imagine large figures lying beneath the earth. Some of these god-like forms were skeletal and white, so that their bones were revealed beneath a thin coverlet of green sward. Other gigantic titans had been frozen in stone for eternity, and reached up towards the light that had been stolen from them for ever. On occasion, these figures woke from their long imprisonment, stirred, rolled over and caused huge sections of the cliffs to fall away to expose clean stone to the steady erosion of the wind, the rain and the never-ending pounding of the sea. One day, Arthur imagined, these buried gods would rise from the earth with a huge convulsion of soil. Then the tribes would be judged for their husbandry of the land that had been given to them, and Arthur had the grim feeling that he and his kind would be deemed unworthy.

War had no place in this landscape of magic. From the huge white chalk horse on the cliffs in the south to the Giant's Dance on the sweeping plains, gods had walked on this earth, playing games with pebbles which they left behind like abandoned toys. Bran, Arthur and the survival of the west were minor irritants to the body of the land.

After a slow, early-spring ramble through the countryside, broken by nights spent in tents under the stars or in small inns full of gaiety and good ale, Eamonn turned their mounts towards the sea. Now they found themselves in a new landscape where trees leaned away from the ocean breezes and were transformed into twisted old creatures out of legend. The grasses were long and green, blown into curls and smooth humps like long hair combed back from the faces of the cliffs. The wind stiffened, and teased their hair with strong fingers so that it constantly required their attention. Here, their fires were lit in hollows and securely bound in circles of stone lest the wind set the flames free to rage their way through the countryside. Finally, the landscape changed once again to something that was wild, pure and alien, so that even the Arden of Arthur's memory was eclipsed by the spare beauty of this gnarled coast.

The three riders came to a fold in the landscape that led down towards the sea, raging over a hundred feet below. A strong, well-kept road made this downward plunge possible to negotiate, and the cliffs on either side meant it could be easily defended. Arthur could finally imagine a disguised Uther Pendragon leading a troop of cavalry down the treacherous, icy surface of the roadway leading into Tintagel. Until now he had doubted the truth of the tales woven around the birth of the Dragon King. How could any place be so difficult to attack that it was deemed impregnable, yet still allow the Dumnonii guards to be duped by a simple disguise? Now, as another winter loosened its iron grip on the west, and the first flowers stirred the grasses, the warrior in Arthur saw the gatehouse ahead wreathed in an imaginary fog. He heard the scrabble of iron-shod hooves on the stones and imagined the Atrebate warriors, clad in Dumnonii armour, cloaks and jerkins, passing guards who could barely see their faces.

'Yes, this is the route that Uther Pendragon took when he inveigled his way into Tintagel. Some of the stories suggest that Myrddion Merlinus used magic to blind the eyes of the garrison, but on an evening when sleet was falling and the wind whipping the guards' hair over their faces it would have been difficult to see anything clearly.' Eamonn was speaking with some pride, for Gorlois had been his grandfather's uncle and men still spoke in awe of the dignity and decency of the Boar of Cornwall. His strong right arm was remembered as well, for Gorlois had been a gifted warrior who led his troops personally in all engagements.

Gorlois's courage was not unusual in those days, for most rulers led from the front. Not so today, Arthur thought bitterly, when kings and lords sent their warriors to their deaths from places of relative safety. As he considered the ethical values of rulers such as King Artair of the Atrebates, who preferred to risk losing their kingdoms to placing their lives at risk, Arthur was able to understand the stiff-necked pride of Eamonn and Bors Minor, his uncompromising father. Their family history and the landscape in which they lived made them a force of nature with marked similarities to the beetling cliffs and craggy coasts of their kingdom.

'Can you see, Arthur? The causeway is down there ahead of us. Our people call it the Neck. When the sea fog comes down, it's hard to make out the edges of the roadway above the steep drop to the sea.'

Eamonn's arm pointed out a narrow stone path at the bottom of a steep incline where a six-foot-wide neck of land separated Tintagel from the mainland. The stones were rough, so the surface was treacherous at all seasons and only horses familiar with the fortress could negotiate it with confidence. Fortunately, grooms were waiting for the arrival of the young masters, so their horses were whisked away to stables attached to the watch tower and garrison on the mainland, leaving Eamonn to lead his guests into Tintagel on foot.

Below the causeway, the water boiled with the force of an incoming tide, but only the wheeling of gulls disturbed the stillness of the air on the Neck, for the island and the cliffs on the mainland protected tired travellers from the ferocious sea gales prevalent in the area. But the stillness was full of sound. The wind could be heard, if not felt, as it found every cranny on the island and turned them into flutes of stone. The resultant wailing chilled Arthur's blood as it touched some primal part of his essence. If magic could exist, it would live here where the wind, sea and sky seemed to be living creatures.

Eamonn strode confidently over the slick stones, all with their share of oysters and barnacles growing where the tidal waters reached. 'Watch your step, Arthur, for those huge feet of yours will trip you up. Tintagel isn't kind to visitors who don't take her seriously.'

I'll wager that's true, Arthur thought as he looked beyond the causeway to where a number of horses were stabled in a small compound overlooking a beach composed of smooth stones. These swaths of pebbles had a wild, monochromatic beauty where black, every shade of grey, beiges and whites struggled for prominence. Smashed shells formed uneven beds where the waves had crunched the pretty, living toys of the sea in their jaws, providing colour to eyes that were acute enough to recognise it – pale pink, apricot, amber and green, interspersed with tangles of black seaweed hurled out of the depths to die on the shale, flint and gravel.

A guard saluted Eamonn with a bright grin and a fist placed over his heart. A small gate opened and Tintagel was almost theirs.

Giants had cut stairs into the living rock. A steep set of steps forced everyone who sought entry to the fortress to climb up cyclopean slabs of stone that made even Arthur's long legs ache. With the ease of long practice, Eamonn skipped up the giddy pathway like a mountain goat, never having to grip a tussock of the tough green grass to assist his balance. Just when Arthur thought the stairs would never end, Eamonn gave a crow of joy and appeared to vanish into the solid rock.

As quickly as his struggling calves and thighs would allow, Arthur followed and found himself on a large, flat platform. The fortress rose above them to the highest point of a peninsula that thrust itself like a spearhead out into the Oceanus Hibernicus. Up here, out of the protection of the cliffs and the flanks of the island, the gale force winds were free to tear at Arthur's unbound hair and run their cold fingers through his plaits, unravelling a strand that immediately corkscrewed around his face.

Deep within him, Arthur felt a door open. A powerful surge of recognition flooded through him as if this strange place released a tide of memories that had been buried all his life. For the first time, Arthur felt the thrill of the sea and *déjà vu* so powerful that he almost toppled with dizziness.

'Come, Arthur! Come, Gareth! I can see my mother at the door. We'll find you suitable sleeping quarters and then I'll show you the wonders of Tintagel,' Eamonn shouted over the wind and his face glowed with pleasure and excitement, for he loved his home with the same passion that Arthur felt for Arden. 'If the stones could speak, you'd hear Uther Pendragon, Myrddion Merlinus and the fair Ygerne.'

'I never took you for a dreamer, Eamonn,' Arthur joked, and then his face fell. 'But I know what you mean. Tintagel is so old that I swear it must have existed when the little honey people raised the great stones at the Giant's Dance. Its age has soaked into stones that can almost speak for themselves.'

A buxom, wide-hipped woman with rosy cheeks came forth to greet her guests. Her short stature and grey-streaked black hair reminded Arthur of the hill folk of Cymru, the last survivors of the people who had owned these isles long before the Celts, the legions, or even the woad-blue Picts had come to drive them into the farthest crannies in the land. Her face split into a wide, fond smile and Arthur felt his own lips respond automatically to her evanescent charm, a magnetism that was more powerful by far than her short, dumpling body and her plain unremarkable features would suggest. Had he been older, Arthur knew she would have beguiled him, such was her unconscious glamour.

'Hello, Mother. Well met! You look wonderful to these tired eyes. I have brought my dear friend, Arthur ap Bedwyr, to meet you. He is from the Forest of Arden and has never seen the ocean before, so I have persuaded him to spend a little time with us before he returns to his trees. His father is the last of the Dragon King's lords and the only survivor of the quest for the Bowl of Ceridwen.'

'Do not invoke *her* name within the walls of our home, my son. The dame comes and goes at no man's bidding, but the cup was never hers to give. Happy is the man who could gaze on it, yet live to tell the tale. Welcome, Arthur. Tintagel is yours to do with as you please while you're here with us.' The wife of King Bors clasped Arthur's extended hands in both her warm, tiny paws. Arthur could feel the hard labour of a true chatelaine in the calluses on her fingers, which had been carved by spindle and wheel. He could also feel her life-force, as strong as a river and as flexible as a young tree in the wind, and his boy's heart skipped at the fierceness of her spirit. 'You might like to see the inscription carved on a stone near our entrance. You may even recognise the name, as it is so much like your own,' she went on, with an odd smile like a curved sickle that was sweet, ambivalent and dangerous. Arthur immediately knew that she was imparting secret information to him.

'The Arthnou Stone, Mother? Now that you mention it, it is a coincidence,' Eamonn added, his dark brows coming together in a puzzled frown.

'And who is this fine young man?' the queen asked, adroitly changing the subject. Her eyes were fixed on Gareth, who flushed pink under her frank scrutiny and stepped forward with a courtier's grace to kneel and bow low over her hand. Eamonn flushed with pleasure at the homage paid to his mother.

'This young warrior is Gareth, and I apologise for not knowing his father's name. I am remiss.' For a moment, Eamonn's dark face was genuinely remorseful at his thoughtlessness. 'He tends to the needs of my large friend here, although he's no servant, but offers his service out of love and duty towards Arthur.'

The queen swayed forward on her small feet and her eyes were sunny and without shadows, despite being as black as jet. 'Welcome to my home, Gareth. There is no shame in service, as my scapegrace son will learn one day. Tintagel is open to you, although I judge you'd prefer to be away from the sound of the sea.'

'Aye, my lady. Odd as it seems, all my family love to be close to the waves but me. My father believed it to be a family memory of hunger and shame from days gone by, but I'm no seer so I can only speak for myself. Tintagel is as beautiful as its mistress, wild and lovely, as unexpected as a flower in a desert or a pearl lying on the shore of a muddy lake.'

'When did you become a poet, Gareth, and put us all to shame with your eloquence?' Arthur asked, mock serious, hoping that Eamonn's mother would not be offended by Gareth's fulsome praise.

He need not have been concerned, for the queen laughed unaffectedly and patted Gareth's cheek. 'I am Valda, wife of King Bors and mother of this ragamuffin here. Allow me to lead you to the room that has been prepared for you. Our living spaces in Tintagel are small, for fortresses are not constructed for leisure, but we can offer you soft beds and all the comforts of a great palace – or so we think. If you desire anything further, please tell my servants and you shall have it.'

Both youngsters bowed, touched that she would choose to

honour them with her birth name. Valda! The sound of those five letters caressed the tongue, yet the name was as short and as decisive as she was. Arthur was charmed.

Queen Valda led them to an upper room. It was small and snug, but bright, and well-built shutters, whitewashed so that the wood seemed new and crisp, were closed tightly over the long window opening to keep out every tendril of cold air. Two beds filled most of the space, strange well-constructed rectangles of wood with carvings of seagulls on the posts rather than the usual complex interlace so beloved of the Cymru people. The carver had been a master of his trade, and the gulls had been imbued with personalities. They seemed to watch over the sleepers with sharp, beady eyes that had been rubbed even darker by generations of fingers.

Plump palliasses of coarse, unbleached wool had been laid on the woven leather straps that formed the bases of the two beds; blankets and flaxen sheets covered the itchy wool and proclaimed the wealth of the household. The floor was of raw adzed timber, split many years earlier and polished by thousands of naked feet so that they seemed to stand on old honey, partially covered by a rag rug which had been woven by a long-dead mistress of Tintagel. She had used woad, onion skins and precious tree bark to dye her wool in various shades of blue, clear yellow, deep brown and a single stripe of viridian. From the glazed terracotta jug of water to the soft, upholstered bed, Tintagel offered comfort and luxury, for everything in this small room had been prepared with love and the industry of busy, willing hands.

'My thanks to you, mistress. No king could be better housed than we will be in such a room.' Arthur bowed once more out of genuine respect, touched by Queen Valda's hospitality.

Valda waved away their thanks and left the young men to complete their unpacking.

After ridding themselves of the dirt accumulated along the road and changing into clean clothes, Arthur and Gareth attempted to find their way back to the dining hall. Corridors and small rooms abounded, and although the mistress of the house had placed sweet-smelling oil lamps at intervals along the walls, which had been worn smooth by the touch of countless hands, the lads were lost within moments of latching their door.

'Tintagel is a maze,' Arthur muttered softly, his forehead furrowed in annoyance.

'It's a rabbit warren that has been carved out and added to over hundreds of years,' Gareth added. 'I'd call it a rat-hole were our hostess not such a wonderful woman. Taking this fortress would be nigh on impossible: holding on to it would be so easy that a child might succeed. There is plenty of water, and if the fortress had food stores it would be able to resist an army with only a vestigial force of warriors. I don't think it could even be attacked from the sea, for the water's like a churn. Any direct attack would be suicidal.'

'Aye,' Arthur replied shortly, remembering the circumstances of his father's conception.

Then, as they tentatively entered a passageway that turned suddenly to their right, they met Eamonn coming to find them.

Eamonn spent the rest of the day introducing them to the wonders of Tintagel. The isthmus was surprisingly large, and had its own well in the centre. Eamonn took them to the headland, where a large depression in the exposed bedrock suggested a footprint, as if a giant had risen out of the ocean and bounded onto the land like a Leviathan that had come to free his fellow Titans from some unimaginable fate. Arthur stood at the very end of the isthmus and looked out at the ocean.

'What's out there, I wonder?' he whispered aloud as his eyes searched the distant horizon.

'When I look out of my window, I always wonder that too,' Eamonn replied. 'If I were a braver person, I'd take a boat and sail west. They say the Isle of Heroes lies in that direction, as does the drowned land of Westernesse. Some people say they can hear her bells ringing when storms churn the waters, but I'm sure that's just foolish superstition. Still, there must be something out there.' Eamonn's profile was clean and pure, reminding Arthur that the Dumnonii prince was little more than a boy and good to the core.

As they returned to the fortress, Arthur marvelled at the narrowness of the paths that linked the small stone cottages of the servants with the upper levels of the castle. Hanging over the boiling sea, a hundred feet above the water, these windowless conical dwellings were made of layered slate and snugly thatched to protect the occupants against snow and rain. But Gareth pointed out that one careless slip by a tired homegoer could easily be fatal.

'Look at the children,' Eamonn explained as they watched two little boys chasing each other between cottages. Considering the narrowness of the paths and the steepness of the fall, the boys were as nimble as mountain goats. As in every part of this charmed, ferocious but beautiful place, flowers were thrusting up colourful heads in the long grasses, and small patches of vegetables clung to the cliff face like limpets.

'Here's the carving that Mother mentioned. It says *Pater Coli avi ficit Artognou,* although I haven't the faintest idea what it means. Do you know, Arthur? Gareth told me that you have learned several languages.'

'Hmn. I believe it says *Artognou is the father of the descendant of Col.*' Eamonn looked blank. 'Artor wouldn't have carved this,' Arthur added. 'He lacked the leisure time to carry out the task. But earlier, when Myrddion Merlinus stayed here after the rape of Queen Ygerne, the seer could have left the carving as a sort of puzzle. I think *Col* could be the Emperor Constantine, but other than that I haven't the faintest idea what it means.'

As they stood and reflected on the odd message from the past, a clod of earth sailed past Arthur's ear and hit Eamonn squarely in the back, knocking him partly off balance so that Arthur had to grab him by the collar.

'Ow! What the devil?' Eamonn cursed. He turned, as did his companions, to confront a girl of about eleven. She made a face at Eamonn and scampered away, laughing as she made her escape.

'Who, or what, was *that*?' Arthur asked, for the child had been very dirty and seemed to have been playing in the mud. Her lanky limbs had the poor coordination of someone who is growing too rapidly to maintain grace, and her dress was tied in large, ungainly knots between her legs to create the illusion of trews. To top off this grubby attire, her long, coal-black hair was uncombed, and as filthy as her small, heart-shaped face.

'That, my friend, is my youngest sister. She's called Blaise, which of course is really a boy's name, but under all that dirt she is definitely a girl,' Eamonn explained. 'Once we get close to the walls, she's likely to drop clods of earth on us from above, so look out. She enjoys causing me embarrassment. She resents her name . . . and me . . . for reasons best known to herself.'

'Why has she been given a saint's name? It sounds pleasant enough, but it seems a little odd,' Arthur said, checking the wall above them for missiles. As they mounted the steps he caught a glimpse of a tousled head, and warned his friends to hug the walls as they climbed.

'My father was sure that the baby would be a boy and wanted to call it Blaise. Mother agreed. She said a man's heart was beating inside the unborn babe, and was sure that even if she bore a daughter the girl would be courageous and generous. In the delirium of birth she swore that a vision came to her that the coming child would sail wild seas and rule in far-off places, so they decided to keep the name even when the baby turned out to be a girl.'

'Well, it's an interesting name, but she'll have to be extraordinary to live up to such a vision,' Arthur said thoughtfully.

'She has few good qualities and a vile temper, so she's very lucky to be betrothed to a man of distinction, if we can ever get her to him,' Eamonn added. 'King Geraint of the Otadini tribe has chosen her to marry his eldest grandson, Gilchrist. In time to come she'll be a queen and live beyond the wall where the Saxons will find invasion difficult, so Father wishes to send her off as soon as possible. She's unhappy about it, and you've seen how she responds when she's in a bad temper.'

'She's not happy that she has been betrothed, then?' Arthur asked. His previous experiences had suggested that all girls welcomed marriage to a man born to become a king.

'She's never happy, but she'll obey Father, or he'll send her to Gilchrist tied to her horse. It's time that Blaise learned the ways of the world.' Eamonn stamped up the steps and avoided a handful of dog dung that was thrown with a careful eye, barely missing him as he ducked. 'See what I mean?'

Arthur laughed. Blaise seemed to him to be high spirited and amusing, although she definitely required a bath. He didn't envy the escort who would have to deal with her tantrums when she travelled north. Nor did he have any plans to see much of her himself, for he disliked having dung thrown at his face by a girl who should have known better. He preferred young ladies who were less beautiful but sweeter natured.

The younger children were in their rooms when Eamonn and his guests ate a simple but delicious meal of fish, oysters and a soup concocted from many types of seafood, including seaweed, which Arthur found odd to the taste and chewy in texture. But the bread was fresh and the cheese was remarkable. Even the winter apples were still crisp and delicious, while a concoction of honey and thick cream was both unusual and flavoursome. Arthur and Gareth devoured everything in sight after so long on bivouac with the army. Dried meat becomes boring in time, and the fresh produce provided by the Villa Poppinidii had been eaten far too quickly.

That night, in a bed of such softness that Arthur felt like a Roman sybarite, he swore that he'd like to remain as Valda's guest for as long as he was welcome.

The next day was overcast with grey rain, typical weather for the time of year. Eamonn found a coracle and offered to row his guests round the headland on the ebb tide to see Myrddion's Cave, a prospect which Arthur found exciting, although the thought of sitting in such a flimsy craft dulled his enthusiasm a little. Regardless of Eamonn's confidence in these small vessels, Gareth refused point blank to sit set foot in the circular boat.

'If I'm fated to die young, Master Eamonn, I'd rather meet my maker on good solid land. I'm not meant for sea travel,' he said with sufficient force to convince Eamonn that any pleas were useless.

'I understood you intended to follow your master,' Eamonn joked. 'Even into the jaws of hell.'

Gareth flushed a little. 'I will pass this particular opportunity by if I can only get to your cave by sea. I thank you, Master Eamonn, but I'm not prepared to risk a cold and wet grave.'

Later, with the help of the ebbing tide and Eamonn's expert use of the paddle, the hide-covered coracle slid along the coast of Tintagel, the two occupants enjoying a crazy, dizzying view of the peasants' cottages that were clustered around the fortress like chicks around their mother's breast. Then, as Arthur felt the coracle scrape along the weed-edged rock, Eamonn waited for a count of ten, judged the force of a small wave and shot out into the current. Like a leaf in a downpour, the boat was whisked into clear water before riding the wave into a huge opening under the roots of the promontory.

Arthur realised he had been holding his breath.

'You can open your eyes now, Arthur,' Eamonn said. 'It's only been called Myrddion's Cave during the last few years. Before that, it had a far nastier reputation, and was rumoured to be the entry to the womb of the Mother. Although I'm a Christian, this place always gives me the creeps. According to gossip, Morgan the Fey was part of a very nasty coven of witches that dabbled in human sacrifice – right here in this cave.'

Arthur looked up at the dripping roof and the dank, encrusted walls. 'Is the cave entrance covered at high tide?'

'Of course, but we have hours before that happens. Would you like to see the caves above the high-water line? I've not explored the half of them and I've been coming here all my life.'

'As long as we can't become trapped in here. I've always believed I was meant for something better than drowning in an underground cavern, especially one devoted to *her*.'

'Who may not be named? There's a stone effigy of her here that might interest you.'

Eamonn drew the coracle up to a weathered, barnacle-encrusted post of iron set into the rocks. A brass ring indicated that boats could be tethered there, but once Arthur had clambered out of the flimsy vessel Eamonn picked it up and pulled it above the high-water line where a passage led upwards into the heart of Tintagel's rocky mass. There, an area of clear space opened out before them, wide and dank, with a deep pool at one end containing midnight-black water. The limitless depths were oily and vile in appearance, and the water smelled very different from the turbulent waters outside. As the companions moved further into the cave the smell became stronger.

'Ugh!' Arthur shivered inside his warm tunic, but the cold came from something other than the ambient temperature. 'Old death!' he exclaimed, his nostrils quivering. 'This place reeks of old and unhallowed death.'

'And many other things that are too dark to think about. I'd rather not know what foul acts have taken place down here,' Eamonn murmured. He was uncharacteristically glum. 'I've always tried to avoid this chamber when I explored these underground caves. It gives me the night horrors!'

He had brought fish oil with them in a hide container, and Arthur prepared an old torch that had been left in the cavern to illuminate the dimly lit spaces. The first object that came to his attention was a large flat stone, some seven feet in diameter, which seemed to have been used as some form of table. The smoke was acrid in the enclosed space and reeked of fish oil, but the flickering light showed black stains spider-webbed around an unmarked area of stone that was roughly human in shape.

'I'd swear those stains are blood,' Arthur said softly when he caught the distinctive but faint scent of rusting iron. 'Faugh! I hate these places. The Romans swore they had driven out the old bad ways, but I'm certain this cavern has been used for evil purposes more recently than that.'

'King Gorlois put the entire coven to death when he discovered that his daughter was hoping to acquire arcane powers by taking part in rituals involving human sacrifice. Like you, I have a feeling that this cavern has been used since then.' Eamonn looked distressed, as if the events that had taken place in this chamber had sullied his home and his family, as Arthur supposed they had. 'Anyway, the effigy is in that alcove over there.' He pointed to a dim corner. 'Even Gorlois feared to lay impious hands upon *her*, so she resides in this place of infamy in stillness and perpetual darkness.'

'But not quite alone,' Arthur murmurred as he followed Eamonn towards the strange stone figure. The statue had no arms, only vestigial legs, and no features on its lumpish face. The grotesquely swollen breasts, buttocks and belly parodied the awkward form of a pregnant woman, but it was dehumanised, as if it came from some primal, ancient branch of nature that civilisation had attempted to banish. Sticky blood had coated the figure and dried over her surface many times, until she was eventually glazed with a dull, sanguine coat that welded her to the stone of the alcove. Offerings of rotten fruit, perished flowers, shells and a single child's hand, desiccated by time, lay on a plate before her.

Arthur swore and turned away.

'I'm sorry, Arthur. I didn't expect this place to still be in use. I haven't been down here for years.'

There was no light in the cavern except for the torch Eamonn held above his head. Still, Arthur was able to see a glint of superstition in the younger man's eyes.

'I really want to get out of this place. The air seems to hum, and I'm developing a headache.' Arthur felt that tell-tale itch at the back of his skull come alive, as if something in this dank, dark place was trying to crawl into his body through his skin. He knew that if it burrowed into him, like a tick or a parasite, he would carry its evil with him for ever.

He began to panic; a blind, unthinking fear that had never attacked him when he faced a living adversary. To name this unhallowed place after Myrddion Merlinus was a grotesque parody, for the healer would never have aligned himself with such wickedness. This evil was real, potent and determined to undermine anything good. He needed to run – fast.

'I'm sorry, Eamonn, but I've got to get out of here. Can't you feel *her* presence? It's either the goddess, or something that has usurped *her* place and *her* person.'

'I'll tell my father and older brothers what we've seen here. The caverns along this coast are obviously being used for evil purposes and he must stop the practice before our own name is sullied. Morgan's reputation has obviously led simpler souls into covens that search for her kind of power.'

'Tell me, Eamonn, do you ever have odd experiences? Taliessin told me that those who belong to the house of Gorlois sometimes have strange skills.' Arthur's face seemed casual and unconcerned in the torchlight, but his voice gave him away. Eamonn understood that Arthur's question was in deadly earnest.

'No, my friend. I'm not aware that any of my family carries the curse. It's generally accepted among us that our talent for prophecy came from Ygerne the Fair, who inherited it from her father Pridenow, a man of extraordinary skill and vision. But he was beset by head pains and died when he was still a young man. Why do you ask?'

Arthur had reached the coracle and helped Eamonn to launch the frail vessel before seating himself in the rear of its leather hull.

'When we reach the shore I'll tell you everything I know about the family curse. The time has come when I must share a terrible secret with you. You could betray me through a slip of the tongue and if so I'd probably die because of your mistake – but I trust you. Apart from Gareth and my tutors, you're my only real friend.'

The short journey from the cavern to the shore had to be negotiated with considerable seacraft, since the cavern seemed unwilling to relinquish its hold on the two young men. Eamonn was forced to draw on all his skills and knowledge of the tides, the wind and the water to force their way back to the shingle shore.

Once the coracle was stored away in the garrison they re-joined Gareth, who was looking grey and strained with concern. As they collected their horses, all three men heaved a deep sigh of relief.

'I feel lighter somehow,' Eamonn said as they spurred their mounts to the top of the steep roadway, the wind blowing his black hair into a bush of curls. 'I've never had the strange feelings I experienced just now on previous visits to the caves, and I don't plan to suffer them again. They were vile!'

'Aye, my friend, vile is an accurate description,' Arthur replied. 'The sun has decided to shine, so let's ride to the next headland and remove the air of that hideous place from our lungs.'

On the next headland a large number of sea birds were busy hunting for small creatures that would keep their newly hatched chicks fed. When Arthur dismounted he drew the fresh air deep into his lungs, and felt his headache start to ease in the sweet, salty air.

Once the three had settled themselves comfortably in the long grass, which was beginning to show the first daffodils of spring, they opened the packs of food provided by Tintagel's kitchens. Like all young men, they devoured every crumb.

'What I'm going to tell you could place you in some danger, Eamonn, so forgive me in advance. If you don't want to hear the details, speak out now and we'll say no more on the subject. But I believe you ought to know my secret and how it could affect you in the future.' Arthur stared at his long, powerful hands, still smeared with slime from the cavern. With an oath of disgust, he wiped away all evidence of that inner room with clean grass while Eamonn nodded slowly.

'I don't know what your secret is,' he said, 'but how could such knowledge harm me, provided I don't repeat it? You're a good man, Arthur, and I'm proud that you're my friend.'

'Perhaps you've heard people say that I resemble the Dragon King when he was a young man?'

Eamonn nodded.

'I am his natural son. I was born just before he died at the Battle of the Ford. For obvious reasons, my status was kept secret. My foster-father, Bedwyr, has been the most generous and loving father imaginable and I am proud to be his foster-son, but you can understand how I'm an embarrassment and a threat to King Bran, and also to my friend and kinsman Ector. My existence threatens the stability of the remaining tribes of the west. I have sworn allegiance to Bran, but he still suspects me. In all honesty, I can declare to you that I have no desire to take his place.'

Eamonn's eyes were very wide. 'So we are almost kinsmen, at least by marriage, although I don't believe we share the same blood.'

'No, we share no ties of blood, but I'm technically part of the Dumnonii tribe. I'm also a member of the Atrebate and Cornovii tribes, so my position is rather unusual. I also share Ygerne's gift, but in my case it's manifested as a warning which I hear when I'm in danger. I've been able to survive many attacks on my life when I should have died. Do you understand now why Bran placed me in the front line at the battle of Calleva?'

Eamonn paled. 'But that means that Bran tried to have you killed. It makes sense. He'll not move against you openly, but he wouldn't shed tears if you should die in battle.'

'Exactly! So you see that any friendship with me is dangerous. I'd not have your life threatened by any relationship with me while you were unwarned.'

Eamonn found a forgotten apple in his pack and munched on it reflectively. 'Are you certain that you hold no ambitions to usurp the High King's throne?' he asked carefully.

'None. I have no desire to preside over the fall of the west. I'll fight to the death to avoid our defeat, but I believe the union of kings is finished and it's going to be every tribe for itself. I just wanted you to know why I'm treated oddly at times by those who rule over us. Gareth knows, of course, for his father trained him to take his place as my bodyguard, just as Gareth Major was the Dragon King's companion for most of his life. I'll truly understand, Eamonn, if you choose to terminate our friendship for your own safety. After seeing the cavern today, an evil place which is part of my aunt's legacy to both of us, I knew I had to tell you everything.'

'Say no more, Arthur. Your sire is only of minimal importance to me. I would hope I'm a good judge of men, and that's all that counts. Now, how about a week or two off the leash? I know a series of inns where we can find some willing girls and have a proper holiday away from mothers and difficult siblings. You'll see trouble enough in the years that lie ahead of us, and I have no gifts to bring to you apart from good common sense. So for today, let's just enjoy ourselves while the opportunity is here. We should all have fun, even Gareth, who seems unwilling to ever crack a smile. Damn it, man, how was it possible for you to be born so old?'

'I take my duties seriously, Master Eamonn,' Gareth replied, a little tersely. He was affronted, but neither of his companions noticed.

The friends remounted and returned to the castle, where they packed their few belongings and informed the queen that they'd be away for a week. Then, with Valda's motherly warnings ringing in their ears, they rode away with all the enthusiasm and excitement of young men who have no cares or duties to restrain them.

CHAPTER XVIII

JOURNEY INTO DARKNESS

In nature there are neither rewards nor punishments – there are consequences.

Bernard Ingham, *Some Reasons Why*

The courier reached the three travellers in a fishing village well to the south of Tintagel. King Bors required his son and his guests to return to Tintagel, post haste.

The three friends had enjoyed a leisurely journey through the sweet early spring where the villages, no matter how tawdry and poor, had been washed clean by fresh showers and the fields were green with spear-points of new growth. Cows stood up to their udders in new, sweet-smelling grass, and the milk they produced seduced the senses as effectively as wine or cider. The young men drank rather more than was good for them, but they also ate well and used their combined muscle to assist war widows with repairs to their cottages, or ploughed the fallow fields to sow crops for the sustenance of bereaved families. Sadly, they found enough charity work to occupy their time well beyond the single week they had initially planned, and a month flew by on floral feet.

The young men worked for nothing. Eamonn took his obligation to his people seriously, and Arthur found pleasure in meeting the needs of those who needed his help. Gareth was happy just to keep Arthur out of trouble.

In the early evenings, they dined like kings on fresh, homely fare and drank sweet cider and strong ale with other men, or danced impromptu ring dances from the ancient past, heads garlanded with flowers from the girls who were more than willing to share the joys of springtime with pleasant young men of quality. Eamonn and Arthur wallowed in the generosity of sweet young things with rosy cheeks, unbound hair and soft, downy thighs. Pillowed on firm young breasts, Arthur found a blessedness of physical sensation that gave him happiness, for it was untouched by the exchange of coins experienced in Aquae Sulis.

Gareth was a special favourite with the ladies, perhaps because he was a little diffident and was unwilling to spend his seed randomly. The three had decided at the start of their journey that they'd not seduce virgins or hurt good men by accepting the subtle blandishments of wives, but there were enough willing girls for all. Arthur wondered a little at their popularity, until Gareth set both young nobles straight with his characteristic bluntness.

'The girls and their families court pregnancy,' he said. Arthur and Eamonn paled at the thought of fathering bastards, but Gareth explained the peasants' points of view succinctly.

'Who would you rather have to father your child or your grandchild? A village man, a fisherman or a farm hand? Or would you prefer to have your progeny sired by tall young noblemen who will give the family strong sons or clever daughters? The old granddams aren't stupid. Girls and boys will always meet and mate, so it's better for these people to have the best for their daughters. They won't demand anything of you, for you are the givers in this case. But don't get swelled heads, because any tribal warriors would meet their requirements. Even Mareddyd would be welcome here, although they would probably find him less likeable.'

So Arthur luxuriated in physicality throughout the early spring, acquiring many skills that had not been possible to master in Arden. He learned to swim far better than his few early experiences in rivers and tarns had permitted. He helped the fishermen and became adept at cleaning fish and repairing nets. His skin was soon as brown as old honey, his eyes vivid in his tanned face. He was completely and thoughtlessly happy during those sweet days and long nights. He learned how to give and take for mutual pleasure and discovered the sensitivity and blunt practicality of women for the first time.

Only one cloud blotted his final lessons in what it was to be a man. An old woman asked them if they could repair the thatch on her roof, which was thin and mouldy with age, so after some simple tutelage from a village elder they clambered over the roof and covered it with sweet-smelling rushes cut from a patch of marshy ground near the river. Arthur in particular enjoyed making the wooden pegs that held the rushes firmly in place. In thanks, she gave them wonderful baking from her simple clay ovens and fed them like kings, treating them like her grandsons, who had all died in Bran's wars.

One by one, she took their strong young hands in her own shrivelled palms and turned her eyes up into her head. Her face was wiped clean of the years and the suffering that had scored her features, revealing the strange otherness that characterised the glamour shared by all wise women.

'Master,' she said to Eamonn, 'you will travel far and visit lands where the Celtic people have not been seen for a thousand years. During your absence, many changes will occur in your homeland, but you will perform heroic deeds that bring honour to your tribe. Your kin will continue to rule in Tintagel, and your line will endure down the centuries, even after your fortress is abandoned.'

Then she turned to Gareth, who would have pulled away had Arthur not insisted he stay lest he hurt the old woman's feelings.

'And you, son of a great father, and father of a great son. You will also journey far as you search in the wild places to find that which you have lost. Do not despair when the days seem darkest, for you will find what you desire and settle at last on the soil of your own land, where you will start anew and keep many of the good ways alive. Do not forget the garden that has sustained you, although the old one will have disappeared and you will have to rebuild to enjoy its fruits again.'

Gareth thanked her courteously, although the tingling in his hands disconcerted him. The old woman had meant well, although her appearance reminded him more of a witch than a simple woman of the countryside.

Then, with an odd sigh of resignation, she turned to Arthur. At her first touch, he felt a shiver start in his toes and rise through his whole body. Her bead-like brown eyes seemed very distant as she began to speak.

'You, master, are the Last Dragon. You are the last of the Great Ones. Because of a traitorous whisper, you will be forced to labour like a slave with your weapons torn away from you. But fear not, Lord of Mother Sea, for you will go to far-off places where the cold is a living thing. There you will regain your weapons, because the gifts from the Mother have prepared you for a special purpose. You are destined to lead men in great wars where you will win high renown and much gold. Then, when you return to your home and find that your forests are cut down and everyone you knew and loved is dead, you will make something new and bright out of your losses. Your star will shine throughout the centuries and your children will change the north for ever.'

'I thank you, Mother,' Arthur murmured with a rueful grimace. 'I can't say that your prophecies sound very cheerful. Will I find love? Or will I be the Last Dragon in truth and perish alone?'

'Have no fear.' She cackled with an odd girlishness. 'You will win the heart of a woman too good for you and beget sons on her. Your kingdom will be powerful down through the ages, long after the Celts have become a shattered people who will never recover from the disasters that will befall them. You will hold your faith, and all that lies before you will be as I have predicted.'

That night, inevitably, the companions spoke of the widow's prophecies. Eamonn was inclined to scoff, but Arthur could tell that he was impressed by the old woman and had been comforted by her predictions.

The next day, the courier from King Bors tracked them down. The brief holiday was over.

Stopping only to rest the horses, the three companions rode to Tintagel as if the devil were at their backs. Eamonn was anxious, for only a matter of some urgency would have prompted his father to send a courier to recall them. As always in these dangerous days, he automatically expected the worst, from family sickness or death to warning of imminent invasion, so he led the way on his roan hill pony at the best possible speed.

'I would have thought that if there was an urgent problem in Tintagel, your father would have alluded to it in the message he sent with his courier,' Arthur murmured as he tried to reassure his friend. 'I don't feel any warning signs in my head, and I know I'd have signals of apprehension if we were riding into danger. You'll find your father just wants to see you and sent a courier to bring us back into the fold. After all, we were enjoying ourselves far too much to hurry home of our own accord – you especially.'

Arthur grinned, and Eamonn couldn't help but respond. His lips twitched at first, but then he smiled widely. 'I was just collecting your left-over women, Arthur. Between you and Gareth, a normal-sized man doesn't stand a hope of catching the attention of any pretty maids.'

'I hope those nubile girls were attracted by our brains rather than our . . .'

With a muffled laugh, Eamonn tried to cover Arthur's mouth from the saddle, almost tipping both of them into a hedge. Gareth joined them on his grey horse, an indulgent smile on his face. 'We'd reach Tintagel a lot faster if we stopped comparing the length of each other's appendages,' he muttered with a smirk. The tone of Gareth's voice showed that he had unbent considerably during their impromptu holiday. No longer as quiet and servile as he had been, he was now an equal in Arthur and Eamonn's eyes and had gradually begun to act like a young man rather than a superior servant.

On the late afternoon of the second day, the cliffs surrounding Tintagel hove into view. The fortress was lit from the west by the last of the sun as it sank towards the horizon, bathing the stern battlements and towers in a roseate glow. A fast trot down to the Neck was easily achieved and Eamonn decided that on this occasion they would ride over and stable their horses on the peninsula itself, in case there was a need for them to make a hurried departure.

As day turned into night, the rocks became black and the sea turned to the colour of molten lead in the dregs of the daylight. Even the stairs seemed easier to mount, as all three men knew that warm beds and loving arms awaited them at the top, provided

Blaise hadn't taken a supply of mud and dog turds into the fortress with her. Arthur decided that even a wilful, spoiled child might think twice about pelting her brother and his guests in the presence of her father, the Hammer of the West.

Bors was waiting for them in the main hall of Tintagel where, uncharacteristically, the whole family was at dinner. At five feet eight inches Bors was not a tall man, but his demeanour was charged with the old Roman quality of gravitas, so that he seemed like a giant who had been forced to fit the scale of his fortress. His face was neither fair nor ugly, while his hair was neither curled nor straight, and was a midnight shade of black. But his features were firm and his clipped beard was so vigorous that any warrior meeting him for the first time instinctively deferred to him as a master without the need for introduction. Like Tintagel, Bors was a force in the British domains, and men spoke of how Gorlois had come again to keep the Dumnonii safe in these parlous times.

Arthur knelt to him immediately, with Gareth also on his knees at his side, his head lowered.

'Well, Eamonn, you've decided to return to your home after sowing your seed all over the south, I don't wonder. Your mother has told me about your friends. Rise, Arthur, Gareth, and let me take a good look at you both.'

The king's voice was deep and gruff, rather like stones grinding together, but Arthur heard no anger or resentment in it, so he rose to his full height. As he examined his guests, Bors was forced to look up into their faces, although such was the force of his personality that he lost nothing by his lack of inches. But if Arthur had been able to read the king's mind, he would have been disconcerted by what he found there.

By Ban's head, this young man is the living image of the Dragon King, Bors thought to himself. Because of the filial ties between his family and King Artor in days gone by, Bors Minor had spent many years at Cadbury Tor, where he had observed the High King dispensing justice, and had served with the loyal forces in Artor's war with Modred.

This boy has the look of Artor, without the sadness that was ever present in the High King's eyes. But would this young man have the strength to rule if the opportunity presented itself? Would he tear apart what little is left of the tribal structure? We can scarcely survive another civil war. If he has an inclination to usurp Bran's throne, it might be best to kill him now, Bors thought. But no trace of his ruthless conclusion was revealed on his craggy face.

Arthur was no tyro in the game of secrecy. Since entering his teen years he had been forced to negotiate dangerous conversations, always watching every word lest he should display some trace of ambition that would be sufficient reason for a knife to find a gap between his ribs in the dead of night. No one had ever needed to teach Arthur how to hide the innermost thoughts that lay behind his grey-green eyes, which seemed so deep and clear yet actually revealed very little of what went on below the surface.

So when the king of the Dumnonii, the Hammer of Cornwall, stared deeply into Arthur's eyes and examined his features for the faintest hint of falsity, all he saw was a mild, agreeable young man who was blessed with great strength and attractiveness, and possessed an amiable nature to match.

And only the faintest sign of an itch warned Arthur that Bors was a man who should not be underestimated . . . or completely trusted. Bors would protect his lands and his people, regardless of the cost to others.

'Eamonn, Gareth, I ask you to sit and eat, for I'd like to speak privately to our young guest before he and I take our ease. We will join you shortly. Will you come with me, Arthur of Arden?'

'How could I deny any request from the Hammer of the West?' Arthur replied.

'You were right, Valda, my beloved. He speaks with the courtesy of a king,' Bors said cheerfully to his wife, kissing the top of her neat head as he passed her place at the long table. At the door, he stood aside to allow Arthur to leave the room before him.

'You are doing me an unearned honour, your majesty,' Arthur murmured as he entered the short hallway. Bors led him to the flagged courtyard outside, where a servant hurried to place a lit torch in a wall sconce created by the blacksmiths for that purpose. The night still had a slight chill of winter upon it, as if the Winter King were unwilling to loosen his aged blue hands from the sea winds, but the light from the narrow, unshuttered windows of the hall sent cheerful bands of gold over the flagged surface, despite the nip of cold.

Bors began to pace and the wind lifted his black hair to expose small, almost womanish ears. One lobe had been pierced to hold a golden ring with a cabochon stone set into a small basketwork setting. The simple decoration caught the light and the red in the stone's heart glowed like a single drop of blood.

'I'm aware of your parentage. No man who knew the Dragon King in his middle years could fail to recognise his offspring. I was only a boy at the time, but I remember those days of blood and glory with some regret.'

'I am the foster-son of Bedwyr, the Arden Knife, who has all my love and loyalty. I want nothing more, regardless of my birth father,' Arthur replied, careful of every word he uttered.

'There's no need to tell falsehoods to me in this house, boy, for I will recognise any fabrication. I wish to ask you some impertinent questions, and you would be within your rights to consign me to the devil. But consider your answers with care, if you do comply.

It is important that I know whom my son calls friend, although he will not inherit Tintagel unless the Lord Jesus sees fit to take his two older brothers from us. Will you answer me fairly, Arthur of Arden?'

'Willingly, my lord.'

'Then, my first question is whether King Bran knows of your true relationship to him?' Bors was frank, and this question struck deeply into the tangled politics of the remaining kingdoms of the Britons. Arthur understood his concerns and was as truthful as possible.

'Yes, my lord, he does. He has known since I was seven years old and King Gawayne, my cousin, was still alive. My sister Anna and my kinsmen Bran and Ector are all well aware of my birth and have accepted my oaths of fealty. I would die before I betray my kinfolk, Lord Bors. So, before you ask, I will state that I have no desire to be aught but what I am, the foster-son of Bedwyr of Arden. Such distinction should be enough for any man.'

Arthur's jaw jutted out with his passion, and Bors could see the shark eyes of his old master clearly enough to know that this younger man spoke the truth as far as he knew it. His eyes fell to Arthur's sword belt and he saw the Dragon Knife.

Arthur's eyes caught that quick glance and he knew, without being told, what the king was thinking.

'Before King Artor died after the Battle of the Ford, Artor gave this knife to Father Bedwyr to pass on to my mother and, eventually, to me. He owned it before he became king of the Britons, so it was truly his own to do with as he wished. This relic is all I need of the past, Lord King. I am the son of two fathers, and I make my own way in this world, not lust after the possessions of my kinsmen. I was raised by Elayne, my mother, and her husband Bedwyr, the Arden Knife, two of the wisest people in Britannia. With them,

Taliessin has watched over me all my life. I speak the truth, Lord Bors, although you have only my word for it.'

'Give me your hand then, young man, and I'll know what is within your heart by the clasp of your palm in mine,' Bors said equably. Arthur complied without hesitation.

'I'm satisfied,' the king said softly. 'A man's hand is the only oath worth giving. I see nothing false in you, and Valda swears you're true. She comes from the hill people who are . . . sensitive in the ways of the spirit. I also like to think that Eamonn is a good judge of character.'

The silence drew out between them as Bors seemed to consider some matter that required a decision on his part. Then, brusquely, he walked towards the parapet that hung over the dizzying black drop to the shore below.

'Would you be prepared to commit to a service for me that is very important? Would you be willing to journey to the Vallum Hadriani at the head of a small band of warriors to deliver a very special package?'

Arthur thought quickly. He had never travelled to the north. Nor had he seen Hadrian's Wall, which was built to hold back the savage Picts. Between the wall and Arden, Saxons had built settlements that would need to be avoided, not to mention the new kingdom of Mercia. Only narrow strips of country on the east and west coasts allowed for safe passage, but tribesmen could still travel if they were careful, although only God knew how long that state of affairs would continue.

But it was an adventure – a real quest! What better thing could a young man profitably do with his time?

'Aye, Lord Bors. I would be willing to do as you ask, as long as I can make two detours along the path to the north.'

The king's eyes gleamed with curiosity, although he nodded

calmly enough. 'Where would you wish to go, Arthur? It's none of my business, but I'm curious.'

'I'd like to visit Glastonbury to see King Artor's grave. My mother was told by Nimue, Enid and Anna that they took his body to Glastonbury, where the bishop agreed to bury it in the grounds of the church. I know the site of his grave is unmarked and is supposed to be secret, but I'm almost certain that the bishop will oblige me.'

'That's a natural curiosity. And the other?'

'I would like to travel via Arden Forest. My father is a very old man, despite riding off to serve in the siege of Calleva Atrebatum with King Bran. That hideous encounter was probably his last battle, so I wish to pay my respects to the one man alive whom I truly love.'

Bors shot a penetrating glance at Arthur. 'You have no desire to visit Bran, who is your kinsman and liege lord?'

'No, Lord Bors. King Bran and I have always treated each other with courtesy and dignity, but there's little liking on either side. That makes no difference to my loyalty, but truth is truth.'

'You avoided mention of respect, Arthur,' Bors observed, with another penetrating glance.

Arthur sighed. 'I have never faced the pressures and frustrations that Bran is experiencing, so I have no right to pass judgement on him, or to criticise his decisions. I don't have to walk in his shoes.'

'But . . . ?'

'I don't understand how he could have used Marine Fire in the battle, knowing what it did. Nor can I have any respect for rulers who don't lead their men from the front. Artor led from the front . . . and that's why he died. Please, my lord. Ask no more of me, for I might compromise my honour with unwise words.'

'I watched you at the forefront of the battle lines at Calleva, Arthur. I rode with Bedwyr and Ector on that day because, as you say, I couldn't allow good warriors to fight without their leaders. But King Bran had to try to stay alive or, once again, we would have been faced with the vacuum that followed the death of Artor. He is, to all intents and purposes, the last of the dragon kings.'

Bors stared at the stars with a sudden surge of insight.

'But you're the last dragon, Arthur, aren't you? Although most men may not know it, you are the last remnant of a bitter time in our history. Poor Bran! When he looks at you and sees his grandfather born again, he must be cut to the quick. To have seen you in battle, as the Dragon King born anew, must have cast him into the throes of jealousy and despair, especially when he was forced to stay out of it in a position that was relatively safe from attack.'

Arthur's lips moved as his mind digested the words of wisdom spoken by the Dumnonii king. 'His feelings must be worse than wounds or death, for he has suffered the loss of all that was good in his world,' Bors went on inexorably. 'And such suffering is worthy of your respect, Arthur. You'll not grow into the man your father was unless you begin to think beyond your own concerns.'

'I believe I see, my lord. Perhaps I should respect Bran more and try to understand him better. It's time I stopped being childish.'

'Good. I can only ask you to try, and to thank you for your promise to take my package to the wall. Come, then. It's time for us to return to the hall. We'll talk about your journey after we've eaten.'

Bors seemed satisfied, so Arthur heaved a sigh of relief and followed his host back into the hall where they rejoined the family and began to eat with gusto. The meal seemed more elaborate than the usual fare served in the fortress, and Arthur deduced that a family celebration was in progress. Bors confirmed this impression when he rose to his feet and addressed his five sons and three daughters, a large family by any standards, for happy was the mother who could care for so many living children.

'My dear wife! My honoured guests! And my children, who are the dearest possessions that any man could have! I would happily die for any one of you. Bleddyn, my heir and my pride, Pedr, Eamonn, Owain and Nudd, my youngest baby – you are the sons who fill me with pride as I watch you grow. What man could be more blessed than Bors of Tintagel? And my daughters, fair and good to the core. Mair, who is visiting Tintagel with her little one, is now the mistress of her own broad acres to the south. Blaise and Ineda, who carry the blood of my heart, are dutiful and good girls. This day has come too soon, but for safety's sake I must forgo the company of my darling Blaise, who is betrothed to Gilchrist, heir of the Otadini tribe, who lives to the north of Hadrian's Wall. Blaise will grow to maturity far from the love of her parents and siblings, but she will grow safe and happy in the bosom of her new family, who will soon love her as much as we do.'

Bors turned and gazed directly at his daughter. 'Although your mother and I will weep to lose you, you must depart for Onnum, where King Geraint will meet you. He will guard you for the remainder of the journey to Bremenium, where you will live safely with his people. Circumstances decree that you must leave in two days, so let us all drink to the great good fortune of our lovely Blaise.'

As the diners stood and raised their cups in a toast to the young girl, Arthur examined her face. A smear of mud had escaped her toilette and her hair was dragged back into a horse's tail and tied with a thong. Arthur wagered that if he could see her feet under the table they wouldn't be very clean. When these indicators of carelessness were added to her sullen expression, the young girl's appearance was anything but regal.

'I don't want to go, Father,' Blaise responded with angry eyes. 'Why must I go there?'

'Remember that we have guests, Blaise, and mind your manners.' Queen Valda's tone was scolding, but Blaise ignored the order.

'But I don't want to go to the lands of the Picts,' Blaise snapped, working herself up into a tantrum. 'I don't want to marry anyone, so why can't I stay here?'

'In two days you will set forth on the long journey to the north in company with your servant girl, your bride's chest and your dowry. Your brother, Eamonn, will accompany you and Arthur ap Bedwyr has agreed to lead five of my warriors as your personal guard. Don't bother to cry or to sulk, Blaise, because you're going, regardless of what you wish. I'm your father and your king, so you will begin to pack as soon as our meal is consumed.'

Rather than argue, for even she recognised the determination in her father's voice, Blaise leapt to her feet, sending her stool flying, and stomped out of the room.

'My apologies, Arthur, but Blaise has always been a handful. She will be Geraint's problem soon, and meanwhile I'm grateful that you've accepted my offer to deliver this little package. We never spoke of payment for the task, but when you have lugged my recalcitrant daughter to the border you will have earned a reward.'

Arthur flushed hotly. Two spots of high colour formed on his cheeks, while the skin around his mouth whitened with anger.

'You insult me, my lord. When I agreed to help you I did so without any expectation of payment. No, I do this for my friend Eamonn, and for you as his father. I also do it for young Blaise, who may need our guidance during the journey before her.'

Queen Valda could tell that their guest's feelings had been hurt at the mention of payment, so she laid a small, short-fingered hand on his arm to console him. 'Then accept our thanks and love as your reward, Arthur. They have no monetary value, but they do have much worth.'

Despite himself, Arthur smiled and raised the queen's hand to his lips.

'You are the wisest woman in the land, my lady, save only for my mother, Elayne of Arden. I accept your reward with gratitude.'

The party was beginning to tire after five days of travel along the roads leading from Tintagel to Glastonbury. Blaise had used every strategy she could think of to delay their journey and make it unpleasant. With a child's viciousness, she had turned Tintagel into a small hell with her tantrums, her rages, her demands and her rudeness. Bors and Valda were embarrassed by her behaviour and Bors eventually threatened to bind and gag her over the saddle for the entire journey to the wall. Blaise finally submitted.

After some minor difficulties, a long, green valley finally stretched out before the riders, bounded by rows of hills on either side. Arthur could imagine this swath of land as an inland sea, for it was criss-crossed with waterways and every shade of green blended with the glistening streams to give the illusion of a huge platter, glazed with shiny emerald glass and decorated with a web of silver. Only two huge, natural features stood out on the fair landscape – the earthworks surrounding Great Cadbury to the south, which the riders had avoided, and the massive tor at Glastonbury with its single tower that pointed upward like an impudent finger. Arthur admitted to himself that he was looking forward to a clean straw pallet and some relief from Blaise's endless complaints.

Valda had been true to her promise, and had resisted the impulse to shower Arthur with gifts. However, even in the two short days available to her, she had found two items to show her appreciation. The first was a cloak, for she had noticed that Arthur's red woollen cape and hood were worn at the edges and unravelling at the seams. The cloak she handed to him was woad-blue and scarlet woven plaid, which mirrored the colours worn by her husband's warriors, but its hood was lined with part of the pelt of a winter wolf that Bors had slain. Its white fur provided protection and warmth for Arthur's head, although he protested that the spring weather didn't really warrant such a garment.

'It's for the north, dear Arthur. The weather there is always cool, even when the rest of the country is looking forward to summer. I'd not have your mother believing we'd allow you to travel without warm clothing.'

She blushed when Arthur kissed her palm in gratitude after trying on the vivid cloak and preening like any young man judging the effect of attractive clothing. 'I'm touched by your generosity, my lady, but there was no need to give me such a valuable gift. Still, I will happily accept it and will wear it with pride because the mistress of Tintagel made it with her own hands.'

It was the queen's turn to blush with embarrassment as she reached upward to hang a small pendant round his neck. Among her jewels, she had found a small iron dragon which she had looped through a thong for him to wear over his heart.

'This trinket is to bring you good luck, young Arthur. The dragon is the sigil of your house and will protect you in times of danger.' Arthur was too touched to argue with her and found himself on the verge of tears. He realised that his time among the kind people of Cornwall had been as happy as any in his short life, and he accepted the largely valueless emblem in the generous and loving spirit in which it had been offered.

The gift that Bors gave him later that day was much harder to accept. The king had produced a gold and ruby earring from a package and then, with his own hands, had driven its spike through Arthur's ear lobe. The king was so quick and deft in his actions that Arthur didn't even have time to yelp in pain. 'I can't accept this gem,' Arthur protested, while the king cleaned away a few errant drops of blood from the hole in Arthur's ear. 'It's far too valuable.'

'You have refused payment for the task I have foisted on you, my boy, but you've been honest with me and my family, and for that I thank you. I'm also aware of the sigil that my wife has already given you to mark your position as the last of your bloodline. I should be kneeling at your feet and offering you the homage that is your due. But your father sired you at the end of his life and I understand why he chose to protect you from the ugliness of high office. He gave you a great gift, you know, and what you win in this life will be earned rather than granted by an accident of birth. Like the Dragon King himself, you will carve out your own future. Remember that when you turn this ring in your ear. Remember too that you are free to make your own future, and are not bound like Bran to fight a desperate struggle that I fear will inevitably become a lost cause. Take my daughter to safety and then make your own way in the world. Like Bran, I'm not free to help you or to acknowledge who you are, but I sincerely wish you luck in the life that awaits you. I also ask that you take care of my Eamonn. He's not my heir, nor even second in line, but I've a fondness for the boy. He's true, if you understand me, like a well-crafted arrow. Send him back to me alive, and my house will be forever indebted to yours.'

So Arthur gave the king his word and his hand as the party left Tintagel. If Eamonn wondered at his father's ring in Arthur's ear, he made no mention of it, although the same could not be said of his sister. On the second night on the road, in dreary spring rain which turned their campsite to mud, she vented her spite in the only way she could.

'I see my father's paid you to sell me to the Otadini. I hope you received plenty of gold from him, because I intend to make sure you earn every grain of it.'

'Do shut up, Blaise, there's a good girl. You might impress some people with your tantrums, but to me you're only a dirty little waif with a vile temper, a horrid attitude to everyone who comes in contact with you and an undisciplined, foul-mouthed tongue.'

'How dare you! I'm a princess and you're just a dirty upstart from God knows where. I intend to say and do what I like.'

Arthur grinned like a wolf and, for the first time, Blaise felt a frisson of uncertainty.

'You will obey me, Blaise, or I will personally gag you – and keep you gagged! My agreement with your father doesn't require me to tolerate boring behaviour that is better suited to a whore than a princess. If you continue to bleat, you may expect a worse response.'

With wide, astounded eyes, Blaise fell silent and remained so all the way to Glastonbury. She sulked in silence, but left Arthur in no doubt that she was plotting her revenge.

When Glastonbury appeared before them Arthur felt the peace of the holy place descend into his soul. He had been raised to venerate this valley, where so much of his family history had been forged. Bishop Lucius of Glastonbury had arranged for the infant Artor to be taken to the Villa Poppinidii and then paid Ector Major to foster his new charge. At the end of Artor's life another bishop had buried him in secret and prayed for his soul. Desperate to find some connection with his birth father which did not involve pain and disappointment, Arthur had come to see the resting place of the last High King of the Britons.

For the sake of the brothers of Glastonbury, Arthur left the party on the outskirts of the village that had grown around the religious enclosure, itself centred on a small, dilapidated wooden structure that had been bound together in places with straps of iron and sheets of lead to keep it upright.

Here, according to the legends, Joseph of Arimathea had built a church and planted the holy thorn from either the Cross of Calvary or the Crown of Thorns. When he died, the Cup of Lucius, rumoured to be the Bowl of Ceridwen or even the Sangreal, or Holy Grail, had been stolen from his grave. True or not, legends filled the sweet air of Glastonbury that weaved its way around the tor and all who lived below it.

Arthur and Gareth trotted their horses up to the rudimentary gatehouse and Arthur asked if he could speak to the bishop, apologising that he was unfamiliar with the name of the current incumbent of this important position. He gave his own name and that of Gareth before explaining their pedigree to a priest, who folded his hands inside his long sleeves as he memorised their message.

'Brother Peter will take you and your companion to the quarters we keep here for pilgrims who visit. I must ask now that you put away all weapons in this holy place, for they are not permitted. Then, depending on the decision of our bishop, you and the rest of your party may be permitted to remain in the quarters for the night. We see many pilgrims who come to Glastonbury for the sake of their souls, but in these uncertain days even God's house is not free of threat from the pagans. They would burn Joseph's House without a qualm, so I will take your message to the bishop myself.'

The two men followed Brother Peter to a simple two-storeyed structure of wood some little way from the church, the priests' quarters, the fish ponds and the gardens in which men were labouring despite the light, drizzling rain. The building for pilgrims was close to the smithy and the snug stables, and Arthur's experienced eye saw that these rooms had been set up like a plain and serviceable inn for travellers. He quickly realised that the clean pallets were filled with sweet grass and the wooden floors had been scrubbed until the planks were almost white.

The sun was lowering in the west when three robed men arrived at the pilgrims' quarters nearly an hour later. The priest who had met them at the gate was one of them, while another was a huge old man, white haired around his tonsure but obviously powerful. Arthur and Gareth assumed that he was a bodyguard of sorts to the frail, slender man who accompanied him. All three were dressed in heavily cowled robes of unbleached wool, tied at the waist with simple cords. Each carried a crucifix and beads at their waist for their prayers, and each had obviously been hardened by toil because the hands they offered were callused from years of labour in the fields. The smallest man stepped forward and both young warriors inclined their heads in gestures of respect.

'I am Father Philip, the treasurer of the Glastonbury community,' he said in a mild, scratchy voice that was ragged from lack of use, and Arthur wondered if this inoffensive man had taken a vow of silence in the past. 'You have already met Father Septimus, who cares for the needs of all our pilgrims. This is Bishop Mark,' he added, indicating the elderly, burly priest whom they had taken for some kind of protector.

Arthur and Gareth knelt and asked for a blessing, which Bishop Mark gave with gnarled, age-spotted hands that still retained traces of beauty. When they rose to their feet Mark looked up at Arthur, and the warrior could see recognition in the clear brown eyes that were still young and burning in the old man's face.

'So rumour does not lie. The Dragon King has left a hatchling behind him,' he said. Arthur blushed scarlet, and assured the priest that whoever his sire might have been he was the foster-son of Bedwyr, the Arden Knife, and had no wish to be addressed in any other way.

'I knew Lord Bedwyr well, although he couldn't bring himself to return to the Church. I remember him and Mistress Nimue with fondness. He must be very old now, is he not?'

'Aye, master, he is quite frail. He wearies of life, except for my mother, and waits with anticipation for the day when he will re-join his beloved king.'

'You may tell Bedwyr that I will pray for him. The days when he could use the roads to travel to Glastonbury died with the High King, I fear! Now, what can I do for you, son of the forest?'

Arthur blushed again. 'I wish to see the grave of the High King, Bishop Mark. Nimue has told me of her journey here, and she is certain that he will come again at a time of great need. She told me that the body lies near the church, and I am hoping that it is in your power to show me the place so that I can offer a prayer for his spirit.'

Without a word, Mark turned and led the way to the church and its small graveyard, while Gareth waited for Brother Peter to return with the rest of their party. One grave mound was a little separate from the others, situated to the right of the church wall. The sod had been disturbed during the past few years, and although the grass had grown back over the slight concavity in the earth, the cross looked a little askew, as if it had been hastily replaced in the ground. Mark saw Arthur gazing at the grave and divined his thoughts.

'Near to four years ago, an ancient man rode up to the church, surrounded by a heavily armed band of warriors who were strange to us. A pack beast bore a small wrapped bundle and I believed at first that they wished to bury a beloved child in our graveyard. The old man was King Gawayne, whom I had not seen for decades. He was very frail and desperately ill, but his will shone through his eyes as strongly as ever. I heard later that he died shortly after he returned to his home, and I said many prayers for a man who displayed such loyalty.'

'Whose was the corpse?' Arthur asked despite himself.

'When we opened the wrappings, we found the body of Abbess Mary Martha, whose name in your world was Wenhaver, High Queen of the Britons.'

Arthur felt his chest constrict. He had heard much of her fabled beauty, her faithlessness with Gawayne and her ultimate courage as the last High Queen of the British people.

'What did Gawayne want, Bishop Mark? This is not idle curiosity. As you know, Gawayne was my kinsman, and I would dearly wish to know how his story ended.'

'I understand your desire, my son. Gawayne believed that the last High Queen of the Britons should lie with her husband, as she had wished, and we abided by his request. We opened the grave, removed the stone that covered the High King's remains and placed the queen's body on top. They are now together in death, deep in the ground where we had first interred him after he was brought to this holy place.'

The bishop stared into Arthur's eyes.

'Before returning home, Gawayne asked us to carve a final message on the reverse of Artor's gravestone. One of our artisans did so, and the stone was replaced in the grave before it was refilled. The prayers for the dead were private and short, but all was done as Mother Mary Martha would have wished. Artor and Wenhaver will rest for ever in peace within this holy place.'

'Can you tell me the message ordered by Gawayne?'

'The words came straight from the heart of the great warrior: *Here lies Artor, King of the Britons, and Wenhaver, his second wife.*'

'Thank you for your kindness, my lord. I would like to pray now, if you will excuse me.'

Bishop Mark moved some little distance from the grave and watched as the beautiful, extraordinarily tall young man knelt in the grass and abased himself at the foot of the grave. Then Arthur sat on his heels with a bent head.

Mark smiled sadly to himself. Somewhere in his devout heart some trace of the old Roman ways that had coloured his youth was retained, so he imagined a great wheel being turned by God rather than Fortuna, and the figures of mighty men rising and falling as judgement was meted out to those powerful manipulators of human life who had reigned supreme until their deaths.

'I hope the king sleeps well,' he murmured. 'In the aftermath of his death, his sins have been forgiven, for he gave everything for his people and the Church. He was not a true believer, but his son is cut from finer cloth and seems to be noble to the bone. However, his eyes are still innocent, and he has yet to experience the cruelty of life, so I pray the Lord to have mercy on him, if only for the sake of his father.'

The last rays of the sun caught Arthur's amber curls and turned them into a halo, or a crown. Mark shivered. There lay the past, and there knelt the future. 'Ah, Lord, what you have decided will come to pass. We foolish souls cannot understand your divine purpose.' He looked up, and saw that Arthur was gazing at him with eyes that were everything and nothing.

'Thank you for your courtesy, Bishop Mark. I believe I shall not pass this way again, but I pray that Glastonbury remains safe from the Saxons.'

As they walked back to the pilgrims' lodgings, where even Blaise had been silenced by the atmosphere of this sacred place, Mark realised that he was weeping, but in the days and years that followed he could never explain the reasons for his tears.

Arthur's Trek from Tintagel to Onnum

CHAPTER XIX

THE LAST OF ARDEN

Man is the shuttle, to whose winding quest
And passage through these looms
God orders motion, but ordained no rest.

Henry Vaughan, *Silex Scintillans*, 'Man'

After weeks of travel, Arthur felt as though he had been on the road for ever with the bitch-child, Blaise, who more than lived up to her name with its echoes of fire. Nothing was ever right in Blaise's world, and everyone suffered because of her misery. Arthur was prepared to concede that being torn away from everything that was familiar and comforting at such a young age would have caused him to experience fear, feelings of rejection and displeasure, but he hoped that he would have acted with more grace than this girl displayed. She had never left Tintagel except for brief visits to Isca Dumnoniorum, so she should have enjoyed new places and people as a relief from the tedium of her childhood. But the journey from Tintagel to Glastonbury, and then by easy stages to Lindinis before joining the old Roman road to the north, had been agony for everyone involved.

At first, Arthur had sought to amuse the girl with the strange sights and the local legends. She remained sullen and, if she spoke, was devastatingly rude. Whenever he tried to show any empathy for her situation Blaise cut him off, until he despaired of finding any common ground where they could meet. Blaise was only a child, a difficult little girl, and she had no concept of what it meant to her family to have her safely married and domiciled in the relative security of the north.

Then, at a no-name, unimportant village in the hills above Corinium which they detoured towards after noticing a pall of smoke rising into the clear spring air, Arthur and Blaise came to their first fragile, tentative understanding.

The village had been attacked and destroyed on the previous day, and the remnants of its stone cottages were still smouldering, criss-crossed by fallen timbers that had been burned almost through by the heat of the conflagration.

'Keep the girl back,' Arthur ordered brusquely. He could still recall the remains of Crookback Farm all those years earlier, so he had some understanding of what they would find when they entered the village. He and Eamonn rode ahead into the small settlement, which had been so poor that most of the cottages were built of wood and thatch, obviously scavenged: materials that allowed the structures to burn like dry leaves. All that was left was stamped earth, ashes and a few broken pots. And the bodies.

Behind the cottages, empty pens showed that these villagers had scrabbled to earn a living with black-faced sheep and goats, because the soil was clearly a mixture of shale, flint and clay that was far too heavy for most crops. Water was plentiful, but life must have been hard for the inhabitants before the Saxon raiding party took everything of value, including their lives.

Unseen by the two warriors, Blaise had disobeyed their

instructions and ventured into the shell of the first cottage on the edge of the circle of ruins. Her piercing cry drew their immediate attention, and with swords drawn they turned to face what they thought was an imminent threat to their safety.

'They're dead!' the child wailed, her eyes staring and very dark in her chalk-white face. 'The little children – even the boys! They've been . . . hacked to pieces. Who could do that to five-year-old children?'

Arthur stepped towards the ashen-faced, shaking girl. 'I told you to stay with the guards. When will you learn to obey?'

'But they're all dead!' she protested, two tears escaping unnoticed from her eyes. 'What was the point of killing children, Eamonn? They couldn't fight back. They were no threat to anyone. They were no older than little Nudd. Who would kill someone as young as little Nudd?'

Arthur gripped the girl's shaking shoulders and noticed that she was tall for her age and gangly with her growth spurt. She seemed on the verge of hysterics, so he put one arm round her shoulders and gently steered her back to the guards and her pony.

'These Saxons weren't necessarily warriors. Their fighting men aren't always monsters, just different from us in too many ways for us to live together peacefully. But every race has its outlaws, creatures who prey on weaker victims. This band lacked the courage to mount an attack on any group stronger than unarmed villagers who only had spades and hoes to protect themselves. Such men grow fat on the chaos of war and nothing is too vile for them to do. Do you see?'

'Yes,' she whispered, gulping and beginning to cry again in the shelter of her hill pony's mane. Arthur returned to the circle of buildings, ordering the five Dumnonii warriors to accompany him.

'Seek out all the bodies and bring them to this hut. We'll use the stones from the wall to surround them and then cover them over with whatever timber we can find,' he ordered crisply. 'We'll burn their remains.'

The men fanned out immediately, each entering one of the pathetic ruins.

Eamonn stepped over the threshold of the cottage Arthur had selected and looked at the partially burned bodies within it. A number of children had been driven inside before the doors had been shut and the thatched roof set on fire with a flung torch. The doors and walls had sagged under the assault of five small bodies as the children had tried to escape the flames that were devouring them. Fortunately, they appeared to have died from inhaling the black, oily smoke which still stained their mouths and nostrils in the minutes before the fire engulfed their tender bodies. Eamonn turned away, sickened by the mental image of their last moments. As the bodies of ten adults and several more infants were gathered and placed in the hut with the children, he conferred with Arthur.

'Are you sure we're doing the right thing?' he asked.

'Yes,' Arthur murmured. 'We don't have the time to bury these corpses, or even cover them, so we must burn them right here in their village. The outlaws could still be close, and we don't have the luxury of time to hunt them down. Besides, we'd be risking the safety of the girls, which King Bors wouldn't tolerate – or forgive. No, we have to allow these animals to remain free.'

'How do you know these murders weren't inflicted by a war band? I've always been told that the Saxons will commit almost any sin,' Eamonn said softly. He was piling wood from a shattered animal pen on top of the pitiful tangle of dead flesh, and his face was twisted with suppressed, impotent fury.

'Bedwyr has often told me that the northerners of bygone days acted in this way, but he swears that many of the current Saxon lords were born here in Britain, just as we were. Today's Saxons don't seem to be quite so senselessly cruel; they only attack settlements to further their land holdings and their power. Of what use is this village to the Saxon warrior class? Was there really so much wealth here that a war band would be tempted to attack it? Besides, what group of settlers would want holdings as poor as these? No, logic indicates that this is the work of a rebel group, men who have been cast out of their own villages as outlaws and so prey on small, unprotected places like this for food and what few precious objects are owned by the farmers. Think, Eamonn! We live in lawless times, and we are far from Mercia or the kingdoms of the east. The one good thing to result from this senseless ruin might be that Blaise will give us an easier journey. She's badly shaken by what she has seen here.'

Eamonn nodded, but his dark eyes were bemused. 'Sometimes you can be so matter-of-fact and so cold that I can hardly recognise you, my friend.'

'Put it down to my parentage, Eamonn. No one in my family is particularly soft hearted,' Arthur replied wistfully. Under the layer of practical analysis, he felt the deaths of these children acutely, but time was passing too quickly for the party to spend too much time here. Spring would soon be over and summer would be upon them. He had no intention of being caught in the north during the autumn, and the prospect of winter's grasp was totally unacceptable. If they were delayed here, they would all suffer.

So Arthur used his flint to strike up a fresh spark and consigned the poor farmers to a cleaner burial than their murderers had intended. In the sudden leap of flames, the bodies seemed to move as if they were intent on rising out of their winding sheets of fire and coming forth from the funeral pyre. Arthur turned and left the victims, carefully closing the door and latching it to conceal the sad corpses, although the hut was open to the sky and any attempt to protect the bodies from airborne predators would be futile.

After that, the road leading to Arden was long and exhausting. Even with their spare mounts and the good food they purchased as they travelled, the party was ragged and tired when Arthur finally saw the river and the road to his home branching away to the right.

'See, Blaise,' he said, pointing at a green smudge of trees beyond the water meadows. Although she rarely spoke to him directly, the girl had taken to staying very close to him as if his presence ensured her safety. 'Those trees mark the boundary of Arden, my home, and they are the only barrier that protects us from the Saxons.'

On the surface, little had changed in Arden Forest in the months Arthur had been absent. The route into the heart of the forest was as tortuous as ever, but now a well-placed arrow whizzed across a clearing ahead of the party to bury itself quivering in the trunk of an old alder tree not far from where Arthur sat astride his horse. Then, from the treeline, a voice demanded to know who he was, and the nature of his business in Arden Forest.

'I am Arthur, first son of Bedwyr, the Arden Knife, and Lady Elayne. I am accompanied by a party of Dumnonii warriors led by Eamonn pen Bors, third son of King Bors, the Hammer of Cornwall. The party includes Lady Blaise, the daughter of King Bors, and her serving woman. I beg shelter and hospitality from my father for these Dumnonii nobles. Are we now so lacking in trust that we turn guests away?'

A head appeared high in a venerable oak tree, where the bowman was comfortably ensconced, while another voice boomed out of the thickest part of the forest edge beside the narrow trail. Arthur noticed that Blaise's fingers trembled as she held her horse's reins.

'We did not expect to see you for some time yet, Lord Arthur. Your noble father has been worried about you. He has alerted all the scouts to watch and listen for any word of you.'

'May we pass?' Arthur shouted. 'I wish to join my family in Arden by tomorrow. Please send word on ahead, good sir.'

A muffled shout indicated that the party could move forward without threat. Arthur explained to Eamonn that this type of security was most unusual and probably meant that Arden had experienced some breaches in security, probably from the east, where it guarded the two Roman roads that protected the north.

'Will this problem affect the route we take towards Hadrian's Wall? I had thought we would travel along the Roman road that runs through Venonae,' Eamonn said. His voice and expression indicated his concern, for the most dangerous part of their journey would begin as they skirted the Saxon kingdom of Mercia, hugging the mountain chain to avoid old Eburacum, now call Eoferwic, which had been held by the Angles and Jutes for twenty years. The High King had crushed the Saxons at Eburacum and the British had experienced a period of relief, but as the Dragon King had aged the eastern coast had become too difficult to control, until even Artor, in all his stubborn pride, had known that the city would ultimately fall to his enemy. Eamonn knew as much of the history of the north as any well-educated son of the nobility, so he was alarmed to hear that Arden might no longer control the roads which were the arteries of Britain.

'Don't fear, Eamonn. Father will know all the details of any Saxon incursions into the lands to our north. If need be, we'll divert towards the west coast, but let's not worry too much about our route until we know what we face.' A feeling of gloom washed over Arthur as he began to think ahead. Yes, he could take a western detour, but it would lengthen the journey by weeks, perhaps months, and autumn would catch them unprepared and far from safety.

For the first time in their travels, Blaise showed some interest. Having grown up on the coast and been lulled to sleep by the sound of waves for all her short life, she missed the constant rhythm of the sea. But here, deep in primal forest, the wind soughed through the trees with a sound that mimicked the waves with a little extra added – the smell of life, of rotting vegetation, of deep leaf mould, lichen, tree bark and aromatic leaves. Somehow, the combination stimulated Blaise's senses and reminded her of home, so she knew she would be able to sleep.

The girl had skin of an unnatural whiteness, even when compared with the pallor of the women of Cymru. Perhaps to take her mind off the long and difficult journey, Blaise had begun to show a belated interest in cleanliness, causing Arthur to notice that her black hair and eyes were in dramatic contrast to her pale skin. Sun, dust and wind burned it and made travel a misery, with the result that she sweltered under layers of clothing to protect herself from the traitorous sun. To make matters worse, hours in the saddle chafed her childish flesh. No wonder the child was so miserable, Arthur said to himself. But deep in the forest, where the sun's rays were filtered, she cast off the cowl of her cloak with a crow of pleasure and raised her face to the muted green light.

For the first time, Arthur began to admire the early signs of beauty in her. His heart softened automatically, and he slowed his horse to ride beside her. 'This forest is my home, Mistress Blaise. When I was younger than you I knew all the great trees in these woods. I even used one forest giant as a special place where I could go when I was troubled.'

She looked up at him then, and the urchin who threw mud and turds at her brother was eclipsed. Her lashes were abnormally long and thick, like those of a fawn or fallow deer whose eyes reproached him when the time for butchering had come. Her hairline was straight and true, and her brows were finely feathered and turned up at the outer edges. Arthur decided she was a perfect miniature of the best of the tribal traits of womanhood, although her eye colour spoke of earlier, more ancient peoples who predated his own race.

It's strange, he thought. I only remember Valda as a woman who has borne eight living children and is long past the age of physical beauty, but this child reminds me of her. But Valda had charm and glamour aplenty, and she spoke of the sensitivity of her people with conscious pride. Does this daughter of hers have voices that speak to her inside her head? Does she fear the unknown, being the most like her mother of all the siblings? I should watch her closely.

Something squirmed in his head, scolding him for thinking of Blaise in such an analytical fashion, as if she were an interesting sword or a fine horse. He shook his head in amazement at the realisation that this girl, who had been so monumentally rude to him since their first meeting, had captured his attention, and he sighed in exasperation.

'I know the hollows around Tintagel in the same way as you know Arden. I've watched the sea birds my whole life, so I know which ones nest on the cliffs and which ones live nearby at Saint Brigit's Well. How can I live in a place where I don't know the birds?'

Arthur thought quickly, because the child needed reassurance. He'd not expected that she would love hunting birds, a strange preoccupation for a young lady.

'Perhaps Gilchrist will give you merlins of your own. I've been told that some northerners love to train birds of prey to hunt for them.'

Arthur had intended comfort, but the child's eyes grew wide with horror.

'I would never choose to possess a bird. It makes me sick to think of it. I'd be forced to free it so that I could pretend that I was flying with it, high above the earth and all its troubles.' Then Arthur recalled a long-buried memory of Ector's young wife, who had been in Arden when Maeve was born. She had dreamed of flying like a bird and escaping to far lands where she was free of the demands of her sex and her position in life. He had always liked Gwyllan, who had been the daughter of King Gawayne.

'Is being a wife and mother so grim a future, little one? My mother is very happy and she is the cleverest woman I know.'

'I'd rather travel and hold a sword. I'd like to learn to write and not be forced to spin and weave all day. I have no wish to be married to anyone,' Blaise whispered, and her passion could be read in those jet-black eyes. Had Arthur ever known his aunt, he would have recognised something of Morgan in Blaise's vehement denial of the female role that was laid out inexorably before her. After all, Morgan le Fey and Blaise were kin, although much removed.

Unfortunately, Eamonn picked this moment to join them. Blaise's enthusiasm died and her eyes became flat and expressionless when her brother guided his horse to ride alongside her. From long practice, she masked her feelings under a sullen expression.

The troop rode on, resting that night under the trees. In the morning they would reach the palisades, and Arthur hoped that his companions would be rested and look their very best when they paid their respects to his parents.

In the weak light of a new day, Arthur combed and plaited his hair with Gareth's assistance. Like all warriors, Arthur assisted Gareth with the same homely task, and he wondered, as always, how hair could vary so widely from man to man. His wild corkscrew curls crackled with energy while Gareth's long straight locks were smooth and straight, like rare cloth or fine thread.

During the night, they had polished their heavy leather travelling tunics, reinforced with metal plates of iron, until the metal shone brightly. When the sun came over the horizon, the two young men quickly packed their saddle bags and assisted Blaise and her servant to mount their horses. Bors's troop of warriors had also seen to their toilettes, realising that they would be meeting the famed Arden Knife, a man of legend who had seen the Bloody Cup with his own eyes. Bedwyr was especially venerated among the common soldiery, for he had served on the front line at Moridunum and had helped to bring down the fortress of Caer Fyrddin. The old man had ridden in the footsteps of the Dragon King, and the warriors dreamed of meeting this great man, of hearing his voice and recapturing those days of glory.

An excited, disciplined band set forth after a hurried meal of cold porridge and a handful of nuts. A spirit of fervour and anticipation hummed through the ranks as the men mounted and the party greeted the day as something new and special.

Arthur was glad they had eaten the meagre breakfast, for their journey was slowed by regular guard checks, although the Cornovii warriors never broke their cover in the fringes of the trees. 'The Saxons and Jutes must have been on the prowl recently if our identities are being checked so often when they know we are coming,' Eamonn muttered after they had been stopped for the fourth time in less than an hour.

'Father speaks the Saxon language fluently, as I do, but he has pointed out that if he could pretend to be a Saxon, then they could learn our language and pretend to be tribal warriors,' Arthur replied. 'My father is a very cautious man, so he thinks ahead and trusts few people other than family and close friends.'

But all journeys come to an end. A little after noon, Arthur saw the crown of his own oak tree through a gap in the forest and knew that the palisades were near. So suddenly that the newcomers were left blinking, the forest released them from its heart into the open meadows around his home. The fallow fields were thick with grass and wild flowers, and grazing cows watched with incurious eyes as the troop passed

'There they are! The palisades of Arden,' Arthur shouted, and pointed. Bedwyr's hall lay at the centre of the cleared meadows, most of which were under cultivation: another indication of Saxon raids in the area of Arden, since it must mean that trade was much reduced. The gates were open and there was Bedwyr, grizzled and bent, but grinning through his beard like a crazy man. Arthur could also see Elayne, her face streaming tears and a new streak of white in her red-gold hair. His siblings were waving madly, their faces glowing with health and the boys capering like acrobats at a fair.

'They've grown so tall!' Arthur marvelled in a whisper. Then he realised he had been gone rather longer than he had intended, and his brothers and sisters were almost fully grown.

One small form stood separate from the others. Maeve, the youngest daughter, stood off to one side. Even from this distance Arthur could see that, at eleven, she was tall for her age and her hair was crimson-red, a strange colour that flamed in the afternoon sun.

'You have returned, Arthur,' Bedwyr said softly, his eyes moist with tears. 'I am so very proud of you. Look at you! You are a man by any measurement. Come, introduce me to your friends and then you can join your mother. She has longed for your return, my boy, fearful that some disaster might have caused you lasting harm.'

Eamonn dismounted. 'Go to your mother, Arthur. I can introduce our party to Lord Bedwyr with pride, for he is the greatest living man in Britain.'

Arthur nodded, and hurried through the gates to where Elayne waited with her heart in her eyes.

'I didn't think I'd see you before the onset of winter, if then.' There was not the faintest trace of self-pity or complaint in her voice. Instead, Arthur saw a great relief and joy that he had come, no matter how brief the visit. As he picked her up in his strong, manly arms until her feet dangled and she wound her arms round his neck, Arthur was amazed at how small and light she had become, as if a breath of wind could blow her away like thistledown. His heart beat faster when he saw the greyness in her hair, and he suddenly realised that his mother had grown old.

'All things eventually come to an end, my son. I'm just so happy that you've returned home, even if it's only for a short visit.' Tears formed in her eyes, and it was as well he had no way of knowing what her true feelings had been when she had seen him striding towards her with the sun behind him.

My Artor has come again, she had thought tremulously, her heart in her mouth. Oh, my beloved, it has been so long since we spoke together.

Then she looked at him again with her sun-dazzled eyes and realised it was her son who was holding her, her son who was kissing her soft wrinkled throat, and the spell was broken.

'You've grown, Lasair,' Arthur said cheerfully as he turned to the seventeen-year-old boy who hovered at his mother's shoulder. The lad stood as tall as Bedwyr and his shock of brown hair showed a corona of red from the sun. The young man flushed and gripped his brother's hand until Arthur put his mother down, laughed, and ruffled Lasair's hair from his superior height. He began to regret the many months he had been absent, for time had transformed them from children into young men and women hovering on the brink of adulthood.

Only Maeve remained apart from the group. Like Blaise, she was only eleven years old, and she waited patiently to speak to her oldest brother in private. When the group walked towards the hall across the roughly flagged courtyard, she followed like a pale wraith, her eyes enormous in her small, triangular face.

As they crossed the threshold, followed by Bedwyr at the head of his guests, the Dumnonii guards were escorted to the Cornovii barracks where ale and good food waited, along with the opportunity for boasting about the Saxons they had slain. Maeve's was the only serious face among the laughing, milling throng, and as Arthur tried to make his excuses to go to her he saw Blaise stop beside her. The two girls spoke quickly to each other, dark head close to red one, until Maeve nodded and took Blaise's hand to lead her away to the children's quarters.

'Blaise has found a friend,' Eamonn said as he approached Arthur from behind. 'How very unusual!'

'Yes. That's Maeve, my youngest sister,' Arthur replied thoughtfully as the young girls disappeared from view. 'She's a strange little thing. She's very clever, but she's so shy that you hardly notice she's with you most of the time.'

Then Arthur forgot his sister and his Dumnonii responsibilities as his family demanded to hear everything about the marvels he had seen in the south. The boys were particularly eager to hear his news, for they longed to know the gruesome details of the battle for Calleva Atrebatum. The afternoon flew away on winged feet and Arthur experienced that most comforting of all supports, the closeness of a loving family.

And so night came.

* * *

'Is it wise to travel to the wall at this time of year? The hive around old Eburacum will be stirring with Angles and Saxons aplenty. This Blaise is only a young girl, but she's very clever and she's already quite thick with Maeve.' Elayne looked fondly at her son, who was sitting cross-legged on the plank floor and watching, engrossed, while she coaxed the washed wool onto her spindle. The sight of the spinning wool and the wooden wheel was entrancing as she pulled the wool upward while twisting and lengthening the fibres into a strong, slightly nobbled thread.

'Oh, damn!' she swore mildly with exasperation. 'Nuala already outstrips me. Her thread is even and perfect, while mine . . . Still, your father says he likes my knitting and weaving precisely because it has imperfections. He says he knows it is my hands that have worked the cloth and the flaws that come with it.' She smiled as she thought of her husband. 'He's a dear, isn't he?' she murmured, and Arthur nodded. 'But the dear man's very old now. He's even older than the High King was when he died, and he's outlived every man he loved during his long life. The bone swelling is crippling him now, although he tries not to limp.' Elayne's face was sad, and yet beneath her worry and sorrow she was inured to the idea that her beloved husband would soon be lost to her.

'Many who served my dear Artor have now lived far beyond the normal life span. I don't know why this law of nature has been suspended in Bedwyr's case. Perhaps the Dragon King imparted to him some of his own zest for living, and he's certainly needed, just as the High King was, to lead our people through these troubled times of the Saxon invasions. Perhaps the good and quiet living that he enjoyed here in Arden has blessed him. But I do know that he is trying to send the children and me to his new settlement outside Deva. He's been preparing for our move for years now, knowing that Arden will eventually be infiltrated and that our people will be forced to retreat to the west. The forest on the borders of the Deceangli and Ordovice lands is similar to our home here. Bedwyr says the change would be seamless, and although we'd still be guarding a frontier it would be some time before the Saxons penetrated so far west.'

Artor nodded, unable to speak for the lump in his throat.

'But I'm going to stay here. He needs me, Arthur. I have no fear of death, because I'll simply leave one room, pass through a door, and enter another. I should have died in the snowstorm when you were conceived, so I owe my life to God and that debt must eventually be paid.' She brushed away a tear. 'I have tried to use the years God has given me to help others and I plan to ensure that our people are kept safe here in the dangerous years that will soon be upon us. But they will need guidance and a strong right hand to protect them, and Lasair will have little time to gain the experience he needs to accept the responsibilities that will be placed on him as his father fails. Perhaps the younger children can be moved to safety, which will give Bedwyr some relief. But I'll not leave him, and will support him always.'

'Why are you confiding in me, Mother? What do you want me to do? I'm proud that you trust me, but I believe you need me to do something of importance for you. Am I correct?'

'Yes, you are. You must convince your father that my plan will be the best course of action, complete your mission, and then hurry home. We will need your strong right hand, your courage and your steadfastness here in Arden Forest. Your brothers will have a desperate need for you if anything should happen to your father and me. They are still too young to understand the harsh realities of life, and even Lasair will need a guiding hand at first. Your greatest skill is your ability to see through to the heart of any problem, especially if you know the situation is critical. That skill will be sorely needed when Arden finally succumbs to the Saxons and your nephew's kingdom is open to attack from the east.'

'Bran will never listen to me,' Arthur replied regretfully, his mouth clenched tight.

'But Bran isn't immortal. Ector will eventually rule in his father's place, and he thinks of you with fondness. He has assured me that he admires your loyalty and your martial skills. You'll be able to protect my children at a time when no one else will have the capacity or the desire to do so.'

Arthur thought for a moment. His mother was asking little of him, and it would be an opportunity to repay Bedwyr for his unqualified love and trust.

'Of course, Mother. I'll do everything you ask. I'll defend my brothers and sisters with my heart's blood and I'll do anything to ease Father's last years. I promise that I'll be back by winter, and only death will keep me away.'

Elayne shivered as if a goose had walked over her grave, for the old cliché might have had some truth. 'I hope your heart's blood won't be needed, but I'll sleep better knowing that you stand with us. Hurry on your journey. I envy Bors, being able to send his daughter to a place that is so well protected, but our situation can't be helped and I think my plan is the best of several unpleasant options. Lasair will need persuasion to accede to my wishes, but together you and I will convince him.'

Then she reached up and kissed her son on the lips. 'Bedwyr has told me of your exploits on the line outside of Calleva, Arthur. He said he saw Artor fight one last time when you were at the forefront of the battle, and he was so proud of you that he thought he'd burst. I'm proud of my son too, as is Artor from beyond the shadows. I can feel him sometimes, as if he watches over me from the corner of the room. He would have been so happy to see the man you've become.'

Then mother and son parted to go about their various duties. The Dumnonii party had only been in Arden for one day, but Arthur was already eager to depart. But first, he had some old friends to see and his mother's first request to fulfil.

Germanus and Lorcan were due to arrive that afternoon. Germanus had retired from the life of a warrior and taken up a farm on the western edge of Arden with his wife. During the best part of a year since they had parted at Calleva Atrebatum, Germanus's wife had borne a son who was the arms master's pride and joy. He was coming for the evening family meal to see his erstwhile pupil.

Father Lorcan had distinguished himself among the wounded and dying after the battle of Calleva. No man perished in the tents of the healers without Lorcan by his side. He gave extreme unction to men who were Christian and heard the confessions of men who were not, interceding for them with their gods although, technically, his church frowned on the dissemination of such comfort. Always compassionate and prepared to make the rules of his order a little more elastic than was intended, Lorcan went from man to man, offering solace and writing letters, where possible, on pieces of vellum that he begged, borrowed or stole as the mood took him so that he could pass final messages from husbands and sons to widows and parents. Along the way, he worked hard with the healers, holding the hands of shattered, burned men and giving the most precious thing he possessed, his heart, to dying men, who went to their god or gods with cleaner souls as a result.

Since his return to Arden, Lorcan had divided his time between the people within the forest and those farmers and small villagers who sheltered on its margins. Imbued with new energy, he offered comfort as well as practical assistance to the frightened communities that depended on Arden, often assisting with the spring lambing if a farmer was unwell or helping with ploughing or farmyard tasks, especially for the older persons in his flock. But he was happy to assist anyone who needed his skills, even pagans. In the process, despite his disreputable appearance and rough tongue, he became universally loved.

Lorcan arrived early, so he and Arthur shared a mug of ale as Arthur explained his mission and recounted the experiences from which he had learned so much in the recent past.

'You've had yourself a high time then, Arthur, and now you're off to deliver a young girl to her betrothed. Good lad! By giving, we receive. I regret that I've been slow to remember the lessons I should have learned from the monks when I was still a young man, but I'm trying to rectify my deficiencies now.'

Arthur thanked his old teacher, but Lorcan was far from finished.

'I worry about you sometimes, Arthur, because you are a good and trusting young man. Don't bridle, lad, because it's no insult to call you good. Before you protest, I know you were hurt by the disillusion of Calleva and your nephew's use of you on the line, but that's not the same as losing everything you have. You haven't lost your innocence, and while that is your good fortune it could also cause you to become prey to wicked or amoral men.'

'By the gods, Lorcan,' Arthur swore. 'You make me sound like a babe at the breast. I'm well past the age of the nursery, and I don't need other people to look out for me.'

'But you still take men at their word until they prove false, Arthur. It's not a fault, I assure you, but in the world you inhabit, and especially considering the delicacy of the task you are currently undertaking, such a trusting nature might get you into trouble. Be careful of other people, Arthur, regardless of the faces they present to the world. In particular, you should remember your experiences with Mareddyd. I heard news of him recently, and I immediately remembered that you can't trust a fair face or sweet words. By our actions we are known.'

'I understand, Lorcan. But surely you're worrying unnecessarily.'

Lorcan examined his hands carefully, as if the key to heaven lay within the long fingers with their sprinkling of fine black hair. Several had been missed when he washed his hands, so crescents of black loam were clearly visible under his nails. He used a small knife to clean out the detritus while Arthur waited patiently.

'I've never spoken of my experiences in Rome because I was ashamed, but I was redeemed at Calleva, and through the terrible suffering of both our people and the Saxons I've come to realise that my own poor trials of faith helped to make me the man I am, for good or ill. God's purpose is not always easy to understand, but there is reasoning behind his structure of the universe.'

'I suppose so,' Arthur murmured. He was more confused than ever.

'I told you that I was taken to Rome because I had a gift with languages, especially Latin and transcription. The cardinal who mentored me was called Septimus, and I thought he was a cleric of great culture and piety.'

Arthur kept silent, because Lorcan's reminiscences were obviously painful to him.

'At first, Septimus seemed to be the perfect master. I was set to work copying ancient religious texts, using all the skill and beauty I could muster. His praise was lavish, and he made me believe that I was serving God when I worked for him. His home in Rome was palatial, a true palace in the Roman style, but I was hard at work with other young prelates and never saw the very unpriestly behaviour that took place in darkness. Nor did I give any credence to the other lads who spoke of Septimus with fear and loathing. Like you, I still trusted in the essential goodness of the people around me.'

Arthur sensed a deliberate direction in Lorcan's reminiscences and he began to protest, but Lorcan placed one twisted finger over the younger man's lips.

'You'll find it hard to believe, but I was a beautiful boy when I was a youngster, until life put creases in my face and blurred my understanding of right and wrong. By speaking now I'm placing my life in your hands, so, against my own advice, I'm placing my trust in another person.'

Arthur winced, for he was beginning to divine the ending to Lorcan's ugly story. But he also saw a certain cathartic relief in Lorcan's face, as if voicing his pain lessened the power it held over him. Arthur held his tongue.

'Cardinal Septimus was a voluptuous sybarite. Both girls and boys were unsafe if they were placed under his control, for he didn't really care about the sex or the age of the young people he assaulted. His depravity had no bounds, for he lived like a dissolute Roman emperor while he continued to espouse poverty and obedience. He raped me after one of his feasts, and I couldn't believe what had been done . . . or why. I chose to believe that I was the one who was at fault.'

'What happened?' Arthur croaked. 'Did you report his attack to the authorities?'

'Would they have believed me? Probably. But would they have censured him or saved me? Never! I tried to protect myself and remain beyond his reach, but I knew no one in Rome and I had no means of gaining money. I endured seven months of rape and torture before I eventually suffered a bout of madness.' He grimaced with distaste. 'I remember the night very well. Septimus's personal bodyguard had come for me – he actually had to drag me – and, to my shame, I was weeping. I was thrust into an antechamber and the door was locked behind me. There was a little girl there already, dressed in a flimsy, transparent robe. I could see the buds of her breasts and she had yet to grow pubic hair, so she couldn't have been any older than eleven. Someone had painted her face with cosmetics. She was struggling not to cry, for that would ruin the black lines painted around her eyes.'

'I don't understand how such things can be done in God's name,' Arthur whispered. 'If that makes me an innocent, I'd prefer to remain so than live in a world where such sins are accepted as commonplace.'

'Yes, perhaps so. I'd grown taller by then and hair had begun to sprout under my arms and in my groin, so although I didn't know it at the time I was less attractive to my master. He took the little girl first and I was forced to listen to her shrieking through the inner door. I was incensed, but what could I do? He sent for me shortly afterwards and told me that he found my hairy body repugnant and intended to have me shaved from head to foot. The little girl was curled up in a corner of the cardinal's bed, weeping quietly and bleeding. Her cosmetics had run and I felt disgust burn through me. Septimus then ordered me to take the girl for his pleasure. He sat naked in a chair beside the bed and his little paunch and flaccid penis disgusted me. But my disgust was exacerbated by the look of lust, greed and triumph that burned in his eyes. His look of anticipation still haunts me. When I reached for the child, she cried and cringed away from me and something snapped in my mind.'

'What did you do?' Arthur whispered.

'I strangled the cardinal with my own two hands. He never

expected me to attack him, so I had his throat under my thumbs before he understood the murderous intention in my eyes. I had been a blacksmith's son in my youth and had spent years copying and painting manuscripts since then. My hands were very strong and I squeezed the life out of him slowly, even as he struggled. His face became congested, then blue and bloated; his tongue lolled out at the end and his eyes popped and became red as the blood vessels burst just under the sclera. He had thought himself to be a handsome man, but Septimus had lost his beauty by the time I was through with him.' Lorcan grimaced. 'I wasn't quite suicidal, but I didn't much care if I lived or died. I decided to run. I tried to take the little girl with me, but she screamed and hid from me in Septimus's bed. Coward that I was, I left her behind, and told the guards that my master didn't want to be disturbed. No one doubted me or believed me capable of violence, so I had several hours before the cardinal's body was found. I robbed his rooms too, so I was now in possession of some of his gold. I was out of Rome within days and heading north. The rest of my life you know.'

'I'm sorry for what happened to you, but I'd hope I will never be placed in a situation like that,' Arthur murmured, for he was revolted by Lorcan's tale.

'So you say, lad, and I hope you're right. Just take care when you're with strangers, even if you consider they deserve a modicum of your trust. That's all I ask. I'll pray for you while you are leading your party to the north, a place where men cannot be trusted a single inch.'

When Germanus arrived, the three friends joined Eamonn and Gareth to boast, to share experiences and to give and take advice on the best routes to Onnum, their ultimate destination. The decision was made to head to Venonae and Ratae along the Fosse Way, but then to leave the main road and head overland towards

Vernemetum. From there, they must skirt Mercia and Eburacum by cutting through Sherwood Forest, passing under the old fortress of Temple and thence through the marshlands of Calcaria. Arthur was familiar with this area from the battle he had been involved in during his fourteenth year when he had won acclaim for his protection of the healers' enclave. All they must do here was remain close to the badlands, using the ancient paths of the hill people until they reached Danum. Then, at speed, they would bypass Isurium, Lavatrae and Vinovia, for the road then led them straight to Onnum.

'Easy,' Arthur murmured sardonically, and his companions laughed. Eamonn was dumbfounded by Arthur's use of a rudimentary map on which he made notations, until Lorcan explained about Myrddion Merlinus's passion for maps, and the examples he had made from his own travels. Because the boy was interested in his father's cartography, Taliessin had given Arthur copies of his father's charts of Britain many years earlier, and the citizens of Arden took great pride in using such valuable tools when they travelled outside the boundaries of their forest homes.

Arthur had already decided that the party must leave in two days' time. The journey before them would be long, arduous and fraught with danger, but men who possessed woodcraft skills could cope with the tribulations that lay before them, for most of the Saxon activity was currently centred in the south of Britain. Few of the invaders looked towards Arden with avaricious eyes.

Once the plan was decided, Arthur had time to relax and enjoy the peace of Arden, or so he hoped. From the palisades, as he looked towards his favourite tree, he saw Maeve and Blaise walking through the fallow fields picking wild flowers. The girls had made daisy chains for their hair, so white coronets glowed on their twin heads, one black as jet and the other as red as flame. Their joy in each other's company was clearly evident, for their arms were full of flowers and they were laughing uninhibitedly, making Arthur wonder at the wisdom of turning little girls into wives at such young ages.

Then he shrugged. After all, such a decision was none of his business. Eamonn was eager to leave, but Blaise set the hall alive with her laughter. Even Bedwyr took an unexpected liking to Blaise, calling her a *pretty little dove* to her face so that she blushed prettily whenever he addressed her. His avuncular manner was accentuated around her and Arthur wondered if his father wouldn't be a better commander of the party as it headed into the north. Then Bedwyr rose to his feet and groaned with the pain in his hips. Arthur castigated himself for even considering transferring his responsibilities to his father, an elderly man who was tired and sore from swollen, painful joints, a man whose face reflected his constant aches and pains.

Bedwyr is an old man, Arthur thought sadly. How could I consider passing on to him a task that I find onerous? I'm being selfish.

So he patted his father on the back, noting the bony protuberances on the old man's spine with alarm. They spoke of the days ahead and Arthur proposed his mother's plan bluntly, finding to his surprise that his father agreed with the proposal.

'I'll be back to help you before the end of winter, Father. I'm confident I can reach our destination and return by that time. Only death or capture will stop me.'

'Don't say such things, boy. My heart would break if anything were to happen to you. When I watched you fighting two-handed in the line at Calleva with such ferocity that even the largest Jutes couldn't reach you, I knew that your father had returned, just as Nimue promised.'

Arthur smiled tremulously. 'I'm not the Dragon King, Father. I'm just Arthur, and you deserve the credit for any honours that have come my way.'

'You're kind to say so, boy. Yes, I agree that I've watered your roots and kept down the tangling weeds that would have stunted your growth, but you've become what Artor should have been if he had been nurtured better as a boy. I can see your mother's influence on you as well, both in your calm logic and in your pleasant nature. I hope you never become bitter, my son. I did, and I wasted many years in a fruitless search for revenge against the Saxons who had used me. Any wrong that's been done to us can't be changed, so why should we spend our lives trying to find some kind of balance? Bad people won't change either, because they believe their actions can be justified.'

'Please don't speak as if we'll never meet again, Father,' Arthur murmured, patting his father's shoulder as he would an infant's. 'You sound as though this is the last time I'll be in Arden. I'll return, I swear it.' He laughed. 'I'll be like Odysseus! If I get sidetracked along the way, I'll turn up when you least expect it.'

'You talk about things I don't understand, Arthur, but I don't care. I'm a plain man who knows he's incapable of kingship. Unlike you, my boy! What a king you'd have made!'

Before Arthur could protest that there was nothing he wanted less, Maeve and Blaise came tripping into the hall and brought the scent of flowers and sunshine with them. Maeve's face was transfigured with joy. Her usual pallor was stained with rosy colouring and her green eyes were emerald bright with excitement. Like a cat, she had a small triangular face and a certain lanky grace under a head of thick, bright red hair. Unlike most red-haired tribeswomen, her face was free of freckles, but a faint dusting of gold reflected the time she had spent in the sun during the last few days.

Her manner today was also out of character, the self-contained reserve replaced by an elfin animation.

'May we talk to you for a moment, Father?' she asked, her eyes sparkling. She glanced at Blaise for support and confirmation, and the Dumnonii princess hurried into an obviously prepared speech. Arthur quickly understood why the girls had been together, head to head, all day.

'Master Bedwyr,' Blaise began. 'As you know, I am to be wed to the heir of the Otadini tribe. I will be a queen in time,' she added with unconscious pride. 'My father sends me to the north because it is safe from Saxon or Jute attacks. Maeve and I have become friends.'

Both girls held up their thumbs, which bore identical cuts across the ball. 'We mingled our blood, Father, so we could become sisters,' Maeve explained. 'It hurt, but I didn't care, and I didn't cry, did I, Blaise?'

Her friend nodded eagerly. 'We would like to remain together, so I'm asking your permission to take Maeve with me to Onnum as my friend and companion. She will be protected from harm in the bosom of the Otadini tribe, and she will find a good husband there, especially when it becomes known that she is the daughter of the Arden Knife.'

Gape mouthed, Bedwyr looked at his son, who seemed as surprised as he was, and then back at his youngest child.' 'But, lass, you can't just go riding to Onnum as if you were going to a fair. Your proposal is absurd, and your mother would weep to lose you,' he said. He was desperately confused, for he had never really understood Maeve, with her odd little face and quirky, restrained personality. 'Have you considered what your mother will say? She'll be heartbroken that you don't want to remain with her.'

'But you intend to send us west soon,' Maeve replied earnestly. 'I know you do. And Mother will never leave you, so I'll just be an added responsibility to my brothers and sister when we arrive there. Wouldn't I be safer if I travelled with Arthur and Eamonn to King Geraint in the north?'

Bedwyr was unsure how to respond, so he sent for his wife in the hope that she could persuade her exasperating young daughter to see some sense. Of course, Bedwyr could simply refuse Maeve's request, but her early brush with death had created a certain mystique around the girl, and few people were prepared to deny her anything. Arthur sent a servant to fetch some herbal tea for his father, whose complexion had paled from the stress of his daughter's surprising request.

Elayne hurried into the hall. She was accompanied by Eamonn, and her children were hot on her heels. The gentle susurration of her woollen skirts on the flagging made a soft counterpoint to the clicking of Maeve's hard-soled sandals as the girl impatiently paced across the floor. Four sets of eyes looked up as Elayne entered, her own eyes reflecting her anxiety. She gazed at Bedwyr's face and her hands went out to him with concern and love.

'My darling! Girls! Arthur! Why has the peace of the house been disturbed at a time when we should be at rest?' As always, Elayne's voice and manner were calming, and Arthur watched as Bedwyr's agitation lessened and his frown gradually cleared. Mother has a special gift that can turn chaos into peace, Arthur thought. No wonder Artor turned to her when everything around him was falling apart.

A servant entered with Bedwyr's herbal tea, and Elayne nodded at her son with approval. 'Sit down and take your drink, darling husband. You'll feel better when you do, and no matter what has upset you we'll find a way to make all well,' she soothed in her gentle voice.

Quickly and with passion, Maeve repeated her request. Elayne listened calmly as Blaise added the same arguments she had used earlier. The mistress of Arden treated the girls like adults and gave all her attention to their proposal.

'I understand your desire to travel with your friend, Maeve. A true friend is very hard to find, especially one with whom you feel comfortable and who intends to be your sister for ever.' Elayne smiled up into their faces as they held each other's hands with the natural grace of the very young. 'But you must accept that such a proposal would cause concern to Bedwyr, who understands the difficulties of travel in lands controlled by our enemies. The Otadini tribe is far away, and the Saxon numbers are thick between Arden and Onnum.'

'But Arthur will be with us, and he and his warriors will be protecting our party,' Maeve assured her mother as if their roles were reversed.

'True, Maeve, but Arthur is only one man,' Elayne said calmly.

'My brother will be travelling with us as well,' Blaise put in. 'And we have a whole troop of my father's warriors under Arthur's command. We are as safe as my father could make us for my journey to Onnum.' Blaise could understand Elayne's negative response to their request. She was a clever girl and she knew that Elayne would comply with Bedwyr's wishes. She is my enemy, Blaise decided, although the thought didn't anger her. In Lady Elayne's place, Blaise knew that she would have taken the same approach.

Discussion continued to rage for some time. Eamonn understood his host's concerns, but he thought the new Blaise a vast improvement on her old self, and if this change of nature was Maeve's doing he'd cheerfully welcome her into their party. He said as much to Bedwyr, his wife and Arthur, although he acknowledged that they had reason to be concerned about the dangers of such a journey. Cunningly, he raised the valid point that Arden would soon become unsafe for Maeve and the other children because of the threat of Saxon invasion, incursions that would probably be successful.

Eventually, Maeve's siblings were sent to supper and an early bed while the decision swung first one way and then the other. Arthur admitted that the journey would be hazardous, but he and the rest of the party were travelling north anyway. If they reached Onnum safely, Maeve's future would be secure for now.

'Can we really protect any of our children?' Elayne wondered. 'What do you say, Father Lorcan? Is there any merit in considering Blaise's invitation to Maeve?'

'Of course there is. There is a certain amount of danger, but the gains are long term and would be considerable. Is she safer here? Or would she be safer in the borders of Cymru? I would consider what Maeve needs, rather than what she wants.'

'You're being oblique, Father Lorcan. Kindly say what you mean,' Bedwyr snapped. 'Word games are irritating.'

'Maeve is a very lonely little girl, isn't she?' Father Lorcan responded. 'If she journeyed to the north, would she be happier? You must be prepared to balance one future against another; one threat against another threat. You are her father and I wouldn't like to make your decision for you, but logic indicates that Blaise's proposal has great merit.'

'I will sleep on the problem,' Bedwyr decided gruffly. 'To bed, all of you. Everything will seem clearer in the morning.'

As they lay in bed, Bedwyr and Elayne regretfully made the final decision to allow Maeve to travel towards an uncertain future in the Otadini tribal lands. They had never understood their strange, fey daughter, and both knew that she would vanish one day like the Otherworld creatures she so resembled. Both parents concluded that they would have to keep the girl under lock and key for months if they were to be sure of keeping her at home. And so Bedwyr decided to bow to the inevitable and let Maeve go with Arthur and her new-found friend.

The girls were ecstatic at the news, while the rest of the household set about their duties with long faces. Maeve packed her bags so quickly that Elayne was forced to completely re-do the whole task, while selecting a servant girl to accompany her daughter on the journey. The number of persons in Arthur's party seemed to be increasing by the minute.

Two days later, the party rode out of Arden to tears, regret and wild joy. Maeve scarcely looked back at her parents, who wept at being parted from their youngest child. For her part, Maeve was chattering so happily with Blaise that Arthur wanted to slap her for her indifference to the feelings of her parents and siblings. Then, with long embraces and tears, he tried to fill the gap that Maeve was leaving.

The road that lay ahead would be long, but the girls appeared to be happy to undertake their perilous and tiring journey. Arthur hoped they were, and turned his horse's head reluctantly towards the north-east, twisting his body round in the saddle to wave fond farewells to his parents.

He continued to wave until his arm ached and the palisades disappeared from sight among the shadows of the great trees. Only then, when the last traces of his home had vanished, did he face forward again and begin to think of the uncertain future that lay before them.

CHAPTER XX

BETRAYAL AND LOSS

There is only one eternally true legend – that of Judas.

Joseph Stalin, at the trial of Radek in 1937

Mareddyd sat at his ease in a hostelry just outside Vinovia, just past the river that cut deep into the landscape. His booted feet rested on top of the beer-stained table and he had tilted his stool back at a precarious angle so he could rest against the wattle and daub wall behind him. His facial features reflected none of the turbulent thoughts passing through his brain as his mind calculated the amount of time that had elapsed since he had seen the Dumnonii party, quite by accident, at Cataractonium. Now, by assuming the travelling rate of a group of its size, he could make a rough estimate of when they should arrive in Vinovia, which would tell him how long he had to put his plan into effect. He'd only caught a glimpse of the Dumnonii warriors at a distance, but there was no way that a hundred yards could deceive him. He knew Arthur, the Cornovii bastard, by his hair, his height and his fucking arrogance, for he was riding through neutral territory as if he were safe from Saxons, Jutes and the many packs of outlaws that stalked the Roman road between here and the wall.

'God damn his eyes! If there was any justice, he'd have died at Calleva instead of becoming a hero,' Mareddyd whispered into a mug of inferior ale. Putting his thoughts into words fanned his slow-burning, never-quenched fury.

The indignities of the argument at the Warriors' Dyke sprang, fresh and bleeding, into Mareddyd's mind, for the details were still sharp and appallingly clear. He would never be able to forget his shameful defeat and the backs of all those sons of the nobility that were turned upon him, even if many of them had since learned to think better of their stance. Those suggestions of cowardice had driven him to run for home like a yellow dog with its tail between its legs. For once, he knew his father had been mortified, and Mareddyd had moved heaven and earth to ensure that his father remained ignorant of the full details of the family shame. Tewdwr didn't want to be cut out of the succession because his son was a laughing stock, and he never tired of telling Mareddyd just how much he had damaged the family name.

'The damned family name!' Mareddyd exclaimed drunkenly.

Several unshaven cut-throats looked in his direction with careful, hooded eyes, but none of them were the men he sought, so he curled his lip and ostentatiously turned his head away from them. Somewhere deep inside his gut, Mareddyd carried a lump of hot lead that burned and burned, and grew fiercely hotter with the passage of time.

He stared at his fine, princely boots. He had worn these same boots in the cavalry charge at Calleva at a time when he hoped to win glory and wipe away the collective memory of his shame. That prick Eamonn was in the same troop. The boy had suddenly been elevated to manhood because of the pressures of the war, but the Dumnonii brat had had the effrontery to stare at Mareddyd and mouth the word 'coward' in his direction. What did Eamonn pen Bors know? He was a third son, as useful to his tribe as a tit on a bull, and just as ugly. Frustrated, Mareddyd drank deeply from his mug and bellowed at a harried serving girl to bring more of the tasteless brew. She nodded her head in acknowledgement and averted her eyes as she hurried to obey him. Mareddyd didn't see the contemptuous gesture she made with her fingers, but he heard the muffled laughter of two peasants of indeterminate race and he glared in their direction.

'Who do you think you're looking at?' he snarled, and the cluster of dung-stained farmhands looked away, their faces wiped blank of any emotion.

Like Eamonn, Mareddyd had been given little opportunity to distinguish himself in the charge at Calleva. Despite his upbringing, Mareddyd was an indifferent horseman, mostly because his mounts tended to shy away from his cruel hand on a straight bit and his liberal use of a hardened hazel whip. The young warrior had wounded only one man, a stroke he achieved with an underarm sweep of his sword. Then, in his anger and frustration, he had deliberately veered to ride down a wounded Saxon who was being helped to his feet by a tall blond slut, obviously one of the camp followers. He had enjoyed the thud and crunch of breaking bones under his horse's hooves and the scream of the woman, high and thin, like the cry of a distant hunting bird.

Then he had felt cold eyes on him as the cavalry troop re-formed, and he turned in the saddle to see Lord Bedwyr watching him with eyes that were cold with undisguised contempt. What had the Cornovii whelp told his father? Mareddyd was indignant. How dare a mere master of trees look at him as if he were a turd that had fouled his boots? But somehow Bedwyr had contrived to ensure that Mareddyd was given no further opportunity to distinguish himself.

'It was Arthur's fault,' the young man murmured to himself. 'The bastard always made sure that any credit that could be earned would go his way.'

'Sir?' The serving maid was standing before him with a clutch of filled mugs in each hand. She was very careful to keep beyond the reach of Mareddyd's fists and feet.

'Nothing, bitch,' he snapped. She placed the mug on the table top, served several other customers and scuttled back to the plain bar with a blank expression tattooed firmly on her work-soiled face.

What does she matter anyway? Any man desperate enough to fuck her would have to do it in the dark, Mareddyd thought with an appreciative grin at his own wit, but his memories soon wiped the grin off his face.

He'd no sooner returned from the far gate of Calleva, his ears assaulted by the screams of burning men, than he'd seen the front line of the Atrebate defence still holding firm against a determined Jute attack. And there, in the front of the defensive line, and without a shield for protection, that Cornovii bastard was slaying any man who came within reach of that sodding Dragon Knife and his new sword. Mareddyd was forced to listen to the open admiration of cavalrymen praising that glory hound for his supposed courage as the Jutes broke and ran. For the first time in his young life, Mareddyd had prayed with real passion for the destruction of his nemesis, Arthur of Arden.

But the bastard wouldn't die. He survived the Marine Fire and the trap that should have seen all the Atrebates either cut into bloody sides of meat or burned alive. He had seen the awe and veneration in the faces of common warriors and nobles alike, and had ground his teeth in frustration.

The only virtue in that endless day had been Mareddyd's

realisation that Arthur couldn't be Bedwyr's son. Seen side by side, Bedwyr and Arthur were completely different in every aspect of their physical features.

'So Arthur really *is* a bastard,' Mareddyd had whispered to himself. That was when he began to scheme how he could use this observation to his own advantage.

Then he had overheard the muffled whispers in the latrines and learned something that drove him wild with jealousy and anger. To this day he could recall the stink of faeces that made him gag in the confined space, and picture the coarse lengths of raw torn cloth that separated the facilities for the common warriors from those used by nobles and women.

'Not that there was any real difference. Both stank like a badger's armpit,' Mareddyd muttered under his breath.

Two warriors had been talking beyond the fragile wall. By rights, considering the substance of their gossip, they should have been more circumspect, but as Mareddyd was the only person to hear them, and he was invisible, he was glad of their indiscretion.

'Did you see the warrior on the line in the red cloak?' one disembodied voice had asked, his voice hushed with awe. 'Bedwyr's lad?'

'Aye. It was a pleasure to see some real swordcraft. I've not seen such skill since I was a boy in my first battle at Moridunum,' the second man answered in a gravelly voice that suggested advanced, but still vigorous, age.

'That was a fair time ago,' the younger voice answered with a trace of humour. 'I would have thought your eyes would have given out by now. Bowmen need good eyesight.'

'It's been near enough to thirty-five years, I think, because I was only fifteen at Moridunum. They were the days, boy, for that was a real line we held. Three days! And my eyes might be old, but they still work well enough. I'm still a master of the long bow. In these bad times, even old farts like me are needed.'

'Aye, Grandfather,' the younger voice replied with respect. 'So who was it who fought like Bedwyr's boy? Bedwyr was at Moridunum too, if I recall correctly, having escaped from the Saxons who held Caer Fyrddin.'

'Yes, you're right. When the battle was over he was stiff with blood from the crown of his head to the soles of his ragged sandals. He was covered in blood the whole three days. I recall he told me afterwards that he saw enough blood at Moridunum to last him a lifetime.'

'But you still haven't told me who fought like the boy in red,' his companion repeated.

'It was the Dragon King himself, my boy. I saw him standing and fighting as close to me as you are now. And the boy out there on the battlefield today was King Artor's twin. If I didn't know better, I'd say that Lord Bedwyr's wife played the game of the two-backed beast near to twenty years ago. But you didn't hear that from me.'

That had been many months ago, and no opportunity to use the information had arisen since then, but when Mareddyd had recognised his enemy in the party he had seen at Cataractonium he had realised immediately that this was his chance to achieve his longed-for satisfaction at last.

He'd ridden out of Cataractonium as if the Wild Hunt was hot on his heels. Uncaring for the value of horse flesh, he had nearly killed two beasts in a desperate dash to reach Vinovia before the Dumnonii party arrived. Then, anxious to set his plans in place, he had sent a message to a renegade Saxon trader he knew, a man who had influence with Saxon war parties.

Mareddyd had come north to forge links with the Saxon traders who valued the cider, wool and pork that was produced in the Dobunni lands. The young prince was no fool when it came to matters of business, and he realised that only those kings who built strong connections with the Saxons would survive the catastrophes that were to come. His father and grandfather refused point blank to have dealings with the enemy, considering that any tribesmen who did so had forgotten their honour and were traitors to the British cause.

Mareddyd scoffed at his kinsmen's arguments, but he was too wise to openly express his plans. What his grandfather didn't know wouldn't hurt him. People who lived in the past tossed around words like 'traitor' without understanding what was necessary if you wished to survive and prosper. For Mareddyd, the meeting with this particular trader was useful, for the northerner's contacts would make a great deal of money out of their association, ensuring that the Saxons *owed* him. That much he understood about Saxon pride.

Mareddyd drained his mug again and felt the warm beer curdle in his gorge. He had some difficulty believing his luck. After a few words, coins had been exchanged at Vinovia's best inn and Mareddyd had discovered that Eamonn had come north with his sister Blaise. The red-headed slut was called Maeve and she called the leader of the party 'brother'. The group was a fine clutch of Celt nobility, far from the comfort and protection of their tribes. When he wanted to do so, God showed his favour in strange ways. Mareddyd grinned happily, allowing his white teeth to flash in his tanned face. Finally, Fortuna was turning his way.

Arthur tried to keep the party moving quickly along the Roman road. They travelled by daylight, and Arthur insisted that they moved well off the road and the open ground that ran beside it when they stopped to rest. As a further precaution, all fires were banned at night. At first, Blaise complained about cold porridge and dried meat, but Maeve proved to be Arthur's unexpected ally and convinced the Dumnonii princess that to warn outlaws that a party, including four females, was travelling on the open road would be foolish. With surprising tact, she persuaded Blaise that any deprivations they suffered turned each meal into a picnic, and the girls and their maidservants competed with each other to find the most interesting ways of serving cold food.

'Your sister is a treasure,' Eamonn told Arthur cheerfully, nodding in Maeve's direction. 'Blaise is far more pleasant now that Maeve talks sense to her. If I have any say in the matter, I'll recommend to King Geraint that he treats her like the princess she is. Congratulations, Arthur. Maeve is a sensible girl.'

'I can't take any credit for Maeve's virtues, Eamonn. I really don't know her as well as I should, but you're right when you call her a treasure. I've never known her to be so animated.'

Arthur refrained from sharing his most pressing worry with Eamonn. The itch at the back of his skull had returned. While he was taking every precaution within his power to ensure their anonymity, something in Vinovia had set his extra sense on edge, despite the fact that nothing in the grimy, multi-racial town had given him any obvious reason to be on his guard.

Vinovia was a frontier town where interaction and trade were engaged in by Saxons and Celts alike. As an erstwhile Roman garrison, the abandoned fortress had always had a village around it that catered to the basic tastes of the legionaries. In its prime, women, drink, trade and amusements had robbed the soldiers of any spare coin they might have had on those occasions when the army bothered to pay them. While the Roman soldiers had sworn that Vinovia was the arse-end of the world, their absence had caused a financial loss to the gambling and whoring establishments that relied on their patronage.

But frontiers always need a Vinovia. The small town was situated on the road leading to the wall, so it was the perfect meeting place where Saxons, Jutes, Angles, Jews and Celts could set up deals, make trading alliances and exchange coin for a range of practices.

Some interaction and communication was necessary between the peoples who shared this bitterly divided country. Farmers on both sides still produced wool, grain and other commodities which needed markets if the population was to survive and, with luck, prosper. Goods still filtered into the north of Britain from the lands of the Franks and the Visigoths, and this trade too was necessary to both sides in the conflict. Vinovia had its own special dangers, but they were less obvious than those of many of the hamlets, villages and towns that Arthur's party had successfully passed through during their journey.

But Arthur had developed an inordinate belief in the accuracy of his inner voice, so he was determined to take every precaution he could.

Blaise continued to remain close to Arthur, as if she had belatedly recognised that he was central to the party's security. Since they had left the nameless village far to the south where she had, for the first time, confronted the realities of life in dangerous territory, she had developed a healthy respect for her brother's friend, although she was still unsure whether she liked him very much.

'He's nothing like your father or your other brothers, is he?' she had whispered to Maeve as they hovered on the edge of sleep, while still three days' journey from Cataractonium. Both girls were exhausted after weeks in the saddle, and both were suffering from the dust and heat of summer.

Maeve rolled over, wincing as her tender thighs protested at the movement. Leaning on one elbow, she examined her friend with the clever, owlish expression of a very tired girl.

'No, he's my half-brother, and his father was a very important man. No one talks about it very much, but we all know that Arthur has skills and raw talents that the rest of us will never possess. We don't care, though, because we love him. Arthur's a very special person, Blaise. Lasair worships him, and Nuala says he's her ideal man. Yet he's the kindest brother anyone could ever want, considering he can't be expected to treat younger siblings as amusing company.'

'Eamonn says he's an exceptional warrior,' Blaise replied, chewing over Maeve's praise with her meticulous, detail-obsessed thought processes.

'I couldn't say about that. But I have watched him all my life, and in every type of weather he'd be out in the courtyard, bare-chested, exercising and practising movements with his knife, sword, bow, spear, shield or any other weapon of death you can think of, including a sling.' Maeve yawned delicately, like a slender tawny cat. 'You should see him with a sling – he's death on legs.'

'How can you speak of him so, Maeve? You say you love your brother, yet you refer to him in such a manner?' Blaise's face lit up with anger at her friend and her black eyes were sharp and glittering with something a little stronger than annoyance.

Unfortunately, Blaise was an angry girl and had been difficult from birth. God, or Satan, or Fortuna, it didn't matter which, had played a cosmic joke on her. She should have been born a boy, just as her name implied. She hadn't been intended to wear skirts, play the whore with a seductive fan or work at domestic duties when she wasn't gravid with child. Blaise knew that she had been destined for a life where she could be more active and self-determined than her female sex permitted. And so, regardless of the season or the celebration, she remained permanently at war with her world.

Suddenly, Maeve recognised the warrior behind the black eyes of her eleven-year-old friend. 'I'm beginning to think you like Arthur, Blaise, or at least the idea of him,' she gasped with sudden insight. 'I think he's your ideal man too. Heavens, Gilchrist will have some hard work to do to keep up with my brother.'

'There you go, Maeve, reminding me of the purpose of this journey just when I was feeling content with life.' Blaise giggled endearingly. 'I don't know why I'm laughing, because my situation might become dire. I've never even seen Gilchrist. He could be ugly, or short, or unmanly, for all I know.'

'Or he might like boys more than girls. He might like to sew and weave, or be a farmer, or wear women's clothing.' Maeve was listing the most outlandish and ignoble traits she could think of, and both girls collapsed into a series of helpless giggles. At that moment they were children, but for the most part the girls spoke and thought like little adults. Within two years, by the time the moon blood first came to them, both girls would be married. In three years, they would be mothers or they would be dead. Too many young women died in childbirth, and the odds were that one of them would perish in a welter of blood and pain after hurried sex entered into to produce the children who would perpetuate the tribal structure. In the unenlightened world of the tribes before the arrival of the Romans, the lowliest male slave had more freedom than a noblewoman, but Boudicca, the Iceni bitch-queen, had begun a slow change in male attitudes. Now the Saxons, who were patriarchal in the extreme, had set back the status of women once more.

Maeve's mind must have danced ahead to the same conclusion. 'Do you ever wish that you'd been born a man, Blaise?'

'Ever? Always! I used to say it wasn't fair, but half of all babies are girls so childbirth is always a game of chance. I wish I was Eamonn. I'd be grateful every day, just for the freedom to wear trews.'

The girls giggled again at the thought, which would have shocked their mothers and brought down the anger of the Church upon their hapless heads. But they didn't care.

'To run without skirts tangling round my knees,' Blaise whispered longingly.

'To be able to climb a tree without risking death,' Maeve added.

'To go fishing in a coracle.'

'To learn to swim in a lake.'

'To get my hands dirty, growing trees and building my own tree house.'

'To go hunting.'

'We could go on forever, but everyone, including our families, would think we were moon mad.' Blaise looked sad and defeated. 'That's why we like each other, Maeve. Both of us hate living the way we must.'

'I have a huge list of things I don't want to do, starting with spinning,' Maeve said.

'And weaving, sewing, mending, darning, knitting . . .' Blaise grinned in the darkness.

'Cooking, cleaning, planning menus, preserving fruit, drying fish and meat, collecting eggs . . .'

'Sitting down to pee, wearing so many clothes, being polite at all times . . .'

'Smiling until my jaws ache.' Maeve was now well into the spirit of the game.

'Being sold off to the highest bidder like a cow,' Blaise added bitterly.

'Never learning to do more than basic counting and simple

reading, and pretending that all men are better than we are, no matter what oafs they might be.' By now Maeve's tone was almost, but not quite, venomous. She finished the litany of ills with this decisive, cynical statement and Blaise nodded her agreement. 'I have read in Arthur's scrolls of a society of women in Greece who lived without men, finding all their pleasure in each other.'

Blaise's eyebrows shot up. 'I don't think I overly fancy that prospect,' she decided. 'It would be fine to live and work together, but I don't know about the other parts of it.'

'There always seem to be drawbacks to the way we are expected to live our lives, don't there?' Maeve's voice was sad.

The girls settled down in their simple leather tent, which was barely big enough for two. Outside, the wind sighed quietly in the coppice and an owl screeched as it killed something small in the enveloping darkness.

Arthur stepped away from the shadow of the trees. While not spying, he had heard every word the sleepy girls had uttered inside their tent, and he had a mountain of unfamiliar emotions to consider. Like most men, he had never really considered the plight of women, having been raised to believe they lived the lives that they desired. What Maeve and Blaise had described was a form of slavery. With something perilously close to shame, he looked skyward and thanked the Christian God who had seen fit to have him born a male.

While Arthur was experiencing his new appreciation of the nature of womanhood, Mareddyd waited at the inn for the messenger that he had been told to expect. The go-between did not appear, and as he was unused to waiting for anyone or anything Mareddyd's temper was stretched to breaking point.

Out of a dearth of choices, the young prince took his pleasure with the plain serving woman who lived at the inn. Typically, he never paused to consider her status. She was just another female, conveniently close to hand, whose plain looks and servile manner made her a non-person in his eyes, simply a convenient receptacle for his juices.

As he was staying in the best room of the inn, it required only an order to the innkeeper for the woman to present herself at his room. She soon arrived, shivering, and trying to look as small and inoffensive as possible.

'Strip,' Mareddyd ordered from the grimy, flaxen sheets on the bed. 'Have you bathed recently, girl? I'd like to stay clean.'

'I wash every week, master. My hair was cleansed only yesterday.'

He had wondered what was different about her and now he saw that her hair had the fluffy look of freshly washed locks. It was golden blond, speaking of northern heritage, but the amber lights in the lamplight reminded him of Arthur, so when he took her roughly on the coarse mattress he made no effort to be gentle or to spare her. Before she was kicked unceremoniously onto the floor, her body was covered with bruises and bites, and her quiet weeping had left runnels of tears and snot on her plain, high-boned face.

When she fled from the room, he caught a glimpse of the innkeeper waiting in the corridor with a woollen blanket, which he draped around the girl's shoulders as soon as she appeared. But Mareddyd barely bothered to wonder why a man of substance would care about a serving wench. In fact, he was asleep within moments of blowing out his candle.

On the morrow Mareddyd was feeling a little better, especially when he had broken his fast with a bowl of unsalted porridge, new milk and a boiled egg. It was served by the same girl, whose swollen face and livid throat showed the marks of his fingers, leaving him with an odd feeling of mixed shame and triumph. In his mind, he had defeated Arthur on her body in some weird exchange of human desire and transmutation. By the middle of the day, however, forced inactivity and a sense that he was being treated with a marked lack of respect had blunted his pleasant mood.

As he left the inn to face a day of heat and steamy rain, a disreputable man in a dirty grey cloak, hooded to disguise his face, came up behind him.

'Master Mareddyd?'

The Dobunni prince nodded tersely.

'The man you enquired after will meet you at the cross of Saint Fidelma, two miles to the north. One hour from now – right?'

Before Mareddyd could answer, the man had disappeared into a narrow back alley. Mareddyd was disinclined to follow him, since he reeked of the distinctive smell of the piggery. Besides, the alleyway was dark and forbidding.

An hour later, the Dobunni was pacing impatiently on the only road leading north which boasted a crossroad of sorts, if the track that crossed the paved Roman construction could aspire to such a lofty description. Its only mark of distinction was a single standing stone, decorated with Celtic interlace, that formed an ancient rustic cross.

Suddenly a group of four very tall men appeared out of the long grass at the side of the road. They were as silent as ghosts. One moment the road was empty; the next second they were ranged around him on the shoulder of the passageway. The men were very fair, robust and white of skin. They were armed to the teeth and he was at their mercy.

'Are you Mareddyd, the so-called tribal prince from the south?' the tallest man asked in guttural, halting Celtic. He was clearly uncomfortable with the language, but as Mareddyd had never bothered to learn a single word of Saxon he was forced to persevere.

'Yes, I am the heir to the Dobunni throne. I am Mareddyd, but names are unimportant considering our business together.' His arrogant tone failed to impress the warrior, who merely raised one pale eyebrow and looked down at him with pale eyes that said nothing, but lacked the respect that Mareddyd felt was his due. As he gazed at the warrior, he saw the suggestion of a sneer around his bearded, thin-lipped mouth.

'What business could we possibly have together?'

'One involving mutual profit,' Mareddyd replied crisply. 'You'll earn a large cache of gold from our exchange, and I'll get satisfaction from taking my revenge on an enemy of note.'

'I like plain speaking,' the northerner answered. 'What coin can I earn, and how must I earn it?' He leaned negligently on a long, single-bladed axe, one that was quite unlike the normal Saxon weapon. By its long handle and the warrior's casual use of its shining length, Mareddyd registered that he was a man of some importance among his race.

'I cannot accept that you're a Saxon,' he said bluntly, and the tall man narrowed his eyes with suspicion.

'What could a man like you have heard of a man like me?'

'I asked certain mutual acquaintances if they knew of a band of northerners who would have the balls to capture a group of aristocratic British tribesmen and women for the certainty of the gold involved in selling the prisoners back to their kin for a ransom. Preferably alive. If you go by the name of Stormbringer, you were recommended to me by a mutual acquaintance.' Mareddyd chose his words carefully, glad now that he had taken the precaution of placing a bowman from his entourage in the crown of a nearby oak. The slightest turn of Mareddyd's eyeballs in the direction of the tree would result in an arrow firmly embedded in Stormbringer's back. Mareddyd felt a moment's disgust and contempt. Did this oaf think that an obvious alias like Stormbringer would make him anonymous?

'Don't look for your bowman, Mareddyd, or whatever your name is. Your archer is now wearing an extra grin. I'm not fond of men who plant assassins at my back. It indicates a lack of trust on your part.'

Mareddyd suddenly felt alone and unprotected, so he hurried back into speech. The promise of coin might save him yet. 'In a few days, a party of eight men and four young ladies will be riding in this direction. They are bound for Onnum in the north. The party is distinguished, although you'd scarcely know it from their mode of dress. Two of the women are barely of age and are of noble birth. The black-haired bitch is the daughter of King Bors of Cornwall, and she is betrothed to the son of King Geraint of the Otadini tribe who dwells north of the wall. The red-haired piece is the daughter of the Arden Knife, the master of Arden Forest. You may have heard of this man, who goes by the name of Bedwyr.'

'Yes, I have heard of Bedwyr. These girls will be good for ransom, or as noble slaves. And . . . ?' Stormbringer realised that the fate of two prepubescent female children meant nothing to the prince, certainly not enough to turn him against his own kind. Careful to keep the distaste out of his expression, Stormbringer waited patiently for the real point of this meeting.

'The leader of this party is a tall, red-haired lad not yet out of his teens. He's an excellent warrior, so don't treat him casually. As the eldest son of the Arden Knife, he is ripe for ransom, but you may want to consider using him in another way. He is the unacknowledged son of Artor, the Dragon King, who was the last High King of the Britons. My heart will not weep if you sell him into slavery beyond these lands, or kill him. I leave the decision to you. But I must warn you that he carries Artor's Dragon Knife and wields a sword wrought by the best metalsmith in our lands. He will not be easy to capture.'

'Is there anyone else you'd like me to assassinate or send into slavery?' Stormbringer asked sarcastically. Such was Mareddyd's vanity that he missed the contempt in the warrior's voice.

'A shorter, dark-haired warrior travels with them. He is the third son of the King of the Dumnonii tribe, who protects vast acres in the south-west of Britain. His name is Eamonn pen Bors. Whatever you decide to do with him is up to you.'

'Who else travels with them? Such important personages should not travel unguarded.'

'Arthur's bodyguard is a blond-haired warrior called Gareth. He will not be easy to subdue as he is oath-bound to his master, who is known as the Last Dragon. Five Dumnonii warriors accompany them, along with two serving maids for the girls. You may do with them what you will, because I don't care if they live or die.'

'Why are you giving me this information, Mareddyd?' Stormbringer asked.

'Do my reasons matter? I have given you information that will bring you gold. Surely I can keep my motives to myself. Why should you care?'

'I am Dene. I like to know why I'm hired to kill someone.'

Mareddyd caught a trace of Stormbringer's disdain. The man's use of the term Dene puzzled and wrong footed him, for he had never heard of the Dene. Puzzles normally made him nervous, but his desire for revenge continued to burn inside him and caused him to give the man a little more information than he had intended.

'Arthur and I have been enemies for years. He has shamed me, but he has so much power and reputation that I would never be permitted to meet him in open combat so I cannot retaliate, no matter how he insults me.'

Something of Mareddyd's passion overrode the lie, and convinced Stormbringer that this Arthur had already proved too powerful for this Dobunni cur to overcome in mortal combat. This pact was a dirty business all round, but it could prove to be profitable on many levels for Stormbringer if he was successful. Mareddyd, on the other hand, could rot for all he cared.

'Very well. You may expect that this party will not reach its destination. Ride on to Onnum, and await word from me there. Your . . . friends and countrymen will not arrive.'

'Good.' Mareddyd would have mounted his horse and ridden away, but the Dene stopped him with a guttural command.

'I take nothing without payment,' he muttered. He tossed a leather bag towards Mareddyd, who was forced to catch it awkwardly. Something inside the bag clinked dully, but by the feel it wasn't coin. Mareddyd pulled the drawstring open and found five large rings of pure silver, linked together, inside the bag. Each of the rings was large enough to be worn on a man's wrist but they were obviously a means of exchange, and not for decoration.

'I want no payment,' Mareddyd snapped. 'What do you think I am?'

'I know exactly what you are, Briton. I choose to pay my debts as they become due.'

Every mile travelled northwards sent the itch in Arthur's brain into increased urgency and soon interrupted his sleep. Attuned to his master's every expression, Gareth confronted him once they had left the relative safety of Vinovia. They had just crossed a Roman bridge over a wide river when the itch turned into a hard, painful moan that added to Arthur's woes. Ahead, hills led into the mountains, and Arthur knew the heights offered greater safety. The lowlands provided greens, berries, fruit and a plentiful supply of small animals for the cooking pot, when Arthur permitted it, but until he reached the hills the leader of the party would be unable to rest.

'What's wrong, Arthur? You're pale, your eyes are never still and your hands remain painfully close to your sword hilt.' Hesitantly, Gareth reached out to touch his master's shoulder. Normally, Arthur would have shrugged off the small gesture of comfort, but this time he accepted the sign of affection and concern. 'What do you know that we don't?'

'I don't know anything, Gareth, but I can sense that danger is very close to us. If anything should happen to me, I want you to protect the women. Promise me.'

'Of course, Arthur, but I don't understand.'

'I do,' Eamonn muttered as he loomed out of the darkness from the direction of the picket lines. 'It's that voice in your head, isn't it? It tells you that something dangerous lies in the hills ahead of us.'

'Yes, but I can't for the life of me understand what it is. Our path through the North has been unremarkable, so I'm at a loss to understand how anyone could have divined who we are or where we're going. All these weeks on the road have made us a ragged lot.'

Eamonn grimaced in agreement. Their clothing had lost their sharp, vegetable-dyed colours in the summer sun and even the simple act of washing it in the river water had weakened the fabric in places so that many of Arthur's tunics had split along the seams.

'I won't be happy until we reach those mountains. They'll provide some protective cover that we don't have here. We're exposed in this flat country.' Arthur thought for a moment. 'Tell the girls to rest well tonight, for we'll be riding hard and fast tomorrow until we reach the foothills. We'll only take enough rest to keep the horses alive. I know it will be hard going, especially for the women, but needs must. We'll sleep easier when we reach the mountains.'

Mareddyd was drunk and belligerent. He had kept to his room, taking his food there and keeping out of sight from the time he had heard from one of his warriors who had been tasked to watch the gates of Vinovia and warn him of the arrival of the Dumnonii party. Mareddyd knew he must not be seen by Arthur or his friends.

He never went anywhere without a troop of ten armed guards. One man had been executed by the Dene at the cross-roads, but the other nine were ordered to remain in their quarters until such time as Arthur and his travelling companions had left the town. Once they had gone, everyone heaved a sigh of relief.

'Innkeeper,' Mareddyd shouted over the hubbub in the small bar. 'Hoi! I want to talk to you.'

Alarmed by his tone, and eager to lessen his belligerence, the innkeeper left his accustomed place at the bar to personally serve his noble guest.

'Sit down with me, innkeeper,' Mareddyd demanded in a voice that was just a little too loud because of his fuddled wits. 'What's your name?'

'Of course, sir,' the innkeeper replied soothingly as he eased himself down onto a bench seat. 'My name is Ossian, son of Ottar, and you know my daughter Myfanwy, who has served you many times.' The innkeeper kept his face servile and pleasant, but his heart surged with resentment.

'Little deer!' Mareddyd scoffed, choosing to sneer at the meaning of the girl's name. He had never possessed an understanding of other people and had never exerted himself enough to try. Had he bothered, he would have wondered why the father of a ravaged daughter could sit so easily with the man who had assaulted her.

'Yes, my lord, it is an unfortunate name. How may I help you?'

'Who and what are the Dene? I've never heard of them until I met one today. I'm curious.'

Ossian paled a little. Enough Jutes passed through this northern town to give him some familiarity with a race that even they feared.

'I've heard that the Dene came to Jutland from places even further north. It's said that their homeland is a place where half the year is dark with no dawning, and the remaining half of the year is light with no sunset. Perhaps these tales are lies, because I can't imagine such a place, but the Jutes swear it exists.'

Mareddyd mumbled drunkenly and nodded his head like a man on the verge of unconsciousness.

He won't remember a word of what I'm saying in the morning, Ossian thought sullenly. I wish I was a braver man. I'd cut this animal's throat for Myfanwy's sake. This brute seems to enjoy inflicting pain on the powerless.

'The Dene invaded Jutland some hundred years ago and, mile by mile, they've taken all the decent land. They're great sailors and fierce fighters. Their excessive height makes them almost impossible to defeat in combat and they worship Ice Dragons and northern gods that are very much like those revered by the Saxons. The Dene and the Saxons are distant relatives, although the Saxons are shorter.'

'Shite!' Mareddyd focused on the innkeeper's face. 'They value dragons, do they? Let's hope that admiration doesn't extend to the human variety.'

'I don't understand, my lord.' Ossian's confusion was written clearly on his face.

'Don't worry, Ossian.' Mareddyd drained his mug and struggled to his feet, patting Ossian's head as he weaved towards his upstairs room. 'You serve good beer!' He leered across at his landlord. 'My thanks for the information, Ossian. Oh, and you can send Myfanwy to my room, right now.'

'Of course, my lord,' Ossian replied, his voice both servile and sullen.

As usual, Mareddyd didn't notice.

The next morning, as Arthur's troop rode at a steady trot along the straight road through the late-summer countryside, Eamonn spurred his horse to join Arthur at its head with a raw-boned warrior at his side.

'Arthur, I have just gleaned some information that makes me distinctly nervous. Trefor here saw something in Vinovia that could be the source of your nervousness.'

Arthur glanced up from under his leonine brows and Eamonn noticed that his friend's eyes were very pale today. They were almost wholly grey, while the whites were red from lack of sleep.

'Trefor, my good fellow, tell us what you saw.'

Trefor was thin and dark. Not overly tall for his people, he probably owed much of his ancestry to the Picts who had been driven out from the tribal lands many generations before the arrival of the Romans. During their long journey, Eamonn had come to respect the warrior for his obedience, flexibility and observational powers. If Trefor saw something that caused him some concern, it was worth repeating the tale to his leader.

'When we rode into Vinovia from the south and passed through the gateway, I thought I saw a man whose homespun cloak was lined with the Dobunni squares. They're distinctive in colour, as Leodegran chose the closest colour to purple he could make from vegetable dyes and mixed them with squares of a rusty red. I'm sure it wasn't my imagination, and I've thought and thought about a reason for a Dobunni warrior to have travelled so far north. I know they trade widely, but this man was not a trader, although I only caught a glimpse of him. I should have told Lord Eamonn earlier, but I wasn't sure. I hope I've caused no harm by keeping silent.'

'That can't be helped now, so I thank you, Trefor. If you see any more of that distinctive check, let me know at once. Let all the men know, for that matter. And the girls, because forewarned is forearmed. You can resume your position in the line now.'

'You're not angry with me, my lord?' Trefor asked nervously.

Arthur smiled and shook his head, so Trefor drew rein and retraced his steps back through the line of travellers, passing the message as he went.

'You don't think Mareddyd's around here somewhere, do you, Arthur?' Eamonn asked, a line creasing the skin between his brows.

'I can't think of any reason for his venturing this far north, but I can't discount it. That man wants both our heads. Meanwhile, there's a knoll ahead of us that's a perfect spot to rest the horses and have a meal. We'll stop there for a few hours.'

The horses were urged into a brisk canter. The trees grew much more thickly along this part of the road and some spreading branches met overhead, turning the light of noon as green as grass, or the skin of a dead man. Then, suddenly, the hum in Arthur's skull began to keen and a sense of urgency exploded through every vein in his body.

'Ride! Ride! Ride! There are enemies here somewhere! Keep tightly together and ride like hell for the top of the knoll.'

Obedient and disciplined, the warriors obeyed. The girls' faces whitened at the unaccustomed speed they were forced to maintain as they raced along the rough track. The knoll was close and they had almost cleared the thickly encroaching tree line when a section of rope netting sprang up across the track, directly in front of Arthur and Eamonn who were leading the troop. The web-like obstruction swept both warriors from their saddles and brought their horses down in a tangle of legs and screaming, open mouths.

Huge bearded men swinging long-handled axes sprang out from their hiding places and felled the horses of the warriors at the rear of the column with the same stroke that women used when wielding twig brooms. Shaking his head to clear it as he struggled to his feet, Arthur's last view of the brief battle was seeing Trefor suddenly beheaded. The warrior who performed the execution stood at Arthur's height and used his single-bladed weapon with exquisite economy of movement. Arthur was still staring in surprise when Trefor's head sprang from his shoulders and rolled away into the brambles beside the road.

Then something struck Arthur on the side of the head and he felt his senses start to slide away. The screaming in his head was so loud that it seemed to fill the whole world as Gareth sprang over the tangle of horses and gutted the man who had struck Arthur with the blunt hilt of his sword.

'Ride, Gareth, and find help,' Arthur ordered with the last of his wits. 'God damn you, Gareth! Ride – and ride fast! We're done here, so go.'

Then the darkness embraced him with sounds that were full of raucous noise and a voice that cried and cried.

'Stay alive, Arthur! No matter what happens, you must stay alive. Stay alive!'

* * *

In Vinovia, Mareddyd awoke with a vile headache and a taste in his mouth of bile, vomit and something rotten. He gagged as he sat upright, because the pain in his head from the ale he had drunk seemed to fill the universe with its sharp, blinding totality.

To avoid disgracing himself, he quickly found the pot that was kept under the bed for guests to use during the night. Then, embarrassed, he vomited into the malodorous receptacle, whose reek caused him to sicken still further until he felt raw inside and out. His stomach was completely voided.

An uncontrollable thirst claimed him.

Mareddyd sought out the jug of water for washing that sat on a rickety table in his room, but the ewer was almost empty. He drained the lukewarm water in it at a single draught and then bellowed for more.

'What happened last night?' he asked himself aloud. He was sick, dazed and unable to remember anything after his conversation with the innkeeper. 'Just my luck to pick the one group of cut-throats who are likely to admire Artor and Arthur because of their links with dragons.'

The afternoon had the steady heat of an unusually settled summer's day. The bedding stuck to Mareddyd's naked back and sweat pooled in his armpits, his groin and the hollows behind his knees, while the reek of vomit made him dizzy. His head ached sullenly and his thirst was unbearable.

'I need water!' he bellowed again, careless of the hour and the display he was making in front of other guests staying at the inn. 'Myfanwy, you bitch, get your lazy arse moving and get me some water. Now!'

The simple latch opened and the door swung gently inwards. Myfanwy was standing tentatively on the threshold with a jug of water in her left hand. Her right arm was splinted and bandaged.

'What did you do to your arm?' Mareddyd asked casually as he snatched the jug from her and began to drink.

'You broke it, my lord. I was a little slow to undress you.' The girl's expression was flat and colourless. Mareddyd decided that she looked half witted.

'Get me another jug, woman. This one's empty.'

In obvious pain, she padded away on silent feet.

Mareddyd lay back on the bed and sighed. He felt better already because he had realised even as he drank that Stormbringer's thugs would already have dealt with Arthur and his enemy's future would have been decided, for good or ill. Oh, the sheer pleasure of that thought, and the revenge he had achieved. The Dobunni heir groaned with exhilaration and absently scratched at his testicles.

The door opened again and Myfanwy entered quickly. This time, she had brought a bowl of fruit, a mug and a large pottery jug filled with water. She balanced the tray on her bandaged arm, but took most of the weight on her good hand.

Before she could place the tray on the rickety table, Mareddyd grabbed at an apple and bit into it. The taste was wonderful, for it was flavoured with his new-found freedom from the quest for revenge that had consumed him for so long. Myfanwy had poured a mug of water and set it on a stool beside his bed, so he drained the contents swiftly, and his brain began to work again.

'More water!'

Then a ghastly, frightening nightmare surfaced out of the tangle of thoughts that had been so pleasing a moment earlier.

He knocked the ewer from her hand, causing the heavy jug to fall onto the rush mats on the floor and spill water over the planking. But it didn't break. Absently, the girl picked it up.

'Are you half witted, you slut? How could you let me drink water? If I get bellyache I'll string you up by your hair – and your father with you. And I'll burn this fleapit to the ground. You know that water is poison in these parts, so if I suffer for it I'll make you suffer ten times worse. Do you understand, bitch?'

'You told me to bring the water to you,' Myfanwy said dully. 'If I hadn't brought it you'd have beaten me anyway.'

Mareddyd knew she spoke the truth. Oblivious of his nakedness, he sat upright on the bed, and found himself filled with a God-like feeling of power. 'Don't you understand, that's what you're here for?' He leered across at her. 'You can get me some decent ale now, and something better to eat than this shit.'

He threw the apple core at her with his full force. It hit her bruised cheekbone with an audible thump. Then, disgusted at her bovine expression, he turned his back on her.

The ewer was in her hand. Seemingly, it developed a life of its own and she swung it up and brought it down across the back of Mareddyd's head with a soft, mushy thud.

Mareddyd fell back onto the bed, his eyes full of the last sight he would ever see: the ewer, already stained with blood and hair as it flashed down towards his head again.

Myfanwy struck at Mareddyd's handsome face again and again until the heavy earthenware finally broke in her hands. She looked down at a reddened, shapeless mass of broken teeth, splintered bone, pulpy eyes, and a fractured skull. Fluid leaked from both ears and grey jelly oozed from a deep split in the forehead which finished at the crown of the head.

Then her vomit joined the reek of Mareddyd's voided bowels and bladder, until she forced herself to cover his body with a ruined sheet. She stared at him one final time, and then walked through the open door where her father was already waiting.

And so the heir of the Dobunni tribe perished. A rudimentary investigation was conducted but no one seemed to know any details about Mareddyd, or why he was so far north of the Dobunni lands. Nor could anyone in the town have profited from his death. Perhaps robbery was the motive, although five silver rings were found on his person.

An urn carried his ashes home to his father, who made token shows of tears for reputation's sake, but it soon became the talk of the Dobunni tribe that Tewdwr immediately commenced a search for a younger wife on whom he could sire a new heir and so maintain the succession after the death of King Ifor.

After all, Tewdwr was only forty years old and the tribe must have a new prince. Tewdwr soon found a girl of the Dumnonii tribe with a good pedigree. Fortunately, this voluptuous young princess swiftly earned King Ifor's approval now that his contentious grandson, Mareddyd, had gone to meet his maker.

Everyone was rather pleased that Mareddyd was no more.

God, Fortuna or Satan had once more turned the wheel, and life went on.

POSTSCRIPT

'Education made us what we are.'

Helvetius, *De l'esprit des lois*, 'Discourse 3', chapter 30

'I feel sick,' Arthur said suddenly in a voice that was gravelly with disuse. He opened one eye, because the other was still stuck together with blood, and proceeded to vomit weakly into an old pot held by Blaise's shaking hands.

'Thanks to heaven, Arthur, we thought you were dead,' she whispered. 'Drink a little of this. The hulk in charge told me this stuff would set you to rights if you ever woke up.'

Like a child, he drank obediently. The plank on which he lay pitched and tossed so that his head swam, while the liquid burned through him like fire. A cold, wet cloth was pressed against his face and the cooling sensation was so pleasurable and eased the persistent agony in his skull so much that a soft moan escaped his dry, cracked lips.

'Now you must have some ale. Try to keep it down, Arthur, or I'll be cross. You'll die if you don't get some fluid into your body.'

'Aren't I dead already?' he asked seriously.

'Not quite, brother.' It was Maeve's voice that answered him. Her words gave him boundless relief.

'Silence!' a voice barked in a strange tongue, but Arthur had no concept of what was said. He desperately wanted to sleep. His eye closed and Maeve, Blaise and Eamonn feared he had returned to the death-like unconsciousness that had claimed him for four days.

'Don't worry, children,' Stormbringer boomed in a voice that easily made itself heard over the sound of the wind, the regular slapping of the sail and the groan of the ship as she breasted the waves. 'Your friend will be better when he awakes. The Last Dragon has a very hard head.'

Taken by a neat trap that they had almost avoided because of Arthur's sudden turn of speed, the four nobles had been slung over horses and the long ride to the river's mouth not far from old Pons Aelius, now firmly in Saxon hands, had followed. Stormbringer had pressed his troop to ride hard, for none of them were truly comfortable with horses, and their ship was vulnerable and could be discovered by enemies at any time. Without their ship, they would become marooned in an unfriendly land.

At one point, with the horses resting, and both Celtic males still unconscious, Blaise and Maeve were questioned by their captors. Stormbringer, as the only one of his party who spoke good Celtic, had to calm the terror-stricken fears of the young girls before he could make sense of their answers.

'Why did your Arthur order your troop to gallop?' he asked at last. 'Did he see us?' Like any good commander, he was concerned that one of his men had inadvertently betrayed their position.

Blaise shrugged in her ignorance, but Maeve saw a red glow in Stormbringer's blue eyes and readily explained Arthur's secret. After all, the whole family was aware of the gift that had kept him alive in several potentially dangerous situations.

'My brother says he has a voice in his head that warns him of trouble. It starts as an itch, he says, and then it becomes a scream until finally he hears actual words of warning. He was almost killed by Saxons when he was seven, and I was a babe in arms. You can still see the scars if you want. That was when he killed his first man. Please let us care for him. My mother would die of sorrow if he should perish.'

Stormbringer had looked at Arthur oddly at that point and permitted the girls to clean the wound on his head and several nasty bruises on his chest. The commander saw Arthur's impressive array of scars with his own eyes.

'How old is your brother by your reckoning?'

Maeve thought carefully. 'I'm nearly twelve now, so he's nearly nineteen. Eamonn is seventeen.'

Stormbringer became even more thoughtful, and then ordered that the two young men should be force-fed ale so they didn't die of thirst before regaining consciousness. The commander of the Denes was a superstitious man, and he began to wonder what kind of odd fish he had caught in his net.

By the time they reached the sea, Eamonn was conscious but Arthur still lay like one of the living dead. Stormbringer was fatalistic. 'I've seen men in these trances after they have suffered from head wounds. Sometimes they never waken and their lives slip away through starvation. Sometimes they waken, but their wits are addled. Occasionally they are unchanged, although they can't remember how and where they received their wounds.'

With that cold comfort, the three conscious members of the party were forced to follow the Dene chieftain as he rode carefully along a stony, inhospitable coastline until they came to a secluded cove where a strange and lovely ship rode at anchor.

Leaf shaped, with a huge prow like a serpent's head rising high above the decks, the vessel was a thing of great beauty. Adze marks decorated the strong planks that held it together. Eamonn looked at the craftsmanship and carving of the strange vessel and compared it with Saxon ceols he had seen, and knew instinctively that this ship was built with an incredible construction technique. Comparison with the Saxon vessels was crass, for the ceols were mongrels compared with this aristocratic work of art. No nails were used in its construction, only pegs of superbly crafted wood coupled with an amazing understanding of timber, pitch, the action of the sea and flotation. Eamonn thought of his tiny coracle and winced at the comparison.

Once on board the ship, Arthur was unceremoniously dumped on an unused section of the deck. The other captives, awestruck by their surroundings, were warned to remain silent and compliant or they could expect to be dropped overboard to drown.

As they prepared for their departure, the night sea was wild and rough with a powerful current and a huge tidal effect. Eamonn could tell that this Oceanus Germanicus was as unpredictable and as cruel as the waters that surrounded and embraced Tintagel. Phosphorescence edged the waves with a rime of white fire and the full moon caught the lines of the ship, turning it into a thing of shadows and mists. The warriors sat at huge oars and Eamonn discovered immediately why they were such powerful men, because they rowed the ship until it was beyond the breakers. Out, out, out they went, beyond easy sight of land, until they felt the pull of the night wind and raised a single, vast sail which they erected by muscle power alone. As it caught the wind and filled, round bellied like a woman due to give birth, Maeve saw a long serpent with vast wings emblazoned on its surface.

'All will be well, Blaise, you'll see. The dragon rises above us to protect Arthur and his people.'

Stormbringer heard the child's words and clutched at the runes that hung on a tablet of walrus ivory round his neck. These four young ones were strange, like godlings, or creatures of chaos. He was yet to decide which, but he trusted to his king and his woman to read the truth in the eyes of these children, for they were little more, even Arthur who was the focus of them all, and as tall as a fully grown Dene.

Maeve's green eyes gleamed in the moonlight and her blood-red hair was a cold flame. 'Where are we going, Lord Stormbringer? Do you plan to rape us or kill us? Or will you sell us as slaves? I have heard tales of the travails that you barbarians place on your captives.'

'I don't rape children,' Stormbringer answered in an insulted voice. 'Nor will you be killed unless I am forced to do so by your actions. Ultimately, my master will decide your fate.'

'What happened to the others who were with us?'

'Who was the white-haired warrior with the Roman armour?'

'That was Gareth, Arthur's sworn guard,' Maeve replied, with hope in her voice.

'Your brother ordered him to run, and he did. He took with him a tall, dark man who seemed to be badly wounded. The dark one had a scar across his cheekbones. I decided that such bravery as he had shown was worthy of mercy.'

'That was Deddwyd. As soon as he arranges care for Deddwyd, Gareth will follow you and he will find us, wherever we are, because his oath to Arthur and Arthur's house is to the death, if you understand such concepts,' Maeve replied, her tone oddly conversational considering that she was insulting this huge, powerful man to the core on his own ship.

With a grunt, the commander ignored her insult and grinned through his curling blond beard, baring strong white teeth and pronounced canines. In the blue moonlight, Maeve thought she saw traces of red in that beard, but she rejected the evidence of her eyes because it seemed so unlikely.

'You know nothing, little one. But you'll learn. Aye, you'll learn, or you'll die. We sail for Dene Land, that place which you call Jutland, which lies across the sea. Only Father Serpent himself will stop me from keeping my oath. We go to the Folketinget, and when we arrive I will tell my king what we have seen in your lands. I'll bring him gifts as well – you three and the Last Dragon, if he's fated to live. Then, perhaps, you will learn something.'

As Blaise and Maeve wept silently for family and the scent of home, Eamonn looked out over the vast, inscrutable sea. No land was visible. Only moonlight gave a clue to the way they would travel. They were going to far-off places, just as the wise old woman had promised, beyond the sight of land, which was more than Eamonn could contemplate.

Only heaven knew if they would ever find their way back to their homes.

AUTHOR'S NOTES

This book is the seventh in my Arthurian series, so any serious student of the Arthuriad is entitled to ask, 'Why have you chosen to extend the story past the death of King Arthur?'

The legend has to come to an end sometime and my original plan was to follow in the footsteps of other Arthurian writers and end the saga with the death of King Arthur himself, the original *Le Morte d'Arthur*. However, as I delved deeper and deeper into the lives of the characters that inhabit the Arthuriad, I felt constrained to explain to our readers what I believe happened to the kinfolk of Arthur and the Celtic peoples after the High King's death. Not one of the many authors who have chronicled the life of the great man has bothered to explain what happened to Arthur's kin or, for that matter, to the descendants of the Celtic peoples after King Arthur's death.

I have always believed that legends cannot be built out of nothing, so I researched the old sources in detail once again and came to the conclusion that Arthur left at least one son behind him, and it is quite feasible that there were more descendants who have been lost in the mists of time. We are given the name of one son and a trinity of mistresses, but what happened to the children of these high-caste women is unrecorded.

Secondly, the various historians who gave us the early sources and developed or translated the legends into an intriguing, coherent form have often pointed to the fact that there might have been several Arthurs. For instance, speculation has occurred over the works of Gildas, raising the possibility that this great historian confused Arthur with Ambrosius, or amalgamated the two into one person. Other distinguished writers suggest that a father and son could easily have been combined in the legends as one man. Similarly, different men with similar names, such as Arturius and Arthur, could have been confused in an era from which few written records have survived.

I thought about these factors for some time. Arthurian legends are usually centralised in Wales and the south-west of Britain, but other sites crop up, extending from Scotland right down through England, including the southern counties, and across into France. These sites, with their local legends, are always fiercely defended as accepted truths, even after the passing of fifteen centuries. My initial reaction was to discount most of these sites because I had difficulty in believing that a Dux Bellorum from the Dark Ages could cover such vast areas of the country. But what if Arthur was actually two men? What if the time period covered a number of decades? The unbelievable aspects of Arthur's story then become more credible, and the many sites from Scotland down through the east coast of England could easily be more than wishful thinking.

The northern Celtic tribes such as the Otadini and the Selgovae, to name only two, lived between two defensive walls. Most present-day tourists hear about the Vallum Hadriani (Hadrian's Wall), but the Vallum Antonini (Antony's Wall) that isolated the Picts is scarcely mentioned. The Saxons made very slow inroads into the north. York was a Scandinavian city named Jorvic for many years. In fact, Harold had been fighting outside Jorvic at Stamford Bridge when William the Conqueror landed in 1066. A later Arthur could easily be found in the north in the sixth century as the south-west was gradually infiltrated by large numbers of Saxons and Angles. It was inevitable that the British tribes were forced to flee north and west as the barbarians flooded into the country from the east. The Jutes colonised those sections of Britain that possessed cooler climates after their people were driven out of what we now call Denmark by the Dene, a tall, warlike race who came from Scandinavia. They would later be called the Vikings, in company with the warriors of Norway, and these great seafarers would harry the rulers of England and Scotland throughout the seventh, eighth and ninth centuries, almost without opposition from the defenders. In Dublin, Normandy and the Scottish isles, successful colonies were set up where their influence still endures.

The Dark Ages are not easy times to unravel, but certain factors remain constant, so I tried to include them in this novel. The Wansdyke was built during the period I refer to in the novel under the name of the Warriors' Dyke or the Ditch. Expert opinion is divided as to whether the construction was built by the Saxons or the Celts, but as the Celts had a more pressing reason to build it, and the ditch itself faced the direction from which the Saxons would attack, I decided to credit the Celts with its construction. The area it protects is one of the easiest natural paths leading to modern-day Bath, Bristol, Wells, Glastonbury and the many villages of this fecund area of Britain. Just as pilgrims used this route for thousands of years, so would various armies during their advances into the south-west.

The use of chains as a defensive device to block the river seemed perfectly logical to me, given Myrddion's experiences of the entrance to the Golden Horn in Constantinople. Iron was a precious commodity, so the Saxons would have plundered the metal as soon as the south-west became theirs. But the ditch and the mounds remain as a tantalising reminder of the ancient past.

The neckpiece worn by Germanus is real. When I was last in Glastonbury, the innkeeper was busy building new apartments behind the Market Place Inn on Magdalene Street. One day, one of the young men working on the construction site found a fossilized shell as Germanus did and I, like Arthur, soaked it in water for days, picking away at hundreds of years of mud. At the time, I was surprised that something so old was found close to ground level, until I discovered that a hole had been bored through its centre. That nice young man gave me the shell, and my friend Pauline, who lives in the artists' community of Montville, Queensland, made it into a neck piece for me. It's devilishly heavy, but I love it.

As for Greek Fire, most modern wisdom credits the Byzantines with its invention during the Crusades, but these claims ignore the fact that something very similar was used many times in the distant past. That the recipe for Greek Fire was a closely guarded secret is beyond doubt, but it was also considered a hellish weapon, and its infrequent use suggests that it was a weapon of last resort. Pots of an odd combustible substance were recorded as being used by the Assyrians in the ninth century BC, while Thucydides writes of tubed containers of a strange flammable substance in the siege of Delium in 424 BC.

One emperor of the Eastern Roman Empire, Anastasius I, used Greek Fire during a naval battle. He is also reported to have used the substance in quelling a revolt in AD 515, and claimed to have been given the recipe by an Athenian. The name Greek Fire was not in use until centuries later, so it was initially called Liquid Fire, Marine Fire or Roman Fire (a reference to the Eastern Roman

Empire in Constantinople) in the years prior to the Muslim invasion. After visiting Constantinople in AD 454, it is feasible that Myrddion managed to access the recipe and puzzle it out, just as it is possible that he decided never to use it. But the Bran I created as a British king is a fallible man, for all his usual honesty and his attempts to conduct himself with nobility. My Bran is capable of forcing the secret out of Nimue with suggestions of the inevitable destruction of the Britons in the south-west. The older, disillusioned Taliessin could have colluded with Bran for his own reasons.

The first rule of fiction for most writers is to create a believable set of circumstances as the plot-line. The small details that follow should be feasible and realistic, but I am ultimately a novelist, so my books are inventions rather than histories. Yet accuracy is still important to me, especially in the small details of daily life.

For me, characterisation was central to my version of the legends. Having invented an infant son who grew to manhood in the period immediately following Artor's death, I decided to call him Arthur, because that name came into common usage within noble households during the years following the High King's death (if the great man actually existed).

As writers often do, I wondered what it would be like to be the bastard son of such a famous and powerful father. The twentieth and twenty-first centuries are thick with examples of tragic children attempting to live up to the qualities of an extraordinary parent. The heirs of the Kennedy clan provide a number of examples, as do the late son of the actor Paul Newman and the many troubled children of actors, singers and celebrities from all levels of fame and talent. The difficulties encountered by these children are listed in such painful, intensely personal sources as *Postcards from the Edge*, by Carrie Fisher, the daughter of Debbie Reynolds and Eddie Fisher. Such relationships are frequently difficult for children, as they try to equal or surpass the achievements of their famous parents.

So my Arthur would be born with several strikes against him. Coupled with his lack of status was his difficult relationship with his kin, because no one in the same situation as Anna, Bedwyr, Bran or Ector could be comfortable with such a potentially threatening child/man, one whose very existence could fracture the political allegiances of those troubled times.

A number of correspondents have asked me why there are no clear records of this period. After all, we know all about the life of Caesar, and he died long before Arthur. There are several pertinent reasons for this lack. The fifth and sixth centuries, and the decades that followed them, were times of wanton destruction. The Christian church had inherited the task of record keeping, and the monasteries were under constant attack from the barbarians as they extended their control over the tribal lands of Britain. Most of the manuscripts, painfully created and copied by individual monks within the confines of the abbeys and monasteries, were totally destroyed by parties of Saxon and Angle raiders. In one century, they burned the accumulated knowledge of a millennium. Ironically, by the seventh century, many of the invaders had themselves become Christianised and were placed in the position of trying to re-invent the history of the people and the institutions that they had destroyed. That the Saxons resurrected the legend of Arthur is remarkable, considering that victors always portray their own versions of any conflict. The stories of Arthur were adopted and elaborated on in their totality, and were then buried deeply and permanently in the spirit of the English people, regardless of the racial backgrounds of the men and women who were essential parts of the legends.

And so the character of King Arthur's son would be fraught

with negative influences from birth. I attempted to mitigate the inevitable conflicts through the personalities of Elayne and Bedwyr, because they are honourable and loving parents. Artor, his sire, had grown without real love, but his son experiences the affection that lay at the root of his relationships with his foster-father and mother. They provide the solid base necessary for the boy's character to grow.

To add to the difficulties inherent in kinship, I also gave Arthur similar physical characteristics to those of his birth father, making him dissimilar to his foster-father in both appearance and character. Because very few men still lived who had known Artor in his youth, Arthur's physical likeness would only be a minor distraction, but his likeness to Artor would none the less feed the rumour mill.

As for the characters of Cissa, Cerdic and his son, we know little of their personalities, except for the fact that they must have been superior warriors and leaders. I invented Cissa's sterility, but the many years of civil war in the south actually happened after his death. I chose sterility as an explanation for the absence of a clear line of succession in an age where men married many times and fathered huge numbers of children.

The rise to power of the state of Mercia effectively crushed the Brigante tribe forever. Although the Otadini lands seemed safe from invasion, they were the basis of the Northumbrian state that would become enormously powerful during the Saxon years. In the southern parts of Northumbria, the Venerable Bede was a part of a great concentration of science, literature and history. This twist of history was ironic, because Eburacum, which would become York, was one of the prime cities of the north, and yet its history is scarcely Saxon.

I have tried to imagine the uncertainty of this century and the violence of the culture clash. Even considering the chaos that occurred during World War I and World War II, the sixth, seventh and eighth centuries were arguably more destructive in the displacement and movement of tribes and races throughout Western Europe, although our current methods of transportation and mechanisation are far superior to those available during the Dark Ages.

I hope you have enjoyed my tale of what could have happened after the death of the Dux Bellorum. I enjoyed writing it, and I adored having the opportunity to research the early and fragmented Saxon kingdoms and the men who wrested power from the old tribal lords. Perhaps, with the current European fluidity of movement, the English people are experiencing a totally new form of culture clash. Only time will tell.

GLOSSARY OF PLACE NAMES

Abone	Sea Mills, Bristol
Aquae Sulis	Bath and North-East Somerset
Arden (Forest of Arden)	Warwickshire
Bannaventa	Norton, Northamptonshire
Bravoniacum	Kirkby Thore, Cumbria
Bremenium	High Rochester, Northumberland
Bremetennacum	Ribchester, Lancashire
Cadbury	South Cadbury, Somerset (site of Cadbury Tor)
Caer Gai	Llanuwchllyn, Gwynedd
Calcaria	Tadcaster, Yorkshire
Calleva Atrebatum	Silchester, Hampshire
Camulodunum	Colchester, Essex
Canovium	Caerhun, Conwy
Cataractonium	Catterick, Yorkshire
Caussenae	Ancaster, Lincolnshire
Corinium	Cirencester, Gloucestershire
Cunetio	Mildenhall, Wiltshire
Danum	Doncaster, South Yorkshire
Deva	Chester
Durnovaria	Dorchester, Dorset
Durovernum	Canterbury, Kent
Eburacum	York
Glastonbury	Glastonbury, Somerset
Glevum	Gloucester
Isca Dumnoniorum	Exeter, Devon

Isurium	Aldborough, North Yorkshire
Lavatrae	Bowes, Durham
Letocetum	Wall, Staffordshire
Lindinis	Ilchester, Somerset
Lindum	Lincoln
Londinium	London
Magnus Portus	Portsmouth, Hampshire
Margidunum	East Bridgford, Nottinghamshire
Mona	The Isle of Anglesey
Morgidunum	Bridgford, Nottinghamshire
Moridunum	Carmarthen
Noviomagus	Chichester, West Sussex
Onnum	Halton, Northumberland
Petrianae	Stanwix, Cumbria
Petuaria	Brough-on-Humber, East Yorkshire
Pons Aelius	Newcastle Upon Tyne
Pontes	Staines, Middlesex
Portus Adurni	Portchester, Hampshire
Ratae	Leicester
Rheged	Eden Valley, Cumbria
Sorviodunum	Salisbury, Wiltshire
Spinis	Newbury, Berkshire
Tamesis	River Thames
Temple	Templebrough, Yorkshire
Tintagel	Tintagel, Cornwall
Vallum Antonini	Antonine Wall
Vallum Hadriani	Hadrian's Wall
Vectis	The Isle of Wight
Venonae	High Cross, Leicestershire
Venta Belgarum	Winchester, Hampshire
Venta Icenorum	Caistor St Edmund, Norfolk
Verlucio	Sandy Lane, Wiltshire
Vernemetum	Willoughly-on-the-Wolds, Nottinghamshire
Verterae	Brough, Cumbria
Verulamium	St Albans, Hertfordshire
Vinovia	Bishop Auckland, Durham
Viroconium	Wroxeter, Shropshire

GLOSSARY OF TRIBAL NAMES USED

Atrebates
Brigante
Catuvellauni
Coritani
Deceangli
Demetae
Dumnonii
Dobunni
Iceni
Otadini
Ordovice
Selgovae
Trinovantes